THE
RIDDLED
NIGHT

THE
RIDDLED
NIGHT

Valery Leith

VICTOR GOLLANCZ

LONDON

Copyright © 2000 by Valery Leith
All rights reserved

The right of Valery Leith to be identified as the author
of this work has been asserted by her in accordance with
the Copyright, Designs and Patents Act 1988.

This edition first published in Great Britain in 2000 by

Victor Gollancz
An imprint of Orion Books Ltd
Orion House, 5 Upper St Martin's Lane,
London WC2H 9EA

To receive information on the Millennium list, e-mail us at:
smy@orionbooks.co.uk

A CIP catalogue record for this book
is available from the British Library

Typeset at The Spartan Press Ltd,
Lymington, Hants
Printed in Great Britain by
Clays Ltd, St Ives plc

For Kathy

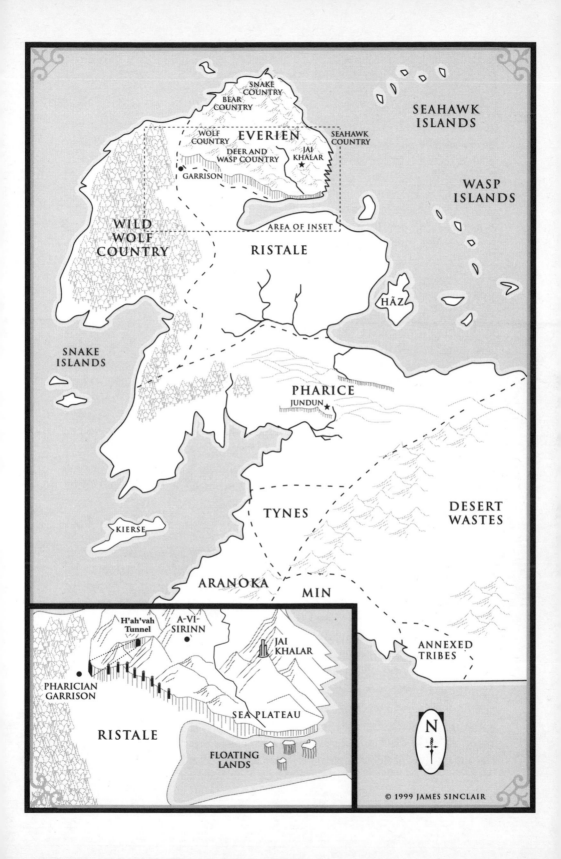

SNAKE
COUNTRY

BEAR
COUNTRY

SEAHAWK
ISLANDS

WOLF
COUNTRY

EVERIEN

SEAHAWK
COUNTRY

DEER AND
WASP COUNTRY

JAI
KHALAR

WASP
ISLANDS

GARRISON

WILD
WOLF
COUNTRY

AREA OF INSET

RISTALE

HĀZ

SNAKE
ISLANDS

PHARICE

JUNDUN

DESERT
WASTES

TYNES

KIERSE

ARANOKA

MIN

ANNEXED
TRIBES

H'ah'vah
Tunnel

A-VI-
SIRINN

JAI
KHALAR

PHARICIAN
GARRISON

SEA PLATEAU

RISTALE

FLOATING
LANDS

N

© 1999 JAMES SINCLAIR

Contents

The Pelt of a Snow Lion 1
A Red Cord 7
Buried 9
Responsibility for Goatshit 15
Ixo 21
I Would Rather Be Chief of the Dung Beetles 25
The Skyfalcon's Error 30
Byrdland 31
A Dried Footprint in Silt 43
Seahawk 58
Poison Pass 66
Ice, with Fingers 71
The One-Sided Road 79
A Deaf Whore's Recounting 84
Courage 93
I Can See Your Bones 103
Her Hair Was Red 108
Like Heavy Rain 111
Wolves at the Door 114
Spice the Lion 122
Winterfever 128
Noses Bent Out of Shape 135
The Torture Artist 141
Your Smallest Finger 147
A Few Skeins Short of a Full Sheep 151
She Smells Kind 154
Faces That Speak by Touch 160
Someone to Talk To 171
Mousetrap 187
A Whole New Definition 195
A Good Snake 206
A Good Sword 212
The Problem with Invisibility 218
Deep in the Ruse 232
The Maw of Time 236
Within Sight of Home 244
Remove the Bear Tompien 256
Grietar 267

A White-Haired Warrior 271
Hunting the Sekk 282
Tyger Pass 287
Humans Always Bleed 296
Do Not Steal 301
Founded on a Cloud 315
A Mystery Language 322
Moral Ambiguity 328
Invisible Flower 340
Liaku Spy 345
A Sculpture in Ice 352
The Rebel Camp 359
The Wasp's Arrow 363
Eteltar 368
Or 376
Listening Walls 385
A Reunion 388
Jaya's House 392
Night Is Here 398
Black and White Stallions 405
Night's Eye and Poison 409
The Trial 417
Trust 421
Learning to Fly 423
Medicine 426
Sledgehammer 438
The Good Son 442
Returning to Stone 448
Losing His Head 452
You Can't Build an Animal 454
Water of Night Sky Glass 459
The Rescue of Istar 464
Four Parallel Waves in Silver 472
A Snake by Any Other Name 475
Istar's Army 477
Yanse-Not-Yanse 479
An Unexpected Retreat 486
The Stars That Shake 489
Lake of Candles 496
Don't Let Go 499
Li'ah'vah 506
Falling 508
Music 509
Into the Neverbefore 511
Who Really Shot Ice 514
Free 516

The Pelt of a Snow Lion

Thietar and the Sekk faced each other across the white void. Falling snow blew over the icy crust with a scoffing sound, like dry laughter. Thietar closed his eyes.

'I will not love it,' he chanted to himself. 'I will not love it. I do not have to hate it but I will not love it. It is only a stone. It is only a piece of shadow on the snow. I will not love it.'

Yet he couldn't take his eyes off the distant figure. The Sekk did nothing. It was out of earshot anyway, although Thietar supposed it might possibly be influencing the tenor of the wind with its song. It had not moved for hours; neither had Thietar. He kept hoping the others would realize what had happened and come up Tyger Pass looking for him. Surely they could put two and two together: the ruined caravan lying half buried in the gully, the absence of any enemy, the silence of the hills and the whiteness of the sky. Now, of course, it seemed so obvious to him that the Sekk had been watching him all along, maybe had even been calling him. It seemed so obvious. It had taken the caravan and then lain in wait for whoever would come along next. Sekk didn't need food like people. They didn't need heat like people. They could lie underground for years, like corpses, like hidden pools of water, unknown to light or time. And now this one had him in its sights, and he would either freeze to death or be Enslaved. It was only a matter of time.

O great Hawks of my ancestors, thought Thietar, who was relatively unversed in the Animal Magic and usually disinterested in spiritual matters. *O killer Hawk saviour, O taloned one – please let the cold come quickly. Please let my heart be frozen. Do not let me love it. Please!*

His toes and fingers had no more feeling. It was said that when you froze to death you felt warm and comfortable and sleepy, but he was shivering violently, and he was hungry, and his teeth ached. Death was not close enough to rescue him from the Slaving spell. Suicide was a possibility but he didn't think he had the will to do violence to himself. Did that mean the Sekk was getting to him, even at this distance? Why could he not move his hand to his dagger, draw it swiftly across each of his own wrists, bleed himself to death here in the snow? Was he Enslaved already? No, it was merely that he could not move his arms. He could not move anything, but his teeth chattered.

I

I will not love it. I will not love it. I will not love it.

Like a ceremonial chant he repeated it. If you said something enough times you had to believe it eventually. Right?

The expedition had been ill-advised from the start. Thietar and his brothers had been hunting snow lion in Tyger Pass for the past several days. It had been his brother Birtar's idea. Birtar was besotted with Lyntar the outbreed, who was going to be rich now that the Elder Mintar's fortune was passing to Lyntar and her twin sister Pietar, already all but promised to Grietar whom nobody wanted to cross. So, like every unattached Seahawk man with eyes in his head, Birtar was applying his whole imagination to the problem of impressing Lyntar.

He had recruited his younger brothers to his cause, saying, 'We will bring back the pelt of the snow lion, and when I spread it across her shoulders and arrange her braids on its fur, I will say, "Here is the most elusive, the rarest, the most beautiful of creatures. I found her in the lonely snows, and I told her that I was your hunter, and she threw herself upon my arrow that she might adorn you rather than live." Then I will look in Lyntar's eyes and say, "Do not let this snow lion's death be for nothing! Make my words true, Exquisite One. Make me yours." '

After Birtar's brothers had finished groaning and throwing their socks at him, Birtar had reminded them that if bound to Lyntar he would be one of the wealthiest men in the Seahawk Clan and could repay their favours ten-fold. So it was that they had gladly set out through the ice and snow in search of the shy snow lion. Three weeks later, they were still looking. Thietar was the youngest but also the best hunter, and on a hunch he had gone off on his own up Tyger Pass. He had seen no tracks, and he knew it would be a long shot finding a snow lion so close to a trade route. But it was the dead of winter, and the snow lions would know that weather closed the pass from October to April or May every year, making the territory safe for them. Thietar always played his hunches, and Tyger Pass seemed to be calling to him.

It was almost noon when he came across the remains of the caravan overturned in a gully halfway up the Seahawk side of the pass. It was not a large vehicle; probably the tail end of a longer train crossing back to Snake Country from Seahawk Country last autumn. It was laid deep in this year's snow, and at first Thietar thought it had merely been emptied of its cargo and abandoned. He headed toward it, being careful to stay downwind in case a snow lion had chosen it as a place to shelter; if one had not done so, Thietar himself might use the caravan as a hide. He shuffled toward it across the icy crust on his snowshoes, head down and eyes half closed against the midday glare.

There were no tracks anywhere near the caravan. He could not get at the doors for the snow was too deep, so he cut the ropes that held the hide roof to the frame and peeled it back. The cargo was still there: sacks of whalebone carvings, a couple of casks of the best Seahawk mead, tins of fine lamp oil and even finer caviar, and enough mink skins to make cloaks for an entire family.

Thietar let out a whoop. He capered in the snow, then ate some caviar and thought about breaking into the mead. But it was too cold up here for drinking. Instead he focused his mind on how to remove all the plunder. It was not a fortune, to be sure, but it was better than one blessed snow lion skin, especially when they hadn't even *seen* a lion in three weeks, much less caught one.

He couldn't understand what had happened. Surely if the traders had come back down the Seahawk side of the pass after abandoning their caravan, he would have heard the tale. The style of the vehicle was Snake, but when Thietar searched further he found Pharician coinage, and he thought it more likely that Pharicians could afford such a haul than the Snake Clan. Besides, the Snakes would never be caught up here once the snows were falling.

Then again, Pharicians usually did their trade with Seahawk by ship. Why labour over the pass when they could sail up the coast from the Floating Lands? It was a puzzle. Thietar thought about going straight to the rendezvous and waiting for his brothers with the news of his find; but he was curious. He got a spade out of the caravan and began digging through the snowdrift, wondering what other treasures might have been left behind.

Things started to make a little more sense when his shovel hit frozen bone.

The scavengers had not left much. There were skeletons of men and mules, and pieces of armour and clothing; but it could not have been the case that the caravan had been halted by snow, or the bodies would have been frozen and covered, protected from the buzzards until spring.

Thietar could not stop digging. He worked up a fine sweat, and the noon hour passed, but he kept finding things. The men had been Pharician according to their equipment. He was compelled onward by a macabre curiosity. After a time he uncovered a wooden chest, and although he was tired and hungry, the sight of it excited him so much that he cleared all the snow around it. Then he pried it open.

The bird that flew out was big enough to set him tumbling by the force of its wings beating the air alone, and it exploded out of the box in a blinding flash of light. Thietar spun ass over head and saw the bird silhouetted against the sky, wings fully outspread and threatening with their great span. At first he thought there was some trick of the shadows, and then he thought he'd seen lightning, for the feathers on the falcon's wings seemed white for a moment, and then just as quickly they were black; and then, as if the bird itself had rent a hole in the sky, he saw no feathers at all, but a distant view of a green and sunlit forest cut out in the shape of the falcon. It was a small perfect world, utterly incongruous in the snow and wind, and it drew his gaze like a gem. He stumbled after the bird as it ascended, trying to see what was moving in the trees of the unlikely vision, for he thought he'd glimpsed a figure, possibly a horse. But the falcon rose into the air as quickly as other things could fall, as if gravity were reversed for it alone. Thietar watched the falcon becoming a glittering mote and then disappearing altogether. His eyes ached with the effort.

Someone said his name. It was his own voice, saying 'Thietar.' He turned.

'Who's there?' he said, unnerved. As he turned back toward the empty box, the snow before him rose up in human form and confronted him with eyes that dragged him toward their own emptiness.

'I am here,' said Thietar's voice to himself.

There was no hope now that the others would come for him before he froze. And if they did, what would he do? What could he do?

I want to live, he thought.

But he must pray for the cold to take him quickly. The Sekk, motionless, worked its spell. Invisible, silent, still, the Slaving spell must surely be descending on him. Just because he couldn't feel it didn't mean it wasn't happening.

Thietar tried to stir. His vision was growing dark. Was it night settling in? Was it storm? Was it the frost? Was it the Slaving? Did it matter? Why did he persist in having to know what was happening to him when he was so obviously doomed?

He had done everything he could to resist. As soon as he had taken in the Sekk's white face and white hands, its white braids and white cloak made all of snow lion pelts, its green eyes and its silver voice and its wavering form that made it seem no more substantial than a candle or reflection on water, he had ripped his sword from the scabbard on his back and charged. Thietar had lived all his life with the threat of the Sekk an ever-present, shadowy possibility. His father, his uncle, and his two eldest brothers had joined Ajiko's army and were marched off to their deaths, all of them, in the thrall of Night. None had returned from Jai Pendu.

He screamed as he attacked. His heart was hard as he drove the sword into its belly.

The Sekk did not cry out. It was bleeding. It looked at him.

4

As his sword came back toward him, it somehow swung wide and cut across his own leg. He didn't feel pain at first, but he was surprised and angry at his own clumsiness, and he was afraid. He went after the Sekk again, but it had fallen into the deeper snow and when he tried to pursue, his snowshoes got tangled and he almost fell.

He looked down and blood was gushing from a deep gash in his thigh. The sight of his own blood made him want to faint. Thietar hid his eyes from the Sekk and began to run, clumsy in the snowshoes. His sword was dripping. His leg screamed at him. Blood soaked his fur boot inside and out. The Sekk should be finished after that blow. Any man would be mortally wounded. Oh, but it had been waiting in the snow, it had risen before his eyes like smoke, like material light. What was blood to a Sekk?

He had not run very far before his leg gave out a second time. He broke through the crust as he fell, lying in the soft, deep snow that had been protected by ice. He looked back.

From this distance he couldn't see any blood on it. The Sekk was crouched in a hollow in the snow just as Thietar was: his opposite watching him across a chessboard. But all the squares were white, and the other pieces were gone. Thietar bound his leg as best as he could, desperate to stop the bleeding. He intended to get up and keep going, limping, staggering – crawling if necessary to get away from the Sekk.

But he didn't move.

He didn't know how much time had passed in the stalemate. Too long. Too long. He could not end it. He was angry. An animal would never panic like this. An animal would not equivocate. It simply would not think. If it was given to an animal to die, then it would die; and if it was given to it to fight, then it would fight. There would be none of this miserable inner debate.

Oh, but he was cold. Would his companions really leave him to the elements? Were they so stupid that they could not find his tracks? Or did they not care?

It was getting so dark, soon he would not be able to see his enemy. Would he then be released? Or would it move in to finish him?

Voices. In the stillness they sounded metallic and strange, but he recognized them all the same. They had come for him!

His brothers were approaching him from behind and he began to panic again. What was he going to do? An animal would not give its soul. An animal would fight. *I will not love it*, he said to himself again but they were only words; it was too late. He belonged to the Sekk.

They were almost upon him. Turning in the greyness of his own vision, he reached out feebly with his knife and tried to slash it at Birtar, but the other man took the knife away, grabbed his hair, and hauled him to his feet.

5

'Look into my eyes!' commanded Birtar brokenly, and Thietar saw that tears were streaming down his cheeks. 'Oh, Ysse, tell me you are not Enslaved, my brother! Look into my eyes.'

Thietar had no choice; he was half frozen, and Birtar used the hold on his hair to jerk his head into position. When he saw the expression on Birtar's face, Thietar knew he was lost. Birtar, crying harder now, turned Thietar's own knife around and cleanly slit his throat. As Thietar fell into the deep, warm snow, he heard Birtar say to the others, 'Let's get out of here before it has us, too.'

And as he was dying the sound of wings beating came to him, as if he were with the silver skyfalcon on its flight above the dizzy snowfall and the massed clouds, where everything was light and clear. Going home.

A Red Cord

It was late morning in Jai Khalar when the bird delivered its message. Its wings thrummed with a deep whirling sound as it came diving into the aviary in a madness of silver feathers, its eyes like raindrops, its talons extended. The Pharician messenger doves had risen up in a white-and-grey panic before the predator, which grasped the wire roof of their cage and gazed at the doves hungrily. The message was tied to its leg with the red cord of urgency. The bird itself was a species now disappeared from the world, the Everien skyfalcon.

The Pharician handler knew nothing of this pedigree, of course – he had never heard of the skyfalcon. He was a byrdman imported from Jundun a few months after Tash's conquest of the Citadel, a skinny, shifty-eyed, dark-skinned little fellow called Hrost who could imitate the sound of any bird but spoke only a broken dialect of Pharician with a thick accent. He could not read the message but he examined it anyway, as it had all but come apart in his hands: the hide was brittle and frozen. There were a few lines of text, then running around the edges of the square were symbols that he didn't think were words. They looked more like pictures.

The bird was screaming in hunger. It was a beautiful thing, but Hrost did not feel safe in its presence. It might not be large enough to prey on humans as a matter of course, but the animals of Everien did unnatural things sometimes. Hrost provided a box of live mice and watched almost reverently as the raptor devoured them. He waited until the skyfalcon was settled and grooming itself before turning his back on it. He trotted down the stairs from the aviary to the grand concourse, deserted at this hour. From here there were any number of routes to Tash's audience room, but thanks to some caprice of the castle – curiosity, perhaps – the first available door admitted Hrost to an antechamber of the main hall. He had never actually been inside.

He put his ear to the panel. Like everybody who lived in Jai Khalar, Pharician and Clan alike, he was terrified of Tash. Now he was torn between the red urgency identifier on the message, and the fact that he had never entered Tash's presence in this way. Belatedly, he realized he should have found a servant to take the message. Someone whom Tash knew. For if this were Jundun, Hrost would never even walk on the same ground as his ruler, let alone enter a room when he was present.

7

Yet he felt urged on by a kind of compulsion. The floor almost seemed to propel him forward, nudge him toward the door separating the deserted antechamber from the audience hall. He leaned on the door and pressed his ear to the wood. He could hear a soft voice speaking. It was a girl's voice, and her accent was neither Clan nor Pharician.

His fist had been raised to knock; now he thought better of it. Red cord or no red cord, he did not want to walk in on Tash uninvited. He turned to go, but the door leading from the antechamber to the main gallery had disappeared. *Jai Khalar!* It was a frightening place. He looked at the door again, but did not dare enter. He sat down and put his back against the place where the exit should have been, but wasn't. He could wait.

Buried

It is a night like every other night, riddled with stars. My horse's crystal white breath explodes the dark way ahead while his hooves make a soft bass beat on hemlock needles thick with seasons and rain. I do not know where I am and maybe I never will again. In my memory something itches and I feel sure I ought to be carrying scrolls, or scribestones, or some other medium inlaid with the messages to you that I have composed year in and year out, never failing, never forgetting. But the messages exist only in my mind: I have no saddlebags and no luggage, nor ink, nor even language I could say with certainty that you would understand. All the careful filigree of my love is wrought in nothing but time, and tonight in the counting of these hoofbeats, in the tilt of the visible constellations, in the indefinite darkness I have come to inhabit like skin, now I feel sure time is running out.

Where are you? I am searching everywhere, but it is you who must find me, and I am buried in a night I cannot part with.

Once I was bold, but now I am afraid. Please come.

Tash snapped his fingers and the Impressionist fell silent. She was only a girl, and an ugly one that that: Her straw-coloured hair hung lank and lustreless from her thin skull, and her features were bulbous and ruddy. While she had been speaking, a kind of dignity had crept into her scratchy, Snake-inflected voice, and she had stopped shaking and sniffling. Now, that dignity was gone. She wiped her nose with the back of her hand.

'She whines too much,' Tash said. He stabbed a forefinger at the Carry Eye cupped in the Impressionist's nail-bitten hands. 'She will break it in her adolescent stupidity. I asked about the firethrowers. What is this nonsense about scribestones and love?'

The girl would not meet his gaze. Another tremor went through her, and a glimmer of moisture appeared below her left nostril. Kivi was hovering protectively nearby, as if the Impressionist were a baby sparrow and not a receptacle for Everien's greatest power, the Knowledge. Tash refused to feel guilty for merely expecting the girl to do her job, and he resented the implication that he was abusing her. He was not a tyrant!

'What's the matter?' he queried, forcing himself to make his tone more gentle. 'Come on, explain your meaning, girl!'

9

She sniffled again and seemed to shrink, her white fingers catching at the edge of her cloak. Kivi twitched a helping hand in her direction and then caught himself. Tash glared at him and muttered, 'Twit.'

'She's cold,' said Kivi quietly, and Tash exploded.

'Cold? We're all *cold*, damn you, Kivi! If she's cold, imagine how I feel. At least you two are born to this frigid climate.' The Pharician surged from his seat, fur cloak billowing behind him like a tawny wing as he strode down the length of his audience hall. An enormous fire had been built on the hearth at the far end, but the oval windows that looked out on the cultivated valley of the Everien River kept mysteriously blowing open; or rather – Tash corrected himself, for in Jai Khalar nothing was ever so simple – the coloured glass in the windows intermittently appeared and then disappeared, admitting the icy alpine wind. Outside, a splinter of sunlight had pierced the soupy clouds on the southwestern horizon, casting Everien in a range of deep greens and purples and blue-white that made the landscape seem vivid and alive. This wouldn't last. At most the sun would grant an hour-long respite from the long winter night and its grey cousin, day.

'We are all fighting the gloom!' Tash shouted, as if volume could make his words more true. 'I have not called this child here to remind me of what I already know: that it is always night. Tell her to forget her own miseries and conjure a true vision of the making of the heavy weapons firing mechanism, as I have asked. And if she cannot do that, then she will have no fire or soup, and I will give her something to cry about.'

The outburst improved his mood. He reached the hearth where the heat struck him in a burst, like a soft blow from an enormous pillow. He picked up the goblet of mulled wine he had been drinking prior to the entrance of the two wizards and quaffed the rest of it, aware that he had become rather too dependent on his spirits in recent weeks. He didn't care. This place was so frustrating at times, and yet he was forced to hold it in order to keep it from the rebel Clansmen, who had been a thorn in his side since the initial coup that had given him Jai Khalar. The Clans had few men and fewer resources, and they had no system of Eyes at all to help them – and yet they managed to put Tash under constant pressure. Until he thoroughly cowed them, how could he hope to possess Everien? The valley with its backward people and tortured geography had resisted him almost as much as this mad castle. But the Knowledge of the ancient Everiens could make him strong. No Clan could stand against that. This conviction had become the fire in his belly, the flash of certainty in his dark eyes, the source of the smell his skin exuded that made other men instinctively fear him and race to do his bidding.

He turned to judge Kivi's reaction to his threats. The Seer had thrown his own cloak over the ugly girl's shoulders and was helping her to her feet. The Carry Eye that had once been Kivi's rolled unnoticed on the floor as the girl stumbled and caught herself, falling against the Seer. It had suddenly gone dark two days ago – that was when his troubles had begun.

'What's the matter with her? Is she sick?'

'She is not a trained Seer,' Kivi said. 'She is only an Impressionist, a child. She does not understand how to use the Eyes.'

'I would not have to use young girls to do the work if you *trained Seers* could do it properly yourselves.' Tash didn't trust the Seers, and had purged their ranks of all but the most essential personnel when he first took over Jai Khalar. He needed them to manage the Water of Glass and monitor the ground across Everien, but he had a low opinion of them generally. He had retained Kivi because, of all the Seers in Jai Khalar, he seemed the most capable when it came to tasks other than lurking around the Eye Tower being pompous and flatulent. Anyway, Kivi was willing to explain things to Tash without being patronizing, and Tash wasn't so arrogant as to think he could run Everien without some kind of understanding of how its Eyes worked. He had even taken Kivi's Carry Eye for a time, hoping to spy on the Seers at their work; but it had only had the same bizarre effect on him as the first time he had tried to use it. A kind of swoon had come over him and he could remember nothing of what he'd Seen.

Then Tash had experienced a great piece of luck, in that a young girl he had taken to his bed had picked up the Carry Eye one night and idly looked into it. Within five minutes she had completed an exact sketch of an object such as Tash had never seen. When he showed it to one of his engineers who was working in the Fire Houses making crossbows, the man had become unreasonably excited.

Four weeks later came the prototype of a flamethrower to be used from horseback. Tash's chest swelled at the prospect of sweeping across Ristale with a cavalry force armed with such demonry. Who could stand in his way?

The girl had forgotten the episode entirely and denied having drawn the sketch. Subsequent efforts to make her repeat the feat ended in failure; but Tash was fascinated. He began to collect pliant young girls who, though inexperienced with the Water of Glass, soon proved their genius with Kivi's Carry Eye. Before long the Impressionists were inventing weapons and other machines that could be built in the Fire Houses, seeming to pick their ideas out of the very air while they looked into Kivi's mysterious Eye. Tash had come to count on the flow of information from the Carry Eye to the Impressionists to the Fire Houses to provide him with the necessary weapons to command Everien.

Until the day before yesterday, when in mid-Impression, the girl he had been using had made a choking sound and begun to cry, 'No, no! I can't see. Leave me alone! Help!' Tash recalled her distress with disgust. She had pretended to be blind, but later had startled when a mouse ran across her path and her fakery had been exposed. Yet, when he replaced her with a newer, fresher, even younger girl, the new Impressionist could not finish the diagram of a war machine component that her predecessor had started. When she gazed into the dark Eye, she, too, had collapsed after utterances similar to this blond chit's in both tone and substance.

'She's faking,' Tash accused, scuffing the flagstones with a booted toe. He had few compunctions about killing other men, as was necessary for discipline and control; but it ill suited him to bully a helpless, pathetic creature such as this. Yet the Impressionists had the power he needed, small and weak though they might be.

Kivi said nothing. By now he knew better than to argue with Tash when the Pharician conqueror was in such a mood. Kivi had taken to keeping his mouth shut except to answer direct questions. So Tash asked one.

'What's the big problem? All she has to do is See into the Eye and write down or draw the weapons she learns how to build. Why does she have to go all funny and get sick? I'm not putting her to work in the mines! I'm not having her beaten or raped or tortured! Yet she behaves as though suffering the most cruel violence, when she is in truth among the luckiest of my subjects.'

Kivi began to lead the girl toward an antechamber separated from the main hall by an unobtrusive door tucked between frescoes depicting the Everien Fire Houses. Tash moved to refill his goblet, but the skin was empty. 'Answer me, Kivi.'

'It is difficult work,' Kivi said shortly.

'I will make it more difficult if I don't see some results soon! This is unacceptable. Ah, I can feel it in my guts – something is wrong in Everien.'

Kivi's face drew tighter with concern. 'It is deep winter. The Eye has gone dark, but the days, too, are disappearing. Mayhap in the spring these things will move again.'

'No excuses!' Tash flared, whirling and flinging the empty goblet into the flames. It clanged and rolled out again. The glass came back into the windows and suddenly the wind died. Tash lowered his voice in the abrupt silence. 'How hard can it be to get to the bottom of this? Even I have looked into your Carry Eye.'

Kivi stopped, turned with the girl's head lolling against his shoulder, and cast a piercing look at the dark Pharician warlord.

'Yes,' he said. 'I remember.'

Tash ignored the irony in the Seer's tone. 'I was not afraid! Perhaps when I spoke I made no sense, but I was not afraid to try.'

'Nor is she,' Kivi answered, indicating the swooning girl. 'It is for you to interpret what she says. She cannot control the Impressions she receives.'

'But what she says is not interesting,' protested Tash, now pursuing the pair across the hall toward a side door near the far end. 'It has no military value! It gives me nothing I can use, not against the damned rebel Clansmen who beleaguer my men, nor against the Sekk and their fell deeds. I *will* rule this country and I will *not* be made impotent by *that*!' He tossed his head at the Carry Eye once again. But the expression of frustration had broken the back of Tash's anger, and now his tone bordered on the pleading when he added, 'What do *you* think it means, Kivi?'

The Seer glanced away. He reached for the door but Tash was quicker, planting one large palm on the wood to hold the panel shut. The girl moaned and sagged in Kivi's arms. His expression was pinched and pale.

'I don't think she has the strength to penetrate the darkness,' Kivi said at last. 'It's not the girls, it's the Carry Eye itself. I don't believe we are wise to use it, now that it has gone dark.'

'But why does the darkness come? Was it something we did in the Fire Houses? What has changed in this last day and a half? I suspect you Seers of somehow aiding the rebels, and using the Eyes to do it.' He studied Kivi intently as he spoke. Tash knew that his personality was excessive, and he shrewdly used his own flamboyance as a cloak with which to hide the fact that he was always observing the people around him. He knew that Kivi thought himself more intelligent than Tash – thought Tash childish and rash and self-centred. Tash could be all of these things, but also he had five good senses and they were connected to his wits at all times. He could sense Kivi thinking that he was not cerebral enough, that there was something he didn't understand, but the Seer was obviously not about to contradict the Pharician warlord in order to point it out.

'Out with it, Kivi! What have you heard today that worries you so much?'

The Seer hesitated. 'I don't know what has changed in the last day or two, but . . .'

Tash felt the hot breath race out through his nostrils.

'I'm not going to eat you, Kivi!' But he felt like a dragon. His anger at the Seer's fear of him was only making Kivi even more frightened, but he couldn't stop himself. 'Kivi! Answer me. Stop quivering and answer.'

Kivi gulped and blurted, 'I think there *is* a meaning to her words. I think she may be connecting to something in the Liminal.'

'Like what?'

Kivi took a deep breath and said, 'Accounts of the scene at Jai Pendu all agree that the Company was freed from its Glass and returned to the Floating City. But the fate of Night was never determined. Nor that of Tarquin the Free. Both were lost in the wake of Jai Pendu.'

'So? So what?' Tash said sharply. He had that suspicious look that he always wore when Kivi referred to some aspect of the Knowledge that Tash didn't understand.

The Seer said, 'I'm not sure of this. But forget the interpretation for a moment. Only listen to the actual *words* this girl uses. To the words of all the Impressionists since the Carry Eye has gone dark. These girls all talk about the same thing. They all talk about Night.'

Responsibility for Goatshit

Tash's hand slipped down the surface of the door to hang slack at his side.

'Night . . .' he murmured. 'Night.' He shook himself and, looking up, fixed Kivi with his eyes. 'You will be careful to remember that you live or die by my word, so if it emerges that you have been manipulating these Eyes or these Impressionists in order to aid the rebels in the woods, then you will not be surprised when I find the most elaborate means I can think of to slowly torture you to death. For there is another explanation for why every strategic objective I identify seems to run afoul by the Sekk monsters, and every campaign against the Clans is spoilt, and that is that you are somehow using the Eyes to warn them of my plans.'

'The Clans have not profited by the interference of the Sekk. If anything, they have been worse hurt than Pharice's troops. They are being slain on their own ground, and they have precious little of that to begin with.'

'You do not answer my question.'

'Did you ask one, my lord?'

'Are you true to me, Kivi? Do you and your Deer Clan accept my authority, or will you betray me to your wretched ditch-sleeping rebels?'

'I am true. I cannot speak for my Clan.' Kivi clenched his jaw to keep himself from swallowing nervously. He did not like the idea of Tash having doubts. It was the Pharician's habit to kill first and consider the alternatives second. Kivi knew the only thing saving him was the fact that no other Seers of any rank or competence remained in Jai Khalar. They had all either fled or been purged; or, like this young girl, they had been ruined before their training was complete. Oh, but he wished Mhani were here. Even if she didn't know the full meaning of the situation, she would have an idea what to do. But it was useless wishing for what couldn't be. Mhani had vanished, just like Hanji, the traitorous seneschal who had opened the doors for the Pharicians.

'Go, then!' said Tash abruptly. 'I am vexed. I have not slept, and yesterday and today have been the most vexing of all my vexed days in this castle! Kivi, get your damned Carry Eye working again. And get rid of this stupid girl. Bring me another. Ah, vexation, what is this?'

Kivi, eager to slip away before Tash changed his mind, had opened

15

the door. An awkward brown parcel of limbs with a thatch of black hair was huddled on the other side, pressed against the other door of the antechamber with his knees drawn up against his chest. He startled and scrambled up, then glanced over his shoulder at the door he'd been leaning against, and startled again. Kivi recognized the Pharician byrdman.

'What is it, Hrost?' Kivi asked with thin patience. The man gabbled something incomprehensible and practically threw a piece of disintegrating hide at him. It fluttered to the floor as Kivi reached out for it, and he had to let go of the girl to stoop and pick it up. She swayed and he caught her again just in time, struggling to unroll the leather with one hand. It was icy cold.

Kivi read the message and puzzled for a moment over the symbols drawn around the perimeter of the page. 'This can't be right.'

'What does it say?' Tash was hovering impatiently behind him, like a cyclone brewing.

'It's addressed to Ysse – Hrost, where did you get this? Have you been snooping around the records chamber?'

'Ysse!' Tash scoffed. 'What kind of joke is that? What does it say?'

Kivi seemed reluctant to answer. 'It's a warning against using the Fire Houses. And something about Tyger Pass.'

'Ah, chickenheads! Don't tell me you think this is an omen, Kivi.'

'I don't know what to make of it.'

'I don't want any part of omens and Everien superstitions. You will fix the Carry Eye, Kivi, and we will get back to work in the Fire Houses! Do not be swayed by such nonsense as this. Some dissident in my house is playing games. We will soon find him, and sure as men have bones, I'll have some new crockery for my table!'

Kivi said to Hrost, 'But this message is old! Decades old! Where did you find it?'

The byrdman pantomimed a predatory flier and pointed up to indicate the aviary. Kivi glanced over his shoulder. Tash had turned his back and walked to the other end of the hall. One of his slave girls had slipped into the room and engaged Tash's attention. Kivi sighed.

'Ah, I'll have to see for myself. All right, just a bleeding minute. Here, take this and hold on to it. I'll be up to the aviary shortly.' He handed back the message and Hrost scurried out before him. He watched the byrdman take his bearings as if surprised to find himself in that particular corridor, before rushing off in the wrong direction. Kivi could not be bothered to correct him. These Pharicians were so slow at learning their way around Jai Khalar! The castle hardly ever gave Kivi any trouble at all.

He looked back at Tash and saw that he was now practising throwing his dagger into a wooden beam at different angles and making the slave girl retrieve it for him while he ogled her.

'Bring it to me in your mouth,' he was saying to her as Kivi surreptitiously shut the door. 'On all fours, like a hound.'

Kivi took a better hold of the limp Impressionist and set off. He had to get her away from Tash and hand her over to someone else – someone who would know what to do with her. She had not been faking the shakes or the faintness, and in truth he was not finding it easy to support her. Tash's private apartments were at the other end of his audience chamber, but this corridor led past a series of kitchens and pantries before ending in a balcony that surrounded a large gallery, where a glass roof admitted what little daylight there was. The balcony overlooked a tiled courtyard with a fountain in the centre, where Tash's women usually gathered to decorate each other or sew or make music. The balcony ran around the outside of the courtyard past several doors, most of them bedchambers occupied by whatever girls or women were in favour at the moment.

After Tash had killed Ajiko, Sendrigel, and most of the council, and disbanded whatever remained of Lerien's order in Jai Khalar, he had made himself some eunuchs from among the male captives, and these now guarded the women, together with three tame wolves and a seahawk. The seahawk was perched on the railing of the balcony grooming its tail feathers in the weak sunlight, and one of the eunuchs, a fair young man called Doren, nodded to Kivi as he came in with Gialse.

'Another one?' he said, a flash of humour brightening both his features and Kivi's mood: If Doren could live as half a man and manage to smile, how could Kivi let his troubles weigh on him? Doren added, 'I think we have some Bear whiskey around the place somewhere. That usually does the trick when Tash overworks them.'

Kivi looked over the balcony and saw that the wolves were in the main courtyard, sprawled around the chair of Grandmother Mistel, the Wolf Clan elder who had settled in Jai Khalar as a refugee after the ruin of her country by Night. He had been hoping to find her here, for she would know what to do with the Impressionist, and possibly she would have some ideas about what to do with Tash, as well. It was Mistel who had negotiated with Tash for the return of her people's lands, for the women had all been refugees in Jai Khalar and the men had been either killed or Enslaved by Night at Jai Pendu. The Wolves were not known for diplomacy in matters outside their own Clan, but thanks to the efforts of Mistel they had managed to make a relatively peaceable return to their country in the west of Everien. She had arranged with Tash that she would stay behind in Jai Khalar to vouchsafe her own people. Tash had learned enough about Clan ways to recognize that the Wolves would never misbehave as long as he had possession of their Grandmother.

'Does Tash know she's in here?'

Doren shook his head. 'He only forbids men to enter this area, so we allow Mistel to come and go as she will.'

'What do they talk about all day?' Kivi asked, seeing that Mistel had a semicircle of avid listeners gathered about her, young women of all Clans riveted by what the Wolf Grandmother was saying.

'Ah, that I cannot say,' Doren replied. 'Nor should you ask, lest you end up like me – or worse, lest you end up dead. You may leave the girl here with me. There is no need for you to go further.'

Kivi accepted the warning and let go of Gialse, who cast panicky eyes at him as the eunuch led her away. The Seer began to walk lazily back down the corridor, opening a door that led to the back of one of the kitchens, intending to beg a pastry or two before tackling the problem in the aviary. He was still preoccupied by what he had heard Gialse say during the Impression, and when a soft voice called his name from behind he startled a little. Turning in the doorway to the kitchen storeroom, with the Carry Eye held in one hand, he saw Mistel coming toward him at a brisk pace. He should have known he would not escape so easily.

Mistel was a deceptively small woman. She had silver hair, small hands, and a petite, pear-shaped figure that had birthed ten sons and six daughters, of whom all but three had grown to adulthood. She had forty grandchildren and had rather lost track of their progeny. She knew how to take care of people, which – since the advent of Tash and concomitant disappearance of Hanji – made her the most important woman in the castle.

'Is she an Impressionist?' Mistel now asked as she came toward him, slightly out of breath after climbing the stairs from the courtyard. He held the door open for her and then closed it behind her so that their voices would not echo back into the harem. It was quiet in the storeroom, but from the adjoining kitchen he could hear pans ringing and he smelled something savoury baking, possibly with cheese. Mistel added, 'Shall I expect to sit by her bed and hold her hand at night when she dreams?'

Kivi looked at the floor. 'I am a Seer and a Scholar,' he said. 'I don't claim responsibility for Impressionists or understand what they do.'

Mistel sighed. 'Aye, no one accepts responsibility for goatshit any more. Even' – and she had to shift to one side as the door behind her became a smooth wall – 'even the Citadel itself refuses to commit to being here or there, this or that.'

Kivi couldn't argue with this, but the way Mistel said it made him feel personally accountable. As if he had any control over Jai Khalar. People overestimated the abilities of Seers.

'What is Tash doing, Kivi? Tell me only this. Maybe I can help the girl.'

Kivi thought about the wisdom of answering her question. Mistel was technically a prisoner, and Tash might let her move about freely, but she was the enemy of his regime and could make plenty of trouble for Kivi if she chose. Yet Kivi was sure that her intentions were good. Mistel had only ever cared about caring for others. He could not imagine that she had political motives. She was too old and gentle for that.

'He has her looking into my Carry Eye, which has just lately become darkened,' he said at last, wearily. 'She is tapping into something, to be sure, but Tash can't make any sense of it and I . . .' He stopped because he didn't know what he thought.

'What?'

'. . . I don't know what to make of it, either.'

'Very well. We'll leave it at that, Kivi, if you wish.' Mistel turned around as if to leave, then remembered that the door wasn't there any more. Suddenly she became angry. 'Stop it, you wicked wall!' she cried in a shaking voice, kicking at the stone. 'I'll have none of your fucking tricks!'

Kivi flinched at the Elder's profanity. 'I have to go,' he said. 'Shall I find you a guidemouse and then you can take your time? I am sure a passage back to the women's gallery will open soon.'

Mistel's wrinkled face softened, and she laid a warm hand on his arm. For all her diminutive stature, her touch was heavy and firm. It said, *There will be no nonsense*, even as her smoke grey eyes gazed kindly up at him. 'Oh, you mustn't trouble yourself with a bad-tempered old woman. I expect that Tash gives you enough grief with his moods and demands. I only hope he doesn't have that little Impressionist working in the Fire Houses. Creating weapons.'

'Who told you that?'

Mistel took her hand away and blinked, dissembling. 'Told me what?'

'Come then, Mistel. Don't play games. Who told you about the Impressionists and the Fire Houses?'

Mistel smiled. 'No one did. I was only guessing. But now I see that my guess was correct, or you would not be looking so angry.'

Kivi took a step back from her. The damned Wolves! Half of them could see the spirits, and the rest were pretending to. What was the point of engaging in mental gymnastics and disciplined Scholarship to master the Knowledge when with no training at all someone like Mistel could pluck your thoughts out of the very air?

Mistel showed no sign of pleasure at having outwitted him, though. Her face became sunken with concern. She whispered, 'It is a terrible thing he's doing. Gialse is only a child! What can Tash be thinking?' Mistel was shaking, not with the tremors of old age, but with outrage. 'Kivi, wake up! Think what you are allowing to go on!'

'*Allowing?*'

'Shh! Never mind.' She rapped on the wall with her knuckles and it obligingly became a door again. 'Guidemouse, my foot! I can find my own way. This miserable castle doesn't dare fuck with me.'

Ixo

Mistel saw to it that Gialse was fed and given warm clothes, and she herself played the harp to the girl and sang the only Snake tune that she knew. Gialse dropped off to sleep on a pile of soft cushions in the quarters of Tash's concubines, and Mistel left instructions with the women that she was to be given some work to do when she awakened.

'There is to be no talk of serious matters; and try not to speak of Tash in her hearing, either. She is in a fragile state. Keep everything light, and make sure she is busy.'

The girls seemed puzzled by Gialse, who was far from beautiful by anybody's taste. Mistel hoped this meant she would be treated kindly and not perceived as a threat or rival within the ever-shifting power network of Tash's harem. But Ixo, Tash's long-standing favourite, was a little more intelligent than the rest. She was not fooled by the girl's pathetic appearance, and at the first opportunity she drew Mistel into her bedchamber and directed a fusillade of questions at her.

'What is that *thing*? Why have you brought her among us? And is it true she is the one he sends for now?'

Tears filled Ixo's brown eyes. Her breasts heaved beneath the tightly laced velvet bodice she had sewn to show them off. Tash liked his women buxom and fiery, and Ixo had been his best mistress from the first night he spent in Jai Khalar. Having killed Ajiko personally, and quickly dispatched with his handful of loyal followers, Tash had ordered their heads displayed on spikes in prominent locations about the castle and then sent his men to bring him the best women they could find. His second-in-command, Illyra, had rounded them up, making sure none of the men touched their flesh disrespectfully before Tash had taken his pick. When the women were brought before the fire in the hall that Tash was later to adopt as his audience chamber, the Pharician warlord had ordered each in turn to come and sit on his lap so that he might choose which he liked most. When it was Ixo's turn, Tash gave a pleased laugh and nodded approvingly at Illyra. Then he ripped her gown open and seized her breast. Milk spilled from it.

'Where is your child?' he had asked her softly. She struggled. 'Shall I have it killed? I will tolerate no rivals, great or small, unless they come from my own loins.' And he bucked suggestively beneath her.

Ixo spat in his eye. Tash caught her about the waist and stood up. 'You savage!' he said, but he was smiling. 'Do you fight for your babe?'

Ixo cursed him loudly in Wasp, scratching and biting, and Illyra moved to lend a hand, but Tash tossed her on the rug, where she crouched defensively, her eyes darting about the room seeking escape. Tash said, 'Let us see whether you are intelligent as well as beautiful. Tell me, will you fight thus for *my* children? Will you?' He knelt on the rug beside her and fixed her with his eyes. She hesitated, panting, confused. Tash whispered, 'I am not a brute. I will refrain from killing your child, but it will nurse from another, and you will have no part in its rearing. Do you understand? You belong to me now.'

Then he had taken her hand and drawn her to her feet, and she had been docile after that. Relatively. Or so the story had got about, and Mistel had been the first to hear it, for she was the one who had arranged a wet nurse for Ixo's baby and who had counselled the girl ever since. Tash liked having many girls at his call, but he used only two or three favourites at any time, and Ixo was the only one who had kept his interest for more than a few weeks. Quickly she had become conversant in Pharician and spoke with Tash in his own language, and her intimacy with him had made her a source of much good information and useful influence to Mistel.

Now Ixo was in a panic, seizing hold of Mistel's hand and shutting the door behind her. 'I have not seen him these three nights, and the last time we were together he stopped before climaxing. He said he was saving himself. Who does he save himself for? Why does he not want me? Is it that I am not yet pregnant? How am I to get with child if he withholds his seed?'

Keeping hold of the young woman's hand, Mistel sat down on Ixo's bed. It was covered with furs and trimmed in silk, and perfume rose from it. Ixo had done well by Tash. No wonder she was a wreck at the idea that her time had finally come. Mistel knew the way of these things. Ixo would be in love with Tash by now. She no longer saw him as an oppressor or even an opponent. Mistel must bring her back to her senses. She made a quick judgment call and said,

'Ixo, I need your help.'

The girl blinked, sniffled, and blotted her eyes with the back of her hand. '*My* help? What's going on?'

'Tash is up to something.'

'Yes, I know! Bestiality, it seems, to judge by that little lizard he's got himself.'

'Hush. Gialse is a Clan sister, not an enemy.'

'She's no sister of mine, the Snake!'

Mistel looked at Ixo sadly. 'You and I are not the same Clan, Ixo, yet

22

we have always trusted one another. Am I to understand that deep down you think of me as the enemy Wolf, and not your own friend and advisor?'

Ixo squeezed her hand apologetically. 'Of course not! But it's different with you.'

'Maybe. Still, Gialse is not your problem. Your problem and mine – indeed the problem for everyone in Jai Khalar and possibly Everien itself – lies with Tash himself. And the only one who can do anything about it right now is you.'

That got her attention. Ixo's tears were forgotten, and she composed herself on the bed to listen, folding her legs over one another in the Pharician style. Tash had taught her to sit this way in order to make her body more limber and gymnastic for the games they played together.

Mistel said, 'Now. Has he called for any of the others since last you lay with him?'

'No. Only that little—' She bit off the remark.

'Good.' Mistel patted Ixo's hand. 'It is as I suspected.'

'What? Tell me! Mistel, do not be so mysterious! Can't you see I'm dying?'

Mistel sighed. 'You are not *dying*, child. Grow a little patience in your garden. I must think what to do.'

Ixo sat radiating frustration while Mistel thought about Tash.

'He is afraid of something,' she murmured. 'But what does he fear? This is what we must learn. Ixo, you must not take personal insult that he does not sleep with you. A warrior will behave this way sometimes, before a duel, for example. Think of his words to you when last you saw him. Is there a rival to his control of Jai Khalar? Illyra is away in Wolf Country – and anyway I can't imagine that Tash feels threatened by him. But could there be someone else, someone we don't know? He uses the Eyes, remember. It may be that he is involved in a confrontation with someone far away, and it is about to turn bloody. It may be many things, but I suspect that this little Seer and her Impressions play into it.'

'He could not be sleeping with her,' Ixo acknowledged sheepishly. 'I don't know why I was so jealous.'

'He is clearly obsessed with whatever business is associated with her. His obsession does him no good; and I fear it could do all of us great harm if he isn't stopped.'

'You have not said what you think he is doing with the girl,' Ixo said.

'Nor will I. It is only speculation. Anyway, you will find out soon enough if you can only get him back into bed.'

'But how? What if he does not send for me?'

'Probably he has just forgotten about you among all his troubles. Go

23

to him about some trivial matter. Be gentle and unassuming. Let him see that you miss him. He will soon send for you again.'

'And then what?'

'You will make him *very* happy. And then you will listen to whatever he wants to tell you.'

Ixo smiled. She felt powerful again.

I Would Rather Be Chief of the Dung Beetles

Hrost and Kivi got to the aviary almost at the same time, for Hrost had gotten lost on the way, as Kivi could have predicted by watching him scurry from Tash's presence. It seemed that everything in Jai Khalar obeyed Tash, with the fortunate exception of the castle itself, which obeyed no man. The change of lifestyle from the days of Lerien, who had been king throughout Kivi's adulthood, was a dramatic one, and not only because Tash was Pharician.

In fact, Kivi reflected, the Pharicians themselves got little joy from Tash. To his own company of horsemen he was both good-humoured and generous, but his animosity toward the rest of Pharice had become apparent in the first weeks of his rule, when the armies had begun to come in from the Floating Lands. Hezene, pleased that the forces of the Ristale garrison he'd thought routed were still largely alive and fit, promptly assigned their commander, Rovene, to Jai Khalar. He relayed orders to Tash for the deployment of Rovene's men in occupying the high valley. The Pharicians must have taken heart, Kivi thought, thinking Tash their friend, for not only had he done their job for them by taking Everien, but he would surely welcome their help now that the Clan armies were returning from the sea plateau. While the dispirited Clansmen returned to their home countries in straggling groups (Lerien, it was said, had been killed, and a number of his top men had vanished, leaving the rest leaderless and at the mercy of Pharice), the Pharician army marched toward the gates of Everien in cheerful files. They were to enter the country as conquerors, though they had beaten no one. Tash, it was expected, would desperately need armies both to manage the influx of Clan soldiers and to civilize the weary and conflict-torn valley. Therefore Rovene, a lieutenant-general and the acting commander of the Ristale garrison invasion force, expected to be welcomed with honour by Tash, at which point he would bestow, as directed by his emperor Hezene, the title of Cavalry Chief of Everien upon Tash the barbarian's son. Then Rovene would occupy Jai Khalar and begin administering Hezene's new territory.

Naturally, Tash had other plans for Rovene.

Kivi had been instructed to invite the Pharician lieutenant-general and all his officers into the invisible castle using the most cordial of phrasing, which Kivi did in all good faith. Once inside, however, the officers had been arrested and Rovene slain in a bloody duel with Tash on the ramparts, in full view of the army.

'He was still a Slave!' Tash cried. 'How many of you are similarly afflicted?' He then tossed Rovene's body over the ramparts. It took several seconds to fall from the Citadel and when it landed it was crushed by gravity in the most astounding way, greatly impressing the foot soldiers below. Few of the Pharicians, Kivi later realized, would have had experience of heights such as the land of Everien possessed.

The arrested officers had been assembled in the old military training ground, then inhabited only by falcons and mice as all of the Clan soldiers were gone. There it was soon clear to the baffled officers from Ristale that Hezene's authority was too distant to save them. Tash's men encircled them with spears, their weapons having been taken at the door. They might have been hoping to find hearth and loaf and jug, baths after a long journey, women, camaraderie, and drink; they might have been hoping for a chance to talk and make sense of their time under Night's Slaving spell; for sanity after madness. None of these was forthcoming. Tash treated them worse than pigs. He stalked up and down before them, and spat.

'Cavalry chief!' he mocked. 'If you are to be my officers, I would rather be Chief of the Dung Beetles! What manner of fool was Rovene as to offer me such a sop, he who had nothing to offer but his pathetic death on my sword?'

He turned to the highest-ranked officer, the major who had narrowly avoided a one-on-one against Tarquin the Free, Kivi recalled, during the fracas when the latter had instead fought the great black bewitch-webbed captain with Night looking on through its Glass.

'Khartou!' Tash addressed this unfortunate. 'Have your honour and testicles shrunk so small that you managed to outlive your superiors?'

'Luck befriended me,' Khartou replied carefully, and Kivi was later to learn that the deaths of his commanders counted against his honour.

'Fickle luck! But she never lies with losers, not once, not ever. Once you have lost, you will continue to lose. It is the way of luck.' He took in all the men with his gaze. 'Therefore do not blame luck for her absence, for you are losers and luck would no sooner come to you than a horse to a jackal. You even lost in your own postings in Ristale. You let yourselves be defeated by a Company of a mere dozen!'

He paused before a captain built like an oak stump and about as emotionally responsive. 'What say you about that?'

The man didn't answer. Khartou said,

'They were not mortal men. They were phantoms.'

'All the more your shame. I can see it still in your faces, in your eyes.' Tash paced on, pantheresque, mesmerizing in his movements. Suddenly he stopped, and the lieutenant closest to him startled violently, his eyes rolling like a mare's when a stallion approaches from behind.

'Hah! You see it, Khartou? Your men's balls are mouldy with unuse. And you yourself – what did you think you were doing, marching beneath an Everien standard, led by some night-host of Clan demons? Were you pleased with yourself? Did you think yourself grand? You whore. Where was your loyalty to your emperor then? How easily you gave it away.'

'You never saw Night,' Khartou challenged, his face animated, his blood up. He must sense, Kivi thought, that his end was nigh; so men became frank and bold at the most unlikely of times. 'He was like a god! The air of him, all full of starlight. Oh, he was not Clan, he was no barbarian like these.' And he gestured round contemptuously, but Kivi saw Tash bristle, for Tash was considered a barbarian in Pharice. 'He was something higher. And *she* . . .' There was rapture in his face as words failed him; then suddenly, as if remembering where he was, he snapped his mouth shut and began to babble like a maniac. 'My lord Tash, the emperor Hezene in all his Greatness is my ruler and lord. As his servant here I defer to you irrespective of your rank or mine.' But Tash was already laughing as Khartou continued what he thought was an apology. 'A foul madness took me. I will kill myself now if you will not accept my loyalty.'

He fell silent and Tash just looked at him. There was a snuffling sound as one of the junior officers actually began to cry. The butt of a spear in his kidneys produced a grunt and then quiet.

'You have earned no such honour,' Tash replied at last, and Khartou's grey-green eyes rolled up in his bronzed face and held fast to Tash's. Khartou swallowed. 'As for your loyalty, it does not exist. Twice you have broken faith. I do not intend to be your third victim.'

The commander bowed his head. 'Here is my neck.'

Tash laughed.

'How disgusting. It sickens me to taint my sword with your blood; and my hand will not do this deed, for the honour would be too great for you. You will not die by the hand of a warrior. Kivi!'

The Seer came forward, eyes darting from Tash to Khartou. He was expecting Tash to make *him* kill the warrior; yet no matter what Tash might say of lost honour, Kivi had no wish to go within ten feet of such a man. Some of these Pharicians were giants, and they smelled dangerous.

'Kivi, send for Ixo.' Tash grinned at Khartou. 'My concubine will kill you.'

Kivi had not watched the act itself, but he remembered the thud of the head on the sand, and the sight of Ixo trembling with fear and exultation, the sword dragging on the ground beneath her clasped hands. The blood spattering the hem of her gown and how she stared at it. He remembered Tash telling her to clean the sword and bring it back, and there was a shuffling lull as his men smoked pipes and stretched their legs, the prisoners milling like sheep under their charge. He well remembered how Tash had gone through the ranks after that like a storm. Some officers he killed and some he spared, for no apparent reason. When he was done, he spoke.

'Those who thought Night was a god, I have done this to cure you of your illusions. If you wish to understand the gods, understand what has just occurred. For I have treated you as a god would treat you, though I am a man. That is how the gods are – unpredictable and senseless for all that we may try to tame them. Anything else is a lie. Those who are standing, swear loyalty and show it. Forget Night, forget Jai Pendu, and answer my commands with everything that is in your power. If you cannot or will not, I will soon know it and you will be killed.'

They fell on their knees as one.

Their first task had been to butcher and burn the bodies of their dead comrades. When this was done, Tash offered them a feast from the stores of Jai Khalar. Kivi looked on in distaste, thinking of the famines in Snake Country and the Bear highlands. Tash was already posting his new officers, who by now were so drunk with sensation that they responded to him like dogs.

'Your wits will return,' he told them. 'See you always use them for my cause, and I will reward you. Now go to your men and make them feel the same.'

Sometimes Kivi thought that a little of Tash's attitude might have rubbed off on him after all this time. For when he reached the aviary and saw that Hrost had not yet followed his orders, he was incensed.

The aviary was in chaos. The skyfalcon was gone. A hole had been ripped in the wire cage, and blood and feathers were stuck to its edges. The Pharician birds had all fled . . . all but one, trapped in between the cage and the feed room in a narrow alley from which panic would not allow it to escape.

'What a mess,' said Kivi, shuddering. 'You should have found a boy to bring us this message. Now look at this. Get it cleaned up, Hrost. I will notify the Eye Tower that we need more birds sent from Jundun with the next convoy.' He turned on his heel and started to leave. Then, over his shoulder, he added, 'If this killer bird returns, send for me immediately.'

There was some satisfaction in stalking away, knowing that the little Pharician byrdman would have to scramble and rush to do his bidding. Some, but not much. For Kivi knew in his heart that he was not made of the same stuff at Tash, and Hrost probably knew it, too.

Hrost coaxed the Pharician flier out of hiding with the offer of some grain. Eventually four more birds returned, but the rest had probably flown home to Jundun. The skyfalcon was gone completely. The spurned message lay on the floor of the cage.

Hrost picked it up. *Tyger Pass.* He knew someone in Pharice who would be interested in this information. He collected the Pharician bird, fastened the message to her leg, and, whispering instructions, threw her into the air.

Kivi came later in the day to question Hrost further about the falcon, but the byrdman played stupid. He was good at that.

'And where is the message? I told you to keep it for me.'

Hrost threw up his hands, gestured at the chaos in the aviary, scratched his head.

'Ah, you fool! I will be blamed for it if it turns out to be important. You had better find it, Hrost. I will tell Tash that several of his birds were killed thanks to your negligence.'

Hrost fell on his knees, sobbing in a practised manner.

'Damn you, Hrost. You are a nuisance. I don't know why the birds like you so much. Listen, I will find you an assistant. Next time you have an urgent message, leave someone up here to mind the birds while you are gone. And get someone to teach you the protocols in case you have to go before Tash. And for the love of Ysse, take a bath!'

Hrost opened his mouth and wetly shrieked his joy and gratitude at Kivi's mercy.

'Don't be disgusting,' Kivi said. 'Stand up! Find some work to do, will you?'

As soon as he left, Hrost wiped his eyes and went among the birds, pleased. An assistant! Now he could sleep all day if he wanted. The advent of the skyfalcon might not have been such a bad omen after all. He soothed his remaining birds and then went to wash off the blood of their flockmates. They would settle down in a day or so. And he would keep his slingshot handy in case the silver falcon returned.

If Hrost was in any doubt as to whether he had done well, Jai Khalar soon saw to it that he was rewarded. Later that day, Hrost found a group of mice working as a team, dragging something from a drainpipe into his sleeping area: a cloth-wrapped lump of Tash's most favourite cheese. He ate it by darkness, and their many eyes watched him.

The Skyfalcon's Error

The skyfalcon could fly five miles above the earth, and at speeds that made the fastest horse appear to stand still. Although the vast city of Jundun looked no larger than a diamond-shaped stain on the dun earth of the Pharician plateau, the skyfalcon could see the messenger pigeon labouring its low, slow way toward its destination. The predator had found his prey in the nick of time, for he had wasted precious days circling Jai Khalar at a great height, trying to work out what had happened to the place he remembered. He had returned to Everien at the wrong time; he could not deliver his message to its intended recipient; and the birds he had tried to speak with in the aviary were all stupid Pharician slaves, no use to him in his time of need. When he had finally deduced that his message had been sent on to Jundun, the skyfalcon had shot across Ristale at a great height, cutting the dove's lead from two weeks to five minutes. Even so, he was almost too late, for the messenger had reached Jundun, and finding one dove in all the airspace above the plateau of the city was akin to finding one krill in a whale's mouth. The skyfalcon began to descend, his silver eye fixed on the mote that was his prey, singling out the bird from the confusion of others that surrounded Jundun like an ever-present, moving cloud. He held to his target and began his dive.

He caught the pigeon only fifty feet above the rooftops, too close a shave at such speeds. Triumph filled him; but he had misjudged his angle. In another instant he would crash. He corrected his wing position and pulled out of the dive at a steep angle. In doing so, he inadvertently opened his beak. Such are the errors of birds, who resemble men in only a few small ways, but this is not the least of them: that such a great one could make such an unnecessary and costly error. For all its talent, the Everien skyfalcon could be a foolish sort of bird. He had dropped his precious cargo.

Byrdland

When the skyfalcon's shadow fell on Liaku she was standing on the roof
of the Kukuyu in the middle of a pane of chala as thin as paper and
flexible as skin, baiting a crow trap, for the ravens had been thieving her
doves' eggs and depriving her of food. It was the middle of the day, and
the sunlight was clean until suddenly the wings came between the sun
and Liaku and stopped there, engulfing her in their shadow. She
dropped to her knees and covered her head with her arms in an
instinctive act of self-preservation, heedless of the fact that the chala
could easily tear even under her slight mass. There was a deep *whoof* of
updraft and the frame of the chala shuddered against the pressure.
Something light but solid hit the stretched chala near her head,
bounced once, and was still. She knew that the shadow still covered
her, for without the sun her back actually felt cold, as it was the middle
of winter and the air up on the roof of Jundun could be chilly. She
opened one eye.

About a foot away lay a dead Pharician flier, grey-brown against the
muted gold of the chala roof. It wore a message scroll and a red cord.
She recognized the bird; it was one of Ral's, sent to Everien almost a
year ago. It must have just made the long winter journey home only to
be killed in its native airspace.

She didn't reach for the bird. Its killer still hovered over her. She could
now see the outlines of its form in the sharp shadow it cast on the chala.
Its wing type was that of a falcon, but it was much larger than any
falcon she had ever seen. Also, its body was more bell-shaped than a
typical predator's. It hung in the air as though glued to the sky,
wingtips making minute alterations so as to hold its position, its head
turning slightly from side to side, watching her.

'Skyfalcon,' she breathed. It didn't matter that she had never seen a
real skyfalcon; the long-lost species had been described to her so many
times that she couldn't fail to recognize its shadow, however impossible
it might seem. She wondered how high it was. If it was low, then its
shadow would be near to its true size – but she would have no chance of
escape in that range. If it was high, then she had more time, but it
would mean the bird was as big as a horse. Either way, she had a
problem. There was no time to calculate. In a sudden, unpremeditated
movement she snatched up the dead bird and took a flying leap to the

next chala pane, deliberately driving her legs downward with a powerful stroke in an effort to break through the fine, papery skin that formed an overceiling for Jundun's Byrdland.

It didn't work. For once the chala was too strong, or Liaku was too small. She skittered across the surface, the bird's shadow coming after her like a blown garment. The nearest hatch was three or four seconds' run from where she was, and she heard the long shriek of her desperate inhalation as she made for the hatch, plunged through, and slithered down a series of poles until she came to rest in one of her own nests, unharmed.

She looked up. The bird blotted out all the light. She could see its beak where its head peered in after her. It was not as big as she'd feared, but it had a face so strange that she froze, mouth open, until the cast-off feathers of the dead flier drifted into her mouth and she began to cough. As soon as Liaku and the falcon made eye contact, she knew that it was more intelligent than she was.

'Hello, beautiful,' she said. 'What you want?'

She knew he wanted his bird back, but Liaku was very hungry and knew that by the bird code, it belonged to her as finder. She decided to bring the message to Ral as a courtesy, though, for the red cord was not to be taken lightly.

The skyfalcon was still watching her.

'Ah, no you look at me like that!' she scolded. 'It your fault you drop him right where I see him. You catch other one. Easy for you.'

Perhaps he understood her, for the silver skyfalcon withdrew his head from the hatch and his shadow could be seen moving across the translucent paper ceiling, then growing smaller as he ascended. She waited with her breath held in case he was about to plunge through the hatch to steal back his prey. But nothing happened, and the skyfalcon did not return. After a while she remembered the red cord meant 'urgent', and dutifully she set off to look for Ral in the patchwork of shadows and sky that was Byrdland, her home.

Jundun was a city of paper boxes; a city of cranes; a city of air. Birds had visited this plateau for thousands of years, migrants in teeming flocks that stopped to roost and feed here in successive waves, spring and fall, each one locked into place in the turning seasons' wheel; you had no need of calendars in Jundun, when the colour of the daily featherfall could tell you so much. The old city was built of clay and sandstone and it had risen up as a way post for traffic from the twin river valleys that stretched to the eastern ocean and the western sea, respectively. The agrarian civilizations to either side of the Jundun plateau had fought for control of the high ground from time immemorial, for whoever ruled the plateau not only surveyed all the lands below, but tithed whatever trade passed from one side of the continent to the other. Because of its position as a land bridge, the Pharician highland also guarded the passage from Ristale and the Wolf forests to the north, and the deserts and tropic kingdoms to the south.

But it was not the endless stream of human supply trains visiting the plateau that gave Jundun its character; nor did the lines of sails that plied the twin rivers the city overlooked; nor the irrigation patterns so visible from the height that lent geometry to the seasonal floods. These signs of disciplined, premeditated human settlement were distinctive, and to the eyes of the unschooled nomads of the south and the hunter barbarians of the north they undoubtedly appeared impressive. Yet none of these sights captured the essence of Jundun. That was created by the birds. The birds, in their own way, were the true builders of the capital city of the Pharician Empire.

If you lived in Jundun you aspired to be pale and fat, because this meant you were rich. The thin struts of the overcity where the poorest caste lived would not support anyone who carried extra flesh, and the sunlight that scorched the byrdmen inhabiting Jundun's highest reaches never touched the wealthier classes beneath, who enjoyed the coloured shade cast by hundreds of thousands of paperlike chala shields stretched between frames of wooden poles that enveloped the city in a honeycomb system of bird traps. For the superstructure of the city was as ephemeral as its underground roots were deep, and had been designed to both celebrate and exploit the winged migrants.

Byrdmen lived on the heights, slept there, ate there, and conducted their work there: collecting bird dung, feathers, and eggs, and – according to a rigid system of quotas set by the emperor Hezene and enforced by the Imperial Air Police – killing the birds. A byrdman's feet were allowed to touch the earth on only two occasions: first, during the predawn and nightfall exodus down a series of ladders to the sewage pipes at the city's perimeter, where he was obliged even to defecate on schedule; and second, during the annual Down celebration, when for a day the undercity's residents fled the metropolis to allow for a symbolic bird invasion in which the byrdmen ran about the empty clay streets, looting houses, throwing shit, and leaving feathers everywhere. Otherwise, byrdmen were relegated to the paper boxes that cloaked Jundun, and they enjoyed an existence that was in many ways free of the stifling restrictions borne willingly by all other Pharicians, especially the urban classes who filled Jundun. And they did possess the special protection of the emperor. Reviled by mainstream society, the byrdmen knew virtually everything that happened in the maze of the city, for much information drifted up to them from windows and courtyards, and many of the buildings were roofless but for their paper ceilings. The rustling of birds and byrdmen above was taken for granted, and because the byrdmen spoke their own language it was widely – and falsely – believed they could not understand Pharician. Yet in truth they understood not only Pharician, but the languages of numerous other countries and all dialects of Everien Clan, as well as some of the rare island tongues; for in all the hordes of fliers that passed over Jundun on their way to mate, nest, feed, or flee winter, every so often of one species or another there came a few Speakers. And Speakers were critical to the equation between the byrdmen and the emperor.

For the only way you could ever hope to become pale and fat, if you were a byrdman, was to catch a Speaker and present it to the emperor. This was precisely the feat which had been accomplished by Lor, former byrdman and now freeman of the city and chief informer for Hezene's Imperial Air Police. For Lor had given to Hezene Byrd, his favourite of all the Speakers, as well as Byrd's mate Chee, thanks to which act Hezene now owned a whole flock of tame Speakers of exceptional wit and imagination. Lor now lived a quiet life in a well-watered villa coloured pink and gold like a birthday cake, where he sat by a fountain eating fruit and playing a lyre most days, looking after his pet birds and his pet byrdmen. There was nothing which occurred up there in Byrdland that Lor didn't hear about sooner or later. But no one had seen the skyfalcon descend suddenly from a thousand feet to snatch the Everien flier out of the air; and no one had seen him gift it to Liaku. So Lor had no idea why Liaku came to see him in such a rush that morning; but he was pleased to see her nonetheless.

She arrived on the roof of his courtyard with an urgent message between her teeth, looking for all the world like a large brown crow with her bent-legged stance on the crossbar and her ragged garment shedding feathers in the wind.

'What have you got, my love?' Lor said to the urchin, yawning and setting down his lyre. Liaku was one of the best – at less than four feet tall she could fit into any crack, weighed less than a loaf of bread, and feared nothing provided she had somewhere to run. He had seen her up there among the birds, swinging like a chimp and shrieking as loud as the darkwings from Wolf Forest. She was a gifted mimic and would repeat entire conversations, including every inflection and cough, that she had overheard at night with her ear to the paper floor. Now she held a dead flier in her hand. With the other hand she took the message scroll from her mouth.

'I find him on roof of Kukuyu,' she said, meaning the place where all the pigeons gathered; Kukuyu was an onomatopoeic byrdman term. 'He Ral bird and I see he has message. I no read, so I take him to Ral and Ral take him away exchange for Pastry Rights. So I go lie on roof of patisserie, steal four chocolate breads when bakers go outside for noon smoke, then I go spy Ral. He take little dove to Scrollmen in the boomhall, and they go to the wooden room, with rolling things.'

She meant the office adjacent to the main reading library, where the seats were on rollers. The inmost den of the imperial scholars, in other words. *Hmm*, thought Lor.

'Ral give message to Yanse and Yanse give it back. Say, "I am not Ysse! What kind of granule-grained walnut brain are you, white-shitting fleahouse sniveller. I will pay you nothing, and take your bird out of here before it or you shit on something antiquated and valuable."'

She giggled and resumed her normal voice. 'So Ral come back with dovey, and he still has message. Ral mad at me, so I give him one chocolate bread and tell him to fuck himself. I keep message, but nobody know where to find Ysse. So I come to you.'

'Clever Liaku,' Lor praised, wanting to stroke her head but knowing it would be full of lice. 'It is a very good thing you did, too.'

'I remember you say name Ysse many time. When I was little. "Lerien will never be worthy of Ysse's trust." You say, "Why would Ysse leave her country in the hands of someone so indecisive?" You say—'

'But you were only a babe then!'

Yet the look she gave him said she had never been a babe, but possibly had hatched, complete with connivance, directly into her present form. Lor laughed, laying his hand on her head now just to shut her up. 'It was very clever to remember that I knew who Ysse was. Now, I know you have had your chocolate, so tell me what I can give you. Would you like something for your hair, perhaps? A bit of silk for your neck?'

But she was too young to care about those things. She gazed hungrily at the fountain.

'Ah,' he said, understanding. He glanced around furtively. 'Well, I wouldn't want to make a habit of it, but I suppose just this once you might play in the fountain. But only for a quarter hour! And tell no one you brought me this dove, do you understand, Liaku?'

Liaku whipped off the rag that passed for her only garment and flung herself into the water.

'Well,' said Lor philosophically, 'I suppose she needs a good cleaning. Baqile! Remind the yard boy to clean the drains of the fountain this afternoon. And scrub the tiles. Just in case . . .'

Then he opened the message. It was scribed in the new Everien tongue, which was itself derived from a patois of Clan languages spelled in the Pharician characters.

35

April moon, two days old, the year past Smoke Year

Lor paused and looked at the sky. By the standard reckoning, years only got their names after they were over, so dates were always rendered 'the year after' whatever the last year had been. Smoke Year . . . why, Smoke Year had been named after the fires that raged across Ristale that summer – but that had been forty years ago. Doves only lived half a dozen.

April moon, two days old, the year past Smoke Year
Ysse:

I am taken by the White Road. All my hope goes with you.

If you return, you will be great. You will have no more need of me. But before you take up your mantle, honour one last instruction from teacher to pupil: Do not use the Fire Houses, whatever happens!

I left something for you in Tyger Pass. Seek it not too soon, but find it before you die.

Eteltar.

Lor studied the message for the entire quarter of an hour in which the child made merry in his fountain. When her time was up, Baqile made to chase her away; but Lor stopped him and beckoned to the child. She was bright-eyed now, thrilled, her skin gleaming and her white teeth shining as she grinned her pleasure. If Lor didn't know better he might have said that her cunning had left her for a moment, and that she was just a child like any other, poorer than a mouse and destined for almost as short a life.

'Liaku, smallwing, if you find any more like this one, come straight to me – understand?'

'You offer good deal, fat man? Ah, of course I come, my friend. I take dovey, yes? Make good supper and other things.'

Before he could answer she picked up the corpse and was gone, shooting up a support pillar and disappearing across the paper ceiling leaving no trace but a faint scampering noise. Baqile stood over the yard boy, supervising while he began to scrub the fountain.

Lor held up one finger and Tol jumped onto it obediently, regarding him from one eye.

'Go to Byrd, and bring him here as soon as he can come,' Lor said. 'No stopping on the way to mate, either. This is important.'

He glanced at the paper ceiling, thinking: *I know that child is watching all this. May she keep her wits and not do anything foolish.*

Liaku was indeed watching. It was a rare event for Byrd to venture forth from the Imperial Palace, and a testament to Lor's influence that he would follow Tol to Lor's home without being told anything of the matter at hand. Of course, Lor and Byrd were old friends; but Byrd was Hezene's favourite creature in all the world, even above his own children, and he seldom left the emperor's side.

Lor read the message aloud to Byrd, and Liaku, who was illiterate, heard and understood it for the first time. When Byrd queried, 'Smoke Year? Are you sure?' she didn't understand; but Lor said, 'Ah, Smoke Year was only two years before the beginning of Ysse's reign as Queen of Everien. If the message is to Ysse, it could very well have been sent during Smoke Year.'

'Where is the messenger?'

'Er . . . dead.'

'Show me.'

'The byrdchild who found it took the body. It was a young bird, fat enough to eat.'

'A young bird? You should have kept it. This makes no sense. Could the message have been attached to his leg more recently?'

Lor shrugged. 'I know not its history, only that it arrived here last night. One of my helpers brought it to me.'

'Has anyone else seen it?'

Lor hesitated, then said, 'Only the byrdboy whose property it was. He apparently misunderstood Ysse for Yanse, and brought it to a Scholar by that name, who sent him packing.'

'And then he brought it to you.'

Lor didn't hesitate this time. He gave a definite nod. 'Yes.'

'That is well,' said Byrd. 'What was the name of the boy?'

Liaku held her breath. Why had Lor not mentioned her part in it? She bristled angrily.

'Ral,' Lor said, looking sorrowful.

'Ral and Yanse. Are they the only ones who saw the message?'

'Yes. But the boy could hardly have understood what he was reading. They are illiterate, most of these byrdmen. That's why he got the name wrong.'

'I am sorry,' Byrd said, 'if he is a favourite of yours. But he will have to go. This information is very important. I will take it to the emperor at once. But you must not mention it to anyone. Hezene well remembers your past loyalty, and I will speak highly of you to him at the next opportunity I get.'

'Any small favour I can do, anything at all, I beg you only to name it,' Lor blurted.

'You have done enough for the time being. Only give me a servant to bear this message back to the palace.'

'Of course!' Lor said, and clapped for his boy.

'You yourself, of course, have no memory of any message to Ysse.'

'I know nothing of such a matter,' Lor said hastily.

'That is well,' Byrd replied, and launched himself into the air. Liaku slid deeper into the crevasse of the palm tree, trembling. If she was caught spying on this conversation, she would be killed. Ral was already as good as dead.

But why? Queen Ysse of Everien had been dead for years; even an ignoramus like Liaku knew that. So what was so important about a lost message – if it even was authentic?

Liaku knew she should return to her nest and think carefully about her next move, but she couldn't resist following Byrd back to the palace. He was well ahead of her, his red-gold wings moving him much faster in flight than she could ever hope to do on foot, especially over the uncertain surfaces of the paper boxes that comprised her city. But although he was the emperor's prize Speaker and therefore privileged to fly among humans on the streets of Jundun, for some reason he chose now to duck in among the paper boxes where the byrdmen trapped less intelligent birds, and where Liaku plied her spy trade. His progress was slowed and now Liaku was able to keep up with him on a parallel, always making sure that he could not see her shadow through the chala walls or hear any sound she made. Her smell, she knew, was thoroughly birdified, and mixed with so many odours from the city below that it was not likely to alarm the Speaker even if he did get wind of her. She half expected him to return to the bazaar, but instead he flew back to the palace, entering it through the open window of one of the reception rooms.

Now Liaku knew what he was up to. She had seen Byrd play this game before, but she had never understood what it was about. She spread herself flat and crept across the chala ceiling. It was stained and crusted with droppings, for its only purpose was to prevent the imperial rooftops from suffering insults of this nature. No one of any real size could hope to make such a crossing without tearing the paper, but Liaku was tiny for her age, and life among the birds had taught her to be greatly patient; for birds were nervous creatures and did not like to be rushed. Liaku could hold one position without moving for hours. Even her eyes would not move. When she was still in her father's nest, her brothers and sisters had thought her fey, but what did they know? She had stashes of barter notes and favours secreted all across the imperial scaffolding, in hollowed-out poles and glued to the undersides of paper joints where no one would ever think to look. At the age of nine she was on her way to being rich; but she could not afford to be fat. Not yet.

She was already nearly over the window of the reception room that Byrd was in the habit of visiting. She had been following the conversation between Byrd and Se for some months, initially using it to teach herself the fine points of the vocabulary of the Object Language. But soon she became caught up in the drama that was unfolding in these secret messages, and now she checked the room after every function in which Se or one of his associates might have a chance to enter and read the signs. Se was a member of the Pharician nobility, a privileged man who did nothing in particular for a living yet somehow got invited to every party. Liaku had spied on Se extensively in an effort to understand the relationship between him and Byrd, but also in a purely recreational way, for he was very interesting to observe. He was a dangerously skilled gambler, an amateur Scholar in his own right specializing in medicines and tonics, and a player of psychological games. He seemed to thrive on the ebb and flow of scandal, power, and position in the Imperial Court, while never being touched by it personally. Se knew everyone. He went everywhere. He was a big man, broad-shouldered and powerful yet surprisingly graceful, with eyes the colour of weather-greened copper and a soft, suggestive voice. He was charismatic, but in a slightly unwholesome, dark way. Liaku knew there was to be a reception tonight and guessed that Byrd had been busy leaving his message for Se while she tracked him. As she looked through the skylight, she saw that Byrd was still there. He was flitting from one piece of furniture to another, making his adjustments.

Liaku took in the changes in the room's topography. For every object in the room there was a potential set of secret meanings, and when objects were adjusted in certain ways, a coded meaning was created, intelligible only to a visitor who knew how to read the room. When Se came to a party, he looked at the signs and then made his own alterations. Over the years, Liaku had painstakingly leaned how to read the code that passed between Byrd and Se, and as she made a clockwise scan of the room starting from the door to the hall, she noted several positional changes in the room's decor. Some of them were minute: the turning of an ornamental figurine by fifteen degrees; the removal of one pink silk flower from an arrangement. She did not understand all the signs, but she was able to read enough that a shiver of comprehension went through her.

She was disappointed. It wasn't about the skyfalcon at all. The message said, 'Wakhe bodyguard Scholar, Yanse. Target. Immediately. Details at bazaar.'

This information would be tricky to pursue, Liaku realized as Byrd hopped out of the room, leaving it in stillness. The bazaar was open-aired, and as a byrdman she was forbidden to set foot on the ground. What details? What was meant by target? Was Yanse a target for murder as well as Ral, simply because he had read the message of the skyfalcon? Ah, the skyfalcon. As she looked out across the dusty blur of pale colours that was Jundun, all she could think of were the rumoured snows of Everien. As white as the moon, it was said, and as cold. The air was clear there, and the heights were open. What would that be like? Birds never left the sky in Everien, said the stories. They never wasted their time roosting and shitting and shedding feathers; they only flew. Liaku dreamed sometimes of their flight, when she was very lucky. The dreams were like exotic flowers, and they withered quickly, leaving only a scent memory.

Well, she could not enter the bazaar; it was the one section of the city off-limits to the byrdmen, being kept open to the air. Liaku suspected the reason for this was to prevent excessive theft from the caravans, but she had gotten round it by teaching some of her best birds to fly in and steal for her. She had once or twice broken the cardinal rule of byrdmen and set foot herself in the bazaar, but only in the dead of night, and mainly only as a way to scare herself when she was feeling bored. She wasn't going to be able to spy on the rendezvous between Byrd and Se.

She was nervous. What was Byrd up to? What if they found out that Liaku had picked up the message? She was glad she had lied about the skyfalcon. At the time it had been a routine lie, for it never did to tell the truth unless forced by circumstances to do so. Elusiveness was more important than morality. Now it occurred to her that her lie might have saved her life, for if he had known about the skyfalcon, Lor would have had to tell Byrd, and he would not have been able to keep her name out of it in that case. Still, she had better be careful.

So after she'd hung the dead flier in a secret hide for eating later, Liaku decided to retreat to one of her nests and wait quietly until dark. At sunset she went up to the Kukuyu, on the top level of paper roofs as she did every night, to watch the birds swirl in on the breeze. The support poles extended from the city like masts, scoring the red sky with dark lines, while the taut chala lay in a patchwork below, each section reminiscent of a sail swollen with wind so that from certain angles the city resembled some strange ship that never went anywhere. Each Watch pole that reached into the sky was reserved for a different byrdman; Liaku had inherited hers from old man Hoos when he fell into the bazaar from three levels up and broke his neck – he had been trying to steal a gold bracelet from a caravan parked on the edge of the bazaar, using a fishing hook and line – and Liaku, witnessing his fall, had hastened to his Watch pole to secure it for herself before anyone else could climb it. She had had to defend it from other aspirants for the first few weeks, but now it was recognized as Liaku's Watch and she seldom had any trouble. She shinnied up it like a brown eel, her bag of treats bouncing against her back, and smiled into the rush of wind as her special birds flocked to her. They always came to her at this hour for the treats she had collected for them during the day. Some among her favourites were actually former members of the Imperial Air Police whom she had lured away from the palace and homed to her person. They looked exactly like the imperial birds, down to the fine striping on their wings that distinguished them from common fliers; but Liaku's renegades preferred her to their palace home, and they came to her wherever she was, for as trained police birds they were skilled at finding and remembering people. She didn't know why they chose her, unless it was that they understood that Liaku liked *them* more than she liked her fellow men, women, and children, and the birds were simply returning the compliment.

Liaku's pole commanded a view of the river, where on most evenings the field workers could be seen carrying bundles of the chala harvest rolled into long tubes. The chala would be boiled, then each leaf patiently unrolled and glued to the next using a pitch made from the stem of the chala plant. In this way the city could be repaired, rearranged, and added to with great ease, and the chala grew so quickly in the hot climate that there was always plenty of it; in fact, it was occasionally burned as fuel simply to keep it from invading the cultivated terraces where food crops were grown on both sides of the river.

But tonight, there were no chala bearers of any kind on the road. There were no workers at all. The road was totally empty. Liaku ducked her head from side to side, trying to look through the blur of wings and bodies of her birds, but she could not see any reason why the road should be deserted at this hour. She wanted to ask someone what was going on, but the only Watch within earshot of hers was Ral's, and he was not there. Word must have gone out that he was dead, for the juniors were wrestling at the base of his pole, shaking it in an effort to bring down the other byrdchildren who were already climbing it in a battle for control over Ral's Watch. Liaku felt a vague unease at the thought of Ral's death, but it quickly passed. Byrdmen didn't often live into adulthood.

While she looked on, Ral's Watch was successfully occupied by a slick-fingered boy called Grint, who threw darts at anyone who tried to get up the pole and depose him. She saw a girl go down with a dart in her eye, and then the others gave up.

'La!' she called. 'Grint!'

The young victor turned his head just like a seagull and sniffed in her direction. She pointed to the road and cupped one hand around her mouth to make her words carry.

'Why nobody on road?'

41

He grinned. 'Army come. Many spear. We good stealings at barracks roof tomorrow, yes?'

She squinted and in the distance she could see something blocking the road in the direction of the sea. It was out of season for soldiers to return to Jundun, but Grint appeared to be right.

'Why army come here?' she shouted.

'Reposting. To Everien, they say. Many furs brought, and barrels of butter, I taste some . . . mmm, so good.' He rubbed his belly. 'I be sick, eat any more.'

Liaku frowned, annoyed that of all the days that the army supply caravans might arrive, they had to choose the day she had spent in hiding. She loved butter. Sometimes she dreamed about it.

Having consumed her supply of gifts, the birds left her one by one to roost, but Liaku stayed, clinging to her post with an ease that showed she had been born in Byrdland. Night quickened. After a while she realized that she was anticipating seeing the skyfalcon again, but he did not come. She remembered so clearly how he had pursued her, and the look in his eye when she had spoken to him; but he was not a Speaker, for he hadn't answered her. Yet when he had stared at her she had received the distinct impression that he was curious about her, and that he was trying to communicate. The other events of the day seemed to fade into the background whenever she thought of the falcon. With a rare yearning that was not connected to food or water or treasure, she wanted to meet this bird again.

But though she waited until dark and beyond, the falcon did not come.

A Dried Footprint in Silt

In the morning there was a new message in the reception room. From Se to Byrd it read, *No kill Yanse. I no bodyguard Wakhe!*

To show Se's scorn for the proposition, a sparrow turd had been left on the windowsill. Not an official element of the code, but difficult to misinterpret.

So Se didn't want to kill Yanse. What would Byrd do now?

And where had the skyfalcon gone? She began to ask around among her contacts for someone who had seen the falcon, but everyone responded as though she was crazy, until at last she spied on Lor and heard him confiding to Tol that he was worried about the recent capture of the Everien skyfalcon by Hezene's guards. Liaku had to stifle a gasp when she heard this, and her heart turned black. No one should capture a wild bird. It was wrong.

'I fear that this skyfalcon will depose Byrd in the emperor's high favour, and then where will we be, Tol? Ah, skyfalcons are creatures of legend. I have never even seen one. Would that it had flown to me! I would have fed it without turning it in.'

'I would not wish to see a skyfalcon,' Tol answered. 'They are said to be of evil disposition and they can fly so high that the world looks small to them, and still pick out a beetle on the end of a stem.'

'Yes,' said Lor morosely. 'I have heard the same.' He fell into a glum reverie and Liaku did not learn more of the skyfalcon for all that she spent the morning shadowing Lor.

Liaku began to have foolish thoughts. She kept recalling the sky-falcon's curious gaze, and because of this, in her mind she named him Quiz. He liked her; she knew that, or he would not have let her take the flier away from him. He had killed her a meal; therefore, did she not now owe him? Perhaps she could rescue the bird, she thought. Once the idea was in her mind, she couldn't get it out.

So she plucked up her courage and began spying on the emperor. It was an activity she only pursued when she had a good reason, for the palace was heavily guarded and it was not a good idea to be seen anywhere near it more often than absolutely necessary. That was why it had taken Liaku almost a fortnight to place her spy mirrors so that they would go undetected by the palace police. The first two had been easy: the largest, pilfered from among the scrap tin brought by horse merchants from Or, had been placed by Liaku at an angle convenient for her viewing while reclining in one of her nests above the palace; and the second, a small glass mirror stolen from the back of an oxcart at the bazaar, she had stuffed in the joint between the chimney and roof, climbing down the chimney in the very dark when even the mice were sleeping. But the third mirror – the essential one, which was to offer a vantage of the emperor's sitting room itself – this had been the hardest. It was not that there was any lack of places to wedge it among the elaborate coppices and ornamentations of the stone fireplace; far from it. The trouble was that the smoke from the fire tended to fog the mirror and make the successive reflections blurry; and when there was no fire on the grate at all then no image could form, for it was too dark. But at last, one morning when the cleaners were clanging and rearranging the soot, she managed to spot a hidden recess offering an angle that not only gave her a smokeless view, but included the chair where Hezene was accustomed to sit, one adorned with a special perch for Byrd and Chee, the emperor's favourite pair of Speakers.

Liaku liked Chee. Byrd's mate seldom spoke (and when she did her observations about people were dead wrong), and never did anything useful, spending her days grooming herself and studying her own reflection in Hezene's black stone mirrors. But when she was in the mood, she could sing like a sunset over Kierse – a rare talent in a Speaker, especially a female. And she was beautiful, her feathers the deep molten colour of true gold except for striking turquoise wingtips and a red throat. Beauty was not a coinage Liaku herself possessed, and so she valued it all the more when she saw it in others. Anyway, beauty would be only a burden to Liaku, who was obscurely proud of her smallness, her anonymity. It was all she had, and it served her in the incessant scramble for crumbs up here in the paper city.

Besides, the flamboyance of Hezene's palace soaked into her on sight. She didn't have to own it to appreciate it, and her view on its splendours was unique, for she could look right into the imperial home.

Hezene himself was not splendid to see, especially in private. Liaku thought he looked like a dried footprint in silt. His edges were sharp and there were sculpted shadows about his cheekbones and eyes, as if he was already mostly a memory even to himself. He was small, lean, and strangely inquisitive for all that he kept his eyes half closed as a sign that what transpired within was more important than any crisis his subjects could design. Beside him his retinue of female attendants hovered, rounded and luscious like berries paled by mist and jewelled in dewdrops. Their sheer clothes barely hid the darkness of their nether parts, the pale colours accenting the sultry shine of their eyes. He touched the women only a little but loved to have them around, and they posed like dolphins in waves at sunset, unaware of themselves, thinking: *This is life. Flashing my breasts for the emperor is its substance. There is nothing more.* At least, this is what Liaku imagined they thought, and what a luxury it must be! But Hezene confided only in Byrd.

'My friend,' he said to the Speaker, 'Everien sits on my mind like the pit of a fruit remains in the gut. I cannot spit it out, I cannot break it down. I cannot even let it go.'

'The shit of the emperor is profound in all its manifestations,' remarked the Speaker. 'Can I help?'

'Am I doing the right thing by annexing Everien? I wonder sometimes whether I should go on this expedition myself. How else can I ensure that my will be done?' He snapped his fingers and one of the posing girls floated to his side with mincing steps. At a gesture from the emperor she slid the robes away from his shoulders and began kneading them, her fingers white and tiny on his ropy neck. Byrd watched her for a moment and then said diplomatically,

'Surely the messenger bird has not troubled the Lord of the Birds so much as all that! It is a matter of history, best left for the Scholars.'

'The injunction against using the Fire Houses is not a matter of history. You know as well as I do that Tash is using their secrets to beat the Sekk.'

'The message has not even been authenticated. No bird is old enough to have borne it for forty years, and anyone could have written the message. Probably it is a joke!'

Liaku's ears pricked. Byrd had not treated it as a joke with Lor . . . nor with Ral, dead as a consequence of merely having heard the contents of the message. Was the emperor's own Speaker lying to him?

'Some joke,' Hezene said darkly. There was a long silence. The girl who was massaging him carefully replaced the silk cowl that trailed down his shoulders. She moved to his feet and presently began sucking his toes.

Byrd puffed his feathers and shook. 'Anyway, has no one thought to ask how came an Everien skyfalcon to Jundun, when its home is surely Jai Khalar and that is where it was sent?'

'The Scholars had better answer that one,' Hezene declared, throwing his head back and closing his eyes as the pale-skinned youth placed the sole of his foot on her bare breast and began massaging oil into the skin of the arch. 'Or they do not earn their bread and wine. Yet I cannot wait for their analysis before I proceed.'

'It is winter in Everien,' Byrd remarked. 'A long, bitter winter.'

'Indeed, and I wish to possess that country on the quickening of another spring. I have waited long enough. I spent ten years slowly building the garrison at Ristale and opening trade routes with Lerien, hoping to walk through the front door and take the place easily. And yet, on the eve of my attack, my garrison was overwhelmed!'

'But the Clans did not do this act,' Byrd said. 'The Sekk did.'

'Still, my plans were all for nothing, for then Tash, whom I loved and hoped to make a prince of, Tash seized his opportunity to get Jai Khalar – and who can blame him? Were I a young hothead I might have done the same.'

'He did it in your name, Great One.'

'Ah, but he slew my officers, the ones who returned alive from the Floating Lands. He said he could not trust those who had once been Enslaved. But they had recovered, the Company of Glass was gone, and what more can he require of an army other than that they follow commands? Already he speaks like a Clansman!'

'He is a barbarian's son from Or,' Byrd suggested.

Hezene snorted. 'So they say, and I once knew the man he calls Father. Well, it's true that the horses are strong in him. I must rein him in. Everien will get out of hand too easily with Tash in charge; this I read in the attitude of the Clans. In Lerien I encouraged the civilizing influence, tried to court him to our ways, but since this last visitation of Jai Pendu the old ways of the Clan are returning, and soon there will be anarchy. This does not suit my purposes. I have no choice but to send a large force to tame Everien. If I lose Tash in the process, this is a price I must pay.' Yet his tone made it plain that he was not satisfied with his own rhetoric. He waved at the servant girl and she flitted away, taking her bowl of oil with her.

'Tash may be glad enough of help.'

'Or he may fancy himself king already.'

'A king among the Sekk,' said Byrd. 'Who would desire such a burden?'

Hezene fell into another brooding silence. Liaku moved closer to the mirror, trying to see him better. He was slouched in his chair, skeletal within the heavy robes sewn with silver and gold. Nearby on her perch Chee was busily grooming her left underwing. Hezene stirred. 'The Sekk can reach us, even here. This Night has shown us. And such an even-tuality must be prevented, however distant it now seems. But I don't trust Tash to remain subordinate. He is dangerous, no matter what I do with him. I know I should try to win Tash to my side, use him to control the Sekk and let him shoulder that responsibility – but I am uneasy to give him so much, lest he take it and run away with it.'

'Who else is strong enough to subdue the Clans?'

'Lerien was not, as even Sendrigel came to see. But it isn't the Clans who worry me, it is the Knowledge of the Fire Houses. Whence came this Everien skyfalcon, I ask you again? Has one been seen anywhere in living memory? They are extinct in Everien, yet this one arrives here, almost at the same time as this strange message which you tell me to ignore.'

'I did not make a connection between the two,' Byrd said, and Liaku sensed that he was lying. 'What is Your Brightness suggesting? This humble Speaker does not understand.'

'I'm suggesting that maybe Tash is experimenting with the Knowledge and has somehow revived this antique bird from the remains of Everien. If that is so, then the sooner I establish control of Jai Khalar, the better. Yet I cannot simply invade, or he will fight me. He is a warrior, not a statesman.'

'He is a man,' said Chee suddenly.

Hezene laughed. 'Yes,' he said. 'Yes, Chee, he is a man. I will have to think on this.'

He left the room then and the two birds looked at each other but did not speak. Liaku sat debating with herself whether to venture off and look for the skyfalcon elsewhere in the palace, or whether to stay and learn more from the emperor. In light of what had happened to Ral, she decided to stay, and her patience was rewarded when Hezene retreated to his sitting room for a light meal and a nap. When he woke he said to Byrd, 'I have made up my mind what to do. Send for Ukili.'

Byrd flew off, and a little while later a beautiful girl slipped into view of the mirror. Liaku almost cried out in pain that anyone should be gifted with such looks. Chee stopped grooming herself and made a jealous chattering noise, shifting closer to Byrd's empty perch.

Ukili's eyes were the colour of polished bronze, deep and subtly shiny and a little surprising in the context of her pale, olive-shaded skin. Her face was a perfect oval, and her lips swelled like flower petals. The haughty curve of her nostrils reminded Liaku of a stallion she had once seen, trained in some extraordinary way to stand on his hind legs and hop like a dancer. Ukili's waist was slender and long, but her form was full and her breasts mirrored the firm mounds of her buttocks such that her young body appeared to be exempt from the law of gravity. Gold dust had been scattered on her cheekbones and collarbones. She smiled gently at her father.

'My daughter,' said Hezene. 'I have a job for you.'

There was a pregnant pause. Liaku saw the flare of the girl's nostrils as she braced herself for what her father was about to say. Hezene, obviously accustomed to taking his time to say what he wanted to say, scratched his head in a leisurely manner and drummed the arm of his chair with the fingers of his left hand before suddenly announcing,

'You are going to be wed to Tash, whom I shall make Prince of Everien. I have prepared troops to send to Everien to secure it from the

Sekk and make it part of our empire once and for all. Were the matter less urgent I might summon Tash here and give you a royal wedding with all the splendour that Jundun can display; but times are troubled in Everien, and the matter cannot wait until Tash has fully settled into power. He will only do so once wed to you and secure in his position with us. I do not expect you to understand this, but you will comply with it.'

'It is my honour and privilege to offer myself and my life for any need of the emperor's.'

Rat tails, thought Liaku. *He's sending his daughter into a war zone as a trophy. What a fink.*

'To ensure your safety I shall send with you a personal guard who is to be your servant and advisor in all things. Shiror is his name, and he is trained in all the arts of war and statesmanship. He has assisted me greatly in establishing Pharician ways among the barbarians of Aranoka and he is experienced in civilian administration. He has recently returned from duty in Kierse, where he excelled at putting down a slave rebellion.'

Liaku noticed that Byrd was now grooming Chee with an almost manic intensity. She wondered what he was so nervous about.

The emperor continued, 'You may put your trust in Shiror. I know you have little experience of men, especially soldiers, but Shiror will never lay a hand on you. He is not that way inclined, do you understand?'

The girl nodded. 'I thank my father for his generosity and marvel at the grace that offers me this chance to serve him.'

'It will be cold in Everien,' said the little man, pantomiming a shiver within his metal-heavy robes. 'They do not have the same amenities you have known all your life. But Jai Khalar is said to be a wondrous place. Byrd has been there, have you not, my friend?'

'I hatched there,' said Byrd quietly, looking up from Chee's wing that he had been combing with his beak. 'Princess Ukili will live in the highest castle in the world, and she will See all Everien from its Eye Tower.'

Ukili smiled and looked at the floor.

'You will leave in two days,' Hezene said. 'Therefore—'

'Two days?' Her head shot up and then her hand went to her mouth to check the inadvertent outburst. She blushed.

'It is enough time to gather the essentials, and you can send for the rest later when it is clear to you what you will need in your new home. You may select three girls to bring with you for companionship. Choose those who will be useful to you in practical ways, those who are levelheaded and strong. Once you are settled you may have more in

48

your court, but there may be danger in the early days and Shiror should not be asked to be accountable for too many. Now, if there is anything you wish to ask me, ask it now, for I will be too busy after this. Do you wish any special favours before you go?'

Ukili gathered herself, shifted her weight a little, leaned forward in her chair. Liaku admired her sandals' golden thongs that passed between shapely toes with their nails painted pale green. Ukili even had lovely feet.

'Can I bring my cat, Sheerwater?'

Byrd bobbed his head uneasily from side to side but said nothing.

'I think that a military expedition is unsuitable for a lap cat, child. However, I had it in my mind to send with you one of my very own birds, as your companion and helper, and to remind you that the thoughts of your father the emperor go with you everywhere.'

Ukili caught her breath.

Hezene held up his finger and Chee flew to it.

'She is my most favourite darling,' he said, and held out his hand to Ukili. 'She will Speak my blessing over you at your wedding, hear your thoughts, dress your hair, sing any song you command, and be a friend to you.'

Now he turned to Byrd.

'Do you have the list of Scholars?'

Byrd brought him a scroll in his beak and Hezene read it. 'Bast. Kan Qika. Wakhe and Yanse. Kodol Sen. Akiva. And of course, our friend Evra Kiss. Byrd, this is a long list. You were to choose only five.'

'We will strike Kan Qika, then,' said Byrd.

'Why not strike Wakhe and Yanse, since the one always goes with the other. Surely a mathematician is not needed – particularly one that no one can communicate with.'

'I beg Your Brightness,' Byrd said. 'Kan Qika is a special friend of mine, and I will pine enough without my mate Chee. Do not take them both!'

The emperor sighed and stroked Byrd's comb. 'I cannot refuse you when you put it to me this way. Very well. Kan Qika stays, Wakhe goes.'

Not long after this audience, the Speakers left the palace together. Liaku tracked them to Lor's courtyard, where Chee alternated singing with mournful complaints about her situation.

'Lor, why does he send me away? I trusted you, and I served the emperor always. I thought never to leave his side. Now he sends me to a cold land where my kind never go. I will freeze. My beak will fall off.'

Lor pursed his fat lips and said nothing. Byrd ducked his head under his wing and gave a musical moan.

'He trusts you, Chee,' Lor said. 'This is a matter where he should trust no one, but he trusts you. What do you know about this expedition?'

Byrd answered the question. 'It is to bring Tash into line and secure control of the Everien Knowledge.'

'Who commands it?'

'Evra Kiss is the leader in name, but since he is only a Scholar, Shiror is being sent to guard Ukili.'

'The emperor is up to something here. Kiss is just an administrator, an organizer – all mouth, that's why he was given the name. Shiror . . . an interesting choice.'

'Never mind that, Lor. I am losing my mate. It is the ultimate test of loyalty to the emperor.'

'Ah, now. Of course you must obey the emperor. Tell me, though, for I am curious. Who else is being sent, aside from the soldiers?'

'There are a number of Scholars.'

'Scholars? Which ones?'

'Bast. Kodol Sen. Akiva. Wakhe and Yanse.'

'Wakhe? You must be joking. He will wither in the sunlight. He can't tie his own sandals.'

'There will be attendants and helpers.'

'But why? Ah, Byrd, your judgment surprises me. Wakhe.'

'I heard he is a cripple,' said Chee.

'He is less than a cripple, fluffy one. He's a simpleton, barely able to tolerate a loud noise without going into a catatonia. He can't speak, he can barely dress himself, and when he's upset he pisses in his robes like an old man.'

'But he is a Scholar, they say!' Chee said. Liaku thought she would have said more, but Byrd actually closed his beak over hers to shut her up!

'Ah. He is,' answered Lor, not seeming to notice. 'He communicates by a unique tapping language that only his intimate handlers and a few other Scholars can understand.' Lor rubbed his chin thoughtfully.

'Then what good is he? Why let him live, let alone make him a Scholar?'

'Because he's good at puzzles. If you give him any kind of a pattern or riddle or mathematical dilemma, he can solve it. Instantly. Seen him do it a thousand times, when I was a boy and he was a boy and I used to go on my information-gathering rounds.'

Chee fluffed her feathers and wrinkled her enormous forehead. 'Tapping language?' she said, pecking lightly at the back of the chair. 'Like this?'

'Yes, I suppose,' mused Lor, deep in thought. 'So he will go all the way to Everien. To solve a puzzle. And they say Tash lives now in an invisible castle, where there is an artifact of Glass from Jai Pendu. Chee, if I were younger and had wings like you, I would envy you. I have always wanted to look on Everien.'

'You can don furs and drink hot wine. I shall freeze solid,' said Chee miserably. 'What will I do without my mate? I know I am not so intelligent as Byrd. I know Hezene loves me only for my song. This is all too hard for me. When you tamed me you told me I would always be well kept. I have served him well in my way. I don't understand why I have to go.'

Lor sighed. 'Because the emperor decrees it,' he said sadly. 'Who knows what his true reason may be?'

'I just remembered I have an urgent errand. I must go,' Byrd said suddenly. 'Lor, comfort her if you can. I will return shortly.'

Operating on her habits, Liaku quickly left the Imperial Zone lest she be caught by the Air Police. They were fumbletons most of the time, but it didn't do to tempt fate. She crawled quickly toward the south side of the city, the side overlooking the Khynahi Mountains and the desert sky. There the painted lands to the south lay as distant and powerful as dreams, their red-and-green sculpted outline rending the blue sky as sharp as a blade.

If Liaku were a skyfalcon, she would go there. She would never go near a place like Jundun with its stink of humans and its traps and alleys.

'Quiz, you mystery,' she said to herself, still gazing dreamily on the mountains. 'Why you come here? Why drop bird to me? Why go to palace, get caught? Why, Quiz?'

There was something sad and strange about it, and Liaku did not like to think of the skyfalcon, who was better than anything, locked up as another imperial possession.

She picked herself up and returned to the palace.

There was the message in the reception room. From Byrd to Se, it read: *I fix everything. Target Yanse. You become Yanse. Wakhe go Everien. Two birds, one stone. Repeat: Target Yanse. Tonight!*

Liaku climbed up the side of the guard tower and slipped onto a tongue of chala. Byrd had been very coy, she thought. *He* had recommended Wakhe for the expedition. And he had done it to satisfy Se, so that Se would go after Yanse. *You become Yanse.* That, Liaku thought, would surely be difficult. She really didn't understand the point of any of it.

Then she looked up and did a double-take. The guard tower had windows on every wall, and sitting on the open sill looking out calmly into the murky gold of Byrdland was the skyfalcon Quiz. When Liaku slipped from the main structure of chala to a support strut and then arrayed herself on the side of the tower itself, splayed out flat with her fingers gripping the stone, the skyfalcon did not stir. Panting and sweating, she inched up the side of the tower until her fingers could hold the lip of the windowsill. Then she dragged herself onto her elbows and addressed the bird, her two eyes to its one eye in profile – for they never looked at you square on if they really wished to see you.

'Quiz, what you do here? Why no you leave? Look, the mountains! Why you come to this bad place?'

It was not like Liaku to be so emotional. Nor did she consider the unwiseness of the bullying tone she used with the animal, who was much bigger than she, and well equipped to do her harm, even through the iron bars. Yet the bird's response was not hostile. It was . . . again, it was a questioning response, as if the bird were putting hooks into her mind and seeking some hidden information about her. Liaku felt tears in her eyes and she couldn't understand why.

'You must leave,' she hissed urgently. 'Fly away! They use you if you let them! Go home.' Quiz opened his beak and hissed like a snake. Liaku shrank back, frightened.

'I only try to help you. Stupid bird. Listen, they gonna put you in cage, and then you very sorry, Quiz.'

The skyfalcon just sat there, ensconced in his voluntary captivity. Liaku thought: *Ral is dead, Yanse is a target, and Lor knows I heard the message, even if he doesn't know that Quiz brought it. How long have I got to live?*

It was time to move her stashes and change nests. But when she went to the nest, which was not far from Lor's place, the Air Police were already there, rifling through her possessions with their clever beaks and claws. She retreated silently the way she had come, wondering what had happened to Chal and what she should do about her other locations. She was wondering who had informed on her when she glimpsed a tiny peacock feather, and then another, making a trail from her nest. The Zu brothers, she thought. They were her rivals for the best peacock feathers in the Imperial Gardens, and they had probably seen her hanging around the palace, and informed on her.

'Ha! I get rid of mitebags,' Liaku muttered. Just because she was preoccupied with other business, she didn't want the Zu brothers to think she was out of the feather game. So she gambolled over the top layer of chala, the weathered and shit-stained over-roof of Jundun. She galloped in quick bursts with a monkey's gait, reaching down and stooping from time to time to gather black crane shit, the explosive of choice for shitbombs. When she had got as much as she could carry, she slithered no-hands down a pole to one of her secondary nests. Quickly she dismantled the booby traps that guarded it, and then under the store of seeds and dried pomegranates she found her stack of boom-glue. She shaped the crane shit into a rough ball, embedding a knob of boom-glue in the centre and threading the sticky sap through and around the loosely packed shit, weighting the whole package down with a couple of rotten eggs. Crane shit was not the most violent explosive you could imagine, but the main purpose of a shitbomb was to cause olfactory distress. Liaku didn't have time to get fancy by adding sulphur or other exotic volatiles.

She raced back toward her destination, the nest of the Zu brothers, flitting through the late afternoon golden light as it filtered through chala. Byrdland looked like a giant irregular honeycomb filled with pale amber delights, and the beating of Liaku's heart, her breathing and foot patter and the erratic flickering of bamboo shadows over her face as she ran, would later return to her, evoked by the rhythms of Wakhe and his strange and secret speech.

When she passed Lor's house, she could see through a gap in the chala that he had guests awaiting him in the street. She paused, cradling the shitbomb. Decisions. To settle the score with the Zu brothers or to spy on Lor? A difficult choice.

When she observed that the men were extremely rich, she decided to stay. They wore velvet caps and exotic feathers. One's mouth flashed gold when he smiled, and another wore dangling sapphire earrings. Lor welcomed them effusively. Liaku carefully shadowed them from above as they sat for tea in the garden. Lor was laughing and talking too much. She watched the four men arrange their cups and plates and perceived a code. She did not know the meaning of the gestures, but the principle of object positioning to express an encoded thought was no different here than in the palace reception room where Byrd and Se had their secret 'talks'.

Her suspicions were confirmed when Tol on Lor's shoulder contributed to the conversation at one point by adding an extra lump of sugar to the leader's tea with his beak.

'I doubt your information is as sweet as all that,' said the man to Lor, leaning back and relaxing, and Liaku sensed that some secret test had been passed by Lor. 'Still, we are happy to hear what you know of Tyger Pass.'

Uh-oh, thought Liaku. *They are the Circle, and Lor is going to spill to them about me and Quiz. Does that mean Lor is Circle, or only kissing them?*

Lor fiddled with his rings and said, 'It is in Everien, is it not?'

Kissing, Liaku decided.

'Yes, it is in Everien,' said the leader. 'Now, what of it? For I may have a proposition for you.'

'My information,' Lor said, 'tells me that there was to be some tryst between Ysse and Eteltar in Tyger Pass. As I know that both of these historical figures are of critical importance in the history of the Knowledge and its recovery, I thought it might be of some interest to your Scholars. It means nothing to me, of course.'

'What kind of tryst?' said the most reserved of the three, leaning forward gracefully.

'Perhaps tryst is the wrong word. I believe that Eteltar had something to tell Ysse – or perhaps something to give her. And it is not the first time his name has been mentioned in connection with Tyger Pass. Some believe he kept a stronghold there, or a retreat of some kind.'

'Your information is vague,' said the leader, taking in the others with his eyes. 'In fact, we may well be ahead of you.'

'Oh?'

'My associates and I have been dealing with a man in Seahawk, and he promised us an item of great antiquity which he had found in Tyger Pass. We sent a team to collect it and they have not returned. Now, what we require is a highly skilled spy bird to fly there and determine for us what has transpired.'

'Ah,' said Lor, placing his chin in one cupped palm and ruminating for several seconds. Liaku's bomb was slowly disintegrating in her hands. If it went off here, it would blow a hole through several layers of chala and would not only destroy her best spy position on Lor, but probably pollute his fountain as well and certainly arouse his suspicions of her. Liaku's black crane bombs were widely imitated but none could duplicate her signature smell, of which she was inordinately proud. She hesitated.

'Let me come to the point,' the rich man was saying. 'What are the chances of stealing the emperor's skyfalcon and using it for reconnaissance?'

Liaku stayed rooted to the spot. Steal Quiz? *Use* Quiz?

'None whatsoever,' Lor said firmly, shaking his head. Liaku breathed a sigh of relief.

'Why not?' snapped the rich man. 'Se thinks it can be done.'

'Se is a rogue . . . er, begging your pardon,' Lor said. 'Fel Brekk, Linz, Guel—'

'Shh!' said the leader. 'No names, fat man!'

'*Gentlemen,*' Lor corrected smoothly. 'Gentlemen – you know that I am the emperor's loyal subject. You know that our conversation therefore has certain . . . limitations.'

'Yes, yes,' said the nobleman impatiently. 'And?'

'And even if I were interested in abetting such an escapade, I doubt it could be done. The skyfalcon was a wild bird. It could not be tamed. It could not be controlled. And, frankly, it was a dangerous animal, unpredictable and vicious.'

'Money is no object,' the third man was chiming in.

'You need more than reconnaissance by bird,' Lor said. He proceeded to tell them about the message.

Liaku's time was up. If she didn't go now, she would give herself away. She shot off through the chala, dumping the bomb in the nick of time and then fleeing the stench that rose from the Zu brothers' primary nest. That would teach them to turn her in to the Air Police.

She worked through the permutations of the conversation she had overheard as she climbed toward the guard tower where Quiz was. And suddenly a voice said,

'Hello, Liaku.'

She stopped and there was Byrd, sitting on a crosspiece of the chala. 'So, you think to get a look at the skyfalcon. What I would like to know is how you know about him. And why you talk to him, and what he says back to you.'

'I know nothing!' Liaku protested, rolling her eyes in an expression of stupidity.

'You are one of Lor's helpers. Don't play dumb, Liaku. You know something. This skyfalcon seems to recognize you. Have you befriended it? Did it meet you before it came here? Come, you can tell us. We are byrdkind. We can help you.'

Liaku didn't know what he meant by 'we', and she didn't trust anyone, byrdkind or humankind. 'I never see him before.'

'That's funny. Because Ral told us that Liaku gave him the message from Eteltar to Ysse, and that it had been taken from a dead flier. So we have followed you, you see.'

She knew what this meant. Liaku clamped her legs together and willed her bladder not to release. In a shaking voice she confessed, 'Skyfalcon kill flier. That all I know. I take flier to Ral. That all.'

'Why did you come here, then?'

She shut her mouth and looked down.

'Liaku, answer me! Why are you here? Who are you working for?'

'No one! I not working.'

'Then why are you here?' repeated Byrd insistently. She held the words in, imagining herself saying them, but not saying them. 'Liaku!'

At last she blurted, 'I want to set him free. He no like cage.'

'He flew into it willingly. Skyfalcons are not easy to catch unless they want to be caught.'

'What they do to him?' she demanded.

55

'That remains to be seen. Now, about your life.'

'No kill me! I good spy. I help you.'

'Do you know who we are?'

'You Speakers, emperor's favourite. I know that.'

'And have you heard of the Circle?' The eye Byrd fixed her with was not human. Byrd's purposes were inscrutable. She didn't know what to say.

'Scholars.' She licked her lips nervously. 'The Circle Scholars. And . . .' She swallowed as the implications began to hit her. 'And killers.'

'Not just killers. Assassins. Join us, and you will always have our protection, wherever in the world you go. You may even get some of our Magic. Oppose us and we will kill you.'

Byrd was a member of the Circle! But Hezene had outlawed the Circle. They were a secret society; so secret that they could only recognize each other by a series of ever-changing signs transmitted by fingers in a handshake, or the wearing of a scarf in a certain fashion, or the subtle particulars of drinking tea. Belatedly Liaku understood that this was what Byrd and Se had been doing when they communicated in the reception room. Therefore Se was part of it too. And what about Chee? Her brain whirled. What about Lor?

She realized Byrd was expecting her to reply.

'What you want Liaku do?' she asked, thinking of her inventory of treasures and wondering if she had enough to buy her escape. A word in the ear of the Imperial Air Police and she would be the quarry in a hunt within a matter of hours.

'You will provide to us a number of your own birds, ones who will return only to you. They must be strong fliers, hardy for the winter, and totally loyal.'

'I can do,' Liaku said. A little belligerently she added, 'No need threaten Liaku. I do it for you anyway, ask nicely and pay.'

'But you will keep your mouth shut, Liaku, on pain of death. Your creativity and intrepid nature have served you well so far. But you work for the Circle now. You will not get creative with us. You will follow instructions precisely and never speak of it to anyone. Do you understand?'

'Yeah, yeah. Understand. How many bird you want?'

'Twenty.'

'I get twelve, no problem. Twenty, forget it.'

'Twelve is not enough. Do not bother trying to bargain. You will deliver twenty before dawn. Leave them at the fishmonger's in the bazaar – he is there early, when few are about, so you may descend without penalty.'

Liaku shook her head, terrified. 'Liaku no set foot on ground until Down Day! Death is punishment.'

'You will pose as a proper little girl. The garments you will wear are already stored under a paving stone beside the fountain in Lor's courtyard. Fetch them tonight, and clean yourself up while you are about it. Then you will go to the skylight on the roof of the Scholars' building and await my signal. Do not make a sound, and do not let anyone observe you. When your task is done, you will proceed to the fishmonger's before dawn and deliver the birds.'

'What if Lor catch me?'

'Lor has been warned to sleep deeply tonight.'

Liaku looked him square on. 'You kill Ral. Why no kill Liaku?'

'Because, runt, you could be useful. But don't give me cause to regret my decision, or I'll change my mind.'

Liaku swallowed. 'Which paving stone?'

Seahawk

Everyone has something they don't talk about. If you're lucky, no one knows what it is and you can sidestep its existence. If you're unlucky, it follows you. You don't speak of it because this thing, whatever it is, made you look over the edges of words and their meanings, and you saw the abyss that lies beyond – and that was enough for you. You backed away quickly and shut up. Everyone does. It's how we live.

Istar never spoke of the seahawk. She had not forgotten her ancestor totem screaming from the sunshattered heavens – whether trying to harm her or warn her she would never know, for she had slain it with one joyous, perfect swordstroke, in Jai Pendu in a high place inhabited by nothing. She was famous now, but not for what she had *really* done at Jai Pendu – not for the secret act of killing that would always haunt her. She was famous for her visible deeds: breaking up the stalemate between Night and Tarquin and taking the Company of Glass away from Jai Pendu, its prisoners finally released to rout Night's host of Slaves. She was also famous for who she was: daughter of Chyko, the wild Animal warrior and prisoner of the Glass, and Mhani, High Seer of Everien who had lost her mind when, roving the Liminal seeking the White Road, she had Seen too much. And finally Istar was famous because she was an Honorary like Ysse, Everien's first and only queen, pledged to a warrior's life in the absence of a male protector in her own family – because the man who should have been her guardian was Tarquin the Free, lawless and Clanless, his freedom purchased with the coinage of her femininity. Tarquin was gone now, vanished in the magic waters around Jai Pendu as it retreated from the world. All she had of him was the Clan he had adopted her into and then abandoned; the Clan whose Animal ways were meant to define and guide her; the Clan whose moniker *tar* she carried within her own name. Tar . . . Seahawk . . . it was a word which aroused a mixture of difficult emotions in her. Even though no one had witnessed what she had done in Jai Pendu in the tower called The Way of the Sun, Istar knew what she had done. The seahawk she had killed never left her memory.

Now, when she looked up and saw the great wings silhouetted against a searingly blue October sky, she felt her throat close, and she went still.

It had come for her.

The bird was a tiny grey blip in a landscape both immense and acutely colourful. The sky was reflected in the waters of Fivesisters Lake, bitingly blue against the surreal, molten red of the maple leaves spectacularly dying on the shore. The bright trees were contrasted by a dark march of firs guarding the high ground to their backs, where snow already sugared the bare stones above the treeline. Even the peaks were dominated by the intense autumn blue where the bird floated, far from its ocean home in the East. The sky was a stillness undisturbed by cloud or creature – except for the seahawk.

Istar kept her eyes on its long, curving descent as all the while her body reacted to its imminent arrival: her heart began to race, her belly tightened inside, and sweat burst out under her arms and between her legs.

It was too late to hide. Even if the bird had not seen her yet, it had surely seen the camp. Her men had pitched their tents on an open hillside where fire had cut a wide swath through the trees. Long grass and scrub had begun to recover the ground, but it was an exposed place and one chosen deliberately in hope of baiting the Sekk that Istar knew to be hunting in these parts. There were Snake lodges down at Fivesisters Lake – once a thriving if rustic community, now decimated by the constant attrition of the Slaving. The Sekk seemed to ooze from some unknown source in the cave-riddled hills hereabouts, Slaving their way from village to village until they reached the more thickly populated regions of Everien within the central valley. Xiriel was convinced the Sekk came from a cave described by Hallen of the Bear Clan, who spoke of an underground lake with floating lights, and beautiful faces inside the lights.

Istar and Xiriel had been looking for this cave since early summer, combing the hills and exterminating any Sekk they found; but they had yet to locate the source. Now, with winter drawing in, they were under pressure to complete their mission. A week ago they had been called to a meeting of the Clan rebels in Wasp Country, where the next stages in the ongoing resistance to Pharician rule would be set; but they had agreed to make one last push to find the cavern before departing Snake Country. It had been Xiriel's idea to make their camp visible from the peaks, in the hope that if they acted as bait, they might flush out the Sekk and trace them back to their subterranean origin. So far, the humans had been alone except for the foxes and bears gathering their winter stores, with nothing to remind them of Pharice or the war or the Knowledge of Everien.

Here came the seahawk. Its glide took it past the camp's tents at the edge of the wood and across a small stream. Shading her eyes with one hand, Istar held up her other arm for the bird to land. In a rush, the impression came back to her: the impossibly strong sun, the bird diving at her out of the light, seeking to rip out her eyes and throat; the fear that had made her thrust her sword into its body and, with it still impaled on her blade, fall into the chaos within Jai Pendu. Here in the ordinary world, it was all she could do to hold her arm steady. The seahawk was eyeing her sidelong as it tilted its body back, its five-foot wingspan casting a shadow over her like a cloak. In a smooth movement it transferred the package it carried from its talons to its beak so that its feet could grasp her forearm; even through the tough leather of her braces she felt the claws bite.

The bird weighed a fraction of what its size suggested. Istar lowered her arm and it shifted toward her elbow, making its weight easier to bear. Cautiously she brought her left hand toward its head and it surrendered the message. Then, pressing down on her arm, it launched itself up again, winging a short distance to the nearest tree, an aspen sapling, where it perched rather unsteadily on a slender branch.

Istar let her breath go out. In those fleeting moments when the bird had been close to her, Istar's fear and guilt had been driven away by the sheer thrill of communicating with something so wild. She shivered, for the first time in a long time thinking that the Seahawks truly were a great Clan, and feeling proud to carry their name even though she was really only an outbreed. Then she opened the message.

To Istar, daughter of Quintar, Honorary
From Hiltar, Grandmother Seahawk

It is my sadness to tell you Ranatar is dead. Your sisters now reside with Ostar, half-sister to Quintar, who will marry them to her sons if she is not prevented. By law you are their guardian until they are wed. Also the fortunes of Equitar and Mintar, good and ill, now pass from Ranatar to you. I most urgently advise you to mind your duties at home. Grietar is ambitious.

Seahawk daughter, I have never called you back before. I do so now, for your own sake and your sisters'.

May she fly well and find you swiftly.

Hiltar

Istar read the note four times. She touched her face where she used to wear the Clan paint, and now didn't; for the rebels had agreed to carry no family markers in case of capture by the Pharicians. Ranatar. Tarquin's sister, herself childless, had raised Lyntar and Pietar almost from birth, and Istar herself had had much care from her during her early childhood, before she had been sent to Jai Khalar for military training. Ranatar had been more of a mother to her than Mhani, even though technically Ranatar had been under Istar's protection since Istar had come of age as an Honorary male. Istar had never worried about Ranatar before, thinking her well guarded at A-Tar-Ness, where the broader circles of the family resided, Grandmother Hiltar among them. Istar's immediate family were a barren lot: Tarquin had no children that were known, Ranatar's had died with her mate of winterfever some years back, and the other offspring of Mintar and Equitar had not lived to adulthood.

Istar's thoughts began to race. Hiltar's note was urgent but vague. The Grandmother was no alarmist. What was Grietar up to? Who would look after her sisters' honour? They were yet children, only fourteen by her reckoning. In the past Mhani had exercised some influence over Ranatar, who had sympathized with the Deer woman's plight in losing her children to another Clan; but now Mhani was out of her wits, and living in Pharician-occupied territory besides.

The hawk's head swivelled toward a gap in the trees above the camp, and Xiriel emerged with two other men, one carrying a pair of wood pigeons over his shoulder. Behind came Pentar carrying a load of firewood on his back. He was the first to spot the seahawk, and his head came up abruptly. He said something to Xiriel and the Seer halted.

In the two years since the passing of Jai Pendu, Xiriel had maintained the shaven head and overall presentation of the Snake Clan even though he had not renounced his status as a Wolf, nor been acknowledged as a Snake. Because he was a Seer as well as a rebel, he could get away with this indeterminate stance, passing it off as a camouflage tactic; but Istar thought that, like her, he was really just confused. Now he took a look at her and then came on, his body moving with an effortless precision granted by hard living. He had made up for all those sedentary years of Scholarship by roughing it with the rebels, and it showed. Alongside him came Pentar, sweating with exertion, his black braids slapping his cheeks. Pentar nodded his respect to the seahawk messenger as he passed, then dumped the wood on the ground outside one of the tents and jogged to catch up with Xiriel.

Istar's gaze had returned to the message. It was easier to look at the scroll than at Xiriel's probing eyes.

'News,' he said, making it a statement, not a question.

'I have to go to Seahawk.' She looked at him then.

'Now? The convocation at A-vi-Sirinn . . .'

'It's my sisters. They are without protection or advocate, and my Grandmother has summoned me.'

Xiriel's exasperation at family matters showed in his face. 'Can no one else stand for you?'

She shook her head. 'Quintar's line is not a strong one. They are rare creatures, the true Seahawks.' She knew that irony coloured her tone, for she was half Wasp, half Deer: both prolific Clans that, in Pallo's words, 'bred like bunnies in summer'. Yet she owed her allegiance to the Seahawks, and Xiriel knew perfectly well that she could not refuse such a summons. Not from Grandmother Hiltar.

'Never mind that now,' Xiriel said, waving a hand dismissively. 'I have news! Jakse has found the cave.'

'The cave?'

'The cave, Istar! The lake of candles! If his description is right, the location would gybe with the last two Sekk we've tracked through this area. It would also match Hallen's description of the lake of candles.'

On any other occasion, Istar would have been almost as excited as Xiriel, who was obsessed with finding Hallen's cave, supposedly linked to the Floating Lands by some unknown mechanism of displacement. 'Great!' she said with an effort. 'But you can do that without me.'

'*What?* You are the best Sekk hunter we have,' Xiriel protested. 'You seem to sense where they will go and what they want.'

'And have no compunctions about killing them,' added Pentar. Istar met his dark eyes, thinking that Pentar would probably never get over having been Enslaved. She felt a cold thrill at the memory of her own encounters with the Sekk. At the knowledge that they had sung to her and she had slain them all the same. Istar might be an outbreed and a weakling compared to men, but her mind was good: keen like Mhani's, indomitable like Chyko's. It was her one great power, and even the murder of the Seahawk had not broken it. As long as there were Sekk, Istar would not be written off as a low-status Honorary.

'Istar, can't you understand what this means? We could exterminate the Sekk. If this cave is what I think it is, we could get rid of them once and for all.'

Exterminate the Sekk. That had been the guiding principle of her life since Istar was old enough to understand the meaning of the words. But so far it had proved an illusory goal – overambitious, to say the least.

She laughed. 'Xiriel, we are reduced to a handful of Clan warriors living in tents in the hills while the Sekk prey on our villages and the Pharicians rule our Knowledge. I cannot think of anything more unlikely than that we should suddenly develop the power to do what generations before us could not.'

'You don't understand the implications of finding this cavern, Istar. Think about it. The Sekk have to come from somewhere. They don't breed, their bodies disintegrate when they die, and yet they keep appearing.'

'Exactly right,' Istar said. 'How can you kill something that isn't alive? How can you get rid of something that isn't even really all there?'

Xiriel said, 'Remember the Floating Lands? Remember how a thing could be in one place and then in another for no reason? Remember how we were displaced? Remember how weird the Everien doors were?'

'How could I forget?'

'Well, what if the Sekk are using Everien doors to come and go? What if that's the key to their elusiveness?'

'You think they come from the Floating Lands?' Istar's brows knitted with the effort of understanding him.

'I don't know where they come from, but the fact that the Floating Lands exist must imply that there are doors where there don't seem to be doors.'

Istar said, 'I still don't see how this gets us any closer to extermination. I mean, I'm glad about the cave, but . . .'

'If the Sekk come from some other place, some hidden place, then they need a door by which to enter Everien. We know that they favour underground places, that they can lie in hibernation like bears, not for a season, but for years. And we know that they feed on human violence even though they are not violent themselves.'

He paused and Istar had the impression he had been distracted by another train of thought.

'Yes? Your point is?'

'But the main thing,' Xiriel continued, recovering the thread, 'they are usually found underground. We describe them as rising from the earth. What if we found the place they rise from? What if we found their door?'

'We could stop it up like a rabbit hole,' said Pentar quietly.

'Yes. We could destroy them before they could emerge.'

'How do you know there is only one place?' Istar asked.

'There could be more than one,' Xiriel conceded impatiently. 'But once we find one, it should be easier to find the rest. And then they cannot do as they do now: rise, have a killing spree, and then return unpunished to wherever they come from only to rise again when next the mood strikes them.'

'Xiriel. How do you propose to close the doors?'

The Seer shrugged. 'One problem at a time, my friend. But think of it! Everien without the Sekk!'

'I cannot think of it,' Istar said. 'My imagination will not stretch that far.'

'You must try harder, then. You have become such a pessimist of late.'

63

'Maybe. But it's no good finding the Sekk's doors if you can't close them.'

'Come on, Istar. Give me some credit,' Xiriel wheedled. 'You know I have a knack with Everien doors.'

There was a long silence. Eventually Pentar said, 'Istar is obviously preoccupied with matters in Seahawk. This is understandable.'

'Thank you,' Istar said. In truth a feeling of doom had come over her when she read the letter, although she didn't know why. Her sisters ought to be well protected, but she was unreasoningly afraid.

Diplomatically, Pentar continued. 'There is a convocation in A-vi-Sirinn, anyway. Xiriel, you cannot hope to close up all these doors, or use Istar in a relevant way, until after you have gone to the convocation and met with Kassien and the king.'

Xiriel didn't look happy.

'I still want Istar to be there when I go into this cave. Jakse was very impressed.'

Istar said, 'If it is what you think it is, there will be time enough to deal with it in the spring. When I have finished my business in Seahawk. Xiriel, do not tear me in two this way!'

'She's right,' Pentar said.

'Ever the stout Seahawk,' Xiriel grumbled in his direction. 'Very well. But if you will insist on going, you should make profit of the time and raise yourself an army while you are there. The Seahawks have long held themselves aloof, thinking their lands too inaccessible to be threatened by Pharice; but sooner or later the fear of displacement will pass and Hezene will send his ships up the coast.'

'I know it,' Istar said shortly.

'You must convince them to join us.'

Istar did not answer this directly. 'I have much to plan.'

'You will bring back an army, then? When I go to the convocation I will tell Kassien you intend to take them across Tyger Pass in the spring, and we can plan their disposition now. It will give us some leverage with the Snakes. They may be bolder in aiding us if they know they will have support from Seahawk at their backs. All the Clans must contribute if we are to drive away Tash.'

Istar was looking at the seahawk, and it at her. Xiriel kept talking, reiterating plans for recovering more artifacts in the Floating Lands over the winter months and whining about the ineffectual espionage attempts of the Deer within A-vi-Khalar – for it burned Xiriel that he had lost the use of the Eyes and their ruler the Water of Glass, all of which were now controlled by Tash. She wasn't listening, but Xiriel had never been a keen enough student of human nature to perceive subtleties of emotion in other people. Pentar, however, snapped his fingers in her face.

'What else does the letter say?' he asked. 'They are all right, your sisters, are they not?'

Istar passed him the letter. 'I don't know. I'd better write a reply immediately. We will set off tomorrow.'

She said 'we' because she had long ago accepted Pentar's insistence on remaining by her side; it was dishonourable, Kassien told her, to do anything else. Sooner or later, she figured, Pentar would get bored of his bond and leave her for higher aspirations – for, unlike Kassien, Istar had not returned from Jai Pendu with ambitions of ruling Everien or winning herself renown, and Pentar could look forward to precious few perquisites for being attached to her. Still, he wasn't bad company, and in this case it couldn't hurt to have him tagging along with her, for he knew the customs and geography of Seahawk far better than she did.

'Good,' Pentar approved. 'For once you are doing the right thing. We will send a message to Hiltar to arrive at A-Tar-Ness ahead of us.'

And he held up his arm, summoning the seahawk Istar feared.

Poison Pass

Istar's best route to A-Tar-Ness from Snake Country would have been Tyger Pass, if it were summer. As it was, she and Pentar would have to ride southeast along a Snake Country valley until they came to a lower pass over the Everien Range – Poison Pass. Once across the mountains, they would be at the head of Poison Fjord, which they could traverse by ice sail until they came to the open sea. Then would come the journey up the largest of the Seahawk fjords, Tyger Fjord, to A-Tar-Ness. It was a long trip; but then again, once she was in A-Tar-Ness there would be no point in leaving until spring, so Istar did not entirely mind the delay.

Until Ysse had come along and pushed for the union of Everien, there had never been much contact between the Snakes and the Seahawks, even though the two Clans occupied adjacent territories in the northeast of Everien. This was largely because the Seahawks were sailors originally, not mountaineers, and therefore reluctant to venture across Tyger Pass, one of the few safe ways to cross the peaks to Snake Country. The Snakes, for their part, were reluctant to interact with the steel-armed Seahawks lest the latter begin to covet Snake Country, which included some fine highland grazing and rich forests – not to mention excellent hunting. The mountain range that extended north from Jai Khalar along the east coast of Everien and then curved slightly west at the terminus of the continent was essentially a no-man's-land, serving as hunting grounds for the boldest Seahawks, and in places tapped for mines by the Snakes and then abandoned, for the winters were too savage to support earthworks. Tyger Pass had only come into use a generation ago, when at Ysse's command Seahawk swords began to go west into Snake Country, and Snake medicines began to go east. Around this time the occasional Pharician supply train also ventured across, although usually the Pharicians restricted themselves to sea trade. Generally, though, the pass was closed eight months out of twelve, and even in summer it was no joy to traverse because of its altitude.

Poison Pass, by contrast, was an easy link between the sea and Snake Country, and snow blocked it only during the worst of the winter storms. It was little used as a trade route, however, because the waters of the fjord as well as most of the streams that fed it had been poisoned by leakage from the old Everien mineworks in the area. There was no fishing and an old Snake injunction ruled against farming; and because the Everiens had mined the area so thoroughly, the Snakes could not profit by excavating its minerals, either. Still, it was a way to get to Seahawk without marching past the survey of Jai Khalar. To be sure, there were Monitor Eyes in Poison Pass, but there were few Pharician troops in the area to obey any orders that came from Jai Khalar via the Eyes.

Istar liked mountains. She was not (like Kassien, who sometimes mistook himself for a goat) an expert climber; but she preferred the crags and crevices and ice shafts of the mountains to the stomach-turning, confining, smelly, unpredictable ocean. Nothing reminded her that she was not truly Seahawk like being in a boat.

They were a week on the road and at the base of Poison Pass when they came to a town where the Sekk had been. The incident was fresh, probably only hours old, but already the damage was done. Pentar saw it first.

'Why is there a pig in the middle of the road?' he asked innocently, a laugh crowding into his voice until he perceived that the pig was feeding on a human body lying by the roadside. Crows rose and fell in the wind.

They drew their weapons and led their ponies into the town, where more bodies and more marauding livestock met them. There was an unpleasant silence except for the sound of pig trotters on stone and the rattle of dry leaves in the gutters.

'Revenge of the pigs,' Istar said to herself as Pentar went off in another direction. She sidestepped an eager carnivorous sow. 'There will be no slaughterhouse for them.'

She had seen this too many times before. It would never be funny and she would never be able to laugh, but she made the comment anyway. The sight of the pigs and the crows feasting on the humans who would have otherwise consumed them imparted an earthliness and a kind of foolishness to a scene that was otherwise eerily without reason. In Istar's mind, nature in the form of the pigs was asserting itself upon an inherently unnatural event.

'It only just happened,' Pentar informed her, trotting down the steps that led from the town's one fortification, an old Everien storage tower adapted by the Clans for military use. 'Maybe it's even still going on.'

His face was white and there was blood on his boots, hands, and the knees of his trousers, but none on his weapon. He was breathing shallowly and his voice shook a little on the last phrase.

'What have you seen?'

'Their Pharician guardsman,' Pentar answered. 'Disembowelled and left to die. He told me it started with some children who went into the forest to gather fern.'

'Is he still conscious?'

'I cut his throat. He was in agony.'

Istar suppressed her annoyance at this news by chewing her lower lip. 'Which way did the children go to get this fern?'

He led her up the steps and pointed across an ancient, arching footbridge. Metal lions chased each other across its handrails, unworn even by so much time: Everien craft. 'Their tracks should be visible in the snow.'

'I'm going,' Istar said. 'Search the houses.'

She almost added, 'Be careful,' but didn't. She saw from Pentar's look that he understood the risks.

'As soon as it's clear I'll start a fire,' he said.

'Drug the survivors.'

He nodded. He knew.

Istar set off through the snow, which was only a light sugaring on the fallen leaves. The beeches overhead were still decorated with pendant gold leaves, and the late sun cut lazily through the forest in pale amber ribbons. The forest was white and gold as a festival cake, and she imagined the group of children racing through here only hours before. Their tracks scattered among the trees in erratic lines, converging and diverging as they played. She could see where they'd taken fern, and the drag marks where they'd hauled bundles of it back home. She couldn't see any tracks big enough to belong to the Sekk that was said to have cast its spell on them.

The children had reached a clearing where the fern grew thick, and here the markings became confused. They had doubled back on them- selves, run in circles, dragged things, and possibly even rolled in the ferns. When she traced the perimeter of this clearing she could see a single line of prints entering the clearing from the hillside above. They were small, like a child's, and barefoot. They had entered the clearing, but they had not left it.

She stopped and stood, listening. Her breath swirled in the air before her. In the distance, jays chattered. A squirrel leaped a gap between branches and sent a shower of snow from above. She looked up, thinking that these trees might bear the weight of a small Sekk, but she could see no such sign.

She wanted to follow the prints all the way back to their source in the forest. Sekk laired in caves and abandoned buildings when they could, and this area was rich in deserted Everien structures. She would like to see where the Sekk had come from.

But there were more pressing concerns – such as where the Sekk had gone. As she checked the area thoroughly and found no more evidence of the barefoot Sekk, it became clear that the Sekk had not cast a Slaving spell and then waited for the results. No. The footprints had been small, and they had only gone one way. The Sekk had not returned to its lair.

No longer being careful to avoid disturbing the snow, Istar set off the way she had come, running through the trees for all she was worth. She charged over the bridge and into the village, drawing her sword as she came to the centre square. Pentar was building a fire and the survivors were sitting in several rough huddles around the perimeter of the square. An old woman moved among them, administering potions with the resigned look of someone who has seen this too many times before. Two other women were splinting the leg of an adolescent boy who bellowed in pain. A baby squalled and was silenced at his mother's breast.

A little apart from the rest sat a child with white-blond hair and flushed cheeks, making a sculpture in the snow. Istar slowed, breathing hard, and checked every part of the square for hidden figures. Pentar prodded his fire and glanced up questioningly. She shook her head no to indicate she had not killed the Sekk, and saw his shoulders sag.

Istar began to walk toward the stunned survivors. Pentar would have organized the men to remove bodies. She did not allow herself to think about how this incident would affect the lives of the townspeople; how they would be scarred; what they would do after she and Pentar left. She made herself cold on the inside as her mind calculated possibilities and probabilities. This was no time for passion.

The blond child was singing under his breath. In her guts Istar felt a spasm begin. The tune was not Clan. It had semitones unknown to Snakes or any other Clan. It was not Pharician, either.

The child was barefoot. She knelt beside him.

'What are you making, my love?' she asked. He looked back at her with dark blue eyes that were round, sincere, and thoughtful. Or so she thought as she waited for him to answer. She glanced at the sculpture and saw that it was a pig. It was very well rendered, too. Behind her back, Istar drew her sword.

The child opened his mouth and sang.

She rammed the sword through the child's body. Someone started screaming. Pentar tackled her from behind and she landed hard in the mud. She said goodbye to herself fleetingly, knowing that her next sensation would be that of Pentar's dagger cutting her throat from behind. Instead he barred her neck with his forearm and rolled on top of her. She smelled mud; inhaled mud; and his weight pressed fiercely into her kidneys. She didn't try to fight back. What was done was done. He would have to kill her. She heard the screams of shock and rage that the people had let out. They suddenly stopped. Pentar's weight lessened marginally. She saw his fist clench in the mud as he pushed himself off his knuckles. His other arm slipped away from her throat and she turned her head. The broken snow was soaking up brown mud like a sponge. She saw no blood. Pentar's tackle had carried Istar two yards from the body of the child where Istar's sword was stuck. The mist of her own breath made the air pearly as her eyes fixed on the child's bloodless body. It had begun to shrink as though dissolving into the air itself.

Pentar was off her now. She rolled over and got halfway to her feet. Their eyes met. His were black and snapping with anger that was more than anger.

'What did you think you were doing?'

'Killing the Sekk,' she answered defensively.

'You could have been wrong.'

'I wasn't.'

'You could have been. I could have killed you, storming in here like a man Enslaved yourself.'

'I was prepared for that possibility.'

'You should have warned me. What if you had made a mistake?'

'I didn't.'

'You could have.'

'But I didn't.'

'Have you a death wish? Mother of Ysse, let the H'ah'vah witness it – Istar, you have gone too far.'

'See your fire does not go out,' Istar said. 'There are many people hurt and in shock here.'

Pentar spat in the snowmelt and turned away. He did as she said.

Ice, with Fingers

'You,' Tarquin said to the boy, 'are supposed to be a horse.'

'Horses don't have fingers, do they? And look at what mine have caught you.' The boy proffered a stack of fish cakes bundled in great spade-shaped leaves the colour of rare jade. He could scarcely contain his elation, and he made a bizarre picture as he jigged up and down in place, unheeding of the earth that stained his black skin red or the flower petals caught in the shock of white hair that radiated from his skull. The sight of this unlikely creature standing over him confused Tarquin, and he nearly flopped back down on the warm rock; then the aroma of the food penetrated his daze.

'I beg your pardon,' Tarquin corrected himself. 'I forgive you for not being Ice.'

He finished sitting up. He had more or less passed out as soon as the boy dragged him from the water, bone-weary from what had seemed an endless swim, and dispirited in the aftermath of the great battle at Jai Pendu where he had lost and found and lost again his beloved Company. The boy had disappeared and Tarquin had lain for hours in a delirium while the sun burned through the clouds, dried his clothes, and began to sear his exposed skin. He roused only when the rattle of loose clay pebbles heralded the arrival of his unlikely helper. Now that the smell of the fish cakes was reaching his nostrils, he had to admit that at the moment a boy with thieving fingers was more use to him than a whole herd of magical horses called Ice.

'I have already eaten,' the boy said. 'I hid behind a fat woman while she was breading the catch. I slipped the odd one off the fire when she wasn't looking. She ate so many on the sly herself that I am sure she didn't keep track of the ones that went missing.'

He licked oily fingers and nodded eagerly at Tarquin to eat. The latter had the feeling as he appreciatively chewed the flaking cooled flesh that the boy was taking a keen vicarious pleasure in watching him wolf down the meal. His unusual features, not *quite* human but close, twisted quizzically, and an innocent sympathetic lightness came over his eyes. The candour of that gaze made Tarquin uncomfortable.

'Woman? What woman?' he said. 'Are we near to a port?'

'It's just a small village,' answered the boy, and he pointed. 'A few miles that way. They cook the fish out on the beach, wrap it, and send it upriver by canoe. The jungle is dense. I would not want to run through it.' He frowned slightly and Tarquin inferred that he was imagining himself as Ice. The thought made Tarquin feel disoriented. Certainly no human would dress himself as this creature did, for he wore only a belt with a couple of pouches hanging from it and a loincloth woven from material that bore a suspicious resemblance to a saddle blanket.

'You had better explain yourself,' Tarquin said. 'Am I to believe that you are Keras's son and also the horse Ice? How can this be?'

In a matter-of-fact tone the boy said, 'Ice ate me when I was a baby.'

'What?' Tarquin stopped chewing. Although his stomach growled and groaned for more, the food had become a tasteless paste. He wanted to spit it out but forced himself to swallow, knowing it might be a long time before his next meal.

'The tales are true, then,' he said slowly. 'I had heard there were cannibal horses in Pharice.'

'In the deserts of Or there are many wild horses, and they will turn cannibal against their own kind under certain conditions. But the strong ones prefer human children to their own.'

'You are a changeling, then.'

'We share time, and we share bodies. It has been many years since Ice permitted me to take this form. The last time, I was only a small child. I needed my mother constantly. How she wept when Ice took me over again!'

'So this is the secret of Ice's longevity.' Tarquin shuddered. 'What happened this time? Can you become Ice again? Where are we? And how is it that Ice – or you – can call the White Road? I still do not understand Mhani's words.'

Suddenly the boy seized one of the fish pies and began to eat it with the shameless ardour of the young. Chewing, he launched into a garbled tale and before long Tarquin's head had begun to pound, whether from the heat or the sudden intake of food or confusion or all three he couldn't tell.

'We can only use the White Road if we are both fully present and cooperating with each other. Which we don't always do. It's very tiring for us both. Ice fulfils the Animal aspect and I . . . I tap into the Knowledge as you like to call it, and between the two of us we walk this tightrope. Ice prefers to be a horse but it is precious little fun for me. I hoped I could tire him out by making him run the White Road, so that he'd have to rest and I could be human – and it worked!' He paused, rolled his eyes upward, and licked his lips appreciatively. Then he held up a forefinger to ask for patience, belched gently, and continued, 'At least I *think* that's why he's tired, although I suppose it could have something to do with his shadow and that thing Night that lives on the other side of the road. It doesn't matter, though, because I'm free now. I'm very happy, Tarquin. Ice is strong but he can't outsmart me. Now I can finally find out what it's like to be a man, not an animal. So far it's good fun. Shall I go and steal some more things, now? Hands are a wonderful invention, aren't they?'

He held his own out before him, fingers splayed, and looked at them as if they were made of gold. Tarquin shook himself a little and said, 'That is not an explanation!'

'That's all I know,' answered the boy brightly. 'I told you – I don't even know my name. What shall I call myself by, now that I'm in the world? I wish I knew my father's name.'

'Beres,' Tarquin replied, having called up the trivium without even trying. The boy's sleek dark eyes fell on him hungrily. There was grease on his protuberant lips, and his neck was dirty, and more than ever Tarquin thought he looked atavistic. Fey. 'He was a Pharician nobleman. I know nothing else about him. My acquaintance with your mother was necessarily brief.'

'Beres,' repeated the boy. 'And Keras. They are similar in tone, are they not?'

Tarquin wasn't really listening. The question of the boy's name was the last thing on his mind. He popped the last piece of fish into his mouth and stood, shading his eyes. He was thirsty. He began to clamber across the sculpted red clay stones toward a series of freshets that trickled from above. They had worn curving channels in the smooth rock, through which they glided noiselessly. The boom of the sea sounded through his body all the way down to his heels. Pitched higher, he detected the pips and squeals of many shorebirds that drifted on the waves or scouted the cliffs. But there were neither gulls nor seahawks, and he wondered where the currents – and Ice – had taken him. A long way, surely. The air was much warmer than Everien's, and the light was far more intense. In fact, his nose was burning.

'I think I'll call myself Kere,' the boy shouted after him.

Tarquin knelt and drank. His stomach was now pleasantly full and his mind began to revive; but also the myriad cuts, bruises, and aches that he had picked up unnoticed along the way had begun to announce themselves and make various demands for succour or rest or both. His chest felt heavy and strained and he suspected he had inhaled some water. He coughed experimentally. No permanent harm, probably.

The boy had followed him to the stream. Now he said earnestly, 'Yes. Kere. It is not a Clan name and so will cause no confusion when we return to Everien.'

'Where are we?' Tarquin asked. He looked out across the sea whence they'd come and saw two islands in the southeast smudging the horizon, which cut a clean line across a now cloudless sky. The water in the cove below was turquoise, and would have been inviting under different circumstances. The breeze carried a floral smell.

The boy shrugged. 'Who cares? It's not where I am that matters to me – it's *what* I am.'

'Jai Pendu is gone, then,' Tarquin murmured half to himself. 'I wish I did not have to send them away. I wish I had thought of something better.'

The scabbard Ysse had given him seemed none the worse for its immersion in salt water; it had seen many years' hard travel already, and Tarquin had mended it again and again. He had strapped his sword to his back as he floated, so that it would not dangle loose in the sea and interfere with his legs. Now he took it out and wiped it down carefully to be sure it was not corroding. All of his other equipment was gone, except for the small knife he kept strapped to his ankle. He sighed.

Kere was bouncing around picking up rocks and throwing them, pointing at features of the jungle and remarking on them ('Tarquin, those mushrooms look like orange turds!') and generally being a nuisance. He made it impossible for Tarquin to enter into any sort of reverie or reflection. Tarquin felt ancient.

'Come on,' he said irritably, and started climbing toward the wall of green, catching at the first vines that tumbled over the edge of the rocks like hair. 'We'd better figure out where we are. I'm starting to feel like the knight in a game of chess, always jumping from place to place. I hope our enemy has not followed us, because I do not think I could fight a gnat at this point.'

Kere raced past him, climbing with utter gracelessness but great energy. He disappeared into the foliage, displacing two bright green birds. They swooped over the waves, circled, and returned to the jungle. Kere imitated their cries and Tarquin instructed him to shut up.

'At least we won't starve,' Tarquin said, eyeing the birds. 'I'll teach you how to make a wrist slingshot like Chyko used to use.'

Even as he said it, he knew it was a ludicrous idea. Kere was as likely to learn to hunt as a buffalo was to juggle. Few boys of twelve or so carry themselves gracefully, and Kere was of that gangly type who grow in awkward spurts and seem to hang disjointedly from their own bones. More than that, he had a tendency to hold his hands as if he didn't know what they were for, his long spatulate fingers half curling, like startled sea creatures. He was nervous and often turned his head or his whole torso to see what was behind him, carrying his shoulders high against his skull as if trying to protect himself from rear attack. Tarquin thought, not for the last time, that it would be tedious to make a journey of any length with a travelling companion such as this. Despite his enthusiasm, there was something not right about Kere, as if he had never had a proper dose of sunlight, or had never played rough, or had never heard an unpleasant truth about himself amid the teasing laughter of friends. Tarquin felt repelled, although he knew he should have more pity, and he wished again for the magnificent Ice like a volcano beneath him instead of this strange boy.

He is not a boy, Tarquin reminded himself. *He has been Eaten. Whatever that means.*

'There is a path,' Kere remarked cheerfully. 'Not far. It cuts through the trees about a quarter mile from here.'

Tarquin was sweating liberally only a dozen paces into the jungle. The undergrowth was dense and viny, and although he could see where the boy had trampled through it, his own way was not made easier by the precedence of someone so much smaller than himself. Progress was slow. Everything was slow. Insects hung in the humid air like particles suspended in fluid, and when Tarquin glanced overhead he saw an enormous snake draped over the branch of a great tree. Its scales rippled as it very gradually eased along the branch. After that he avoided looking up.

'Does this path lead to the people you stole the fish from? I need to know so that I can explain on your behalf.'

'Yes, it does. It looks as if most of the coast has cliffs where you can't bring a boat, but there's one little sandy place where the river comes out and that's where the path goes to. But they all left the harbour once the food was finished. They drew their boats onto the beach and went up the river in canoes. The women went along the path in the other direction.'

'Only one sandy place to land boats, and they didn't build a village there? That's odd. Surely *someone* stayed behind. To guard the boats at least.'

Kere shook his head. 'There was nothing in the boats to guard. Just sails and oars and water bottles. And rope. And tackle. And maybe some bait. And—'

'I get the idea. What about canoes? Did they leave any of those behind as well?'

'No, not one. I was hoping they would because I would have liked to paddle after them, but they took them, every one, and the fishing boats are too big for one to manage. Each boat held eight men at least.'

Tarquin considered this, wondering if it was worth going to this beach of Kere's. 'And the dwellings? Did no one remain there? No one?'

'I don't think so. There were only pits dug in the sand, and some simple tents, and fresh-water barrels.'

'How did the women cook the food?'

'Big iron skillets. They left those behind.'

Tarquin sighed. 'At least you are observant. How long did it take you to walk there?'

Kere shrugged. 'An hour or so I guess. It took longer coming back because I was following the women and I didn't wish to be seen.'

'Ah,' said Tarquin. 'Then we will go the other way, and find the village that they come from. I wonder why they do not live closer to the beach.'

At last they reached the path. It must have been frequently used, for its floor was bare dirt and its edges were free of vines. Yet spiderwebs had already formed across it even though Kere had said the path had been traversed just this morning. Tarquin had pulled up his hood, donned his gloves, and tucked in his clothes as best as he could in an effort to keep out stray spiders – which probably explained why he was so hot. The boy had no such option.

'Stay behind me,' Tarquin said. 'I will break the spiderwebs.'

He had already decided to follow the path inland. He had no wish to get into a boat and set back out to sea after the night he'd spent in the water, and anyway he needed to find out where he was. Sure, Kere had stolen a few fish, but there was no reason to believe these people would be hostile. And the boy had said nothing about weapons or guards.

About a half mile up the trail they came to a flight of steps rising to the northeast. The path widened here and the packed mud was reinforced by logs laid into the hillside. At the top of the stairs, the vegetation had been cleared away in a semicircle to the right side of the path. Set in the earth was a large area of metal partially covered by the clay earth, and within the metal were two oblong panels. At first Tarquin thought they might be trapdoors, for he could feel that there was a hollow space beneath as soon as he stepped on the metal. But there were no handles on the panels, and no other indications of what the construction was for.

Tarquin examined the ground carefully. There were smudged footprints in plenty in the area around the seam in the metal. He pried at it with his fingers, with a dagger, with a stick. He couldn't make anything yield. He wiped the sweat off his forehead. Overhead, monkeys were screaming and setting the trees into erratic motion. Through small gaps in the leaves he could see that the sun had gone in, and the air lay thick and yellow-green under the hot clouds.

Kere said, 'I wonder if it's something to do with those mounds.'

Tarquin hadn't noticed, but when Kere pointed it out he observed that the jungle floor made a kind of plateau with the stairs leading to the top, and the flat area where they now stood was dotted with earthen domes the size of small tents. The domes were so covered with vines and flowers that you had to look quite carefully to see them; but now that Tarquin had caught on, he counted half a dozen within visibility of the path.

'Maybe that's where they live,' he muttered, and strode toward the nearest one. But when he got there he realized it was only about three feet tall and five across, and seemed to be solid – not at all like a tent. 'No. Maybe they're graves.' His skin crept a little; and then he noticed a chink of darkness within the foliage. He slid his gloved hand in carefully and tapped a clear panel.

'Glass?' He knelt and put his eye up to the aperture, which was smaller even than an arrow slit. It was dark within. He was tempted to start tearing the mound apart to find out what was beneath, but overhead the monkeys had gathered and were hurling fruit and imprecations at him.

'Come, Tarquin,' Kere called. 'They look nasty. And I think it's going to rain.'

Tarquin desisted. 'This is a weird place,' he told the boy. 'Tell me if you see anything else unusual. You have sharp eyes – I'll grant you that.'

He took a good look around at the lay of the land. They had begun to climb, and when Tarquin looked up into the spaces between the trees he could glimpse the shoulders of a mountain farther inland. It was completely green-clad, but had the look of a volcanic cone. Memories of his years spent travelling tugged at him but did not satisfy.

'This is puzzling,' he said under his breath. 'I can't work out where we are.'

As they followed the path, its twists and turns became more dramatic, for it was winding amongst complex rock formations overgrown with moss, lichen, and flowered vines. Also the ground began to rise and fall steeply as the path led across folds in the land and up and down gullies. There were wooden footbridges in some places and flights of stairs reinforced with logs in others, and Tarquin knew enough about plant growth rates in warmer climates to appreciate that if no one had tended this path, it would have been all but invisible in a matter of a few weeks. He didn't know whether to be relieved or wary at the idea that other people were about, nearby. The jungle sounds were so loud and its foliage so dense and complex that he was well aware how easily they might be ambushed as they walked along the path. Yet to travel any other way would have been impossible: he had no boat and no machete and his sword would soon be blunted on all this green wood if he tried to use it that way. Besides, he was afraid of the snakes and spiders.

After a while Tarquin found himself entering into the familiar journey mode of idle thought that he had learned to wear the way others wear their clothes. Beside him, Kere was stumbling and jolting as if he scarce understood the workings of his own legs, or as if he expected monsters to leap from the jungle at any moment. Tarquin was accustomed to maintaining a constant scan of the environment, an alertness to danger or its forerunners, while freeing the rest of his mind to daydream; Kere had no such facility and behaved as though seeing everything for the first time. He was, Tarquin thought, not unlike a high-strung horse who shies at the least anomaly in his normal environment, even if it is only a rake propped against a wall. Unfortunately, that was the *only* way in which he could be said to resemble a horse.

Tarquin's feet were blistering. The boy was breathing loudly through his nose.

Correction: one more equine attribute, but useless.

The sky grumbled and it started to rain. Kere twitched and shied. Tarquin shrugged into his hood and hooked his thumbs into his belt, thinking staunchly that if the natives could come up and down this path often enough to keep it maintained, he would soon reach a settlement – or meet other travellers. The path couldn't go on forever. It just seemed that way.

The rain stopped and insects appeared. Now it was muggy, and the boy kept jerking his shoulders whenever an insect or a drop of sweat touched him. Tarquin growled under his breath and tried to think of snow. Kere tripped over a puddle and caught himself on a thorn bush, which cut his hand. Tarquin paid no attention as the boy made a show of sucking away the blood. Then the youth slapped hysterically at mosquitoes that were settling on his neck. Tarquin ignored him. Kere began to whistle off key.

'Enough!' Tarquin roared, turning on the white-haired boy. 'Let's have Ice back. Immediately!'

Startled, Kere halted and edged back a pace from Tarquin, who had a hand on his sword. He had no intention of drawing on the boy, or even of giving him the smack and two kicks he so richly deserved; but Kere reacted as though his life were forfeit. His nostrils flared, his hair seemed to stand up even straighter, and he began to hyperventilate. Before Tarquin could reassure him, his eyes had rolled back in his head and he had collapsed on the path, his body stiff as wood, twitching and frothing at the mouth and kicking the dirt like a rabid dog.

The One-Sided Road

Kere writhed and jerked, digging furrows in the red clay of the path with his heels before flipping over spontaneously like a fish out of water and coming to rest facedown, where he lay stiff and unmoving. Tarquin cast about for some way to help, but he had lost his pack and the few simple medicines it contained. None of these would be any good against poison, anyway. It had probably been a spider. He would have to see if he could find the bite mark and bleed it out.

He knelt beside Kere and examined his skin carefully, trying to recall everything he knew about venomous insects. It didn't add up to much. Chyko had possessed a lexicon of information on insects and their poisons, and he had shared the occasional tip with Tarquin, but unless Tarquin could find out what kind of spider or insect had bitten Kere, he had no hope of identifying the poison, much less counteracting it. And he probably didn't have enough time. Kere was breathing and his skin was still warm, but his eyes were glazed over, open yet unseeing, and froth bubbled at his parted lips.

There wasn't a single mark or imperfection on Kere's skin; Tarquin turned him over and studied his body inch by inch, but there was nothing. He began to search through Kere's thatch of white hair, but found only a few fleas. Then Kere stirred.

'Hey,' he said, offended. 'What are you doing? Don't touch me. I'm not inclined that way.'

Tarquin rocked back on his heels as the boy sat up, wiping mud from his mouth and jaw.

'I thought you were dying!'

Kere looked away.

'What bit you? Did you see it?'

'*Bit* me?' Kere clambered to his feet.

'Didn't you even feel a sting?'

Now the boy was looking at the ground – sheepishly, Tarquin thought, standing up himself and following Kere, who had started to proceed along the trail as if nothing had happened. The boy hunched his shoulders against a spatter of rain. Tarquin grabbed his arm and turned him around.

'What was that all about? Didn't you get stung?'

'I . . . uh . . . sometimes that happens to me. Never to Ice, only to me.'

'Happens? What happens? What were you doing?'

Kere shrugged and looked so forlorn that Tarquin let go of his arm.

'I dunno. I just – sometimes I just go funny. I can't control it, you know,' he added defensively.

'But why? What's wrong with you?'

'Nothing's wrong with me!' Kere started walking again.

'Then why does it happen?'

'I told you I don't know. When I get upset, sometimes.'

Tarquin rolled his eyes. 'When you get upset? When you get upset? Oh, great! So I'm supposed to treat you like a girl, like a delicate little flower? What do you mean, *when you get upset?*'

Kere didn't answer, and Tarquin restrained himself from continuing. He didn't wish to witness a second performance on the part of Kere. The first had been disturbing enough.

'Well,' he said after a minute, 'just keep your mouth shut and do as I say, and you'll have no reason to *get upset*. All right?'

But he could tell by the set of the boy's shoulders that he was sulking.

'Children,' Tarquin muttered. 'What is the damned use of you?' Almost as soon as he'd said it, he caught himself and realized that he was already on the road to inducing another attack in the boy. Very carefully, he said, '*Kere.*'

The boy looked up at him with molten eyes like his mother's.

'Kere, why do you think Ice came here? If he was tired, why didn't he go home to Snake Country in the north where your mother and the other horses are? Or return to the deserts where you were both born? Why would he come to this volcano, probably an island, where there isn't enough room for a horse to move?'

Kere didn't answer at first. He began to walk in an uneven, spiralling circle on the open path, bumping into the occasional tree. It was the behaviour of a four-year-old, not a boy approaching the beginning of manhood.

'Or was it your idea to swim all this way?' Tarquin watched the boy carefully, wary of the moment when he might lapse into another nervous taking, and studying the physical signs of stress. Kere had stopped and was pulling a palm frond from its branch. He took one of the single leaflets and peeled it free, focusing all his attention on his hands and the strip of leaf as he manipulated it. Tarquin sighed and tried to be patient.

'The White Road has only one side,' the boy said. 'But it is infinite, and appears to have two.' Kere licked his fingers, took some sap from the bole of a nearby tree, and daubed it on the leaf.

80

'What? I don't understand you. Will you put that down and talk sensibly?'

Kere, satisfied with the operation he had performed on the leaf, held it out to Tarquin, walking toward him.

'Look,' he said, stretching the strip of leaf out like a string. 'See, the leaf has two sides.'

'Of course it has two sides, you idiot.'

'We know this because on one side it is pale and the vein stands out, and on the other side it is dark and smooth. See?' He so earnestly presented the leaf that Tarquin inspected it just to humour him.

'Yes. I see. But—'

'Now look.' Kere held up the leaf, twisted it, and joined the ends, sticking them together with a bit of sap. 'Pick a side and run your finger along it.'

Tarquin complied.

'Your finger is on the dark side. Now trace it all the way around the leaf. Now which side is your finger on?'

'Well . . . it's on the light side. Wait. Let me do it again.'

Kere stood back, smiling. 'You see? Now it has only one side.'

'But that's impossible.'

'I know.'

'Kere, this is a stupid game. It's raining, and you're giving me a headache.'

'When we left Jai Pendu, Ice was tired, but it's more than that. We can't get to the White Road, Tarquin.'

'Why not? Why don't you just turn into Ice? He'll know what to do.'

'I'm afraid.'

Tarquin held the strip of leaf aloft and let it drift to the path.

'Useless toy,' he said. 'Don't waste my time trying to distract me from the fact you are afraid. I could tell you more about fear than you'll ever—' But the boy interrupted him.

'We are not alone on the White Road. There's something on the other side of it, but it's the same side, and we have to slow down or catch up to it. And it's making Ice sick and I have to find the cure, and the whole thing's making me dizzy, Tarquin the Free.'

'But how can this be?' Tarquin glared at the leaf. 'You're just playing games. You're trying to trick me, but it doesn't mean anything. It's only a leaf. It has nothing to do with anything.'

'You are not very intelligent,' Kere said. 'Ice is a horse and even he understands this principle.'

Tarquin felt a snarl forming and turned his back.

'Come on, you wretch. I've had enough of this chatter. Don't talk to me any more.'

The rain had left the air even hotter and more oppressive. The path continued to deteriorate, plunging steeply down, and wound through and over another series of gullies, crossing several whitewater streams as it went. Tarquin began to lose hope of coming to a settlement, but doggedly pursued the increasingly difficult way. They came around a series of bends, crossed yet another stream, and then suddenly arrived at the sea again, this time from a considerable height. Steep cliffs plunged to the breakwater, completely overgrown by jungle. The path ended in a roughly circular clearing that was well on its way to being taken over by weeds, vines, and saplings.

'This puzzles me,' Tarquin said. 'Why would they fish on the other beach and then walk all the way across the jungle only to come to the sea again? Where are their dwellings? And what is the purpose of this inland path?'

As he took in his immediate surroundings, he noticed that the path had not entirely ended, it had merely been overgrown to the point of obscurity. When it reached the clearing, it made a sharp turn to the left, where rough stairs had been cut in the mountainside. If Tarquin bent double he could just crane his neck enough to peer up a long tunnel in the foliage. The steps seemed to rise endlessly. Far up, where the leaves admitted a sliver of blue sky, he could glimpse a mountain peak: black, bare, and sheer as a wall.

'Well, I'm not bloody well going up there,' he said with a laugh. 'Eh, Kere?'

But Kere, evidently having taken Tarquin's instructions to heart, said nothing. He hung back, messing around in the bushes while Tarquin explored the area, climbing a little way toward the cliff edge where he could see the sea, cool and inviting and too far down to get anywhere near. Tarquin let him go, loath to speak to him lest he induce another fit – or be given another lecture on circles that were really square, or the lightness of rocks, or something equally silly. He looked out over jagged and difficult shoreline. The sea was wild and white. By its constant licking at the red-and-black stone, it had carved out deep overhangs in the cliffs as well as in the sides of the seastacks that broke the surface like jagged pillars. Looking up the coastline, Tarquin saw no relief from this pattern, no beach like the one Kere had described this morning. He could not see how anyone could land here; but there were ships ranging across the deep only a mile from the shore. From their design he would not have recognized them. They used rows of oars as well as red sails set on three masts, and Tarquin guessed they were more or less flat-bottomed, and ill suited to ocean crossings. They must either come from the islands, or somewhere up or down the coast. He would have guessed from the sail colour that they were Pharician, but they seemed too simple to be imperial warships, and rather too small as well.

'I wouldn't mind knowing where the hell I am,' he said, knowing that Kere probably couldn't hear him. 'There are volcanoes among the Seahawk Islands, but they are in the far north. The island chains beyond Hāz are flat and sandy atolls by all accounts, and there are no jungles along the east coast of Ristale or Pharice. Even in the southerly regions the lands are dry. And whose boats are those? I would like to tie that boy to a tree and dump army ants all over him and make him tell me everything he knows, but he would probably faint and choke on his own tongue, and then where would I be? Ah, I wonder if Keras knew this would happen. She must have seduced me on purpose.'

Thinking of Keras with her lean thighs and her smouldering eyes cheered him. He wasn't done for yet, anyway. His stomach was reminding him he owed it several meals, not merely a few bites of fish and hasty swallows of water. At least, he thought, he could camp in this jungle and recuperate for a while, gradually exploring the island until he learned who were its inhabitants and how he could get back to the mainland.

He sat down on a stone in the shade, watching the waves make their patterns below. What was the rush, anyway? What was done was done. It was over. Wherever he was, whatever had happened, Jai Pendu was gone, Chyko was gone – everyone was gone. It really didn't matter what he did now. He chuckled. And he had been so rough on the boy. It was habit formed after years of hardship. But the sky here was blue and what was there to fear?

'Kere!' he called over his shoulder, thinking he really ought to try to be kinder . . . Ice had probably saved his life, after all, and anyway without the magical horse he would still be up in Snake Country, making his tortuous way back to Jai Khalar by foot. 'Kere, come and sit down. We'll have a rest until sunset, and then we'll see what fish we can catch honestly.'

There was no answer. He turned, shading his eyes as he looked back up the path.

'Bloody hell,' he said, and got to his feet. 'What have you got yourself into now?'

Kere's head appeared from behind a stumpy, awkward-looking tree. He emerged with a piece of oblong yellow fruit in each hand.

'They look silly, but they're good inside!' he exclaimed with his mouth full, waving a rubbery yellow skin.

'Would that we could say the same of you,' Tarquin retorted. In a low voice, he added, 'I hope you come true in the end, Ice. Where am I?'

A Deaf Whore's Recounting

The beach was deserted when they reached it late in the afternoon. It was just as Kere had described it. Tarquin was disappointed when he saw the chasm through which the stream ran. Steep cliffs surrounded the beach on all sides. The accumulation of sand had been formed from the runoff of the stream, but the stream emerged from a deep cutting in the volcanic rock. The sides of the chasm were sheer and virtually without greenery, which did not speak well of their ability to be scaled. The water was deep and swift. It would not be possible to wade upstream. At the top of the chasm, jungle arched overhead on both sides.

Tarquin made an attempt to cut through the forest from the path uphill toward the cone of the volcano, hoping to perhaps follow the watercourse inland from the top of the chasm and so eventually come to its source. But the jungle only became denser the deeper he tried to penetrate it. The areas they had already crossed, between the shore and Kere's path, seemed open country by comparison to the thicket of thorns and vines that prevailed inland. Tarquin was not about to blunt his sword on green wood. Sweating, thorn-scratched, and frustrated, he decided to forget finding the source of the stream for now, and concentrate on the fact that the fishermen had to come to the beach to ply their trade.

Working on the assumption that they fished by night, Tarquin trusted that no one would be coming here at this hour and descended to the sand as the sun was flirting with the horizon. The light was the colour of honey and the breeze had begun to kick up. His sunburn ached and he thought how glad he would be of darkness; but for now he needed the glaze of golden light that drenched the beach, so that he could examine the beached fishing boats of the locals.

They were simple craft, with only rudimentary sails and no navigation tools at all, but they were painted and decorated with carvings around the bows and at the bases of the masts. The carvings depicted lizards and flowers but no men nor symbols. The tiller of one had been carved so that a snake seemed to be winding around its length, its forked tongue protruding from the end like a pronged spike. There was cunning and craft in the make of the boats, but Tarquin was surprised to think that anyone would venture on the ocean in one of them. They looked more like river or shore craft except for their long rudders. Yet the fish Kere had brought this morning had been a deep-sea type; the flavour had been unmistakable. And Kere said the fishermen had used canoes to get up the river into the jungle; so these had to be their ocean-going boats. Tarquin grunted and Kere came up behind him, hovering.

'What is it? What have you found?'

'Nothing. I thought I told you to keep lookout.'

'I am. Look at the sky behind you, Tarquin. Have you ever seen such a sky?'

Tarquin had not. The sun rose over the ocean in Seahawk Country, but although the clouds sometimes made dramatic displays in the silvery northern light, sunrise was seldom a colourful affair. When he looked back to the west, the edge of the sun was nearly touching the water, which was so calm it formed a perfect mirror for the sky above. Colours such as he had never imagined, let alone seen, were spread across land and sea in a seamless gloss. There was only one cloud formation, and it looked like an island in the sky made of gold and the pinks of tropic flowers.

Tarquin shuddered and turned away.

'It reminds you of the Floating City,' said Kere.

'Keep watch,' Tarquin grunted. But he said nothing when the boy followed him. He had not had time to assimilate what had happened at Jai Pendu; in fact, the experience was still so fresh he knew it could probably be smelled on his very skin, some unworldly perfume. He twitched again a little and stepped over to the last of the boats, the smallest one but more highly decorated than the rest. The sail of this one had not been properly furled, and it stirred in the evening breeze. Unlike the other sails, it was black. Tarquin picked up the edge and noticed that it was inlaid with stones, white crystals sewn into its fabric. He unfurled it and stretched it out on the beach. The black sail was meant to be a night sky, and the gems had been set in it like stars, forming a constellation. Tarquin had been taught all of the stars as a child in Seahawk; he could roughly navigate by their movement if pressed, although it had been years since he last had sailed. He did not recognize this grouping, though. He looked at the constellation from two or three angles before he saw what could be an outline of a figure on a horse.

There was no such picture in the sky he knew.

'Ice!' he called. 'I mean, Kere. Kere, come here and look at this.'

The boy had wandered off toward the water and now came rushing across the sand. The tide was low and the beach stretched out well beneath the level of the boats, occasionally broken by a rock or sand pit. As his spindly legs took him over the smooth expanse, his gait was so graceless that Tarquin had to look away. Kere was out of breath when he arrived in a spew of wet sand. His hair was flattened and sticking to his neck in damp clumps, and Tarquin surmised he had been in the water.

Tarquin pointed at the sail. 'What do you make of this?'

'It's a lady on a horse.' Kere wiped his dripping nose with the back of his wrist. 'There are some strange creatures down there, in the tide pools—'

'Keep away from them!' Tarquin answered sharply. 'How do you know it's a lady? Have you see this group of stars before?'

The boy shrugged. Wet, his head looked small and curious. 'No . . . maybe it's a man. I was only guessing.'

He ignored the suspicious glance Tarquin cast in his direction.

Tarquin rolled up the sail and looked around. The sun was almost gone. The last of its light sparkled and shone off the bodies of sailsnakes leaping from the water in the distance. Tiny, ephemeral rainbows glimmered for an instant each before vanishing.

'Let's get some crabs,' Tarquin said. 'And try to sleep a little while it's early. We have a long night ahead of us.'

But he could not sleep. There were wild noises in the jungle; it was louder than market day in A-vi-Khalar, Tarquin thought, jumping within his own skin for the hundredth time as a series of screams pealed across the night. The ocean pulled soft and steady at the sands in a background rhythm. Nearer to hand there were slithers and shrieks and rustlings, and insects of every variety seemed to be biting him or crawling on him. Kere quivered and jumped and made snorting noises, whimpering to himself – but in the end he slept. His hands and feet twitched and he jerked in his slumber as if shocked. He snored.

Tarquin wrapped himself tightly in his cloak and leaned against the smooth roots of a tree. It would be safer to stay awake, he thought.

Then Kere was shaking him. He opened his eyes and it was utterly dark.

'Come!' Kere said. 'Look at this.'

Tarquin stumbled after him, not feeling his feet engage beneath him until they were on the path. It was deep night. He must have been sleeping dreamlessly for some time, for there was a half-moon high over the sea, and in its light could be seen ships just beyond the entrance to the bay.

Tarquin did a double-take. The little snake-carved boats still rested supine on the sand, but the tide was coming in strong and threatening their position. The ships he had taken for Pharician were now a bow shot beyond the breakers. Their masts were down and the double rows of oars were out. Boats hung from their sides, ready for launch. Triple masts with multiple sails sliced the sky into neat sections.

Kere tugged at his sleeve. 'Those are not the men I told you about,' he informed Tarquin unnecessarily, whispering hot breath into Tarquin's ear.

Tarquin put a hand on his shoulder to silence him and kept looking. He knew whose ships they were. There was no mistaking a Pharician warship.

They moved out of the trees and halfway down the rocks that led to the beach. There were vines covering the rocks but no trees, so they could hunker there out of sight and obtain an unobstructed view of the beach and the bay.

'Too bad it's not a full moon,' Kere observed. 'We'd see better.'

Tarquin started to nod and then realized something.

'*Why* is it only a half-moon?'

The boy's face couldn't be read in the darkness. 'Eh?'

'When we were at Jai Pendu the moon was full. Even if we were on the ocean more than one day, we could not have drifted for as much as a week.'

Kere said nothing.

'How long was I lying on that shoreline?' Tarquin asked in alarm, forgetting to keep his voice to a whisper.

'Only a few hours, I told you.'

'I don't trust you. How do I even know you are Ice? You could have been sent to trick me.'

'Sent by who? And why?'

Tarquin gave the boy a shake. 'Where are we, Kere? Damn you, tomorrow you will call Ice on pain of death! Go on, have a seizure if you want. I don't care. I won't be lied to this way.'

'I'm not lying to you. I don't know what happened. We must have slipped in time.'

'Slipped in time?' Tarquin mocked in a harsh whisper. 'Is time now a rare oil that we have slipped in it?'

Tarquin's sarcasm didn't faze the boy. 'No, no. I forget how little you understand.'

'How little I—Don't pretend to be so wise, pip. Tell me what you know.'

'Uh . . . well, it's like the White Road. How could it carry you so far, so fast, unless it slipped underneath time and took a shortcut? Like a fighter slipping a blow.' And he bobbed to illustrate, but his imitation of a fighter was hopelessly lame.

'Just tell me where we are, when we are, Kere,' he growled. 'Metaphysics are for the Scholars.'

'I'm trying to but I can't simplify it enough.'

'Try harder.'

87

In a high voice Kere babbled, 'I can't! You'll be mad. You'll be mad and you'll scare me and I'll . . . I'll get sick like you know I get sick, and then the Pharicians will come and discover us and we'll be captured.'

'I won't be mad, Kere.' The boy was already trembling and Tarquin was afraid he would have a fit just anticipating Tarquin's reaction. 'I promise.'

'Oh, yes, you will.'

'Kere!'

'No! No! I don't know anything.'

Tarquin forced himself to lower his voice to a whisper. He leaned close to Kere and said in his ear, 'You don't want to be captured by the Pharicians, do you? If they come for you, you'll have to change to Ice. Wouldn't you rather be a horse than be dead?'

'I'd rather be a boy and alive and that's why I'm not telling you anything.'

'You insubordinate, sneaky little brat!' Tarquin snarled.

'You're not clever enough to understand my answer. No. I can't put it into terms you would understand.'

'You snivelling, clumsy, useless, arrogant intellectual bean sprout! Don't tell me what I'm clever enough to understand, you—'

'Shh!' Kere grabbed his arm and pointed. Two canoes had emerged from darkness where the cutting disappeared into the jungle. They glided across the beach until they reached a shelf in the rock, where the men inside climbed out and tied them up.

'All right,' Tarquin whispered. 'Don't tell me. I'll find out for myself. But I haven't forgotten your deceitfulness.'

He directed his attention to the scene on the beach. There were two men in each canoe. Their skin had been stained dark, but it was striped with something that made it glow bright yellow, and when they moved they appeared unreal. Tarquin felt a shiver go through him as he watched them disembark, for they moved sinuously, and the eerie colouration heightened the impression that they were never still, always connected as if a thread of activity passed through each one like a current. They carried no weapons that Tarquin could see, but one of them had a bag slung across his back. They wore loincloths held in place by belts that looked as though they were made of many tiny bones stitched together, and there were pouches attached to their belts and hanging around their necks. Otherwise their skin was bare.

One was significantly bigger than the rest, broad-shouldered and powerful where the others were tall and lean. He was a dangerous-looking customer, his skin black as oak loam but painted in thin spiralling stripes of phosphorescent yellow that made him seem to weave elusively from side to side as he moved. He led the others down the beach, and a boat was lowered from the Pharician vessel. Tarquin touched Kere's arm and they darted to a new position in the rocks. He wanted to get close enough to hear their voices.

Now he could see that the leader had fluorescent stripes crossing his face, reminiscent of Vorse's Snake Clan paint – although that had not glowed the way this stuff glowed. He put his hands on his hips and Tarquin saw that he wore a codpiece decorated with a cobra, its hood in full spread. Delusions of grandeur, or a real threat? Tarquin wondered, and was glad for his sword. He wouldn't wish to tangle with this specimen, especially if he was as well versed as Vorse had been in the arts of throwing and wrestling.

The Pharician boat reached the shore and its occupants jumped out into the white surf. In the moonlight Tarquin saw the Snake leader reach up and take something out of his ear, which seemed to be misshapen and exaggeratedly large, and pop it into his mouth. His jaw worked and then suddenly he stepped forward, gesticulating as he spoke.

'You are late,' he said in Pharician tinted by some odd accent. The figures that emerged from the waves wore the characteristic red cloaks and round, spiked helmets of the Pharician military, but their armour was not made of metal but rather, Tarquin guessed, some type of banded wood. They carried spears, not swords, although long daggers hung at their belts. He counted twenty, but they didn't openly display their rank and their leader made himself known simply by stepping forward to meet the other. Oddly informal behaviour for a Pharician, Tarquin thought.

'Your luck it is for we are here,' he replied, and Tarquin frowned at his strange usage of Pharician. 'It yielded no useful thing to us which egg you last gave us. Is it Wasp that the great Snake God is playing as a game on you? Or us Wasping you are?'

The large man stopped in his tracks. Even the way he stood still was menacing, Tarquin thought, his mind working double-time to unravel both accent and manner of speech. He guessed it was something like: *You're lucky we came. The egg you gave us was useless. Is the Snake God playing games with you like a Wasp, or are you tricking us?*

'That is no answer. If you our poisons steal and give to your emperor them as though brewed by yourselves they are, the surprise harsh will be at the time when ends our supply to you of them.'

Tarquin blinked, struggling to understand.

'When the emperor comes with his entire fleet harsh your surprise will be, and your minute and tiny enclave he destroys. Do not treat the serpent-who-eats-itself as your enemy, for find you faced with a worse enemy it is possible.' The Pharician's voice sounded shrill by comparison with the Snake's. It seemed to Tarquin that his voice was overloud, and when the large Snake answered him, his tone was mellow and calm by comparison.

'Another egg receive you will not if no information by you to us is offered for the one to you we last gave.'

'That we have no information the words were not mine, only that useless the poisons were.' The Pharician waggled a finger in a classic gesture of negotiation. 'For by truth our Scholars certain patterns which interest them have discovered.'

The Snake man laughed. 'That is vaguer than a deaf whore's recounting of world history.' Tarquin muffled a laugh, as this was the first sentence he clearly understood. 'Say more, or we will to the Snakes return and to them of your failure tell.'

Tarquin, looking at the four luminous, naked men facing twenty well-armed Pharicians backed up by two ships bristling with spears, thought they must have boulders for balls. He did notice that the man carrying the bag stood behind the others, closest to the canoes that waited, ready to slip away again upstream.

'Eggs . . .' Kere whispered. 'I wonder what kind of eggs the emperor would send two ships for.'

'Shh!'

The Pharician had been elaborating on the 'patterns' that he said the Scholars detected in the egg. Tarquin was not able to follow what he was saying; the meaning slid off him like rain, and he shook himself a little just as though he truly had gotten wet. 'To the Fire Houses the eggs must return,' the Pharician concluded. 'But beneath the waves sank many years ago Everien.'

The reaction of the other was violent.

'Is this all you have to say? It does not behoove you to fail us, for if they die you will lose your supplier. What will your emperor say then?'

'I know it well, Snake man. So give us another egg and we will try one more time.'

'No. You are cheating us.'

Kere murmured, 'That's strange. Snakes don't lay eggs.' Then he silenced himself before Tarquin could do it for him. Tarquin was starting to catch on to the strange way they had of speaking, and he found himself turning the phrases the right way round in his mind even as they were spoken.

'You will lose your supply of poison, too, Snake man. You will not walk about as gods, and you will not brighten the darkness as you do, if your Animals die before they produce a viable egg. You need our Scholars. Your Snakes need our Scholars.'

'We were only ever slaves,' said the Snake. 'My people created themselves out of nothing once before, and we can do it again. Go away, then. You will not get another egg. I know you are cheating me.'

The Pharicians shifted in place behind their leader; they were not very well disciplined for Pharicians, Tarquin thought, to move without being told.

'I give you one more chance to hand over the egg,' the Pharician leader said.

'No.' Even as the Snake answered, the man carrying the bag had already darted toward the canoes and dropped into one of them, paddling away at a furious rate. The Pharician soldiers jostled as if to get past, and again Tarquin thought they weren't acting much like Pharicians. But they did obey their leader, who held up a hand and gazed steadily at the glowing man, who seemed to be moving and weaving in place.

'Very well, Mavese. But the wrath of Cirene will fall on you. There will not be a second chance.'

'So be it,' Mavese replied. 'The Snakes were here long before Cirene. Pharice was a place of mud huts and the Feather King ruled over two rocks and a puddle when the Snakes were born.'

'Insult him and Cirene will surely move even faster. The Nightbird has heard your words.'

With that he flung up his arm, and the strange-looking bird that had been sitting on his shoulder launched into the sky. Its wings gleamed iridescent blue where they caught the moonlight, and for a moment the men on the beach were still, watching it disappear into the darkness over the sea. The Pharicians kept their spears pointed at the yellow-painted men while their leader boarded the boat; then they filed in after him and began to row away, while Mavese and the other two stood silently on the empty beach.

The waves drew higher on the shore. Lights flared on the Pharician ships as they changed sail and began slowly to move away from the coastline. The three men remained. At last, as the sky around the shoulders of the black mountain began to pale, Mavese said in a clear voice, 'By Jaya, you will not vanquish us.'

He raised his arm and canoes began to slip out of the darkness of the chasm.

'The fishermen,' Kere whispered helpfully. 'It was around this time yesterday.'

'We'd better get under cover,' Tarquin said, and stealthily they moved back to their original position in the brush. But the Pharician boats were still quite close, and Mavese did not permit the fishing boats to launch yet. Instead, the men milled around the beach. They didn't speak, but Tarquin saw them touching hands and tapping each other's faces and bodies with their fingertips.

'What a funny way to talk,' Kere said, and Tarquin wondered if the boy could be right. They were talking by tapping on each other. Kere's odd intelligence – about some things – was perplexing. The boy added, 'Can they go to sea now? It's almost morning.'

'No,' Tarquin answered. 'It's too late for a night catch. Not unless they stick close to the shore. I don't see how they can catch deep-sea fish in those little boats, anyway.' He yawned.

'A serpent who eats his tail is just a circle,' Kere mused. 'What's that supposed to mean?'

'Just a circle.' Tarquin yawned again. 'Could it be *the* Circle?'

'Could be,' Kere said nonchalantly. 'Who is Cirene?'

'What? I don't know. The name is familiar, but . . . wait! Did they said Cirene was the emperor? But Hezene is the emperor of Pharice.' He tapped his forehead, crunching his brows together in an effort to concentrate. 'Cirene . . . Cirene . . . Who? – Oh! Ysse, make it not be so.'

'Ouch!' Kere cried suddenly. 'Something bit me.'

'Don't try to distract me, ragamuffin. You know who Cirene was, don't you?'

'I think it was an ant. Ooh, it burns!' Kere shifted.

'You are a little bullshit artist, Kere. You know perfectly well that Cirene was the first emperor of Pharice, and that he lived a thousand years before Hezene. And that's why their armour was wood, and why they didn't use swords, and why they acted like men, not machines . . . Oh, it all adds up!' He laughed. 'And the moon. To think I worried about losing a week! I am living in a world that passed a thousand years before I was even born.'

Kere was writhing in place and slapping himself, making little muffled squawks. He scrambled away from the ant hole and ran stumbling up the path before plunging into the jungle. Tarquin yawned deeply and rubbed his temples.

'All my Company, I have traded for this?'

Courage

The clothes that the Circle had left for Liaku in Lor's courtyard were spectacular. They had been cut to fit her, and when she drew them on in the safety of her nest and looked at herself in the mirror, she was astonished. If she tied her knotted and straggly hair back from her face, she looked every inch the young aristocrat. Well, maybe not an aristocrat, but a merchant-class child at least. She had taken them off at once and carried them on her back for her mission. Now she hugged her own arms. Although it was a warm night, Liaku was shivering. The voice of the Speaker made tinny echoes in her memory.

'Go to the skylight on the roof of the Scholars' building and await my signal. Do not make a sound, and do not let anyone observe you. Not even your own birds.'

She had done as he said. Three times she had stopped to urinate nervously, careful to leave no mark by which she might be identified. She didn't know what to expect, but she was sure it wasn't going to be pleasant. The urge to leave the city at once was strong: Just slip down the ladders on the border of Byrdland and steal away through the sewers until she was free. But as she made her way across the city in the lonely moonlight, she knew that to leave without making preparations would be her undoing. Survival was hard enough when you had built your nests and hides and your network of contacts and bird relationships; survival on the ground, without these things, would be impossible without money and planning. She couldn't flee. She had to go through with this.

When she reached the skylight all was silent and still. Somewhere, way down near the river, a nightingale was singing. Liaku crawled to the edge of the chala and stepped onto the stone roof of the Scholars' building. It was shaped like a loaf of white bread, a long hall with a convex roof pocked with glassed-in skylights. The central skylight was the largest, a curving oval dome. Liaku padded across the cool roof until she reached the edge of the glass. She looked down into the boomhall.

There were many rows of shelves, each divided into boxes like pigeon nests, but instead of birds they contained words and words and words on scroll after scroll. Some of the words were in flat tomes, imitations of the ancient Everien writing method, she had been told. Liaku wasn't sure what was meant by that, for she could read not at all, although she

93

liked looking at the pictures which sometimes illustrated the scrolls or decorated their borders. She was a practised artist herself, for all that her only materials were the chala and a quill pen and some cheap ink that she occasionally bartered for when her spy trade was going well. She had done many sketches of birds and one or two of Lor, in exchange for bathing in his fountain. If she had time, she would have loved to draw a picture of Quiz – but she didn't have time.

The library was almost dark. An oil lamp glowed orange in a wall recess near one of the private offices; Liaku knew that only the most accomplished of the Scholars rated private rooms on the top floor of the building. Most of them slept in communal barracks in the basement and worked out in the open, at the long tables that ran down the centre of the room. These tables had been mostly cleared for the night, with only a few of the largest volumes remaining on surfaces that would, during the day, be strewn with documents. The stone floor had been swept clean. Liaku could see a loaded mousetrap near the end of one of the bookshelves. Even mice, she thought, would have to be very quiet indeed to pass through this room unnoticed. It was not called the boomhall for nothing – the echoes were tremendous.

One of the double doors leading to the hall and stairwell had been left ajar. Liaku's eyes picked up the sliver of darkness that passed through the aperture, but she lost the figure once it was within the library. She tensed. Rumour among byrdmen placed members of the Circle second only to ghosts in elusiveness and secrecy. The Circle were spoken of with awe, and the fact that their true purpose was unknown made them even more frightening to the byrdmen, whose sideline in spying brought them closer to the Circle than any caste in the undercity save perhaps the pharmacists. And now she was about to witness their stealth firsthand.

She didn't see the man cross the library. She didn't see him climb up a bookshelf and catch onto one of the smaller skylights, for that was what he must have done. All she saw, out of the corner of her left eye, was the silent opening of one of the skylights, like an invitation.

She waited. Nothing happened. The nightingale was silent and then began singing again. Liaku scurried across the roof to the open hatchway and looked inside. Nothing.

She slid into the aperture, hung by her fingers, and, by swinging her body, jumped to the top of one of the bookcases. When she hit the wood, she made a much louder noise than she expected, and she immediately flattened herself and lay still, listening. She was sure her heart could be heard echoing through the wooden frame of the bookcase. Liaku went to the end of the bookcase, dropped to the floor (silently this time), and hesitated.

94

There was a slight draft and someone grabbed her wrist. She caught her breath but didn't make a sound.

'Good,' whispered a voice, and a black-clad figure slid from around the corner of the bookshelf and stood before her. 'In this situation, screaming would not be a good idea. Do you know who I am?'

He reached up and peeled away the scarf that covered his face. She instantly recognized the aristocratic mouth and the set of the eyes. He was much taller when standing before her this way than ever he had appeared when she had watched him through the window of the palace. She should have expected this.

'Se,' she breathed.

'Yes. Now, this is not going according to plan. I expected Yanse to be in bed, but he is not. Therefore, we improvise. You are my lookout. Follow me, and be very quiet.'

He left her, moving so fast and so surely across the cluttered room that she lost sight of him, but she saw the door to the hall move until it was wide open, and a little light from the hall came into the library. She could hear water running in an echoey space, and when she peered around the edge of the doorjamb she could see the opening to another room across the stairwell. Liaku knew that the bathing rooms were on the ground floor, but because there were pipes laid outside the building rising to this level, she deduced that there must be some kind of secondary facility on this floor. She regretted not knowing more about the layout of the place, but Scholars were notoriously poor and therefore largely neglected by byrdfolk.

A rattling noise came from the other room, like a drumbeat only more complicated, blurred by the echoes of its stony surroundings. The sound died away and a man spoke. She disliked him instantly on the basis of the grating, nasal tone of his voice.

'No, we're not done yet, as you well know. Ah, I wish you would take your therapy in the day like you used to, Wakhe.' As the man spoke, he was tapping on something hollow. The words were muttered as if to himself, but they reverberated so that Liaku could hear them. 'It is a chore trying to see what I am doing at this hour. Here, don't squirm.'

There was a loud splash. Emboldened by the noise, Liaku slipped into the hallway and flattened herself against the wall outside the bathing room.

'Just paddle as usual, please. That's it. And five more. Now turn over, please.'

She positioned herself carefully and then peeked inside for just a second. There were two men in the dim room, which contained a sunken tub with various bars and handles attached to it as well as a mat on which were arrayed a series of weights and other physical training

95

equipment. One of the men was wearing a black Scholar's robe with the sleeves rolled up and the hood thrown back. He had his back to her, and he must be the one who had been speaking, for the other man was in the water, floundering around to what purpose Liaku could scarcely imagine. There was something wrong with the second man's face, especially one of the eyes, but she allowed herself only a brief glimpse lest one of them see her before she retreated to her original position.

The tapping noise was repeated, but in a different cadence. Liaku wondered if the swimming man had drummed on the side of the tub in an effort to communicate, for she now remembered that Lor had spoken of a 'tapping language' associated with Wakhe.

'You will have to get used to cold water,' said the Scholar in a wheedling tone, tapping back in turn. 'Probably in Everien they roll in the snow to bathe. Ah, but do not worry.' He began whistling tunelessly. Suddenly the whistling cut off. There was a loud splash. Liaku looked quickly inside, just in time to see Se lowering the body of the Scholar to the ground. She saw the gleam of a strangle-wire as it slipped from around the Scholar's throat and into the sleeve of the assassin. Then her attention focused on the man in the pool. He had dived underwater and stayed down.

Se turned and beckoned to her. She spun and had begun to run back the way she'd come, but his voice stopped her.

'Liaku! Come here! Don't be afraid.'

She went back, horrified and fascinated. The assassin was already dragging the body across the floor toward her. Wakhe was still underwater. The breath caught in Liaku's throat.

'Help me,' Se hissed, heaving the dead body into the hallway and dropping it. 'Get him undressed, quickly. Call me if you hear anyone coming. I won't be long.'

Liaku had stripped a body before, and she did this one in record time, disappointed that there was no gold on it anywhere. The assassin had returned to the therapy room and could be heard splashing in the pool. She watched him haul the crippled Scholar out of the water and deposit him on the stone floor. He pressed on Wakhe's chest and Wakhe began to cough and jerk spasmodically. Se stood up and began peeling off his black garments. He ran to Liaku, who proffered the dead man's clothes. Se threw the robe over his head, jerking it down quickly, shaking his head to settle the folds. He faced her. Liaku looked from his face to that of the dead man. Now they were the same.

She took a step back and tripped over a foot. She couldn't stop staring at him. He was no longer Se. She made a small, strangled noise.

'Shh! Listen in the stairwell in case anyone comes. Don't let Wakhe see you.'

But she couldn't resist looking around the corner, so she witnessed Wakhe struggling to sit up while the assassin, posing as his assistant, rushed to his side, seizing up a towel on the way and making a show of rubbing him down with it in an apparent effort to distract the crippled Scholar, who kept trying to grab him. She didn't know what Wakhe was 'saying', but she could see him tapping frantically upon various parts of the imposter's body, his mouth working as if he would speak if he could. After a moment, Se gave up and let go the towel, holding the distraught Scholar by one shoulder and speaking aloud while with his other hand he tapped on Wakhe's forehead.

'It's all right,' he was saying aloud. 'Can you breathe? Were you frightened when I lost my balance and fell? It's all right. See? I am fine. You are fine. Come, let's get you to bed.'

The crippled Scholar resembled a terrified goat, Liaku thought. He was ugly and horrible and she wanted to feel sorry for him, but it was impossible. Both of them, Wakhe and Se pretending to be his helper, both of them were horrible. She wished she could leave but didn't dare. There was no time to analyse what had happened, or speculate as to how Se could transform himself so that he appeared to be a completely different man. Instead, carried along in the moment-to-moment progression of things, Liaku found she could not really think at all. She simply followed orders. Se took Wakhe away down the stairs, and when he returned he still resembled the dead man, but his voice was sharper.

He made her stand guard while he cut up the body of his doppelgänger. When she hesitated, he rebuked her.

'If I leave you here, they will soon find you. You are a byrdman. The penalty for standing in this place is death,' he said. 'Moreover, you are in the secret quarters of the Scholars. They would torture you before they killed you, just to find out what you are doing here.'

'And Liaku speak what she know,' Liaku said defiantly, and enjoyed the anger in his face. Byrdmen were not supposed to talk back. But this man had dismembered one of his own species with no sign of disgust or remorse. Watching this had convinced her of her superiority to him. When he struck her, she ducked too late and went spinning across the stone. She got up and ran from the therapy room out into the hall. She made it through the door to the library, where a gust of air reminded her that the skylight was still open. Escape.

Something hit her head and she lost her balance, tumbling dizzily toward the carpet. On the way down she crashed into a bookshelf, aware that her two front teeth were loose following the punch. One of them had only just grown in. She swallowed warm salty blood and rolled to her feet. She studied the assassin's figure as he came toward her out of the darkness.

'You are a stupid child. This is a great opportunity for you. Do as I say, and do it quickly before I decide to fuck every hole in your body, cut you up, and sell your organ meat in the marketplace tomorrow morning.'

Liaku just stood there. She was trying to remember the exact heights of the bookcases and their placement in relation to the skylight. Even if she scurried straight up the side of this case, she didn't think she could make it out without the aid of some kind of rope or prop. The ceiling was just too high.

'Well?' he said. 'Have I got your attention now?'

She nodded.

'Take this bag. Put the head in it and take it to this address. Do not let yourself be seen, and do not even think about touching ground again.'

She took the slip from him, together with a large empty oilcloth bag. 'What I do when go there?'

'A woman will meet you. She will say she is my sister. Give her the bag, and the paper, and return at once.'

Liaku nodded assent.

'Don't even think of trying to run. If you aren't back in an hour, I'll have you hunted down and then there will be some fun. Remember, the skyfalcon is still a captive.'

She swallowed. 'No hurt bird. I come. Promise it.'

He led her back to the therapy room, where the body lay in parts, its reeking guts coiled at its feet. He busied himself cutting the spine into sections, all the while humming the same sea shanty that his pre-decessor had been whistling so poorly in the moments before his death. She did not understand his calmness. In time, Se picked up the head, scalped it, drew the brain out with wires (Liaku looked away when she realized what was happening, and kept looking away until he called to her). When he was finished, the Scholar's head was a bloody, featureless lump.

'Open the bag,' Se told her. He dropped the skull inside and she staggered a little, surprised at its weight. He pointed out the door in the direction of the skylight. 'Go. Hurry.'

Out in the cool air, Liaku raced with the moon. It kept ducking and diving among the clouds, and her blue shadow went sharp and then indistinct among the bristling lines cast by scaffolds and the semitrans-lucent walls of the bird traps. Everything was asleep. She didn't even hear an owl. There was no blood on here anywhere; the smudge on her face where he'd hit her she'd made sure to wipe off on the pages of a book written in a language she'd never seen. Some essence of the dead man would thereby remain forever the rooms of the Scholars, even if no one knew it. Liaku believed in such things; it was for that same reason she collected feathers and eggshells.

She reached the house on the piece of paper and saw that it had a courtyard not unlike Lor's, open to the sun. A woman was pacing up and down within the yard. In the centre a bright fire was burning in a pit. Judging by the number of blackened logs around the edges, it had been burning this way for some time. Liaku marvelled at the wealth that made such things possible. They weren't even using the fire to cook, and the night was not cold enough to need it for the heat, most of which was being lost to the sky, anyway. The moon was drinking it, Liaku thought, glancing over her shoulder at the white orb that had almost caught up with her.

'I coming,' she whispered to it, and gave a birdcall. The woman looked up sharply. Her eyes were decorated with golden dust and her cheekbones painted with delicate traceries of henna.

'Did my brother send you? Come down, come down.'

Liaku stayed where she was. There had been nothing in the agreement about risking touchdown again. She upended the bag and let the head fall out. The woman let out a cry of disgust and dismay.

'You evil creature! Come here and put it in the fire at once. I don't want its blood on my hands!'

But Liaku had shrunk back into the moonshadows. She sat there in total silence until the woman gave up calling out for her, assuming she had gone. When Se's sister at last approached the lump of bloody bone and gingerly picked it up in her hands, Liaku remained stoically silent. She watched the woman run across the court with small mincing steps and toss the head into the blaze, which blackened and smoked and released a nasty smell. The woman could be heard hissing and moaning in horror. Liaku let her teeth show, knowing the moon would be shining on them. After a few more minutes, she unfolded herself and darted away, the bloody bag trailing behind her like a flag.

When she returned to him, Se made her dispose of the rest of the body part by part, taking it to the Carrion Place near the edge of the city where the crows and gulls gathered to dispose of Jundun's unwanted remains. Se took the organs and genitals and eyes for some reason of his own, stowing them in a tightly woven basket. Liaku had to make seven trips to carry the entire man. By the time she had finished there were portents of dawn in the sky. Suddenly she remembered the birds she was supposed to bring to the market. She sagged against the chala, exhausted and sick to her stomach. Se in his guise as Yanse did not look any happier than she did.

'It is a stupid plan,' she heard him mutter. 'Just because I can speak the tapping language doesn't mean I want to be saddled with this old

99

fool all the way to Tyger Pass! Ah, Byrd-Shit-for-Brains Speaker, I could wring his neck and roast him on a spit with chilli sauce. Two-birds-one-stone, my cock! There must have been some other way to shut Yanse up and leave me free to get to Tyger Pass on my own steam.'

Liaku let out an involuntary groan as she pushed herself into action. She still had a job to do. Se glanced up and looked at her, emerging from his reverie.

'I will not offer you food,' Se told her. 'It would do you no more good than it would do poor Yanse. But change into your fine clothes, and I will let you go deliver your birds.'

Liaku spat on her hands and rubbed them over her face, and danced up and down in place to keep warm. Se was laughing.

'You have done well,' he said. He extended a hand and she saw that he offered her a vial of dark liquid with a cork in it. 'You will feel high and restless after this, but save your strength, for I will call for you again. Be ready. Take this, and when you have got to a place of safety, drink it all down.'

Liaku took it and looked at it. 'What is?'

'It's called Courage. You will feel much better when you have had it; but no matter how good you feel, I want you to stay by yourself and rest until I call for you.'

'All right.' She would have said anything, just to be released.

'Go on, then.'

For the final time she pulled herself up the drape cord and through the open skylight. Mist and rain were starting to come in after her, and the paper beneath her feet was treacherously soft. She put on the fine clothes and went to fetch her birds. By now she just wanted the sun to come up so this could be over. Once she was through at the fishmonger's, having left her prized fliers without a backward glance, she numbly made her way for a feather-section among the common bird-boxes and hid there till she was sure Se had not followed her. Then she slept awhile; then she went to one of her hides and got some dried fish she had secreted there, and choked it down. She was very hungry and could have eaten much more, but was too nervous to stay in one place for long. She looked at the vial he had given her. She'd heard Courage spoken of. It was extremely valuable. What other treasures might come her way, now that she was connected to the infamous Circle?

But she didn't drink it. After the market had opened, she brought the vial to one of her contacts there, an old deaf woman who had once been a byrdman and had graduated to becoming the third wife of a fat islander who sold salt and poisons.

'Who'd you steal this off, child?' the woman asked in the weird accent of the deaf when she'd tasted a bit on her fingertip. 'What you want in exchange? I got good silk, you want that?'

'Food,' Liaku said. 'Me and birds. Plenty food.'

Lip-reading, the old woman laughed. 'You can have enough food for a month on this. Maybe two. I'll get you coffee and chocolate, too.'

'No coffee. No liquor. Just lot of food.'

She collected one sack at a time, dragging them very carefully up and down levels, past bird traps, around Imperial Air Police patrols. She scattered the packages all over the heights and told her birds where they could be found. It was all she could do. She couldn't look after them forever, but she could get them started. They would need to make their own way after this, as she would need to make hers.

Because the Circle would not leave alive a witness to such a murder. If she were Se, she would kill Liaku posthaste. She could not go to Lor; Lor had already betrayed Ral and he would betray her, too, as soon as was necessary for his own protection. Liaku knew her only chance at survival was to leave Jundun.

It seemed as if it was no time before night fell again. She fell asleep under the bare and cloudy sky. To the city dwellers this was the mark of the impoverished and damned – to sleep without a roof was a curse. Even a tent roof protected you from the emptiness of the sky; but Liaku lay beneath the occluded stars with a kind of defiance. The rules and ways of Jundun soon would not apply to her. She felt a touch of vertigo, just imagining a life without the routines of Byrdland. She was afraid; but she had no choice.

At dawn she set off. She would slip down the ladders with all the other byrdmen to relieve herself, but she would not return. If she followed the sewage pipe downstream, she could emerge on the riverbank and there make her way from Jundun, shedding her byrdgirl persona as she went. It would not be pleasant, but it would get her away from the murderous Circle.

She joined the mob of byrdmen as usual, and like one member of a gull colony soon was rendered anonymous in the crowd. Everyone pushed and shoved and cursed each other, and they all smelled like birds and dry heat. Liaku found the routine so reassuring that for a moment she forgot that it was her last day in Jundun, that she was to leave it all behind. At the first horn call she climbed down the ladder and found a place to squat, flapping and screaming at some boys who got too close. She urinated and then, as she stood up, surreptitiously adjusted the thin sack she had slid between her skin and her ragged tunic, where it would not be noticed among the loose folds of the garment. She checked with her fingers. Everything was there: knife, folded water skin, poison, fat-stuffed pastry to eat, lucky feather. The second horn call sounded. She glanced furtively to her right, where the sewage pipe curved and passed beneath one of the nearer buildings, the Ministry of Transport, she was pretty sure. That was where she would go, and hide in the gap between the pipe and the wall of the building until she found a way to slip down to the river.

But when she reached the sewage pipe, someone was waiting for her. She let out a soft, involuntary shriek.

'*Quiz!*'

I Can See Your Bones

The Pharician ships pulled away, their lanterns still visible across the water even as the locals set out in their small fishing boats. By the time the beach was clear, the sun had started to burn away the mist from the forests. Tarquin counted sunrises and his mind reeled.

A thousand years.

Only seven women passed along the path today, and they were furtive and quiet. After they had gone by, he and Kere followed as silently as they could. Fortunately, the jungle sounds were loud enough to cover the sound of their feet, and the women were hacking branches out of the way as they walked, anyway. They seemed more at ease now, and spoke a little among themselves. Tarquin guessed that with the Pharician warships safely removed, they were relaxing.

Tarquin grew bolder as they approached the stairs, cutting the distance between them so that he was just out of view around the bend in the path. When they got to the stone panel in the ground, he crept forward so that he could actually see them. Their bodies were now sweat-soaked and they mopped their shaven heads with the backs of their hands. Some were eating fruit they had picked on the way.

The one in the lead put down her bundle, stood on the stone panel, and with great vigour began dancing a stamping beat upon it. She paused, and there was silence. From within came a faint tapping, again in a specific rhythm. She danced again and waited. Again there was a tapping, and this time the other women looked at each other and laughed. The lead woman danced a final time, putting a flourish on her last few phrases. Then she picked up her net and backed away.

The panel disappeared.

Kere gasped. Tarquin cuffed him lightly in the gut and he started coughing, but fortunately the women had already descended what seemed to be a flight of stairs leading underground. Tarquin's mind was still reeling at the way the stone had vanished. It must be a trapdoor, he thought; but then he realized that a door could not fall away suddenly if there was a staircase beneath. It was physically impossible. He watched carefully, and after all the women had disappeared, the panel *slid* across from the side. But it moved so quickly it seemed to just appear. Tarquin blinked. Who was strong enough to move a stone so quickly – or so silently?

'They live underground. Why? To escape the Pharicians? There must be another way to get down, Kere. We're going to have to go up that river somehow.'

'I don't understand what's going on,' Kere moaned.

'I can't explain it to you,' Tarquin replied in a snide tone. 'It's too *complicated*. It's too *sophisticated* for a simple horse like you.'

'I'm not a horse.'

'Sorry. That was just wishful thinking. Come on, boy. It's been a long morning. Let's find some of that upside-down fruit you like.'

'Banana,' Kere said.

They lived in the jungle for a couple of days, resting, eating, and – in Tarquin's case – thinking. He pilfered small items from the boats, using and then returning them before they could be missed, except for a length of rope, which he outright stole. He made a simple bow and some arrows and tried to teach the boy to use them, but despite great enthusiasm, the boy had the attention span of a bumblebee. Tarquin managed to shoot a bird, but it didn't prove very tasty and after that they stuck to crabs, mussels, and the occasional fish trapped above the tide in the rock pools. Kere gorged himself on fruit and his digestion suffered accordingly.

'Grass is simpler,' he admitted, clutching his cramping belly.

'Any time you want to change back to Ice, I'm game,' Tarquin answered, but the boy was adamant. Tarquin had tried threats, bribes, and everything else short of actual begging, which he couldn't bring himself to do. All Kere wanted was to be a human, and the threats always reduced him to seizures, which frightened Tarquin. He was afraid the boy would hurt himself thrashing around, and then he'd really be stuck.

He had to find a way out of this place. And out of this time.

'I wonder what it was about when the Pharicians sent that bird,' Tarquin mused once. 'They didn't write a message or anything. I've heard legends that Pharicians had talking birds, but I travelled widely in Pharice and never saw one.'

'It was an unusual bird,' Kere agreed. 'Its head was not shaped like other birds.'

'No, it was not. That's observant of you. It had a lump on its forehead, didn't it? Like it was carrying something on top of its beak, only that was its head. Now, if I knew where we were I might be able to calculate how long it will take for the bird to reach Jundun, and then for Cirene's ships to come here and attack. How will they invade? They can't get up the river any easier than we can. They could build small boats and go up the river, but it would be hard to get an advantage that way. I wonder if they can dig up the tunnel where the door and the stairs are.'

'If they have birds,' Kere said, 'they can fly over the river and see what lies beyond the chasm. They might then beat a way through the jungle and invade from another angle.'

Tarquin grunted. 'I'm surprised they haven't done that already. Hezene would have set the whole place afire and smoked them out. These Pharicians are different, though. They almost seem to be afraid of the Snakes.'

'Snakes?'

'Well, obviously these people are some branch of the Snake Clan.'

'But Snake Country is in the far north of Everien.'

'And Snake legend says that their people came from the south, where they escaped slavery and learned seamanship. Judging by the seamanship we have seen so far, these people could travel to Everien by boat if they wanted to.'

'Why don't we make a boat and go up the river?'

Tarquin stared at him. 'Make a boat? Out of what? With what tools?'

Kere picked up the bow. 'You made this. You're Seahawk. You must know how to make a boat. You could teach me.'

'Teach *you*? I might as well teach a worm.'

Kere shrugged and Tarquin knew his feelings were hurt. Sulkily he tore a blue flower from its stalk with his teeth. His eyes lit up at the taste. Kere loved eating flowers. He claimed they were delicious and tried to convert Tarquin to sharing his passion, but Tarquin was convinced it was all a vestigial Ice trait. Now he looked at the boy and sighed.

'Kere . . . Look, I know you want to be human but honestly, you have spent all these years as a horse. Don't you think – well, don't you think it's what you're made to do now? You can't go around as a human startling every time you hear a noise, or eating every five minutes as if you are a chewing machine. Look at your belly, you're always eating.'

Still chewing the blue flower, Kere put his hand on his bloated abdomen. 'But that's what I always do.'

'No, that's what Ice always does. You're not Ice. At least, that's what you told me. But I think you are Ice, and you're just playing games. When are you going to get tired of the game and realize that you're happier with four feet and sharp teeth and this – this time-slipping ability or whatever you want to call it.'

'No. I won't change back, Tarquin. Don't even start that again.'

Tarquin fell silent. He was sure that if Kere was really, genuinely scared or in true danger, the self-preservation instinct would take over and Ice would return automatically whether Kere liked it or not. The trick was figuring out how to trigger this reaction without actually taking the risk of killing Kere. The threat would have to be real, and life-threatening. That sort of thing couldn't be manufactured.

'Why don't we just talk to them?' Kere asked. 'They can't be all bad. You speak some Pharician, and I speak . . . I speak things, too.'

'Talking to people has never been my strong suit,' Tarquin said wryly. 'And two against an entire tribe – maybe an entire civilization? Only as a last resort.'

'If we climbed up the volcano, I bet we could see where the river leads. Maybe we could get into their stronghold from above.'

Tarquin didn't answer at first. He had already come to the same conclusion, but he couldn't seem to work himself up to actually attempting the long climb through thick vegetation, among spiders.

Kere licked his fingers and threw away the flower stalk.

'Oh, Tarquin! I can see your bones.'

Suddenly Tarquin took heed. Kere's pupils were dilated, and his face was flushed.

'What have you done? This flower-eating is foolishness.'

Kere grabbed his hand and stared at it. 'Incredible,' he whispered.

'Stop it. Now we know we are dealing with the Snake Clan. This must be their origin, the source of their magic. They have strange sexual practices and even stranger concoctions that they eat and drink and paint on their skins. You should not experiment on yourself this way, Kere.'

'But I can't help it, Tarquin. The flowers are beautiful, and they taste so good . . .'

Tarquin took the boy by the shoulders. 'Go to sleep,' he said. 'Tomorrow we are going to have a talk.'

'I want to go up the mountain. I want to go up the mountain. I'm bored. I'm bored.'

Tarquin gave him a shake and tossed him to the ground. Kere continued to mumble, but was quieter. He didn't think Kere slept that night: He could hear the boy singing to himself and wandering around. But in the morning he was sober, and although he would not sit still for Tarquin's lecture and insisted on bouncing around in his usual nervous, ungainly way, he did seem to be listening.

'If you want to be human, there is a lot to learn. One thing that is essential, Kere, is self-mastery. Meaning that just because you see a flower that looks good, you do not pick it and eat it without thinking first. That is the difference between men and animals.'

'That is why you try to put bridles on us,' Kere said.

Tarquin gazed at him sternly. 'You will be killed. It's that simple. If you want to be human, you must use your wits. You cannot rely on your teeth and hooves. Do you understand me, Kere?'

'Yes, I understand you!' Kere sang in a sarcastic tone. 'I am not stupid.'

'Then stop acting that way.'

'I could see all your skeleton. I could see the fruit pits in your stomach, like black eggs.'

'Kere!'

'What?'

'I am warning you. Be more wary, clamp down on your impulses, or you will find yourself in real danger. Sooner or later we will encounter some of these Snakemen. If you act like a stupid animal, you'll get killed.'

'You'll protect me,' Kere said.

'Up to a point.'

'Yes, you will! Because you want to get back to Everien and your own time.'

'Maybe I do, and maybe I don't. But there are some things I cannot protect you from, and I won't give up my life for you. What a wretched brat you are. If Keras could see you like this she would clock you one or two, I'm sure of it.'

'Shut up about my mother.'

'You know it's the truth.'

'Shut up, Tarquin. You're not my father.'

'Thank Ysse for that. On second thoughts, you can stay here while I go up the mountain. I'm getting sick of you, Kere.'

'No! Don't leave me! I want to come.'

Tarquin sighed. 'You act like a boy half your age.'

'That's because I've never had a chance to be a boy. Give me a chance, Tarquin. Please.'

Tarquin wanted to hit him. It wasn't fair the way Kere used those soft black eyes and that sad expression, just like a dog locked indoors on a bright day. It was a depraved trick.

'All right,' he grunted. 'But if you cause me any trouble, I throw you over the edge.'

Her Hair Was Red

The climb didn't prove as bad as he expected. Sections of the path had actually been maintained by someone, for when the staircase crossed flat sections or ledges in the stone, there were sometimes other paths intersecting it, and these were kept free of vines. Several times Tarquin and Kere broke from their climb to explore these terraces. Sometimes they found only doors similar to the sliding panels below, with no clue as to how to enter. In other places, they came across whole open fields of terrace gardens where cereal crops and vegetables were being cleverly grown on the steep mountainside under the intense tropic sun. They spent their second morning of the hike spying on the field workers, who came and went through the mysterious doors; but Tarquin did not approach them. He didn't want to alert anyone of their presence, for now that he had glimpsed the relationship of this insular culture with the aggressive Pharicians, he anticipated that they would not be welcoming to strangers and, if they were aware they were being watched, would either retreat underground or attack. Neither result would please Tarquin, at least not until he knew more about them. So he insisted that Kere accompany him to the top, even after the boy had discovered a field of cultivated beans where he would gladly have spent his whole life eating.

In time the trees disappeared altogether and they passed through open country of blowing grass and rock. An occasional lookout terrace could be seen, but the cross-paths vanished once they were above the farming level, and the verdant foliage gradually decreased. By the time they reached the cone, the path sputtered out, appearing and disappearing according to whether stairs were needed, but otherwise indistinguishable from the smooth black volcanic rock. They camped there, under the open sky for the first time since Jai Pendu, and Tarquin found himself searching the stars for the constellation he had seen on the black sails of the fishing boats. He did not find it.

It was cold that night, and neither was prepared for that. Kere shivered, chattered, mumbled to himself for a few fitful hours while Tarquin sat stoically awake; then they were off again. They spent the better part of a day scrambling up the side of the cone, changing directions, descending and starting again, and often stopping to rest in the shade of overhanging boulders where the shale lay in pastrylike layers. When at last they came over the edge of the cone and looked down inside, the day was ending in a cloud-crowded blur of grey.

The land was dead, ashen, and bleak where the cone curved inward. The wind was chilly and dry. The jungle teeming with diverse and persistent life seemed only a faint memory, and even their more recent glimpses of well-tended terrace gardens bright with crops were rendered foolish and hopeful up here, where the black earth met the sullen, cloudy sky. The volcano had become a moribund extrusion, like a gangrenous limb deprived of vitality from below. There was an unhealthy odour in the air that drifted out of the deep concavity, and from the piles of sooty stone eked tendrils of grey steam. The terrain within the cone, though bare of tree or grass or even moss, was nonetheless complex, being scored with fissures, pocked with holes, and decorated with swirls of once-molten stone, like black cream frozen in the midst of whipping.

Tarquin leaned on the walking stick he had cut for himself miles back where young trees were plentiful. He wiped sweat from his eyes with the back of his forearm. His gaze had fixed on a small man-made structure near the bottom of the pit in the centre of the cone. Its polished metal was free of ash and, even in the grey light, it shone a little. The sides were black, incised with a silver design, and its edges were silvery. It looked like a tent or, seen sideways, like the sail of a Pharician boat.

'What a strange thing,' he murmured, noticing that there were a number of fault lines running across the bottom of the cone's interior. 'This mountain has not been still for so very many years, and yet that building sits there, undisturbed. Let's take a look.'

Kere wobbled after him as they worked their way down the inside of the cone. The boy was clumsier than usual as his legs were being asked to suddenly work going downhill after days of climbing uphill. At times he broke into an involuntary run. Tarquin looked at the way his joints connected to each other and marvelled that he could stand up at all, much less run. His muscles and tendons were undeveloped and unpractised. Tarquin reminded himself to be careful with the boy lest Kere be injured or killed; then there would be no hope of getting Ice back. Yet, he thought, surely the magical horse from Or knew what he was doing. This whole thing was probably Ice's idea of a joke.

The impression of a tent had not been so far off, for as Tarquin approached the structure he saw that it was not a complete building, but rather two slabs of a metal-like substance propped against one another to make a triangular shape open at either end. Drawing closer, he realized that he was looking at a hinged set of double doors meant to cover a rectangular aperture in the earth; but the activity of the volcano had apparently forced them up and outward, and they buckled slightly where they leaned together. The pattern of cracks in the black stone reinforced this impression, and Tarquin gathered that the opening had once been larger than it was now. Some kind of dark shaft could still be seen leading down. Although there was no smoke, the air was foul.

As he came within arm's reach of the doors, he noticed two things which, taken together, made him stop, hand outstretched. The first was that the material was neither metal nor stone nor wood, but a substance that the Clans had never been able to replicate – an Everien material. The second was that etched into the material of the double doors, meant to form a single picture when the doors were shut but now partly interrupted where the doors buckled up sharply, was a design that he recognized. The outline was the same as the one studding the black sail on the beach below: a woman on a horse. But this rendition was more detailed, and it was vividly coloured. The horse was black, and decked out in the Pharician style. The woman was more of a girl, and she had long hair and very fair skin that showed against the green of her eyes where she half turned in the saddle as if to glimpse something behind her. Her hair was red.

Like Heavy Rain

'It must be an alternate entrance to their underground stronghold. Judging by the condition of these doors, it's not used. There won't be any guards, either. This is perfect.'

Kere was kneeling on the brink, his head and shoulders wedged into the space created by the warped doors. His voice echoed.

'It's hot down there. It doesn't smell so good, either. There's no light. How will you know where to go?'

'I'll go in the morning, when the light's better. I'll just climb down far enough to get the lie of the stone. If there's a clear way, then we'll have to make some torches or something. First I want to be sure that the passage hasn't been blocked by whatever wrenched up these doors.'

Kere said, 'There has to be an easier way. All those entrances by the garden terraces. We saw only women. How hard could it be to get in that way?'

'No, I don't want to do that. I still don't know who I'm dealing with. This Mavese could be a hard character, and we know nothing about the layout of their city or what weapons they may have. The Snake Clan are famous for their poisons and drugs. Even a small woman can use these to deadly effect. I'd rather go in by the back door.'

'And what am I supposed to do? Wait around and sit lookout?'

'Exactly.'

Kere sighed.

In the morning, Tarquin ate sparingly, then removed his boots and shirt and sword belt and gave them to Kere. He took a long drink and instructed Kere to stay put and listen for him to call up. He showed the boy how to wrap the rope around a rock and brace himself so that he could take Tarquin's weight if necessary.

'I'm only going to be gone an hour or two, and I'll probably be in voice range the whole time, so don't get any ideas about wandering off.'

It was a long rope, but slender. He secured one end around his waist and began his descent. At first the rope was more of a nuisance than a help. The shaft was narrow and he was able to chimney-climb it, bracing his back against one side and walking his feet down the other. After about a hundred feet, he came to the first blockage. The earth had shifted and the shaft had cracked and moved over against itself, so that there was only about two feet of width in which to manoeuvre before the opening resumed, several feet below, displaced to one side. This left Tarquin with very little space, a sheer drop, and the sharp edge of the rock to fray what he'd already felt was an inadequate rope.

'Kere!' he called up, and a shadow appeared in the blurry light, above.

'I can't see you,' Kere said. 'Are you all right?'

'There's a blockage here. I can't see what's beyond, but I'm worried about the rope fraying. Can you move it over so it doesn't rub against this edge?'

He waited while Kere repositioned the rope. Then he slithered through the crack and felt carefully for new footholds below.

'All right,' he called. The shaft had gotten wider and there was plenty of air moving around him, but now he was in complete darkness and he began to think of suffocation.

'I can't hear you,' Kere answered. Tarquin repeated himself. After three tries Kere said, 'Good. But I can't really hear you. Your voice is just noise, there's so much echo.'

Tarquin kept going. He got through a second block without trouble, but just below it the tunnel widened yet again. There was no way he could brace against the shaft and chimney-climb it. He switched to free-climbing, face against the increasingly smooth stone and working only by feel since there wasn't one iota of light. The air had begun to get hot.

'Kere!'

There was a faint noise in answer, but no recognizable words.

'Hold the rope secure, Kere,' Tarquin whispered to himself. Then he kicked free and slithered down the wall. It was a good four or five seconds before the rope came tight and caught him. There was still nowhere to catch hold. He dangled there bouncing off the wall from time to time, and shouted up to Kere to get his attention.

'Kere! I'm coming up. We're out of rope and I can't find a hold down here.'

There was no answer. Tarquin emitted a brief curse and began to climb up the rope, thinking that this had been a colossal waste of time. He couldn't see anything. He'd come over a hundred feet down into the volcano, and despite the presence of the doors at the top of the shaft, there was nothing down here to indicate the presence of humans. Maybe Kere was right; maybe he should build a boat and go up the chasm.

He stopped climbing and swung closer to one of the walls, reaching out to check it for roughness. It seemed to him that he should have reached the point where last he had been able to gain holds, but the rock was still smooth as glass. He drew up his legs and stretched one arm up to pull himself higher and suddenly all the tension went out of the rope. He was falling.

He bounced off the wall twice, grabbed for a hold and skinned his hands on the rock before coming to a jarring landing on his heels where a protruding ledge caught him. He stood there motionless, heart racing, blood afire with the rush of fear, while the limp rope slapped him in the head and proceeded to drop progressively onto him, pound after pound of safety landing on his head and shoulders like heavy rain. It tumbled over him and continued down, soon dragging at him and threatening his position on the ledge. Hastily he untied himself and pushed the coils off him even as they fell. He couldn't see anything, but he could hear the slither of the rope as it disappeared into the unknown depths. He couldn't help but think of snakes.

'Kere!' he screamed. 'Kere!'

There was no answer at all, not even a peep.

Wolves at the Door

'Honour,' said Tash to the mice, 'is a myth. Were I not so short of supplies, I would spray you all with oil and strike a match. I don't care how small you are. You are numerous, and you watch me. One day I will leave this castle and its eyes – the Eyes of Knowledge and your Animal eyes – oh, don't think I am ignorant of your schemes, mouse! Taking this castle was too easy, I know it. I watch Everien, and you watch me. Watch me, then!'

He sprang up and made a dash across the hearth, the poker extended like a sword, cutting daring strokes across an imaginary opponent. His shadow fell over the mice and passed, wavering as the wind he created fanned the flames of the lamps. He spun and laughed, for the mice had been set scurrying, taking up new positions under different shadows. Tash strode to the low table with the remains of his meal and picked up a handful of pastry. He tossed it across the flagstones and the crumbs went tumbling in many directions.

'Come out!' he called in a wheedling tone. 'Come out, come out, micelings. Come to your mice lord. Scheme away, but I am your ruler now.'

There was a slight stirring from the edge of a heavily tasselled carpet, and a single mouse shot forward, seized a crumb, and vanished again. Encouraged, more of them began to come forward, until all the pastry was gone.

'There,' said Tash. 'Now you will advise me, little bastards. I have fed you and you owe me. Tell me what to do about this dark Eye, for you cannot be any worse than shit-for-brains Kivi.'

But the mice fled. Even their eyes disappeared from the room's dark perimeter.

'Bloody beasts,' Tash murmured. 'Rejected even by the damned mice. Now I have no one to talk to but myself, and I am worse company than a dead camel.'

He started to laugh at his own joke and caught himself up, suddenly falling silent and taking a half step toward the far end of the hall, where one of the doors stood slightly ajar.

'Who's there?'

For two heartbeats, nothing moved; then one of the velvet curtains covering a draft at the end of the hall stirred, and Ixo peeked out.

'How did *you* get here?' he asked, his face lighting up. She twisted the edge of the curtain between nervous fingers and bit her lip. 'Did you sneak out of the women's quarters? Ah, my bold Wasp. Come, turn and show me your bottom – I must check your stinger, honeybee!'

Ixo stepped out from behind the curtain. Her hair was unbound and she wore a shift of red Pharician silk that Tash had given her in their first weeks together. Her feet were bare. She was shivering. 'I missed you,' she said softly.

Two hours later, Ixo stretched her arm across Tash's back and buried her face in his fragrant skin. He lay prostrate on the black bearskin rug, and firelight glazed his sweating skin with highlights of gold and red. She trailed a languid hand down the length of his body.

'The fire burns my skin,' she whispered. 'Is it like this all the time in your country?'

'The heat is good,' he murmured. 'I would lie right among the flames if I could, but I am too lazy to move.'

'You have outdone yourself this night,' Ixo said, and his back shook with amusement.

'I hope you are satisfied,' came the reply, muffled by the rug. 'For I can do no more.'

Ixo draped herself over him and kissed whatever she could reach of his face and neck.

'Stop it!' he said in a mock growl. 'Do not arouse me. I have to think.'

'Is that what you have been doing without me all these nights?' she chided. 'Thinking?'

He rolled over beneath her and grabbed both her hands, which had begun to do mischief. 'You are a distraction,' he complained. 'How am I to solve all these problems when you have made me so relaxed and useless? Take care you do not make me soft with your attentions.'

She wriggled against him, frowning. 'I have tried to make you soft but it doesn't seem to be working, and I will be split in two if we do not stop.'

He stroked her hair and regarded her through liquid, dark eyes.

'You look sad,' she said.

'I am a war leader. I never look sad. I only look stern, angry, or threatening.'

'What if one of your men dies?'

'Then I look vengeful.'

She kissed him. 'Well, I think you look sad . . .'

He blew out a long breath and his full lips fluttered. 'Ah, well, I suppose you are too old anyway.'

'Too old? What do you mean, too old?'

Tash laughed. 'For the Impressions.'

'Oh. Well, yes, I am too old.'

'But have you ever had one?'

'Not a one. Ever.'

'Too bad. For I must get that Carry Eye of Kivi's working again.'

'I know nothing of such things, Tash,' Ixo began cautiously.

'But?' He laughed. 'Clan wildwoman, say what you will.'

'I was only going to ask one stupid question. Why is a small Carry Eye so important when you possess the Eye Tower itself, including the Water of Glass and all that are connected to it?'

'That is not a stupid question,' said Tash, stroking her cheek and smiling. 'But Kivi's Carry Eye has not been like the others, not since it looked on Night on the plains of Ristale. Even I have looked into it, and the experience was very strange. I can remember nothing. I lost control of myself for a time. It was deeply unpleasant.'

Boldly, Ixo remarked, 'We hear rumours that you send the Impressionists to work in the Fire Houses.'

'I do,' said Tash. 'Only not to hammer and sweat in the forge pits.'

'To do what, then?'

'Never mind. To answer your question, Ixo, the Carry Eye is special. I need what it can give me.' He let out a long sigh, and Ixo stroked his back, nuzzling his skin.

'Tell me what is wrong,' she whispered. 'You will feel better if you speak to little Ixo.'

'Ah, I don't even know, honeybee Ixo. Maybe it is good news, but in my heart I fear it is the beginning of the end.'

'What news?'

'Our emperor Hezene, he plans to send troops to Everien. He says they are to support me, but I suspect he intends to replace me with some effete administrator. You would not like to live under Hezene's rule, Ixo. I tolerate your Clan ways. I let you keep your language and I am far less harsh than Hezene would ever be. Yet if I cannot hold Everien fast within my hand, he will take it away from me.'

Ixo wrapped her arms around him.

'Even a week ago, before this event with the Eye, I was confident of my future here. For the work in the Fire Houses outstripped anything Hezene has ever done, in its own way. Now I have no such confidence. If I do not follow through on my boasts about the Fire Houses, I cannot fight Hezene if he tries to depose me. And if he truly does intend to support me, then he will only do so on the basis that I make Everien profitable. For Hezene, that means producing Knowledge and weapons. Do you understand, Ixo?'

'Where I come from, to be spared from attack by the Sekk is

considered success. To have a good harvest of honey and medicines to trade to the Bear Clan is a great blessing.'

'Ah, all women will say this. "We need no war, we wish only to nurse our babies in peace." Yet watch them crowd round a fight. Watch them throw themselves at the winner. Look at you, for example! What are you doing here tonight? I did not send for you.'

Ixo looked hurt. 'I missed you,' she said. 'I came to see who you have been with these past nights.'

'No one, as well you know, for you rule the women's quarters. I lie with no one, for I must think, and sex drains my mind.' He pinched her thigh.

'Can I do anything to help you? I will make Gialse talk. I can brew drugs that will remove her will.'

He smiled and touched her lips with a fingertip. 'I'm sure you can. But she is one of many, once useful, now used up. I will find another way. I have already sent to Hezene asking for more engineers, loath though I am to put my faith in Scholars. You see, I have powerful weapons already in the Fire Houses, Ixo. But they are unproven in battle, and I don't know whether I should make more. If the blacksmiths work double shifts developing the plans we already have, then there will be no time to make tests. Yet if I am to meet Hezene's army with a strong force of my own, I have no choice but to build more machines. For he has many, many men, and I have few.

'I'm running out of ideas,' continued Tash. 'I have been struggling to get this Eye to speak to me, but it seems to be no use. Is it any wonder I grow frustrated and short of temper? Ah, Kivi, he is so useless, now he accuses me of frightening his precious Impressionist.'

Ixo kissed him. 'You probably *do* frighten her. She doesn't know you like I know you.'

He slid his hands down her back and pulled her buttocks apart. 'Maybe *you* should listen to the runt Impressionist,' he said. 'Maybe you can get some information out of her. I suspect Kivi of coaching her.'

'You think she's not really Seeing what she says?' Ixo said incredulously. Everything she'd ever been told about Impressionists suggested that they had no control over their experiences in trance.

'I don't know. But Kivi is a do-gooder, everybody's friend and benefactor, and I don't like that.'

'I don't think Kivi is a match for me.'

Tash spanked her playfully. 'No, he is not! Not when you are in a temper anyway, you little hothead. Come here. I will suck your tits now.'

'No,' she moaned feebly.

'Yes,' he contradicted with his mouth already full. 'But you must be quieter this time. Look, you have awakened all the mice! They are watching us.'

Ixo looked past the circle of firelight and saw dozens of tiny eyes.

'Ugh! Ugh . . . *Oh. Oh*, Tash, please don't start again. *Ohh* . . .'

Kivi was not pleased when Ixo informed him that she was going to take charge of the Impressionist Gialse, and that he should hand over the Carry Eye to her. It was not that Kivi relished the responsibility – far from it. But he did feel sure that in the hands of a girl as ambitious as this Wasp, whom Tash already favoured too much, both Gialse and the Carry Eye would quickly come to grief.

And he said so – loudly. He woke Mistel up from her late afternoon nap, as a matter of fact. The old Wolf came out of one of the salons accompanied by her silent grey familiars to find Ixo standing in the bottom of the women's gallery. She was wearing a red gown that made the most of her splendid figure; Kivi on the balcony above was getting a good view of her, but was blocked by Doren and a second eunuch from approaching. He leaned over the rail to shout his replies to Ixo. The other girls watched silently from doorways and alcoves. When Mistel arrived, there was further evidence that the argument had grown heated in the form of silk cushions littering the balcony, as well as part of an uprooted plant which decorated Kivi's hair just above his left ear. He did not appear to have retaliated (yet) and it showed: His face was red with suppressed anger.

'There you are, Kivi,' Mistel said sweetly, peering up into the gloom. Rain was beating on the glass roof. Ixo snorted and tossed her head.

'Doesn't Kivi have something else to do?' she asked regally. 'Tash has instructed me to question the girl, and Kivi will not give me the Carry Eye though I told him it is Tash's express wish.'

'Kivi?' Mistel said. 'Is this true?'

'Tash would never entrust such an artifact to the hands of Ixo, Mistel. As soon as I can find him, I will ask him what role he means for her to have in the Seeing of Gialse. But I have more serious problems to worry about today, and so does Tash. I cannot guarantee an immediate answer.'

Mistel began to climb the spiral stairs leading to the balcony. Wheezing a little, she said, 'Kivi, why don't you be sensible and let Ixo get on with it? Surely you have no lack of Eyes up in your Tower.'

'It's more than my life is worth, this Carry Eye—' Kivi began, and Ixo shrilled,

'Aye, it is ten times the value of your life, you fool!'

Kivi's lip curled, but Mistel gave Ixo a silencing wave. She went to Kivi and put her hands on his shoulders, gazing up at him with her warmest expression.

'Shh, never mind, Kivi. Ixo is getting too full of herself. Go on, go back to Tash and find out what he really wants Ixo to do, and in the meanwhile we will see to it that no harm comes to Gialse.'

Kivi subsided. 'Very well,' he said. 'I will talk to Tash. But I would advise you to stay out of it, Mistel. There are reports coming in through the Eyes in Wolf Country, and I gather there is trouble there.'

'What kind of trouble?' Mistel asked, alarmed.

Kivi shrugged. 'The rebels, I assume. You must keep quiet, Mistel, if you don't want to be hurt. I hope your people have not forgotten their pledge to you.'

Mistel put a hand to her forehead and swayed against Kivi, for all the world like Gialse after the trance. Kivi caught her and supported her, and a moment later the old woman recovered.

'What have they done?' she whispered, clutching at Kivi's robes.

'I'm sure it will be all right,' he stammered, not very convincingly. 'Come, now. Ixo, stop being such a raving bitch and help Mistel.'

Ixo was already running up the stairs, her face pale with concern.

Doren peeled Mistel away from Kivi and pushed him out into the corridor as the girl approached.

'I think you should leave,' he said firmly.

Ixo and Mistel returned to the women's gallery. Ixo took her into her own bedchamber, seated her in the red velvet Pharician chair Tash had sent as a gift, and ordered wine brought. She lit a scented candle and fanned Mistel's face.

'I won't let him hurt you! What bullies men are. How can they punish you for something your Clan has done, far away?'

Mistel patted her hand, but her voice was weak and did not match the bravery of her words. 'Hush, little one. It would not be the first time I survived a skirmish in Wolf Country.'

'I hope it was only a skirmish,' Ixo said. 'No one tells us anything! I wondered why Kivi was in such a bad mood.'

'Kivi bears the brunt of Tash's demands with Illyra out in the field.'

'Oh – speaking of Illyra, *he* is in Wolf Country!' Ixo exclaimed. 'Delivering medicine against the winterfever, I think.'

'Illyra is not a healer.'

Ixo pouted in concern. 'Do you think it could be Illyra? Do you think *that* is what is bothering Tash, and not the Eyes at all?'

'I don't know,' Mistel answered, sighing and closing her eyes. 'The inner workings of the mind of Tash are a mystery to me. But if Kivi is upset and refusing to share the Carry Eye, and if Tash told you to help Gialse with the Impressions, then that is his biggest concern, for whatever reason. It is always the Fire Houses, with him; and yet none but Kivi and his Clan know what transpires there, and the

Impressionists can never remember what they have Seen. We are all in the dark.' She fell silent.

Ixo poured wine and begged her to drink it, holding the glass to Mistel's lips as if she were an invalid.

'It is all right,' Mistel said, opening one smoky grey eye that sparkled with humour as she took the glass. 'Do not feel sorry for me. I have tried to help the Wolves resettle, but if they choose to fight Tash in the end, it is their decision. I do not hold my life ahead of theirs, and they know that.' She closed her eyes again meditatively. 'I am not afraid of Tash.'

'You should be.' Ixo shuddered. 'I saw him do terrible things when he first took over Jai Khalar. You don't know what he may be capable of.'

'Let's not waste time,' Mistel said. 'I expect Kivi will be back soon. Fetch the little Impressionist to me.'

When Gialse was brought she looked much recovered, but still nervous. Mistel smiled at the skinny girl, but she hid behind a fringe of brassy hair, her eyes downcast and her fingers twiddling. She sat on the edge of Ixo's bed as if prepared to spring up and run away. It was no wonder: the guardian wolves had followed Mistel in, and one lay at her feet, the other two sitting before the door as though preventing escape. Ixo lounged on the rug by the fire much as she was in the habit of doing in Tash's room, observing the girl with a rather predatory eye.

Mistel felt sorry for Gialse to be in such a position. She selected her words to the Impressionist carefully.

'Do you understand, my dear, that we all must use whatever talents we have to help Everien? I will not betray you to Tash. I will tell no one what you tell me. You must realize that you are in a unique position to know what Tash plans. You look into the Carry Eye and See as he commands you.'

'But I couldn't see anything.'

'Why not? What happened?'

'I don't know. I don't remember. But he became angry with me, and he threatened to send me to the mines, I think. Kivi protected me. I do not think Tash will use me again, Mistel. I hope he will not. He said my words were foolish.'

'What did you say?'

She shrugged. 'I don't remember anything. It was like being asleep, only colder.'

'What if I told you that even now there is something going on in Wolf Country, that the Clans were making trouble for Tash there? Could you look into a Carry Eye and See what is going on?'

'I am not a Seer, Grandmother Mistel. I only feel things, and don't remember them afterward. And even a Seer would need the Water of Glass to See all the way to Wolf Country. Kivi could do it.'

'Ah, but Kivi belongs to Tash,' Ixo said. 'Never mind Wolf Country, Mistel. We will find out what the rebels are doing there soon enough. Tash wants to know what she feels in the darkness of Kivi's Carry Eye. Ask her about that, Mistel. Ask her to explain. Then maybe Tash will trust me with the Eye, and if I tell him you helped me maybe that will make him softer toward you, if the Wolves have made some aggression.'

'I can do better than that,' Mistel said. She smiled at Gialse and clasped her hands. 'Could you show me what you do? Could you do it right here, right now, for me? If I promise not to do you any harm, no matter what you may say in the trance?'

'No, for I would still need the Carry Eye, Grandmother Mistel.'

Mistel slipped a hand into her robe and pulled out the Carry Eye she had pickpocketed from Kivi when she grabbed hold of him. 'Will this do?'

Spice the Lion

You come creeping beneath the darkness beside me, like a cat slipping under the bedclothes for warmth. You want to know what I know.

I don't know whether I am a child or not. I know the size of my hands and feet, and that I have not grown into them yet. I know that though my breasts have budded they do not yet weigh on me as my mother's do upon her. And I feel uncertain in many things that before I felt sure of; but also I see that I was stupid then, and I'm glad I am older now. My heart aches for home. Yet when I was there, I wanted to be outside, free. These are too many contradictions for me to bear, but I bear them just as the black horse bears me, and wonder.

It is a perplexing forest. The sound of owls fills it every hour of the day. There are cloaks and curtains of moss that hang from the oaks, and the roots of things are often exposed like great uncoiling snakes made all of bone. I see it all by moonlight or not all, and the place perplexes me, for Jihan taught me enough that I understand plants require sunlight. There is never any of that here, but much mist, and the slither of suggested creatures who never make themselves fully known. The horse killed something once, attacked it with his hooves, stamping it and slashing it into oblivion. I don't know what the thing was: some kind of slug or snail I suspect from the glimpse I had, but it moved fast, which is not ordinary. I have often felt after that that the horse protects me from this place and that I would be unsafe if I were to tread among these trees on my own.

And yet I grow tired of being a passenger. This horse never tires, but I do. I want to feel my feet on the earth. I want to break bread with my fingers, and swallow water, and lie down. I want to be still.

I must leave this forest. I must.

But they are following me.

I cannot think of that. I must think of something happier, while you are making your way toward me as I know you must be, for you would not forsake me. I know you would not. I will think of something long ago, from the time of daylight, but only if you promise wherever you are to smile, at least a little.

In the house of my father there were many books. I used to sit in a high western window late in the afternoon, when the day is spent and awaits the falling of the sun as some mere formality, and the smells of dinner are beginning to waft from the kitchens below. Half listening to the music of birds and water from the garden, I would prop my father's books on my bent knees and turn the pages. There were few pictures in his books, and some of them were writ in languages I couldn't even name, much less understand. One among these I looked at anyway, for it was written by hand, and I loved the way the light fell across the creamy pages with their thick, textured surfaces and ragged edges, and the smell of the leather and silk and paper and ink and age was precious to me. I turned the pages in wonder, gazing at the magnificent hand that had written a story in symbols and characters whose meaning I could not divine, save for the series of pictures that were laid in the very centre of the tome. They were line drawings in coloured ink, and each was of a different animal. My favourite was a lion whose mane was a blend of colours, ginger and cinnamon and nutmeg: When I was very small and first able to open this book, I named him Spice and we had many secret talks. When I grew older I began to see sadness in his eyes, and later I noticed that he was ribby and lean as if he had been hunting for a long time with no success; and eventually it became so that when I opened to his page I could see nothing of him but his claws, blackened with old stains, sharp, and overgrown.

Even at the age of nine, I knew better than to run to my mother and tell her this. By then I knew that in such a circumstance she would only continue stirring her soup and tasting it, or gently raking the earth between the rows of young lettuces, or perhaps squeezing a cheese through a cloth. And she would say, 'We are given imagination so that we may understand our world, Jaya. This world.' Taking my hand she would press it to the cheese or the earth or the wooden spoon so that I had to feel her warm flesh and the firm surfaces of the objects she was handling. 'Imagination was never meant to be a horse that runs away with us. Put a bridle on yours, Jaya.'

She never spoke harshly when she said things like this. My mother was simply so firmly rooted in her garden, her cellar, her pantry, her kitchen, and her sewing room that even the winds that lifted the elms one winter and dumped them on their sides could not dislodge my mother from her practical tasks. I remember playing in their branches, marvelling at last year's robin's nest turned on its side, while through the kitchen window my mother could be seen serenely kneading bread dough.

Jihan had to cut the tree into pieces and drag it away, and how he moaned about it. I was a child in those days, and I was allowed to laugh and run around while others did the work. I was the centre of everything. Now I'm the centre of nothing. I'm older now, but I feel so young and foolish. It seems to me there was a time when I knew more, when I could see more. I can't imagine how, but I must once have been wiser. I try to remember how I was in the days before I rode away, the days before the night that came alive and hunted me. How I thought, how I felt, what I did. I try, yet it's becoming so *that sometimes I forget those days entirely, and all I remember is riding and riding, here in the misshapen half-dark. It seems like forever.*

My mother didn't like to speak of my father. I had to infer what he was like from the things he had left behind. I suppose this is why I spent so much time in the library, sitting on the window ledge with the vines outside curling just as I curled my hair round my fingers. My mother never came to the library. It was almost as if she blamed the books for my father's absence. She stayed among the living things, in the garden or the cellars or the aviary. She kept his birds long after he was gone, though she feared them. I could never tell whether she was angry or happy when I went to the aviary to see the falcons, or afterward when I began to hunt with them. She did not like me hunting: I knew this much. Nor did she stop me, seeming to feel this was an area somehow outside her province.

'The wild woods are unsafe,' she would say. 'You must consider your duties here.' Yet all I knew of my duties was that I was meant to stay in the silence and eventlessness of the house and garden, and 'keep' them, as my mother said. 'One day, all this will be yours,' she told me; but all I could think was how one day I would saddle my horse Midnight Blue and ride him down the hill and into the forest, and only return when I had discovered what else the world I'd read of in my father's books was made of. It was not to be, my mother told me.

'One day, if you are patient, a man will come to you and then you will have your own children. He will have had many conquests and accomplishments in the world without, but he will choose you, and this place for a sanctuary, and stay here with you. That is what you must hope for.'

'I want to leave,' I said. 'Why can't I go away, just for a while, if I promise to come back?'

'You would not be able to get back if you left,' said my mother. 'Do you not think your father wishes to return?'

Her mouth was small and bitter when she said this, and there were tears in her eyes. I wondered whether my father wished to return. I didn't like the idea that anything could keep him from returning to us if he wished to; nor did I like the idea that he would leave us. He was a conundrum to me, but I never asked about him. I wanted to fold my mother and her dress up and stuff them into the back of a closet so I could get on with my plans, but I could not, so I merely stalked off, sulking. I grew practised at biding my time. Sooner or later, I knew something had to happen. It always did. Like when I found the key to the imagination room. Like opening the deck of cards. Like waking them *and* having to run for my life. Like falling into the fountain. Sooner or later, in the house of my father, something always happens.

'This house requires careful attention,' my mother would say solemnly, 'to maintain its order. That is why we are not allowed to leave.'

124

That is why you are not allowed to leave, I wanted to say, but I thought it would be cruel, and she didn't really deserve that. Still, I wondered what she meant and I asked Jihan about it. He took it all less seriously; but then again, that is Jihan and although he was as familiar to me as the walls themselves, I don't know how to talk about him. I suppose you could say he was my teacher. He taught me to fly the falcons, to fence, to understand the principles behind the world: what is in it and what is not in it. He explained to me that my mother was not a true steward of the house: that that duty was meant to be my father's, and my father was gone.

'She needs an ordinary house to run,' Jihan said of my mother. I watched him with round eyes: I was half in love with Jihan, not in a sexual way exactly but in some other way I can't quite pin down. He was lithe and red-haired with cornflower blue eyes, and every move he made seemed a form of jest. He could imitate anyone and anything and his face seemed infinitely pliant, and he was never sour or tired that I could ever see. He walked about in a blue cloak with a silver braid on its hood, and he treated everything as a great game. Also it seemed to me that as I grew older, he grew younger, although he always knew more than I did and could frequently trick me in all sorts of matters. It was rather like having a cat for a tutor, he was so clever and self-possessed, and my chances of ever impressing him, much less becoming like him, seemed about equal to my chances of ever becoming a cat; yet I never stopped trying.

'What do you mean?' I said. 'What do you mean, an ordinary house?'

'Ordinary houses are . . . ordinary,' Jihan answered, and began juggling jam jars, for it was the middle of the night and we were in the kitchen raiding it for a snack.

'If our house isn't ordinary, then what is it?' I asked.

Jihan tossed me a jar of apricot conserves and the lid spun off it as it flew. I caught the lid but missed the jar. It smashed on the flagstones, and jam splattered everywhere.

'Clumsy!' he accused, shaking his head. 'I despair of ever teaching you anything. Our house is a timewalker, of course.'

Gialse fell silent. Neither Ixo nor Mistel had noticed how much time had gone by; for it was always dark and the shadows didn't move across the room. One lamp burned out but they paid no attention, hypnotized by the voice coming out of Gialse that sounded so different from her own.

There had been a timid scratching at the door which everybody took to be mouse-related; then, a few moments later, four soft knocks. The smallest of the wolves, asleep with his head on Mistel's feet, growled softly without waking. Ixo opened the door and one of Tash's younger harem-girls stood there.

'Tash commands the presence of Mistel,' she said without looking at anyone. The wolves' eyes all came open and they stared at the girl. Ixo paced to the window and back in agitation. No one spoke.

At last Mistel gave an annoyed snort. 'We're right in the middle of something,' she said. 'What the fuck does he want me for now?'

The girl clasped her hands in front of her and swayed from side to side submissively. 'I don't know. I gather there's been a messenger from Wolf Country. It must be an emergency. He is in a very bad mood.'

Ixo flung herself at Mistel's feet. 'You mustn't go!' she said. 'We'll hide you somewhere. In Jai Khalar there are a thousand hiding places – why, think of it. Hanji has been gone for years and no one can find him. You shall do the same. Quickly, out the back with you.'

Mistel stroked the girl's silky black hair, smoothing the loose strands away from her flushed cheeks. 'No,' she said sadly. 'He would only punish all of you, and anyway that is not the way I conduct myself. I am the Grandmother of my people. I will go to Tash if that is what he wants.'

She stood and arranged her cloak. As one, the three wolves lifted their snouts and began to howl.

Ixo was sobbing as Mistel led the messenger girl out and across the gallery. 'Do not let her go!' she cried out to the harem at large. 'He will slay her, I am sure of it! Stop her!'

The others stopped what they were doing and stared, but no one interfered with Mistel, and even Ixo, though she stretched out her arms imploringly to the old woman, did nothing to restrain her physically. There was something about her bearing that made them stop. It was the kind of dignity usually possessed only by very old trees and even the stones of the world themselves; or maybe it was as if Mistel had already crossed over where they could not reach her. As if she were already a ghost.

Helplessly Ixo watched her go down the corridor to the door leading to Tash's audience hall. As the wooden door closed behind Mistel, Ixo began to wail and cry out, but Doren blocked her way and would not even let her see what was going on. She sat down cross-legged on the balcony, intending to wait, and listen, to what was happening in the room beyond. Soon other girls and women had joined her, and even the kitchen staff who had gotten wind of Tash's summons had begun to trickle into the back passage, curious. The eunuchs commanded the girls to return to the gallery and stop making trouble, but no one listened. Ixo was about to insist that they all march in on Tash en masse and demand Mistel's release, when suddenly she remembered that the Impressionist was still in her own bedchamber . . . and that she had Kivi's Carry Eye.

Suddenly Ixo was on her feet and addressing the imposing chest of Doren.

'Very well,' she said, her eyes still full of tears, although her mind was now making calculations at a furious rate. 'We will comply for the moment, but do not think this is over.'

She marched herself down to her chamber and the others took her lead, returning to their occupations with much talk and grumbling and continued crying, especially on the part of the young Wolves, who had heard there was trouble in their homeland.

Doren watched Ixo disappear into her room and leaned on his spear thoughtfully. He turned to his companions and remarked, 'She is up to something, that one.'

Winterfever

Snow loomed over the Pharician riders like a long-spun hex about to be let loose upon their heads. They sat their horses ill at ease, looking out of place and overwhelmed by the relentless grey-white of the dead winter landscape. Surefooted as goats, the furry Everien beasts scampered headlong up and down the folds of Wolf Country, unheeding of the occasional cry of dismay from their riders, who expected a spill at any moment. But these horses needed no paths and little guidance, for if they lacked in the speed and ferocity of the Pharician warmbloods, they made up the deficit with intelligence. An Everien horse remembered where he had been, no matter how long ago; and his sense of the weather and the passage of predators had not been domesticated out of him. The Clans had been well served by these animals for generations, but the Pharicians were used to neither their independence nor their unusual gaits. Now the horses were hurrying, aware of the gravid sky and the rising wind. They wanted shelter.

Illyra squinted at the sky. He might not possess the natives' knack for reading the weather, but it did not take a genius to see that snowfall was imminent. He couldn't believe the Clans travelled at all in such weather, no matter what the emergency. The Deer representatives had trudged on their snowshoes for miles alongside the mounted Pharicians, and no matter what the wind did, the ponies put their heads down and walked into it, though their coats were aglitter with ice and snow. At first Illyra had watched the Deer consume lumps of butter and twists of dried beef jerky on the march with the disgust of the civilized for barbarian ways; but a week into the journey and the rations his men had packed for him seemed to run through him like water. He was hungry and cold all the time, and he soon tired of taking constant precautions against the loss of fingers and toes – yet he could not show it. He had to set an example for his men.

For their part, his men grumbled that they had forsaken great careers in travelling and fighting and pillaging and drinking and whoring, and for what? Delivering medical supplies to a distant Wolf village in the dead of winter, so that all their babies wouldn't die of winterfever. Who cared how many Clan babies died, Illyra thought. His troops were Pharician Imperial Guards, not wet nurses. But Tash had sent them here, and Tash would have no compunctions about killing them if they didn't perform to standard. Illyra only hoped there was some bigger strategy of Tash's than simply taking and holding this forsaken valley. Why he would rather be ruler of such a shithole than the most notorious of wandering warrior princes was a mystery too deep for Illyra's frostbitten mind to penetrate. He shifted his weight in the saddle to ease his seat bones. Even the leather was frozen, and these little ponies weren't much to have between your legs – at the moment it was like trying to ride a goat made of granite. How he missed his faithful destrier Laika, now eating hay somewhere in the depths of the stables at Jai Khalar. Assuming the stables still existed and had not been replaced by a fishpond.

Thinking of Jai Khalar cheered him slightly. Better to be out here, even, than in that horrible place. He raised his eyes to the horizon, still squinting hard, for the snow and the pale sky created a glare that made it almost impossible to keep them open. The dark splotches of the Wolf caves that were their destination could be seen breaking the monotony of white. As he counted them and tried to judge the best path up, he saw a dogsled emerge from the lowest of the caves and hurtle down toward them. It was followed by two more; but Illyra did not wish to make the transaction on the open trail, especially if the Wolves enjoyed the advantage of elevation.

'Make sure we meet them outside their own caves,' he instructed Joni, the Deer physician who was nominally in charge of the mission. 'Give them nothing until we are secure in our position.'

Joni looked surprised, but Illyra didn't care. He dispatched four of his men to secure the slopes above the caves. The track was icy and steep, and in three or more places it passed between jagged rock formations before finally mounting the final slope to the visible caves. There were many points of ambush. Also the Wolves could have set pit traps in the snow and ice. Or there might be White Screamers nearby. With this much snow lying on the hills, an avalanche was possible even without the instigation of White Screamers, and Illyra was very nervous, although he couldn't think of a special reason he should be. Many little factors seemed to be adding up in his mind to make his stomach churn with something more than the mountain sickness.

The rebels, after all, had been very quiet lately. They were pre-occupied dealing with the Sekk, which was well because it saved the Pharicians from having to fight the strange creatures. Of the men whom Tash commanded, only his core force of horsemen could really be trusted against the Sekk. The rest had all been subject to the Slaving spell of Night that had swept through the garrison at Ristale last summer. They might have survived the experience, but it would have rendered them vulnerable to Sekk for ever after.

Illyra called a rest and let the dogsleds approach. He watched his men climbing slowly up the icy hillsides off the path, seeking to get a superior view of the cave entrances and whatever other holdings the Wolves might possess. It would be some time before he felt safe in his position.

The Deer were grumbling about the halt.

'We are almost there,' Joni protested. 'Why are we stopping at this exposed point?'

'Tactics,' Illyra answered shortly.

Joni was losing his temper – unusual for a Deer, Illyra thought. 'Tactics?' The Deer pointed to the sky. 'Do you see those clouds? We're going to be buried in an hour. Let's get into the caves before we can't even see the caves any more.'

Illyra ignored him. 'Look after your people,' he said. 'See to it they eat. And keep quiet. It is not asked of you that you should do more than this.'

Joni was plainly furious, but it had been clear from the beginning that the Pharicians were in charge, not the Deer, for all that it was precious Deer medicine, brewed in the cauldrons of the smallest Fire House from the purified egg of the H'ah'vah, which was being offered to the Wolves today. Tash had ordered the medicines dispensed even though their cost was astronomical. H'ah'vah potions were precious and the Deer were being compensated for them with nothing more than pelts, craftwork, and a bit of Wolf silver. In truth the medicines were a gift. But the Deer did as they were told by Tash. They didn't dare do otherwise. Virtually all their lands were patrolled by the Pharician army. Alone of the Clans, the Deer lived predominantly in the lowlands, where Pharician horses could easily travel, especially given the network of abandoned Everien roads.

The dogsleds drew near. Illyra suppressed a jolt of fear at the sight of the 'tame' dogs of the Wolf Clan: they looked like creatures out of his worst childhood nightmares. They were huge and silver or black, and when they panted their teeth gleamed white and curving. Barrel-chested, with huge paws and deep-throated barks and growls, they seemed barely contained by their harnesses, straining at the leather and whining urgently. They gazed at the trading party with eyes that ranged from grey to blue to yellow, but all hauntingly intelligent.

The two men who stepped off the first sled were both big, and their heavy furs made them look bigger. Behind his black beard the first said, 'Declare yourselves who bring weapons into Wolf territory.' He pointed at the Pharician rocket-launcher that had been designed by Impressionists and built in the Fire Houses: It had taken four ponies and six men to drag it up here, and Illyra had regretted bringing it as soon as the terrain grew steep – but Tash wanted it field-tested, and almost all the terrain in Everien was as rugged as this. The Wolf looked more puzzled than threatened by the device. By contrast, Illyra observed the Wolf's weapons: two of the biggest axes he had ever seen hanging from either side of the man's belt. Illyra relaxed fractionally as he had the thought that they would be too unwieldy to succeed in a fight against anything more mobile than a tree.

Joni glanced once at Illyra and said, 'I am Joni of the Deer Clan. We bring medicines with the grace of Tash at Jai Khalar, who sends greetings and offers what assistance he can.'

'I am Norrel and this is Xeel. Are you now the servant of Tash, Deer Clan man?'

Illyra wasn't catching every word, but he understood the hostility in the tone of the Wolf, and the matching offence in Joni's.

'A storm is coming, Norrel Wolf. We bring aid, and the weather is the enemy of all men. Can we not do our business by the fire? We have our own provisions and need not short you.'

'The Wolf Clan is not so poor as to refuse food to travellers,' said Xeel in a booming voice. He nodded to one of the others, a young man by his slim girth and light beard, and a deer carcass was dragged from the back of the sled and tossed in the snow in front of the party. The dogs barked and whined. Xeel spoke to them softly and stroked their heads. It had begun to snow.

Even Illyra, a foreigner and unfamiliar with many Clan customs, was not blind to the insult in this. So his troubled stomach had not lied. The Wolves were looking for a fight. Why?

He glanced uphill; his men had disappeared. Some signal from them was called for. Illyra was now thinking of nothing but dropping his cargo and getting out of there. He really didn't care what the Deer Clan got in return for their trouble; he just wanted to reach a more sheltered position before the snow destroyed what little visibility the gloom afforded.

He tapped Joni on the shoulder and the Deer turned, glancing up at him in alarm.

'Why do they offend you? If they want to fight, we will fight them. Don't let them keep you talking if they only intend to attack.'

Joni put a finger to his lips and shook his head. 'No, no. You don't understand. They're insulting us because they can't afford to pay.'

Illyra guffawed. 'Of all the foolish, self-destructive—'

'Wolves are notoriously proud,' Joni said. 'I was afraid of this. I had thought as a physician I would be immune to this sort of treatment, but apparently they don't care.'

'Hurry up, whatever you do,' Illyra said. 'I give you ten minutes and then we leave. We can return after the storm if you wish, but I won't be caught out in this.'

Again Joni shook his head. He smiled and laid a reassuring hand on the pony's bridle. 'We should be invited inside and given hospitality. There is no need to camp out in the storm.'

Illyra tossed his head at the sky. Already half an inch of white had settled on his fur collar, and the wind was picking up.

'Ten minutes,' he repeated. When Joni returned to the conversation, he again scanned the mountainside above the caves but saw no sign of his men. Joni was saying something about having exhausted men who were too inexperienced in the hills to handle the storm. He sounded as if he were trying to make the Wolves feel more secure; but Xeel only looked angrier.

'You cannot come up!' he shouted. 'There is a plague in our houses. If you come in, you will only infect your own people. Are you an idiot, Joni the physician, that you cannot see this?'

'Mountain fever cannot be carried by those who are not infected,' Joni said calmly. 'We are all adults and immune.'

'The Pharicians aren't,' Norrel said darkly. 'What blindness have they cast over you that you allow them up here with you? Are they so stupid in the south that they do not understand about infection?'

Joni was tongue-tied. 'But – they insist on coming,' he said. 'It is their country, after all.'

'You slime-lickers!' screamed Xeel. 'Get rid of the Pharicians and come up yourselves if you want, but we will give you only venison and melted snow. You are a faithless people.'

Now Joni was angry. 'We offer you freely the purified heart of the H'ah'vah egg as only we can prepare it in the Fire Houses. We offer you Knowledge, wealth, charity, and we are to get only a few pelts and other oddments in payment, that you not think we take pity on you, wildings. You do not want the medicines? You want an entire generation to die this winter? Go on, then! I will hear no more insults.' He turned away. Illyra gripped his sword, ready to fight; but Norrel looked like he was going to laugh and Xeel, though beet red, said nothing at first. As Joni turned around he winked at Illyra and mouthed, 'It is all part of the game.'

'Wait!' called Norrel in a conciliatory tone; but at that moment there was a cry from above and one of the Pharicians fell off the cliff. The Wolves suddenly had their axes out, and another group of Wolves could be seen from above, arrayed in a rough phalanx and wielding the deadly spin-blades. They had come off the fastness of the heights and had apparently discovered Illyra's scout party and attacked it. Now they were cutting a lightning path down the mountain toward the Pharician party. The attackers had no wings, but they flew down the mountainside with the speed and smoothness of diving birds, hurling spin-blades

132

all the while. Illyra just about worked out that they were standing on smooth pieces of wood that allowed them to slide across the snow at high speed, when a spin-blade struck his pony at the crest of the neck and it squealed and plunged sideways, dumping him ignominiously into the snow. He scrambled to his feet in the midst of sudden chaos. Xeel in his black furs was coming at him with one great axe gripped in two gloved hands; Illyra could barely feel his own fingers as they closed on his sword.

Xeel had let his dogs loose.

There were two men between Illyra and Xeel, and they moved to defend their leader. But the fight was not fair; the dogs were all over the men, and their swords were actually too long and unwieldy to use against the animals. The dogs got one soldier by the throat, dragging him to the ground, even as Xeel's axe came in to threaten Illyra.

Illyra had secretly been wishing to use the rocket-launcher in real combat, but had not yet had the opportunity, and this occasion seemed unlikely to provoke it. Yet he had brought the thing, always hoping . . . and now the time was nigh. How else were they to deal with such fell hounds? Fire in a blizzard seemed impossible, but not with the chemicals that had been implanted in the rockets. They could explode in anything short of full immersion in water – and on impact they would shower their vicinity with flammable oil that would burn whatever was left of their target. Illyra could not wait to see the rockets in action.

Now he was almost incoherent. 'Kill them all!' he shouted at his men. 'Kill them and take their dwellings before we all perish in the storm.'

He turned to face Xeel, and out of the corner of his eye he could see the flames shoot from the rocket-launcher, blue and white and an unreal yellow. Xeel paused, momentarily rooted to the spot by the roar and horror of the fire, and Illyra charged in and cut him down. Covered with Xeel's blood, he screamed his pleasure. 'Kill them all!' he repeated, laughing.

The squeals of the burning dogs brought out the entire Clan. Women came flying down through the snow, furless and hair unbound, carrying blankets to smother the flames. The dead and injured dogs were picked up and carried toward the dwellings as if they were children. Illyra's men shot at the women, but in the raging blizzard their arrows went astray. Joni began to clamber up the path toward the safety of the caves, clutching the bundle of medicines to his chest.

One of the snow-sliders clipped Joni with a spin-blade, and Joni in turn slipped and began to slide down the ice. The packet containing the precious medicine flew from his hands, skidded down a piece of frozen runoff from what must have been the Clan's water source, and disappeared in the deep powder of a snowdrift some thirty feet beneath.

Joni cried out, '*No!*' and began to run toward the place where the packet had landed, only to set off a small avalanche. He was picked up off his feet and carried down the gully by the snow and boulders that were suddenly set free, taking the whole side of the hill with them. Illyra didn't spare him further thought. The entire village had been mobilized and was attacking the party. A woman was coming at him with an axe raised in her two hands. Blood was streaming from the axe haft and coated her forearms.

'You killed our dogs!' shrieked the woman. 'You are worse than the Sekk. You will pay! Come have some winterfever, Pharician monsters. Come! Come! Eat our babies and die yourselves of winterfever, foul ones. And you dare call us barbarians, dog-killer!'

Illyra was stunned that the woman could show so much emotion over a dead animal when the Clan leader lay decapitated in the snow and the medicines that could have saved her children were now buried beneath the snow – although this did not stop the sliders from trying to find them, digging even with their hands in snow that was well over a man's head in depth.

'Calm yourself, stupid wench,' he said, and stepped toward her. 'Put the axe down, or die.'

She didn't heed him. The axe was already coming toward him in a movement driven by every sinew in her body. Her eyes bulged and her face was distorted into a grotesque mask. To see a woman thus ruined, even a barbarian woman, was an offence to every sensibility Illyra possessed. He took her head off cleanly, and before the rest of her body had hit the ground, he was already shouting to his men.

'Kill the lot of them and torch everything they have. Make the Deer clean out the caves but do not enter them yourselves. We will set our tents outside where the disease cannot find us.'

Joni had climbed from the snow. He stood still, too horrified to speak or act.

'Move!' Illyra cried. 'Move, and move your people as well! If the storm doesn't kill you, I will!'

Noses Bent Out of Shape

Beneath the snow, the rebels' tents looked no different from the boulders and the sheep. The dingle had been chosen because it was out of view of the monitor towers in the vicinity, as were a number of routes to it. A very careful Seer who used the Eye Tower to observe the paths and roadways of this region of Deer Country might possibly notice that travellers were passing in and out of the blind spot rather more often than they should, and infer that there was a rebel camp hidden in the hills. But either the Seers were not very careful, or the camp hadn't been there long enough to attract attention. The fells all around were empty and bleak in the midwinter darkness, but inside the tents there were lights and fires and the voices of Clansmen who had gathered from far and wide to exchange intelligence and make plans at Kassien's convocation near Pharician-held A-vi-Sirinn.

Command suited Kassien, even if it was a pseudo-command in which his king hid disabled in the woods surrounded by a few loyal followers, issuing orders and receiving information while trusting the younger generation to do the groundwork. The king's camp in Bear Country was well concealed and looked after by the Bear people, who had returned in droves from the borders of Everien when it had been learned that most of their men had been only captive to the Sekk, not killed. Kassien's high position in that Clan made him the automatic leader of the rebellion – and it didn't hurt that Lerien came from the Bear Clan as well, even though Ysse had placed no stock in such family associations. Besides, Kassien had passed through the Floating Lands. Even if he had not made it to Jai Pendu, he was still a hero, and looked it. In fact, Xiriel thought when he saw Kassien for the first time in a year, it was almost as if Kassien had been born with the looks and bearing of a heroic figure and had only been waiting for circumstances to name him one. The Seer, threadbare, cold, and a bit malnourished after an overlong journey on little-frequented hill paths from Snake Country, could not help but feel a bit inferior when he got an eyeful of Kassien.

The new leader of the Bear Clan had filled out considerably, and he wore his dark brown hair long and unbraided. He was clad in a tunic and trousers of dappled grey-brown spider silk that shifted colour when he passed from light to shadow, providing camouflage and making his movements subtly deceptive. Well-toned muscle moved easily beneath this fabric, and seeing the chain-woven gloves Kassien wore, Xiriel thought immediately that he would not care to be on the receiving end of a blow from one of Kassien's fists.

These same hands came out to clasp his and thump his back as Kassien gave a pleased laugh and greeted him.

'You look cold and ill fed, Xiriel,' he accused. 'Come, and I will get Dhien to feed you. She eats constantly herself nowadays – it will be no trouble.'

Xiriel went with him to a log house set in a grouping of others among the pines that lined the side of the glen, where a heavily pregnant Dhien was to be found mending saddle-leathers in a patch of winter sunlight. The dogs at her feet raised their heads when the two men approached, but to Xiriel's relief they did not charge. They stayed by Dhien's side and milled around wagging and sniffing.

'I must get what light and air I can,' she argued when Kassien reproached her for being outdoors in the cold. 'I will go out of my mind, cooped up in the darkness with himself kicking me all the time! Xiriel, is that you? I almost didn't recognize you. I haven't seen you since you came to our camp on the sea plateau.'

'It's been a long time,' Xiriel mumbled. Social graces were not his strong suit, and his mind was on the smell of venison stew wafting from within the house.

'Don't mind him. He'll perk up when he's been fed. Fetch us some stew, eh, Dhien?'

She got to her feet with an effort and lumbered inside. Xiriel thought how pleased Istar would be to see the beautiful girl so heavy and ungainly. He also thought that Istar would not much like fetching meals for Kassien's friends, and made a mental note to tell her that she was lucky Kassien did not fancy her but had instead bonded with Dhien. For Istar was surely destined for glory in the Seahawk Clan.

The talk was all about the disaster in Wolf Country, which had raised the hackles on them all. Bad enough that the winterfever had been so severe this year and that people had died needlessly; but to hear the manner in which the deaths had occurred brought some to depression, others to fury. Stavel had conveyed the news by bird scout in advance of his return from Wolf Country, where he had been doing his best to rally support for the rebel banner. Until recently there had been little enthusiasm for fighting from the men who were only too glad to return to their homes after the long march to and from the Floating Lands – little enthusiasm, that is, until word had spread of the incident up-country between the Pharicians and Xeel's family. As an uncle of Xeel,

Stavel had found himself with no lack of able-bodied men volunteering to set the Pharicians straight by any means necessary. He brought them in force to the convocation.

'I am going to send Dhien home to Bear,' Kassien confided in Xiriel. 'This has become a military camp. Things are going to start moving soon. It is inevitable, now that Tash has begun to aggress on our villages.'

Xiriel was uncomfortable with the whole business. For one thing, he no longer considered himself Wolf, yet his Clan looked to him as a hero ever since the passage of Jai Pendu. Furthermore, the Wolf demands for an end to the domination of Everien by the Knowledge did not sit well with him as a Seer and a Scholar. He wanted to get rid of Tash as much as anyone – but not at the price of destroying the Knowledge. So he arrived at the camp only too glad to leave the matter of revenge in the hands of Kassien and the other Clan leaders. He had many other things on his mind, not least of which was the discovery of the lake of candles, which he had had to leave in the hands of Jakse so that he could attend Kassien's convocation. He was eager to return to it and explore, but Kassien waved the subject away.

'There will be time for all that, I promise you,' he said. 'But not now. It is a great accomplishment that you found it, but you must now let Jakse watch over it and lend us your services here.'

'My services? How?'

'The fire weapons,' said Kassien. 'We will talk about it more in the meeting. Are you finished eating?'

Pallo turned up just then, and Dhien was called upon to provide more food, which she did, albeit with a strained smile on her face. Kassien went off to check on the main tent where the Clan representatives were to meet.

'Did you hear about Wolf Country?' Pallo said, and bit into a roll.

'I would like to have been present at this incident myself,' Xiriel replied. 'If only to see these weapons that were spoken of. I am poorly versed in the arts of the Fire Houses, but I did not think that terrors such as these could be produced there.'

Pallo shivered, looking worried. 'I hope Istar's mother will be all right. I have been travelling around in the guise of a Pharician Scholar, and I have heard a few rumours about the Fire Houses that trouble me. Istar should have removed her to a quieter place, where she would not run the risk of being recognized.'

'She was satisfied that Mhani was being well cared for by her youngest brother Dzani. If she were here, I'm sure she'd be saddling a horse for A-vi-Khalar to get Mhani out of there right now.'

As he spoke, the tent flap moved and Kassien returned, shedding snow. 'We are almost ready in the big tent,' he said. 'It's crowded, but then again, it's warm.'

Pallo caught Xiriel's arm, grabbing a slice of pie in his other hand. 'Where is Istar, then?'

'She went off with Pentar to Seahawk Country. Family problems. And she is raising an army.'

There was a shout from outside.

'Let's go,' Kassien said. 'Let's get in there before they start fighting.'

The Clansmen had been in the tent long enough to start arguing even before the meeting had formally started. Kassien entered and signalled for quiet.

'We have had time to be angry,' Kassien began.

'Not enough!' cried Stavel, who sat across from Xiriel and Pallo in a tightly controlled rage. Burel was beside him, looking white and terrible. He had been away from his village on the day of the massacre, hunting. He had returned to find the place destroyed and his entire family dead. It had been Burel who first brought the news, even ahead of the snow-bound Pharicians who camped throughout the storm before returning from upcountry with the story of the incident. Pallo tried to imagine what he must be feeling, and could not.

'It is their use of the Fire Houses that alarms me most,' Burel said in a low voice. 'These weapons they are making are capable of the most horrific damage, and none of the Clans possess their equivalent. It was hard enough when the Seahawks came with swords' – and here Joren the Bear grumbled slightly, something muttered under his breath along the lines of, *What about when the Wolves came with their steel axes and subjugated the Bears?* – 'but there is no way we can pit our weapons against these. The Deer are lying through their teeth when they say they are not warlike, but wish only to farm the land and explore the Knowledge. Any Knowledge they explore while under the guidance of such a man as Tash is bound to lead to more terror for us all. Maybe they are betraying us deliberately in order to get more power under the new Pharician regime, or even if we are charitable and say that their intentions in bringing the H'ah'vah medicine were honourable, still we have no choice but to conclude that they are deceiving themselves if they think they can play with the Fire Houses without being manipulated by the Pharicians. Now that the Deer have more than sticks to fight with, what is to stop them from using these new weapons? And even if they do not use them themselves, they seem to have no compunctions about giving them to Tash.'

'Yes, Burel,' Kassien interrupted as he drew breath to continue. 'You have made your point, and we all share your shock and grief. I suggest—'

Burel stood up. 'I'm not interested in your platitudes, you witless Bear. I want action for my Clan. Do not come to me with sympathy, for my mate is dead and so are my two youngest children, and it is senseless, and I will go single-handed against Tash if I have to—'

Two Snakes had moved to flank the Wolf, and at a nod from Kassien they laid a hand on each of his shoulders. Burel shook off their hands. He would have done violence to the Snakes if he could, but before he knew it they had skilfully neutralized his weapons and immobilized him. They picked him up and carried him out, still ranting.

There was a silence.

'Grief,' said Kassien diplomatically. The Deer Clan representatives, Raki and Elissi, were not meeting anybody's eye.

Xiriel was sitting a little to one side as though he didn't wish to draw attention to himself. He identified himself as neither Wolf nor Seer nor Snake, so he had no allegiances but also no supporters among the rebels. In a low voice he said, 'Perhaps it is time we took the Fire Houses away from them.'

Everyone looked surprised to hear him speak.

'We cannot,' Pallo said, looking at his friend in shock. 'There are innocent people in A-vi-Khalar. It is true that Tash abuses the Fire Houses, and perhaps there are some in the Deer Clan who comply—'

'Some?' cried Stavel. 'That entire Clan is Knowledge-addled, and traitorous besides. They will keep the best of the farmlands for themselves, and they will keep the comforts of the Knowledge, and they bow to the will of Tash while we freeze our backsides off in the barren hills and fight the Sekk.'

'It is not only the Deer. The Wasps are just as bad,' argued Elissi, glancing at Miro. 'They have done well enough by the Pharicians, yet they are happy to raid their new lords and steal what they can. They kiss up to Tash and then turn around and aid our rebellions.'

'My people are cunning,' Miro said defensively. 'We have gotten much good information for the rebellion, and if we serve our own Clan first, who can blame us? Who would not do the same in our position?'

'We are not blind,' said Elissi, 'to the fact that your Clan would like nothing better than to wipe out the Deer once and for all, take our holdings including the Fire Houses, and control all the agriculture in the valley for yourselves.'

'We are good farmers,' the Wasp said, waving a preemptive hand at Kassien when the Bear began to agree with Elissi. 'What do the Bears know about growing grain and raising milk cows? I suggest you keep to what you know.'

'Let's stick to our purpose,' Stavel put in. 'We must stop this perversion of the Fire Houses. It is unfortunate that the Deer Clan have settled their families in the village around the workings, but they know how strategic an objective the Fire Houses are. If innocents are killed when we take the Fire Houses back, the Deer Clan are as much to blame as we.'

'You call that logic?' Pallo muttered, but he could not be heard over the babble of voices: agreement, protest, the throwing forth of suggestions. Raki and Elissi walked out in a huff.

Kassien spoke over the din.

'Taking the Fire Houses for ourselves, or at the very least disabling their activity, is inevitable if we are to continue to resist Tash. Does anyone here want to stop the resistance? Peace with Pharice, anyone?'

Silence.

'So I thought. We are resolved then. Let's get down to details.'

Pallo said desperately, 'What about the Deer Clan representatives?'

'Let them go. The Deer Clan are effete Scholars and cowards, one and all,' Stavel interrupted. 'I say we storm the Fire Houses and take back our own. Quickly, before Tash makes even more of these terrible fires.'

There was no lack of approval for Stavel, who leaned across the table to shake Xiriel's hand.

'Now, how are we going to do it, young Wolf Seer?'

Kassien said, 'Yes, Xiriel, this is where we are going to need your help. You must get us into the Fire Houses secretly.'

And Xiriel in turn looked at Pallo. 'This is where I am going to need *your* help,' he said.

The skinny blond Pharician resembled an alarmed chicken as he squawked, 'Me?'

'Yes. You.'

The Torture Artist

'So Illyra has bungled the medicines in Wolf Country. What a waste, sending him to help those ingrates. He would have been better off here, where he could support me in my troubles.'

Tash groaned, stretching out on the velvet recliner he'd had sent from Jundun to remind him of home. He reached out and tossed another piece of wood on the fire, making the logs rattle and spark. Kivi no longer jumped in his skin when Tash did things like that; he had been well broken in to Tash's disruptive behaviour. Tash laughed at the explosion and added, 'At least the rockets worked.'

The Seer said nothing. He kept thinking of Joni and how he had sincerely intended to help the Wolves. But he had been misused.

'I don't trust you, you know,' Tash added, glancing at the Seer and nodding to emphasize his point. He said this once or twice a week, almost as much for his own benefit as for the Seer's – for it would not do to become too dependent on the counsel of one whose people he had conquered. Kivi had the emotional receptivity of a good woman, but unlike a woman he knew when to keep his mouth shut. Now he stood just within the circle of light created by the fire, hands clasped behind his back, toes pointed slightly outward and feet shoulder-width apart, his carefully combed brown hair glazing his shoulders like a sheet of falling water. Although it was deep winter his complexion remained bronze, a testament to some distant Pharician blood mixed with the plains people of Ristale, and thence with the Deer Clan that had migrated to Everien only a dozen generations before. Tash was not given to self-analysis, or he might have realized that part of his affinity for Kivi could arise from this sense of common ancestry. Most of the Clansmen had been bleached white by the snows of Everien; they struck Tash as bloodless. Maybe it was the need to prove they bled as freely as other men that caused his compulsion to cut them as often and as deeply as he could.

Or maybe it was their continued resistance.

'The Wolf Clan have always been difficult,' Kivi remarked.

'Ah, fuck them. It's only a small incident. I have bigger problems.'

Kivi was puzzled, and Tash looked gratified. Because Kivi controlled the Eyes (if you could call it that), he thought he was on top of all the intelligence in Everien; but of course he was not, for he did not have the privilege of reading Tash's sealed messages from Jundun, and he did not know what was happening inside Tash's head. He found himself playing catch-up, wondering what Tash knew that he didn't.

'What ever became of that message?'

'What message?' Kivi blinked, unable to follow the train of thought.

'The one with the red cord. The one you said was absurd.'

'Oh, you mean the old one.' A cold sweat broke out between Kivi's shoulder blades. 'Hrost lost it, and the bird that brought it killed several doves. It was a disaster.'

Tash grunted.

'Do you think it was important?'

'How should I know, Kivi? You've gone and lost it, so whether or not it was important is irrelevant now.'

'I remember what it said. It said that Eteltar had left something for Ysse in Tyger Pass, that she shouldn't use the Fire Houses, and that he was going away on the White Road. Something like that. It was dated Smoke Year. That was a long time ago. Probably the bird was trapped somewhere in Jai Khalar. In a time whirl or something like that.'

'The message should not have been lost.'

'I know. It is my fault. I had to supervise Gialse, and I could not watch her and Hrost at the same time. I chose to take care of the girl. It was the wrong choice.' Kivi was always apologizing for something. There was a long silence. Tash was evaluating whether or not Kivi was lying. Kivi was familiar with the process, and he felt a panic come over him as he remembered that he had also misplaced the Carry Eye. What would he tell Tash when Tash asked for it, as he was bound eventually to do? But in the silence, Tash's mind had turned a different corner. Apparently the Pharician was satisfied that Kivi was truthful, for he dropped the subject of the skyfalcon. Instead, in a doleful tone he said,

'Well, what can I do? It is all fucked up. Hezene's army is already on the way.'

Kivi was taken aback. 'Don't you think this is *good* news?' he asked cautiously.

'Ah, why am I talking to you?' Tash sneered. 'You do not understand the way of these things! Ixo my concubine is smarter than you, Kivi.'

The Seer didn't flinch under the abuse. He was accustomed to it.

'Shall I spell it out for you? Hezene never authorized the takeover of Everien. I saw an opportunity in Lerien's weakness and the armies all tied up in Jai Pendu, and I capitalized on it. Everien is mine, but now he will try to supplant me with some pet administrator, some toady of his own who brings enough forces to overwhelm my small band.'

'Maybe he is sincere. The reinforcements he sent from the Floating

Lands at the end of the summer gave their allegiance to you as Hezene's representative here.'

'And I quite rightly rejected them! Those men were fools. They had been Enslaved – what did he imagine I was going to do with them?'

'Make peace with the Clans, perhaps,' Kivi said in a small voice; for they were bold words.

'Ah, your precious Clans. All of you have gotten above yourselves, just because your king lived in Jai Khalar and your heroes went to Jai Pendu. None of you know what's good for you. How can I consolidate my holdings when these miserable rebels oppose me at every turn, spreading out my men and ruining my profits? It's folly! They are only hurting themselves. Why will your countrymen not see this? When they are not fighting me, they are fighting each other—'

'Or the Sekk,' Kivi put in quietly.

'—or the Sekk,' he admitted parenthetically and plunged on, 'but no matter how you look at it, your people lose. I have control of the Knowledge, such as it is. I have the Fire Houses and the wind towers. I am the strong war leader they should have had instead of Lerien, and if I had been in command then, perhaps they would have done better this last pass of Jai Pendu. As it stands now, they haven't a leg to stand on. The Company of Glass is gone. Tarquin their hero is gone, and all his men. Yet they will persist in behaving as though Everien belongs to them. It does not! Your people were only ever stewards, Kivi, and now they will ruin the land rather than live off it under my just and fair rule.'

Kivi stirred a little at these last words, and Tash snapped, 'What? I am not a tyrant, Kivi. I am more just than many in my land would have been in my position, and I will not stand for corruption or robbery. Your people should have no complaints about me.'

'Just or not, they do not wish to have a ruler from outside the Clans,' Kivi said.

'But they must!' Tash sputtered. 'In my country, if you have a good king, you keep him! You don't undermine him so that someone worse can come along! I have not made slaves of the Clans, though I might well have done. In fact, that may well be Hezene's intention in sending so many Pharicians hence. He will put your people in chains and give the land to the Pharician gentry. It is the normal pattern.'

Kivi swallowed. 'The Clans all came here as outcasts or wanderers or explorers from their own lands. They are not lawless, but they do not take well to rulership outside their own families.'

Tash threw back his head and laughed. 'Ridiculous! Everien was ruled by a woman!'

'Perhaps that's why she was successful,' Kivi answered seriously. 'Women are more diplomatic, and a heavy hand is not suffered for long by the Clans. That's why Lerien was so cautious. He knew his people were only inches from revolt at any given time.'

Tash frowned. 'They will be cowed, or hunted down and killed, every last one. That is inevitable, Kivi. If you cannot tell me how to win over your rebel kinsmen, you must at least help me use the Knowledge to hold Everien against this usurper from Pharice.'

Kivi caught the change in his tone. 'What usurper? You are not telling me everything.'

'The leader of the forces Hezene is waiting for, so that he can send his men. I have never heard of him. He is called Evra Kiss. What kind of a name is that? It is not a warrior's name. I know every man of consequence who is close to Hezene, every warleader by name and reputation if not by personal experience, and I have never heard of this Kiss. What name is that for a warlord? Yet Hezene has placed him in command of a large force. I am nervous, Kivi, as I have never been before a battle. I suspect intrigue – Jundun is full of it. I may have to kill him and take his men.'

'Will that not bring Hezene down even harder?' asked Kivi in alarm.

'Hezene appreciates balls,' Tash said. 'Anyway, if I can take Evra Kiss's forces out from under him, and if I could just make a little more progress with the Fire Houses, then I will make Everien too strong to brook interference by the emperor. It can be Hezene's in name, but I will have this land for me and my sons.'

Kivi rocked back on his heels. Tash began to laugh.

'Yes, I think we will have to turn defence into offence,' he said. 'If Hezene will throw his weight against me, then I will have to make my power play. But *you*' – he pointed at Kivi – 'must do more for me. If I had had better control of the Eyes, I might have been able to stop this absurd incident in Wolf Country. Now there may well be real trouble, and I need close surveillance over the Clans more than ever. You must get your Carry Eye working, or find some other way to get at the Knowledge we need for the Fire Houses. If I don't get a result on this soon, I will kill the Seers and the Impressionists and the clerks with their damned documents. I'll kill you one and all and fly your scalps from the towers of Jai Khalar.'

'But I've already tried everything I can think of. What more am I supposed to do?'

Tash pointed a forefinger at Kivi as though it were a lance and regarded him from behind it. '*You* are a Seer. *You* told me you think Night is causing the problems with your Eye. *You* figure out what to do.'

Kivi was so unnerved by this proposition that he forgot his inhibitions about speaking to Tash. He wrung his hands. 'But I don't even know if the Sekk called Night is in this world!'

'Whatever world it is in, I will vanquish it. I will not allow anything to stand in between me and my kingship.'

He stretched like a panther and rubbed his eyes. 'What else, Kivi? What other news do you bring me, for I can feel you hovering and fretting.'

'Reports from Snake Country,' Kivi said. 'Soren has Seen a village overrun by the Slaving in each of four different monitors. It cannot be one Sekk alone. There must be a few of them all coming at once. They are working their way down from the heights.'

'Illyra is too far away to be of use,' Tash muttered. 'Anyway, his men are tired and I wish to confer with him in person.'

'We have not seen an infestation so severe since the year before Jai Pendu,' Kivi said. 'Wax Year. And in that year, we found that a small outbreak soon spread like a disease.'

Tash scuffed at the flagstones with his bare foot. For all he complained about the cold, Kivi noticed that he still had the habit of walking around in little but his skin. His ceaseless motion must keep him warm, but it had always made Kivi jumpy.

'We can send Clan fighters,' Kivi said. 'We have enough men here in Jai Khalar who have sworn loyalty to you. If the emperor's troops are not far off, then the Clan warriors will not long be needed here.'

'I had thought to save them, anyway, for I do not trust them with my Fire Houses weapons lest they think to turn against me.'

'Such weapons may not be needed against the Sekk. They can go on patrol village by village and engage the Sekk and their Slaves hand-to-hand. It's the old traditional way of fighting the Sekk. It's not exciting, but it works.'

Kivi held his breath, aware that his suggestion carried more force than he usually used when addressing Tash; but past experience had made him keenly concerned about the dangers in Snake Country, and he knew that Tash had little understanding of the Sekk or how they worked. The hills had been quiet in the aftermath of Jai Pendu. Kivi had the uneasy sense that they were only now beginning to wake, and it made him speak up before the Pharician leader.

'Very well,' Tash said. 'I will think on it. But under no circumstances are they to have rockets or any other devices other than their usual weapons.'

'Of course not!'

'And leave enough Clansmen here to police the castle. I cannot waste my own men to patrol endless corridors and disappearing stairwells.'

'Yes, Tash.'

'And give them a Carry Eye if one is to be found. I want to keep tabs on them. Who will command them?'

'I was thinking of Dario. And Bellen and Uven, the Wolf brothers.'

'Wolves! After that episode?'

'Better to keep them away from Wolf Country, I thought,' Kivi suggested. 'Then they cannot be drawn in by the rebels. And Dario can control them, I'm sure of that.'

'Dario, eh? Well, I hope he is good.' When Tash said this, Kivi swallowed but did not correct him as to Dario's gender. 'I will hold you responsible for his deeds, Kivi. You are to keep them in your Sight, understand?'

'Yes, Tash.' Kivi began backing out of the room before Tash could think of any other conditions, but just as he'd reached the door, Tash let out an almighty yawn and waved at him to stop.

'Oh, by the way. I will need to see Mistel. Send for her, and bring me a Carry Eye. A *working* Carry Eye, Kivi. I wish to send a message to the Wolf chieftains at A-vel-Hira.'

'That I can do,' Kivi answered, relieved to be given an order he was able to fulfil.

'Oh,' Tash added almost absently. 'Also send for old what's-his-name.'

'Old what's-his-name?' Kivi repeated, studying Tash suspiciously. He could tell the Pharician was playing some sort of psychological game, but he didn't understand what it was.

'You know the one. Jaqal, is it?'

'Not Jaqal,' Kivi said in horror, thinking of Mistel.

'Yes, that's his name, isn't it? Jaqal, the torture artist. Tell him to come and to bring his finest carving knives.'

Your Smallest Finger

The Grandmother looked at the torture artist and laughed.

'There is no need for you to be here,' she said. 'I am too fucking old to keep secrets. What do you wish to know from me?'

'It is the treachery of the Wolf Clan that concerns me,' said Tash.

'I am not in communication with them,' Mistel answered calmly. 'If they have committed treachery, I have no way of knowing about it.'

'You arrogant little hag,' Tash snapped. 'Why did I ever listen to you? I was trying to help them, the bastards. I sent them expensive medicines from the Fire Houses, and your people attacked my men. What repayment is this for my mercy? For all I care, they may all die this winter. I will only send to Pharice for men to work the land – loyal men who are glad to have me as their ruler.'

'My people are proud,' Mistel said. 'If you gave them medicine in your typical haughty, high-handed manner, then no wonder you were attacked.'

Tash drew himself up, his face stunned.

'How dare she speak to me so?' he called out to the room at large. 'I will have you killed, Mistel.'

The Grandmother shrugged.

'Oh? You think it funny? You are forsworn, Mistel, for you told me your people would comply with my policies.'

'Apparently they have not. Therefore my life is forfeit. So I swore.'

Tash sounded nervous, as if it were he being backed into a corner and not the little old woman in her grey cloak and hood, so small and composed in the great, chilly hall. 'If you think I will spare you because you are weak and old, think again.'

'You must do as your conscience dictates. I am ready to die.'

'What do you know about Tyger Pass?' Tash asked suddenly.

Mistel blinked a few times. 'It's the pass between Seahawk and Snake. I've never been there. It will be snowed under at this time of year.'

'How long would it take a bird to fly from there to here?'

'I don't know! Why don't you look at a bleeding map, Tash? Why ask me?'

'Mind your insolence,' he growled. 'Take a guess.'

'A few days, maybe a week, depending on the bird. I mean, it's a long journey by road but if you could fly over the mountains, it wouldn't take very long.'

'There are no monitor towers there.'

'As far as I know, all the monitor towers are on the border of Ristale. I guess the Everiens weren't afraid of attack from within their own mountains.'

'Someone is fucking with me,' Tash said.

Mistel snorted. 'It's about time.'

He whirled and pointed a finger at her. 'Do not test me, crone! You should know better than to play around when I am in a bad mood. One day I will forget myself and lop off your head.'

'You're always in a bad mood, lately,' she observed, drawing her shawl closer and sliding her hands up her crossed arms for warmth. 'Why don't you speak plainly and maybe I can help you.'

'As if I would trust you.'

'You know I want peace. Do you think it easy for me to watch you kill my children and then speak civilly to you? Go on, kill me! I don't care. If you are going to refuse to hear good sense, then I might as well be dead. There are only worse days to come.'

'Enough! I didn't bring you here to preach to me.'

'That's right. You brought me here to torture me. Come, Jaqal! Do your worst. Let's see what terrible secrets I possess that will help Tash.'

Tash waved a hand at the blank-faced Pharician. 'Oh, him! You know that's just for show.'

'Like your drinking bowls are just for show?' Mistel asked wryly, gesturing at the row of erratically shaped bowls on the mantelpiece. They were bone white for a good reason.

'What? You mean Ajiko? My, but his skull is big. No wonder I am intoxicated all the time.'

'You killed Sendrigel as well. My nephew. He might well have helped you.'

'He was trading with the Circle even while his king administered treaties with my emperor! He admitted as much to me himself. I will have no truck with the Circle. They are nothing but a band of intellectuals and assassins – the worst possible combination.'

'Anyway,' said Mistel, 'I don't see what Tyger Pass has to do with what just happened in Wolf Country.'

'Huh. You do not. That is because you don't know that the Seahawks have been quiet lately . . . too quiet. Or that Snake Country is a hotbed of rebel activity. The pass between them . . . I wonder if that ridiculous message was really some kind of a code. They could all be massing against me in Tyger Pass—'

'Not at this time of year.' Mistel laughed. 'Not unless they are snow lions! All those mountains are a whiteout, probably worse than A-vel-Jasse.'

'Well. I will let you live, Mistel. For now. But I am at a loss for what to do about your foolish people.'

'Illyra is not a very good representative for peace. You should have gone yourself. If you want the loyalty of the people, you must do something for them.'

'I cannot go riding out shaking men's hands and distributing blankets! I must stay and control the Eyes.'

'That is the mistake Lerien made.'

'I will send them help when the supplies from Pharice arrive. I will send them protection against the Sekk, and Pharician goods to get them through the remainder of winter. But the Wolves must cease their hostilities.'

'Let me talk to them,' Mistel said.

'I cannot do that and keep you hostage at the same time, you silly bat.'

Mistel threw up her hands. 'I cannot think what else to do.'

'Is Ixo getting anywhere with the Carry Eye?'

She looked at him sharply, then quickly covered her surprise that he knew she had Kivi's Eye. 'Not really. I mean, there is nothing more about weapons coming through, but the girl is still talking.'

'Damn. I had hoped it might right itself. Isn't it strange that the darkening of the Carry Eye is followed so soon by the arrival of the mystery bird bearing a message about Tyger Pass? The message Kivi has conveniently lost.'

'Is that so?' said Mistel in a suspiciously bland tone. 'Yet there is nothing about Tyger Pass in what the girl says. I have a scribe taking it down.'

Tash turned gleaming eyes on her. 'Good! Good, Mistel.'

'Tash . . .' For a moment her tone was plaintive, almost yearning.

'What, Grandmother?'

'If only you and I would work together this way all the time, there is much we might accomplish.'

'Indeed. We are working together, are we not? For now, my partner, I must direct you to brace yourself. I will have to confine you. Do you understand?'

'You are throwing me in prison so that I cannot corrupt young Ixo.'

Tash laughed. 'Yes.'

'I fucking well expected it.'

'Watch your mouth, Mistel.'

'What else, Tash?' she asked tensely. 'Brace myself for what?'

Tash frowned, his fun spoiled because Mistel was perceptive enough to see through him. 'I am sending a message to your Clan and I will require you to be a part of it.'

Her eyes grew wary again. She knew she had been tricked somehow.

'What do you want, Tash?'

'Only a token that you are in my power. For now I will take your smallest finger. Jaqal? I must ask you to go against your nature. Make it as painless as is reasonable.'

A Few Skeins Short of a Full Sheep

'Auntie Mhani!' Enzi's whisper crackled in the still air of the Fire House. Though dormant for a few hours in the dead of night, the structure's walls radiated ambient heat and there was a slight but detectable vibration in the floor. 'Auntie Mhani! Hurry! The guard is coming back.'

The guard was not moving very quickly, but her mother had schooled into her an unreasoning terror of the Pharicians, and Enzi was not about to take any chances. This was only their third attempt to penetrate the seals of the underground city, and Enzi did not quite have a bead on the timing of the guard's nightly rounds. Normally at about this hour he went for a piss and a look at the sky, returned briefly to his post, and then began a circuit of the exterior of the Fire Houses, aboveground. Enzi had worked it out so that when he went for his piss, she and Mhani stole into the Fire House and hid in one of the forge pits, and when he locked the door behind him before going to make his rounds outside, they would attempt to open the seal to the adjacent Fire House, the one containing the Fire of Glass, which was always locked after midnight – or whenever the last and most diligent of the smiths had left. If they failed, as they had done on their first two attempts, it became a matter of dozing at the bottom of the forge pit amongst the machinery, until the guard went for his second piss and they could slip out before the day workers arrived and fired the equipment.

But Enzi did not intend to fail tonight. She needed Mhani with her because the taller woman could manipulate the large wheels that controlled the doors to the works, but it was Enzi who had worked out enough of the code to unlock the bolts. She had watched her father do it time enough to have memorized most of the combination, and the rest she had figured out by trial and error. Last time they had run out of time before the guard returned; the door had unlocked, but they could not risk making a noise while he was at his post outside. Tonight they would need to get the combination right on the first try, open the locks, and slip inside before he had finished his rounds upstairs. Enzi was confident; but as of yet they had not gotten inside the first Fire House where the weapons were made, and Mhani was nowhere to be found.

That was the one problem with Mhani. She wasn't stupid like most adults, and you could talk her into almost anything, and she mostly did as she was told for she'd been trained that way during the months of her tenure at A-vi-Khalar – but the one problem with her was that she was, of course, a few skeins short of a full sheep.

The guard was weaving along the passage lazily. If Enzi had not known better, she would have said he was drunken; but the Pharicians would never drink on duty. They were unnatural that way.

'Psst!' she risked one more time, and then darted into the Fire House as the guard's torch suddenly jerked.

'Who's there?' he said in Pharician, and Enzi slithered into the forge pit just as he reached the entrance to the main chamber. She stepped on Mhani's hand on the way down and sank against her aunt, trembling with a mixture of fear and relief. Mhani must have snuck in while she was looking after the guard. She slipped a hand over her aunt's mouth as an extra caution, but she could tell by the way Mhani was breathing that her aunt's mind was elsewhere entirely. She only hoped the exiled High Seer would not begin speaking in tongues while the guard was actually in the room.

He circumambulated the forge pit without shining his torch down inside it, seeming satisfied that there was no one in the Fire House. Enzi's eyes fixed on his stiff leather boots with their metal trimmings. How cold his feet must get in the winter snows, she thought. She herself was buried in a rabbit parka that left only a smidgen of her cheeks exposed, and a slit cloth covered her eyes. Her mother insisted on such garb in the winter, when chill winds blew snow off the frozen river with the same scouring effect as sand. But the Pharician was ill dressed for the cold, and the metal that dominated his gear would surely make him miserable wherever it touched his inner garments. She decided that he was dragging his feet because he had no wish to go aboveground this frigid night. He gave credence to her suspicions when he lingered in the main chamber of the Fire House, warming his hands against the wall. Enzi prayed Mhani would remain silent.

At last he departed, walking down the entrance tunnel with a brisk, determined stride. Enzi wasted no more time. She darted out of the forge pit, went to the door to the central Fire House, and began spinning the locks.

'He'll be back in no time,' Enzi whispered to her aunt. 'We've got to be very quick tonight.'

Mhani said nothing, but held the lightstone for her while Enzi worked. At last the locks were undone. Enzi threw all her weight into the smallest wheel, and Mhani seemed to rouse from her torpor and lent a hand. The first wheel loosened with a shriek. Enzi stopped and cringed, but there was no answering sound from the guard.

'Quick!' she hissed, and Mhani helped her open the second wheel. It was quieter than the first. The third wheel was too high for Enzi to reach, but Mhani threw all the strength of her legs into it and at last it gave. The door could now be pushed open manually. Enzi tugged the makeshift strap she had seen her father use and it opened a crack. Warm air came out.

'Help me, Mhani,' she whispered, aware that their time had probably run out – but they had no choice now. They could not return the wheels or the locks to their closed positions before the guard got back, so they would have to go inside and stay there until the next watch, hoping that none in the morning shift would notice that the door had been left unlocked. Mhani gave her a hand once again and they opened the door enough to slip through into the red-lit vault of the biggest Fire House. They closed the door behind them and Enzi leaned against the wall, heart pounding, panting a little.

Footsteps sounded in the chamber they had just come from. The guard was singing in Pharician – a love song. A minute later, he had gone, leaving the two trembling Deer alone with the Fire of Glass.

'Now,' Mhani whispered. 'Now we shall see.'

She Smells Kind

No matter how many times the emperor, Hezene, laid his hands on the head of one of his commanders and sent him and all his troops into battle, he never grew bored of the ritual. To Hezene every campaign was like the first one that had driven back the barbarians in the northern forests and brought him first to the notice of Pharice's then-king, Ntubiet. Hezene had been fifteen years old at the time; now sixty, he had gained only two inches and twenty pounds on the wiry frame of his youth, and his black eyes sparkled with the same intensity they always had. People found it disconcerting, his gaze – but then, very few were permitted to look at him full in the face. Hezene interpreted eye contact as a challenge, and seldom tolerated it from any but his most favoured of wives and children.

He surveyed the columns and rows of soldiers arrayed before him, their armour capturing the golden sunlight and sending it back watery and dreamlike. The ancestors of these men had once been barbarians scraping a living from their respective lands in between squabbling with one another over women and property; now they were subject to his word. Thanks to his lineage, they had been organized to build the walls and fountains and sky bridges of Jundun; thanks to his lineage they spoke and wrote the same language, observed the same feast days, sang the same songs. And they spread his name and his accomplishments far and wide. None now would ever forget Hezene, Forty-ninth Emperor of Pharice, no matter what came after his death.

The same could not be said for the Everiens, whose abandoned holdings he was at last to add to his trove of conquered or annexed territories. He was pleased. The debacle at the forest garrison in Ristale last year was turning out to have certain advantages. For one thing, the drawing out of all Everien's troops into the Floating Lands had informed Hezene of their numbers and weapons makeup; also the commanders whom he had recalled directly to Jundun had much to say about the attitudes, hopes, and fears of the Clan men whom they'd been in such close contact with. Until that time, Hezene had been pursuing what he called a policy of envy with the Clans: trade vigorously, show them how good things were in Pharice, and maybe they would submit willingly to imperial rule when – as it was bound to do, for the Clans could never agree on anything – their own central government broke down. He had thought to use this policy to soften the ground for his eventual takeover, now delayed by Night's escapade. Recently, he'd begun to question why the Clans should be interested in the advantages of Pharician civilization so long as the Knowledge lurked in the forgotten byways of their own home.

Hezene was haunted by the fact that the Everiens had been so great, and were now forgotten. He didn't want anything like this to happen to him – perhaps this was why he had always shied away from the high land to the north with its mysterious boundaries and its monstrous denizens that resembled no other creatures in all the world. When he looked out on his city, with its subtly curving boulevards and its water gardens and its windblown flags proclaiming him Lord of the Seasons, Father of the Elements, and Keeper of the Numbers, he could not help but imagine it being devoured by assimilators or carved up by H'ah'vah. He could not help but imagine the Sekk ghosting through its predawn streets, softly calling.

But that would not happen; he would insure it with his own blood. Just below his dais rested Ukili's tent, where she was waiting to be formally introduced to her travelling companions and helpers. Hezene was grateful that his wife was dead, for he need not listen to a woman's complaints that Ukili was being bundled off to be raped by barbarians – married to a bastard, anyway.

Shiror was late. Hezene snapped his fingers and Byrd said, 'They are looking for him. Meanwhile, the Scholars you asked for have arrived. Do you wish to speak with them first, Greatness?'

'Very well,' said Hezene in a flat tone that meant he was annoyed.

It was not like Shiror to be late, and the delay did not sit well with Hezene. Schedules were important to him: everyone in Pharice knew this. One of his other titles was Hezene the Bird Emperor, for it had been the flocks of migrant birds passing over his homeland in the veldt of central Pharice that had inspired his conception of a kingdom. True, his people were agrarian and did not migrate like birds or like the pastor-alists of Ristale or the deserts to the south; but all people followed patterns, and Hezene had long ago discovered that if you could convince them to follow the patterns you set, then the people belonged to you. Organization was his genius, and his empire was modelled according to a hierarchy of detail that gave everyone a pattern to follow, and the patterns changed very little except in their scale.

In the north, in Everien, the Clans believed in their Animal founders or archetypal spirits. Hezene was more practical than this. Why should his Scholars confine themselves to the study of only one animal? Why not know them all? Why not take an aspect of this one and wed it to an aspect of that? Why not use the organizational principles of ants and the wariness of the hyena? There was no mystery to animals in the end; and that meant there was no mystery to men, either. People didn't like meeting Hezene's gaze because it cut through their mystery, broke them down to their constituent parts, and communicated to the mind behind those dark eyes the precise information necessary to render them obedient.

Hezene absentmindedly drummed his fingers on his thighs, idly turning over several problems at once in his mind while his soldiers stood sweating in the sun, awaiting the arrival of the princess's bodyguard. His birds chortled and cooed to themselves in the darkness of his tent, shifting from foot to foot and probably thinking of their dinners, now delayed. The Scholars sat at their ease in a small group. They were not speaking, but some of them were reading. Hezene did not mind. He liked to own brilliant men just as he liked to own fast horses and beautiful women. And they looked at him usually quivering and flustered, for genius and status never seemed to coexist in the same man in the same lifetime, and Hezene's status far outstripped the Scholars' genius. Star counters, he called them, and it was not the insult some took it as. For Hezene believed in counting stars: Why should they be so special? Some men thought counting stars was irrelevant and an insult to stars; but those men were romantics who usually died in duels.

Here came Wakhe the cripple, supported by two soldiers and yet astumble as though drunk. Superstition about the cosmic meanings of physical deformity could not cloud Hezene's judgment, but he was beginning to wonder whether the Scholar could make such a long journey, even were he carried in a litter like a pregnant girl.

'He comes from the desolate Snake Islands,' Byrd said in his ear. 'He climbed cliffs every day to get water. He cannot walk, but he is hale.'

Hezene nodded and stroked Byrd's comb affectionately.

'What will Tash say when he sees this?' the emperor mused, smiling.

'Tash! Tash!' chorused the birds. 'Two balls and a cock don't make brains Tash!'

'Shh! Of course he has a brain. Just points it at all the wrong things.' Hezene sighed. Tash thought himself son of Griasj, the barbarian horse lord of southern Or, and no one had trouble believing it, for Tash was fierce and dark and rode like a burr in October. But Griasj was not his father.

Had anyone but Tash so impudently seized Everien for himself without approval via Hezene's chain of command, the emperor would have had his body parts rearranged and sewn together inside out.

'Murder!' cried Byrd, reading his mind.

'Yes,' Hezene murmured. 'He gets away with it. Ah, to see his face when Wakhe arrives. Chee, go with the Scholar. Be his friend, and show me Tash's reaction.'

The canary leapt from her perch and flew toward the Scholar, singing.

'The emperor bestows his blessing upon the Scholar Wakhe and all the men who escort him to Jai Khalar. Let the Imperial Flier be your guide and the Eyes and Mouth of Hezene in the North.'

Hezene smiled.

'I shall miss her,' said Byrd sadly.

'I will find you another chickadee, my friend,' the emperor replied. He turned to the assembled crowd. Shiror's young son, sublieutenant Duor, had slipped in unnoticed and was now speaking to Evra Kiss, who shifted uneasily from foot and foot in the presence of the desert warrior's bastard. That Shiror had a son was thought to be a miracle, for he had never been known to so much as glance at a woman; for that reason, the boy would never have any status but that he fought tooth and nail to gain for himself. The emperor knew Evra Kiss was not comfortable in his leadership. Hezene had hoped to protect both Shiror and Kiss by giving official control of the army to neither; for he was sure Tash had killed Hezene's other officers out of fear of being usurped by them. As a Scholar in all but name, Kiss would never be a threat to a man like Tash, and by assigning Shiror to be Ukili's bodyguard, Hezene hoped to place him within Tash's intimate orbit. It would be Shiror who delivered his daughter, and therefore Tash ought to trust Shiror, whom Hezene could use as a wedge into Tash's control of Everien.

But Shiror was late, and it had been a strange day already.

He had met with Byrd in the predawn stillness of his apartments to discuss the arrangements.

'No messages are to precede the army. I don't wish to give Tash too much time to prepare for our arrival. I want him nervous.'

'Very well,' said Byrd. 'And Chee's Speech?'

'Chee will Speak My Words to Tash. I have already given them to her.' He smiled. 'You will learn what they are soon enough, Byrd! If you are very clever, you may even have guessed by now.'

That had shut Byrd up. Hezene liked to have secrets from his favourite Speaker. It was good for Byrd and kept him in his place.

'Finally,' said Hezene to Byrd, 'I will send the skyfalcon. It must be kept on its tresses at all times.'

'*The skyfalcon?*' That had shocked the little bugger.

'Indeed. It is my wedding gift to Tash. It is fitting. A symbol of me, the Bird Emperor, ruling even over Everien in its ancient greatness. I am sure that this creature coming to my roof from out of the distant past is a sign that I will soon triumph over that land and return Everien to its former glory, in the name of Hezene.'

'But did not Tash send the bird to Your Brightness?'

'*If* he has sent it here to frighten me with his power, I shall send it back that he may know I understand his game, and I am not frightened. On the contrary. My astonishing generosity will catch him off guard. He will not know what to make of it. Softness can be strength, Byrd, and my softness is Ukili. I do not think Tash will resist us in this. Now, have you the skyfalcon to hand?'

Byrd's feathers twitched.

'No, my father. He has flown off.'

'What's this, Byrd?'

'I did not wish to bother you with it,' Byrd said, 'until after the troops were gone. But the bird left the palace last night, and when we tried to seize him from the chala, he would not be caught.'

'He will be caught now! Go get him.'

'But my lord, no one can touch him. He has killed seven men in the effort to catch him.'

Hezene never raised his voice. He just said, 'What kind of an answer is this, Byrd?'

'I will bring the falcon to you,' said Byrd fervently, and flew off in a rush.

When Byrd returned, it was only moments before Hezene was to address the army and bid farewell to his daughter. Byrd flew escort over the heads of a squad of Imperial Guards, each with a member of the Air Police on his shoulder. Among them all walked a scruffy female child of the byrd persuasion, and sitting upon her shoulders like a gigantic cape was the skyfalcon.

Hezene had been too shocked to take offence at the fact that the byrdchild walked on the same ground as he.

Byrd said, 'Profound apologies, Your Great Bright Winged Goldenitude! The only way to catch the skyfalcon was to catch the byrdgirl, which it has taken an obscure shine to, and the skyfalcon would not suffer her to be bound or carried. This was the only way to come here in time.'

He hid his head under his wing as Hezene stared.

'Is that true, byrdgirl?'

Liaku nodded. They had woken her from deep sleep and she had had no chance to relieve her bladder. Her knees were clamped together with her effort not to pee. In her mind she chanted to herself, hold on, hold on, holdon holdonholdonholdonholdon hold on! but her bladder and back ached and the fine muscles of her groin even cried out for relief, quivering with the effort of holding back the gush of urine. She dared not speak.

'What's the matter with her?'

'She is awed and terrified, Your Greatness.'

'I thought this skyfalcon killed seven men.'

'Ten as of this morning, my emperor. But the byrdgirl asked it to stop, and it did.'

'Chee! What do you think of her?'

Chee flew to a nearby shelf and eyed Liaku, who turned her eyes toward her and managed a pathetic whistle. Chee whistled back, fluffed her feathers, accepting the compliment.

'She smells kind,' Chee said.

Just then Liaku wet herself.

Fortunately, the byrdgirl was now being kept amongst the baggage and servants out of his sight – and out of Ukili's, for the princess was nervous enough already. But the skyfalcon presided over the blessing of the troops, and when the delay of Shiror became pronounced, the great silver bird began shifting its weight from foot to foot and stretching its wings. Maybe sending the skyfalcon hadn't been Hezene's most inspired notion, but when one was emperor one was allowed to indulge in the occasional grand gesture without being obliged to explain oneself. And it was an extraordinary bird. Let it kill a few of Tash's guards, Hezene thought, pleased.

'Ah, at last!' cried Byrd. 'It is Shiror!'

His voice rose to a surprised squeak. Hezene had never seen his First Speaker in such a taking and attributed his nerves to the imminent departure of his mate.

'Of course it's Shiror. What has happened to him? He's bleeding.'

Shiror ascended the dais and obeised himself before Hezene. There was a thin cut across his exposed chest and his hair, which he had been growing out in preparation for the cold, was in disarray. He was full of apologies for his tardiness.

'A bar brawl? It is almost unto midday, Shiror. I would not have put it in your character.'

Shiror looked up at the emperor, surprise at the informality making him candid.

'I was attacked,' he said bluntly. 'But I dispatched the would-be killers. I believe you will find they are Circle: Linz and Fel Brekk and one other. It would seem they don't wish me to go to Everien.'

Hezene raised one eyebrow and, leaning forward, pressed something into Shiror's hand where no one else could see it.

'Give this to Tash,' he said. 'Do not be put aside by anyone. Care well for Ukili, and every reward in my power shall be yours, Shiror.'

Faces That Speak by Touch

There were advantages to having lived a life that had consisted of getting into and out of tight spaces. It meant that sometimes time was short and every survival instinct had to be mobilized fully. It also meant that most of the time nothing happened at all, and there were quiet patches of reflection, which in Tarquin's case had been accentuated by his constant peregrination since leaving Ysse's guard. Yet trouble could come at any time, from any direction, and catch you completely unawares. Therefore you learned how not to panic. You learned to separate emotion from pragma – because when you had to act, you had to do it fast, and that meant thinking fast, or, more often than not, not thinking at all, but acting on instinct.

For if you were smart, during the quiet periods you had not been idle. You had relived in your mind every dangerous situation you had ever been in, calculating the possibilities and probabilities. You asked yourself questions: What had you done wrong that you would correct if you could? Where had you been saved by luck and where by skill? How could you have anticipated better? What if one single thing about the situation had gone differently – how would the outcome have been affected?

Tarquin's long hours in the saddle and on footpaths, his roadside snoozes on stone walls in the sun, his evenings alone in the wild hills, they might appear to add up to a life of bone-idleness compared to the labours set before men of more conventional responsibilities. But every situation was to Tarquin a laboratory, a chance to pick up new skills and discard bad habits, an opportunity to test himself. He had been working this way for the thirty years in warfare that had elapsed since his boyhood. He knew himself.

He was not surprised when he fell. The rope had been more of a psychological crutch, an obligation to the concept of safety, than a real element of security. Kere had probably had a fit, or been captured by the Snakes, or perhaps he had, horselike, simply spontaneously run away. There was no point in speculating. Tarquin knew he had to forget the rope and concentrate on his problem. And his problem was that he had just come down a section that couldn't be chimney-climbed nor even free-climbed without support. Without a rope, he wasn't getting back up it. He reached overhead anyway, slithered from side to side as far as he could in hope of getting a better position, hoping for a hold overhead that his feet had somehow missed on the way down. The lava was slippery smooth and purely vertical. He would have to keep going down, and hope.

Maybe it was an hour; maybe it was ten hours. He descended steadily and carefully, relating to the rock but otherwise not thinking about anything. There was nothing to mark the passage of time, until the clicking noise started.

It was a cricketlike clattering, a summer insect noise only magnified, yet regular and unfaltering. The echoes carried it up the shaft he was climbing, making it difficult to pinpoint the source. The sound got louder as he went lower, and he began to hope that at last he was getting somewhere. Perhaps the Snakes were communicating to each other. Perhaps he had found one of their thoroughfares. He descended quicker, sweating. A warm draft hit him and he gathered that the passage was opening into a larger cave, but the shaft was vertical now and too wide to chimney-climb. The clicking echoed and reechoed in the larger space. Below, he could see a faint, cold glow – probably a patch of phosphorescent cave moss. He stood on a tiny ledge with the toes of his left foot, clutching the rock with his right hand while his right foot groped for purchase. He found a small niche but had to stretch to reach it. When he swung his weight onto the right foot, it touched the foothold and then slid off, repelled by something slimy growing on the ledge.

With that, he was falling. He caught at the stone, but his hands slithered off and he could not stop himself. For a breathless couple of instants he was dropping through total darkness except for the blobs of greenish luminosity that came rushing up at him.

He hit deep sand. The wind went out of him and he lay prone for some time, commanding himself to breathe. When he could inhale again, he began coughing uncontrollably. His whole body felt as if it had been crushed by a hammer. He lay still.

The clicking had stopped. Everything was dark. The moss lay on the walls and ceiling in streaky designs, but it didn't shed enough light to show anything of the cave. When he began to crawl over the sand, his breathing echoed with a rushing noise.

The clicking started again, slower and in a different time signature. He made himself small and flat against the sand and tried to slow his laboured respiration. After a while he came to a wall, and standing, he felt his way along it until he came to what he judged by the air currents to be the opening of a tunnel. The clicking was coming from behind him, but also, in a fainter off-rhythm counterpoint, from the tunnel he was now entering. He began to rush along the tunnel, desperate for light and beginning to feel disoriented. The clicking followed him, growing louder. He was not alone.

Something fluttered near his face and he recoiled. His hand came up to swat it away but met only air. He went still, listening, and with an amalgam of his senses perceived that the tunnel ahead was filling with a great, hot, living bulk – it was arriving like an ooze, formless in the dark. There was a series of insectlike clicks, very fast and cunningly articulated, and again the air before his face moved as though something had nearly touched him.

He began to crawl backward the way he had come, hoping to escape into the larger cave where he'd landed. He knew it was only a little way, but his body was getting mixed up as he tried to reverse. He fell into a shallow pit that he had not encountered before, for he'd been following the opposite wall. The pit led to a smaller, wormlike tunnel that felt just big enough to accommodate him; but he was afraid of the small space and remained where he had tripped, craning his head up toward the hole he'd fallen into, listening for whatever was pursuing him. There was a long, silent pause.

Then from the passage above appeared a wan, yellow, sickly light that had not been there before. At first he thought he was imagining it, for it was very faint and seemed to disappear for a moment when he closed his eyes. He could hear a large body, stealthily moving. He could hear the thing breathing. The clicks came again, a tattoo like the dance-drumming of the Snake Clan; a wordless language, a language of time.

If only he had his sword.

Greatly daring, he drew himself up a little and looked over the edge of the pit, into the original tunnel and the almost imperceptible glow. The air stirred again; something soft and warm and moist touched his face ever so briefly, light as a bird's wing. In the same instant, a cloying smell rushed at him with a hiss, and he suddenly deduced that the Snake must have opened its mouth to swallow him. He ducked back into the safety of his pit and groped for the small tunnel, almost ready to squeeze into it no matter how claustrophobic he felt.

'What thing are you?' he cried, and in the next instant his bowels loosened. From the tunnel above flared a strange light, which moved as the creature emitting it came down the hole after him. It had a mongrel face, humanlike but ten times human size and surrounded by a cobra's hood that angry arousal had flared wide to reveal a lining of luminous yellow. Its jaws yawned open and two transparent fangs each the length of an arm dangled from its upper jaw to guard the entrance to its mouth. Between the human lips a reptilian tongue stiffened, and behind that Tarquin could see the long snake throat, glowing faintly from within. But the most disturbing feature of the monster was its eyes.

He knew perfectly well that even the most luminous eyes of wildcats and other animals didn't really give off their own light: they only reflected what little light was already present, and intensified it. But there was no light at all in this cave, so how could the eyes be glowing at him? Their light was unholy, a cold yellow-green. Some of it came from the irises themselves. Still more must be coming from the skin around the eyes, but there was not enough of it to delineate an outline, no way to separate the creature from its surroundings. The impression that Tarquin received was that the darkness itself had manifested eyes and a mouth, and both were coming to get him.

He flattened himself tight against the farthest wall while the glowing eyes came questing toward him and the tongue again flickered out, tasting the air. Tarquin felt for the escape hole he'd been so loath to crawl inside and recoiled as his hand slid over the smooth contours of what felt like a human face, only petrified, hard as stone. Then his fingers found the lip of the hole and he jammed himself into it even as the attacking monster widened its mouth still further. The fangs whipped through the air with a sound not unlike a sword swinging. Tarquin felt the breeze but didn't wait to determine whether he'd been bitten. He slithered round a bend away from the creature.

After a few seconds he realized he hadn't been grazed, but he kept going as fast as he could, passing a side tunnel that was even narrower and then climbing up a steep section where a draft from the right told him there was yet another passage. He barely indexed these facts, fixated as he was on simply getting away. He could no longer see the creature's light, but he heard something thumping above him. He was confused; he had thought he'd ascended, but maybe he'd missed something in his hurry. He felt unnerved; he was sweating and shaking, and his head pounded. After a moment the thumping stopped; then the clicking resumed.

Tarquin rubbed his temples and kept pressing inward, praying that the tunnel was too small to allow the monster to follow. It was a very close passage. Someone or something had smoothed its surfaces so that it felt like marble, yet it was as twisted as the inside of a gut. He had to crawl on his belly. He passed a couple of tributary passages, and then he came to a junction where he had to decide which way to go. Three other tunnels split off, going at odd angles. One went straight up. Tarquin braced himself in the cross-space and concentrated on building a mental picture of his orientation. Already he felt lost, and the absence of light was starting to weigh on him. He decided to wait awhile and go back the way he'd come. See if the human-snake was still there.

He rested a little and then turned around and began to go back. But he was soon lost. He must have taken a turning when he thought he'd gone straight, for he now found himself doubling back on his own track. He pictured his route in his mind, but the tunnel was so tortuously twisted that it was impossible to be certain how high or low he was, how far he had looped to the right or left, or whether he had crossed his own path somewhere without realizing it. Warm, sulphurous air sometimes blew past him, making him wonder whether the volcano was still active – but the eruption seemed the least of his problems now. He would die of thirst and exhaustion within a matter of days if he didn't find a way out, and he had no means of tracking his progress. He suspected he was going in circles. Then he began to suspect that someone had deliberately designed these tunnels as a maze.

It didn't take Tarquin very long to discover that there is a difference between the free and open darkness of the most moonless night, and the butter-thick darkness of the earth's belly. The passage was big enough to permit him to crawl, yet he felt crushed, as if his lungs couldn't draw in enough air, as if his skin was being touched by the darkness like strange fur. Though he kept choosing the turnings that led upward, they always seemed to turn down again later, twisting and plunging so that no matter what, he sank deeper than he had been before. The air was breathable, untainted by poisons; yet it seemed ever to grow warmer.

He had to keep going. Well aware that he might wander endlessly in circles until he died of thirst and exhaustion, he nevertheless shoved that awareness out of his way. It did him no good. He tried to be systematic but it was impossible to build a mental map of this place when everywhere he went he went by feel and no other sense.

He had already guessed that the entire section of the island which they'd crossed must be riddled with tunnels: it would explain the hollow metal panels, the domes in the forest, and lastly the double doors in the cone of the volcano. Yet if the Snakes possessed the capability to build an entire city underground, why could they not beat back the Pharicians? Tarquin couldn't understand it. According to legend, Snakes were the descendants of a slave class from Pharice who had broken free of their masters and tried their luck in the wilderness. Yet these Snakes acted like more than a mere band of renegades, judging by their attitude to the Pharicians, anyway. *Eggs*, Mavese had said. *We won't give you any more eggs.* Tarquin assumed that the eggs belonged to the creature he'd just encountered. Maybe it was angry about the theft of its eggs. Or maybe it just ate anything that came near it. Or maybe it was guarding the Snake people's stronghold. Or maybe – he cut off the rush of thoughts. None of this was helping him. Better not to think. Better to find his way out of here.

Sweat rilled in the creases of his skin and coated the grit and grease deposited there, flattened the hairs of his body. Crawling almost flat on his belly made him conscious of the tail he didn't have. He felt naked, incomplete without it. The back of his jaw moved from side to side as he quested along the tunnel. His hands became levers, weak assistants to his feet; but it was his head, his nose and his smell of the air which dragged him forward.

Sometimes he passed a patch of phosphorescent moss or slime on the stone, never enough to give real light. Yet quantities of it must grow down here somewhere. He had seen the Snakes decorated with it, and now he wondered whether the smudges he saw from time to time weren't simply that paint, rubbed off by somebody's passage. But he found it hard to believe that anyone had passed this way lately. Every time he found some of this material glow, he stopped and fingered it, smelt it, tried to convince himself it was real and not a trick of his light-starved eyes.

There was a feeling after a time that the earth all round him was alive, elemental and impersonal in power and yet conscious nonetheless. Its unconcern for him made him feel frail and sorry for himself, and then, after that, angry. Alone in the dark with no direction he thought, *Of all the ways to finish my life. No one will ever know what's become of me.*

It was around this time that he encountered the skeleton, and it scared him rational. Crawling on hands and knees, he cut his palm on what turned out to be a piece of sharp bone – he deduced this when he found the rest of the skeleton, more or less undisturbed. He determined by feel that it was human. It took up most of the tunnel, and he ended up breaking up the rib cage in order to get past it. There were no weapons or supplies near the body, but after that he got in the habit of feeling very carefully along the floor in front of him just in case he should find something useful.

By Ysse, he thought. *How many others have died down here?*

He armed himself with a human femur, thinking it might function as a club, a hammer, a lever, or even a choking bar. Having even this one tool heartened him, especially when, creeping along with his left hand feeling for the way, he encountered a human face buried in the stone.

His heart lifted momentarily as he associated it with the face he'd touched near the entrance he had used when escaping the Snake-monster; but this one was in a different place entirely. It didn't feel the same, either. It could belong to the same person, but its surface was rougher and less distinct. If his fingers had not been searching so carefully, he might not have recognized it for what it was. He had been halted by indecision in a crossways, groping around assessing the dimensions and angles of the various choices, when his hand moved over something bumpy in the left wall of the passage. He guessed that it either had been carved in the stone deliberately, or embedded in the molten lava. The thought of the latter possibility made him shiver a bit. These tunnels might well have been carved in an eruption. What if people had been buried alive in here?

Buried alive as he was about to be if he didn't find a way out. The skeleton had found its way into this maze of tunnels, but it had not come out.

He ran his fingers over the face again. The features were delicate. It was small, probably female. The nose and ear were chipped. Maybe it was a sign. He decided to choose the passage that it was carved in.

For a little while he felt hopeful, but like all the others, the passage marked by the face led only to more of the maze, and he seemed to have no gift for guessing the turns right. At last he stopped, sagging into a prostrate position. There was a tunnel going up, a tunnel going left, and a little farther ahead, a shaft going down. He did not think he had been to this junction before, so maybe he wasn't going in circles after all. But there had to be a way out. Someone had used these tunnels . . . They must have. How were they directing themselves? Did they do it purely by memory? Did they possess special senses? He fell asleep trying to figure it out, and woke up hungry and thirsty and hot.

The face was the only thing that could mean anything, but for the life of him he could not understand *what* it might mean. He decided to feel every inch of the passage from now on, just in case he managed to somehow find another carving. In this way he made very slow progress. He started to think about madness and how thin a membrane there seemed to be between sanity and insanity, and he realized he was on the verge of screaming hysterics. Then he found another face.

This one was in profile, carved on the right wall, again at a junction of ways. What did it mean? He decided to choose the passage that the nose was pointing to and see where that got him. He was slithering along on his belly, feeling carefully for more signs, when an echoing noise came rushing along the tunnel toward him.

It was a human sneeze.

Tarquin went still. He didn't think he'd been making much noise, and probably the other man hadn't been, either, but the sneeze had given him away. Tarquin froze and waited for him almost gleefully. He heard the man come sniffling and snuffling along the tunnel, dragging himself slowly and, Tarquin thought, awkwardly. Some Snake. Tarquin felt his blood begin to race as he lay in wait. He could smell the other man. He could feel his heat.

Tarquin sprang.

He got hold of the skull and brought down several smashing blows with his forearm and clenched fist, wanting to use the femur bone but lacking the space to swing it. He had been meaning to crack down on the back of the neck and render his victim unconscious, but the blows came down on the exposed throat instead. He realized an instant too late that his victim had been lying on his back. Belatedly he grabbed the jaw, pulling the head back to expose the throat, and wrapped his right arm around the neck to secure a hold. The man was thrashing and kicking, but Tarquin held him firmly in the crook of his elbow. He slid his left hand around the other side of the head and grabbed his own forearm, enclosing the neck snugly. He applied pressure, choking the man until he went limp. Then Tarquin let go. While the man was momentarily unconscious, he quickly searched his body for weapons by feel. He got a small serrated knife, the sort used for utility purposes rather than fighting, and a strangle-wire: a Snake weapon. The man's head was shaven and he was clad as a Snake, but he had no luminous paint to announce his presence in the dark.

Tarquin took the weapons and used the leather thongs that had held the equipment in place on his bare torso to tie the Snake's hands so he could control him as he revived. He was pleased with himself, for now he could make the other lead him out of the maze.

But the Snake's breathing wasn't right. He made terrible choking and wheezing sounds, and his body began to convulse. He flipped over, grabbing at his throat. Tarquin felt across his face. There was bloody foam coming from his mouth. He made strangled noises. When Tarquin's fingers crept over the other's throat, he realized the trachea was crushed. Blood and saliva sprayed as the man tried to breathe and inhaled fluid.

This was not an injury that Tarquin could fix. He finished the job brutally and then backed away from the dead body superstitiously. He was furious and guilty. Mostly he was angry at himself for getting it wrong and killing his one chance at escape, but he was also angry at the other man for dying and blocking the tunnel.

'You stupid Snake bastard,' he thought. 'I thought you were crawling on your belly. Why were you on your back, fool? If you'd been on your belly you'd be alive right now.'

He fumed for a while, and then he began to think. Why was the Snake lying on his back? Who crawled on their back down a hard tunnel? Unless . . . unless they were trying to feel for something overhead.

Tarquin turned around so that he was oriented just like the dead man and began to feel along the roof of the passage. It was smooth. Maybe, Tarquin thought, the man had been looking for one of those carvings. The faces. He continued along the passage on this supposition. After about twenty feet there was an opening in the ceiling. Maybe that's what he'd been looking for, Tarquin thought, excited, and climbed up into the shaft. It was tight, but climbable. Just inside it he found a carving. He felt it carefully. It was the right profile of a head.

'Strange,' said Tarquin, and his voice echoed. 'This means something.'

The sibilant echoes of his voice reminded him of the echoing clicks of the adder pit. Were these carvings some sort of clues – would they tell him which way to go? But how?

He returned to the body and clambered over it with some difficulty. He crawled back along the passage the way the dead man had come. He went very slowly on his back, feeling all the while for more faces. He passed several turnings to the left, but when he felt their walls, there were no carvings. At last he came to a right turning. In the ceiling where the two passages met there was a bump. Tarquin passed his hands across it several times. It was not a face, nor a profile, but it did feel a bit like the back of someone's head.

'Ho,' he said softly. Now it was staring to make sense. The dead man had crawled along the right-hand passage until he came to this junction, and then he had felt around until he found the bump. The back of the head told him that he needed to adopt that same position, so he got on his back and went along until . . . until when? How did he know what the next turn should be?

Tarquin tried it. If he was on his back, then he had to be feeling for a shaft going up. The dead man had been attempting to reach an upward-turning passage when Tarquin sprang on him and killed him. All right. It was a theory, but how to be sure? He returned along the passage and took the right-hand turning that he suspected the dead man had taken. If the bump meant that you were lying on your back and the next turning was up, and if the man had made a left turn to enter the fatal passage, then he must have been crawling on his right side at the time, facing the left wall, and somewhere back there along his route there had to be a head signalling the way he had come. Tarquin tried finding it, and sure enough, after only a short stretch, there was a hole in the floor, and near the hole a face in profile.

Excited now, Tarquin followed the pattern, sure that this was the key to finding a way through the maze. However, he took only two more turnings before he came to an intersection of several passages. There was no way to know which way the man had come from – only which way he had gone. Some of the passages might well be blinds, or might lead to adder pits.

Tarquin stopped, defeated.

Then it dawned on him that he might not be able to trace back the way the dead man had come, but he should have no problem continuing on the way he had been going. He knew the code. He was saved!

In good spirits, he reversed and returned yet again to the corpse. By now he had had a chance to think the thing through, and he realized that wherever he emerged, he had better be prepared to contend with the Snakes. So he robbed the corpse of what little equipment it possessed: a flask of water, some leather thongs that might come in handy if he got bitten and had to make a tourniquet, and a small tin of yellow phosphorescent paint. He thought about using this to mark a trail and decided he didn't have enough; anyway, if he got out of the maze, he would need it in order to pass himself off as one of them. He couldn't steal the man's body tattoos, but the face paint would at least help in a pinch. He stuck it in a pocket, put the knife in his belt, and considered the corpse again. If there was traffic of any kind down here, he could not risk its discovery. He decided to take the time and effort to drag it to the nearest pit and shove it down. He made sure he chose a tunnel that had no markers on it, hoping that this meant the passage would be unused by Snakes and reserved for those who were lost and couldn't read the signs. He wasn't sure whether he had quite grasped the full logic of those signs, so he supposed it was possible he had only pushed the body into a different part of the good route. Still, if he had left it lying where it was, he knew for a fact it would be on a usable path. He could not possibly make matters any worse by moving it.

He drank some water and set off, deeply pleased with himself. He was sure now he would live, and nothing else mattered. He was inexplicably content. In the darkness his body felt vivid and strong. He could sense his skeleton and how it was joined together; he could detect gravity and heat and their influence on him. He was aware of his own fingerprints, of the grease and grit trapped in the fine hairs that grew along his spine, of the burned skin on his nose and cheekbones already beginning to peel. He did not believe his senses had ever been so acute. While he was riding Ice and the spectacle of the White Road was revealing itself to him, he had felt high and awed and *changed*, as if he could never go back to an ordinary world with its boredoms, non sequiturs, disappointments – for he would somehow have transcended it.

What a stupid delusion that had been. Here he was again, hungry, tired, scared. Alone. But his body would not fail him. Not yet. He could trust it as he had never trusted the Knowledge.

In the end the maze led him to an area he judged to be more frequently used than the others, for he could feel the grooves in the floor made by the repeated passage of bodies, and some of the faces were even worn down by touch to blurred, lumpy reductions of what they had been. He was nearing the populated city. In fact, there were times when he could feel or hear the vibrations of activity as if on the other side of a wall. He could almost believe that the maze had been constructed directly adjacent to the inhabited regions of the caves, winding amongst the chambers and halls of the Snake people. Sooner or later, he would come to an entrance. Then, he would have to be ready.

He pulled himself into an unmarked passage and systematically cut off his braids. He fingered them with some affection for the years they represented before stuffing them into a crack in the rock. Gritting his teeth, he then scraped the knife across his scalp, stopping frequently to blot the blood and allow it to clot before he continued shaving. When he was done with all this, he rubbed the leftover blood into his skin to darken it, and then he began painting his face and forearms and chest with the phosphorescent colour, copying from memory the patterns he had seen on the Snakes.

He could hear people close by now, but he couldn't get to them. He was hungry, and tired, and he wanted to use his eyes again. He felt animalian and strange. He no longer felt like himself, like Tarquin the Free – a man who was anything but free as long as his memories defined him. The lonely twisted journey without his sword or its fateful scabbard had made some subtle change. Now, he didn't even feel like a man. He felt like a darkness.

Someone to Talk To

It was the middle of a snowstorm when Pallo reached A-vi-Khalar, and the bright frescoes in the street were completely obscured by clinging white. His pony trudged along to the blacksmith's house and clopped into the swept yard, where geese were pecking at corn and scraps of bread and swede under the shelter of the stable awnings.

'I am a friend of Istar's,' he told the blacksmith, who came out of the kitchen wearing a fur coat and carrying a pike. Pallo held up his hands in a show of peace.

'Are you Pharician or Clan?' demanded the man, narrow-eyed and red-faced in the blowing snow. 'Your gear describes you as Pharician if your accent is a mixture, and we have had enough Pharician harassment here for one day.'

'I am a friend of Istar's,' Pallo repeated patiently. 'Is there trouble? Can I help?'

'No,' answered the smith, not very convincingly. He added, 'You had better come in. It's a terrible night. Where is Istar?'

He beckoned Pallo into the stable, where he stood the pike against the wall and pulled himself into the loft. He began tossing straw down into an empty box, arousing hopeful whickers from the horses.

'You've already had your hay,' he informed them in an aggrieved tone, dumping thick yellow straw almost on Pallo's head as he attempted to spread the bedding out. 'Sorry about that.' Good green hay followed the straw; then the blacksmith threw some more hay into each of the other boxes, saying the horses might as well have extra in this cold, 'the poor bastards'. He also got a spare blanket for Pallo's pony, whom Pallo had untacked and begun to rub down with straw. The smith was a kind sort, he thought, and gratefully accepted a bucket of sweet feed for the tired animal.

'Your legs are too long for her,' the smith observed, leaning on the stall door and assessing Pallo's mount. 'Why don't you get yourself a horse from your own country?'

'I had one,' Pallo said, 'but he could not manage the cold as well as your Everien mountain ponies. I do a lot of travelling, and on the whole I find the pony suits me better.'

The blacksmith was eyeing him thoughtfully. 'My name's Dzani,' he said. 'What do you call yourself, friend of Istar?'

'Pallo.'

The blacksmith held his gaze for a second before beginning to smile.

'Ah . . . Pallo the swordsman?' he laughed, pantomiming a fencer, and Pallo blushed, knowing Istar would have told any number of funny stories at his expense. Dzani reached out and slapped him warmly on the shoulder. 'Pallo, indeed! Well met! Istar spoke highly of you, for all she said you were a clown. Let's go inside and get comfortable. I've had a terrible day, but it may end well after all.'

A gust of snowy wind preceded Pallo into the hall, where he gaped at the brightly coloured walls. Irregular blocks of strong, rich colours decorated walls and floor, while the ceiling was dark, almost black. The air felt extremely warm and rather dry; he had the uneasy sensation that he was inside an oven.

Dzani saw him staring and laughed. 'Go on, touch it. The colour doesn't rub off.' Pallo touched the wall and observed that the designs he'd first taken for frescoes evidently were not. The colour was laid deep in the stone, or perhaps natural to it, if this were possible.

'Glyni tried hanging tapestries over the walls, but it never quite looked right. And this stuff won't hold paint or plaster. After a while you just get used to it. Come on in where it's really warm. Glyni's made a stew. We've finished ours but there's plenty in the pot.'

Pallo trailed after the young blacksmith into a large reception room with an open hearth and windows shuttered against the night. Rapidly he peeled off several layers of clothing, for a fire was roaring, and three cats and two children were cast out on a rug before it like religious supplicants, soaking up the heat. He was introduced to Glyni, a sturdy brown-haired girl who didn't look old enough to be mother to the strapping youth who sat doing leatherwork in the corner. When the lad managed no more than a nod and a grunt for the visitor, Glyni apologetically said, 'My son has been manning the Fire Houses for four days running. It is draining work – he should be asleep, but I think he is too tired even for that.'

'Aye,' Dzani concurred. 'Even I can't manage more than a day at a time in the big Fire House, especially—' He cut himself off abruptly, as if he'd spoken too openly before the stranger.

Pallo said, 'I know almost nothing about forgecraft, but I gather it is a difficult art. I should not have arrived so late in the day; I beg your pardon.'

'You sound Pharician,' Dzani said bluntly. 'And you dress and ride as a Pharician, too, for all your fair hair.'

Glyni looked embarrassed and hurriedly left before Pallo gathered his wits to answer.

'I am half Pharician by birth,' he said quietly. 'But my loyalty is to Everien as a nation, and specifically to Istar. I advertise my Pharician blood because it is easier to travel about the land as a Pharician since Tash took over Jai Khalar.'

Dzani nodded his acceptance of this, but Pallo noticed he did not apologize.

'You have done well by Tash, I take it?' he inquired. Dzani still looked uncomfortable.

'We might have done worse,' he admitted.

'The Fire Houses are overworked,' said the elder son from the corner without looking up from his handiwork.

'You are tired, son,' Dzani said firmly. 'Go to bed.'

Just then Glyni came in and set down a tray on a trestle table close by Pallo. There was a large bowl of stew, a basket of hot, crusty bread, a wedge of soft yellow cheese veined with blue, and a rhubarb tart smothered in cream. Pallo fell upon the feast delightedly.

'Istar sent me to check on Mhani,' he said with his mouth full. 'She had to go to Seahawk and will be away until spring at least. She's concerned for Mhani's progress in recovering.'

'We don't like for it to get about that my sister even lives here,' Dzani said carefully. 'A lot of people know she was the High Seer, and even in my own Clan there are those who might be tempted to sell that information to Tash's men. He goes through Seers the way I go through polishing rags, and he'd do anything to find out where Mhani disappeared to. He's probably still ransacking the cellars of Jai Khalar in hope of finding her there.'

'I understand,' Pallo said. 'That is why I have come dressed as a trader. No one need know the reason for my call. You may sell me some trinkets for Pharician coin, and I will be on my way as soon as I have had a few words with Mhani.'

Glyni said, 'She isn't a great one for talking nowadays.'

'All the same,' Pallo insisted, chewing. 'I promised Istar.'

He was in a tricky situation and he knew it. If he didn't tell these people why he needed to get Mhani out of here, they might refuse to let him get near her. But he couldn't tell them of the attack the rebels were planning, or they would raise the alarm and ruin the surprise.

It was obvious that Dzani didn't trust him, either way.

Pallo broke apart some bread with a spray of crumbs and spread soft cheese on it before mopping up the remains of the stew.

'Where is Enzi?' one of the children by the fire said suddenly, sitting up and poking the cat.

'Go to bed,' Glyni said, rising to herd the children out of the room. 'You, too, Ravi.'

173

'But where's Enzi? Why doesn't she have to go to bed?' repeated the younger child, whom Pallo made to be about four.

'Shh,' Glyni said. 'Come.'

Pallo now remembered that Enzi was the favourite niece of Mhani's, the one who, Istar said, was the only person able to talk to the mad Seer. He watched Glyni closely. She was becoming flustered as the child refused to stop questioning her about Enzi and had to be dragged across the room until Dzani barked, 'That's enough, Chiami. Close your mouth and listen to your mother.'

The door closed behind them, but not before Glyni had shot a frightened glance at Dzani. He turned to Pallo and explained.

'My daughter is missing. The Pharicians accuse her of some crime and come looking for her, but they will tell us nothing. Meanwhile we know nothing of her whereabouts, and the weather gets worse and worse. The High Seer also is missing, and I fear they are together.'

Pallo's heart sank. 'Istar's mother has gone missing as well? For how long?'

'Since last night. They took no horses, but nor have they been found here in the town, and Mhani is as mad as a marmot on a hot day, and Enzi full of mischief from the day she was born. I wish Istar had taken her mother away from here while she could. But I suppose it is not her responsibility, her being Seahawk and Lerien's laws no longer in force.'

Uneasily, Pallo said, 'Istar still considers Mhani her relation, and if she were here I'm sure she would be very concerned. She's in Seahawk on other business and I cannot contact her. But perhaps I can help Mhani without giving away her identity.'

Dzani thought a moment. 'If you maintain your posture of Pharician trader, you can get into the Fire Houses and possibly into the undercity. I suspect that is where they have gone. Enzi is unduly fascinated with the Fire Houses. She's even faked the Impressions a time or two in the hope of getting to work there like some of the girls they bring here. But I am happy she has no such talent. Tash abuses the Impressionists, and look what happened to Mhani!'

Pallo opened his purse. 'I have Pharician gems,' he said. 'Don't ask me where I got them. Is this enough to interest the men who run the Fire Houses?'

Dzani looked at his open palm, picking up one of the stones and gazing at it critically. 'Do not ask them about weapons. They are cagey about such things. Ask them about metalwork. Say you want these gems set in the ancient fashion. Say you have heard that Everien Impressions can be stored in gems and you want a demonstration.'

'Very well. What about payment?'

'You can haggle that with them. They will expect goods shipped from

Pharice in spring, so you will not need to show them more up front, other than these stones themselves. I will not ask you where you got them, but I hope you know you hold a fortune in your palm.'

Pallo had not known it, and now he gulped.

'I will try to find out what Mhani is accused of. Don't worry, I won't ask questions. But I can eavesdrop. My Pharician is flawless.'

Dzani refilled Pallo's cup and clicked his own against it.

'It is good to have someone to talk to,' he said.

For his part, Pallo felt like a shit. Xiriel had sent him here to scout out the city, determine its weaknesses, the complement of men, the number and nature of its weapons, and – if possible – the most vulnerable times and places to attack. It had been Pallo's idea to get Mhani out before the invasion, but he had not planned on becoming personally acquainted with the rest of Istar's family – nor on helping the blacksmith to recover his lost daughter. Xiriel would not approve; but it was not Xiriel who was being asked to deceive people who had put their trust in him. Pallo resolved that before he finished his mission and left A-vi-Khalar, he would do or say something to warn Dzani without spoiling the surprise effect of the attack.

What he would say, he didn't know. But he would think of something. It was the only way he could live with himself.

Pallo slept on a couch by the fire that night, and the entire family was up before him. He was awakened by the rattle of the front door and the hoarse shout of a Pharician voice.

'Open up, blacksmith! Answer now, or we will break down the door.'

Even in his half-sleep Pallo knew that it was not so easy to break down the door of an old Everien house, and he staggered out into the hall to see Dzani and his oldest son exchanging glances as they considered the threat.

'Have you found my daughter?' Dzani shouted back, and was answered with an elaborate curse followed by more pounding. Glyni came running from the kitchen.

'They have Pallo's horse.'

'What criminal do you harbour? Open the door!'

Dzani's eyes on Pallo were cold, and Pallo realized that to these people he must look like some sort of betrayer. He went to the door and opened it himself, speaking in formal High Pharician with its exaggerated vowels.

'What in the name of the Most Promiscuous She-Leopard are you making so much noise about at this hour? A man's heart could stop, his sleep thus arrested. Has the northern winter frozen your senses, you inane provincial border guard with breath like a graveyard rat's?' His

Pharician came back to him effortlessly, and he clutched the blanket around his shoulders, shivering – it had been warm by the fire and now the cold shocked him. This unconscious gesture as much as anything must have convinced the sergeant outside that Pallo was genuine, for he shoved his way into the house and gestured for his two assistants to close the door behind them.

'Who are you?' the sergeant demanded.

'I am Nazar of the House of Amn, and I am about to be your enemy unless you have a good reason for disturbing my rest. This weather you keep here in Everien, it is enough to deter even the most intrepid man! Where is your inn? Where are your trading houses? I was obliged to shelter here from the storm and sleep with these . . . these natives!'

'I apologize, Amn Nazar. If these barbarians have treated you poorly—'

'Ah, they are all right, poor miserable souls.' Now he spoke in a lower dialect, as if letting down his guard. 'They are only common people, but you, you should know better. Tash beckons Pharician merchants to come and partake of the glories of Everien, and this is what greets the weary traveller? Threats from a . . . sergeant and his frigid men-at-arms? I want your name and that of your commander, I want better digs, and I want breakfast instantly. I think I shall go straight back to Ristale as soon as the storm breaks. If this is Everien, I am not interested.'

As he spoke the blanket had slipped from his shoulders, and when he stooped to pick it up the gems fell in a glittering shower to the floor. The sergeant's eyes all but popped out of his head.

'Damn it,' Pallo said. 'They are always doing that.'

Everyone scurried to pick up the stones. The sergeant sweated and stammered to make amends. Within an hour, Pallo was drinking mulled wine in the office of the captain of the guard of A-vi-Khalar.

'I have had a time of it,' Pallo told the commander. 'First my party was ambushed by a band of Clan barbarians. They killed my men and stole the gifts I had intended to bring to Tash. They stole my horses and I was obliged to continue on foot until I could pick up this pony at a village near your borders. That is why I have so little with me, other than these few bits and pieces I carry on my person.'

'You are very lucky,' said the captain soberly. 'I will have my men escort you to Jai Khalar. I am sure Tash will want to make reparations for the losses you have suffered.'

'Yes,' Pallo agreed. 'When the weather improves, I would like to go to Jai Khalar. While I am here, though, I wish to see the legendary Fire Houses. For gems and stonework are my specialty and the desired objects of my master, the Most-High Lord Amn.'

'That is easily arranged. I will see that you are given the full tour.'

Pallo, of course, had been in the Fire Houses many a time. Because of their close proximity to Jai Khalar, and because the Fire of Glass, which was housed in the central Fire House, was thought to be closely associated with the Water of Glass in Jai Khalar's Eye Tower, the Fire Houses were frequently attended by students and Scholars from Jai Khalar. Pallo knew his way around well, and had to make an effort to act both awed and ignorant when every detail of design and function was explained to him. Not that he was prepared for everything; for the Fire Houses were being used for entirely new purposes now that Tash was in power, and Pallo was surprised by some of what he saw in the first of the three Houses.

'This one is given over entirely to Tash's weapons now,' said the old Scholar, a man so brown and bent he looked more like a root than a human. 'Before your people came, we used it for swords and armour and arrowheads, but there is little need for such items these days.'

Pallo wrinkled his nose at the smell. In the central pit a white fire was burning, assisted by jets coming out of the walls of the pit. It reminded him of the cave of quicksilver in the Floating Lands, but to have said so would have exposed his identity. The old man explained how there were reservoirs of this fire deep underground.

'Do you mean in the undercity?' Pallo asked. The Scholar shrugged.

'We cannot get into that part of the undercity. It has been completely sealed.'

But Pallo didn't dwell on this fact. He was observing the activity of four men in the pits. They were working on welding a metal frame roughly the size of a beer barrel. They were stripped for the task, their skin stained with ash and gleaming with sweat. Each had a three-day growth of beard and none looked like they had had a good meal lately. One of the four squatted to one side before a rectangular slate, on which was chalked a diagram and some symbols.

'Is he the designer?' Pallo asked innocently. 'A Scholar such as yourself?'

The flattery worked. 'Alas,' said the old man. 'Would that I had such expertise, but I do not. Neither does he. The design was made by a slip of a girl, a refugee from the Snake Clan I think she is. Gialse.'

'An Impressionist. I had heard of them. Can I meet her?'

'*He* has taken her. Up to Jai Khalar,' replied the Scholar, glancing in that direction. For the first time in their conversation something dark and wary crept into his manner. It was almost as if he had said the girl had been taken to be fed to Freeze Wasps.

'Well', said Pallo briskly, pretending not to notice. 'I am not a military man, or I'm sure I would have a better understanding of what they are working on, yon. As it is I had better not comment, lest I reveal my ignorance.'

The old man smiled. 'I don't understand it, either, lad. These newfangled weapons are beyond my ken, and I don't mind telling you I don't like them. But that Tash, he's a hard man and he pushes everyone. Now, it's not for me to say, but between you and me, I think this land is more productive and safer now that he is here, for all that those rebels keep making trouble for everyone.'

Pallo nodded. 'Sometimes a strong hand is needed,' he said cautiously.

He followed the Scholar out of the first Fire House and into the third, skipping the largest in the middle. There was a distinct change in atmosphere within the other structure. It was identical to the first Fire House, but instead of having a large fire going in each pit, this house had a tiny fire available to each worker. The workers inside were mainly women – due, the Scholar informed him, to the loss of so many men in the Slaving – and they sat or stood at benches working on objects too small for Pallo to identify. The fires burned different colours, and they reflected from the glass-lined walls of the cone, making the air seem to swirl with brilliant hues. Pallo hadn't noticed whether there was any glass in the first Fire House; he had had the impression that everything there was covered with soot. Here, the atmosphere was full of light.

'It's beautiful.'

The Scholar beckoned him over to where a heavyset woman with short grey hair presided over an intricate piece of jewellery. Pallo noticed that her tools were dangling from an overhead rack by flexible wires, so that she could pick them up and let them go without looking or cluttering up her workspace. The jewellery itself was a platinum diadem set with emeralds and raw eyestones. It was so bright, it hurt him to look at it. She was wearing a dark visor and using a pencil that seemed to paint on the metal with light – until she removed it from the surface and Pallo saw that she had incised a design in the platinum. His mind began to race as he considered the source of that cutting light, which came from a pencil attached to a wire that disappeared in the ceiling far overhead. Then he realized the Scholar was eyeing him expectantly, and he remembered to keep up his front.

'Ah . . .' he said with an awe that was not entirely contrived. 'Never have I seen such magic at work.'

'It is not magic,' the Scholar answered smugly. 'It is the Knowledge.'

Pallo took his cue to ask, 'But where does the . . . the light, the heat for these tools. Where does it come from? I see no fires powering them.'

The Scholar smiled. 'Come with me,' he said. 'And I will show you something as you have never seen.'

Pallo followed him outside, although he could not resist turning and gazing back longingly at the sparkling things suspended in their work frames, catching the light. Over the last year or so he had grown practised in the role of not-too-bright-but-rich Pharician merchant, and he found himself slipping into character without even trying.

'Do you never feel like a whore, old man?' he asked.

'What?'

Ha, that had got his attention.

'You were Clan until Ysse; then you joined Everien as a confederacy; now you accept the rule of Tash. Yet you have such wonders here at your disposal. Why do you serve anyone?'

The old man cleared his throat, momentarily unbalanced. Pallo had the impression he was running through his file of stock responses and trying to cobble together something plausible.

'Er . . . listen, what you must understand is that I am a Scholar. My pursuit is the Knowledge. Some among the Deer Clan are farmers, some artisans, but the Scholars from my Clan and every other Clan are . . .'

'Separate? Like a guild in Pharice?'

'Guild? I don't know. I've never been to Pharice. The Scholars in Everien try to understand the things that were left behind. All of that came before the Clans, or the rule of Ysse and Lerien, or Tash. We consider ourselves . . .' He seemed to be searching for a phrase.

'Above all our petty internecine conflicts? Too wise to meddle in politics?'

Pallo was baiting the man deliberately. He had to find out how far he could push this two-faced Scholar. Was the man's cooperation with Tash genuine, or were he and his cronies pretending to help Tash but really pursuing subversive ends of their own? The only way he could find out was to force a glimmer of truth by tickling the Scholar's emotional hot spots.

'Not above,' corrected the old man. 'Beside. For the Fire Houses were here before the Clans, and they will be here after.'

'So were the bones of the dead,' Pallo retorted. 'Yet those we leave undisturbed in their graves.'

'Ah, but would you do so if you found they could assist you in your wars?'

'They are not my wars!' Pallo cried defensively. 'I am only a petty merchant.'

'I beg your pardon,' said the Scholar, retreating into his shoulders like a turtle.

Pallo gave a magnanimous laugh. 'Ah, I see what you are saying. I benefit from the wars, though I am not a warrior. Therefore I am caught up in this, too. Well, you are right. But I know whose side I am on: my

179

own. What I don't know is whose side you are on. It seems you go any way the wind blows.'

'I am on the side of the truth,' said the old man. Pallo snorted derisively.

'I think you are lying to me. But respect for your advanced age saves you. What about the third House? So what do you do in there?'

'We do not use it. It is the power source, no more. It is a strange, noisy place and it often vibrates and flashes light when the other Houses are working. Some think that it is there to absorb the overflow of the vibratory emissions from the other Houses.'

'Vibratory emissions? I don't understand.'

'Ah, but you are Pharician, my lord. Begging your pardon, but there are some mysteries that must be studied for many years before they yield fruit. I cannot explain the vibratory emissions this morning!'

Pallo wanted to laugh.

'I would like to see it anyway.'

'Very well,' said the Scholar, looking smug. He led Pallo to a heavily locked and bolted door and went about opening it. 'I do not think it will fail to impress.'

Pallo was nervous. He had heard many descriptions of the Fire of Glass, both in Pharice and in Everien, but he had never seen it and wasn't sure how he ought to react. After all, he was meant to be a Pharician jewellery merchant, but in fact he had seen sights in the Floating Lands to curdle the mind, puree the rational, to overcome all that people took for granted about the world. Since that time, he found it difficult to feel amazed by anything.

But he gasped all the same. It must be the sound, the throbbing he could feel in his breastbone. Or maybe it was the vertigo he felt when he looked up and saw the fire, and the way it reminded him of the volcano that the rope bridge had taken him past, and its awful heat and immensity. But it was not hot here, and the place was empty, and the red walls looked more like the vaulted interior of a tree than a building made by people.

The Scholar didn't move, but Pallo walked into the centre of the space, where in a checkered jigsaw pattern of black-and-white marble a pit was set in the floor. He walked around it and it seemed to him that he felt a faint hollowness beneath his boots, but he kept his expression neutral. Around the rim of the square, which was roughly ten feet by ten, ran a strip of red stone inscribed with symbol characters. He had seen their like in the Floating Lands, but unlike Xiriel he could not read them. Nor could he commit their pattern to memory as he knew the Seer would be able to do. He wondered if Xiriel had ever been in here, and what he thought.

'I see you do not know what to make of it,' remarked the Scholar. 'No one does. Yet if I tell you that all the art of the Fire Houses comes from that fire up there, you must take what I say as the only truth we know.'

Pallo hitched his thumbs into his belt and wished he had a belly to stick out. He was enjoying baiting the old man. 'Is it true what they say about Queen Ysse? Did a barbarian woman truly handle such an artifact of power? It is inconceivable.'

For the first time, a flicker of real emotion crossed the Scholar's face.

'She was more than a barbarian woman,' he said. 'She was a person of eminence. And yes, she brought it here in her hands, and set it up there with the help of her birds.'

'And is it true,' probed Pallo, enjoying himself now, 'that if that Glass up there is removed, Jai Khalar and everything in it will disappear?'

The Scholar's lips pursed and his sagging jowls tightened.

'Yes,' he answered, and after that he clammed up.

'Not that anyone can see it anyway,' Pallo yammered on cheerfully. 'What are those stripes on the wall?'

When the Scholar didn't answer right away, Pallo went and inspected the bands of dark glass that ran around the walls in concentric circles. The floor panels were also made of glass that was scored with thousands of irregular lines, like a puzzle, and it seemed to him when he stepped on the cracks that they sang ever so slightly into the balls of his feet, as though charged with a current. He approached the band on the wall that was closest to eye level and saw that it flickered with light. When he touched the wall in which these glass stripes were laid, he felt bumpy lines, like veins underneath the surface of the Everien smoothstone. He looked over his shoulder at the opposite wall and thought he could see faint patterns in the walls between the concentric stripes.

'Are those symbols in the walls?' he asked, and was surprised because one of the bands flared to life, shooting a little current of light from left to right across the glass band. The pattern darted like a wasp in erratic flight, incredibly fast and delicate, then quickly faded.

'They respond to sound,' said the Scholar, and when he spoke as well, a jagged line of light seemed to rise within the band like a rough wave, wriggling and then subsiding when he stopped speaking. 'If you look in the centre of the floor you will also see that there are musical apparatus.'

There was a waist-deep depression, a dimple in the centre of the floor. Pallo couldn't see any strings or horns, but when he stepped into the well he found a set of panels that he could stand amongst. When struck, their surfaces made pitched sounds that reverberated through the entire space.

'These are like jungle drums!' he cried. 'Talking drums that they use in Aranoka to communicate across the impassable bush! I have read of these and seen pictures, but I have never played them. What are they made of? I see no skin, and they're too thin to give such a deep sound.'

'They are Everien,' said the Scholar as if this explained everything.

Pallo began beating a ferocious rhythm on the drums. The Scholar covered his ears.

'Do not play on them, you might light up the symbols!'

Pallo stopped, perplexed, for he had noticed that the lights which shot across the walls like little waves did not respond the same way to his drumming. 'Why doesn't my drumming make little waves?'

'It is too gross and loud,' answered the Scholar, and Pallo saw that the waves returned when he spoke. 'It overpowers the little waves.'

'What does all this mean?' Pallo said. 'What's it for? And what do you mean, light up the symbols?'

'There are symbols in the walls, you can't see them until they are lit. And they are only lit when certain rhythms evoke them.'

'Really? What rhythms? Show me?'

'I cannot. I have not the Knowledge. Please, come out of the pit now.'

There was a tuft of fur stuck between two of the rhythm panels, Pallo noticed. 'But why would you want to light up a symbol?'

'It is time for lunch,' said the Scholar nervously.

'Ah, I would not try to steal your secrets,' Pallo said magnanimously. 'I was only curious.'

On the pretext of tapping a final, soft rhythm, he bent and tugged at the fur. It was otter.

'The truth is, we don't know,' the Scholar said. 'But you must not let this worry you, for the Fire House that concerns you is the second one, and the first is working at full capacity. In fact, the smiths work there all night making weapons.'

'Why such a hurry? Are the Sekk so bad?'

'Tash has ordered it. They are shipping large quantities of fire-throwers and other Everien weapons to Jai Khalar.'

'Jai Khalar? Why do *they* need weapons? They're impregnable.'

'That is not for me to say.'

Pallo was torn between caution in maintaining his disguise as Pharician trader and the urgency of knowing that an aging woman and a young girl were missing. After his tour of the Fire Houses he returned to the room he had taken in the Pharician-run inn, where he blended easily enough among the other traders. The inn reminded him of a miniature Jundun, so diverse was its clientele and so crowded the accommodation. Pallo had grown accustomed to the vast echoing space of Jai Khalar – and the even bigger bed of the ground itself, where he had spent many nights since returning from Jai Pendu. To be crammed into warm smoke-filled rooms dense with Pharician accents and the smell of exotic food recalled him to his youth in Jundun, and he found Pharician ways returning to him easily. He knew how to eat a Ghissa stew with flatbread and dried fruit. He knew what to say when someone sneezed. He didn't have to think about any of it; in fact, he was enjoying himself.

But the mystery of Mhani clouded his mind. He heard nothing at the inn, so before dawn he stole outside and trudged through the un-ploughed powdery snow to the blacksmith's house. His horse still being stabled there gave him an excuse to return without arousing suspicion, and he simply collected the beast and dropped a scribestone in the animal's feed tub, trusting that Dzani would notice it there. In the scribestone he had recorded, 'The weapons house. Midnight.'

He returned to the inn and began making arrangements to leave for Jai Khalar the next day. 'I have seen all I need to see,' he let it be known. 'Now I wish to speak with Tash, for his family are the friends of my master's house, and I have news to exchange with him.'

Meanwhile he packed a light kit for himself, which he carried in a slim rucksack that slipped beneath his cloak without making too much of a bulge. Once he had entered the undercity, he had to assume he could be there for quite some time. When he met Dzani outside the Fire House, production was still running, the smiths taking the work in shifts. Dzani came along in an otter-fur hat and a heavy cloak.

'That looks a warm hat,' Pallo remarked.

'Yes, all my family have them,' Dzani said absently. 'What have you learned?'

'I have a few questions. Were the Fire Houses searched thoroughly?'

'Yes, of course. But they are always guarded and locked.'

'Does Enzi know how to get through the locks?'

'She might,' Dzani conceded. 'But why would she want to? What are you accusing her of?'

'Nothing! But think on it, Dzani. A mad Seer who in the Liminal once had access to information we can only guess, and a headstrong young girl. They could get up to some mischief.'

'I suppose.'

'What's under the floor tiles of the big Fire House?'

Dzani looked surprised. 'There is equipment down there – but how did *you* know?'

'It's hollow. You can hear it. Are there any doors to the undercity?'

'Now that you mention it, yes.'

'Show me?'

While they walked fully wrapped through the sleeping undercity, Dzani explained how most of it lay in ruins and the rest was sealed off by Everien doors with unbreakable locks. The city lay in a circle all round the Houses, and the only way through the diameter was a single, deep corridor running north to south – beneath all of the Fire Houses, Dzani told Pallo. There was an Everien door on this cross-corridor.

Dzani said, 'This is the door to the forge pit of the largest Fire House.'

Pallo consulted his maps and his frown deepened.

'I make that door to be off centre, to reach the centre Fire House,' he muttered, then half glanced at Dzani and fell silent.

'Where did you get those?' Dzani hissed.

'That is a trade secret,' Pallo said. The maps were the remnant of the book given to him by the insect-woman in the Floating Lands. She had burned the book, but not all of it had been destroyed, and Pallo had copied out what remained, leaving white space where the burned parts were. He had possession of maps of parts of the Floating Lands, A-vi-Khalar, Jai Khalar, and one or two other Everien sites that he had not yet identified. 'That door is not in the right position.'

'We never use it. It is Knowledge-locked and no Scholar has ever broken the code.'

'It just goes to the forge pit? That's all?'

'Aye. It must have been put there as a convenience in the old days, to save people going above ground, but it doesn't matter to us – we don't live in the undercity and therefore don't need direct access to the Fire Houses from below. Shall we carry on?'

His tone was patient, but firm. Pallo had been examining the symbols on the door panel, but now he quickly folded his map and followed Dzani.

'Has anyone been in the fire pit since Mhani disappeared?'

'Sure, yes.'

'Did anyone try to open this door recently? Since looking for Mhani?'

'Not that I know of. It is always locked, and there was no sign of anyone in the forge pit. Anyway, why would they want to open it? It only leads to this corridor.' And Dzani indicated the Pharician guards posted at either end of the cross-corridor, just visible by the light of the oil lamps they carried on the ends of their spears.

'Did you try opening the door from that end?'

'No. Like I said, it's always locked.'

'Mhani is a Seer of great repute. She may know more of codes than you realize.'

Dzani was growing impatient. He repeated his argument.

'But we have sealed off the undercity. Even if she had gone through this door, we have blocked all of the other exits. And anyway, why would she go this way? The Fire Houses are guarded. If she wanted access to the undercity, she could have gone through the public entrance in the main square.'

'That would not have been secret enough.'

'It is not patrolled in the middle of the night. The Pharicians are not so oppressive as all that.'

Pallo grunted enigmatically.

'I don't know for certain where she is. But I think I know why you haven't found her. Come, Dzani. Let's go to the big forge pit.'

'These are not Everien locks,' Dzani said as he spun the wheels that controlled the door to the central Fire House. 'They are actually of Pharician design, installed in the early years of Lerien's reign. In Ysse's time the Fire Houses were open, but when the Sekk began to threaten it was necessary to install security. Only the Scholars and the smiths know the codes you need to get in. Of course, now the Pharicians know them as well, so the area I'm admitting you to is really not so secret after all. Still, the guards are there as a second level of security. Some of the things being made here now are very secret indeed. Not that you would know what you were looking at if I thrust it right in your face. Everything in the Fire Houses is coded, one way or another.'

Dzani went to the well in the centre of the room and pried up a tile with his knife. Within moments, he had disassembled the drums, revealing a dark, hollow area beneath. Pallo followed him into a warm, dry room. It reminded him of the interior of the Floating Lands, and some of the design features of this structure were almost the same as those rooms; but the walls were written over almost entirely in Everien symbol-language, glowing yellow-white against a dark blue background. And there were waist-high panels like desks or tables, made of a hard substance that shone. Lights moved across them when they were touched.

'That old bugger said this place wasn't used,' Pallo breathed, amazed.

'It isn't. We leave well enough alone. No one has the faintest idea what any of this is for.' Dzani busied himself replacing the panels from the inside. They were now effectively trapped in the pit. 'Keep your voice down, in case someone comes in. Now, there's the door to the cross-corridor.'

He went to a trapdoor and tugged it open, revealing a shaft with struts sticking out of the walls where there had once been some kind of structure, possibly a spiral staircase. At the bottom was a faintly glowing Everien door.

'Did you bring rope?' Pallo said.

'No.'

'Well, then, we'll see whether it's climbable. The girl might manage it, but I wouldn't have thought Mhani nimble enough.'

Pallo actually did climb down the side without any great trouble. He went very slowly, for he had a terrible head for heights and was intimidated by the depth of the shaft. The handholds were regularly spaced and had almost certainly once supported either stairs or a ladder of some kind.

At the bottom, Pallo shone his Knowledge light on the door.

'You're right,' he reported. 'She didn't unlock it.'

Dzani sighed. 'I told you s—'

'She forced it.'

Mousetrap

Pallo covered his ears as Dzani came barrelling noisily down the shaft. The lock had been melted, probably with a tool from the Fire Houses themselves. When Pallo shone his Knowledge-light into the open doorway, they could both see that it did not open onto the cross-corridor where they'd stood earlier.

'I told you it was off centre,' Pallo crowed. 'See, look at the map. This cross-corridor that cuts across the diameter of the city is asymmetrical where it bisects the circle. That means it bypasses the exact centre for some reason. And look at the way the three Fire Houses fit together. See the space between the three circles, sort of like a triangle? I bet you any money there's a shaft there, and that's why the cross-corridor is off centre. So as not to intersect that shaft.'

'You're a genius,' Dzani said. 'Truly.'

'Thank you. I wish you would tell that to some people, particularly Istar. Now, I'm going to ask you to go back and wait. I may be gone some time, but on no account are you to follow me or tell anyone what we have found. I have instructions to give you, and you must trust me. Dzani, your second son is much the same size as me. He will leave the town disguised as me. He will be wrapped against the cold and no one will know the difference, nor dare speak with him. When he reaches the next village he will take ill and take to his bed, and stay there until you have word from me what to do next. With the winterfever as bad as it is this year, no one will go near him.'

'But how am I to explain his absence from the pits?'

'Same thing,' Pallo said. 'Winterfever. The whole house will come down with it. As the father, you will work on bravely, but everyone else is to stay in and put up the sickness signs on the doors. By the time medicines arrive, I should be finished and your family can be cured.'

'It is a great risk you ask me to take. Already I have lost my little one . . .'

'If you want to get her back in one piece, you'll do as I say. I think I can find her, Dzani. And if I can't, I'll cover you no matter what. I give you my word.'

'All right. All right. I trust you, my friend.'

Pallo thought about what Stavel intended for A-vi-Khalar and resolved that, though he deceived Dzani for now, he would tell him the truth about the invasion before it was too late.

There was no doubt in Pallo's mind that he had entered one of the sealed sections of the ancient undercity of A-vi-Khalar. Equally, he was sure that Mhani and the child were here. There was no dust down here, nothing to mark their passage: the place was sterile and soulless, and the air was stale and hard to breathe

He walked around for a while, trying to orient himself in relation to his map, which was frustratingly blank in a lot of important places. After about half an hour of this, he heard a voice. He stopped and stood stock-still. It was a feminine voice, speaking very softly. He could not make out the words at first, but he moved toward the sound until he came to a junction of passages. The echoes were thrown in such a way that he couldn't be sure where the speaker was. But now he could hear her words, and in a higher pitch, the girl's words answering her.

'Enzi, I have Seen it. Just as I have Seen the Making of the mice of Jai Khalar. Well, not the Making, but the collection of the mouse impression.'

'What's a mouse impression?'

'It's a way of catching mice.'

'Oh, you mean a mousetrap. We have those! There are lots of cruel ones, but my mother uses a glass bowl balanced on a thimble full of goat's cheese. The mouse goes under the bowl to eat the cheese and when he disturbs the thimble, the bowl comes down on him. Actually, it only works about half the time.'

Loquacious child, Pallo thought, turning slowly to try to pinpoint the location of her voice.

'Ah, the Deer Clan!' Mhani cried. 'I know it well. The obsession to build a better mousetrap. It will be our downfall. Well, the Knowledge is the best mousetrap of all because it can catch any mouse. The Everiens solved the problem. And it solved them!'

'If the Everiens solved it, how come there are so many mice in Jai Khalar?'

'Because when they caught one mouse in the Making equipment, when the recorded the very writing on its being and translated it into a rhythm and ultimately a symbol such as these mysterious symbols you see all over the place down here, when they did that it was the Everiens against one small mouse. But this very act of pattern-saving meant that now they were dealing with Mouse. With all possible mice everywhere. And that is a big number. It's a number big enough to eat you and me. And don't forget the wild element that segregates life from death, which is a mystery to all. What's the difference between a live mouse and a dead mouse, Enzi?'

'I don't know.'

'Time. Between an unborn mouse and one that eats out your larder. Time! And the spark that is without substance or code.'

'Mhani, Auntie, I cannot understand you. Are you rested enough now? Can we go on? I'm hungry.'

'But I have Seen it!' Mhani wailed.

'Shh! Stay quiet. You must think! Think backward. How did you pass through the city?'

'We entered near the river. We walked through the city. Then we went down deep, and finally we came to the spiral stairs and then the forge pit.'

'But the details, Mhani. Close your eyes and try to see it. We have got past the forge pit and the stairs. Walk yourself backward. What then?'

'I'm trying. My mind, child, it is weak.'

'All right. Rest then. Just rest.'

Pallo heard shuffling noises and followed them to a dead-end passage with a hole in the bottom. There was a shaft going straight down into darkness. Could the voices have been echoing up the shaft? He hesitated. His stomach protested at the idea of dealing with yet another height.

Then he heard a sneeze from below. He shone the Knowledge-light down the hole.

It was too dark to see her face clearly, and anyway she had crammed her body deeply into a recessed well in the wall of the shaft, her fingers catching on the dank stone and her feet drawn up so that only the soles protruded from beneath the drapery of her robes, which were of the sort meant for the bedchamber and not the underground passages of a long-dead city. Her feet were bare.

Pallo lowered himself as far as he could until he was practically on top of her. He braced himself against the narrow shaft with his back and legs.

'Mhani, how did you find this place?'

She didn't answer, didn't even seem to register the question. He shifted position and she looked up at him. Her face was pallid and there were dark circles beneath her eyes. Her mouth was half open and she was breathing through it.

'Thirsty,' she said.

'Simpleton!' Pallo cursed himself and fumbled for his water bottle. 'Are you hungry? Here is some cake.'

But she was occupied with drinking, her eyes closed as she tilted her head back leaving her throat open in an entirely unselfconscious way.

When she had finished she gave back the bottle and looked at the wedge of yellow cake he proffered. It was studded with fruit and its top was sugar-glazed – Pallo had a weakness for such delicacies and had used his Rich Pharician Merchant clout to acquire it, then had not had time to eat the full round and had packed the leftovers with the idea that he might fancy a snack at some point. Here in this dark place the cake looked not merely incongruous, but almost offensively luxurious. Mhani stared at it in disbelief.

'The girl,' she uttered in a grey voice.

'Enzi? Where is she?'

'The girl,' Mhani said again.

'Oh, hell,' Pallo said to the air. Then: 'Mhani, come with me. You have to come out. They're looking for you up there.'

And yet he was torn. Here was a veritable warren of passages that he was sure weren't known to anyone. Where did they go? Would they lead to the inner workings of the Fire Houses? And what about Enzi – he couldn't return without her, not after all Dzani had done for him.

'I wish Istar was here,' he said, and Mhani blinked at the mention of her daughter's name. 'She'd go down that mouse hole faster than you could say—'

'Mouse,' Mhani said.

He laughed uneasily, not sure of her meaning. 'Yeah. Mouse.'

'Come on, Mhani.' He reached out and she took his hands. He tugged at her, but instead it was he who was pulled down. The aging woman might not be strong, but she knew where and when to apply what weight she had so as to tip him off balance. It was a struggle to get her out of the shaft. When they were standing in the corridor again, he rubbed his forehead, trying to decide what to do now.

'Did she escape in time?' Mhani asked with sudden urgency.

'Enzi? Were they chasing her?'

'They will always follow her. Until . . . tell me, did she get out in time?'

'I don't know. In time for what?'

'The breaking. Or was it tearing? A kind of horrible birth. Tell me she got out.'

'Show me which way she went and I'll see,' Pallo replied cannily. 'I'll make sure she's safe. Which way did she go?'

But Mhani was ignoring him, absorbed in some internal drama. He wasn't even sure he and Mhani were talking about the same thing, or the same person. Suddenly Pallo had an inspiration.

'Here!' He pulled from his kit a sheaf of vellum leaves bound in soft leather and tied with a silk cord. He opened the book on his bent knees and showed it to Mhani.

'Xiriel made me copy these out,' he said. 'Most of it was burnt when the Wasp-woman lost her temper, but there were vestiges of the original maps, and some parts I added from memory. Mhani, could any of these maps apply to the Fire Houses? This place.'

She flipped through the pages with a neat efficiency at odds with the rest of her manner. She stopped. Inhaled slowly.

'Yes,' she answered.

He helped Mhani to her feet and they moved off, Pallo holding the Knowledge-light and the bent woman weakly holding the maps. She stopped at a door and said, 'Eteltar.'

'What?'

The door slid open and Mhani slipped inside. The room was very much like the one hidden under the floor of the third Fire House, but it was smaller and more cluttered, and there was a huge, gaping hole in the far wall. The tables and walls were tiled in an extraordinary manner.

'What are these things?' asked Pallo, touching the tiles one at a time and recoiling each time, as the images lit up and moved within their frames like living creatures in cages. 'Some are animals. But others . . .'

'They are abominations.' Mhani's voice was so low and scratching that he might have mistaken her for a man. 'Some are kind to men, some cruel, most are indifferent. All have haunted Everien since times long past. The Assimilator, the sailsnake, the distancc-spider who folds the earth, the freeze wasp, the time serpent, the dreamflower. Every one an abomination that cannot now be recalled to nonexistence.'

'What about this tile?' said Pallo. 'What's supposed to be here?'

'That is man's vision of man,' Mhani said. 'That is our downfall, pitch-black and hidden to us. It is the Sekk, our hunter, the predator designed to make food of us with our own passions.'

Pallo said, 'How did they come here, to Everien?'

'The Everiens made them,' said Mhani.

'And where did the Everiens go?'

'They never left.'

Pallo took a deep breath. 'Okay,' he said, walking across the rubble to the gaping hole. 'Where does this go?'

'I don't know. It wasn't there. It looks like there was an explosion.'

'*Mhani? Mhani?*' The girl's voice echoed from without, and Pallo realized guiltily that he had completely forgotten about her. She came into the room, her eyes wide, and stopped when she saw Pallo.

'Who are you?'

'A friend of Mhani's. I've come to help you.'

Enzi smiled. 'Are they looking for us everywhere? Are they worried?'

'Of course they are! But we're going now.'

'Okay.' Enzi shrugged. It was all just an adventure to her.

Mhani said, 'I'm not leaving.'

Pallo chose to ignore this, for he was thinking aloud. 'I don't see how we can leave via the Fire Houses. They're looking for you, and by now they may well be looking for me. We need to get out of A-vi-Khalar altogether, and quickly. I'm to find the best way to attack; but if I don't return, the Clan rebellion led by the Wolves will attack anyway. I was not permitted to warn the Deer Clan, but I'm here to get you out. Istar could not come.'

'I don't care,' Mhani said.

'I care!' Enzi cried. 'My parents. My sister and brothers! What do you mean, you were not permitted to warn them?'

'Shush,' Pallo whispered peremptorily. 'These passages are complex. We do not know who may hear us.'

'I'm going back! I have to tell my family.'

'No, you're not.' He grabbed her arm. 'It's too late now. You'd only be captured, and probably killed once they learned you'd been spying down here. The Deer Clan is not being deliberately targeted and your family have a good chance of making it out – or even aiding the coup.'

'You should have warned them.'

'I could not risk it. The Pharicians were ready to pick up your father for questioning any moment. Because of you, Enzi, so quiet yourself and do as you are told.'

The girl obeyed, sulking. He turned to Mhani.

'Can you use these maps? Can you get us out of here?'

'She is not in her right mind, you know,' Enzi said. 'Sometimes she knows what she's doing and sometimes she doesn't.'

'I told you to be quiet.'

'Not this way,' Mhani said. 'That's not how we came. I have to think, retrace my steps. We need to be beneath the centre Fire House. We went there directly from the overcity. So we must return that way, or else find a connecting passage between this area and the centre House.'

'Is there one?' Pallo examined the map again. 'This is the only part that survived the flames.'

'We're here.' Mhani put her finger down with conviction on one of the inked-in parts of the map. The burned areas had been left blank when Pallo had copied the original, and she now traced her finger down a series of stairs and passages and then into the white unknown.

'There. Somewhere. We'll pick a linking corridor and get to the central Fire House. We'll have to go down a few levels, though, before we can cross over.'

'I wonder why they went to such effort to keep the Fire Houses separate underground,' Enzi mused, and then put her hand over her mouth and glanced at Pallo.

'To prevent contamination,' Mhani said tonelessly.

'What?'

The Seer only looked at him. In all innocence, she repeated back to him, 'What?'

'What do you mean, contamination?'

'Contamination? I didn't say anything of the kind.'

'She is like that,' Enzi began again, and again ceased.

Pallo climbed to his feet. 'Let's go.'

They were all tired and Enzi was cranky when finally they had reached a position almost directly below the entrance Mhani 'remembered' from her Impression in the Liminal. They were no longer on the map. The corridor was wide and smooth, with a glassy floor that would have been slippery had it not been coated with several layers of grit and ash. To either side were corridors and barred doors, unused probably for centuries. It was still, pristine, sterile – except for a yawning hole to the right, just before the foot of a wide flight of stairs rising into darkness.

Mhani pointed to the stairs. 'There! I think that's the last flight. It takes us out to the docks.'

'The Pharicians are all over the docks,' Enzi warned. 'If this is our secret exit, it's not a very good one.'

But Pallo was sniffing curiously. The draught coming from the ragged hole was perceptibly fresher – and colder – than the dead warm air that pervaded the undercity.

'That wasn't there,' Mhani said, but by the stubborn way she spoke, she might as well have said, 'That *isn't* there.'

Enzi shivered. 'It looks like a monster's lair.'

It did indeed look rather like a H'ah'vah tunnel, Pallo thought. It was very much the same as the great pit that had opened in the side of the laboratory with the animal tiles. Had something *eaten* its way through here? Pallo shuddered. Then he turned his Knowledge-light toward it. 'I want to have a look.'

The rough passage rose steeply. It was jaggedly cut and lined with scree. There were burn marks along the walls. About two men in height and perhaps wide enough for four to walk abreast, it must have required no small effort to cut, yet none of the finesse employed elsewhere in the building of A-vi-Khalar was in evidence here.

'I don't like this.' Enzi's voice echoed from behind. 'It's evil.'

Pallo had always assumed he liked children, at least as a general principle, if only for the reason that he had yet to really grow up himself.

It came as something of a surprise to learn that Enzi was annoying. Perhaps even profoundly annoying. He wished she would shut up. Especially because she seemed to be right.

He kept walking. He could feel that compulsive curiosity coming over him – the curiosity that everyone who'd ever instructed or commanded him or tried to advise him had said was his second greatest liability (his truthfulness being his first and his inattention to the obvious/over-attention to the not-obvious and usually-irrelevant being the third). Pallo blundered up the passageway confidently holding his Knowledge-light like a talisman before him. Mhani and Enzi trailed uncertainly some distance behind. He could hear them whispering to each other but could not make out the words.

They were probably complaining to each other that he was leading them nowhere; that they would never find the way to the surface. The passage grew steeper and more difficult, and he wondered if he should turn back.

Then, suddenly, a hole opened in the ceiling. White cold flakes of snow blew across the hole and dropped in, like stars melting on his face.

A Whole New Definition

Once he had solved the riddle of the maze, Tarquin was in no hurry. As it turned out, there were several entrances to the Snakes' city, for once he took the final turn which let him out of the maze, he came out into a long tunnel, man-high and dimly lit by phosphorescent moss, which spiralled around the outside of the carved city. From this spiralling highway sprouted numerous entrances, and he spent some time checking them all out and getting to know his way around. Unlike the maze, the spiral passageway was well trafficked, and Tarquin had a number of close calls at first. He had had time to feel guilt for the murder of the Snake in the maze, and he didn't wish to put himself in a situation where he had to kill another innocent, especially since there were at least as many females as males to be found in the passages.

He followed one woman into the city itself. He had no way of knowing what hour of day or night it was down here, but when he smelled the contents of the basket she was carrying he guessed it was late morning and she was bringing her share of the catch back for her family. She shuffled along an internal corridor, humming to herself, and as Tarquin followed he took in the Everien-style frescoes on the walls and the recessed Knowledge-lights that he had never seen anywhere other than in Everien cities. The woman paused at a door and was seen doing something to the wall beside it. She put down her basket momentarily and Tarquin, who sported what felt like at least a three-day hunger, rushed in and seized it up, changing directions so fast he nearly suffered whiplash as he sped up the passage the way he had come.

So began his days and weeks of thieving from the Snake Clan. He enjoyed himself, having no other responsibility beyond his own survival – and after the dangers of the monster and its maze, this was easy, for his social conscience was limited and he'd no qualms about stealing food. There were a great many unused passages in the city, which was complex enough to give him trouble in finding his way around even after many days. Stealing from the Snakes was not so easy, particularly after they began to suspect that a criminal was in their midst. Women soon began travelling only in groups, or walking and climbing with their pet snakes curled around their necks, literally watching their backs. For there were many snakes among the Snakes, and although they showed no signs of possessing a special intelligence, they had a way of appearing when and where you least expected them to. Tarquin grew cagey and wary and sly, and if he missed his sword he also knew that bare skin and bare teeth served him better down here. He ghosted about the city, looking for a way out but never finding one, for he was forced to stick to the less populated regions. The Snakes never seemed to sleep, and there was no way to sneak among them unnoticed.

He learned that the Clan was preparing for the Pharician attack. Warriors came and went. Enormous quantities of food were brought down and stored in vaults and chambers. Then the siege began. Men patrolled the tunnels, sometimes even entering the maze; but Tarquin never let himself be caught. Women still ventured outside, but only with armed guards and, Tarquin supposed, through secret ways. He tried following them, hoping for a way out himself, but the men all carried guardian snakes who hissed if a stranger came near, and Tarquin could never get close enough to keep an effective trail. The incoming supply of fruits and fresh fish grew scant as journey to the surface became riskier.

He ventured deeper and deeper down the spiral, until he was sure he must be getting close to water level. There were more people down here, and he discovered their food routes. One time he found a woman bearing a basket full of things that smelled so good he actually leaped out and tore it from her back, running blindly down a side tunnel with his loot. About half the contents spilled out as he ran, but he managed to close the basket up even as he was losing himself in another, seemingly deserted, section of the city, thereby avoiding leaving a long trail of stolen food behind him. In time he emerged from darkness onto a ledge overlooking a huge natural cavern. Its floor sparkled with black sand, and its walls were honeycombed with holes like the one Tarquin was sitting in, and he could make out patterns of ledges where hand- and footholds had been worn in the rock, which was the glossy black of volcanic lava. Oil lamps were set around the walls and there were several torches on stands scattered across the sand so that the cave was fairly well illuminated for eyes already accustomed to darkness. There was a pool of water near the far wall with several structures of wood and metal and netting alongside it, as well as a round, roped pit. Almost in the centre of the floor had been set a large round wooden frame, like a platform covered with tightly lashed hide. With the exception of this last piece of equipment the cave resembled a sort of gymnasium.

No one was about. Tarquin gobbled down the sticky confections he had stolen and promptly fell asleep, until the sound of high-pitched voices roused him. He jerked his head up and saw a chaotic platoon of little people come rushing into the arena below, flanked by women like shepherds. The children were shrieking and turning cartwheels in the sand. Tarquin stirred grumpily. He didn't think anyone could see him up here, but he made sure to stay in the shadows anyway.

There were a hundred holes in this bowl-shaped cave if there was one, and in its centre was a dirt pit surrounded by netting. It reminded Tarquin of the wrestling pit at Jai Khalar, and he remembered that he had gotten the idea for that from Ysse, who said it was the traditional Snake venue for practice. At the other end of the bowl was a pool of water, to which two women decamped, soon surrounded by half a dozen babies and small children. Although there were wrestling matches going on in the dirt ring, and tests of strength being conducted everywhere for the older boys, Tarquin found himself watching the tiniest children, a little shocked at what he saw. The children were made to grab onto a length of cloth and then the women slung them through the air around themselves, spinning all the while. The children screamed with laughter, and when they were set on the sands again, the women immediately fell on them, cuffing and slapping them lightly and giving them commands. Astonished, Tarquin watched them roll into defensive postures immediately. Praise from the mothers; then it was the next child's turn. After all of the little ones had had a few doses of the swinging, they were tossed in the air every which way so that they landed in the water, where they wrestled each other. He heard the same phrase over and over again from the watchful mothers, and eventually he recognized it as thickly accented Snake: *Don't panic.*

Older children were made to cling to posts of varying widths as though learning to climb trees for pineapples; and there was a wooden climbing frame over a sandpit, where older ones had to crawl out along the 'branches,' hang, and then drop to the sand without making a sound, where they pretended to attack and strangle sandbag dummies.

Every so often a boy or girl emerged from one of the many narrow tunnels that punctured the arena, and after a while Tarquin realized they were being trained in navigation and climbing skills. After that he kept an ear out in case one of them came up his tunnel. He found himself marvelling at the strength and agility of these people, and he realized that he'd been very lucky when he interrupted his victim and killed him with one unanticipated blow. Tarquin was not adapted to crawling around these tunnels or fighting bare-handed, and he might not have done so well had the man realized he was lying in wait. Looking at the Snakes made him feel clumsy and unrefined.

Then Kere walked in and provided a whole new definition for clumsiness. Actually, he more or less fell in, shoved from one of the entrance tunnels by a band of youths who shrieked with laughter as Kere tumbled to the ground, rolled, and got up, shaking his white head in an effort to reorient himself. He staggered a few paces through the sand, dodged a net thrown by a girl younger than himself but possessing thrice his physical coordination, and came to a halt beside one of the posts of a climbing frame. The kids who had pushed him continued to follow him, taunting him in Snake slang replete with body language and the occasional rhythmic tattoo for special emphasis, until one of the adults called for order. Kere slunk into the shadows and hid, but the other children assembled themselves in groups according to age and gathered in a rough semicircle around a slim man decorated in yellow phosphor.

Tarquin's attention fixed on the speaker. He recognized the man as one of those who had accompanied Mavese to the beach that night when the Pharicians had come. It appeared that he was now acting as instructor to the youth of the tribe, for he was assigning different tasks to different groups. The women who were supervising the babies and toddlers were instructed to perform the 'water drills', whatever they were, and the older girls – there weren't many, Tarquin noticed, surprised to see them included in military exercises at all – were assigned to work on the climbing frames and walls, led by a wiry female wearing a few cursory streaks of warrior paint on her back.

'Silence and secrecy are your only defences,' the instructor told the group before they went off. 'This is not for play. Pharician soldiers prowl the island and seek entrance to our tunnels. We must repel them. Next week we will train in the jungle itself.'

Solemnly the girls filed off, and then a couple of the older boys were sent off to teach the younger ones.

'Concentrate on locks and finishes, but don't neglect climbing to get them warmed up,' said the instructor to his young assistants. 'Don't bother with the fancy finishes. Keep it simple and effective. This isn't going to be a mating contest, but a war. Style is unimportant.'

By now most of the trainees had dispersed to begin their tasks, but the oldest boys remained. Some of them had taken advantage of the diversion of the instructor's attention to engage in lighthearted scuffles. Tarquin was impressed with the way they moved. For all that they might secrete themselves underground, the Snakes were no cowards. They took their combat preparation seriously. Nor was their teacher, Pakise, easy to please. He rounded up the older boys and told them to do the 'little bulls' drill. They promptly paired up and began pushing one another in the sand, chest to chest, each seeking to drive the other backward and corner him. Pakise made scornful remarks from the sidelines.

'Go on, *push*! Inise, if your penis is as limp as your spine, you'll never fuck a squid, never mind a girl. No, Brelse, don't let up on him yet. Inise!

Don't quit! Push push push *push*! Ah, that's a bit better. All right, get your breath if you must. Next!'

Tarquin smiled, recognizing the drill, for it was a classic training method he had used himself with Ysse's guard. The object was for each man to brace against the other and drive his weight forward, transferring power from the ground to his upper body. When the exercise was performed properly, the contestants looked like two bull elephant seals fighting by the sheer throwing around of weight.

Then it was Kere's turn. He came forward gamely enough, apparently undismayed by the harassment of the boys even when he was paired with one of his tormentors, who said something inaudible to Kere, and then laughed until Pakise told him to shut his trap. The boy was the same size as Kere, but for all that Kere threw himself into the drill with great enthusiasm, including copious grunting and flailing of his arms, within a matter of seconds he was reeling backward across the sand while the other boy charged him and pushed him to the ground. For good measure, Kere's opponent landed on top of him, wrapped Kere up with his arms and legs, and applied a finishing hold to his neck.

'All right, that's enough, Lise. Kere, get up! Come here. Lise, you work with Binnatse.'

The instructor walked Kere toward Tarquin, lowering his voice to speak to the boy privately. As they drew closer, Tarquin picked up what he was saying. '. . . practice! Much more practice, Kere. Forget sleeping, forget eating, just get down here and train yourself all the time. And another thing. I don't want to see you running away from the other boys. You act like a coward.'

'But I can't fight them, Pakise! What can I do besides run?'

'The more you run, the more they will chase you. You will have to outwit them somehow. If you are as smart as Mavese says, this should present no problem. See Woose if you must; she has the biggest collection of short-acting potions in the whole city. Laxatives are always a sure bet, and they're very difficult to trace.'

Tarquin stifled a laugh at the look of surprise on Kere's face.

'Wise up, boy!' Pakise said, slapping Kere on the shoulder. 'It's no good having a fancy sword and being able to speak a dozen languages if you don't know how to act in your own best interests. Now, don't make me talk to you about this again. Mavese doesn't have much patience for outsiders. You're lucky he didn't kill you first and ask questions later. And the training maze is not easy. Boys have died there in the past. Do you understand me?'

'Yes, Pakise. I'll try to do better.'

'Don't *try*. Just do it, Kere. It's your life on the line. I wouldn't be

199

worth my salt as a teacher if I didn't tell you what you will really be up against.'

'But what should I do? The others, they've been training since they were only small!' Kere gestured to the toddlers being rolled around inside hollow barrels by their mothers in an effort to disorient them. 'How can I hope to catch up?'

'If you want my advice, you'll find a way to make friends with Lise and Brelse and those others who torment you. They're good little fighters, and if this siege goes on, as I think it will, soon they'll be sent out to the jungle as monkey-police in the trees. They could teach you a lot.'

Kere looked miserable.

Change to Ice, damn you, thought Tarquin to himself, for he empathized with the boy, who really couldn't help it if he didn't know how to fight. As exasperating as Kere could be, Tarquin couldn't help thinking that if Pakise or Mavese or any of these people knew what he really was, no one would dare taunt or tease him, much less make him learn a fighting art that could be transcended by one blow of his mighty forehooves – as Tarquin had good cause to know from personal history.

But Kere only swallowed, eyes shining with tears, and pushed his shoulders back. 'I will do what I must,' he said shakily.

There was a rumbling sound that startled Tarquin until he located its source. A man had entered the cavern and climbed atop the hide-covered frame near the middle. He had begun to shuffle and dance on it, beating a rhythm that reverberated and built and echoed again, becoming more and more intricate as he carried on. Tarquin was studying his movement and seeing the fluidity of his muscle control. His body was tattooed in bands of yellow and black, which undulated as his muscles flexed – only his face was free of the tattoos, but was painted instead in a manner not dissimilar to the Snakes Tarquin had known in Everien. He was extremely lean and supple.

To the music of his footfalls, people began to appear from the separate tunnels: men scantily clad but richly tattooed in broad bands and patches of red and green and blue; women less flamboyantly displayed in close-fitting but plain clothes. All of their heads were shaven, and all were slim almost to the point of etiolation. From two or three tiny apertures high in the cavern came children, who secreted themselves behind rocks and looked on furtively, never straying far from the holes they had come from, as if they were afraid.

They are like wild animals, Tarquin thought, and then the drumbeats died. A solitary figure was approaching across the sands, and from the reactions of the others, Tarquin guessed he was their leader even before he saw Mavese.

This time the warrior was not wearing his full ceremonial paint, but his body was unmistakable. He looked like a giant amongst the small and slim Snakes. The drummer stopped.

Mavese said, 'The Pharicians have broken through the water traps just this morning. They do not yet know the gate code, but it is only a matter of time. Soon all of us will be fighting for our lives. For our way of life.

'Those of you who are of an age to come away from your mothers' sides will be tested. For some of you it will happen too soon, but I cannot apologize for this because we can never predict what circumstances will bring us. I can tell you of my own history, which may bring hope to some of you, although in the end your survival is up to you. What I am about to tell you I have never told to any group before.'

He paused and glanced across his rapt audience.

'There are many tests and difficulties in the training maze, and some we are honour-bound not to disclose after we have passed through. I, however, did not pass through all of the training maze. I was defeated by it.'

There was an embarrassed hush.

'As you all know, during the test of manhood if we do not pass through the maze and return with proof of our success, we are cast out of the Clan. This is what happened to me. It is no secret to any of you that there are some very tight spots in the training maze, places where the passage is no bigger than some of your bodies, and grotesquely twisted. One bend in particular has been constructed to test suppleness, static strength, and slipperiness all at once.'

Mavese stood up.

'Look at my build. Look at my shoulders. They are broad, are they not? And even as a boy, I was not slim of form.'

It was perfectly true, Tarquin thought. No amount of dieting would make Mavese's bones any smaller. He stood out among the other Snakes, who were slim and delicate even by ordinary standards, and sylphlike compared to Mavese.

'I could not get through this bend. My instructor had advised me to dislocate one of my shoulders and slide through that way, no matter the pain; but although I performed the dislocation and suffered the excruciation, I still could not get through. It was physically impossible.

'I had to return the way I'd come. My instructor begged leniency for me, begged that I be given some alternate test, but our leader of the time would not be gainsaid. He didn't care that I could understand the time serpents' language better than any of our people and that I should be allowed to live on that basis alone. No, he believed in tradition. To his death-shakes, when I later choked him to death in a grudge match, he would not give in. But I get ahead of myself.

'I was cast out into the jungle. I lived there for some time and continued my training, hoping for some way back into the good graces of my Clan. Other failures had gone to the mainland, or died of poison bites or infections, or drowned trying to swim to other islands. Some gave up and were executed by the Clan. I didn't even consider any of these things. Always I searched a way back, and after many months, when I was even bigger and stronger and tougher and more vicious than I ever had been when I attempted the training maze, I found another way into the cave system.'

'The top of the volcano,' said one of the boys, and Kere looked at him sharply.

'Yes. I climbed down the shaft and fell into the time serpent chamber. They were sleeping and I fled before they could kill me, but I soon found myself in an impossible maze. It was the Jaya maze, and once I got in I couldn't get out.'

Jaya maze? Tarquin forced himself to stay still. *In the name of Jaya,* Mavese had said once. And Ysse had kept Jaya plants, which the red-haired girl had called roses. He shivered.

'I was starving after weeks wandering the maze. I couldn't get out. Sometimes I could actually hear my people through the walls, going about their business in the old city, but I couldn't reach them. I learned afterward that by my cries they'd thought me a ghost. At last I found my way back to the time serpent chamber, hoping to steal some bones or other scraps left behind from their meals, which our people brought to them as live offerings. I knew that if I were truly courageous, I would try to catch one of the animals before the time serpent could get to it, drag it into the maze, and kill it with my bare hands. Or die trying, which was the more likely outcome. I'd been eating the moss simply to fill my belly, and my skin glowed from within even though the moss did nothing to sustain my life. I expected them to see me and kill me, but they were preoccupied. One of their eggs was finally hatching.

'In all the years of our people's history, there has never been a report of a live time serpent born. As far as we know, the pair that live there now have always been there. They are as old as the maze, and probably as old as the city itself. Maybe older. My great-grandfather used to say that they were born with the volcano and that they carved all this, but I do not know the truth. Anyway, the event of offspring was unheard-of. For all my hunger and weakness, I watched in awe as the young time serpent pushed its way out of the egg.'

Mavese paused and the silence was stretched taut with the children's listening.

'It was only about that long.' He measured his hands four feet apart. 'It had a human face, but not the face of a baby, the face of a very small adult human. Its body was yellow and green, banded up and down. It was extremely weak, and when it moved it was uncoordinated. It could only flop sideways in a spiral, like this.' Mavese lay on the sand and demonstrated, and Tarquin had a vivid image of the hapless snake thrashing ineffectually.

'I retreated immediately and watched from the safety of the maze. I was afraid the parents would kill me and feed me to it; but they did nothing. I could hear them talking to each other, and to it. The baby didn't talk back.'

'What did they say, Mavese? What did they do?'

'The male knew immediately that it was dying, and he was right. He said that they were under a curse and that they could never make a viable offspring. The female didn't want to hear it. She kept encouraging the young one, even as it was breathing its last breaths. Then she told him that it was his fault, and he said it was hers, and they argued this way for a time. While they were fighting, I slipped in and stole the corpse of the young snake.'

Gasps.

'It wasn't courage, it was desperation. I dragged it into the tunnels where they couldn't reach me, and I ate it raw. I forced myself to eat it slowly, a little every day, and with the strength I had got from the meat I made a determined effort to find a way through the maze. I was very lucky. I learned the way more by chance than by deduction, but in the end I found myself back in the city by a secret passage.'

'What secret passage? Where?'

'It has since been blocked up, so do not get excited! The Jaya maze is too dangerous for the uninitiated to enter, so do not think about it. Now, my teachers and family were shocked to see me, for I had been presumed dead long ago. I did not explain to them what had happened, and this made them fear me. They told me that the time serpents were angry and refusing to talk to them or accept offerings, and they were afraid for the fate of our tribe if the time serpents decided to attack us.'

'How could they attack if they were trapped in the maze?'

'Good question . . . Kere. But you must realize that although they secrete themselves in there, they have the capability of carving and altering stone with their bodies. If they wanted to come and eat us, they could. It must be the human aspect of them that restrains them. Now, after I stole the body of their young, they were furious. Anything might have happened. I didn't think I could win them over, but I had to try. To my people I was now a legend, and I could not be seen to be cowardly. So I took an offering of a large fish to the time serpents through the Jaya tunnels, and I also dragged with me a drum with which I spoke to them in the time serpent language.'

Now Mavese's speech became more stylized, as if he were reciting his story by rote. Tarquin supposed he must have told this part many times before.

'I told them what had happened. I explained that I meant no dishonour, but that I would help them to solve their problem if I could. I said I would travel to Pharice and seek out Scholars who might study their eggs and see what was wrong with them. I said I would be their servant.'

Again he paused, and the children leaned forward anxiously to hear what he would say. Someone (probably Kere) sneezed.

'They sniffed me over very carefully. The female in particular grew excited. "You have assimilated us," she said to me, and to her mate she said, "Look, he even glows!"

'The male was not so easily won over. "If he has assimilated something, it was a dead spirit. Do not think of him as your child."

' "He is the closest I may ever have. What is your name?" I told her, and she said, "Mavese, I name you leader of the Snake cult and charge you to find a cure for our people. You now have some of us in you, and you will find a way to save our kind. You will do this as if it were your own life, for you know it is."

'So it was that I became charged with the duty which I also pass on to all of you. I have spent my life fulfilling this duty. The time serpents sent me to Pharice, where I encountered the Circle of old Everien, who pay richly for anything to do with the Knowledge. The time serpents have given me their eggs in exchange for an understanding of the patterns of life that lie within them, ever hoping for a cure for their barrenness. With the poison and medical arts of their venom, we have also traded for other materials that will help our people.

'Children, we have grown strong. Remember, once we were poor slaves. Now we live like kings in our stronghold. All of you must uphold that way of life. The Circle is a fickle group of scholars and artisans and other renegades, and they dabble in sorcery and killing. Yet they have been our partners. Pharice is dangerous. Everyone wants what we have. But as long as I am your leader, the time serpents will speak only to us, live side by side only with us. They have many powers which are even unknown to you.

'Tomorrow, each of you who is of age will make his way alone through the training maze. If you succeed, you will come face to face with the time serpents just as every warrior has done since the beginning of our history. You will bring back something from their lair, some knowledge or souvenir that you did not have when you entered. Then you will be taught the secret of the Jaya maze, the secret that I learned almost at the price of my life. And if you fail the test, you will go into the wilderness as I did, and with the Pharicians all over the island, this is a guaranteed death. And a shameful one; remember, we are no longer slaves. We do not bow to the will of the emperor. We are the proud servants of the time serpents and the time serpents alone.'

With that, Mavese's speech ended. Tarquin watched Kere carefully. The boy was shaking. Without even knowing the specifics of the training maze that had defeated Mavese, Tarquin was certain that Kere could not negotiate its difficulties. For that matter, he doubted Kere could prove his fighting skills in even the most rudimentary way. In fairness to Kere, that would be too difficult a task for most boys, for the Snakes had been rigorously and intelligently trained from a young age, and they were impressive to witness in action. Kere didn't stand a chance.

He would have to be rescued.

A Good Snake

After the other children had left and the cavern was empty again, Kere stayed. He roamed from one piece of equipment to another, climbing a bit of wall until he fell, splashing about in the pool to no great effect, and trying to roll the enormous hollow stone balls that the Snakes used for strength training. Then he stood in the middle of the sandpit looking forlorn.

'Psst!' said Tarquin, and his voice echoed from the vaulted walls. Kere jumped and spun around, trying to locate the source of the sound. Tarquin threw a fruit pit at him and then Kere saw him. The boy bounded across the sand like a puppy and climbed up to Tarquin, who had to concede that Kere was marginally more coordinated than he had been a few weeks ago. He must be learning something.

'There you are!' Kere whispered. 'I didn't know what to tell them. They had seen our traces and followed us up the volcano, then when you were down the shaft they grabbed me and let the rope go. They laughed. They said you were Snake food. But I didn't think you'd be so easy to kill. I must say I've seen you looking better, though, Tarquin. You've – well, you've never looked *good*, precisely, but you've looked better than you do now.'

Tarquin eyed the boy, who sat there in a heap of disconnected bones topped by white frizzy hair. 'And you're no diplomat,' he retorted. 'But there has to be something we can do for you. You'll never make a wrestler, that's certain. You should stick to being a horse. Don't you see you'll get yourself killed? Ice can take care of you, but you sure as hell can't take care of yourself, Kere.'

The boy smiled. 'See, it's nice to have a name of my own. When I'm in Ice I don't have a name separate from him. I can't even think about anything besides what he wants to think about. Imagine it, Tarquin! Oh, you think it's bad losing your precious sword, but you've never been a prisoner like I've been a prisoner.'

'Where is my sword, anyway? You didn't give it to them, did you?'

'What choice did I have?'

'You could have let Ice take you and me both away from here. By Ysse, I've been hunted by those snake creatures that live down here, I've been living in total darkness for weeks, I murdered a man, and you're still trying to prove a point with Ice. It's madness!'

206

'It's not that simple, Tarquin. Leave me alone.'

With that, Kere's tears began to flow. He wrapped his arms about himself, getting ready for another fit, Tarquin thought.

'Children!' Tarquin muttered. 'It makes me nervous, when you get all soft and pathetic like that. Stop it. Don't you have a rational bone in your body, you useless little sack of wet salt? Quit sobbing and change to Ice or I'll . . . I'll . . .' What would he do, anyway? He could scarcely do harm to such a weakling as Kere. Then again, all of this was Kere's fault. If the boy had been eaten by a Horse, well, then he had been Eaten and that was all there was to it. This was his lot in life. It was not for Tarquin to deal out better justice.

His rationalizations didn't help him, though. There was the boy, curled up in a ball, not an ounce of potential manhood anywhere, even in his puny testicles. He simply didn't know a thing about being a person.

'All right,' said Tarquin at last, mastering his anger. 'I'm not going to hurt you – for the moment – but you must agree that we can't stay here. What have you learned about these people, since they seem to have welcomed you with open arms? And what do you know about the giant snake hybrids that live in the caves? You apparently speak their language – what did you tell Mavese about that?'

'I said I was your servant, that we were shipwrecked off the coast, fleeing some Pharicians whom you'd angered. I said you were a great swordsman from the far North and that I was your translator because you could only speak your strange barbarian tongue.'

'And the giant Snakes? Mavese intends you to talk to them?'

'They are time serpents, hybrids of men and the Li'ah'vah of ancient Everien.'

'Li'ah'vah!' breathed Tarquin. 'They carved huge tunnels, bigger than H'ah'vah tunnels. The mountains of Everien are riddled with their holes.'

'This pair are very old, and they are dying,' Kere said. 'They cannot have offspring. The female lays eggs, but they do not hatch. Mavese had given the eggs to the Pharician Scholars in hope that a cure might be found, but there is nothing alive inside the eggs. Only a substance that all claim is magical, but none know fully how to use.'

'What substance?'

'It's hard to be sure. I am being taught with the other children, remember. But it seems to be a special poison of great value, and that is why the Snakes are so revered. This is the cause of the conflict with the Pharicians. The Pharicians keep sending people to try to get to the time serpents, but the maze protects them.'

'Is that where these eggs are kept? In the chamber above the maze?'

'Something like that. The time serpents live in an inner sanctum open only to the full males of the Clan. There is an initiation rite which the boys must pass through. It involves climbing through a training maze which is full of booby-traps and other dangers. Only a fully trained warrior can get to the inner chamber. It's said that the eggs are kept there, together with the poisons and elixirs that have been distilled from them.'

'What about the venom?'

'It's deadly. They don't protect it the way they protect the eggs, though. You can find it in the ordinary herbalists' in the residential quarter. There are other venoms that they use, collected from the jungle above.'

'This initiation rite. Is it the only way you can reach the giant Snakes?'

'I don't know. There is the Jaya maze which is said to also lead to the time serpents, but very few know their way around it. I only know that the boys who fail the initiation test twice are given a choice between castration followed by slavehood to the time serpents in the Jaya maze, and guard duty against the Pharicians in the jungle. Most of them choose the latter, but whether it's because of the castration or the time serpents and their maze I don't know.'

'Why's it called the Jaya maze?'

'Dunno. It's a giant maze that surrounds the whole city. It actually passes through the city in some places, and they say if you knocked holes in certain walls you'd break into the maze. It's as old as the city and is used as a defence against the Pharicians. You can only pass through if you know the maze. Otherwise you get lost and die, or end up in the time serpents' habitat where they eat you.'

'Not a kind fate,' Tarquin said.

'Those who act as guards in the jungle outside seldom live long. The Pharicians kill them whenever they come ashore, but they are of use to the Clan because the commotion warns them that the Pharicians are about. Secrecy is everything to the Snakes.'

'Why should they stand guard over a people who have cast them out?' Tarquin asked incredulously.

'Because if they prove their worth, they might be let back in. That doesn't usually happen. Sometimes they give themselves up to Pharice and become slaves like their ancestors, or else they live wild in the jungle; but if they are caught this way by the Clan, they are subject to death on the spot. Most die of despair, it's said.'

'It is a harsh way of life,' Tarquin remarked, and then considered how his days underground, alone, had changed his personality. Darkness did not make one kind, he realized. 'So you are to take this initiation test? Of course you will fail it. Why does Mavese bother feeding you if he knows you will soon die?'

'Because of the language, I guess. I think he hopes that I will prove myself by passing the test, and then I will become a Snake and he can entrust secret information to me.'

'He has a very cool head,' Tarquin said, 'for a man with the legions of Cirene poised to swarm over his island.'

'They are stockpiling food to withstand a siege. It will not be easy to break in here. The river exit seems to be of Everien design, practically impermeable. You need a special rhythmic code to get in.'

'So much for the canoe we were going to build,' Tarquin said, smiling and ruffling the boy's hair. 'It's good to see you, Kere, even if we are in a scrape. I want to talk to Mavese, but on my terms, not his. I have already killed one of their men – or maybe one of the eunuchs, for he was wandering around the Jaya maze – and according to their law Mavese may well have every excuse to kill me on that ground alone. So I must get to him without letting him get to me. What can you tell me about the layout of the city?'

Kere leaned forward and smoothed the loose sand over the ledge before beginning to sketch.

'We are above water level,' he began. 'As near as I can make it, the breeding pair of time serpents live in a large cavern above us and a little bit to the north. But you have to go through the Jaya maze, or the training maze, which opens onto this spiral passage.'

'The highway, I understand. I need to know how to get from the spiral highway to the water exit. I'm not worried about the Jaya maze because I understand it now. I can get us both through it, and given a little time, we'll find the time serpents. What I want to know is how I can get from the time serpent lair to the outside. In a hurry.'

'I can lead you,' Kere said.

'Do you know the door code?'

'Yes, it's simple. It's in the rhythm language.'

'Good. Let's go.'

'Now?'

'Do you want to wait until tomorrow and you're being tested in the maze where you have to dislocate your own shoulder?'

'OK. I'll come now. Is that food?'

'What?' Tarquin saw that Kere was pointing to his stolen basket. 'Are you hungry? Rather save it for when we need it.'

'You're the thief!' Kere exclaimed. 'They've been looking for you everywhere.'

Tarquin smiled and stretched, beginning to stand up. 'Are you going to turn me in?'

Kere started to say something, but Tarquin never found out what it was because someone tackled him from behind and knocked him down.

It did not go well for Tarquin. As he tried to recover from the surprise, he was conscious of the fact that he wasn't as strong as he once had been; that hard going had worn him down and stripped his muscles to their bare essentials; that when he asked for a response from his body it came too little, too late. Grappling was the most exhausting form of combat, and his unknown Snake opponent had every advantage: youth, surprise, polished skill, and home territory. Tarquin had watched the children train and knew that the adults had to be formidable. He was a swordsman, and there was no ego left in him for this contest. A part of him wanted to give up. It was only the faint but deep spark within that struggled on his behalf, the small but insistent need to stay alive.

He found himself prostrate with his knees drawn up under him, elbows protecting his head while his adversary rode him like a horse. It was a bad position, for he couldn't strike out, was vulnerable to strangulation, and, in this case, was too weak to get his feet under him and stand.

His opponent was twenty years his junior, muscled like a physician's atlas of anatomy, and keen to dominate. Tarquin didn't know it, but to the eyes of other men he appeared emaciated and weak, swordless, and most of all, old. His beard was growing in grey, and his skin appeared fragile for all that the sun had darkened it to gold during his time climbing the volcano. In the first moments of the engagement he had responded feebly, lacking his usual enthusiasm to be tested against another man, for he had only lately battled the maze, and before that, the sea itself – and before that . . . well, before that – worse.

A more experienced opponent might have known better than to take these signs of weakness at face value. As it was, the man who tried to subdue Tarquin allowed himself to feel at ease where he should have been wary. He didn't immediately apply a stranglehold to render Tarquin unconscious, but made the mistake of becoming momentarily caught up boxing Tarquin's ears, trying to divert one of his arms from its protective curl so as to apply a figure-four to his neck. But Tarquin had been hit on the head so many times he wasn't troubled by the light blows, and the small waste of time while he was curled up in this manner gave him a chance to catch his breath and gather what little strength he could. He felt the man's weight shift to the right as he tried to get a better angle on slaps and punches that were (Tarquin thought, even in the middle of it all) rather weak for a man of his weight. The shift in weight was a small opportunity, but Tarquin took it. He felt his own bones slither beneath skin and muscle as he subtly repositioned his hips before hurling himself backward, flipping over on the way with a catlike twist. He knocked the wind out of the younger man when he landed on him, then managed to get a crushing knee into his enemy's balls as he scrambled up his body, grabbing his enemy's head and smothering him against his chest as he climbed on top, hooking the man's ankles with his own feet to prevent being bucked off. He rested here for a second, then shoved his upper body up, delivered a couple of punches more or less into the face, and dropped again. His opponent's arms wrapped around his back and tried to crush his ribs, but the grip was not tight enough to incapacitate Tarquin and didn't stop him grinding his knuckles into an exposed earhole, biting, or jamming an elbow into the collarbone where it was particularly sensitive. He heard screaming beneath him, and knew he didn't have much time before the younger man became incensed and scared and began to draw on his own emergency reserves, which were bound to be far more substantial than Tarquin's. He let go the feet and moved his weight higher on his opponent's body, intending to beat his face to a pulp since it was clear the other couldn't punch his way out of a wet sack.

He had only delivered two or three hits when he felt a sudden, piercing bite on his inner thigh, and then retrospectively he recalled that he had felt something moving between his trousers and his skin along his right calf but hadn't perceived the subtle sensation as a threat. Now he didn't even have time to think *damn it*. Poison slipped into his blood like a sudden, irresistible music.

He woke with a headache worse than if he'd drunk barleywine topped by rum and joyweed. He could hear water trickling nearby, and when he opened his eyes he saw a small fountain in the shape of a blooming tropic flower. He was lying on cushions in a dimly lit cave lined with reed mats and fresh flowers, and Mavese was sitting a few feet away. He pointed at Tarquin's leg, laughed, and said something Tarquin didn't understand.

'A good snake,' Kere translated, 'is worth a thousand women. They are loyal, they live off your body heat, and they are a last defence against enemies.'

A Good Sword

Up close, Mavese had the distinctive look of a self-made man. His face could never be mistaken for that of another, nor his voice easily imitated. His gaze was steady and strong, and though he spoke Pharician, he punctuated his words with a drumming of the fingers of his right hand on his own inner thigh, while reaching out with his left to occasionally touch Tarquin's forearm. Tarquin didn't understand the meaning of these rhythms that ran alongside his words, but he was sure that they had a meaning, just as the clicking of the Snakes' tongues did. Occasionally he said something that Kere had to translate, but mainly he addressed Tarquin directly. Tarquin gathered that they were in Mavese's private rooms, for there were noises of women and children in adjacent chambers, and the curtain past Kere's right shoulder rustled from time to time as a child peeped in, sometimes holding a pet adder. Mavese was saying scornful things about Tarquin's plan to infiltrate the time serpents' lair and then escape, but Tarquin had a headache and was in no mood to be lectured.

'You fool,' Tarquin interrupted. 'You don't even know what you have here in this boy. What kind of a trainer would put a neophyte like him through a manhood initiation? It is cruel, and for no reason.'

'The Pharicians will kill him anyway. They may kill all of us if our defences don't hold out. As for the boy, I have no time to train him, if he can be trained, which I doubt. My people are badly pressed.'

'You should not have given the time serpents' secrets to the Pharicians,' said Kere. 'Especially the Circle. They are amoral and ruthless.'

'What do you know about them, boy?'

'More than you,' said Kere with a jaunty wink, and Mavese was so taken aback by the insolence that he could do nothing. 'Hey, it's clever of you to learn a little of the time serpent language, but you speak it with a foreigner's understanding. You don't feel its meaning from experience and you don't understand its figures of speech.'

'Impudent child!' Mavese managed to say, stunned.

'Isn't he,' agreed Tarquin. 'But for some reason he wants to help your time serpents. Fellow-feeling, maybe. I suggest you listen to him.'

Eagerly Kere said, 'They don't want you to take their eggs or their venom or their blood or anything else about them and give it to the

Circle. What they need is for someone to help them rewrite their history, and that can only be done by finding their makers. For they are Made beings, creatures of the ancients. They are not freaks of nature like you and me—'

'Speak for yourself,' said Tarquin.

'They were intended. They were cultivated like flowers.'

'Jaya flowers!' cried Tarquin, snapping his fingers. 'Enough about the fucking time serpents, I want somebody to explain what Jaya means and who that girl on the horse is.'

'How dare you make demands on me? You are lucky to be alive!'

'So is your henchman who attacked me, Mavese.' And Tarquin fixed his gaze on Pakise, who sat behind the leader; he had not seen Pakise's face but he had recognized his body while they scuffled, and Pakise looked back at him now with hate in his eyes. 'Were it not for his guard snake biting me, your man would be dead by my hand. Nor,' he could not resist adding, 'would he be the first.'

Mavese gave a little nod of understanding, his eyes glinting as he assessed Tarquin anew. Tarquin continued in his halting Pharician.

'I have hunted your people and killed them bare-handed. I have haunted your city. I have seen the time serpents, and my friend Kere understands their language. Soon they will be dead, and you will run out of eggs, and Pharice will have you back again for slavery. You have seen my sword that the boy keeps for me, and you may believe I know how to use it. You should be applying to me for help, for I can teach you to make and use weapons that will kill the Pharicians from a distance. I can teach you to make boats that are better than their boats, and I can teach you to navigate them so you can escape their range. You have no future here, Mavese – you see that, don't you? Pharice isn't going to get smaller, I assure you. You need weapons.'

'We do not use the spear. It is a cursed weapon, a tool of our oppressors.'

'I'm not talking about a spear, I'm talking about weapons you can shoot a hundred paces away and more.'

'Shoot? Slingshots? They are only good for hunting birds.'

'That's what you think.'

'Prove it, barbarian!'

'Ah, I will help you, Mavese, but I must know more about this place. Who built it, what led you here, what your people found. Take me to your Scholars if you do not know yourself.'

'No. I am not interested in you. My people are not interested in warfare, and with the Pharicians on our doorstep it is too late to start now. We want only to live as we have lived, side by side with the time serpents. They have taught us everything we know about survival outside Pharice. We have no other common heritage . . . We come from all over, all places and people, we were all slaves, but the time serpents have given us something of theirs. We would not forsake them as long as they live.'

'You mean, *you*, Mavese, would not forsake them. You ate one of their young, didn't you? You are part time serpent, Mavese, are you not?'

'You barbarian!' Mavese erupted, and Tarquin wondered which of his insinuations had offended the man. 'You cannot understand the time serpents. They are ancient. They are dying. Their kind will never come again, unless I can learn to hatch their eggs. Their venom is priceless, their knowledge boundless. They are wiser than men and their tongues are more cunning. But they are built to kill.'

'Your cult is strange to me,' Tarquin said, struggling with a Pharician dialect that hadn't yet come to pass in this age of the world. Mavese was eyeing him as if he were stupid. 'Are all your ways built around the lives of these two monstrous creatures?'

'They are deep and strange. If you knew them you would shit yourself to contemplate what they are. Ah, the foolishness of Cirene and all his legions! They can never touch what I have touched. Only one viable egg, only one of their kind to hatch alive, and I could stand all Pharice on its head. But they are dying.'

Tarquin was unmoved. The time serpents would have devoured him – probably had devoured countless humans unfortunate enough to come down the shaft or through the maze – so why should he care? What did it matter?

Yet Mavese was no fool, and Tarquin did not take him lightly. Here in Mavese Tarquin had found again something like the quality he had lost in his own Company. For his own part, Mavese made it clear that he rated Tarquin not at all. In fact, the Snake leader seemed likely to kill him, sooner or later. So he had better do something.

'You are not as safe as you think here, Mavese. I am an outsider, and I have broken the secret of your maze. Her face guides you through. Mavese, not only can I navigate your puzzle maze, I know the meaning of the face. I know *her*. I am looking for her. So tell me how she came to be carved in this stone, and how the maze has survived the moving of the fire and the shifting of the earth. You may believe it is not an accident that Kere and I are here, and if you like I can even tell you your future.'

'My future! You make me laugh. Speak, then.'

Tarquin cleared his throat, wondering if his guesses would prove good.

'After the time serpents are dead, the Pharicians will drive your

214

people out. Not this time, but it will happen in your lifetime, Mavese. You will take your boats and sail up the coast, past the forests where the Wolf-men dwell with their deadly steel. You will sail through the wastes until you round the tip of the continent in the far north where the sun rides on a steep angle. You will come to shore high in the mountains of Everien, and there you will find wild hybrids like these time serpents you worship, relatives of theirs, only unfriendly and hardly so wise. They will carve you tunnels and halls where you will make your new home. For Cirene is not content to allow your island to go on this way, autonomous. And the mountain is not dead, it is only sleeping. The time for you to leave this place is coming.'

Mavese looked grave. 'You are as like an enemy as a friend. I hate your words. I would never go to the north! If we flee we will go south, to the climes where my ancestors lived before Cirene caught them and brought them to Pharice.'

'All those lands in the south will belong to Cirene, if they do not already. Min, Aranoka, the desert tribes, all will pay him tribute in gold and slaves.'

Mavese started to laugh. 'I think not,' he began, but Kere reached out and touched his knee with one finger. There was something potent in the gesture, even though it was only the lightest touch. Kere said, 'Are you really an Animal now? Did eating the dead time serpent make you a Snake?'

Unaccountably, Mavese regarded Kere seriously for what Tarquin reckoned was the first time. 'The Eating has given me certain talents. I can mimic, for one thing – shed my skin and acquire the features of another. I have keener senses. And the flowers and infusions my people use for medicinal and sexual and combative purposes, they have different effects on me.'

'Can you timeslip?' said Kere.

'I have never attempted it, although I believe it may be possible, using their venom. The venom would kill an ordinary man, but a man who has eaten Snake is no longer ordinary. I believe if I took their venom my transformation would be complete.'

'Why don't you take it?'

'I will not throw my life away needlessly – for what if I'm wrong? And without me, my people would have no leader.'

'The Pharicians are coming,' Kere said.

'If pressed, I might be inclined to attempt the experiment. I carry the venom with me, always.' And he touched a vial around his neck; not unlike Chyko's vial of Freeze, Tarquin thought.

Mavese's rock-hard eyes glared at him and suddenly he was exhausted. His head throbbed. He was thirsty.

215

'My master needs water,' Kere said. 'The guard's snake's poison is affecting him.'

Pakise leaned forward and whispered something in Mavese's ear. Mavese nodded, picked up Tarquin's sheathed sword, and stood. Tarquin glowered up at him, as offended to see another man handle his sword as if the sword had been his woman.

'We have tactical matters to discuss. I will leave you with food and water. When I return, we will decide what to do with you. Come, boy – Pakise says you must take the maze test like the others. This is as good a time for you as any.'

'No!' cried Tarquin, rousing. He leaped up and so did Pakise. 'The boy has remarkable powers. He is wasted in your exercises. What he can do makes your time serpents seem no better than common garden snakes.'

'Oh? What can he do?' Mavese feigned a thin tolerance, his lip curling. 'Show me.'

With his eyes Tarquin willed Kere to do something.

'Kere! *Change!* Come, don't be afraid.'

Kere looked unhappy and hung his head. 'No, Tarquin,' he murmured.

Mavese gave a short laugh. 'To the training maze, boy, before I lose my temper.'

'I would like to speak to the time serpents,' Kere said. Tarquin bristled.

'Kere, enough with the time serpents! Let's go – now!'

'Go where?' laughed Pakise. 'Back to the jungle where the Pharicians can catch and torture you? Or will you build a little coracle and sail it on the high sea?'

'I would like to speak to the time serpents,' Kere repeated.

'Magic Boy wants to visit the time serpents,' scoffed Mavese. 'Well, you will visit them when you have got through the training maze, and we will see whether you shit yourself like the others when you see what is waiting for you on the other side.'

Tarquin threw himself forward, sprawling across the flat blade of his own sword. He knew he had only an instant before both men were on him and his arm would be trapped beneath him, so he kept rolling, kicking Mavese away on his way over and whipping his sword down on Pakise's back as the trainer shot for Tarquin's legs, attempting to drag him to the ground. The spine was severed midway up, and a geyser of Pakise's blood shot toward the ceiling. Kere's stunned fist was in his mouth.

'Run, Kere!' Tarquin screamed. 'Run for the spiral!'

For once Kere obeyed, and Tarquin stepped over Pakise's body to follow. Mavese was standing with his back to the other curtained door, hands spread in surrender. Tarquin's eyes had already searched the room for hidden snakes while they were talking, but he didn't know what was behind that curtain, and thought that Mavese was as like to have poison to hand as not.

'Finer than a thousand women is a good sword,' Tarquin said, and cut the curtain down on his way out.

The Problem with Invisibility

Jai Khalar had always been a restless sleeper, and after the Everien skyfalcon arrived with the cryptic message no one heeded, it became doubly so. Its stones fairly hummed with some inexplicable excitement. At night it tried to remain still but sometimes it could not help but stir and turn over. Sometimes it set the clocks forward when no one was looking, to make the night hours shorter. When sleep eluded it totally, Jai Khalar prowled its own halls like a cat. It visited the aviary with its full complement of Pharician messenger doves beside the Everien hunting birds. It checked the kitchens to be sure the mice were not getting above their station. It ghosted through Tash's audience hall without making a ripple of air or a shadow. The fire was always alive here, banked to embers at night, and it liked to play freely when awakened. One time, Tash had emerged naked and half asleep from his adjoining bedchamber in the middle of the night to see flames leaping from the pit and licking the walls and chimney.

'Fucking death-kingdoms of the poison ants!' Tash had sworn and retreated, flashing the whites of his superstitious eyes. From the safety of his chamber he shouted for servants to come and douse the flames. For the bored and restless castle, the Pharician newcomer had proven a boundless source of entertainment. Even his mind lay wide open like an animal's or a child's, for he was guileless in the way of many great warriors. It watched him climbing a flight of stairs and knew exactly when and where to switch one paving stone so as to make Tash fall on his knees, stupefied and annoyed.

Still, there were pitfalls. The problem with invisibility was that you could lose yourself, and Jai Khalar sometimes did. As it got older, the Citadel found it less easy to maintain self-discipline, especially now that it had had to reabsorb Hanji for his own protection after he let Tash walk in and take over – for the Pharicians would recognize that once a traitor, he was never to be trusted, and kill the old man if they found him. They never had found him. Yet Jai Khalar was lonely without the old man to interact with, in the same way that a caged bird is lonely if you give it a mirror to look at, and then take it away. Without Hanji around, the castle made mistakes. Things fell down. Maybe it wasn't senile yet, but it had memory problems. Its walls had often heard tell that when a man got old he could more vividly remember his youth than what he'd had that very morning for breakfast. This seemed to hold true for castles as well as men. Maybe this was nature's way of comforting you in your last hours: allowing you to relive your glory before you disappeared altogether. For, like an ancient man reduced to slurping pea soup with hand trembling on the spoon, Jai Khalar might prefer not to remember its most recent meal, but rather the banquets of its glorious past.

That is why the Citadel contorted itself as to be always attentive when the young Impressionist Gialse was trancing with the Carry Eye, a practice which Ixo and Mistel encouraged in her. When the Impressionist was speaking, everything seemed to fall into its proper perspective. Jai Khalar itself acted saner. Its walls and windows shrunk to reasonable proportions; its passageways ended in rooms other than the ones they had originated from; its staircases went either up or down but not both ways at the same time. The castle remembered itself accurately, as if the stories of Gialse acted as a tonic for its madness. Tash began to seem less of a threat and more of an annoying itch, like a flea.

Ixo was his devoted servant, though. She coaxed the Impressions from Gialse and scribed them personally in ink on a silk bedsheet, word for word. It became her obsession. Ixo's menstrual bleeding was late but she scarcely noticed, for there was a bright eagerness in her gaze now. She wanted to do something important for Tash. She wanted to win herself a place – and she wanted to keep Gialse and the Carry Eye by her side, where Kivi could not interfere. For if he had missed the Carry Eye, he had not yet guessed that Mistel had stolen it. Things went missing often enough in Jai Khalar that he probably thought it only mislaid, and waited for the castle's tide to cast it up again. Ixo made use of this time. The story that Gialse told was becoming her anchor line in the changing seas as the Pharicians drew nearer, the Wolves plotted silently, and the Sekk waited for their next opportunity.

By night and by day, Ixo and Gialse plied the Eye. Sometimes there was nothing. At other times, Gialse spoke in a voice that was not like her own, and Ixo listened. The walls themselves were listening. The mice were listening. Ixo knew it.

I studied many things. I read physics and exotic languages (I attempted to speak these with Jihan but he laughed himself to stitches at my pronunciation, which had been achieved by a combination of guesswork and imagination) and metallurgy and basket-weaving. I read a whole tome on the flight of birds, and broke my collarbone when I leaped off the barn roof. While recovering from this injury I was made to stay indoors, where I soon proved my incompetence in the kitchen and at the loom, so I made myself scarce. I played with the cats. I looked for trouble, and sometimes I found it.

The house had a turret containing two octagonal rooms, one above the other. The room downstairs was Jihan's workshop; no one went there often, least of all Jihan himself, for the place was a jumble of unfinished projects and their associated tools, and when you entered that room you had the feeling that you might never come out again, but be lost in the clutter, abandoned with all of Jihan's other unrealistic ambitions. The upper chamber could only be accessed by a door on the landing of the staircase that led to the attic where the birds were kept. I had been trying to get in since I was very small, but I never succeeded until, during the course of my study of birds and flight, I found the key in a magpie's nest high in the silver beech tree in the centre of the garden. I was eleven.

Bandaged, bored, and grumpy with the pain in my broken clavicle, I made use of the key to the secret octagonal room. When I entered I was struck by the sensation that I was underwater. Six of the turret's segments had windows on the garden. They were diamond-shaped and filled with segments of stained glass laid in patterns of deep blue and red and green and gold. Sunlight came through them warm and sweet, colouring the floor tiles, which were alabaster and very dusty. The ceiling was dome-shaped, and a skylight at its apex let in clear sunshine; without it, the room would have felt cloistered and drab, for the walls were made of dark wood and the fireplace that was built in the seventh of the eight walls was a large, black maw. I wondered what it would be like here at night, with firelight flickering off the coloured windows, and I immediately began to plot how I could find out without being given away by the light and smoke.

When I shut the door behind me, it snicked closed leaving no visible trace of a seam in the eighth wall of this unusual room, and I had to look carefully for its top edge, running my finger along the wood until I was sure I knew how to get out. There was no knob, only a hole masquerading as a knot in the wood that you could stick your finger into and tug. But I didn't feel nervous at the thought of being locked in. I liked the place immediately. It felt like a sanctuary.

There was practically nothing in the room. In the very centre was a plain table made of purply dark wood with a yellowed piece of linen laid across its surface. Against one of the walls opposite the fireplace was a matching chest with iron bindings. It was unlocked, but its hinges creaked when I lifted the heavy lid.

Inside I found four things: a box made of the same wood as the other furniture and shaped like a large book, a glass lamp half full of oil, a real book with a soft leather cover and a silk ribbon holding it shut, and beneath all of these, a large bundle of fabric wrapped in tissue paper. I didn't remove anything at first. I used the linen to wipe the dust off the table and then laid it on the hearth, for it was grey with soil. I spat on the edge of my skirt and gave the table a quick polish; then I went to the chest and took out the smaller items each in turn, placing them on the table with a ceremonial air. But as soon as I raised the bundle, the tissue paper fell away and a thick velvet cloak tumbled free of its folds.

The cloak was made of a blue so rich that it appeared black, and woven into its fabric were slivers of diamond like tiny stars. When I put the hood up it drooped completely over my face, and the cape dragged on the floor. It was too big. I wondered whether it had been my father's; it hadn't the look of a man's garment, and it was not so huge as all that. Yet I could not imagine asking my mother how tall my father was and getting a straight answer; and Jihan would only laugh at me. So I folded it with its tissue and put it back in the chest.

I turned to the items basking in the sunlight on the table. The lamp was of no immediate use to me, and it was too plain to hold my interest for more than a few seconds. I turned to the box that looked like a book, ran my hands over the satiny wood, and finally opened it.

It was full of rose petals, long dried but still fragrant, and when suddenly released their scent was striking in the empty room. A few drifted up in the air as I lifted the lid, and I saw that something lay amongst them. I gently removed a velvet drawstring pouch the size of a purse, like to the cloak only made of thinner fabric and set with smaller stones. Inside was a large deck of cards.

On the face of each card was a creature, every one different, some familiar animals, some strange to me. On the backs of the cards were designs that seemed to be all alike, but if you looked closely at the patterns you could detect subtle differences.

'Cheat's cards!' I murmured, laughing and wondering if I could use them somehow to trick Jihan in a game. I flipped through all of them. Some were reptiles, some insects, some birds, and some furred creatures. Some were so strange I did not know how to categorize them. Others appeared to be unfinished. Near the bottom of the deck was a human, but only outlined. The pattern on the back of the card was also unfinished.

I looked all through for the horse, but I could not find one. I found a falcon, though, a beautiful silver one like the wild ones that sometimes visited our house but never stayed. I took it out of the deck and looked at it for a long time. I wished I could fly. My collarbone still ached so badly that when I thought about the impact I bit my lip; but it had been worth it, the effort, the moment of being unconnected to the earth in any way, however painful the reconnection had been!

I laid the falcon on top of the deck and wrapped it again in its silk cloth. Then, conscious of the passage of time since I had last been seen doing something useful in the kitchen, I turned to the last item. The leather book was the same colour as Jihan's chestnut mare Chaser, and the edges of its pages were gilded. The ribbon was made of two pieces of silk stitched together back to back, so that it was black on one side and white on the other. It was not tied, but rather a closed loop with a half twist in it, so that now the black side faced outward, now the white. I gently slid the loop of ribbon off and the book fell open. The pages were neither paper nor cloth nor hide. Their substance was soft and smooth as silk, yet it held its shape like parchment, and each page was transparent like glass. There was nothing written there. Nothing at all. I held it up to the light but the pages were blank and clear.

'Jaya! Jaya, your cake is going to burn! Where are you? Jaya!'

Hastily I slid the ribbon over the binding once again, tossed the pack of cards, the book, and the lamp back in their chest atop the wrapped cloak, and bolted for the door. I made the mistake of leaving the key in it.

My mother was waiting for me. By the time I got to the kitchen, my cake had burned on the bottom. My mother sighed.

'I'll be glad when you can get back to your fencing,' she said. 'You're too restless and impatient! Maybe when you're older you'll calm down and I can teach you something.'

I made the obligatory apologies. 'Can't we just cut off the burned bits?'

There was a shout from Jihan in the garden. We saw him go racing up the stairs to the aviary, a crossbow in his hands. I started to go after him but my mother put her hand on my shoulder and I grimaced at the pain.

'Stay here. Let Jihan handle it.'

Jihan reappeared a few minutes later.

'There was a skyfalcon attacking our birds,' he announced. 'I've never seen such a one! I shot at it, but it escaped.'

'It's back luck to shoot a skyfalcon,' I cried, shocked.

'Not when it's out to murder our birds,' he replied. He started to leave and then shot me a sidelong look. 'Where have you been all morning?'

'Nowhere,' I said too quickly. 'I mean, I was visiting Blue in his stable.'

'Blue's in the field,' Jihan said, and quirked a questioning eyebrow at me.

'She's not been with me,' my mother added unhelpfully. 'She burned her cake.'

I refused to disclose my whereabouts or activities, feigning agony in my collarbone. But I was unable to retrieve the key without being observed, and in a little while Jihan tracked me down in the library, waving the silver key in my face.

'Ah-ha! You have been prying.'

I examined the key as if I'd never seen it before. 'Have I?'

'You mustn't go in there!' Jihan said, pretending to be very angry but in truth I could tell he was nervous. 'That's my imagination room. It's very private.'

'But you said it was my father's study.' Secretively I slipped the key into my bodice.

'Did I?'

'Yes, you did. Anyway, you weren't using it. No one's been in there for ages. The dust!'

'Hmm,' Jihan said, and I instantly suspected that he hadn't ever been in there. My suspicions were confirmed when he casually asked, 'Uh . . . so tell me. What did you find there?'

'Come and look!' I said, tugging at his arm. 'It's lovely inside.'

'No! No, I can't. And neither should you. Now give me back the key, little thief.'

I refused. We argued; he chased me around the garden, into the house, through the rockery, and back out to the garden, where at last he knocked me down into the rosebushes. I got stuck in the thorns and my collarbone was wrenched. I started to cry. Mercilessly he ignored my protests and wrested the key away from me. I didn't speak to him for several days. It was our worst fight ever.

Now that I look back on it, it is easy enough to see what a false peace were those years before you came to my house, before you broke the mirror and we looked on each other and did not see. In my memory now I can read the tension in my mother's every word and deed. And Jihan – how I wonder what he really knew, what he was up to, how he felt. For all that he revealed to me, there must have been tenfold that he hid. I would like to meet him now, but I don't believe he is a person any more. He is more solid than that.

There are solid things in the world, after all. Things not like people. Always I have known this. I have come up against the immovable time enough to accept its presence as valid. But I am not one of those solid things. My love, I am vaporous. Whether you find me or lose me determines what I am, and not myself.

I wish Jihan would come and fence me and take my mind from my plight. They say people pass into legend, but do legends ever pass into people? I want to be real.

Six years later, by accident, I found the key lying in the bottom of the fountain. What a stupid place to hide it, I thought. For I often sat by the fountain and stared at the water, and he would be a fool to think I couldn't find it there. Then again, Jihan can be absentminded. My mother says it is a characteristic of genius, but in Jihan's case I think it is a characteristic of idiots, as I am sure that a genius could not possibly misplace an entire flock of pigeons, which Jihan once managed to do. He is not terribly clever with animals, I'm afraid. How else could we have such a perennial mouse problem, despite the presence of six fierce and active cats including the mighty hunter Min, who at age fifteen was seen hurling a large snake through the air as she whipped it to death against the flagstones outside the kitchen?

By the time I found the key again, I had had plenty of time to plan my infiltration of the room and think about what I would do. In my father's library I had read of invisible writing, of the cycles of the moon, of the stars and their constellations, and over the years these many bits of seemingly unrelated information came together in my mind to form a coherent idea. I knew what I would do should I ever get into that room again.

This time, I hid the key in Blue's stall, waiting until the night of the full moon before once again I opened the room, took out the box, and unfolded the cloak, which I had now almost grown into. It swept the floor when I walked. I left the cards alone, although I was surprised to see that the falcon was no longer on top, but rather the snake. Jihan had been in here.

At least, I assumed he had.

The light of the full moon was coming into the room, and I carried the book closer to the windows in hope of reading the invisible writing by its light. I had brought ink and paper with me in case I found something worth copying. I set these on the floor, then knelt and opened the book within the silvery shaft of light.

Fire sprang from its pages, and etched in the fire I saw symbols I didn't understand. I jerked back, afraid that my hair would catch; but there was no heat even when I held my palm over the page. After a moment, emboldened, I began to sketch the symbols on my paper. They were difficult to copy, and I had only done a few pages when a noise without frightened me and I slammed the book shut. I looked out the window.

Midnight Blue was screaming in his stable. I heard him kicking his stall and running in circles. Without wasting a moment, I replaced the items in their box, slipped from the room, and dropped the key back into the fountain where I'd found it. I ran to the stable. Blue was covered with foam, his eyes rolling, and he danced in agitation. I couldn't get near him. I stood outside his stall until Jihan came. In a clipped voice, Jihan said, 'Get inside. Close your shutters and go to bed.'

I obeyed, hiding my notes under the mattress. In the morning the garden was ripped and trampled as if many horses and booted feet had been there. There was mud in the fountain and an arrow shaft sticking in the ground amongst the tulips.

Jihan watched me carefully after that. I denied everything, of course; but then, I always do. I was not allowed to ride Blue and it seemed to me that Jihan had put me on unofficial punishment, even though he could not prove anything. I hid my notes in the drawer where I kept my most private garments, knowing that Jihan's squeamish nature would not permit him to look there. At least, I hoped and trusted that he would not. Jihan had never treated me as anything other than a student, but I was of an age to wonder about men and wish to try out my charms on them, and there was no one else to hand. Besides, Jihan had a sort of glamour about him, and it titillated me to think what would happen if he pawed through my silken underthings.

It took many weeks before I could translate even a few of the symbols I had copied, and much longer before I could come to any conclusions about them. I had begun to feel guilty about my explorations, for as the falcon had appeared when I rearranged the cards, so other strange events seemed to follow in the wake of my exposing the fire-writing to the moonlight. I was eager to see more of the writing, for I was sure these were my father's notes, and I believed they might even have something in common with the symbols I'd seen hidden in the designs on the backs of the animal cards. But when I returned to the imagination room during the first full moon of autumn, the book was gone.

I heard a noise outside. Horses, I thought. And men's voices, very faint. I donned the cloak, picked up the lamp, and slipped down the stairs leaving the door to the imagination room open. On my way through the kitchen I lit the lamp, but covered it with the edge of my cloak so that I would not announce my arrival as I slipped among the topiary of the garden.

I was now not so sure what I had heard. The stable adjacent was quiet; Midnight Blue was not upset, nor Chaser nor any of the others. The chickens were quiet, and we had had no dogs for years as the cats routinely abused them and drove them off into the forest. Still, I remembered what had happened in the garden last time, and I was curious. The moon slanted down through the clouds like a lance, and the garden looked weird in its light. There was no sound. But as I was padding barefooot past the stilled fountain, I thought I saw movement in the water. I went closer, holding the lamp aloft to see better. I saw my shadow on the water and within that a great brightness. I looked closer and saw a hall all alit and full of men and horses and other wondrous creatures. And then, passing through my own reflection, I saw the face of a man. He was wild and I was afraid of him, yet fascinated at the same time.

'Spice?' I said. Then I realized I had been foolish. Spice was a lion, and this had been a fearsome man, not a cat.

Jihan grabbed my arm and spun me around. My cloak whirled over the pool, slid from my shoulders, and obscured the dreamy image.

'Jaya, come away from it. Come away now.'

'No! I want to see!'

There was a great noise within, a noise of battle. I could hear horses' hooves clattering on stone, and men shouting, and the ringing and scraping and rattling of steel – steel on wood, steel on hide. Steel on bone. One man's voice sounded above the others. He must be their leader, for I could hear him calling his warriors. I bent over the pool, trying to see him, but I couldn't, for the cloak had sunk into the water. Then Jihan grabbed me again and forcibly dragged me away. A moment later a whole band of men, mounted and unmounted, had burst out of the water in full battle cry.

They raged through the garden. The earth was torn. Statues came alive, hedges in the shapes of dragons woke and snarled, things appeared and disappeared. There were monsters and shadows and winged things about and upon our home, and the forest was alive with eyes, and the warriors were surrounded.

'Come inside,' Jihan said, throwing his cloak around me and trying to cover my eyes. But I saw. Shaking with fear, I followed him into the house, where we found my mother in her sewing room, undisturbed. Jihan said, 'She is to stay in this room and not come out until dawn.'

My mother pushed her glasses down her nose and looked up at me through watery hazel eyes. 'Sit,' she said simply.

I sat.

'What is happening?' I asked.

'I am doing the corner section of a summer quilt. I can't decide between cornflowers and fuchsia. What do you think would look better?'

I recognized the warning in her gaze. I was not to speak of what was going on outside.

'Cornflowers,' I said sullenly. Then I flopped back in my chair and resignedly closed my eyes.

In the morning, again the garden was torn. The cloak I had dropped in the fountain was nowhere to be seen. Jihan rode off before breakfast and did not come back until I was in bed, and my mother kept me busy all day clearing out the root cellar. After Jihan came home I snuck into the garden, where I found the lamp tilted on its side amongst the rosebushes, apparently unnoticed. I looked up at the sky. The full moon was past, and it was cloudy tonight. Still, if I lit the lamp and shone it on the water, maybe . . .

I waited until I was sure everyone was asleep. Then I shone my father's lamp on the surface of the water. I could see nothing but blackness, but I began to hear music as if from very far away. I thought they were singers, but it was possible they were birds or instruments of some kind, for the voices were not human. Yet they were voices, nonetheless. Their sound was like a sunset – which changes its colour from iridescent pink and gold to the most profound midnight blue without ever alerting you – in the sense that you can look at a sunset and be fooled for hours, until you are standing in utter darkness with your eyes clinging in vain hope to those last poignant flickers of colour, not believing that the light has gone. You have been tricked, lulled – their voices are like that. One can sing and sound like a dozen, or a dozen can sing and sound like one. There is no hint of threat or emergency in anything they do. You soften like a dough to the baker's expert touch.

Out of the nothingness of the reflecting pool a figure appeared. It was not a woman, but I couldn't have said for certain he was a man, either. He was possessed of a grace that seemed to me more catlike than human, and his hair was black and straight. His lips looked as if they had never been soiled by food. They were full and petal-soft, perfect curves to hide the teeth. His eyes were dark yellow and his skin was the colour of a lampshade. As there was no light here but the grey moonbeams, it seemed to me that the face was being lit by some invisible sun that touched only him and left everything else in darkness. He grew larger as he approached me. He was smiling. His throat vibrated with the humming of his song.

I was afraid. For when he stretched out his hand, it seemed to fly toward me much too fast, like a serpent striking, and the rest of the body was left behind but this hand on its arm shot out as if elasticated, and he reached through the water and touched me.

'Daughter,' he said. I shuddered and pulled away, spilling lamp oil on the pool. The reflection wavered and changed, and I saw eyes and tentacles and brilliant plumage and the parts of many animals all woven together, and then there were only swirls on the water.

My hand had been scalded. I put down the lamp and ran inside.

In the morning I confronted Jihan.

'I want to know who I am. Who is my father? Why did he build this house and then leave? What lives in the forest?'

'You had better stick to your lessons,' said Jihan. 'You have mastered trigonometry but not chemicals.'

'Are you my father?' I challenged, daring to ask what I had always secretly wondered. 'Answer me. Are you my father?'

'No.'

'Am I a foundling, then?'

'You should ask your mother these things.'

'She won't talk about it. Was she drunk? Did she not know his name? Why does she believe he will return? Did he leave her for another? I don't even care, but I want to know. What's all this stuff he left behind? Is it for me?'

'He had to leave you here,' Jihan said. 'For safekeeping. You must respect this.'

'Lies!' I screamed. 'All lies, all of it! I need something that's true.'

I wrenched the garden gate open with a rusty shriek.

'Obey, Jaya! I warn you, I cannot protect you if you leave!'

I wasn't listening. I ran out into the field and got up on Blue bareback. I jumped him over the ring fence and into the woods, where we galloped like two demons down paths I had never been on. I will never forget that day, for it was the day I rode to the edge of the forest. The trees never thin, they only stop, and you are left looking out across stark emptiness. It is as if someone has cut the earth and the air and the trees with a pair of scissors. Beyond the edge of this cut you first think you observe sky, but how can the sky be below as well as above? And how can there be a sky that hangs over no earth at all? And what kind of sky bends itself with the sound of their voices? For I could hear them singing, out there, as later I would hear their voices oozing from the very walls of my father's house.

I didn't intend to dismount, but when the horse reached the edge of the forest and stopped, I had to see for myself. My feet touched the ground with a *shock. Still holding the reins. I tiptoed to the edge. There was no wind. There were no celestial objects. It was not a sky. It was a void.*

Jihan found me there, sitting on the edge with my legs dangling over the side. He picked me up and threw me on Blue. He was angry. So was I. More than that, I·was afraid, but I didn't want to show it.

'I don't want you to protect me,' I said. 'I want to know what's going on.'

'Shut up,' he said, and when we got home he shoved me in my room and locked it. I was left with my notes and the occasional meal passed in by my mother, for an entire week. I took to emptying my chamber pot out the window when I saw Jihan passing below. At the end of the week there was a lightning storm, and I climbed out on the roof and stood in it, spreading my arms wide and holding a brass candelabra aloft, the only item in my room that would conduct electricity and was portable.

'Stop trying to get my attention,' Jihan shouted at me over a peal of thunder. 'What if the lightning fries your hair? Do you know what burning hair smells like? Remember when you lit yours in that candle by mistake? Ah, Jaya, come down already.'

I came down into his room, soaking wet and wearing only my nightdress, which clung to me like a second skin. He looked at me.

'Go away, Jaya.'

'Jihan, what are you supposed to be teaching me, anyway?'

'What I'm supposed to be teaching you and what you're learning are not the same.'

'I hate you.'

He poked me playfully in the belly and I swatted him away, scowling. He cuffed at me a few times to make me block, and I slapped his hands away in annoyance for I knew he was only trying to distract me, jolt me out of my mood. But I liked my mood and I did not want to leave it.

'You're not answering my questions,' I complained.

'Yes, I am.' He aimed a light kick at me and I kicked back reflexively. Water flew out from my soaking skirt; I saw its shadow arc across the white wall and the candles flickered. 'See, Jaya, it's shadowboxing!' Jihan joked, addressing his own shadow on the wall. He feinted and dodged the air. 'You can fight yourself in your mind, but you'll never win. Your father put his shadow in a box, and his shadow was you. Whether you practise against an imaginary enemy or a real one, you've got to learn to fight if ever you're going to get out of the box.'

'What box?'

'The shadowbox!' He had stopped prancing and stood, his chest going up and down with fast breaths, teasing me with those sparkling blue eyes. I threw my chin out.

'Word games! Tricks and double meanings!'

Jihan bowed. 'Thank you very much. Go to bed.'

'I want to do something,' I whined. 'I'm tired of always watching and reading and learning and being quiet. When do I get to do something?'

'Hush. Back to your lessons tomorrow. You are beginning to lose your mind, I fear.'

'I want lessons in the things that are in that tower.'

'Possibly. Now go away.' The door closed so fast behind me I had to grab the skirt of my nightdress to keep it from being caught.

It was spring and the rains lasted for several days, and Jihan was busy repairing leaks and managing mice, so it was some days before we did have our lesson – outside for the first time that year. The fountain was overflowing. I had no desire to study. I wished I had not asked Jihan for more lessons; for in our many contests of will and ingenuity, I always lost. Jihan had had too much time to prepare for today, and I was sure he had something unpleasant in mind.

I found myself unwilling to concentrate. I had my eye on the basket of food that my mother had prepared for our lunch, which we would take in between the morning's mental activities and the afternoon's riding instruction. I could just see the shining skin of a dark red apple peeping from beneath a white linen covering. There were few apples left at this time of year, and my mother rationed them carefully, having stored them in her cold cellar all winter to keep them crisp and sharp. I was thinking about how this one would taste when the juice exploded in my mouth, and I was enjoying the feel of the sun on my face and the way the light caught the water as it flew across the backs of the sailsnakes, who were meant to be causing the fountain as they leaped from the sea into the sky. Jihan had showed me pictures of snailsnakes and many other wonderful creatures, and here in the moist spring morning I was wishing I was one of those creatures, free to do as I liked. My mouth was watering at the thought of the apple but I didn't dare show my preoccupation. Jihan could grow very cross if I didn't give his lessons my full attention.

'Now,' he was saying, opening his satchel to reveal a sheaf of papers. I couldn't help groaning.

'Papers? Oh, Jihan, no . . .'

'Have you an allergy to paper? If that's the case, you should keep your nose out of my books. Come, we're going to begin with calligraphy.'

'Calligraphy? On a fine day such as this? Why can't we go out into the woods identifying mushrooms? Why can't we go dig in the creek? Remember those little worms we cut in half and they grew new halves? I was good at that, wasn't I?'

'I can see you're going to be trouble today,' Jihan said calmly. 'But the sooner you get started, the sooner you can eat your lunch.'

He must have seen me eyeing the apple.

'I loathe calligraphy,' I grumbled. I began to scribe at Jihan's dictation. He was describing something ridiculously technical – something about decrypting codes and the physics of sound waves. I was not enjoying myself.

'Wait 'til we get to the technical drawing, after lunch,' said Jihan, delighting in my frustration.

'You're mean,' I said in a mock-childish voice.

'You asked for it, Jaya.'

'I did not!' I dropped my pen and looked up. Jihan was standing with one foot on the edge of the fountain, gazing into the fountain's moving water as if he could see things in there. I shivered.

'You said you wanted lessons in the things in the tower.'

'I do! But I can't understand a word you're saying.'

'Knowledge is not baby food. You can't expect others to chew yours for you and spit it down your throat.'

'There's no need to be grouchy,' I said. 'Why can't you just answer my questions? What about the cards I found?'

'What cards?' he said sharply, turning his gaze away from the fountain as if startled.

'My father's cards. With the animals, and the patterns that change, the cheat's deck.'

'I have never seen them.'

I looked at him sceptically.

'I don't know everything, Jaya. I have never been in that room. I have never seen the cards you speak of. And if you've been playing with them, you've thrown my good advice out with the bathwater.'

I said, 'What about the symbols on the cards? What do they mean?'

'You have to learn to sing if you want to understand symbols.'

'What? Me, sing?'

'Imitate every animal, every whisper, every voice, every change of wind and fall of leaf, every change of water, every noise and creak and groan. Then you can begin to express the symbols. But it won't do you any good because they have no power here. This is a place safe from symbols. That is the whole point.'

'Couldn't you just teach me in a normal way?' I said.

'I'm trying to teach you about sound,' Jihan said. 'Pay attention now. Hear my beat? I can play the same patterns at different frequencies, or I can speed up the pattern as I increase the pitch, or I can alter the timbre, the variation of texture within the sounds. It is all just air fluttering, like a butterfly's wings. You must unravel all these threads to understand the sound. That is why music can hold so much information.'

'I can't even carry a tune,' I moaned.

'There are lots of secrets in music,' Jihan said. 'Lots of mystery languages.'

I said, 'What good is a mystery language if nobody speaks it?'

Jihan sighed. 'Jaya, say if you had a picture you'd painted and you didn't want anyone to copy it. Maybe you didn't even want anyone to see what you'd done.'

'You could hide it.'

'Hidden things have a way of getting found.'

'Like the key to the imagination room.'

'Yes.'

'You could colour over it.'

'You could, but that would destroy the picture.'

'You could cut it up and hide the pieces.'

'Ah! Now you are on to something. Yes, like a jigsaw puzzle. Good, Jaya. And that's what your father has done with his Knowledge. Only he's scattered the pieces across time.'

'Whoa.'

'Yes. Whoa, indeed.'

'He sounds sneaky.'

'He is.'

'Jihan.'

'What?'

'Why are you telling me stuff all of a sudden?'

'Because this is almost the end,' Jihan said. 'Now let's see your penmanship. I hope your letters are less skewed than they were last week.'

There was no getting any more out of him after that; and he was highly critical of my calligraphy to boot.

Deep in the Ruse

Some time ago Mistel had advised Ixo not to use her relationship with Tash to press for special favours. 'It is better to wait until you really need something from him,' she said. 'Even if you make a sacrifice now. Bide your time.'

So Ixo had not asked Tash to let her visit or receive her family, all of whom had returned to their lands in the forests above A-vi-Sirinn. In her heart she knew she was better off remaining incommunicado, anyway. She had learned and adapted to Pharician ways, and to always be reminded of her family and home would have meant a kind of torture. Ixo felt a certain shame when she thought of the way she had given herself to Tash, sexually and emotionally; but she also felt the thrill of vicarious power when she was with him. Perhaps, even, in her efforts to master his language and to please him in every way, she had grown to feel shame at her own Clan beginnings. After all, she and her people were the conquered. That she could feel the desire both to please Tash and also to put him in his place, control him essentially, did not feel like a contradiction. But it was, and there were times when Ixo's mind was no different from Jai Khalar itself in its capricious tendency to change, its faithlessness to one truth or another.

With Mistel gone, she found herself yearning not only for the old Wolf's guidance, but simply for a companionship that was not by nature rivalrous or conniving. She had no intention of confiding in the other girls, not honestly, anyway, and she had no family here to turn to. She found herself restless, filled with a nervous energy, and the restrictions of the women's gallery began to seem unbearable. The days were finally growing longer, and she had a tremendous urge to roam, even if she were to roam no wider than the walls of Jai Khalar themselves and look out from its towers over Everien and its enveloping mountains. She was not quite aware of it, but some part of her mind also felt that it was up to her to find and save Mistel.

'Gialse,' she said to the Impressionist one night as they lay in bed, do you know what a ruse is?'

'A trick?' said the girl, who had become Ixo's servant.

'Indeed. It is the magic of my Clan. I am far from expert in its workings, but I must try.'

Gialse didn't ask questions. Ixo marvelled at how dumb the girl could be when not under the influence of the Impressions. There were times when Ixo looked at the child as she gazed into the Carry Eye and spoke, and saw someone else. Gialse's voice changed dramatically, becoming lower and more melodious, exotically accented. Ixo could even see the rhythmic movement in her body as the gait of the imaginary horse swayed her slightly backward and forward. By *this* girl, Ixo had been quickly mesmerized; for Jaya, too, was trapped, alone, mystified. Ixo felt sure that Jaya would not allow herself to be defeated by a few eunuch guards and an unpredictable castle. Jaya would find her way out.

Ixo had to draw on Wasp Clan magic that she was only dimly familiar with. Her personal magic had always been a sexual magnetism that required little supplement; but here it had got her locked up night and day, and she could think of no way to influence Tash sexually that would gain her any more freedom. The truth was, the fonder Tash became of Ixo, the more protective.

Poisons she was skilled with, and she had some knowledge of healing medicine as well, but as the kitchens were controlled by the Pharicians and the harem women had to depend on carefully rationed supplies for any cooking they did of their own, Ixo's powers were greatly restricted. It was probably possible to get some herbs and other ingredients, stockpiling them gradually over time, but she couldn't think of a way that poison could help her, either, except as a one-off. What she needed was to get out of the harem and find Mistel, and perhaps find herself an escape route as well – for Jaya's situation had made an emotional impression on her and she did not wish to find herself trapped like Jaya.

In the end, Ixo's ruse was simply to turn her sex on its head. She bound her breasts, braided her hair and capped it, and donned the dress of a man. It wasn't so difficult to make the transformation, especially because she managed to pilfer a number of items from Tash's servant boy, and even Tash himself, when she was in the Pharician's quarters. She got a cap for her head, a belt, a fur collar, and an old cloak of the servant's that was only slightly too big. She stole one of Tash's many finger rings and persuaded one of Illyra's women to get her a chain with the imperial signet on it. She made herself a pair of boots in the masculine style, some trousers and a tunic to fit herself, and borrowed a dagger that Mistel had kept hidden behind the painting of a wolf in the main room of the harem. 'It is for emergency use, for any of you who needs it,' she'd said, and winked. 'Don't fucking take it unless you fully intend to cut someone's balls off.'

Ixo was not bent on castration at the moment, but she thought that rescuing Mistel with her own knife would be in the spirit of the injunction. Besides, the knife was mostly for show. Men didn't walk about the Citadel unarmed.

She began making small forays from the harem when the eunuch on guard duty was dozing or distracted – usually the latter, for the other girls were only too glad to abet her and lure the guard away from his post. Ixo's absence from the general harem scene was in keeping with her recent habit of closeting herself for hours with Gialse. Those who didn't know about the Carry Eye thought the two were having some sort of weird affair; Ixo swallowed the insult to her taste because it disguised what was really going on.

Once she had got the hang of the disguise, she confidently went out and about whenever she could, and it wasn't very long before she had deduced where they were keeping Mistel.

She was shocked when she saw the cell, which was tucked away in a remote dungeon not far from the base of the Eye Tower. It was a cold, damp, dark hole far removed from the other prisoners, and Ixo thought that confinement in such a place would drive anyone to despair. There was a rank smell coming from the iron-barred gap in the floor and the pit where Mistel's white face could just be made out in the gloom. Ixo had felt slightly nauseous when she left the harem, but she'd assumed it was only nerves; now a wave of sickness came over her and she covered her nose and mouth against the smell, mastering herself with the greatest effort.

'Grandmother!' she whispered, and lying down flat on the iron stretched her arm down. Mistel stretched up and they were just able to touch fingertips. Ixo began to cry. She wanted to bring Mistel warm blankets and food, but the Wolf refused to accept the former, saying it would only get her in trouble with the guards. Ixo did run back to the harem and bring her hot spiced pastries, which the Wolf devoured. Ixo, smelling the cakes which were normally a favourite of hers, felt sick again.

'I will murder Tash with this dagger,' Ixo vowed passionately, her tears falling from her face and into invisibility.

'You will do no such fucking thing.' Mistel's voice was weak but certain. 'I have not given up on Tash yet. He has not killed me. By Pharician standards, he has been softer than soft – humane in the extreme.'

'He is not an evil man,' Ixo affirmed softly. 'But I could kill him for this all the same. I will speak to him. I will tell him that you must be treated with kindness.'

'No! This is between me and Tash. Do not interfere, Ixo. Listen, tell me about Gialse. What is happening in the Fire Houses?'

So Ixo told her, quickly and in whispers, that the innovation in the Fire Houses was stalled but that Tash was driving the blacksmiths to make all the weapons they could nevertheless. She told Mistel about

Jaya and the secret room, and Jihan, and the strange episodes in the garden.

'Is Gialse all right?'

'She remembers nothing of what she says.'

'That is well. Keep listening, Ixo. There is something in this, although I doubt we can use it.'

There was a noise from a nearby stairwell and Ixo leaped up.

'I will return when I can,' she whispered. 'Keep courage.'

She darted away, slipping down a little-used passage and emerging in the courtyard with a sailsnake fountain. The nausea had returned and with the spurt of fear that had come over her when she heard the guard returning, she suddenly found it had become uncontrollable. She bent over the empty fountain and vomited. Then, shaking, she returned to the harem.

She slipped in while Doren was admiring the needlework of two Bear girls, slipping off her cap so that her hair fell free, drawing the cloak around her as she entered; and it was a good thing she did, because Doren turned and spotted her just as she had her hand on the knob of her bedroom door.

'There you are,' he said. 'We wondered when you were getting up this morning. Are you ill?'

Ixo nodded, drawing the cloak tighter about herself and praying he didn't notice her boots. Just then Gialse opened the door behind her and pulled her inside.

'You should not be out and about,' she said sternly. 'In your condition!'

And Ixo was once again in the safety of her chamber. She turned and looked at Gialse, realization suddenly dawning on her.

'In my condition? What do you mean?'

'I don't know,' babbled the Snake girl. 'I just said anything to get you out of there.'

Ixo put her hand on her flat belly. She rolled her eyes toward the ceiling, her lips moving as she counted. 'I *am* late,' she said. 'I have been so busy with this scheme, I'd lost track of the weeks.'

Gialse took her hands. Ixo was reeling.

'Oh, Mistel,' she moaned. 'Now I am in deep. I will have his child.'

The Maw of Time

Kere knew the way to the spiral highway, and Tarquin knew the way to the Jaya maze, which was still the best place to hide. His sword took care of anybody who was thinking of interfering. In passing he thought how vulnerable the Snakes would be if the Pharicians with their swords found their way into the city. And as they entered the Jaya maze, he reminded himself that the Pharicians were probably already down here. If the time serpents hadn't managed to kill Tarquin, he could assume there were live Pharician warriors wandering around the curves of the maze. He did not take Kere very far in before stopping to rest.

'Well!' he said, strangely exhilarated and thrilled to have his sword back, though he had to strap it to his back in the confines of the tunnel. 'Are you going to explain about Ice, or are you still quite happy to be a boy?'

'I told you not to ask me about Ice!' Kere snarled, his face twisting grotesquely. Tarquin had never seen the boy show anger before, and he was startled.

'Ah, enough games, Kere! They were going to kill us. Being a horse has to be better than being dead. Your stubbornness astounds me.'

'And your thickness astounds me!' Kere shouted, and Tarquin hushed him. When he took his hand off Kere's mouth, the boy was spitting with indignation. 'I was trying to persuade Mavese to help us, for I believe he has the power to do so.'

'We wouldn't need his help if you would *just call Ice.*'

'I *can't* become Ice, Tarquin. I can't, all right? I've tried and I've tried. In the jungle when you saw me having a fit, I was trying to call Ice, because I was afraid and I wanted him to come. I couldn't find him.'

Tarquin couldn't even think at first, and Kere kept babbling into the silence even though Tarquin wasn't really listening.

'I thought maybe the jungle was too thick, or the tunnels too narrow. I thought it had to do with Jai Pendu taking the White Road; but Ice could always run into the Liminal before, anytime he wanted. So the only conclusion I could draw is that he has a reason for bringing me here. I thought it was to teach me to fight, but maybe it was so that I could speak to the time serpents.'

He stopped, and still Tarquin said nothing. He was shaking his head from side to side slowly in the dark; but Kere couldn't see this. At last, he muttered, 'You haven't got a clue, have you?'

'Not really,' said Kere. 'And . . . and I'm afraid. I'm afraid it's none of these reasons. In my heart I have begun to fear that Ice *can't* come.'

Tarquin struck the boy across the face with the back of his hand. Kere began to cry.

'Why didn't you tell me? I bragged to Mavese, I put us in this position because I thought you could escape if you really needed to! You made me think you were only playing games.'

'If I told you the truth, why should you help me? Out there in the jungle, you would have abandoned me. You would have left me on the first day if you had not thought that in me you had passage back to where you wanted to go. Or into the Liminal, to find your Company.'

It was probably true enough, Tarquin thought.

'Miserable trickster,' he said. 'Well, we're truly stuck now.'

'Take me to the time serpents. I can talk to them. I know I can.'

'Kere, you don't know what they're like. They're not cuddly and sweet.'

'Neither was Ice.'

Was? Tarquin felt cold.

'Fair enough,' he whispered. 'But be quiet. There may be enemies in these tunnels.'

Although Tarquin could now find his way, they had to stop to sleep more than once on their way to the time serpents' lair. Tarquin had learned to sleep in blocks of a few hours and no longer had a concept of days. During their rest periods, he tried to glean from Kere what exactly it was that happened when he tried to call Ice; what it was like to change back and forth to Ice; where and what the White Road was; and most of all, how the time serpents were supposed to help them.

Kere was vague.

'It's a feeling,' he said. 'How can you explain a feeling to someone who's never felt it? I tried to show you with the twisted leaf, remember? The leaf with only one side.'

'Aaarghh . . .' Tarquin growled.

'If you punched a hole through that leaf you could be on two points on the same line at the same time. But it is all in your mind. Or Ice's mind.'

'Why am I asking you, anyway?' said Tarquin in despair. 'You eat flowers and cry like a girl.'

'Look, the time serpent is an embodiment of time. They are the masters of acausal nature. They've left time trails everywhere like a snail leaves slime. Maybe they can get us into the Liminal.'

'My Company! Jaya! Do the time serpents know about them? Did they make the picture on the gates?'

'You can ask them yourself,' Kere said. 'I will translate. You may trust me! I'm not a liar.'

'If they eat you, Kere—'

'It would not be the first time for me,' said the boy in a husky voice, and at last Tarquin decided to shut up.

At the bottom of a steep shaft they found the body of an armoured Pharician, dead less than a day, thankfully, for they took his food supply, his dagger, and his belt with its pouches and tools. He carried a dead torch with flint and tinder; Tarquin struck these and pointed the torch up the shaft. The man had fallen half a hundred feet before breaking his neck. Many were the dangers of the Jaya maze.

They were sparing with their food and water, and soon they entered a region where the glowing moss was everywhere.

'I didn't come this way,' Tarquin said before Kere could start asking questions. 'I entered the maze through a small tunnel, but this seems to be the main way through. I don't think we need the Jaya faces any more, but be wary of Pharicians prowling.'

They walked up a wide, smooth cylindrical passage, slippery with phosphorescent moss. There were bloodstains in places, pieces of discarded bone and rotted uniform, and the occasional animal horn. Overhead could be felt the passage of the time serpents' bodies across the sand, a deep shushing that never ceased. Kere raced ahead, unafraid. He picked up a piece of horn and a goat rib and smacked them together in a rhythmic tattoo.

Above, the slithering halted. Clicks. Sweat broke out on Tarquin's back. He remembered that sound.

Kere signalled back, still climbing. Tarquin drew his sword and followed warily.

'They remember you,' Kere said to Tarquin. 'And they greet you.'

'Ask them about Jaya.'

'They say she is a Paradox.'

'A who?'

'The lights aren't going to come on,' Kere translated. 'The puzzle pieces aren't going to float together and click into place. The codes will never be broken and the house will never stop unbuilding itself and one mistake leads to more mistakes. We are trapped for ever.'

'But who is she? The girl on the doors. Riding the black horse. She had red hair. Who is she?'

'She is invisible, for she is a Paradox, and the reasoning ones pursue her.'

'You fucking bastard,' screamed Tarquin. 'She's mine and I can't find her and you know where she is and you speak in riddles.'

Kere rolled himself in a trembling ball. 'It's not my fault,' he squealed. 'I'm only the translator! Don't frighten me, or I'll run!'

Tarquin snorted, suddenly amused. 'Where the fuck are you going to run to, Kere?'

More clicking.

'They like you,' Kere sniffed. 'They're going to help us.'

'Help us? How?'

'It is a reciprocal thing. They help us get into the Liminal, and we help them by seeking the Knowledge that made them.'

'And how are we to do that?'

'They say, "You must go back up the path we made when we came here, to the source."'

'Source of what? Do you mean, go back to Jai Pendu?'

'Sort of. I don't know. Maybe.'

Eagerly Tarquin pressed, 'Does this path take us to Jaya? Ask them about the Company.'

But Kere didn't make another sound. He was staring beyond the Snakes, beyond their luminosity and their great, sad faces, to a slit in the darkness. It was not a slit in the cave, in touchable solid stone; it was a wavering slit in the air, in the untouchable makeup of things.

'What's that?' Tarquin whispered.

'A time serpent trail. It's their excrement, their wake. The time they've left behind.'

'And we have to walk up it?' Tarquin went toward the slit, which was not red or bloody but which nevertheless resembled the opening of a birth canal, and his skin began to crawl. He reached toward it and his hand was repelled as if by electric shock. 'Oh, well. Too bad, it doesn't work.'

'Yes, it does.'

'Whatever you say – but what are we going to do?'

'Time is as alive as you or me,' Kere said. 'Look at a man on the outside and you feel no dismay, but adopt a maggot's view of his body and you will find him far stranger, far more complex on the inside, and probably even unrecognizable as a man. It is all a question of your point of view.'

'What? Aaaaghh, Kere, don't speak that way. You make me feel I have fleas in my skull.'

'Fleas? I said maggots—'

'Shh! Enough. I just meant that I don't understand you.'

239

'Oh.' Kere drew a thoughtful breath as if to try again to explain.

'Never mind. Let's just go. Let's go now, before I have a chance to think about it and change my mind.'

'I have to take their venom with me,' Kere said. 'We will use it to try to cure them, for it contains their code.'

'Take their venom? Don't let them bite you, fool!'

Kere said, 'Have you still got the Pharician's water bottle? Give it to me.'

Tarquin handed it up to him, unwilling to leave his sheltered nook. Just from where he was crouched he could see a severed limb, a moss-grown eggshell, and a pile of what must be regurgitated, indigestible Pharician parts.

Kere approached the male time serpent. It reared back, opening its jaws, and its hollow-nosed human face for a moment became translucent like wax; then the shining teeth appeared as the mouth opened wider, stretching the face to become a parody of itself; and beyond the teeth, Tarquin saw the glowing emptiness of its throat. The Snake lowered its jaw to the floor and Kere stepped onto the threshold it made, slipping his feet into the crevices between its stubby lower teeth. The lower fangs rose to each side of him, half a man high yet sharp as needles, and the upper fangs were even larger. The holes that the poison would pass through were visible even from here, and the poison glands were dark purple, a threatening colour. Kere seemed unafraid.

'What is it with you?' Tarquin whispered, not daring to raise his voice and startle the boy. 'You really have a fetish for letting animals eat you, don't you?'

The other time serpent was hissing and clicking, making complex speech of which Tarquin could understand not one thing.

Kere squeezed the poison sacs one at a time, releasing venom drop by precious drop into the Pharician water bottle whose contents he'd emptied on the black sparkling sand. Between and beyond the two time serpents, the rents and flaws in the fabric of things were beginning to multiply.

'There is a flaw in their code,' Kere said over his shoulder. 'In the pattern of the stuff that makes them time serpents. That's why they can't reproduce. And they can't go back up their own time paths. Between you and me, I don't know why they need to reproduce, since they can live theoretically for ever, but the need to do so seems to have been instilled in them.'

'Mavese said they were dying.'

'Only because they won't travel any more. They won't say why. They are very strange. It is hard to translate how strange they are.'

'That's all right. Never mind that. Just mind what you do with that venom.'

The bottle was full. Kere stepped off the time serpent's jaws and it slid away from him.

'They're really quite docile if you know how to talk to them,' Kere said. He came walking back toward Tarquin, stepping over a Pharician shield that had been bent in half and pierced by a very sharp tooth. He put the stopper in the bottle and tied it securely on his fighting harness.

'Let's go,' he said huskily. In the weird illumination caused by the Snakes, Kere's face looked more awkward and unnatural than usual.

'Go where?'

Kere didn't answer. He was standing still, head tilted to one side, listening. From the shaft overhead there were noises: bits of rock falling, the scrape of boots on rock. Hushed voices.

'Pharice,' Tarquin whispered.

'The time serpents say this is their last stand,' Kere whispered. He slapped his own body erratically, ending with a flourish.

'What have you said to them?'

'I have asked them what will happen to me if I drink the venom.'

'It would kill you,' said Mavese's voice from the darkest part of the cave.

'Shouldn't you be organizing your defence?' Tarquin asked. He had not expected Mavese to bother pursuing them at a time like this. It was disturbing.

'My one defence is of the time serpents. Do not go into their path! It is the one they are saving for me.'

The time serpents went across the cave to greet Mavese, writhing over each other in the darkness, their strange eyes taking in Tarquin and then passing over him. Tarquin's gorge rose in his throat. The time serpents' faces looked like human children with their mouths full of needle teeth.

'I told you you didn't understand their language well,' Kere said calmly to Mavese. 'I asked them about the venom. You heard their answer but you did not understand it.'

'*What did they say?*' hissed Tarquin. A stream of light poured out of the hole in the ceiling that Tarquin had fallen through, and a moment later the end of a rope came tumbling after. He saw it shiver under the pressure of climbers' legs. He moved across the sand with naked blade to a better position in relation to the hole.

'The time serpents say that if their venom enters me, it will take me to the time of my death.'

'What is the difference between death and the time of death?' Mavese scoffed. 'I have seen men die from this venom, trust me.'

'If I were a man, there might be no difference between your translation and mine. But I am not a man, and the time of my death is not simple.'

'Time, time, time,' Tarquin said angrily. 'If we only had more time we could dip arrows in the venom and shoot them.'

'More time,' Kere said and lifted the flask to look inside it just as the first Pharicians leaped into the cavern.

There were four of them, and they landed in quick succession in the sand. Ignoring Tarquin and Kere, they made a suicidal rush at the time serpents, hacking at them with their short stabbing blades even as more soldiers piled down into the cavern. Mavese interposed himself between the time serpents and the hole, but he was soon overwhelmed. Tarquin saw him go staggering across the sand, one arm dangling, bleeding; but the Pharicians were too intent on overcoming the time serpents to pay attention to Mavese. Meanwhile the time serpents were methodically biting and crushing the Pharicians. It was slaughter on both sides, and within a matter of minutes there were dozens of bodies leaking blood on the sand and the time serpents were still alive, their own long and glowing bodies gouged and ripped. The last of the Pharician aggressors escaped down holes leading to the maze.

Then the attack stopped. There was a silence above.

Mavese dragged himself to the bleeding time serpents, sobbing openly.

'The evil of Pharice!' he cried. 'Cirene and all his offspring I curse for what they have done. Now I will go!'

He threw himself at the head of the female serpent. Her mouth lay half open, her eyes closed, her forked tongue hanging lax on the sand. She was taking fast, shallow breaths, the fluorescent edges of her nostrils shaking like a dying candle flame. Mavese lifted his wounded arm and drew the inside of the forearm hard along the time serpent's fang.

'Give me it!' he shouted at her, then callously banged a rapid sequence on the bone of her jaw.

'She has no more,' Kere said. 'Leave her, she is dying.'

'Give me it!' Mavese cried again, and his blood dripped on the serpent's face as he squeezed her poison gland. 'Ah, that's it. Just a drop or two, straight into my blood, it will be enough.'

'What the hell's he doing?'

'He is trying to get into the Liminal,' Kere said. 'Using the time tunnel.'

He pointed to the slit that had refused Tarquin entrance.

'Well, better him than me,' Tarquin said. Mavese, still crying and bleeding, began to limp toward the slit in the air. From above came an

242

echoing, metallic peal of something resonant striking stone repeatedly. Tarquin heard more voices above. Pharice, he thought, and considered the fact that there were already several of them wandering around the maze, lost and hostile. Where could he and Kere run to?

Kere was following Mavese, the blur of his white head reflecting the light of the Snakes as he crossed the cavern. Mavese reached the slit and, as he stepped through it, Tarquin caught a glimpse of something white beyond. The gap in the darkness closed again, leaving only a faint afterglow like a seam where the slit had been.

'Was that the White Road?' Tarquin called, but his voice was drowned out by more clanging from the rock shaft. He smelt oil and stiffened. From the hole in the ceiling was pouring a viscous fluid. It began to fall in the sand and to carve streams along the floor of the cavern.

'Oh, no,' Tarquin said. 'They're going to light it. Kere!'

He began to move away from the oil and toward Kere. He could just make out Kere's figure against the dim light in the aftermath of Mavese's disappearance. The boy was holding the flask to his lips. Tarquin barrelled toward him.

'Kere, no!'

Suddenly there was a flash of bright light as the oil went up. Heat roared toward them, and Kere, turning, caught sight of Tarquin and grabbed him, dragging him toward the slit. A kaleidoscope vision flashed through Tarquin's mind, of darkness striped lurid yellow by the dying Snakes; flames rushing to engulf the huge bodies; the rock shapes of the cavern startlingly illuminated; then he was diving for the White Road, fully cooperative with Kere for the first time.

Everything was silent, colourless, motionless. His eyes were full of useless light, for it illuminated nothing.

'Kere? Kere!'

The white swallowed his voice. The boy was gone and the world itself was gone, but he heard hoofbeats coming toward him.

'At last,' he thought with relief.

Within Sight of Home

Istar and Pentar put their backs to the wind and pulled their hoods close to cut the wind and muffle the teeth-jarring noise of the hull scraping against ice. The wind made a dull, heavy sound in the bowed sail, and the boat sometimes bounced off the surface and slid sideways before the steersman corrected it. They had made good time to Poison Fjord, where an ice sail had been waiting for them, piloted by an ambitious young fisherman from Pentar's branch of the Clan, whom Hiltar, apparently, had hired to fetch Istar. They had come down Poison Fjord, where they boarded a small sailboat that took them along the coast and then partway up Tyger Fjord. Now they were in an ice sail again, deep in the fjord, miles from the sea swells, where the ice was strong and the cliffs tall. A stygian gloom seemed to close round them as they glided farther and farther inland as if entering the maw of a great animal made of stone and snow; or so it seemed to Istar's imagination – but Istar was in a foul mood and prone to exaggeration even within her own mind.

'They cannot be married without my permission,' she said for about the hundredth time. 'It is Seahawk law, and there will be hell to pay if I find my rights have been violated in my absence.'

Pentar said nothing. He had been humming a little under his breath to cheer himself; now he stopped. He had learned that when Istar was unhappy, she liked for everyone else to be the same. Privately he thought that if Istar was so concerned for the welfare of her twin sisters, she should have showed more interest in their affairs up until now. This was Pentar's second visit home since Jai Pendu, and when he had returned the first time with the Seahawk contingent from Ajiko's army that had been freed from the spell of Night and the Company of Glass, Istar's family had expressed surprise and some distress that she had not come herself. She was, after all, one of the heroes of the day; she had been the last person to see Tarquin before he was lost in the sea; and she had been promising to come and settle her sisters' affairs since the previous spring, when Mintar's will had been made public – for Mintar had left the bulk of her fortune to her son Tarquin's adopted daughters. But instead of returning to Seahawk, Istar had chosen to track down her birth mother Mhani and ensure her safety at A-vi-Khalar.

The Seahawks would not approve of such blood loyalty. Istar was lucky to be a part of Tarquin's family: They were wealthy and prestigious, and she was an outbreed, of criminal descent if you considered that Chyko's escapades had only been tolerated (barely) by Ysse because Chyko was Quintar's friend. For that matter, Pentar knew she intended to try to recruit her own corps of fighting men to take into battle against the Pharician occupiers, yet to her own Clan she was little more than a name. Istar should have returned to Seahawk in the summer, and then she would not be in this bind now.

It had crossed Pentar's mind that the reason she had not returned when he had was because she wanted to avoid his company, but he thought this unfair. For one thing, he did most of the hunting and all of the cooking while they were on the road, and during the voyage up the coast from Poison Pass, he had held the bucket for her while she vomited.

'Some Seahawk,' he scoffed. She retaliated by spewing porridge over his sealskin boots.

When they had reached A-Tar-Helt on the coast, they had stayed with Pentar's family for a week before continuing on into the fjord, first by boat and then by ice sail. Remembering the peaceful interlude at A-Tar-Helt, Pentar closed his eyes and sighed, thinking of his mate with her blond braids, her slender forearms covered with flour up to the elbows as she kneaded bread, smiling. When Valtar was sick every morning that he was there, it was for a good reason: She had greeted him with news of her new pregnancy, and though her belly was not yet swollen she had that unmistakable radiance about her.

Istar had been rather quiet all that week, spending most of her time giving Pentar's oldest son sword-fighting lessons out on the shingle, or wrestling with his dogs.

'It is sad for her,' Valtar said to him one night in bed. 'What kind of a life is it for a girl?'

Pentar grunted. 'Istar is not a girl! Anyway, do not let her know that you pity her. She will only exercise her anger upon me.'

'How long are you bound to serve her?' his mate asked in that little-girl voice she used when she wanted something. 'When will your debt be repaid?'

'My life and Anatar's and the lives of those we would have killed if we had descended on the Bear Clan refugees as we were meant to – these do not come cheap.' He kissed her.

'But I miss you,' she said. 'When will you return?'

'When the war is over, of course.'

'Will we be safe here? Will the Pharicians sail up the coast?'

'They have more pressing concerns right now, my love. We will soon drive them out. They will never get this far.'

She pulled him close. Pentar sighed again when he remembered what they had done after that.

Abruptly Istar twisted round to look at their heading. 'There it is!' she exclaimed. 'At last, there it is!'

Pentar turned, squinting into the frigid wind. The walls of the fjord bent and tapered as they approached its root, and in the afternoon gloaming the lights of A-Tar-Ness glowed like candles from the cliffs. The ice below the town was littered with dome-shaped structures made of snow-bricks. Between these, black holes for fishing had been cut in the ice.

The crew began to lower the sail as they approached, coming in on a glide. There were stationary ice sails lined up near the base of the cliff, and a dogsled waited on the shore: The barking of the hounds could be heard on the wind as they were being fed. Figures moved up and down the timber walkways and staircases that had been constructed against the cliff face, connecting the various caves to one another in an intricate network. Gulls floated like paper on the crosscurrents, drifting from one level of the town to another. The social hierarchy matched the geography, with the poorest fishermen housed on the bottom and the majority of the Clan living in various strata within the cliffs. Istar's adoptive family resided in a huge house at the very top, overlooking the fjord and bordering on the hunting grounds and forests that were their ancestral territory. Theirs was not the only such home: Across the fjord were two others, one belonging to the Clan Elder, Hiltar, and her descendants, and the other to Grietar. The ambitious Grietar.

'I will go and see Hiltar tomorrow,' Istar said. 'My relatives will be expecting me tonight. I should go to their house first.'

But when the boat drew in there was a man waiting for them at the dock. Pentar stiffened.

'It's Grietar,' he told her.

Istar studied the whippet of a man who leaned into the wind, the edges of his red velvet cloak soaked with sea spray. His head was covered, but from his complexion and his eyebrows she knew his hair was russet, and his eyes were a watery blue. He wore a well-trimmed beard and two seal-bone rings in his nose. She did not recognize him from her previous visits to A-Tar-Ness, but from his garb and his manner he was a person of importance. He wore a white-gold collar and there was a large sapphire in the hilt of his sword. But the sword itself was of the curved Pharician design. Istar eyed it with hatred.

'My father got it off a Pharician horse-captain in his youth,' he said, following her gaze.

'Your father killed a Pharician?' She looked at him anew. He laughed.

'No, no, he won it gambling.'

Istar suppressed a scornful laugh and leaped onto the dock, turning to catch the pack Pentar tossed her.

'I am Grietar,' said the man, reaching to help her with the pack, but she turned her back.

'I am the Honorary brother of Lyntar and Pietar. I have killed Pharicians and Sekk and Clan alike with this sword. It was Chyko's, my father. I suggest you retire your Pharician blade and take up something more appropriate. Even if you only wear it for decoration.'

She had insulted him several times from different angles, as a test. Pentar stepped on the dock and tried to interpose himself between Istar and Grietar, but it was too late. Grietar had stepped toward Istar, saying,

'The Pharician gambling sword will stand against the sword of Chyko's daughter any day or night she cares to name.'

Istar whipped around, her gauntleted fist raised to strike, but Pentar tripped her up and then caught her.

'She is grief-stricken,' he said. 'Do not take offence or challenge her, Grietar!'

'Grief-stricken?' Istar snarled, trying and failing to sidestep Pentar. Now Grietar was laughing condescendingly. Suddenly he stopped laughing, coughed, and lowered his gaze.

'A terrible thing,' Grietar said. 'I am so deeply sorry. I offered her protection again and again, but she would not take it.'

Istar took a half step back.

'What are you talking about?'

'Ranatar,' Grietar said. 'Killed by the Sekk. I thought you knew.'

'Off you go to your supper,' said a deep voice, and a great hulking figure of a man gripped Grietar by the shoulder and turned him effortlessly away from Istar. Not surprisingly, Grietar did as he was told, and the newcomer – a near giant in Istar's estimation – smiled beneficently on the travellers. Istar didn't remember him from her childhood visits to Seahawk, but Pentar greeted him warmly and introduced him to Istar.

'This is Nantar,' he said, 'Grandson of Hiltar and a warrior of note.'

'Only when pressed to it,' Nantar said with a generous laugh, and held out a hand to Istar. He was the size of a bullock and looked as powerful, with small green eyes set in a ruddy face that looked as if it had seen hard weather every day for some years. Istar guessed he would be about thirty, and wondered if he was one of those who sought her sister's favour. She gripped his palm assertively and met his eye.

'Were you at Jai Pendu?' she asked, and he shook his head.

'I stayed here to fish and hunt for my family.'

'And to fight the Sekk,' Pentar added, and Istar wondered why he was so keen to put Nantar forward to her. The big man acknowledged Pentar's remark with a nod, but didn't take the opportunity to elaborate on his accomplishments.

'It is a bitter wind today,' he said instead. 'Hiltar asked me to fetch you to our house. She bids me see you are warm and comfortable, and then she would like to see Istar.'

Pentar said, 'I am pledged to go straight to my cousin Birtar's house on pain of a thrashing. I have promised the visit for three years running.'

'I will visit you there, then, and we will prevail upon the old man for some of his winter stout. Istar?'

'I will see Hiltar,' she said. *Ranatar killed by the Sekk?*

Nantar carried her luggage up flight after flight of steep stairs to Hiltar's abode. He apologized for the climb, but Istar said, 'I'm well used to steps, being from Jai Khalar, and anyway I've been going stir-crazy pacing back and forth in that little ice sail day after day.'

Nantar shot her a curious glance over his shoulder. She felt suddenly self-conscious. She knew she looked not remotely like the people of her adoptive Clan, who tended to be tall and rangy and fair. Istar was dark and compact, and she wore men's journeywear on a woman's frame. She had muscular legs and strong, callused hands, and she knew she moved and spoke aggressively: She'd had to fight for every ounce of respect ever tendered her. Yet a man the height and girth of Nantar inevitably made her feel like a soft, weak child, and besides she knew she was an outsider here, no matter what rights had been bestowed on her by her relationship with Tarquin.

She wished Pentar had let her slug Grietar, though.

A rush of warm air greeted her when Nantar opened the side door to Hiltar's house. As she was family, he would have been rude to bring her in via the front entrance, and instead he led her through the simple kitchen, where a lingering smell of spices mingled with yeast, and ambient heat from the partially banked fire warmed the air. Joints of smoked meat and netted cheeses hung from the beams, and the only light came from the open hearth where a cauldron was softly steaming over the logs. Istar's stomach began to turn cartwheels with culinary anticipation.

Nantar dumped her luggage in a side hall and led her into a long, low room with whitewashed walls and fur couches. Set near the fire was a low wooden table bearing plates of pastries and a flagon of wine, and beside it, in a stiff wooden chair that looked as old as the house, sat Hiltar the Clan Grandmother. She rose as Istar entered. Istar, remembering her Clan manners though she hadn't had much need to use them in recent years, dropped to one knee and pressed the old woman's dry hand to her cheek, murmuring the traditional phrases of greeting.

Hiltar's white hair was exquisitely braided, drawn back from her face so that its skin was stretched across the prominent cheekbones, making her appear much younger than her ninety-odd years. Equally – though she put away three cream cakes and a berry tart during their conversation – she was a tiny thing, elfin in appearance. With her wide face and tapering jaw, she looked like a child. Yet she moved very slowly and deliberately. Only her eyes were sudden, quick to scan the field of her attention, rivet the subject they selected, and assess it.

She did not spend much time on pleasantries before she said, 'Humour a little old lady and tell me something of Jai Pendu.'

So Istar found herself telling this frail lady what she hadn't been able to speak of to anyone. She told Hiltar about the solitary climb up the Way of the Sun, and of the seahawk that had attacked her at the top. How she had killed it in an unreasoning rage, and how the act had haunted her ever since.

'Is it because I have no Seahawk magic that I could do this act?' Istar asked, distressed. 'I told myself it was wrong, but the anger in my guts was so strong. I couldn't stop myself. It was terrible.'

Hiltar gestured to Istar that she should drink, and the Honorary took a long swallow from the cup of mead. She was shaking, recalling the incident. It was warm and dark in Hiltar's home, and there were smoke stains on the walls, and the rustling of her tame birds could be heard among the bunches of herbs and joints of smoked meat that hung from the rafters. Istar was a long way from Jai Pendu but she didn't feel safe from the memory of that hawk.

After a minute Hiltar spoke in a soft, grating voice.

'We all have within us many Animals, the ones who share our ancestors and the ones whom our ancestors hunted – or were hunted by. It is said in our legends that Astar, who led our people to Everien from the outer islands, was given the key to the Seahawk magic, and that is how he came to find this country. He passed on the key to his descendants, who have preserved it in our traditions. Astar could commune with the birds, fly with them, sail with them, hunt with them. He could call up the Seahawk within himself and use its special abilities that are keener than human senses.'

'All this is no good to me,' moaned Istar. 'I am not a true Seahawk.'

'I know that. But I'm not finished! What I was going to say is that although his descendants tried to repeat Astar's feats and preserve and teach them, they could only do so very imperfectly. For the Animal Magic will never be ruled by human law, or be contained by our conception of what is possible. It runs through some families to be sure, but not as true as do blue eyes or big feet, and in all cases it must first be awakened. Also, there is a difference between the Animal heritage of the Clans or how we identify ourselves to other people, as opposed to the true preserve of the Animal spirit. But the Seahawk Clan has many other animals in its history, just as does the Wasp Clan or your mother's, the Deer. Who knows what may lie dormant in you, Istar? Do not assume the Animal Magic cannot visit you. I have lived long enough to appreciate that Clan law means little to the things that live deep inside your memory, in your brain and bones.'

'You make me think of Xiriel,' Istar mused. 'He was supposed to be a Wolf, but he didn't even believe in the Animal ways, and then he became a Snake!'

'Ah, you see? Do not be fooled by the codes and categories of men, Istar. The sky holds more stars than they can count – therefore the names and numbers men attach to things are of small importance in the end. They will never include everything in their reckoning. Now, will you have another cake?'

'Thank you.'

The old woman passed Istar the platter, then poured mead into her cup and sat back in the chair that dwarfed her. Even in her nineties she preferred the stiff, high-backed timber to the cushioned furniture favoured in Jai Khalar. It seemed to give her no trouble. She sat upright, alert and dainty as a warbler in the bush, poised in constant readiness.

'I don't know why Mintar had to go and die,' Hiltar said suddenly in a scolding tone. Istar, just biting into a pastry, inhaled a puff of icing sugar in surprise. She grabbed her nose to stop herself sneezing.

'They all die so young,' Hiltar complained. 'They seem to just give up!'

'She was seventy, was she not?' Istar asked timidly, recovering.

'I was chopping my own firewood at eighty-five! If it were not for this damned pain in my joints, I still would be. Little Nantar does it for me now.'

Istar checked a smile, wondering whether Hiltar was joking. 'Little' Nantar was one of the biggest, toughest fishermen in A-Tar-Ness. He could probably crumble Hiltar's firewood to splinters in his bare fists.

Hiltar sighed. 'Mintar gave up on life, and I wish she had not, for she was a good friend to me. Quintar was always her favourite, and the one most alike to her. When he did not return year after year, she came to despair. It is an unfortunate trait in that arm of our family – the tendency to melancholia and self-absorption. Quintar suffered it, too, or he would not have withdrawn from us the way he did, after Jai Pendu. Like a sick animal crawling off to die alone.'

Istar was surprised to hear herself coming to Tarquin's defence.

250

'Usually the sick animal is isolated to protect the others. Usually it is kicked out.'

'No one kicked Quintar out. Endurance of hardship and revelling in adversity, these are the Seahawk ways. We are tough! We only tried to snap him out of it, like you throw cold water on someone who can't stop crying.'

She shifted again in the hard seat, and Istar wondered whether her hind-bones weren't aching, after all, and whether she was enduring the pain out of the proud defiance she extolled.

'But it did not work.' Hiltar's lips turned downwards, her bright face sagging and revealing its true age. 'He did not snap out of it.'

'He couldn't explain what he had been through. He felt no one could understand.'

Hiltar's eyes flashed defensively and Istar lowered her gaze to the half-full cup of mead. 'At least, that is what he told me,' she added in a small voice.

Hiltar sniffed and gave herself a little shake. 'I did not intend to discuss Quintar or his demons. It is Mintar, his dead mother, and Ranatar, his poor sister, who concern me – and you – now. Have you made your offerings?'

Istar nodded. 'By A-Tar-Helt at the edge of the sea a few days ago, where the ice is clear. I went at low tide to the farthest spur, and spoke their names, and gave the sea its gifts.'

'Mintar died too young,' she said softly, 'but Ranatar was murdered.'

Istar put down her cup. 'So I have heard.' She did not mention Grietar's name.

'Mintar had lumber and milling holdings in Petrel Fjord, just north of Tyger Pass. There had been trouble there in the summer of Jai Pendu when the Sekk were so bad. Whole families slaughtered, children orphaned. Ranatar used to go check on matters there regularly, for the Sekk was never caught and the land and its people were her responsibility after Mintar's death. While she was there, a Sekk got to one of her men-at-arms, who killed Ranatar before anyone could stop him. It was a terrible blow to us all.'

'Did they catch the Sekk?' Istar said. 'Was it the same one as before?'

'It might have been. No one saw it the second time, and the man who had been Enslaved was killed by his fellows before he could describe it. But the survivors of the first raid said he looked like a Seahawk warrior. White braids, a snow lion cloak, and a fine sword. Yet there is no one by that description that I know of. Snow lions are so rare nowadays that to have an entire cloak of their pelts would be to possess riches almost as great as Mintar's.' She paused, picked up her cup a little shakily, and drank. 'Which brings me to my point. The time of mourning for Ranatar is past. We may now discuss the dispensation of her property, which was most of Mintar's estate. As Grandmother of our family, it is given to me to execute her will. And I must say, Istar, that you do not come a moment too soon. There has been nothing but aggravation regarding this matter, ever since the period of mourning ended and the will was made public.'

'I am here now,' Istar said.

'Yes. Well, you have much to learn about the workings of this family, Istar. We know you not well, nor you us – your little sisters we treat as our own, but even they have scarcely seen you these past several years. Your valour in the Floating Lands and your part in the destruction of the Company of Glass cannot be disputed.'

'That mission was largely a failure,' said Istar. 'I did not return with an Artifact, and—'

'Do not emulate your foster father Tarquin and become a sourpuss who can only see that his cup is half empty when in truth it is also half full!'

Istar said nothing.

'As I was saying, your valour cannot be disputed but your reputation may work against you here. You should expect jealousies and challenges, and you must take care how you marry off your sisters.'

'This is what I have come to stop!' Istar exclaimed. 'It is too soon to think of such things. They are only young.'

Hiltar's eyes were sympathetic.

'And you are no more than a girl yourself – but you are not a girl, you are a man. See you act like one, or you will have a fine mess on your hands.'

'Are my sisters under threat? What is this nonsense of Lyntar being already promised? Who has dishonoured her?'

Hiltar waved a placating hand. 'No, no, it is all quite aboveboard. But the young men – and not-so-young men, truth be told – of this whole Clan have been making fools of themselves since the summer, and the ones who have only lately returned from Enslavement at Jai Pendu have now thrown themselves into the fray.'

'Over my sisters? But why? Whatever are you on about, Mother Hiltar?'

The old woman's manner changed, and she was again the lovely, childlike, flirtatious hostess. She put a warm hand over Istar's.

'Will you have another cake? You have not tried the black-currant . . .'

'No, thank you. They are delicious, of course, but – please, why are you looking at me like that? What's wrong?'

'Poor child,' said Hiltar. 'I've frightened you. A bold creature like you has nothing to fear from this! It is only that I wished to prepare you. Ah, let me be simple. Excepting a few special objects and some servants, Ranatar wills that all her fortune should belong to you.'

Istar dropped the cup. Hiltar's eyes never left her face. The mead splashed on the fur rug and the cup rolled only slightly and stopped. It had barely made a noise.

'Fortune?'

'I can think of no other word for it. Mintar was a wealthy woman, particularly in the last years of her life. We are not Pharicians here. We do not wear our accomplishments on our throats. We would not tempt fate that way! However . . .' Hiltar then proceeded to rattle off the extent of Mintar's property. There were several houses, staffed with servant families who had been war captives from the old days; two fishing boats and a warship, plus assorted small craft; hunting rights over some five thousand acres of forest; livestock of every description . . . Istar began to feel dizzy at this point.

'But what about her sons?'

'Jietar died in battle. Santar is a very wealthy man in his own right. She left him items of sentimental value, and years ago she gave him a house and land, both of which he has added to by his own efforts.'

'And her daughters? Her grandchildren?'

'The grandchildren each will receive a legacy. The daughters are provided for by their mates' families.'

'But . . . why me?'

'Mintar is dead now, so we cannot ask her. She left almost everything to Ranatar, and Ranatar leaves it to you. It is not so hard to see why. Foster child or no, you are the eldest son of the eldest son, and Tarquin is no longer Clan, so his rights pass to you. Ranatar could not leave it to him if she wanted to. And she was always fond of the twins.'

'What of the twins?'

'They are too young to inherit now. Their shares lie with you until their eighteenth birthday, or until they are married, when it passes to their respective mates. But it is your privilege to determine whom they marry, as if you were their father.'

'Does the whole Clan know this but me?'

'More or less. We could not find you!'

'They will hate me,' Istar said bluntly. 'I'm an outsider, an Honorary. I barely knew Mintar and I have not seen Ranatar in years. I should have done something to protect her . . .' And no sooner were the words out of her mouth than she had recalled that Grietar had said very much the same thing. She clenched her teeth.

'That is why I am glad you acquitted yourself so well at Jai Pendu – despite your misgivings about the Seahawk on the Way of the Sun. You should have some status of your own when this falls on you. And you have had a chance now to get your father's wanderlust out of your system.'

By 'father' Istar didn't know whether she meant Chyko or Tarquin. It took a moment before she realized something else was implicit in Hiltar's words.

'Out of my system? You don't . . . you don't expect me to return here?'

It was like a blow to the small of her back, dull and jarring and impossible to see coming. She flashed an image of Kassien donning the bearskin cloak and taking Dhien's hand.

'I believe it is what both Mintar and Ranatar would have wished.'

Istar shook her head vigorously, braids slapping her cheeks. She rose.

'No. No, no. I only came here to find fighting men, and to sort out whoever is harassing my little sister – not to stay! I don't want this, Hiltar. Let my sisters have it. Let Mintar's own daughters have it if they want.'

'That would be both foolish and unfair. Your sisters do not deserve to be abandoned by you, any more than you deserved to be deserted by your father.'

Again, Istar didn't know which father she meant, and hot anger coiled in her stomach as she realized she had been deserted *twice*. She took a deep breath and threw her head back, staring at the soot-blackened ceiling.

'It's simple,' she said after a while. 'I'll give some of it to Mintar's daughters so they won't resent me and my sisters. And some can be sold, and my sisters can go on living where they are until they are married, and then they will have good dowries and no reason to worry. And—'

'Istar. Sit down.'

Istar stooped and retrieved the fallen cup, setting it on the table. Hiltar was still pointing at the chair. Istar sat.

'You have all of this backward,' Hiltar said. 'There is no longer a need for you to go to war. Find husbands for your sisters if you want, and then take one yourself, and concentrate on making your land work for you. We have lost many men. There is much to be done here, and spring is coming.'

'You're mad,' Istar breathed, and then quickly placed one hand over her own mouth and the other upon Hiltar's wrist in a gesture of apology. Hiltar smiled.

'You have much to think about.'

Istar could only shake her head. 'I can't do any of this. Pharice, the

Sekk. What I said to Kassien about commitment. I . . .' Her voice trailed off. Thoughts flowed too fast and jumbled to be spoken.

Hiltar said, 'I suggest you visit your sisters and reacquaint yourself with them before you make any decisions.'

Istar nodded mutely.

'And have a touch more of the mead. No – do not worry about the rug. It has drunk the spilled wine of many a wilder stormhawk than you, little Star.'

Remove the Bear Tompien

Istar would have preferred to stay with Hiltar, speaking of the Animal Magic and eating delicious cakes baked by the precise hand of the Elder herself; but duty sent her to the house of Ostar, Quintar's sister and the foster parent to Istar's sisters. Istar had always been a little afraid of the tall, stoical woman. She was fair, with almond-shaped pale green eyes that could be sympathetic or biting depending on her mood. Big-boned and sinewy, she was a whirlwind of accomplishment and made women half her age roll their eyes with exhaustion. Ostar would go out in the worst storms to help the men drag in the nets from the fishing boats, and she would cook a meal for twenty, do the washing-up in one night, and then be up early the next morning to haggle with the ironmonger over the price of shod boots so that she could climb the cliffs in search of gulls' eggs. No one dared stop her.

She had never been actually harsh with Istar, probably because Istar had never dared cross her. Her husband had got the wrong end of her tongue often enough to retreat to a warm corner of their home in a silence that seemed to have lasted years: He did not look as though he had moved in the time since Istar's last visit, although she saw that he wore a new tunic with fine embroidery. He nodded at her, his eyes catching the firelight. *He reminds me of a tree*, Istar thought, and resolved to speak with him later, after Ostar had had her say. It struck her that not much went on but that Utar saw it; most people took little notice of him there in the corner, whittling or stroking the cats. There might be much he could tell her about her sisters and their suitors.

'Kinsman,' said Ostar, beaming down upon her niece. 'Come to the fire and warm yourself. It is a hard time of the year for travel; all of us have scarcely left our house these past months.'

From the smell of the place Istar was sure she was not lying. To be certain, the house was a fine one, well-appointed with heavy carpets and skilfully crafted tapestries to keep out the draughts, boasting an enormous central fireplace and beautifully carved furniture of dark-stained fir and spruce. But the windows had all been shuttered and barred and draped, and the air was stale. Her aunt's hair was tightly braided in neat brown rows, but it was also greasy and, Istar suspected, full of lice. The furs she wore exuded a pungent aroma when the air stirred them, and from somewhere near the fire there drifted a smell of souring wine.

It was not Jai Khalar.

Still, it was warm, and there were many lights on the walls and in free-standing iron sconces on the floor; children wove in and out among them playing games, one young girl even used the heavy stem of a light-tree to be her partner in a dance. Near the fire sat the harpist, an old man with enormous hands who, though crouched with his legs folded and torso curled, still had the bearing of a giant. He was some relative of Utar's, Istar remembered.

It was this activity that was a sign of wealth in the house, Istar knew. Many Seahawks would be lying in their winter closets, two per bed for the sake of warmth, and emerging only once a day or so to relieve themselves and slowly consume the cheese and dried fish they saved from the summer. If they expended too much energy too early in the winter, their food stores would run short and they would die; but in Tarquin's family there seemed no such concern.

Ostar offered food and the others gathered round, listening as Istar's aunt began plying her with insipid questions about her journey.

'Where are my sisters?' Istar said finally, thinking that she had not come all this way to exchange pleasantries with Ostar when her own blood were nearby.

'They have got in the habit of going up to the tor in the evenings.'

'To the tor? Alone?' Istar didn't like the sound of this. She didn't formulate a specific image in her mind, mostly because she wouldn't have known whether to be afraid of her sisters being eaten by lions or dishonoured by village boys.

'They are not easy to control. But you had better see for yourself. Maritar!' The summons was directed to a boy of about twelve, who until now had been quietly engaged in contemplating a tactical array of toy soldiers and monsters upon a wool rug in the corner. Stepping carefully over his troops and the coiled form of the enemy H'ah'vah, which had been simulated with the help of a grey sock, he picked up a cloak slung across the back of a chair and shrugged into it on his way across the room.

'This is your cousin Istar.' He glanced at her face once and then looked away, either shy or totally indifferent. 'Take her up to the tor and show her where Lyntar and Pietar usually go. And be quick about it or you'll miss your dinner.'

The boy had the lean and watchful look of one who cared little for missed meals – or courtesy, judging by the way he turned his back on Istar and led the way through the front door without a backward glance.

257

Outside it was dark and starless. The boy silently guided her past the beast sheds and along a paved track that led through fenced paddocks and then passed through a stand of firs and began to climb. He said not a word to her. Istar was young enough to remember how annoying could be the fake conventions and small talk of adults, so she didn't try to engage him in conversation. Probably Ostar had interrupted him in the middle of an important campaign.

There was snow on the path the same colour as the overcast sky, smoothed and flattened by diffuse moonlight. The trees shook in the wind, and after only a few turns of the path, the rectangles of light from the harbour and houses had vanished. To their right, along a ridge in the rising land was silhouetted the crooked box of a shepherd's hut, balanced on the first of the heights that would eventually become mountains farther inland. Ahead, the trees parted and the tor appeared, a column of treeless granite upon which was balanced an oval stone the size of a small house. The skirts of the tor were covered with heather and gorse, and Istar remembered coming here in her youth and seeing a vixen standing in the blooming heather, a rabbit clasped limp in her jaws. Istar had halted and stared at the vixen, and the animal at her; but Istar must have blinked because the next thing she knew the fox was gone without a sound, although the yips and cries of her young had rung out from the trees nearby as she arrived moments later with their dinner. Even then Istar had thought the tor a strange place; now, in the darkness and led by the silent boy, that same feeling was recalled to her once again.

Maritar paused and checked the wind. He adjusted their line of approach so that they were downwind of the tall stone; then he dropped behind a boulder and motioned for her to do the same. When Istar had followed suit, he pointed to the base of the tor. Istar could not make out what he was trying to show her, though. All she could see were some scrubby pine trees, stripped and twisted by the wind. Nothing moved.

'It's time for the Hawk Girls to come,' Maritar whispered.

'Who?'

Maritar looked at her like she was stupid. 'Don't they tell you anything in Jai Khalar?' he said bluntly, and she wanted to laugh. He made it sound as though the affairs of A-Tar-Ness were of superlative importance to whatever might be going on in the capital or anywhere else. Istar shook her head, and he explained.

'Lyntar and Pietar always feed them. They try to talk to the Hawk Girls and Pietar says she understands their language, but I think she's lying. Shh!'

Istar hadn't made a sound, but Maritar grabbed her arm and put a finger to his lips. She was still observing the place he had indicated, but she couldn't see a thing on the ground or in the sky. Hawk Girls? She recalled that Pietar had always been fond of hunting birds, but no hawk, seahawk or otherwise, would fly by night. The only flying thing to feed up on the tor at this time of day would be owls.

Then she caught her breath. At the very top of the tor, silhouetted against the clouds, a small figure rose to its feet. Soon it was joined by another.

'What are they doing?' Maritar hissed to himself.

'Are those the Hawk Girls?' Istar asked, feeling stupid but needing to know. He shook his head.

'Those are your sisters. They're stupid to go up there. They'll only scare them away.'

Even as he spoke, the two figures slithered down again, disappearing behind the rock. Istar waited a beat and then stood up. 'This is ridiculous,' she said. 'I'm going to go get them.'

Maritar didn't protest. Now it was his turn to follow as Istar tramped across the snowy heather to the base of the tor, circling around to its far side.

Something stung Istar's left thigh, hard. She dropped to the snow, drawing her dagger even before she had consciously calculated that someone had fired some sort of missile at her.

'Pietar!' the boy called in a voice that cracked from baritone to treble. 'Stop it at once! Don't shoot!'

Understanding, Istar wasted no time in getting to her feet and brushing the snow off herself. Out of the shadows at the base of the tor emerged two identical figures, and when she saw them Istar's voice carried clear across the snowy night. 'You idiots. It's me.'

In the back of her mind, Istar had always hoped that her sisters would turn out beautiful. If she never had a chance to take a mate, at least she wanted Pietar and Lyntar to be able to take their pick, as Dhien had done in the Bear Clan. But while the mating practices of the Bears were more concerned with sexuality and fertility, Seahawk values tended to be less primitive and more commercially materialistic. Beauty was not so important to Seahawks as property. The ravages of the Sekk had taken a toll on the Seahawk Clan, but Istar was now in possession of assets that would be valuable in any time. Mintar's fishing fleet alone would pay for her sisters' keeping in style, leaving aside the rest of the estate.

So it did not matter whether they were beautiful. But they were beautiful anyway, albeit in an angular, feral sort of way. The twins had none of Istar's wide hips or heavy breasts; in fact, either of them would have been ideally suited to life as an Honorary, for they were slender as boys, taller than Istar, and quick and sure in all their movements. Both wore the Seahawk braids, but they did not look like any Seahawks Istar had ever seen. Their complexions were as dark as Chyko's, and they had inherited their father's habit of wearing next to nothing. Mhani had griped nostalgically about the practice when speaking about Istar's father ('Getting shoes on that man was like getting a corset on a tiger'), but she would not be pleased if she saw her little twins dressed as they were now. Their blossoming young bodies were covered only to the bare limits of decency, long limbs and young, high breasts left half exposed, even in the frigid midwinter. The bits and pieces of fur they did wear were mink and white fox, including a matching set of fur boots that Istar envied, for her feet had not been warm in months. Each twin carried a long knife at her belt, as well as a wrist-mounted slingshot of a type Istar had never seen before. Neither seemed troubled in the slightest by the cold, and their eyes, although black as tar, were sparkling. They possessed a quality of intensity that Istar knew well from her brief contact with Chyko at Jai Pendu. She wondered for a moment whether she had any of this quality herself, and quickly discarded the notion.

'What in the name of Tarquin the Free is going on here?' Istar demanded, fixing each of them with what was meant to be an authoritarian eye; but they tolerated about as much of her authority as the typical house-cat. They sniggered without looking at each other, and she knew they were communicating in their own language, their twin language.

The fact that her sisters were twins had somehow made it harder for Istar to get to know them. They seemed complete in themselves, a perfect formation that could stand back to back and face the world. Nothing could get between them; no jealousy, no misunderstanding – nothing. It was not that they were always kind to one another; far from it, they were often unkind and sometimes cruel. But they were also secure in the knowledge that neither was ever alone. Not really alone, not alone like Istar.

Even as the flash of self-pity passed across her, the two girls were moving forward in tandem, flinging their arms around her, kissing her, making happy noises.

'We thought you were one of Grietar's men,' Lyntar said. 'He is always sending someone to guard us. It's so annoying, we can't get even a moment's peace.'

'What?' Istar turned them both around and began dragging them back toward Ostar's house. Each twin wrapped an arm around Istar's waist and leaned into her affectionately; but she was conscious of the fact that she was shorter than they by some inches. No, they were no longer babies.

'How dare he presume? Not that you aren't both fools for being out here at night, and dressed in such a fashion.'

Pietar began to groan and pull away, and Maritar snickered. He had materialized out of the darkness and now led the way back, probably eager to return to his game.

'We had to feed the Hawk Girls,' Pietar said.

'Who are they?' Istar asked. '*What* are they?'

'No one knows their names. We call them the Hawk Girls because they are like baby seahawks. You can't get near them; don't think we haven't tried. It makes Hiltar furious, the idea that children of our Clan should run wild that way.'

'Where is their mother?'

'Dead. The whole branch of the family was killed in a Sekk incident three years ago. They were millers in the forest at the end of Petrel Fjord. You know the place, where the sea goes deep inland and all the good timber is cut and then sailed down the coast.'

'I haven't been there,' said Istar, 'but I've heard it spoken of. Isn't that where Ranatar died?'

'Aye,' Lyntar said, and fell silent. Istar was not surprised that she was so reticent. What was strange was how Pietar kept talking, just as if Ranatar were not recently murdered.

'No one knows what exactly happened the day the Hawk Girls were orphaned. Probably the Sekk got one of the cutters alone in the forest and Enslaved him. The sailors who came to pick up their load found bodies mixed up in the machinery of the mill and the women and children cut down in their own homes. It was a terrible massacre, one of the worst the Seahawks have seen. The village was wiped out in a day.'

'And the two girls? Were they the only survivors?'

'Except for a couple of trappers who saw it from a distance and hid.'

'Didn't anyone find them? Weren't they cared for?'

'No one knew they were alive. They were spotted a year later at the beginning of winter, stealing cheese from one of the hamlets on the south side of the fjord. One of them carried a baby on her back.'

'A baby?' Istar was incredulous. 'But they are only young!'

'Must have been raped during the Sekk madness. Probably . . . ' Pietar lowered her voice. 'Probably one of her own brothers. It happens under the Slaving. The baby must have died, because it wasn't seen again. It's a miracle they didn't all three of them die, living in the wilderness that way.'

'How could anyone let that happen?' Istar was fascinated and horrified at once.

'It couldn't be helped. The girls weren't sighted again that winter. They fled into the woods and wouldn't touch food that was left out for them; they let the wolves get it, instead. Some of the village women tried to find them, to coax them to shelter, but they are shy as lynxes. Then they moved farther south, and that's when our people started to see them occasionally, but only the two, and only up on the heights. Never near the town.'

'And no one does anything?'

'What can we do? We only drive them away if we try to approach them. Some of the lads have spoken to them. They are very cunning, and it's said they know the mountain better than anyone. But they are utterly wild.' Pietar's tone was full of admiration.

'Ranatar tried to help them,' Lyntar said. 'She tried everything.'

Pietar suddenly pulled her braids and then began to run. Lyntar scooped up snow, spitting on it and squashing it into an iceball as she ran, then loading and firing her wrist slingshot. She pelted Pietar on the ass and Pietar went skidding down the icy trail, careering into Maritar, who fell into a snowbank. Istar heard herself shouting to them all to have a care for the cliff, but they didn't heed her. Whooping and shrieking, Maritar and the twins chased each other, throwing snow and insults, while Istar followed after, feeling worried and protective. The three virtually fell into the house, at which point Maritar made himself scarce, slinking around the perimeter of the room like a thieving dog so as to return to his game by the fire before Ostar could rebuke him. Istar tried to enter but caught a leftover snowball in the mouth.

Pietar was laughing manically and apologizing without a hint of sincerity.

'I ought to spank you,' Istar said. Then she caught a glimpse of something out of the corner of her eye – some movement outside in the darkness. She turned but it vanished, leaving her with only a fleeting impression of a small, bare leg and foot. She blinked and tossed her head.

'There, now do you see what I mean?' Ostar wanted to know, pulling her inside. She brushed snow off Istar's collar. 'Ah, it is not your fault, Istar, if they take after their father, but all the same I have to tell you that we are not equipped to control such shenanigans here. Why, it is the middle of winter, and look at them.'

'Yes, I know,' Istar said, frowning at the bare flanks and haunches of her baby sisters as they shed their fur cloaks. 'I will speak to them.'

'And the pranks! They are never home in their beds when they should be, and they lie to us all the time, and they speak to each other in their own language, so how am I to know what they are plotting? Pietar, she eats enough to feed ten sailors, why, it's a terrible habit. She has a beautiful figure now, but in ten years' time she will look slovenly and gross. And Lyntar, though she is no glutton, has been caught with

Utar's dreamweed a time or two or seven. They did not learn such habits from my children!'

'They did not learn them either from me,' said Istar in an offended tone. She wasn't sure who she was angrier at, Ostar or her sisters. The twins were making her look bad before her relatives; and yet she did not envy them here, in this boring place, expected to wait around for marriage proposals and with Ostar forcing her own sons on them.

Istar sat down and accepted a glass of brandy. Sooner or later she would have to talk to Ostar about this marriage nonsense. It might as well be now.

'Does either of them show a preference?'

'I scarcely think their preferences are an issue when they have both proved themselves unable to take responsibility for the slightest duty. That is why I had thought to separate them, and to place them each in the hands of a strong husband, as quickly as could be done. Although,' and she flashed Istar an ingenuine smile, 'now that you are here, of course we will defer to your judgment on this.'

Istar strolled over to the window that looked out over the harbour. She unfastened the skin that covered it and peeled it away, separating the slats of the shutters to get a glimpse of moonlight. Fresh, cold air spilled in; she breathed deep. Where were the Hawk Girls now, she wondered? Where were the seahawks? Roosting high on ice ledges, dreaming of dazzling sunlit days and themselves gliding on the updrafts and watching their shadows slip over the snow? What was she doing here discussing marriage? She knew the least about marriage of anyone. This whole ordeal tired her.

'Who do you have in mind for each of them, exactly?' She asked the question formally although she knew full well what the answer would be and had already formed an impression of each of the candidates Ostar put forward.

'Well,' said Ostar, wiping her hands on her apron and lifting her chest as she took a deep breath. 'For Lyntar I had thought Vortar, and for the other Utar the Younger, who is mild-mannered enough to tolerate her fits of mood.'

This slander of her kindred was beginning to get on Istar's nerves. If these things were being said openly of the twins in the presence of her, their guardian, then what had been going on since Ranatar's death, with no one in this house to speak for the outbreed girls?

'I would have thought you would prefer to see them well away from you,' Istar said. 'It sounds as if they have caused nothing but havoc. Are you sure you wish to see them married to your sons and living here with you?'

'Well, someone will be needed to manage the estates up along the fjord, in the timber country. They have been allowed to lie since Mintar's death, and have been administered only loosely. My sons could revive those businesses and—'

'You aren't talking of sending these two up to Petrel Fjord, where Ranatar was killed? Where the Hawk Girls come from?'

Ostar swallowed. 'There is a huge estate up there.'

'There is a murderous Sekk up there! Think again, Ostar.' She held Ostar's gaze in warning.

'It was only an idea,' Ostar said hastily, and refilled Istar's glass. The brandy, Istar noted, was excellent.

'It *was* an idea,' Istar said. 'Now it is not. Are there other suitors?'

She could tell by Ostar's manner that there were, but she didn't want to inform Istar lest she lose her hold on the twins.

'Grietar presses a claim. He gave us Pharician spirits, and to Utar he gave a panther cloak from the jungles of Aranoka. To Pietar he tried to give a tiara made of heartstones, and Lyntar would have received two bracelets of firebird filigree. I prevented it, of course. He presumes much if he thinks he can purchase the granddaughters of Mintar and Equitar.'

For once Istar agreed with her aunt.

'Since when is Grietar such a wealthy man? He struts about like a king gull at hatching time.'

'Ah,' said Ostar, and poured Istar a third brandy. The firelight had died and her eyes showed slightly bloodshot as she leaned across the leather sofa. Istar recognized this as the point at which the conversation would finally begin to get down to business. At last the Seahawk reserve was beginning to break down . . . Istar snorted a little into her cup, laughing to herself as she thought of the torture of her little sisters, growing up in such a cloistered and austere environment. No wonder they were out in the woods mingling with the wild things.

'Grietar has done well by the Pharicians,' Ostar said. 'He has extensive intercourse with their traders, by ship and by road. A caravan came over Tyger Pass in the fall carrying more riches than you could pile in a tuna net.'

'What does he sell?' Istar asked sharply.

Ostar shrugged, her eyes gleaming with the fascination people have with other people's sins. 'Utar thinks information, but I say if he were a spy, he could not be so open in his dealings.'

'What information could he have to sell, anyway?' Istar asked. 'He knows nothing of rebel positions.' Even as she said it she wondered if he had got hold of a Carry Eye or some other source of information. Or how proficient he was with the birds.

'The birds won't go to him any more,' Ostar said as though reading her mind. 'Ever since the caravan left, he has had to hire a poor fishing family to carry his messages.' She swung her head from side to side like a bullock, disapproving. Then she poured more brandy.

'What's become of the old ways, Istar?' she asked. 'You come from Jai Khalar, you know everything about Everien and Ysse and the Knowledge. Tell me, will the Knowledge ruin our traditions? Is there no room for the Animal ways in the middle of this . . . this storm in Everien?'

'It *is* like a storm,' Istar agreed after a long pause. She looked around the dark room with its smoke stains and its aging furs. 'I don't know what will happen. I only know that unless we get rid of Tash, we will all soon be speaking Pharician and writing in their record books.'

Ostar said, 'Grietar is a man with secrets. I say this to you not as a mother who wishes to ally her sons with a fortune – ah, do not look away, I know what you think, but we all must do what we can for our children, if you had your own you would understand – I say it to you, Istar, because it is the truth. Do not give the twins to him. He will take both, you know, if he can. But it is Hezene who comes to him in the night and fucks him blind, all the way from Jundun. Hezene has got him convinced he will be mighty under the new regime. But a man who lies down for a stranger is not a man any more. He is a beast of burden.'

Istar tried not to laugh. Probably there was some truth in what her aunt was saying, but not much. 'What would the mighty emperor of Pharice want of a nobody like Grietar?' she asked carefully. 'Are you sure it is Hezene?'

'Well, maybe not Hezene personally,' Ostar amended, keeping her voice low as if it were all a great secret (Istar observed that her sisters were lurking just behind her aunt and listening to every word). 'But someone in Pharice is paying a lot of goods to Grietar, and he is blind with lust for what they offer.'

Istar gave in to a huge yawn, and Ostar lurched to her feet.

'It is much later than I thought! I will show you to your bed closet.'

'We want Istar to sleep with us!' cried the twins, and Istar found herself being dragged into a large closet with her two sisters. They dove beneath the furs like a pair of kittens, squirming and giggling as they tossed garments out of the closet one by one.

'It is much warmer this way,' Pietar said. 'And it's so nice not to have to wear clothes.' Lyntar pulled the furs back to admit her older sister and Istar saw that the two were naked beneath the blankets, completely unembarrassed.

'I'm going to see Grietar tomorrow,' she told them as she leaned on the frame of the closet and pulled off her boots.

Pietar spread her legs and made a rude gesture, laughing. Istar gasped.

'Who taught you this?' she snapped, offended, and Lyntar kicked her.

'Ah, Big Brother, take the Bear tompien out of your bottom and relax!'

'Bear tompien . . .' Istar was flustered, and shook her head in incomprehension for a moment before she realized what her little sister had said. 'You rude chit! Is this how you repay Mintar for her decent upbringing? The ocean turns itself over with her shame of you!'

She sounded just like Mhani, but she couldn't help it. For their part, her sisters were gaining no end of pleasure out of baiting her.

'Lyntar does not want a husband,' Pietar said, drawing the fur over Istar and blowing out the lamp; but Istar was still unsettled by the glimpse of her sister's dark-furred genitals and thought how, were she a man, she would have pounced on the girl first and asked questions later. It was remarkable neither of these fools weren't—

'I hope you're not with child!' Istar cried, and then realized she had not been listening to what Pietar had been saying.

'She prefers a woman's tongue to a man's cock, and no wonder, when all men do is take their pleasure and get you with child.'

'*Prefers?* Have you had a man, Lyntar?'

Before Lyntar could speak her more garrulous twin answered for her.

'No, I have. Lyntar watched and decided it was not for her. We drew straws to see who would do it, and I lost. It's not for me, either, at least not now. I would have to be desperate for a baby to endure all that huffing and grabbing! Why, they don't even give your river time to flood its banks—'

'That's enough,' Istar said. The irritating part was that she knew what Pietar meant about huffing and grabbing; however, she didn't like it one bit that her baby sister had gone exploring on her own, not in *that* direction.

Lyntar spoke up at last. 'It is nothing to fear, Brother Istar. We are not interested, truly. It is only a game with men, and we can be more to each other than any man ever will.'

Istar sat back, uncomfortable. She knew Lyntar and Pietar shared everything, but she had never thought of this. She wasn't sure what the Elders would think of twin sisters satisfying each other in bed; was it immoral or only a natural consequence of their basic intimacy? Ah, it only meant they weren't grown up yet, and all the more proof to her point.

'You are not ready for marriage!' she stated categorically.

'True,' said both girls together.

Istar fell silent, confused.

'Then why do you entertain all these suitors, and why do you parade about, dressed thusly?'

Pietar shrugged. 'What else is there to do?'

Grietar

'How was your evening?' Pentar asked her the next morning, winking at her bleary expression.

'Bizarre,' Istar replied, and told him briefly of what had occurred. They walked along the clifftop, Istar occasionally glancing over her shoulder for she had the feeling she was being watched; but there was no one about. Only seabirds.

'I will come with you to see Grietar,' Pentar said. 'As for my planned celebration and reunion, Birtar and his brothers were not there. I am worried. They went hunting two months ago and have not come back. It seems Birtar has his heart set on Lyntar and wants to catch her a snow lion.'

'He will be longer than two months if he persists,' Istar said. 'Snow lions are hardly ever seen any more. They are nearly creatures of legend.'

'I know. I hope he comes back soon, but I fear they have got caught by bad weather and were forced to hole up somewhere until the mountain storms have gone by. They were headed up the pass.'

'Not very wise, I would have thought,' Istar said, frowning. 'All for my sister? It is astonishing.'

'Hmm. Yes, I wouldn't mind knowing what he things of this Grietar and his shady dealings. Birtar is a good man.'

'Well, you can forget putting in a word for him. Lyntar will marry no one, at least not right now.'

'How authoritarian you have become!'

'Become? I always was bossy, and you know it.'

Grietar lived in a fortified tower halfway up Tyger Fjord toward the sea. They had to go by iceboat, for the landscape in between A-Tar-Ness and Grietar's castle was rugged and difficult to traverse. The tower had been in his family for many generations and had been a strategic objective in a number of internecine Seahawk conflicts. Grietar had added numerous buildings: stables for his ponies, guardhouses, and assorted workhouses. Additional facilities were contained in the cliffs below the castle. Given time, Istar thought, Grietar would construct his own city. And she thought it strange that he had troubled himself to come all the way to A-Tar-Ness to greet her last night. What had been his purpose?

Merely to take her measure? Her blood was up even as she stepped off the boat onto Grietar's dock. There were armed men everywhere.

Grietar greeted them in splendour before a well-lit fire. He looked satisfied with himself, and made sure his guests were aware of his wealth.

'As proof of my goodwill and familial intentions, let me offer my services. I have many men in my army, and they are well fed and strong. They are not afraid of the winter.'

'I don't need a force of arms to deal with a Sekk up in Petrel Fjord,' Istar said. 'I can do that personally.'

'After you avenge Ranatar,' Grietar said. 'Take them with you, use them to fight Pharice.'

'What? Will you betray Tash so soon after he has made you rich?'

'I have had a change of heart.'

'I don't believe you,' Istar said bluntly. Pentar grabbed her arm and said, 'Grietar, we must speak privately of this.'

'Of course.' Grietar turned and stalked to the other end of the hall, where he ducked into a stairwell. His boots could be heard ascending toward the ramparts.

'He's lying,' Istar said. 'If he betrays Tash, he will betray us.'

'We need an army, Istar. Has it escaped your notice that in the absence of you and Tarquin and any other male leader, your family is obliged to buy warriors?'

'It is not my fault if they don't breed,' Istar said tartly. 'In Chyko's bloodline, there has never been a shortage of warriors.'

'You mustn't think that way!' Pentar said angrily. 'You are Seahawk now. Why should men follow you if you do nothing to own your own Clan? I don't understand you, Istar. It is a great honour to be the legatee of Equitar's fortune, not to mention the daughter of Tarquin the Free, whom the Seahawks still lay claim to, despite his flight. The Wasps would not have you; they virtually disown Chyko, did you know that? He was a criminal. The Deer are in trouble with every other Clan in Everien because of their complicity with Tash in the Fire Houses and the fact that Hanji let Tash into Jai Khalar, and your mother has no status in her condition. Nor have you any flair for the Knowledge or Scholarship of any kind.'

'Stop browbeating me,' Istar snapped. 'Who asked your opinion? Why do you follow me, then? And if you do not follow me, then go!'

Pentar was quiet a moment. 'Grietar is a suspicious character, I will be the first to acknowledge it. But he commands many men, and it may well be that they would blossom under your leadership. They will not throw themselves behind a traitor, Istar. They will throw themselves behind you.'

268

'You flatter me. It is always the same with you, Pentar. Just because I got you away from the Sekk, I am not a great leader.'

Pentar was blinking and fidgeting. 'What's the matter with you, Istar? Ever since Jai Pendu, something's not right with you. The fight's gone out of you.'

'I have done well enough at exterminating the Sekk,' Istar said defensively.

'That may be, but you have let Kassien take all the glory and you hide yourself away.'

'We've had this argument before,' Istar said. 'It gets us nowhere.'

'Very well,' said Pentar. 'It is your decision. But Grietar sits in the palm of your hand.'

Istar went to the window and sat on the ledge.

'I cannot give him my sisters. It would be cruel.'

'Then do not decide, yet. Take his army and use it, and let him await your word. Istar, you have more power than you know, if only you would take it up.'

'Shh!' she said. 'He's coming back.'

Grietar's boots sounded in the stairwell again.

'It is the midday meal almost,' he called as if to warn them of his approach. 'I would not wish to rush your thinking, but would you honour my family and sit at our table? My grandmother always used to say, "Your decision will be easier made when you are at ease." '

As reluctant as Istar was to accept hospitality, her stomach was growling audibly and she was feeling a headache coming on: last night's mead and brandy, compounded by no breakfast this morning. And Grietar laid a fine table. The Pharician delicacies that he served gave her the opening she needed. She was not subtle.

'What are you doing for Pharice that they send you such riches?'

Grietar patted his moustache carefully with a green linen napkin. His watery eyes steadied on her face.

'They purchased a treasure from me. It was pure luck that I found it, and I chose to capitalize when I learned how excited they were. Only now . . .' His eyes shifted as he thought. He cleared his throat and made a show of throwing his napkin down decisively. 'I will tell you the truth. I sold something to Pharice, and they paid for it, only now it has not turned up at its destination. Something has gone wrong. You are renowned adventurers both—' and his gaze took in the two younger Seahawks admiringly. 'I hoped if I gave you men and made alliance with Equitar's legendary family, you might recover this treasure for me and prevent Pharice from taking revenge.'

Pentar had stopped chewing, listening to this extraordinary admission. Now he spat his food out rudely onto the plate.

'You traded with Tash our enemy?'

'In a manner of speaking, but Pentar, you don't know what it was like. When Pharice got word of what I had found, I was swamped by their birds. They made offers; they made threats; I could scarcely think. If they want this thing so badly, I thought, let them have it! It is of no use to me.'

Istar sat silently, enjoying the sight of Pentar getting worked up into a fine rage. It didn't happen often.

'Clan traitor! Snake! They said you were in the employ of Pharice, but I hoped it was just some clever trick on your part, a way of taking advantage of their stupid merchants.'

'It was! It is! Listen, Pentar, they paid so much for so little that I am now in a position to offer this fine army, and more besides. Our Clan will grow strong on their generosity! But I cannot go back on the deal now. If I do not deliver this thing to the Pharicians, they will descend on me like a plague.'

'Ah, now you think of this!' Pentar said menacingly, slapping his dagger into his palm.

'But they will not discriminate,' cried Grietar. 'They will take revenge on us all.'

'Why don't you give back the money?' Istar asked.

'It's spent! And anyway, they will accuse me of keeping this artifact for myself.'

'Why would you want to do that?' Pentar queried, and Grietar didn't answer. Istar stirred.

'Come, say it. You do not seriously expect me to take up your adventure without knowing what thing it is I am looking for?'

Grietar looked down. 'It is a skeleton.'

Pentar laughed. 'Why would Hezene pay a fortune for bones?'

Grietar shook his head slightly without looking up, as if unwilling or unable to explain.

'Forget it,' Istar said. 'I've heard enough. Let's go.'

Grietar looked at her and the skin between his beard and his eyes had flushed dark pink.

'It is the skeleton of a man,' he said. 'With wings.'

A White-Haired Warrior

'Where?' asked Istar sharply. 'Where did you find such a thing as this?'

'In a gully not far off the main road through Tyger Pass. My men found it last spring when returning from trade with Snake Country. The snowmelt had washed away the earth that concealed it. I told them to leave it there, and I met the Pharicians on the spot so that they could examine it.'

'You carried out this trade in the middle of Tyger Pass?'

'Yes. We arranged what they would bring, and they brought it, by sea. Then I took them up the pass, they saw the thing, and I sent them away with it and some other trade goods we agreed on, in a Snake Clan caravan I had recently acquired.'

'But you did not see them safely over the pass?'

'No. It was autumn by then, and I feared being caught in the snow, so I returned straightaway. They were well armed, and I assumed they had made it through to Snake Country, until I started receiving messenger birds complaining that the caravan could not be found on the other side.'

'Perhaps the Snakes took them,' Pentar remarked. 'Although they would be disappointed to catch a whole caravan and find nothing inside but a pile of bones.'

'To you it is a pile of bones; to Hezene, it is precious.'

'Hezene must be a fool. Wings, indeed. It's a fake, of course. A skeleton doesn't just lie there nicely arranged unless it's been set in a grave. The bones get all mixed, and if all the flesh is gone you can't always tell which piece belongs to who.'

'It was most clearly a real creature that once lived, and flew,' Grietar said. 'For the wings were attached to its spine in a way that you would never see in an ordinary human backbone.'

'Men don't fly,' Istar said. 'It is your wishful thinking and the old Seahawk legends conspiring to make you believe you saw a winged man.'

Grietar shook his head and made a grunt of denial. 'It was checked most carefully and witnessed by one of Hezene's own fliers. Even leaving the wings aside, there were other differences.'

'Such as?'

'The bones were hollow.'

271

Pentar made a dismissive sound and then frowned thoughtfully. *I wish Xiriel were here,* Istar thought. *He would love this.*

'It is not a good enough reason to go up Tyger Pass in the winter, with or without an army. I won't do it.'

Grietar's expression hardened suddenly. 'Do not put bad blood between our families, halfbreed.'

'There will be no marriage blood, that I guarantee,' Istar said hotly. 'Anyway, what would you have me do? Find your skeleton and turn it over to Tash? You must be crazy. He is my sworn enemy. Give me an army to fight him with, and then you and I will be friends and you can forget your ridiculous deal-mongering with Pharice.'

'But that's just it, Istar. I didn't make a deal with Tash. I made it with Hezene's Speaker, Byrd, via bird scout. I'm not even sure Hezene wants Tash to stay here. Hezene wants Knowledge and always has, but maybe he doesn't want Everien. Else why would he pay so richly, treat me so well over the skeleton? He could have come to take it by force.'

Istar laughed. 'Force is not the only way to make a man do your bidding, merely the most honest one. Are you telling me Tash doesn't know about the skeleton?'

'I didn't think so. But he has the Eyes. What if he intercepted it and took it back to Jai Khalar? He can then blame the loss on me and who will Hezene believe?'

'Aye, it's a pickle you've put us in,' Pentar concluded.

Istar said, 'I will have to think about it.'

'You can keep the men. I'll give you fifty, and you can take them right over into Snake Country. Surely that will aid your rebellion against Tash.'

'More welcome aid would be the true rising of the Seahawk people,' Istar said sharply. 'You wait here, biding your time and watching the tide to see whether it is Tash or the Clans who come out on top. You should lend us your swords – all of them, not just fifty – now!'

Grietar made a secret smile and took his time answering.

'The alliance of our families might bring about such a result,' he said.

Istar's mouth worked. *If I were a man,* she thought, *I'd say yes in a second. But the thought of my sisters in the bed of this thug makes my gorge rise.*

'I will have to think about it,' she said again, rising.

She said nothing on the way back to Ostar's house, where instead of entering and facing the rambunctious antics of her sisters, she turned up the path to the tor, Pentar walking silent by her side. She waited until they were well away from the houses and then turned back to look over the sea.

'Pentar, it is deep winter,' she said. 'We will make little progress in this weather anyway, and probably no progress up Tyger Pass unless we take ice picks and snowshoes. And there is something I want to do.'

'I'm listening.'

'I want to see the place where Ranatar was killed. Where these Hawk Girls come from. I want to talk to the trappers who witnessed the first incident, and any among Ranatar's people who were involved on the day she died. It is . . . call it a feeling, but I have to know more. The Sekk that prowls there, it could come here. Knowing that, and knowing Grietar is up to no good, I am reluctant to leave.'

'This is a well-defended place,' Pentar began, and then stopped, recognizing her expression. 'I won't argue with you if that's what you want. I'll ask Nantar to take us to Petrel Fjord.'

'Good.' But she didn't stir. Her nostrils widened as she inhaled the strong sea wind, her eyes focused inwardly. Pentar waited but she seemed content to just stand there and think.

'Istar, what are you not telling me?'

'I don't know. Damn it, I don't know. It's those Hawk Girls. I mean, the Sekk killed everyone but them, and now they've gone wild, and Ranatar tried to help them and it killed her—'

'But she had ventured back into its territory.'

'I know, but Pentar, now the Hawk Girls are here and my sisters are trying to make friends with them, and I have a feeling they are watching my family all the time.'

He suddenly twigged her meaning. His voice rose incredulously. 'You think they are Slaves to this Sekk?'

'I know it sounds impossible, but something isn't right. I just have to go up there and see for myself. Maybe the Sekk will come.'

'Maybe you can kill it and avenge their deaths. I know you, Istar.'

'Not only vengeance. I could assure it can't come after Pietar and Lyntar.'

'All right,' Pentar said at length. 'As you said, we wouldn't get far up Tyger Pass in winter anyway.'

He made arrangements for Nantar to take them to Petrel Fjord three days thence, and Istar decided to use the time to gather more information on the two incidents at the head of Petrel Fjord. One of the two trappers was spending the winter in the harbour caves at A-Tar-Ness, and Istar brought him a cask of cherry brandy and a round of cheese, waking him from sleep in the middle of the day. His name was Chentar and he had a sleeping closet in a communal cave; when she roused him an unidentified person stirred beside him and returned to sleep.

'Come out,' she said. 'I have brought you food and drink.'

Chentar was well over sixty and turkey-featured, but he sprang up

273

nimbly when he got a look at the cheese and piled into his furs. She managed to extract from him a vague description of the massacre at Petrel Fjord, but he could not say for certain whether he had seen the Sekk.

'I was far away, you see, and I could not hear its singing. Also, there were a great many people involved in the fighting. Men was fighting each other and cutting their own women. Some of them was good fighters, too, but they only killed each other in the end. There was one, a fantastic-looking warrior him, with white hair and a big sword. He was laying about like it was all some sort of picnic, but I couldn't tell you whether he was good nor evil, because it was all mayhem. Didn't see anybody kill him, mind you. Maybe he got away.'

Istar asked around in her family whether anybody knew the name of this warrior, thinking that such a description would surely bring recognition. If he had been there, maybe she could enlist his help in learning more about this particular specimen of Sekk. But no one remembered speaking to him or seeing his body among the dead. Istar thought this was strange.

'Maybe he was Enslaved,' someone suggested.

'Maybe he fled into the wilderness.'

Istar then tried to talk to Ranatar's guards. She scoured A-Tar-Ness searching out the relatives of the men, but some of them were away on a fishing trip and the only one who remained had not actually seen Ranatar's death.

'Aye, Rektar went off to check the area before we rode in with my lady Ranatar may the sea sing her to sleep, and he came back acting very quiet. "Did you see anyone?" I asked, and he said, "No, nobody here, not even that damned warrior!" I said, "Pardon, Rektar?" and he came at me just like that! I shouted to the others to look to my lady, and he suddenly spun around and before anybody could do anything, he . . . well, it wouldn't be right to say.'

'You must say,' Istar enjoined.

'He took her head off, just like that. It was so fast. I've never seen anything so fast, and I was in the Floating Lands. I have seen some blood flow, as I don't have to tell yourself, Istar.'

'No, you don't have to tell me. What do you think he meant, about a warrior?'

'I've no idea. We did another search, burned houses, checked everything. Didn't find a soul nor a sausage.'

Istar thanked him. *A white-haired warrior*, she thought. *We'll see about this. Petrel Fjord, get ready for the coming of Istar.*

Istar spent what time she could in the vicinity of the tor, where she found footprints in the snow that must belong to the Hawk Girls. But they had been clever in crossing frozen streams or sweeping away their own tracks, and what good prints she found she soon lost again among the sheep that grazed the steep slopes above the edge of the fjord. She went with her sisters each night to feed them, but they did not appear. Yet always she felt they were watching her.

On the day before they were supposed to leave, Birtar and his younger brother came limping down the road from Tyger Pass. The news of their arrival was brought by Maritar, and soon all of A-Tar-Ness had turned out to meet the dejected procession. Lyntar stood out in the roadway and when Birtar saw her, he fell on his knees in the snow and burst out crying.

'I love you,' he said, 'For you, my brother is dead. I wish it was me.'

Lyntar put her hand over her mouth, gulping back tears. Pietar put a chunk of ice in her slingshot quick as grease and sent it spinning at the miserable Birtar.

'Go away, Birtar!' she cried. 'Lyntar doesn't want you. She never asked you for any gifts.'

But Lyntar ran into the house, and Ostar cuffed Pietar before Istar could beat her to it.

Birtar had frostbite and would lose two of the fingers on his left hand. His brother was not much better off, and both had the haunted look of guilt and fear and most of all, of not understanding what had happened. It was a facial expression that appeared in the wake of the Sekk wherever they went. Pentar and Istar got him alone before the rest of the family could get involved. They explained that it was important they get his story before he forgot it, and such was the respect tendered to the heroes of the Floating Lands that no one questioned them.

'Thietar found it. A caravan, but all the people had been killed and there was a box in the snow. A box of bones. The Sekk, it must have been guarding this place. Ah, Thietar, why did you go digging for caviar? You paid for it with your life!'

'He was Enslaved when you found him?' Pentar asked, knowing that the Sekk habitually singled out one individual and manipulated him or her as a Slave in order to kill the others.

'I saw the Sekk clearly,' he said. 'I killed my brother because it had Enslaved him. But I could not bring myself to face it. I ran. We . . . we both ran. Later, after the Sekk was gone, we came back for Thietar's body, but in the moment of truth, we fled. I am so ashamed!'

'It is a natural enough reaction to the Sekk,' Pentar assured him, 'and it probably saved your life.'

Then Birtar said exactly what Istar knew he would say, for every survivor of the Sekk said something of the kind.

'Why couldn't I have killed the Sekk, and then helped my brother throw off the spell? I was so afraid, I killed him. There was no courage, there was only fear.'

'That is the way of the Sekk,' said Pentar, whose compassion seemed to Istar to be infinite; hers had worn thin long ago. She could only feel hatred now. She was so tired of hunting Sekk, of watching people cry their eyes out, incomprehension making it impossible for them to recover from what they had experienced. 'You cannot try to understand it,' Pentar was saying. 'You must accept it.' Istar thought, *If it was me, I would never accept it.*

'What did the Sekk look like?' she asked, and Birtar stopped sobbing, startled. He wiped his nose and mouth and gathered his words.

'He was a great warrior. Tall, broad. His hair looked to be white and braided like a Seahawk. He carried a sword and he wore a great cloak of . . . of snow lion.' With that he began to cry again. 'We were hunting snow lion, you see,' he explained, making a gesture of apology for his weakness.

Pentar looked at Istar. Istar leaned forward.

'Birtar, listen to me.' She put her hand on his cheek, knowing that he would listen better if she touched him and brought him closer to the present, to reality. 'You must not tell anyone about the caravan or the skeleton. Especially not Grietar. Do you understand?'

'I don't want to tell anyone. I'm so ashamed . . .'

'It was a random Sekk attack. You were high up in the pass, there were White Screamers, you were beset. Say anything you like, but don't bring the caravan into it.'

'Istar, what are you—' She silenced Pentar with a kick.

'Birtar, look at me.' It took a moment and she had to take his poor, ruined hands in hers to get his full attention, but he did. 'I shall avenge Thietar. I shall avenge him. Now promise me you will do as I have said.'

'I promise,' he whispered.

She stood up and walked out. Night had dropped a stark curtain over the fjord, and the chill was so deep she felt it in her breastbone when she tried to inhale.

'I'll find you,' she whispered. 'Kin murderer, I'll find you.'

Grietar was roasting in his personal sauna when Istar came calling. She barrelled through a thicket of servants in the front rooms of his house and jerked open the pine door. A burst of heat and curses greeted her from the darkness within.

'I'll take your damn army,' she said. 'I'll find your fucking skeleton. Put some clothes on and let's talk logistics.'

Grietar, shivering, blinked as he came to the door, hands cupped over his genitals, his skin flushed red like a baby's. Before he could say or do anything, Istar had already spun on her heel and left, settling herself in the kitchen to wait for him. She asked for stew and bread and from down the hallway she heard a thump as he either punched or kicked the wall. Then he began to give loud orders to cover up for his embarrassment.

After she'd left, terms agreed for the use of his soldiers to help locate and retrieve the mysterious skeleton, Grietar sulked into the small hours. The small Seahawk warrior with tits was a gadfly, monumentally annoying and asking to be slapped to death, splattered against a wall.

'Chyko,' he muttered. 'Does she have his sting, I wonder?'

For Grietar had encountered Chyko more than once at the gaming table, and he had been terrified of the unpredictable little man with his violent temper and uncanny skill for inflicting pain. More than anything, it was probably this remembered fear that coloured his dealings with Istar; for he could not think of any other reason why he should allow such a pipsqueak to get the better of him.

Then again, Grietar was beginning to be desperate. The Pharicians who had purchased the skeleton would come looking for their booty sooner or later. This time he didn't expect them to lade themselves with gifts, either.

The fire burned down slowly. Istar had said that Tyger Pass would be so rough this time of year that she might well decide to take the spoils down the other side of the pass into Snake Country, where she reserved the right to use his army for the period of one year, at which point they would be free to choose their allegiance. She promised to send the skeleton and whatever else she found in the caravan back to Seahawk through Poison Pass, which would be open in the early spring. Grietar had put up a good fight and then agreed to these terms, which did not include Lyntar, but that scarcely worried him for the moment.

The terms were not great, Grietar thought, turning the permutations over and over in his mind as the night ground on. But he was placing a set of probabilities that included the good chance that the Pharicians would find Istar with the recovered loot and that she would take the blame for the delay and the destruction of the team Grietar had left up in the pass. For when the Pharicians returned to A-Tar-Ness to demand their treasure, Grietar fully intended to play dumb about where the caravan could be. He would send them up Tyger Pass and into Snake Country, where events would play themselves out. Let Istar and the Pharicians fight each other. And Grietar would be here, with the majority of his men and all of Tyger Fjord under his dominion.

*

Of course Istar would not be allowed to set off without a party first. She was uneasy at the thought of ascending Tyger Pass by dark and winter storm, but the thought of the prowling Sekk preying on her people motivated her. Everyone else thought she was crazy not to wait until spring before taking Grietar's men to join the rebels in Snake Country. Pentar let it be known that Istar, like her famous forebear, was indeed crazy but had phenomenal luck, and that her instincts had to be trusted. It was Pentar's staunch support above all that convinced Istar's family and the men who would follow her that this mission was viable. But Istar didn't let anyone know her true purpose. To Grietar, she was mopping up his problem with Pharice and getting a force of men in exchange. To everyone else, she was going to aid the rebellion in Snake Country and test Grietar's men in the process. Birtar kept his promise and said nothing of the caravan.

It was dark and stormy throughout the day of the party. It seemed all the Clan were gathered in Ostar's house, although in truth it was only Hiltar's family and Pentar. Yet the heat of bodies alone was enough to warm the round central room, and with the great fire roaring in the hearth, furs were quickly discarded and cast onto the couches, which had been pushed back against the walls to form a rough circle.

'There are to be no mating rituals tonight,' Istar had warned Ostar beforehand, prompted by unpleasant memories of the big feast the Bear Clan had put on for her and her comrades right before they assailed the Floating Lands. Ostar only laughed. 'It's dire winter,' she replied. 'We do all our big festivals in late summer, so that children are born in the spring. Not that the family can always control it so nicely; still, it would be bad luck to bear a child in, say, November. Only the very tough ones can survive the cold.'

Istar was embarrassed, and she had come reluctantly to like the blunt-mannered Ostar, so she said, 'How little I understand the ways of this Clan.'

'You will understand them less still if you do not return to take up your holdings,' the woman said gruffly. 'Be careful up there in the snows! But tonight, you drink and eat. Don't think of the moon or the following sea. That's what my father always said to his men before a big fishing expedition, and what's true for the sea must be true for the peaks as well.'

Istar took a heavy goblet from her aunt and drank deeply. She knew she would be the worse for it tomorrow, but she didn't care. She was gripped with that delightful feeling of recklessness which Mhani claimed came from her notorious father, the feeling that she was about to do something rather big and probably very stupid, but nothing could stop her. What would Kassien say when she came down into Snake Country with an army *and* an Artifact, ready to settle grudges with Tash openly? And now she could finally clear her conscience with regard to the Hawk at Jai Pendu, for if it was true that this Sekk that haunted the caravan was the same that had killed the family of the Hawk Girls and Ranatar as well, then she could wipe it out and decisively act on behalf of her family and her Clan.

So she ate. It would have been impossible not to: There were fish stews and platters of smoked meats, chickens on spits turning over the fire; there were loaves of bread, round, long, braided, and square; there were jars of oil and mountains of butter all pale and salted; there were casseroles of egg and greens and roast potatoes; there were pastries baked by the hand of Hiltar herself, dozens of different kinds in raspberry, blueberry, honey, and apple; there were exotic fruits brought by boat from the far south and stored in the cool earth. The evening was ripe with music and dancing and stories that everyone had heard a hundred times but persisted in wanting to hear again, they were such good stories. Istar soon forgot entirely about her road. She was drunk and wove about the room greeting everyone and being patted by them, slapped by them, receiving their advice in her ears or invited to dance by them. The Seahawks were raucous and wild when they let their braids out, and tonight a good many heads were surrounded by wild blond hair that for weeks or months had been tightly contained and now sprang free, frizzy and light in the fiery evening.

'You are one of us,' Nantar told her, making her sit on his lap and squeezing her breast. He laughed as he did it, and when she began to bristle, he laughed harder. 'Relax, little petrel! One day you will grow into a fine woman, after you are done with your adventuring. Meanwhile, you do us honour to be in our Clan. Your father spread his seed widely, but it's best expressed in you. You are an Honorary man and now I say you shall be an Honorary Seahawk, and let no one tread on your rights while you are away!' He stood as he said it, still holding on to her and contriving to raise his glass at the same time, and others echoed the toast in ringing tones.

'Istar Seahawk!' they cried. 'Fly out and return in glory, with blood on your claws!'

Nantar put her down and saluted her – this time, as a man. Istar was blushing.

'My father was Chyko but my father was also Quintar,' she said. 'A warrior who can lay claim to both has no excuse to fail. I wear the paint in joy of a fine death in battle!' She indicated the four silver waves, bowed, and sat down to ragged cheers.

Everyone was drunk. Istar wanted to lie back on a couch well away from the fire, but she was waylaid by the usually somnolent Utar and forced to accept a rich cocktail in a gold cup, and a pastry filled with creamy black chocolate brought all the way from Jundun. She was walking unsteadily through the crowd, stepping over children and fallen cloaks and pausing every now and then to cry out in ecstasy at the taste, when a small voice said her name. Well, not her name exactly . . .

'Starry,' said the voice again, and she turned to see the twins, decently covered for once, feet primly together, heads downcast and eyes peeping at her from beneath thick, dark lashes from their superior height. She thought that Pietar had spoken, but it didn't matter: they were in complete accord. Their twoness made Istar feel small and incomplete. There was only one of her, and where Lyntar and Pietar understood each other, Istar didn't even understand herself, much less somebody else. The thought made her lonely.

'Please, can we talk?'

They were relatively sober, which surprised her. Istar put the chocolate pastry in her mouth, flung her arms around them and propelled them both toward the nearest couch, which was occupied by two old men playing cards and a dog; they scattered when they saw the three daughters of Tarquin coming.

'What is it, my darlings?' Istar asked loudly, having removed the half-eaten pastry from her mouth and being careful not to spread chocolate on Pietar as she wrapped one arm around each twin, pulling them each to one of her hips as she fell back into the leather couch. 'You know I do everything for you. Everything. I would lay down my life for you, I would—'

'We don't want you to go.'

They said it together, one voice in the left ear and one voice in the right. Istar began to laugh.

'It's all right, my doves. I'll come back. And you don't have to get married if you don't want to. Grietar thinks he's getting you, but I assure you this will *never* happen. I'll protect you, don't you see?'

'No. Istar, be quiet and listen to us. This is important.'

Istar rolled her eyes. She leaned back on the couch and licked chocolate off her right palm. 'Have you tried these? What substance is this, it is better than honey and apricots and cream all combined.'

'Please listen,' Lyntar said. 'We know you're drunk, but this is serious.'

'The Hawk Girls are stalking you. We have seen them do it before. I don't know . . .' Pietar lowered her voice to a bare whisper in Istar's ear, leaning close so that Istar could smell the ale on her breath. '. . . I don't know if they have ever killed, but they will stalk and follow a man, and if they believe him to be a threat they will lay traps for him or injure him, or do other things to frighten him. It is not good to get on their bad side.'

'Then why the devil do you feed them and talk to them, if they are hostile? Now I will worry even more about you two.'

'It's not us they're after,' Pietar persisted. 'It's you. They aren't afraid of us. They like us. But they don't like you, Istar.'

Istar laughed again and stuffed the remnants of the sweet into her mouth. 'Huh,' she said, still chewing. She swallowed and lay back, savouring the final taste. Lyntar elbowed her in the ribs.

'Say something.'

'Say something? What do I care whether they like me or hate me? Do you think everyone I meet likes me? I am used to not being liked, downy birdlet. As long as they don't harm the two of you, they can do what they like.'

But in the wooze and sway of the drink, a little bit of guilt was beginning to play its tuneless harp. Istar thought all in a flash that the Hawk girls were connected to the Seahawk Magic. Therefore they Knew. They knew what she had done in Jai Pendu.

Pietar was stroking her braids. 'Don't go,' she said. 'There is money, Ranatar's fortune, and who cares about Grietar? He will not get us, not by jewels nor trickery nor force, for I have the little knife you gave me and I wear it strapped around my thigh, high up, and I know where to cut—'

'Shh, little beast. Ah, Chyko didn't know what he wrought; or maybe he did, and that's why he went back to Jai Pendu rather than return to this world and deal with the consequences of his good times.'

'You're his daughter, too,' Lyntar said, affronted. 'You are free to prance about like a man and do what you want! How dare you criticize us?'

Istar kissed her cheek. 'I do not criticize. But let me do the fighting. You be girls . . . women, be women if you must grow up. I will take the blows.'

Pietar snorted. 'You are as full of yourself as any boy, dear sister,' she said. 'But I wish you would not go. You are drunk now and think yourself invincible, but in the wild with the Hawk Girls and the storms and the snows, what will you do?'

Istar said, 'Have some more to drink, you two. You worry too much. I can take care of myself.'

Hunting the Sekk

Jakse startled from an inadvertent sleep just in time to see the Sekk pass like a shred of moonlight. A hot flash of warning flooded his veins, and the dream of the Floating Lands and the host of Night snapped like a frozen branch and fell away from his thought. The Fivesisters Lake road had garnered a bad reputation for Sekk attacks as far back as the time of Jakse's great-great-grandfather Sanjorse, who had lost an uncle and two brothers in a Slaving ambush only a stone's throw from the cave that it was now given to Jakse to guard: the cave of the lake of candles. Xiriel was nominally in charge of the investigation of the Everien site, but Xiriel had gone to Wasp Country to meet with Kassien, and anyway Jakse had found the cave. This fact, combined with the stories of his great-grandfather about *his* father's failed attempt to hunt the Sekk down in these hollow fells, brought a sense of personal responsibility – possessiveness even – to Jakse's guardianship. And if Xiriel was interested in the globes of light in the cave, in the water-that-was-not-water, and in the anecdotal connection between the lake of candles and the Floating Lands, then Jakse was more interested in the fact that, from time to time, a Sekk walked out of the cave by night and made its ghostly way from the Fivesisters Lake road to whatever human settlement was most convenient.

The Sekk stalked the Snake people, and Jakse stalked the Sekk. Sometimes his efforts took him miles from the Lake; other times, he lay in wait by the cave entrance hoping to catch them going out or coming in, but the Sekk seemed to have an instinct for knowing when he was there, and avoiding him. On this occasion, Jakse was hiding in a thicket in the woods near the bottom end of Fivesisters Lake, waiting to see whether the Sekk he had been studying would follow its usual pattern and pass by this place. It was very dark, and Jakse did not see the Sekk until it had nearly gone by. To his surprise, another man followed it – a Snake warrior, in fact, but not one of Jakse's team.

Jakse watched his kinsman glide across the snow on his skis with hardly a sound. He passed Jakse's hiding place so close by that Jakse could see the icicles dangling from the dagger between his teeth, condensation from his breath frozen in the stark air. Moonlight made his features sharp, and Jakse recognized a younger cousin grown to manhood: Lise, a junior officer of Ajiko's who was apparently now fighting for Tash. Jakse did not remember seeing Lise in the aftermath of Jai Pendu, and assumed he must have been one of the ones who returned – at Lerien's orders – to a home already conquered by the Pharician, Tash. The bitterness of that trade, Everien's young men in exchange for the goodwill of Hezene, had never struck Jakse more personally than now. Lise ought to be with *him*. Or at least he ought to have been assigned to his home village, where he might have helped prevent this Sekk outbreak near Fivesisters Lake, instead of being forced into servitude at Jai Khalar under Tash, who would never understand the Clans. Jakse fought the strong impulse to step out into the path and hail his cousin. Instead, he followed him at a safe distance on a parallel through the young wood.

Lise caught up with the Sekk in a glade where a frozen waterfall now announced its presence only through the faint gurgling of water beneath its still exterior. There were many footprints here in the snow, and Jakse guessed that the Sekk was tired, and this worried him. It was still not clear to him how the Sekk hunted or rested or sustained themselves against the cold, and he had come to believe as Xiriel had that Sekk subsisted on the souls of men they Enslaved for all forms of nourishment. Lise was about to ski right into its den.

The young man stopped on the edge of the glade and hailed the Sekk.

'Brother of Night, turn and answer for your crimes. I was your Slave but I never will be again. I will send you back where you came from, for ever.'

Jakse snorted at the misplaced eloquence, and the Sekk turned and cast fell eyes on his cousin. A glamour came over its expression as though the moon had turned suddenly full on its features; but the moon was now clouded and the night was dark. Its throat trembled and it began to sing.

Jakse went into the mindset he had been taught to employ in the presence of the Sekk, performing complex mental arithmetic so as to distract himself from the effects of its spell, which although not directed at him, could Enslave him all the same. In between calculations he gauged the distance between himself and the Sekk and between himself and Lise. If he didn't move quickly, Lise would turn against him and then the Sekk would have what it really wanted: Snake killing Snake, and it looking on from between the moonshadowed trees.

Before he could move, a flight of arrows came in fast succession from several directions at once. One struck Lise in the calf and he stumbled; the others hit the snow before the Sekk in a harmless scattering. The Sekk moved toward Lise, still singing, one hand extended as if to touch him. Jakse knew that it was hoping to lure the archers out from their positions in the trees, and even as he performed square roots and mental trigonometry, he asked himself whether he would be equally vulnerable if he aided his kinsman now. He decided that he would, and broke from cover anyway.

Jakse was not a good swordsman, but he had a steel net that had not been rusted nor damaged by the cold, and he cast it over both the Sekk and Lise. Even as he did so, another volley of arrows fell about him.

'Help me!' he cried into the night in general. 'I am a friend! Come and kill the Sekk while I hold it.'

The Sekk was still singing; grimly Jakse wrapped the net tighter about it, kicking at Lise to get him out of the way of the barbed strands. Lise's blood soaked the snow and he was groaning and panting, out of his wits as far as Jakse could make out. An arrow hit the Sekk in the shoulder and Jakse screamed, 'Come in and kill it or it will have me, you fools!'

They came then: two Bears wielding swords. The first took off the head of the Sekk and the second put the point of his blade on Jakse's chest.

'Who are you? Are you not a Slave?'

'No, I'm not a Slave! That's my cousin, Lise. See to his wound, and shake him out of his madness before we have real trouble. Are there more Sekk hereabouts? What direction have you come from?'

The Bear fell back before the hail of questions.

'Jakse!' Lise cried, staggering to his feet. 'I thought you were dead.'

'I am with the rebellion,' Jakse said, dragging his net back into his grip and arranging it for reuse. He could get at least two of them with one throw if necessary. The lacerations wouldn't kill them, but they would be tangled up and unable to pursue him if he fled.

An arrow hit the snow at his feet.

'We have four Wasps with us,' said the Bear who had slain the Sekk. He averted his eyes from its body, which was dissolving into the snow as though made of molten wax. 'Do not think of fleeing, or they will shoot you.'

'Where are your Pharician keepers?' Jakse sneered, hoping to appeal to their Clan pride.

'We have been sent out to save the people of Snake,' answered the second Bear. 'I am Uven and this is Bellen. We have more men at the end of this canyon.'

'Tash sent you.'

'Yes. Tash no more wishes to see the Sekk take this valley than you, rebel. Do you know that your activities have done as much harm as good? Do you not think of how our people are to be fed, or who will protect them from the monsters of the Sekk?'

Jakse spat.

'You are a former Slave and a pawn of Lerien in his game of double-bluff. I am a Snake and have never compromised my allegiances. Moreover, if you join my band I will show you the source of this latest rising of the Sekk. I know where it is, but I lack the men to contain it.'

'Show us, then, and we will contain it,' Uven said proudly. 'We will refrain from capturing you if you prove true in your information.'

'Capturing me?' Jakse scoffed. 'We are brothers, at least in this. Have the Pharicians charmed you with their southern herbs?'

'No, but you are outnumbered and I don't like your fresh mouth. Bellen, bind his hands.'

Jakse stood back. 'That isn't going to happen,' he said softly, and the chill air was still with the awareness of a standoff.

A slight figure emerged from the trees, light enough not to break the crust of snow.

'Let there be no fighting among men of the Clans,' said a female voice. 'We can work this out. Come, let us leave this place, for the curse of the Sekk works on us here, surely.'

Jakse stared at the woman. She was wrapped in furs and carried a bow, and Lise, bleeding, turned to her and said, 'Dario, you are ever the diplomat. Very well. Let the Honorary win the day.'

'Dario!' Jakse took two faltering steps toward her.

'Yes,' she said smoothly. 'I remember you, Jakse. I left my children with my aunt's family and took up the bow to defend my people. But Tash mixed us up and reassigned us, so I am in Snake Country now.'

'I don't believe it.'

'Everien is full of Honoraries,' she answered. 'When men die, women must step in and act. Come quickly now, before there is another fight.'

'Come where?' Jakse said. 'Where are you taking me? Will you not consider my offer, and come to my camp?'

'The lion invites the lamb to the slaughter?' Dario laughed.

'No,' Jakse said gently. 'And you know that you and I are not enemies. How could we be? All of us are Clan, and all of us oppose the Sekk.'

Dario thought for a time. 'You say you have found their source?'

'Yes.' He did not tell her that Xiriel had made him promise not to do anything about the cave until he could return.

'Take us there,' she said decisively, and he pointed the way.

She led them off through the snow with a certainty that impressed Jakse: Here was a woman greatly changed from their first meeting, when everything she had had been robbed from her by the Sekk and she had been reduced to hiding in the forest with her children, shooting at everyone who came near. Jakse's initial surprise at the respect tendered the Honorary by seasoned fighting men soon yielded to the realization that she, unlike they, had resisted the spell of the Sekk. In her smaller, weaker body was a more powerful will. She had never succumbed to Night – for that fact alone, they must respect her.

Dario also possessed the tirelessness of true conviction. She led them far down the canyon.

'I assume your men are following us in some way,' she said to Jakse when they had paused briefly to rest. 'Or you would not comply with me so meekly.'

'I hope to convince you to join us,' Jakse answered obliquely.

'Politics do not interest me. I am happy to hunt the Sekk. It is more simple that way.'

'The Pharicians pass out their women amongst each other like men trade horses. Would you like to sit indoors with only other women for company, and none of you having the right to speak or decide your own affairs?'

'I would like to sit indoors,' she said drily. 'But I do not think that will be my fate! As for the company of other women, I am familiar with it, for so many of the men have been killed in Ajiko's wars.'

'Ajiko was a lover of Pharice.'

'Stop trying to make arguments with me. I can still have you shot any time I please.'

'Bellen will not kill me, nor his brother Uven. I saved their lives.'

'We were about to shoot the Sekk when you interfered.'

'You would have been too late. Hesitation is fatal.'

She adjusted her bow on her back and set off again. 'Save your breath,' she advised. 'It's going to be a long night.'

Tyger Pass

Grietar's army were a ragged lot, but at least he had equipped them well against the cold, and his seneschal had packed sufficient provisions for the hardest of mountain journeys. The seneschal had made it clear he thought Istar and Pentar were mad to attempt such a journey, although he was careful not to say so in front of his lord.

Even Istar had to admit that the first few marches were hard. She had not had an easy life since Jai Pendu, sleeping more often that not under the sky or, with luck, a tent, and eating what she could of what the land offered or the supplies of villagers, which tended to be scanty. She was usually either cold or hungry and sometimes both; but the time spent in A-Tar-Ness had put flesh on her frame, pillows beneath her head, and a certain ease in her bearing that came from knowing she was among friends and could let them watch her back. When her feet began tramping up the road at the head of the line of men, she found that her calluses had softened and her back objected to the weight of her pack. The dull ache in her head and neck, a consequence of last night's festivities, didn't help, either. Yet her muscles were fresh and she was uninjured, and after a few hours she had got used to the cold. Pentar exhorted Istar to push the men hard, to feed them little, and to treat them harshly for the first phase of the journey, and she did. She didn't feel at all secure of their loyalty to her, and if anybody was going to drop out or cause trouble, she would rather that he do it now, while they were still in well-known Seahawk lands, than later after they had begun their ascent up the wintery Tyger Pass. But there were no major protests. The men were being well paid.

Birtar walked with Pentar and Istar, his face set in bitter lines that made him seem his father's age and not the bare twenty-five years that he was. He was to lead them to the caravan. When his family had expressed shock at his desire to return after two months of hardship in the pass, he only said that he could help the team make it across, for he knew where the worst avalanche spots were.

'Why could the Sekk not take me?' he asked Istar. 'It was my doing that Thietar was there at all, for all I was in love with Lyntar and wished to rival Grietar in winning her favour. But no woman, not even your sister who is precious to me, no woman is worth the death of my little brother.'

287

'The Sekk are terrible,' Istar answered, feeling as though she uttered meaningless platitudes but unable to think of any words that would offer comfort. 'You must realize how lucky you were to have escaped, and try not to blame yourself for what you could not do.'

He nodded without conviction. 'Istar,' he said. 'If you can kill this Sekk, I pledge all my family to you. Nothing can make us whole again, but to know that this thing which Enslaved my brother still walks, still haunts the snows . . .'

'I will kill it if I can,' Istar answered quietly.

Birtar nodded again, swallowing against emotion this time. Then he fell back and walked with the other men.

Toward the end of the second day, snow began to fall. The days had begun to lengthen again, and the time of endless twilight had passed, but they still had insufficient light most of the time, and the snow-laden clouds flattened what illumination there was, making it difficult to judge distances or even perceive the contours of the snow.

'What a terrible place,' Pentar said to her, hitching up his shoulders and shivering. The mountains' personalities seemed to grow larger the higher the army climbed. It was as if they were entering the territory of giants, and they were now doomed to be forever dwarfed by everything around them: sky, mountains, wind, cold. Nothing seemed to be small, and even birds were rare at this height.

'I like it,' Istar said. 'Ah, Kassien would be happy now. Look at that ice field up there. If I were Kassien, I'd be scaling it right now to get a better view round the side of this mountain, and perhaps even glimpse the place whence the skeleton came.'

At the mention of Kassien's name Pentar didn't blink, but there was an almost imperceptible stiffening between them, for he was disappointed in her for thinking of Kassien. But he only said, 'Do you believe this tale of a skeleton, then?'

'Why shouldn't I? It is well known that the Pharicians gave Grietar a large sum. They had to pay for something.'

'But . . .'

'But what?'

'I don't know. It seems insane that they should care about a skeleton. He must have sold them something else. Or . . .'

'I know what you're thinking,' she snapped. 'That he has only given me this army to get me out of the way, that he may have my sisters. But the rest of the Clan will not stand for it, and I own his men. Anyway, if that had been his intention, surely he could have done it before I arrived.'

'Unless he was hoping to make a true alliance with your house, and changed his tack only when he saw you had no such intentions.'

Istar groaned. 'What are you saying? Have I done the wrong thing? Why didn't you voice these doubts before?'

'No, I don't mean to say you've done the wrong thing. I simply can't understand this business about the skeleton. The location of the caravan where Thietar was killed is only just across the mountains from the head of Petrel Fjord, but how did the Sekk know about the caravan and why did it care? It was busy wiping out Ranatar's milling business and then Ranatar herself. Why did it not sail to A-Tar-Ness and have its way there? Why go over the mountains to the caravan?'

'Maybe they don't know how to sail,' Istar said.

'Or maybe it is wishful thinking for you,' Pentar put in gently. 'Maybe you need it to be the same Sekk, so you can have satisfaction from it. I have never heard of a Sekk dressing as a Clansman. Unless it was an Enslaved Clan warrior, being controlled by a Sekk at some distance.'

'Aye, and what warrior would it be? Have you ever heard of such a man?'

'No, but I don't know every Seahawk. You and I have both spent our years mainly in the valley of Everien, not in Seahawk Country.'

'It doesn't matter what Sekk it is,' Istar said. 'I am pledged to destroy them all.'

He stiffened again. She knew he didn't like the hate in her voice. She added, 'I am not a healer, Pentar. I have told you a thousand times if I've told you once.'

Pentar said nothing.

'You have a wife!' she railed. 'Why fixate on me this way? Let me alone. I am a man or a half man and it cannot be helped.'

Still he said nothing.

'Pentar, do you think Kassien will become king?'

She didn't look at him as she said it, but out of the corner of her eye she saw him turn to scrutinize her.

'Possibly. Lerien supports him. The Wolf Clan supports him. And you . . . It all depends on whether they can take back the Fire Houses, and Jai Khalar.'

'They?'

'We. You know what I mean.'

They made good time trekking up-country, and Birtar led them by the same route that he and his brothers had taken. When the sky was clear Istar once saw a seahawk high over the pass – a good omen, Pentar said, as the birds didn't often travel so far inland. But when it was snowing she sometimes saw other things. She thought it was her imagination at first, for no one else noticed. Sometimes through the curtain of snow she thought she saw a small figure moving; but she could never be sure, and the visibility was generally terrible in the dusky, snow-filled afternoons.

But on the eighth march, while the others were resting, Istar went some distance away to relieve herself in privacy, and then she saw human tracks some hundred paces uphill and to the southwest of the army's trail. They were too small to have been made by any of her men, and too distant from the main track. So now she knew that Pietar and Lyntar had been right. The Hawk Girls were stalking her – or following her, anyway. They were tough souls to survive up here unaided, Istar thought, and began to wonder whether there wasn't something supernatural about them. On the clear days she looked for them intently but never saw them. They seemed only to be there on the days when snow obscured her vision.

As for Birtar and his brothers, their tracks had been covered by snow, and the sky continued to dump on the marchers, but it didn't stop them until they were about halfway across the pass – half a day's march, Birtar estimated, from the place where Thietar had found the caravan.

'The snow up there is too heavy,' he said. 'We saw a couple of small avalanches from the other side where we holed up in a cave, but I think there could easily be more if this snow doesn't stop.'

'What cave?' Istar said, and he pointed to it. 'Is it big enough to hold us?'

'Probably. Or we could break up into two groups. The hills are full of holes, and some of them have heat from underground vents, just like Grietar's house. We keep caches of food and wood up here in case of emergency. We used all the supplies in the cave where we waited for the weather to clear, and I have brought stocks to resupply it.'

She was surprised when she saw the size of the cavern, which had an inner chamber where some fire from below the earth radiated dry heat. It was not pleasant, but she imagined that with enough food you could last quite a long time in here, whatever happened outside.

'Good. We'll camp here until morning, then continue on fresh. Let them have extra rations and fires.'

She and Pentar drew out the brandy Utar had given them. They meant to have only one cup each, but in the relative warmth of the inner cave with torchlight all around and the crowd of men all laughing and joking, one cup turned into six before they lost track.

'Neither of us is thinking about tomorrow,' Istar said. 'I suppose it will come soon enough.'

She couldn't wait, and he knew it.

'Why are you so good at fighting the Sekk, Istar? Come, we are both drunk – tell me how you do it.'

Istar laughed and clicked mugs with him.

'You are remembering how you beat me, Pentar, in swordplay. Is it true?'

He leaned his head against her shoulder and said, 'You know I do not insult you, do you not? But you are smaller and weaker than most men, and as fiery as you are you will never have the drives of a man.'

'I have more drive than plenty of men I could name!' Istar protested. 'I am stronger than some as well, especially in the legs.'

'Yes, but you are only twenty years old, and even the most ferocious female settles down to mate sooner or later.'

'I don't want to mate you, Pentar.'

'I was only going to say that you should not be as good against the Sekk as you are. You have destroyed what others could not. You withstand their Slaving spells. How do you do it? I know it isn't brute strength, but what is it?'

Istar wanted to say, 'Will', or 'The power of the mind', but the alcohol in her blood made her too honest. She shrugged.

'I don't know.'

'Could it be Chyko's blood?'

'Maybe. Or maybe it's sex.'

'Sex?'

'They use sex to lure you, don't they?'

Pentar looked wary. 'It's not so simple.'

'No, it's not so simple. But I am not a man to be seduced by a voice or eyes. I see a Sekk, but it doesn't affect me. Not the way it affects most people. I perceive them, but they don't reach into me. That's the only way I can explain it. I have tried to make love with a woman, and I didn't really mind it – don't blush, Pentar!'

'I'm sorry, I just . . . ah, we are drinking, why not be frank?'

'Exactly. Well, I did it, and it was pleasant, but I wasn't moved. Maybe I have no sex. Maybe being an Honorary spares me that burden.'

Pentar looked thoughtful. 'Sex. That might have been part of it, but the feeling I had with the Sekk I have never had with a woman, though I have heard it spoken of. It was a . . . a brightness, a silence, a—'

'Death,' said Istar ominously, and then burst out laughing. 'Ah, I don't know. I don't know why they can't get to me so easily. But I am happy to fight them, and if I can get closer to them than you, if I can destroy them, then I'm glad.'

But her voice caught and she felt tears in her throat, though she didn't know why.

'All right,' she said at last. 'I'll tell you why the music of the Sekk is really so seductive. It's because it imparts an order, a building up of things to some climax and then to peace. And this order, it's deeply illusory.'

291

'How eloquent we wax,' said Pentar.

'I've never waxed an elephant,' Istar said, puzzled. 'I think my arms would get too tired.'

'Go on! Go on, wiseguy! What about the music?'

'Sekk music,' Istar propounded, 'removes the dirt and the senseless repetition that we are doomed to. You know: wake up, eat, shit, take a bath . . . but the music exalts us. It makes us believe we are more than ourselves.'

'Hmmm. You could be right.'

'I am not more than myself, Pentar. But I wish I was. That's how they'll get me in the end, if I'm not vigilant all the time.'

She spilled brandy on herself and licked her fingers, giggling.

'Always vigilant,' she repeated, and Pentar belched supportively.

'Ah, that's enough drinking, Starry. Let's go to sleep.'

Istar woke from a dazed and drunken slumber to find an animal sniffing her face. She startled, stifling a cry as she jumped back from the creature.

It was close to her face, smiling, and she realized with shock that it was a human being. Its teeth were yellow and black, ruined and broken. Some were the deciduous teeth of a juvenile, and some were full-sized adult teeth. The hair hung in greasy clumps and the body had begun to exude adult smells.

It was one of the Hawk Girls. Istar took in the fact that everyone else was asleep, the fire burned low, and the wind howled softly outside to mask any sounds the girls had made in creeping in here. They were only sketched in the air, these girls, as if they were made of pencil and aquarelles, and they moved fast and jagged.

'Are you hungry?' Istar whispered. 'Are you cold?'

Although she had felt pity for them since the first time she saw them, she also realized that she was afraid. They were as wild as wolves, and their eyes were full of secrets.

The other one had already helped herself to a haunch of meat, and now the two crowded round her, poking her and then jumping back.

'You. No Seahawk.' And the younger one pointed to her braids and paint. She crossed her finger in front of her face. 'No Seahawk.'

The language was not Clan common, but a heavily accented dialect of Seahawk that Istar had to think twice about before comprehending.

'Istar Seahawk,' Istar answered in a whisper, smiling and pointing to her Clan paint.

Then the two of them started running in circles round the fire, singing, 'Chyko Chyko Chyko Chyko.' The older one clasped her hands in front of herself as though cradling a belly and swayed, rolling her eyes back.

'No Seahawk!' she cried again. 'Killer!'

Istar didn't know whether to laugh or take them both by the scruff of the neck and shake them. She was wanting to do the latter, but the two of them had run out of circles and now collapsed together in a heap, giggling.

Why does no one else wake up? Istar found herself thinking. *They are making enough noise for a whole flock of seahawks.*

'No Seahawk,' the younger of the two said again. She stuck her arm out, pantomiming stabbing something with a sword. Then she laughed and both of them ran away.

Istar sat in the dimness, her head aching and spinning from the alcohol, wondering if it had been a dream. Guilt filled her. She had killed the Seahawk at Jai Pendu. She had no Animal Magic and she had no true people. Even Tarquin had left her.

Wasn't that what they had been saying?

She slept again, and when she woke the whole camp was stirring, so she couldn't check for tracks, or missing pieces of meat. And she wasn't the only one with a headache.

There had been considerable snowfall since Birtar had returned from the doomed hunt, and neither he nor Pentar liked the look of the mountainside above.

'Everybody keep as quiet as you can,' Pentar instructed the men. 'It's ripe for an avalanche.'

Whatever was there, Istar thought, looking at the looming white wall, was probably buried deep by now. The sky was clear and hard, but the weather guide Grietar had sent with them shook his head pessimistically when they asked him for his report. 'The birds are getting ready for snow,' he said. 'It looks clear now, but there will be a storm before nightfall.'

'Then let's act quickly,' Istar said.

They decided to approach the area Birtar indicated from the Snake side of the pass, so that if a storm came they would at least be on their way down into safety – and because from the way the snow lay, Pentar said they would be safer from avalanche if they stayed to the northeast side of the crevasse.

'I will go with Birtar alone,' Istar said. 'If there is a Sekk, better to keep the men away from it.'

Birtar led her up through deep, crusted snow and across a steep ice field.

'There are many caves up there. Some of them are hunters' caves that we provision in case we get caught out here in a storm and have to hole up for a month or so. But they are also ideal hiding places for Sekk. Ah.' His voice dropped in pitch. 'There is the caravan.'

The sky was clouding over. Istar scanned the cliff face and saw vertical sheets of ice interspersed with snowy ledges and the dark mouths of caves. The mass of snow that Pentar had been worried about was poised just above the area Birtar indicated. And near its lower edge, just visible behind a white-covered boulder, she saw two dark heads.

'Go back, Birtar,' she said suddenly. 'I'll take over from here.'

'Are you sure?' He was unwilling to leave her alone.

'The Sekk had already seen you. In case it is waiting up there, it is better that you are not here. Go back and wait with Pentar. I will return soon.'

She proceeded, finally gaining some shelter from the wind in a group of ice-clad rock formations. She paused, wiped her nose with the back of her glove, and received a stinging blow to her backside. She whirled.

Istar thought she heard a giggle, but she couldn't see anything move. She carried on, and a moment later four ice pellets hit her in quick succession. They hurt, and she was angry, thinking that they would hurt even more if they had hit her in the face.

'Come out, you little sneaks!' she called, and in answer a chunk of snow slid from a shelf above and crashed onto the ice. Shit. She had to be quiet. From this vantage she couldn't see what the snow-dervishes were doing, but if there were White Screamers about it was best to be silent. So she carried on, dogged by small missiles fired by the invisible and inaudible Hawk Girls.

She came to a deep drift that she would either have to wade through, or climb above, in order to get past. She looked back and saw her men arrayed on the snowfields below. As she turned, she saw one tiny figure set apart. He waved to her. *Pentar.* Between her and Pentar there were whirling dervishes made of snow skating along the surface of the smooth pitch, and she recognized them as telltale warnings of White Screamers. One shriek from a White Screamer and the whole mountain-side would come down on her head. She hoped Pentar would have the sense to stay put, but she had a premonition that he would follow her up here. He was simply incapable of following orders.

She turned and began to climb. The caravan, assuming it hadn't been buried, could not be very far now. Chunks of rock and ice flew at her from above, and she stopped to curse the Hawk Girls.

'Leave me alone, you little shits!'

'No go, Istar Chyko no-Seahawk!' said a little-girl voice, and Istar reflected on the variance between the sound of the voice and the behaviour of the speaker. Now she thought she heard a high keening on the wind, which was not a good omen when White Screamers were in the vicinity. But she did not expect to come around a corner in the rock and find herself face to face with one.

It looked like a blown garment, a virginal filmy negligee perhaps, or a bit of lace. It was halfway between smoke and ice, and it had a voice like breaking glass. It drew breath and screamed in her face, and she felt the whole mountain move in answer to its cry.

Humans Always Bleed

Istar was luckier than she deserved to be. She found herself carried along the crest of the snow and then deposited in a pile of vertical boulders, where she caught and held fast just in time, for the snow around her was carried right off the edge of a cliff. She was wedged in tight and had to squirm out of her pack to get free. Below her, the snow was still moving, and she watched her army rushing down the Snake side of the pass, running flat out to get away from the advance of snow and boulders. Up here, it was curiously still. Istar felt she was not in the same world as her own men, below. She wondered if what she felt was the same detachment that the seahawks felt when they sat on the cliffs and watched fishermen drown. She decided that possibly it was.

She celebrated being alive by squatting and pissing in the snow, then consuming a large chunk of butter and a handful of dried fruit. She stuck some cheese in her pocket and set off up the mountain. She was not seriously deterred. Actually, she felt better for having been broken in a little bit.

The caravan had not been caught by the snowslide. She had no trouble finding what was left of the vehicle and its escort. It had been snowed on, but wind had subsequently blown the snow into drifts, exposing some of the scene.

The body of her kinsman had frozen where it lay, eyes staring, hand still clutching the carved Seahawk dagger. Birtar had been superstitious to leave it, she thought, for the power of the Slaving lay with the Sekk, not its victim. A sadness came over her at the thought of Thietar abandoned here; even the carrion crows had not come for him, and the corpse was frozen solid.

She looked around. She was in a hollow in the snow, where she felt vulnerable for she could not watch the approaches. She had not seen anything of the Hawk Girls since the avalanche, which she suspected them of precipitating. She searched the caravan quickly until she found the box of bones that Grietar had been paid so much for. Without ceremony, Istar gathered up the bones and bundled them into her cloak. Now she was well and truly cold. The sky was white and gravid with cloud, and she was not at all certain that the avalanche was finished, for the snow-dervishes accelerated. Storm was coming.

Istar climbed on top of the caravan to get a better view and there, sitting on the roof, was the Seahawk. Not just any seahawk, not so far from home – no. She knew it with the very first glance. It was the bird that she had run her sword through, the bird that had dragged her from the Way of the Sun and left her in the red crystal where her father fought invisible things.

She was looking at her own act of murder, and it was looking at her. Since Jai Pendu she had had countless dreams about the seahawk, most of them incalculably bad; but she knew she would never awaken from this. It spread its wings and let out a feral, nerve-jarring cry. Istar glanced nervously at the snow wall and wondered if she should put down the bones and draw her sword.

'Don't make me kill you,' she whispered, and as her eyes filled with tears the form of the seahawk wavered and darkened, and the Sekk was there.

He was not like any Sekk she had ever seen. For one thing, she immediately felt she was looking at a person, not an *it* as she had been trained to think of the Sekk. The man was standing on the tilting roof of the damaged caravan half-buried in the snowdrift, in exactly the spot where the Seahawk had perched. He looked down on her from this vantage; but he was already tall, his white hair braided in the style of her Clan and his cheekbones marked with dark green and orange just as hers were. His cloak was thrown back from the powerful shoulders of a swordsman. He wore black trousers, tunic, and gloves, but his cloak was made of snow lion fur, and when it was drawn around him he would be all but invisible in the snow. Now his figure imposed its darkness on the winter scene like an ink stamp on paper. He was big, all muscle – yet streamlined, and although he was standing still he was not static. For all his weight, he seemed volatile, as if a current were flowing through him and at any instant he would be off, moving in some unpredictable direction. He presented himself with legs somewhat apart in a challenging stance, but his blade was strapped to his back and his hands rested on his belt as he watched her. She saw twin puffs of steam flow from his nostrils as he gave a short, silent laugh. He smiled at her. His eyes were ocean green.

Don't look in its eyes. Don't listen to its voice. Don't believe anything you feel. Trust your skeleton and nothing else. The lessons in survival came back to her from childhood. *This is the only way you can survive an encounter with the Sekk. They cannot be resisted any more than a powerful light; but you can shut your eyes to them. You can avoid their infiltration, if you're careful. And lucky.*

He was injured. His tunic was torn in a long gash, revealing blood-stained skin and a vicious wound beneath, oozing blackness. She had

297

never seen a Sekk bleed. She had never seen one that looked so . . . animalian.

Humans always bleed, but the Sekk often do not. If it doesn't bleed, it is definitely a Sekk. If it does . . . it might be human. Or it might not.

Maybe it was the desolation of the landscape, the domination of the snow. Maybe it was the emptiness. But it seemed to her that in the presence of this other living thing, there was something sympathetic.

The facts were laid out before her. The blood on the snow, the bodies picked clean by vultures, the frozen remains of the caravan: These things told the tale as if the events were whispered right into her ear by an unknown onlooker. This Sekk had preyed upon the caravan, and upon the Seahawks who had later come to investigate. It had taken Thietar, kinsman of Pentar, who had managed to wound but not to kill it. Now its eyes were on her like rocks, their gravity weighing on her. The feeling that emanated from it was one of unbearable loneliness. Her breath caught in her throat as he – *it* – as it stepped down from the roof and began to walk toward her. He did not put his hand to the wound, or flinch in pain. Yet there must be pain. Blood was everywhere.

It is a Destroyer, Istar told herself, and knew it was the truth. Yet she could only look at this broken form coming across the snow, at its blood leaking out, at its unsteady gait in which the pain was seen blurring its grace the way rain blurs the view through a window. She kept thinking of a wounded animal. The Seahawk that she once drove her blade through. The snow lion the brothers had been hunting. It wasn't right, this damage. She couldn't have said why.

Somewhere in the part of her mind that could calculate faster than she was aware, she had realized that in the days that it had taken Birtar to return to A-Tar-Ness, and the further days she and Pentar and the men had spent trooping up to Tyger Pass, the wounded Sekk should have either bled to death, moved on to another location, or cured itself. Despite this, it held itself as if freshly hurt. Something was not natural.

Yet this reasoned awareness couldn't change the way she felt. She allowed it to come on. Her boots seems to have frozen in place. Her cloak was still open and the sweat had long since evaporated, leaving her skin to freeze in the dry air. The cold was numbing her body. Something was wrong with her but she couldn't stop herself.

He took another step toward her and she *recognized* him. She knew him but she didn't know from where. She had a feeling of a door swinging open deep into time, as if there were rooms and passages in her life that she'd never explored, and he'd been in one of them all this time, waiting for her to return and find him there.

Behind him she could see the ghostly shape of a White Screamer. She watched as it drew breath. Without turning, he raised a hand to it and it shot off on the wind without making a sound. Istar was stunned. She had never known anyone to command a White Screamer. They were mindless beings.

He was looking at her and he was not a mindless being. His was the Mind that could Understand, and . . . *was this what Slaving was like?*

'It is too hard,' she whispered. She tried to make her hand move toward her dagger. Now she could see who he really was. She could see the face behind the face. In the confused green eyes she saw the honesty.

'I am here,' he said in her ear, though he had moved no closer to her.

She ached. Where was the kill instinct now? 'It's too hard. I can't do it.'

She had already lost. She was falling toward the desperate eyes that couldn't be saved, and the Sekk was singing to her, and the cold all around her meant nothing any more.

From the midst of her daze she heard an awful, blood-freezing shriek – and then, shaking the earth and blotting out the sky, the snow was coming down to the chorus of the White Screamers.

Istar tasted blood.

Someone's hand was around her mouth. She bit down on it and was dragged backward. A knife poked into her belly, not piercing it but threatening to. She felt the sweat and electricity of fear turn all her body afire and she backpedalled furiously, going where the knife forced her, the Sekk forgotten in the metallic thrum of blood in her mouth and the stench of her attacker and the dull arrival of pain as she was clubbed across the face with a length of bone.

'Stupid,' hissed the girl in her ear. She spoke Seahawk. 'Stupid deaf egg! You will be eaten before you ever born, fool.'

She began to struggle and got a thump on the head with the club. She lost consciousness.

She half woke flat on her back, bound across the chest and legs. From the sound of things, the avalanche had stopped. She couldn't move, and for a second she flashed the thought that she was trapped beneath the snow. She began to thrash. Her hands were pinned to her sides and there was a whirring vibration under her head. She woke more fully and realized she was strapped immobile beneath thick furs and that the vibration was caused by the runners of a sledge passing over the snow. Ice had crusted on her lashes and her nose felt frozen. She coughed. The Hawk Girls were towing her at a good clip through fast-falling snow; they had kicked some over her face and this was what had woken her.

'Sekk almost take you,' said the older one in clipped Seahawk.

'He was not a Sekk!' Istar protested. 'That was one of our own Clan, a high warrior of some kind. Did you not see how the White Screamers fled from him?'

'White Screamers belong to him. That Sekk the one we fight. It take many Seahawks above coast. It take father-mother all. It take Ranatar.'

'Shut up, you feather-rat,' Istar said in sudden frustration. 'I know a Sekk when I meet one. He was not Sekk.'

Laughter. 'You Slave already? He Sekk. He Sekk, Istar Chyko no-Seahawk.'

'Why don't you speak properly,' Istar raged. 'What has happened to you?'

'You shut up now,' said the younger one sternly, brandishing a human femur at Istar.

'Fucking beast,' Istar snapped back, helpless and furious. In hindsight, she should have shut up; but she didn't, and to her great shock when she woke up afterward with a bump on her head, the Hawk Girl clubbed her unconscious without the slightest hesitation.

Do Not Steal

Ukili, daughter of Hezene and princess of Everien, reclined in her litter draped in silk, listening to the clever and intricate music of Chee and eating cream chocolates from the rain forests. She was rampantly miserable. The music could not drown out the tramp of hooves and feet or the patter of rain on the litter's covering, which had to be changed regularly to prevent it leaking. She was always cold, and although Chee made her coffee on a brazier lit with hot oil, the drink put her too much on edge and only made her eat more. Ukili was fortunate in that the weight she gained due to weeks of inactivity and bored snacking seemed to deposit itself largely upon her already voluptuous breasts, leaving her legs and belly smooth and neat while adding only a pleasant jiggle to her hindparts – or so her girls told her when she asked them point-blank.

She was in a bad mood, though. They had probably only been saying what they thought she wanted to hear. She popped another sweet into her mouth and swirled the chocolate cream around with her tongue. This whole experience was so boring she felt like throwing something.

'Chee, where is Evra Kiss?' she asked. 'Let us see how his head looks today.'

Chee made a laughing sound. 'It is all black and stubby, the same feeling as a straw doormat.'

For reasons of climate, Kiss had advised all his men to grow their hair out; the shaven pate of the classical Jundun warrior had given way to a coarser look, one which Ukili found unaccountably amusing. It suited some of the men, the ones with straighter hair; but others looked like funny little animals.

'Who is he that he rides on a litter like me?'

'A famous Scholar, yet crippled and stricken with terrible physical infirmities. He is known to Byrd, who says he is a genius. He cannot walk.'

'Give him some of my rations, and send my greetings. A friend of Byrd is a friend of mine.'

After that everyone hated Wakhe. Liaku, who trotted along in the mud of the mule train beside the emperor's birds, had almost fainted when the Scholar was presented to the emperor under the blazing sunlight, for the memory of his servant's molars digging into her fingertips as she handled his empty skull was still a vivid one, and that night of butchery and subterfuge seemed far more real to her than the splendour and fanfare of the imperial farewell. Once under way, Chee had sent for her to instruct her on what rations to bring for her evening snacks, and to demand more mirrors for her cage within the litter of Ukili. Liaku thought Chee a funny, almost perverse bird for preferring a cage to freedom, but then Ukili, too, for all her royalty, seldom peeped out from her curtained litter. When Liaku brought Chee her special requests on that first evening, Wakhe's bodyguard appeared at her elbow and told her to come. She shrank away from the man, knowing that he might not look like Se but he was Se, a cold-blooded assassin.

She could not refuse. Wakhe's litter was bare and dull compared to Ukili's, but the Scholar did have reading lamps and books. He looked up at her with loose, runny eyes like bad eggs, and then he reached out and tapped a rhythm on her shoulder. She leaped back, horrified, and Se laughed.

'You will behave as an ordinary slave,' he said in her ear. 'Trust that when the time is right, I will call on you. For now, do something. When I am ready to send a message, you will know. If one of your birds comes to you from Jundun, bring the bird and the message to me as soon as you can do so discreetly, and not before.'

'Yes.' She didn't look at either of them. She had not been allowed to come inside, but was obliged to scurry alongside the moving litter.

'Do not approach me without some excuse.'

'What about Chee?'

'She is not one of us.'

Liaku glanced at him then, startled.

'She is not intelligent enough. I fear that Hezene sent her with Ukili because he suspects some plot, and he wishes to have a hold over Byrd in the event that Byrd betrays him.'

'Byrd *is* betray—'

'Shh! Mind your impudence. Go now. Keep your head down, and stay out of trouble.'

Liaku did as she was told, shivering, marvelling at her blue fingers and mud-blackened toes, sneezing occasionally and wondering at a world that could turn itself so heartily upside down. Her mother had died giving birth when Liaku was four, and she had abandoned her father almost a year ago now, finding him a useless burden and unfair as well, for he took her egg findings for his own and beat her in the meanwhile. The birds were her allies. And really, they were the best sort of mates to have. Naturally hostile, aggressive, warlike, and cruel, they never tried to trick you into trusting them. They were superior in their way, and

302

they knew it. Liaku preferred to associate with another species if that species, however indirectly, could help her to survive. Nor could she abide human pity, which was simply the blunt end of human mockery but still the same weapon.

Not that she formulated any of these ideas as such. Liaku was nine years old and utterly uninterested in herself except when it came to gratifying her needs. At the moment, she had no sense of security whatsoever, and her old habit of stealing and secreting food or anything else of possible value that she could find was asserting itself. The problem was that she had nowhere to hide her acquisitions. Her beloved chala-and-stick wilderness was far away. Here she was dependent on the handouts of the cook staff, soldiers who laughed at her and cuffed her where she stood in line with her clay bowl and spoon. They talked about her as she gulped down her rations.

'Starveling,' she heard them say. 'Bird filth. Feather ass, flea palace, smelly ghost, darkwing.' She liked the last epithet, for it implied spy. Yet she could not afford to be perceived as a spy, and the nasty old crippled Scholar turned his blind eyes on her always. She wondered if he knew that his real bodyguard had been disembowelled and chopped in little pieces. Yanse watched her also; parting the curtain of his master's litter to check she was walking alongside Ukili's litter as she was meant to, with the result that she began spending more time farther down the line, walking in the beast train beside her avian charges. Then she learned that even Shiror was watching her: He sent one of his special lieutenants to inform her that as a representative of Chee she must be clean and respectful at all times, she must speak Pharician or not at all, she must not steal, and she was to protect the life of Chee above her own, just as Shiror was honour-bound to protect the becurtained Ukili.

Liaku listened to all of this with a blank attitude. The lieutenant, however, would have none of her byrd stupidity.

'What's the matter with you?' he said. 'Presumably you were chosen for this office because you are better than most of your kind. Show some self-respect and answer me.'

Self-respect? It was self-respect that made her steal and lie, avoid humans, and if she had let it, it would have made her kick him in the balls and run.

'Have no other clothes,' she said in a low voice.

'I will have some made for you. Look at me!'

She did. He clicked his tongue. 'You're terrified. There's nothing to fear so long as you can manage to stay honest. Come, hand over the things you have stolen. Come! Shall I turn you upside down and shake you?'

She surrendered her treasures, barely restraining herself from crying bitterly at the injustice: Thievery was her way of life. The lieutenant laughed as the items were produced, passing them one at a time to the boy who had come with him and stood silently a pace behind him.

'Good work, for two days' march.' He put a finger at the base of her neck. 'This will stop,' he commanded. 'If I catch you stealing again, I will kill you on the spot. We are not yet so far from Jundun that another byrd-man can't be sent for. No matter how fond Chee may be of you, and no matter how important the skyfalcon. He may ride in a cage all the way and eat dead meat.'

'He will die if you cage him,' she blurted, shock and resentment overcoming caution.

'Then see it does not happen. If you love your bird so much, and I think you do, you will behave in accordance with the rules of Evra Kiss.'

Liaku temporized at being forced once again to act against her will. She suppressed her anger only by biting her lip and rolling her eyes away, bare feet shifting in place.

'Ah, you are a proud little twig. But you will not steal.'

How could he not understand that thievery was the byrd way – where byrdmen were concerned, there was indeed honour among thieves. You did someone an honour to steal from them, for it meant they had something you valued! Yet she could not explain this concept to the lieutenant. The differences in their social strata prevented it.

'No food,' she said instead. 'No cloth. No nest. Must steal.'

'You will always be fed, just as the soldiers are. No one goes hungry in the princess's retinue. And no one goes about dressed in rags. What else do you need? A bit of gold to make you feel secure? You are not yet a woman and do not deserve it, but I will see what I can do.'

Liaku was so stunned that he was gone and she had walked a dozen paces before she came to her senses. 'Quiz,' she said to her friend, 'this place no right. These people, wrong. Crazy!'

She was even more shocked when, later that afternoon, the boy soldier brought her clothing. He said it had been hastily cut down to her size, but Liaku could see no ragged edges. Everything was beautifully seamed and the fit was only a little too big. In this respect it was useless for hiding stolen trinkets in, actually. She wondered whether she should obey the kind lieutenant. Already she wore more worth on her back than all her nests and hides put together had ever contained. Her food was brought to her by the same young soldier. He had been, Liaku reflected as she sized up his gangly twelve-year-old body and scratched hands, one of those laughing loudest in the mess line. Now he eyed her curiously as he bore food on expensive wooden plates with a silver knife and fork. She resisted the urge to kick him in the shins and run away, opting instead to bolt her food before he changed his mind and tried to takc it away from her. She growled at him as she ate, just as the palace cats growled if they caught a bird and you tried to take it away from them.

Afterward she felt ill. The rich, oily fare given to the officers and household staff of Ukili was unfamiliar to Liaku's stomach, which was accustomed to rice, greens, water, and more often, air.

Do not steal.

It was like saying, 'Do not breathe.'

Yet she looked at Quiz and thought what would happen to him if they killed her, and she stilled her twitching fingers.

The lieutenant was correct about one thing: She was terrified. After the first few days, the cultivated lands of Pharice were left behind. The emptiness of Ristale surrounded her, blunted and reduced by fog but alien all the same. So much earth, so many big heavy bodies around her, and such an adherence to order and routine she had never known. How could the soldiers stand it? They seemed cheerful enough, although when it began to rain they complained.

'Everien – it is a cold and hateful place, the burnt-out end of the world. Its glory is past and it is full of ghosts and monsters, outcasts and runaways, the very worst dregs of the Animal Clans. It is dark and icy. Nothing can grow there.'

And it seemed to Liaku that their words must be prophetic, for rain beat down on the army day in and day out across the plains of Ristale. The cripple Wakhe sat in the litter like a king or a woman, and the soldiers muttered darkly when it was their turn to bear him. Why the soldiers didn't merely abandon the Scholars and let them find their own way without food or protection, Liaku couldn't understand. That was what she'd have done, and gotten a good laugh off it besides. The Scholars got away with everything short of murder, though; and Liaku knew that Se had even gotten away with that!

Se put on an eerily convincing masquerade as Wakhe's bodyscrvant and all-round assistant, a sour-looking middle-aged man called Yanse. Se's job was made easier by the fact that Yanse had apparently been a brooding introvert who kept to himself. At first no one bothered the two Scholars, thinking that each deserved the company of the other; but when after a week the rains had not only failed to abate, but had actually gotten worse, the amnesty toward the pair came to an abrupt end.

The trouble began among the Scholars: specifically, their spokesman and senior representative, Bast, became quite vocal in his protests when he discovered that Wakhe had been allowed to bring his own rations, and they were superior to the standard fare. There had been no fires for several days and Bast was understandably upset at eating stale, cold food on the cold ground in his tent.

'He never should have come,' Bast declared volubly in the middle of the morning's first march. 'The emperor asked for a list of suitable Scholars and Wakhe's name was at the very bottom. Yet whoever amongst the emperor's advisors was assigned to choose the members of the team ignored my recommendations and substituted Wakhe's name for that of my notable colleague, Kan Qika. Now we are without the most skilled of our Everien historians and instead we have to put up with a man who cannot even walk. I ask you, is there sense in it?'

'I heard that Byrd made the decision,' someone said. And in a low voice, another Scholar added, 'Byrd makes most of the decisions at the palace.'

No one said anything for a moment.

'I'm going to complain to Evra Kiss,' Bast declared. 'He should confiscate Wakhe's food and redistribute it amongst us all. And the servant should not be allowed to ride with him, not unless we all ride. My feet are a wreck, and the chill bites into my very sinews. I am sure this was not what the emperor had in mind.'

Kiss came to see Bast when summoned. He listened to the complaints silently. At last, he said, 'I will have to consult with Shiror.'

'Shiror!' Bast cried, getting carried away with himself. 'But surely he is only Ukili's bodyguard. You, Commander Kiss, you are in charge of this army.'

Liaku had been wondering about that for a while. Although Kiss bore a military title in addition to his status as Imperial Scholar, and although he performed all the tasks one would expect of a leader, it was Shiror who possessed the legitimate air of command, for all that he rode alongside Ukili's litter most of the day and was obliged to converse with her.

'That is indisputable,' replied Kiss calmly. 'But with regard to some matters, the wishes of Ukili must be borne in mind.'

'He means, the wishes of Chee and her mate Byrd,' murmured one of the Scholars in a tone that Liaku's well-tuned ears picked up, but no one else seemed to hear. 'They favour that little byrd-urchin, and they favour Wakhe. How ugly are their tastes in servants.'

Being called ugly did not offend Liaku; she was used to it. But she now began to wonder why she truly was here with this entourage. For Chee never sent for her, had little to say to Liaku, and in fact as far as Liaku could tell, barely registered the fact that the byrdgirl existed. The only conclusion that she could draw was that Byrd had arranged for Liaku's presence on the pretext of pleasing his mate Chee. Liaku already knew that Byrd was associated with the Circle, with the murderer Se who now controlled the cripple Wakhe. And Se had not even wanted to accept the mission, or so he had admitted on the night of the murder. It was not really Sc, but Byrd who was using Liaku. But for what? And why?

A week out and Liaku was called upon to send a message. None of her personal birds had come to her, and she was a little worried lest they had become lost in looking for her. The messengers she'd been entrusted with in this journey were simple homing doves, untrained in anything more demanding. But the twenty of her own specials that she had provided to Byrd before she left Jundun were different. Liaku had taught them to find her personally, and they would traverse all the great length and breadth of the metropolis to seek her out. Yet she had never gone so far from Jundun before, nor been absent from them for so long. What if they couldn't figure out where to look? They were smart birds and they ought to understand Byrd's instructions; but they weren't Speakers and they couldn't read minds. Now as she sent the first message from Shiror home to Hezene, she had to anticipate that the emperor would respond. So for the next several days, she was on pins and needles, waiting.

When the familiar silhouette of one of her birds appeared in the sky above, Liaku could have cried. Quiz saw her delight and rose to greet the stranger, who turned and fled in terror. Liaku had to call Quiz to task and run a quarter mile away from the main flow of infantry before her flier would come to her. Then they fell upon each other in an excessive exchange of caresses, and Liaku was so busy feeding the flier grain and praising her that she forgot to bring the message to Ukili. She had caged the bird and it was conversing shyly with Quiz when Shiror's boy came to get the scroll. He was overawed by the sight of Liaku with the magnificent Quiz, and made up for it with extreme rudeness.

'You forget yourself, bitch,' he hissed, and leaped back as Quiz's wings fanned wider than he'd expected. Quiz opened his beak soundlessly to reveal a green forked tongue.

'Here! Here!' Liaku shoved the message at him. 'Don't tell them I forgot and I'll let you stroke him later.'

The boy cast her a look at once angry and hopeful. Then he sprinted off.

He came back only an hour later.

'Chee wants you,' he said, and she noticed that now he looked at her face when he spoke to her, as if she were a person. Liaku fastened Quiz's traces to the byrdcart and blew him a kiss before following the boy up the muddy cart tracks. The boots she had been given were long since mud-caked, but the short-skirted tunic was mostly clean and the brown mud didn't show up much on her bare legs. She spat on her hands and wiped her face like a cat, then examined the bead cap that draped her head, removing a few bird droppings before replacing it and pinning it to her hair. She stuck her finger in her mouth and rubbed her teeth clean, all the while trotting to keep up with the longer strides of the boy ahead. When they reached Ukili's litter, she saw that she need not have bothered.

'Ukili is taking her exercise,' Chee sang. 'See, there she is on her favourite horse, Grassy.'

'Gassy' would have been a better name, Liaku thought, judging by the way the animal was kicking and farting and prancing. Ukili was wrapped from head to toe in white robes that were systematically being altered to match the colour of the chestnut horse as the princess's mount flung up mud and water in great sheets.

'She was bored,' Chee explained. 'And worried about the contours of her thighs. I think she may sleep this afternoon. Come in, Liaku. It's all right. She cannot see you.'

Liaku hesitated. Birds of all kinds, even Speakers, were notorious for neither understanding nor respecting human social symbols or protocols. Byrd was presumably so loved by Hezene precisely because he had a rare perception of status and could lay his compliments on the emperor both thickly and with an astute awareness of what was expected of him. Chee was now showing her true bird colours if she thought so little of inviting Liaku into the princess's litter in her absence.

'Feet dirty,' Liaku begged off. 'Speak here . . . I beg you.' She added the last in an awkward effort to speak proper Pharician as Shiror's lieutenant had instructed her to do. Chee hopped from her perch onto the frame of the litter. She craned her head and tugged a message scroll from between the cushions.

'The main message is on one side. Ukili has read it, greetings from her father. But on the other side are written words too tiny to see. I cannot read, and Ukili's eyesight is not good enough to make out the symbols. Bring the scroll to the Scholars and ask them to give you a glass to make it appear bigger. Yanse surely has one, for his eyesight is atrocious.'

Liaku frowned. She was worrying about Se and wishing she didn't have to go anywhere near him. But Chee thought that she didn't understand the instructions.

'It's just a disc made of glass, ask them to give it to you, or better yet, ask them to copy out the message and send it. Ukili thinks it is secret orders for Shiror, but whatever it is, you must bring it to Ukili first. If the Scholars give you any trouble, send Shiror's boy to me and I will come. Shiror is only a bodyguard, but Ukili is the princess.'

Liaku nodded. She felt duplicitous. Chee was simple and kind, and Shiror had been good to her in his way. She hated Se. If it weren't for him, she might even be able to make a life for herself as an imperial servant.

Then again, it was only because of Se that she was here and not back in Jundun gazing longingly at the waters of Lor's pool. And Chee, for all her apparent innocence, had for some reason waited for that rare moment when Ukili was out before summoning Liaku and giving her this order.

No one was to be trusted. Really, life on the road was little different from life in Jundun.

Liaku could not prevent herself from shuddering when Wakhe looked at her. One side of his face was dragged down as though attached to weights, causing the interior of his right lower eyelid to be exposed, red and shiny. Flies approached the eye and he blinked them away continually in an endlessly repeated random pattern. His body was sprawled unevenly across the litter, taking up a disproportionate amount of space for its size. 'Yanse', his bodyguard, was wedged into the small remaining seat, a food basket balanced on his knees. He smiled as she recoiled at the sight of Wakhe. After the initial, shocked convulsion at the sight of the Scholar's bare countenance, Liaku continued to stare. Wakhe's face was mutilated and his spine was grotesquely distorted, creating the tremorous limp that characterized his movement. For on those rare occasions when Wakhe was seen to move about the camp at night, he looked like a child's post-torture spider, his body parts variously articulated and thrown from side to side like ingredients tossed into soup, bobbing and jockeying for position. Liaku stared and stared. Did Wakhe know that Yanse was not Yanse? Did he remember that night? What had Se told him? Was he now part of the plot, or was he, like her, a helpless victim?

'Enough looking,' said Se in a desiccated voice. 'I did not summon you. What do you want?'

Liaku wiped rain from her face. 'Chee want glass to make writing big.'

Wakhe snorted and smacked his lips. He was truly disgusting. It was said he was a genius, but Liaku had to resist the powerful urge to spit on him and be gone. Within the sleeves of his robe, Wakhe's hands twitched and there was a noise like starlings rattling their beaks against glass. He was trying to communicate. Se ignored him. 'Show us the writing so that we may determine a suitable magnification.'

Reluctantly Liaku surrendered the scroll. In her mind she was riding in the perfumed tent with Chee, and Ukili's horse had run away with her never to be seen again, and Liaku would become princess, as which her first act would be to crucify these two and tan their hides for use as drums in the prostitutes' district.

Se read the message several times, then he tossed a piece of chala and a coalstick to Liaku.

'Send back this reply:

'To Grietar Seahawk,
The Great Scholar has received your message. I will make haste to snake country and take command of the army that emerges from Tyger Pass.
Yours in trust,
Se'

Liaku just sat there. 'I no write.'

'Ah, fuck, give it to me.' Se wrote the message himself. While he was doing so, Wakhe tapped him and went to some effort to get his attention, drumming and poking at Se to no avail. Se made a peremptory signal which Liaku gathered was an instruction to be quiet, but Wakhe soon resumed his demands. Liaku suppressed a smile. After all, Se was supposed to be the Scholar's servant. How would servitude in the bodily functions of this ugly cripple suit a man such as Se?

Finally Se stopped trying to ignore Wakhe and there was an exchange between the two, with Se tapping and so softly Liaku could barely discern his rhythms. Liaku stared at the spiderweb of fine scars that laced Wakhe's throat and wondered what it would be like to be earless and voiceless. No bird could survive that way, she was sure.

Se turned to her. 'Go and send this scroll to Seahawk at once. And here is the translation of the message for Ukili. You are to be silent to her. Tell her nothing.'

Liaku nodded.

'Meanwhile, retain your own bird that arrived today, and send back Ukili's message whenever she commands, but use an ordinary messenger dove. Behave normally and do not deviate from your routine. Shiror watches you constantly.'

Liaku could not help but meet Se's eyes at this. She had thought the surveillance had dropped off. Maybe she was growing soft on rich food.

'Do not befriend Shiror's son, Liaku! It is your only warning. Now go!'

The translation of the tiny print was given to her and she was thrust away, baffled at the revelation that the boy who had been assisting her was the son of Commander Shiror. She had thought Shiror was chosen for Ukili's bodyguard because he was a lover of men, so how could he have a son? The concept baffled her; but more important, her estimation of the rude youth went up just a touch. Liaku came from Jundun, after all. Social standing was everything.

She followed Se's instructions even though her brain was fizzing with questions. She felt unnaturally frustrated and bound in. However precarious her former existence might have been, she had always been free. Now she was merely the well-fed toy of others. Repeatedly she resisted the compulsion to steal, to cut a girth, to jam cart wheels, to pour salt in the beer barrels. She resisted, but she couldn't think she could resist for ever. This good behaviour was killing her.

It was not long before Chee summoned her again, this time to send a message back to Hezene.

'The tiny print, it was a secret message from Byrd to me,' she confided in Liaku, preening. 'Already he misses me and his feathers droop. I have told him to stop whining, for I am cold and wet and have had no fresh insects in all this time.'

Liaku very much doubted that had been the real content of the secret message. Surely it was instead Byrd's instructions to Se. But she soon had other problems.

It was early morning. Liaku was checking on her birds as usual when she heard the chickens' squawking from the back of the pack train change to hysterical shrieking. Someone was killing them. Liaku's messenger birds panicked in their cages, and as she tried to soothe them she craned her head toward the commotion.

Quiz rose from the convoy trailing clouds of feathers. He had a hen in his claws. He rose briefly, then, wings still beating violently, rended it with his talons and beak and dashed in to the ground, where it lay still. Quiz dove in and seized another chicken. The attendants were shouting and pointing, but no one attempted to do anything.

By the time Liaku arrived at the scene and called Quiz down, he had slaughtered six chickens and two ducks. He dropped the final duck at Liaku's feet as if it were a gift, before coming to her shoulder.

'Quiz, why you do this? Troops need food, silly bird. You not even eat these birds.'

Quiz was agitated, but she didn't have time to ask anyone what had precipitated the incident before Evra Kiss was there. Kiss bent and picked up a dead duck, and Quiz screamed at him.

'No, Quiz!' Liaku said in byrd, and clicked at him, begging him to stay on her shoulder.

'Keep that bird under control!' Evra Kiss said sternly, and Quiz gave a feral cry and kept his wings extended. Liaku staggered: Quiz's full wingspan was almost eight feet, and she could barely stand under his weight when he was still, much less if he moved. She saw the fear in Kiss's eyes, and the awe in those of the boy Duor who stood behind him, watching every move the bird made. For the moment it was a standoff between Quiz and Kiss, for Liaku kept her eyes down and said nothing. She had never before had occasion to even meet a soldier, let alone speak to one. Her face was hot and she felt small and squirmy.

Just then Shiror came whistling along down the line. He took in the sight of Evra Kiss with his feather helmet sodden and his silk cloak caked with mud and the dead duck flopping from his hand – the picture of unhappy disarray.

'Mind your manners around that animal,' Shiror called. 'He is an imperial wedding gift and should be treated as such.'

'He is a predator and a scourge,' Kiss answered darkly, and brandished the dead duck. Behind him, Duor stifled a laugh. 'He will kill the other birds if allowed, and he has already slaughtered two ducks.'

'Then we will have duck for dinner. You, byrdgirl! You must hunt him well away from the convoy from now on, hear?'

Liaku nodded, eyes still downcast.

'What's he called?' Shiror asked in a slightly kinder tone, and Kiss rolled his eyes and emitted a soft curse.

'Quiz,' Liaku answered, and when she looked up she accidentally met the boy's eyes. He mouthed, 'Quiz' after her, as if trying to get a feeling for its pronunciation.

'See to it that Quiz causes no harm. It is your second duty, after caring for Chee. I hold you personally responsible for all his actions.'

Liaku looked down again, flustered. How was she supposed to control something so wild? It was foolish of the emperor to think he could make a gift of something like Quiz. It would be like making a gift of the sea, or a cloud. Or lightning.

'Do not indulge her,' Kiss said to Shiror. 'She will get ideas above her station. Duor! What are you looking at?'

'His talons,' Duor answered truthfully. 'They are like daggers.'

'Stay away from them.' Shiror was suddenly serious, laying a hand on his son's shoulder and drawing him away from the bird. 'Liaku, how long before the messengers return from Everien?'

She was not accustomed to such questions and was so taken aback to hear her name used that she forgot to look at her feet when she answered.

'Perhaps one week . . . sir. They should have no trouble to find us on open plain.'

Kiss was staring at her, but he didn't say anything.

'I want that bird kept under control,' he said again. 'Even an imperial wedding gift can ride in a cage if it has a bloodlust.'

'I will mind him, sir, please,' Liaku said in a small, shaking voice.

'See you do.'

With that, they were gone. Quiz hopped off her shoulder and parked himself on the roof of Wakhe's litter. Yanse opened the flap and looked out in irritation, then quailed at the unfriendly aspect of the great skyfalcon. The flap closed and the litter moved on. Liaku trotted beside it.

'You are very foolish!' she said to Quiz in byrd, which she knew only herself and Chee could understand. 'You will get us both in trouble. If you were hungry you should have told me.'

Quiz made a few silent openings of his beak, flexing his whiplike tongue but emitting no sound. She sensed that he had not been hungry; yet there must have been some reason he killed the ducks. Liaku had never seen an animal kill without a reason – except cats, but cats did not believe in rules. She studied Quiz's posture but could not read his behaviour. In a kinder tone Liaku added, 'Don't worry, hatchlet. We will soon reach your first nest, and then you will be happy.'

He watched her with one eye then. One knowing eye, she thought.

Speaking of happiness, Quiz's company brought her more of it than she could make sense of, and she was at a loss to explain it. She had never had any other human with whom to talk about the things that really mattered to her, so she wasn't in the habit of verbalizing her feelings. And so the result of her relationship with Quiz, if relationship was the right word, was a kind of inarticulate joy expressed in everything she did. She walked with little capers and springs even in the icy mud and rain; she selected special tidbits for Quiz with great care, and lavished greater attention than usual on the other birds. She listened to Chee's pointless stories with no sign of impatience, and she even did favours for Se and Wakhe, although it was difficult to hide the revulsion she felt whenever she had to go near either of them.

Quiz never spoke to her. He was not a Speaker. There was nothing of humanity in him that she could see. Yet he had a presence that was better than human. The fact that he existed at all was enough for Liaku, for the skyfalcon embodied everything that was good to her in the world, and it seemed to her that every moment she was near him her breath was half stolen and her heart raced. She even slept with an electrical charge, and she often dreamed of flying, not over the geometrical designs of Jundun, but over the open, tilting heights. She dreamed of places she had never been, and although she could never quite remember the dreams, she remembered the feeling of altitude. She remembered the sensation of freedom.

She wished there could be some way she and Quiz could just leave, make off on their own with enough goods to sustain them in trade until she could find a settlement in need of a bird-tamer – for Liaku was good, and she knew it. Her ego had never been as malnourished as her small body, and even this was beginning to show the good effects of plentiful food. She had more physical energy and better health than she had ever before enjoyed in her life – but there was nothing to do other than walk, and she grew restless. The friendship of Shiror's boy was forbidden to her, and the next time he spoke to her, asking her a question about Quiz in an almost friendly tone, she glared at him and pretended not to understand. Unfortunately this only made him more curious, and she had to apply greater resistance. The boy read her hostility as a challenge, and over the next few weeks the two children waged war on each other with slingshots, theft and countertheft, feigned indifference, and the occasional face-painting-with-horseshit-while-the-other-sleeps trick. Liaku didn't know how to back down from the conflict, and yet her attempts to discourage the boy had the opposite result. Se had said that Shiror watched her. Did he mean, watched her through the boy, just as Se spoke to Byrd through Liaku? Or did he watch her because of the boy? And which side was Shiror on, anyway? Liaku was deeply puzzled. She couldn't figure Se out – for if she had been a shape-shifter who wanted to infiltrate Everien, she would have killed then imitated Shiror, or even Ukili, not the powerless bodyservant of a horrible nasty crippled Scholar who couldn't speak or wipe his own ass and whom everyone hated.

No, she could not figure it out.

Founded on A Cloud

Ristale went on and on, like the drone of a slow dance song played too many times at the end of the evening. Every day that they travelled north it grew colder, until Liaku was walking hip to shoulder with a small donkey for the sake of its warmth. Ukili never came out of her litter, and even Shiror was red-faced and huffing when he rode inspection round the itinerants. Evra Kiss donned furs and paced fastidiously through the mud. He sent and received messages frequently until Duor reminded him politely that Liaku had only a limited number of birds, some of which were reserved for Ukili's personal usage. Kiss turned his gaze on Quiz, who rode on Liaku's shoulders and protected her from wind and rain better than any hat. He even had the grace to take some of his own weight off by flapping occasionally, or sometimes dragging her along with the power of his wings.

'That one should be in a cage. How am I to know he has not been eating the messenger doves?'

Liaku looked at the ground, but Duor answered hastily.

'It is said that the Everien skyfalcon will not suffer a cage. He hunts well away from the camp, now, and scouts ahead to find game for our archers as well. He brings more meat than he uses.'

Kiss grunted and went away grumbling. Liaku swallowed tears. Duor trotted away without saying anything to her, but an hour later he was back with a piece of chicken meat still on the bone.

'Will he eat this?' he asked shyly.

Liaku shook her head, dismayed because now she owed Duor and could not continue ignoring him or tricking him. But if Se found out about their friendship, he would surely punish one or both of the children.

'He eats live creatures only,' she said. 'I no talk you. They say no.' She pointed to Wakhe's litter.

'Ah, stupid old farts. How often does he hunt? What can he kill? A rabbit?'

Liaku laughed. 'Mouse, pigeon, snake, rabbit, dog, small deer, fox, crow, fish . . .'

Duor's eyes widened. 'What about Sheerwater? Could he kill her?'

Liaku shrugged. 'Sheerwater fight back, maybe.'

Duor said, 'I hate cats. They're so sneaky.'

Liaku hated cats, too, because they hunted her birds; but the stow-away Sheerwater was a beautiful silver white with emerald eyes, and she greeted Liaku with a soft miaow when she came to Ukili's tent. Nor did she molest Chee.

'Some people sneaky, too.'

'Yeah, like you! Manure in my shaving kit! I guess you thought that was funny.'

'You don't need shave,' she taunted, and he turned red beneath his walnut skin.

'I do! I've got a beard!' he shouted, and pointed to a huddle of fine hairs on his upper lips. 'See?'

'Oh, that, I thought it dirt.'

He kicked her and ran away before Quiz could retaliate. After that he came to visit Quiz whenever his duties freed him. He kept asking if he could borrow the bird. Liaku refused. Quiz was not a possession. Anyway, an uncomfortable silence had pervaded between her and Se, and she wondered what the shape-shifter would do to her when he found out she'd disobeyed and spoken to Duor.

When he made his next appearance, she told him firmly that she would get in trouble if she talked to him.

'Wakhe is evil,' he agreed. 'They are both evil. Don't be afraid of them, though! My father works for Ukili, and Ukili is a princess. No one will dare harm you or your birds, I swear it.'

She studied his solemn eyes. No one in Byrdland swore anything. To swear was to admit hypocrisy; for everyone had to lie and cheat and steal.

'Is he your father?' she asked. 'They say Shiror boy-lover. Maybe you Shiror boy.'

At that Duor drew back his hand as though to strike her, and she ducked.

'He *is* my father. He married my mother and I am their son. We even look alike. Everyone says so.'

'If Shiror have wife, then why Hezene trust Shiror take care Ukili? Is he eunuch?'

Now he did strike her, and she fell down. No one saw, and she picked herself up with her ears ringing.

'Sorry! Sorry, I take back!' She held up her palm to ward off further blows. Quiz glided overhead and gave a soft croak of warning in the boy's direction. He subsided sulkily. 'Never mind.'

She had half hoped he would stop talking to her after that, but now he rode back and forth between her and Wakhe's litter, giving her reports on the activities of the Scholar and his assistant, for he had picked up on her fear of the two and his fanciful imagination told him that they were plotting to do some nefarious deed to her.

'I will protect you and Quiz,' he announced. Liaku was not reassured by his protection, but there was nothing she could do about it, and for the moment Se seemed preoccupied with Wakhe and the messages going back and forth from Jundun and Seahawk and Jai Khalar. No one saw much of either of them, although much wine was drunk by both judging by the calls on the serving boys. Liaku contemplated poisoning them before they could do something foul to her, but she was too cold and wretched to plot effectively.

The rain turned to snow and ice, and their progress slowed. Duor brought Liaku a fur cloak which she accepted without asking him where he'd gotten it; she was too cold to care what Se did to her now, and for his own part, the shape-shifter seldom poked his nose out from between the curtains of his litter. Shiror had the litters placed on runners and they were transformed into sledges; Evra Kiss stopped laughing as soon as he saw the ease with which the litters were dragged over the flat ground. Ukili was thrilled by the snow at first, but after a week of it, she had had enough.

Liaku agreed with her. Her birds were winter-hardy, and if anything Quiz seemed to thrive on the sharp, diamond-hard air; but Liaku herself was ill equipped for such a climate. She stuffed herself on butterfat and meat in such quantities as she had never eaten in a whole year while living in Jundun, yet she failed to put on weight and her insides always shivered. The slaves took a sickness and a number of them died. No one was allowed in Ukili's tent or litter for this reason. Even her maids were obliged to pass dishes and parcels in and out after they were inspected by Shiror.

'Her life is the most important thing,' he told anyone who complained. Liaku hung on the back of the litter, her feet resting lightly on its frame, so that she was towed across the snow. From this position she heard Chee singing for hours on end. She also received some of the blown heat from within the litter, where the princess kept burning oil in lamps against the protests of Shiror, who feared an outbreak of fire. Liaku listened as he tried to convince Ukili not to use them.

'Wrap up warm, Your Brightness, and you will be safer. When we reach Jai Khalar there will be great fires, I promise.'

'I want to go home,' Liaku heard the princess wail on several occasions. 'This journey is lasting for ever. We're never going to get there.'

'Sure we will,' Shiror answered, but his words were empty until the day the sun came out.

It was afternoon and what was left of the light was behind them in the southwest. The ever-present curtain of falling snow fell away and blue appeared above. Light smashed into the snowfields ahead of them, light so bright that Liaku had to make a slit for her eyes between her cloak, and even then they didn't want to open. Beyond the snowfields, the mountains of Everien appeared suddenly, tall and adamantine. Liaku had seen the gems Ukili wore around her neck and on her forehead, and they were nothing. If you had seen these mountains even once, Liaku thought, no gem would ever thrill you again.

Quiz had gotten in the habit of flying overhead to scout and hunt, and after the initial protests of Evra Kiss, Liaku had not had any arguments about his right to do so. Now he came diving out of the sky and swooped in a large circle over the procession, calling in a wild language Liaku didn't know. Yet her heart was set racing.

At the sound of his cries, everyone turned to look at Liaku, and even Ukili opened her curtains and looked out.

'Is that where we're going?' she breathed. Shiror had to check his horse before he could answer, because Quiz was still spinning out his flight and calling, and all of the horses responded with the same nervous fear. Liaku looked at Shiror standing in his stirrups, working his legs and hands to control the restive horse, and in his flushed face, with the ragged clouds of steam flying from both his mouth and the horse's, and in the show of strength put on by man and mount, she glimpsed how much more of this man there was than the effete bodyguard of a spoiled princess. She wondered what it took for him to defer to Evra Kiss, and remembered the way Duor had bristled over his father's reputation as a boy-lover. Boy-lover or not, Shiror had the magnetism of someone men – and women – would trust. He calmed his horse and bowed to Ukili.

'That is Everien,' Shiror answered with satisfaction, as though he had created it personally. Ukili gave a shrewish little grimace and said, 'Let's hurry up and get there, before it snows again.' Then she pulled the curtains shut.

Liaku looked at Wakhe's litter and saw that the curtains were open on one side. But it was not Yanse who gazed out as she had expected. It was Wakhe the cripple, and his face was twisted in an awful grimace that Liaku could not at first translate. A convulsive wheezing shook his chest and throat with a whistling noise as he sniffed the wind like a dog. At first she thought he was going to be ill. Then she understood that he was laughing.

She was busy after that. Many birds were sent and received in all directions. The mountains appeared and disappeared according to weather conditions, but Quiz indicated that they were nearing the cliffs that led to the sea plateau. Duor explained that the sea plateau was a flat shelf some thousand feet high that could be approached only by a switchback road. Once they had reached the level of the plateau, it would be only a brief journey into the valley of Everien and its guardian Citadel, Jai Khalar.

Despite all their care, Se must have seen Liaku talking to Duor because as they approached the steep trail to the sea plateau and Quiz flew off to reconnoitre, Se summoned her, beat her, told her that all her rations were to be brought to him and that Ukili was to know nothing of the deprivation, and warned her again not to speak to Duor. He then sent her to get Oris, a young soldier of no particular distinction, weedy and cream-tea-coloured with a frizz of dark brown hair and a discreet snake tattoo on his left wrist. She noticed that when they greeted each other, their fingers danced in each other's palms. Another secret language, she thought.

Liaku was instructed to give Oris one of her birds, and she also observed Se slipping a small leather pouch into his hand – a typical purse for carrying gold. Oris grinned and went off. Liaku later observed him speaking to subcommander Inz, and the next day, Evra Kiss and Inz had a meeting in which outriders were assigned to scout the sea plateau. Oris was among them.

Liaku was hungry and sore and seething, so she spared no more attention on Oris (being focused on possible revenges against Se should her opportunity ever come) until the next day, when the main train of the princess's entourage reached the top of the sea plateau. To the right, from the north, a lone figure was sighted walking toward them. Half an hour later, the outriders brought back Oris, covered in mud and with a broken arm. Inz and Oris talked; Inz and Evra Kiss talked. Oris strode down the ranks, a set look of anger on his skinny young face. At the last moment, Liaku realized with shock that he was coming for *her* – and for once she hadn't done anything! She tried to duck away but she was hemmed in by Ukili's guards and before she knew it, Oris had picked her up by the scruff of the neck with his good arm and handed her over to his mates. She was thrown on a horse and ridden off across the plateau in the direction of Seahawk.

She realized that she had grown accustomed to being rescued by Quiz, but now that they were nearing Everien, Quiz had flown off – maybe for good. And if that happened, she would have no protection at all against Se. So when the soldiers reined in their mounts at the sight of a dead horse lying on the plain, Liaku felt panic rising from her guts and seizing her throat.

Then Quiz dropped from the sky and settled on the horse. Skyfalcons are not carrion birds, and Liaku knew Quiz intimately enough to recognize that when he reached his beak into the dead animal's eye socket and swallowed, he was acting purely for effect.

The soldiers shouted curses.

Quiz looked up from the dead horse.

'I'm not hungry,' Liaku said anxiously. 'You no need do this, Quiz.' Her life was worth less than one shoe on the magnificent animal, and now Quiz had killed it because Se had seen fit to cut her rations.

And here came Evra Kiss, moving at a dignified trot on his heavily muscled chestnut charger. From the northeast, the direction of the Floating Lands, Shiror's dark bay appeared, walking. Liaku saw his rider at the same time his rider saw the search party, and the horse broke into a canter. Kiss pulled up and dismounted, adjusting his cloak against the frigid wind that was blowing in off the sea below.

Inz wasted no time in describing how Quiz had attacked the horse and rider. Kiss listened, then nodded in Liaku's direction carelessly.

'Take her and shoot her,' he said. 'Leave the body for the crows, as is fitting. Butcher the horse – the princess can have the best of the meat, the rest goes to the officers . . . and Scholars. Where is the horse's rider?'

'Here, sir.' Oris stepped forward, grimacing from the pain in his broken arm.

'Kill the rider to begin with,' Shiror shouted, arriving among flying clods of turf. He pointed an accusing finger at the young cavalryman. 'I was following you, Oris. You were not riding the patrol you were set. You are ten miles off course at least – where did you think you were going? Seahawk? Or was it just a pleasure outing? That I can forgive, but I saw you jump free and leave your horse for dead. Mayhap the bird was intending to attack *you*. You made no effort to defend yourself or your mount, coward.'

Kiss said, 'It's the *bird's* fault, not the man's—'

'The skyfalcon belongs to our emperor. Therefore it is sacred.'

'Even so, the keeper shall be killed and the bird caged until we reach Jai Khalar.'

'No,' said Shiror. 'I forbid it.'

'On whose authority?'

'On mine,' cried Ukili. Grassy the horse pushed through the crowd, and there was Ukili looking like a pink-and-gold ghost beneath her veils that the sea wind blew so that they whipped and cracked. 'Byrdgirl is under my protection. Bring her to me. And no meat is to go to the Scholars, for they annoy me. Make them walk in the mud. I am sick of you all. I will keep only the company of animals now.'

'Wakhe cannot walk, madam,' Shiror said quietly.

'Who? Oh, the ugly one.' She smiled spitefully. 'Let him ride in his litter then, but no one else. Only he must send me more of his puzzles and games every day, for I require amusement. Hey, byrdgirl! Give me your hand and climb up behind me.'

Fortunately Ukili soon grew bored of Liaku's company, for Liaku never spoke, but she did teach the princess how to make silk webbing with her fingers and how to paint with Chee's shed tailfeathers, and both activities enchanted her for three solid days. Then, for Liaku, it was back to the mud – and Duor's irrepressible interest in Quiz. Now that the hold of Se had been shaken somewhat (for he was obliged to walk in the mud, and although Shiror had not been allowed to kill Oris, the young officer was reduced to walking among the infantry), she was less afraid to be seen with Duor. And their destination was drawing near: white mountains rising out of white fog, so that Everien seemed to be founded on a cloud.

A Mystery Language

'Talk to me, Gialse,' Ixo begged. 'For now I am really afraid. Do I love him? Do I hate him? What will become of this one inside me?'

Gialse had been doing needlework by candlelight, as was her habit. She had developed a squint, and when she looked up in response to Ixo's pleas, Ixo was suddenly reminded of the bizarre contrast between Jaya and Gialse. The latter still looked at Ixo as if she were a goddess, making Ixo feel remote and alone.

'Never mind,' she muttered. Gialse leaped up.

'Do you want tea?' she said. 'Do you want brandy? Shall I draw you a bath?'

Ixo waved her away. 'Sit down, Gialse. Don't pay any attention to me.'

But Gialse, simple though she might be, was not about to give up. She fetched the Carry Eye from among Ixo's silks. She smiled.

Ixo sighed. 'What good will it do?' she said. 'It's only a fantasy. It can't change what happens here.'

Gialse's face was already starting to change as her hands curved around the Eye and she spoke.

In the last days, the weird shapes that were like and unlike animals were coming out of the forest every night. They looked over the garden fence. They looked in the windows. And in some cases, they didn't look because they had no eyes.

I thought about the animal cards and about the symbols I'd tried to understand and duplicate. Some of these creatures looked like animals that were wrong. They had strange aggressions not in keeping with their kind, and they had mixed bodies, and in many cases they did not move like normal things, but in strange jerks and sudden stillnesses. They made sounds that raised the hair on the back of my neck.

And little by little, they were coming into the house.

I had to do something. I got my father's lamp, and I got a knife.

I knew it was my fault.

I had to do something.

There is a long gallery that runs along the courtyard above the sitting rooms. On the inner wall there are paintings and sketches, some highly technical, others artistic. On the outer wall there are windows with large panes of glass overlooking the fountains and grape trellises of the courtyard. I came along this gallery holding the knife before me and calling anxiously for my mother. If I knew my mother, she would pretend nothing was happening even if the earth cracked open at her very feet and fire gushed forth. I had not seen her and I was worried.

The glass shattered and a white, skeletal hand clawed the empty air, missing me by inches as I leaped back with the knife clutched in both hands before me. The lamp flared bright as the winter gusted in and I saw the golden eyes again, irresistible as cool water on a summer's day deep in the silence of the wood where I was meant never to go, but I sometimes did anyway. I felt my lower lip tremble. This creature was unnatural: Its flesh was hard and shining and it moved fast – too fast, faster than earthly things were meant to move and with a precision that made Jihan and all his falcons and even Midnight Blue look like oafs. Yet it was strangely compelling. Almost . . . beautiful, but beautiful like a conflagration, beautiful and awful at once. If I could have watched it from a safe distance, it would have fascinated me for ever. But it was too close, and my bladder threatened to loosen as I flew backward along the passageway, terror-stricken.

The creature did not try to touch me. Yet it pursued me down the gallery. I saw my reflection in the sectioned glass, but not the reflection of the thing that had broken in from the night. I kept backing up, willing myself that I should wield the knife against it if it came too close and invoking Jihan's voice in my mind, instructing me in the fundamentals of personal combat.

'You must attack in between the rise and fall of his breathing, or his movement; and once you begin the attack, you must commit. Hesitation is fatal.'

The apparition had slowed, matching its pace to mine. I backed through the carpeted library and it pursued, silent and inexorable. I could hear myself panting. Cold sweat lined my armpits; I smelt it.

I had reached the other side of the house, the side facing the forest. The thing pointed at one of the windows, and instead of darkness I saw a slanting plane of water, waves tossing and slapping: the sea. I let go the knife with one hand and clapped the other over my mouth in surprise; then, before I could return my gaze to my assailant, I heard a noise behind me. I whirled. There were three more similar to this one, standing quietly in the double doorway to the dining room. As one their heads turned toward the windows, and now all of the windows were filled with daylit ocean, as if we were in the hold of a ship just on the level of the water. In fact it seemed to me that the floor had begun to tilt; the drapes swayed; the house creaked and moaned. I put my back to the portrait of my great-great-grandmother and edged along the wall to my only escape route, the door to my mother's sitting room where she was accustomed to doing her sewing and grooming the cats. As I groped for the handle behind my back, they converged on me, all of them with their bright eyes and their *more-sudden-than-sudden motion and their strange inhuman hands. They had begun to sing. I felt my throat tighten with sympathy, as if it, too, wished to burst into song. I grabbed the handle and turned it, and before I fell back against my mother and her perfume and her exasperation, the nearest of them reached out and touched me, just above the wrist on the inside of my forearm. My mother slammed the door closed and barred it. We could still hear them singing, outside.*

The room was full of brilliant light. The cats were perched on the mantel and bookshelves, two of them huddled in the sewing basket, one kitten hiding under the cold grate in the fireplace among the ashes. The windows were full of illumination brighter than the sun, so that nothing could be seen of the outside, where I knew the garden had to be. I ran to the drapes and pulled them closed.

'Mother,' I said at last, falling into her rocking chair and picking up her knitting, 'it cannot go on like this.'

'I told him not to do it,' my mother wailed. 'He wouldn't listen. Ah, philosophy, I wish I could stab it in the heart. Let all knowledge be dead! We are not safe, not even here—'

'Never mind that now!' I said. 'What can we do? Think, Mother! There must be some way we can fight them!'

She didn't answer, and a moment later the door opened and they entered.

The one that had come through the window and followed me came first. He was black-haired, star-eyed, poetry to see. He stood before my mother and spoke. I will always remember how when he spoke, I could see no tongue, and his lips were expressionless, barely moving. He uttered only three words.

'I am here.'

My mother said nothing. She stood turned in on herself, as if literally in a corner, and she looked up at him with her eyes moving rapidly across his face as if trying to assess something. She began to shake her head in quick small movements back and forth. I could see she was very angry, but I could also see that she wasn't going to do anything.

'Mother! Come, take my hand!' I reached across their cloaked forms, stretching from the rocking chair to reach her. She ignored me. She was shaking. 'Mother!'

He took a step back from her and crooked one finger at her. She shook her head no.

'Mother, come on!' I screamed. 'Why do you stand there? Bite them, kick them, do something, come on!'

At a gesture from the black-haired one, the others moved in. Now they were singing sweetly, a simple melodious tune like a lullaby, only more peppy and cheerful. They calmly took her limbs and began removing them. She stood there like a doll being undressed, only they didn't undress her, they took her flesh away piece by piece, joint by joint, leaving her clothes behind. I saw her lips still set in a hard line as they took her head. One of them threw it up in the air, singing, and it vanished.

I took a poker from the fire and rushed at them, the fencing lessons forgotten and remembered at the same time, for I was not thinking at all about what I was doing, but something of Jihan's teaching must have insinuated itself into the habits of my body because the poker went right into the throat of one, knocking it back and making it shut its bright eyes for a moment. I slipped past it and took a woodsman's swing at the glass door leading onto the garden. There was a bang and the glass cracked but didn't shatter; I whacked it again and again until it broke apart.

Outside in the kitchen courtyard there was so much light that I could do nothing but fling both my arms over my head and run blind. I soon ran headlong into a wall, fell, and then began to feel my way along it, looking for the iron gate that led into the garden. Even with my eyes tightly shut, the light was an agony. Yet there was no heat attached to it. It was a cold brilliance.

I fell again. I crawled. My head bumped into the iron gate and I stood up, clinging to it. I could not endure the terror. I wanted to disappear. I found the latch and opened it, and when I passed through the gate darkness slapped me in the face like a wet cloth waking a sleeper and the nightmare was over.

I was in the dark garden. I could hear crickets and the nightingale. The fountain was trickling feebly and the wind spread rumours of the sea among the leaves.

When I saw Jihan standing by the fountain, I began to cry.

'Listen to me, Jaya,' Jihan said, taking me by both shoulders and gazing deep into my eyes. My heart leaped and I wanted to listen to him, but it was not really his words that I heard, for I was affected by his behaviour, and anyway my emotions were too high-strung that night to begin with. 'You must not flee into your father's books. That's where he fled, and that's where your mother has gone – and probably that is where I will have no choice but to go myself, if they make up their mind to hunt me down and take me. This house isn't safe any more.'

'No!' I cried. 'Jihan, don't leave me here.'

'I don't mean to leave you here. You must cross over.'

'I saw myself in the water! But it was not me. Jihan, I cannot step into that thing. I cannot become it.'

'It was only your shadow, and now you have lost it.'

'What do you mean? I don't understand you, I never have, I—'

'You will live by darkness. Without a shadow the sun can never shine on you. Can it, child?'

'But . . .'

'Go get it!' Jihan urged. 'Find your shadow and follow it, and then the sun will be ever at your back.'

325

I was sobbing. 'You speak riddles. I can't go back into the water,' I said. 'I can't. I'm afraid. I touched the lion-man, and he's chaos! He's . . . he's lawlessness with two eyes. I can't go there.'

'He's only an animal. Only a human like yourself.'

'No! No, I can't.'

'Jaya, if you don't you will make all your father's efforts count for nothing. You are the last one, Jaya. The last human in Everien. All the others are gone.'

'What about my mother?' But I already knew the answer; had known it the moment I saw her among the cats beside the sewing basket. I sniffled. 'What about you?'

'You don't want me,' Jihan said. 'My heart is stone. My hands are stone.'

And suddenly I understood. Jihan reached out and touched a brick, and the house folded up like a pack of cards and he slipped it in his pocket.

'By my father's grave . . .'

'Your father isn't dead. He never existed. He is only a story, but you could be real.'

I clapped my hands over my ears. I backed away, panting, but Jihan just stood there. The garden was full of animal shapes, threatening topiary in the moonless dark. I could hear the music of the Sekk all around the walls.

'Fly!' Jihan said. 'If you will not return to the water, then go find your shadow some other way. Hurry! Fly!'

And then peering at me from beneath the trees I saw my darling, my black charger whose legs and mane and tail had been silvered as if by starlight or something even more refined; but he was ungentle. He was the colour of ice at midnight.

'Blue!' I cried.

And that was how it began.

This.

Whatever it is.

Ixo sighed and put her hands over Gialse's to silence the girl. Gialse woke at once and said, 'Is there any milk?'

Ixo smiled. She found herself gentler when pregnant.

'I feel like a cow myself,' she said. 'And this waiting! Everything is waiting, my life is waiting. How well I understand Jaya.'

She went to get Gialse some milk, but soon after that Tash called for her, and she stayed with him for two days straight. It was not only sex he wanted, but company. He was worried. She tried to get him to talk to her, but he didn't want to talk. He wanted to be distracted. So she sang to him, and told children's stories from her Clan, which he countered with tales from Or. And they sat by the fire eating roast chestnuts and tickling each other. It was the closest Ixo had ever seen Tash come to showing a softer side.

She was with him early in the morning when Kivi came in, eyes averted, bearing urgent news.

'We have sighted Hezene's army in the southernmost Monitor Eye. They have reached the sea plateau and with a little luck from the weather, they will soon arrive. The worst of the storms are over and we will soon have a false spring.'

Tash was in a decisive mood. 'I wish every piece of artillery and military equipment removed from A-vi-Khalar and brought here. Intimidation before the fight is worth many blows during it. We will see to it that Evra Kiss and his men have no creative ideas what to do with so many swords and the blessing of Hezene.'

'What of the unfinished pieces?'

'Let them stay in the Fire Houses, and instruct the smiths to work on them as though everything is proceeding normally. Under no circumstances is Kiss or any of his men to suspect that we do not have full control of the weapons we are creating. I wish the Fire Houses to appear a hive of activity. Keep the men busy building replicas of the weapons we already have! And impress our newcomers with great metal skeletons and bright fires. They will be too ignorant to know that we have been stalled all these weeks.'

Ixo thought this was a clever strategy, and she wanted to tell Tash that she had been working with the Carry Eye and that, in time, she might get Gialse to reveal more of Jaya's Knowledge. For she itched to tell someone this extraordinary story. Yet saying it to Tash would be a betrayal. Mistel was in prison, and her own fate was uncertain.

And she now knew the answers to her own questions. She loved Tash. She hated Tash. Ixo was no longer a creature sure of her place in the world. Everything in her was opposites.

Tash rolled over to get out of bed, and the muscles of his back rippled beautifully. Ixo wondered what it would be like to have such muscles.

Moral Ambiguity

'What is it, Soren?' Kivi knew that his weariness sounded in his tone of voice, and he saw the same concern and worry in the expression of the subordinate who had summoned him. Inwardly he chastised himself for not showing more resolve: It was bad for morale. As he made his way around the elliptical edge of the Water toward Soren, he made an effort to lift his shoulders and extended a hand of greeting, clapping the younger man on the arm as they met, trying to laugh the moment off. 'I must be getting soft. These stairs never used to wear me out so much.'

But Soren was beside himself and didn't seem to even notice Kivi's changes in mood. He kept hold of Kivi's arm and pointed silently at the Water, as if he were afraid he would be overheard by people within the scene it depicted.

'What am I looking at?' Kivi said sharply, and the image wavered. He could see a snowy hillside pocked with black stones and transected by a small stream. There were a number of Clan mountain ponies tied to a stake beside a pile of journey packs, amongst which were bundled a quantity of spears and arrows. One man guarded the ponies, a warrior in the rare silver-white furs of the alpine wolf. He had one axe in his hand and used it to idly slice away sections of snow, then plough them back together. Every so often he glanced up and checked his perimeter; otherwise he was quiet. His dog lay beside him gnawing on a piece of stiff hide.

'It is the border of Wasp Country and Deer Country, not far from A-vi-Khalar.'

'Give me control,' Kivi said, and the image wavered again as he keyed into it, widening the focus of the Eye to include a larger area. 'This is the new monitor tower on the edge of the trade route with A-vi-Sirinn, is it not?'

'Yes.'

'So it used to be a blind spot, and they are using it.'

Soren didn't say anything.

'Have you seen anything else out of the ordinary between Wolf Country and A-vi-Khalar?'

Soren blinked. 'It's a large area. I couldn't say.'

'There are a number of blind spots if you stay high in the hills,' Kivi reflected.

'You think the Clans are sneaking around, avoiding the Eyes?'

'Well, of course they are, Soren,' Kivi snapped. 'It is the only way they can keep their rebellion alive. But it is the middle of winter, and I'm surprised they are abroad.'

'Perhaps it is revenge,' Soren said. 'For what Illyra did.'

Kivi didn't answer. Instead, he said firmly, 'You haven't seen this, Soren. It never happened. If you see future occurrences of this nature, you are not to summon me.'

Soren gaped at him. 'But Tash—'

'I will check in with you from time to time, and then you may speak openly.'

'What about the other Seers?'

'I will assign them to different areas, and I will take over this Eye myself.'

Soren nodded, but there was still an air of indecision in his posture.

'Or do you intend to betray the Wolves, Soren? For I know your people do not love them.'

'My kinsman Kassien is the leader of the rebellion, they say. I would not betray him.'

Kivi nodded. 'Good. I don't think it will come to anything, anyway. You can go, Soren. I'll carry on from here.'

When the younger man had left, Kivi made a sweep of every monitor tower internal to Everien. The task turned up little but snow and desolation, and when he was finished, he was tired. His mind was turning over the question of what the Wolf warrior was doing with so many supplies, alone in a hidden valley that had once been utterly blind to the Eyes but now was partly exposed, since Tash had repaired the broken Eye in its local monitor tower. Returning to the scene, Kivi scrutinized the snow and found tracks leading into the valley and tracks leading out, but all of them buried under the latest snowfall. The side of the mountain blocked a good sized section of the canyon, however, and had it not been for the presence of the guard, Soren or any other Seer probably would not have noticed anything out of sorts.

'Someone's hiding a force of men in there,' Kivi muttered. 'Someone who understand the disposition of the Eyes, and who doesn't know the broken one has been repaired. Someone with Wolf alliances.'

A thrill went along his spine. Xiriel? A giddy sense of admiration came over him, neither of allegiance nor opposition, but more like a professional appreciation for the other Seer's cunning. He wished he could congratulate Xiriel on the trick, and then have the pleasure of showing him that the trick had not worked: The Eye had been fixed.

Then it occurred to him that he would have to choose sides. He would have to go against Xiriel if the rebel Seer was going to threaten Jai

Khalar in some way. Not that this was the only area of moral ambiguity for Kivi. For there was also the matter of Dario, who had reported to him of her meeting with Jakse.

'I think we have the source of the Sekk,' she said. 'It is the lake of candles that Xiriel was asking about far and wide. Jakse knows its location.'

Kivi had urged her to convince Jakse to take her to the cave so she could see the place with her own eyes.

'I need more time,' she said. 'You must not tell Tash. I need to win the trust of the rebels.'

'Be careful with Jakse,' Kivi had instructed her. 'If he suspects you are in contact with Jai Khalar, he will show you nothing but a hole in the ground six feet by six.'

'I will not contact you again,' she answered. 'Not 'til I am sure.'

So Kivi had avoided reporting to Tash about Dario's troop, and he decided that if Tash asked him directly, he would say he had lost contact with them in the snow.

Now he turned his attention to the Eyes placed in the border towers, the ones overlooking the southern part of the plain of Ristale, and the sea plateau. Hezene's army was almost at the gates of Everien.

That, he decided, colluding with himself, was the only news Tash *really* needed to hear. He would keep tabs on the rebel activities, but there was no point in complicating matters now that the army was here. Let Tash worry about one thing at a time.

He left the Eye Tower quickly, calling for an apprentice to replace him. There were preparations to be made for many important guests.

It was midafternoon when one of the runner boys loped across the floor of the audience chamber and hesitated, glancing nervously toward the balcony that looked out over the gates.

'What is it? What do they say?' Tash snapped, and strode to the balcony. The valley seemed to be full of soldiers, file after file of them, mounted and on foot, stretching back along the stream that flowed from the caves beneath Jai Khalar.

'There is a messenger at the cave entrance seeking admission. He says his name is Evra Kiss and he is the leader of the force.'

'What does he look like?'

'Big nose, skin lighter than yours, begging your pardon, my lord, but darker than Kivi's, oiled moustache, about Illyra's age but much smaller.'

Tash considered this, stepping inside and out of view of the assembled below. He paced to and from the fire three times before answering.

'All right,' he uttered at last in a sepulchral groan. 'Let him come up. Let no one greet him, though, and have the leopard escort him in. That should scare him.' He folded his hands across his chest and waited.

'Shall I stay?' whispered Kivi. 'Or—'

'Shut up.'

They did not have long to wait. Ires trotted in silently, and huffing behind him came a slender man wearing furs and a curved Pharician long sword. His face was flushed and his hair was wet.

Evra Kiss fell on his knees before Tash and delivered the scroll that had been given to him by Hezene.

'Hail Tash, Prince of Everien. Your humble servant Evra Kiss delivers greetings from Hezene, Bird Emperor, Lord of the Winds, Guardian of the World and Most Exalted Who Flies Highest.'

Tash opened the scroll and read. Evra Kiss had prostrated himself and awaited Tash's command to rise, but Tash ignored him. He continued to read silently. He reached the end, snorted, glanced once at Kiss, and read it again. Then he tossed the scroll in the air. Everyone held their breath.

And Tash began to laugh. The assembled below, including Ukili sulking beneath the dripping silks of her litter, saw him appear once again as if out of nowhere, spread his arms wide and rock from side to side in mirth. Up in the sky with nothing to either side of him but the snow of Everien's hills, and nothing beneath his feet but the air itself, he looked like a god. Ukili made a sign invoking her father's power.

Tash looked down and beckoned to her.

'Come up! Come up! Welcome to Everien.'

Tash was slightly less pleased when he got a load of Shiror, but Kiss and Shiror had planned this. They had heard what had become of Rovene and Khartou and did not wish to repeat the process. So Shiror attached himself to Ukili, adopting a servile pose toward her that was perfectly appropriate when in the presence of a princess, but would not have been possible had he stood face to face with Tash alone – male honour would not have permitted it.

Tash didn't address Ukili directly, for in Pharice only a barbarian or a rapist addressed a woman he did not know, let alone a prospective wife. So he spoke to Shiror, and there was wariness in his eyes.

'Are you to Speak the Emperor's Words over us?'

'That authority is given to the Emperor's Speaker and the princess's companion, Chee.'

Tash glanced at the bird on the arm of one of the princess's maidens and returned his gaze to Shiror.

'Let it be done as soon as may be. Tomorrow, say. Ask Kivi for anything that may be required for Her Brightness's comfort. If I can provide it, I will. And accept my apologies for the caprice of this castle. I have not yet tamed it. But I will.'

'If I may speak for Princess Ukili,' Shiror said, 'I venture that a bath, and food, and then rest are uppermost upon her mind. Then Her Brightness can prepare herself for the Speaking.'

'Done,' said Tash, and made a gesture that it was finished. 'Chee may Speak His Words tomorrow at break of dawn – which happens quite late here, I remind you – and then we can carry on with our business.' He held Shiror's eyes on this last, and Kivi thought there was an implicit threat in his tone; but Kivi's Pharician was not perfect and he could not be sure of the nuances. Clearly Tash was not easy about the presence of Shiror. Kiss he had fretted over and pondered, but Shiror was a surprise, a real warrior among Scholars and the rank and file.

Abruptly Tash turned away, and if Ukili was offended by his brevity toward her, she had no opportunity to show it. Her veiled face was inscrutable. When Shiror led her away, she simply lowered her head as she would have done before her father, and complied.

The departure of Ukili acted as a signal, and a good many of the folk left the room behind her, with Kivi calling out hushed orders to the household servants and ushering people about. Tash walked to the far end of his hall, turned, and came back. By the time he reached the blazing hearth, the only men left in the room were Evra Kiss and his Scholars, including Wakhe and his hooded servant, and Duor beside Liaku, with Quiz sitting astride her head with one foot on each shoulder. Tash glanced distastefully at Wakhe, then said to Kiss, 'Remove the servant. These talks are secret.'

Evra Kiss cleared his throat. 'Scholar Wakhe cannot communicate without his aide, Yanse. He has no speech, no sight, and imperfect hearing.'

Tash's mouth worked.

'I have heard of you, Wakhe,' he said to the Scholar. 'I warn you that physical infirmity of any kind sickens me. While you are in my presence, you will not remind me of yours. Tell me, Kiss, why the emperor has seen fit to send me such a deformity as this.'

Evra Kiss cleared his throat, and Liaku thought that the glance he himself cast at Wakhe should go some way toward reassuring Tash that Kiss felt the same way he did about the Scholar, though possibly not for the same reason.

'Scholar Wakhe is the foremost code expert in all the empire, and the emperor in His Great Wisdom chose him personally to assist in the development of the Fire Houses as a source of weapons and other useful tools.'

'I need Impressionists who can See, not code experts,' Tash snapped.

'Hezene maintains that Impressionists are native to Everien, but the language and codes of the ancients have long been studied in Pharice. It may be that Wakhe can provide some useful information if he sees the Fire Houses firsthand.'

Tash grunted dismissively. 'How came you by the skyfalcon? They are said to be extinct, and yet this is the second one to visit Jai Khalar this year.'

Se was completely still, but Liaku, with some unknown faculty, could sense the tension in his body at Tash's words.

'It tore up my aviary and terrorized my byrdman,' Tash continued. 'And it had some kind of a message. Could this be the same animal?'

Maybe the message belonged to Quiz, Liaku thought. Maybe Quiz had come from Jai Khalar. It suddenly seemed as clear to her as if the bird had spoken into her mind. Quiz had been chasing the dove, trying to recover the message it carried. Did Tash understand what that message was? Surely if he attached the same significance to the message that the Circle seemed to, he wouldn't speak so openly of it now. Unless he was truly diabolically clever, and trying to draw Evra Kiss out . . .

'This bird carried no message,' Se blurted nervously, and then seemed to disappear within his hood, just as a frightened servant who has spoken out of turn might do.

Kiss appeared unperturbed; turning innocently to Liaku, he said, 'The bird came to this byrdchild in Jundun, who brought it and its message to Hezene. We understand that it is an Everien creature, quite intelligent, and attached to the byrdchild. Both are sent as gifts. The child is somewhat less stupid and deceitful than is typical of her kind, and she has a way with the fliers. She is here to provide special care for Chee, Ukili's Speaker, and to assist with messages.' Liaku was amazed at Kiss's eulogy of her and Quiz, and wanted to spit on him for his deceit.

'Is that all?' Tash laughed. 'I thought Hezene was going to say we must shut down the Fire Houses as a result of that stupid message.'

Evra Kiss said, 'I did not mean for the bird to remain in the room. Duor, take Liaku and Quiz to the women's quarters at once, then return here.'

'Sir, I don't know the way,' Duor said, holding his head high and swallowing nervously.

'Why didn't you follow your master?'

'I tried,' Duor said. 'B-but . . . the door. It wasn't there. I—'

Tash guffawed and waved his hand nonchalantly at Kiss, who was beginning to fume at the impertinence of the young soldier. 'It is all right. Jai Khalar does this sometimes. Stay where you are safe, all three, but sit in the corner and keep the bird quiet. It does not belong indoors at all.'

Liaku and Duor obeyed, sitting with knees almost touching but not quite. Quiz hopped onto the floor and settled, looking about alertly, but, to Liaku's relief, not molesting anything or anyone. Tash motioned for Evra Kiss to take a seat. 'Close to the fire, for you are a long way from the sun. Have some wine.'

Servants came forward and offered Kiss food and wine from heaped platters – coarse food, but rich in fat, as was necessary in the cold of Everien.

'Hezene thinks to use you to get rid of me, but I am not so easy to get rid of. Eat well, for you will be a busy man after this.'

Kiss, whose calm and friendly demeanour had got him far in life until now, tried to appear unruffled, but caught with a chicken bone protruding greasily from his lips, he instead looked a fool, and Tash laughed.

'Are you surprised to find me so direct?'

'No,' answered Kiss, removing the bone and holding it delicately between thumb and forefinger. 'You have a reputation for speaking your mind.'

'Good! For you have a reputation for smiling your way through the worst insults, but you will not smile your way through my sword, and this is my country.'

Kiss said nothing. Tash sat down opposite him and crossed his legs. 'Everien cannot be administered like Pharice, or any of the colonies. And I cannot be placated with a title and a cunt, even if the title is Prince and the cunt is of imperial descent. There are more riches in Everien than in all of the other colonies of the empire combined, for all that the settled land of this valley is smaller than the plateau Jundun's built on. Therefore your fawning dedication to the emperor will stop now, Evra Kiss. You work for me.'

'We have no argument,' Kiss replied calmly. Liaku was shocked. All the fight had gone out of him, and of Shiror as well, the moment they had come within the walls of Jai Khalar. Evra Kiss in particular acted like a whipped dog before Tash. 'Hezene has assigned me to help you, and so I will.'

'And what, in the mind of the emperor, constitutes help?'

'Organizing the Clans to serve us by establishing a landholding and taxation policy. Offering incentives to those who help us understand and ultimately destroy the Sekk. Pooling our information about the Fire Houses and how they work. Establishing Pharician schools and disseminating the Word of the emperor. Finding a way to connect the Everien Eye system to Jundun so that Hezene may be in closer communication with us. Distributing medicine—'

'Hezene wants the Eyes?' Tash's voice leaped an octave and hung there for a long moment before it cracked. 'He's dreaming. If he wants that kind of control, he can come himself.'

'It would be unwise to resist or quarrel with the emperor of Pharice,' Kiss said quietly. 'His hand is offered in friendship. Do not snap at it.'

'Do not instruct me within my own house!' Tash retorted, and the glass in the windows shook, then disappeared. Duor and Liaku looked at each other. 'You know nothing of Everien. I will take you out to tour this country, and you will see for yourself what manner of a place it is. Meanwhile, I wish to inspect the troops.'

Hurriedly, Kiss swallowed his wine and stood. 'I will call Shiror,' he said.

'No! You have a rank, do you not? It was your name which preceded the arrival of this army, not Shiror's. Does Hezene think to hide a wolf among the pigeons?'

Kiss said, 'Shiror was to guard the princess, who has only just made her first journey away from home. It is a great distance to send a virgin daughter. Shiror is bodyguard to her, no more.'

'Hah! Well, then, they are your troops for certain, and you do not need Shiror. Come! We will inspect. And you ragamuffins – ah, Kivi, there you are. Take this crew up to the aviary after you have settled Wakhe in his quarters. We will be in the training grounds.'

Liaku ended up going to the aviary with Kivi alone, for Duor was summoned away by his father, who had been looking for him. Duor had a set, distracted expression on his face, and Liaku knew he was thinking of Tash's words and planning what to say to Shiror to warn him of the warlord's disposition toward him. Meanwhile, Se slid into step with her for a moment and whispered, 'Find out all you can from the byrdman in the aviary. And be careful with Quiz!'

Liaku pretended not to hear, and Quiz hissed at him when he tried to press her. Then they had reached Wakhe's quarters and Kivi was leading her off, to the heights, and the wind, and the sound of wings, and for the first time in many weeks Liaku began to see the prospect of some happiness.

For Kivi, it was a day of endless running and talking and organizing, and by the time it was over he was longing for a week in the Eye Tower with nothing to do but keep watch. But there was no hope of that, for Tash summoned him after the evening meal to instruct him on Pharician wedding custom.

'There is no time for elaborate preparation,' Tash said, 'for if she is under my roof, she must become my wife within three days or my life is forfeit. Hezene will know this and Ukili surely knows it, and she will feel more at ease once the Speaking has been done.'

Kivi remarked that he had never heard of a woman who was pleased with such an abrupt wedding, and Tash laughed.

'Afterward there will be time for her to invent ceremonies and give orders. She will do nothing but make demands for the first six months or so, until she is too heavy with child to cause trouble. It is all right. I had not thought to burden myself with such nonsense, but spring will be on us soon and I will get out of this castle and away from her! I am not worried about that.'

He paused in his endless pacing, flopping onto a couch and picking up the drinking bowl made from Sendrigel's head. He swirled the contents thoughtfully, gazing at the liquid but not drinking it. Kivi waited for him to say something revealing; but someone knocked on the main door and Tash jumped in his skin.

'Let him in,' Tash said, and Kivi had the strange feeling that Tash knew who his guest was. He opened the door to the dark and calm and open countenance of Shiror, who entered the room like a lion to Tash's panther.

'I have come to talk truth,' said Shiror. Tash glanced once at Kivi and then surged to his feet.

'Kivi, my blade.'

The Seer started toward the rack of weapons near the hearth, where Tash's sword lay in repose amongst his collection of spears, knives, throwing blades, and other sharp objects; but Shiror held up a hand.

'I am a friend.'

'Fall to your knees, then,' Tash said, but Kivi knew he was scared.

Shiror said, 'A man of honour does not ask another man of honour to fall at his knees to prove his friendship.'

'A man of honour does not hide among the ranks as a bodyguard when his true intent is to usurp my place. Think you me blind?'

'You see that my true intent is hid, but you mistake the place of its hiding.'

'We will find out. Shall we duel? I am ready.'

Shiror was careful all this time to stay out of Tash's reach. Kivi came near to Tash with the blade, but Tash did not take it. He watched as Shiror reached into his vest and withdrew a silken envelope.

'This is from our emperor. I am the only man who knows of it, and you can kill me for it, but remember that your father did not entrust me with something so precious so that I could die for your hasty temper.'

'My father? But he died in battle, years ago in Or. How comes my father into this matter?' Unwitting, Tash had dropped into an archaic dialect, the kind still spoken in the desert where he'd been born. Shiror did not answer, but only proffered the envelope.

It was red. Tash opened it and removed a lock of straight black hair that had been woven into a plait.

'A fatherhood lock.' His voice was a shocked whisper. 'Where did you get this?'

'Hezene gave it to me to give to you. It was cut on the day of your conception and sent to your father when you were born, to notify him that he had a son.'

'But my father was a tribal chief in Or.'

'With respect, this is not what your mother claims, and the emperor has accepted her claim or he would have destroyed the lock.'

Kivi was just about able to follow the meaning of the conversation, for Pharician mating practices were foreign to him. He gathered from the stunned expression on Tash's face that Hezene was acknowledging him as his son.

'Now I understand,' he said. 'Ukili. This land. He gives them to me! He truly gives them.'

Tash whirled and raced to the far end of the hall, holding the lock aloft before him so that it blew back in the breeze and touched his face. He began to laugh.

'Come then, Shiror, come have a drink and tell me everything.'

The two men were friends so suddenly that Kivi's brain reeled. He stayed to the side, weary but fascinated by their talk. When they spoke too quickly, or in an informal dialect, he understood them only partially; but mostly they spoke good Pharician, and Shiror's accent was easy to follow. Tash asked Shiror about Tyger Pass, and the newcomer said,

'In Jundun there have been whispers of this place. The Circle has been funding the Seahawk Clan, in secret they think, but the emperor has monitored them. I need hardly remind you of the trouble the Seahawks could cause if they decided to rise against us. We think they have found some powerful artifact, but even if they have not, when Tyger Pass opens in the spring it must not fall under Seahawk control.'

'I, too, am suspicious of Tyger Pass,' Tash said. 'For I have lost an army that I sent into Snake Country adjacent to Tyger Pass, and I fear what the Sekk are getting up to in that area. I will ride across Tyger Pass to Seahawk and let them know who is in control.'

'Are you certain you should leave Jai Khalar at this time? Your new wife . . .'

'Illyra can stay. I have had enough of this castle. And if the rebels expect me to cower indoors until the warm weather, they are wrong. If it will be winter, then let me set my shoulders against it and push.'

Before Liaku could get to bed in a large closet off one of Ukili's anterooms, close to Chee, Se waylaid her in the corridor.

'A quick report. What did Shiror say to Tash?'

'He say, Tash is son of Hezene. He go to Tyger Pass. Tash go, too.'

It was so satisfying to watch Se literally reel and catch himself up against a column, which shifted an inch or two as he grabbed for it. He mopped his olive-skinned, shining brow. '*What?*'

'Also,' Liaku continued, unperturbed, 'they take Evra Kiss. Tash hate him, want to watch him.'

Se let out an audible groan. 'Kiss is always in the way. Why the fuck does Tash want to go to Tyger Pass?'

'There bad trouble there,' Liaku offered. 'Sekk, Clan armies, big trouble.'

'Shut up. Is there anything else? What else did they say? What are you withholding from me?'

'Nothing!' Liaku squeaked. 'What I care? I tell everything you.'

'What did you find out from the byrdman?'

'They have a thing, called Carry Eye, it is glass—'

'Yes, I know what it is. Go on.'

'Tash using it to make weapon Fire House. Young girl look inside, she speak many things only Scholar know.'

'Ah . . . Where is this Eye now?'

'I no finish. Hrost say, Quiz come here, with message, same message I find in Kukuyu. Quiz kill other bird and fly away before they catch, and Hrost send message to Jundun.'

'Why?'

'I no know. He say mice tell him.'

'*Mice?*'

'He say.'

'The Eye, Liaku, what about the Eye?'

'Hrost say, Tash angry because Eye go dark two day before Quiz come. Weapons no can make. Fire Houses work stop. Tash very angry everyone. Hrost know why because he hear Kivi and Tash talk, but no he tell, for big secret, he tell me today for I pay him food and candle.'

'This special Eye, it doesn't work properly?'

'No. Not any more.'

'So where is it? Who has it?'

'Don't know. Belong originally to Kivi, Hrost say. Probably Kivi still have.'

'Liaku, I want you to find that Eye and get it for me. Search Kivi's quarters, go up in the Eye Tower, do whatever you must. I need to see this thing for myself.'

Tash was in his element, Kivi thought. With so many of his own countrymen about him, he was busy showing off and sent for the Seer only to obtain his reports from the Eye Tower. Kivi told Tash no more than he wished the Pharician to know, and Tash was too busy to grill him thoroughly as was his habit. Instead, he was planning the winning over of the Clans and the reorganization of Everien according to the principles of Pharician government.

'Let messages be sent ahead of me to every village and town:

'Tash, Prince of Everien and son of the Emperor Hezene, calls for your attention. He will ride among you bringing gifts and aid in token of his pledge to you to rule Everien as it has never been ruled before. Tash will vanquish the Sekk and discover the great treasures that lie within the ruins of the old people. Everien shall prosper under the rule of Prince Tash, and her riches shall make her the greatest land in all the World. The Knowledge is already being rediscovered and soon Tash's subjects will reap its rewards.

'For those bearing old grudges, now is the time to forget them and join with Tash, for the loyal and true people of every Clan will have a place in New Everien, but the wicked and intolerant will be punished. Tash and his officers ride to every territory in Everien to name leaders and distribute land and arms. Each family will be judged individually. Rebels and spies will be executed and their lands dispersed among the loyal. All are to prepare for the coming of Tash, son of Hezene, Prince of Everien.'

The wedding was over before Kivi could blink. When Ukili's veils were lifted, all present breathed a sigh of relief, for she was so beautiful that even Tash could hardly find fault. And when Chee Spoke the Emperor's Law of Marriage, she added a special line or two for Tash.

'Tash, son of Hezene our Emperor and Loqissa of Or, raised by Hezene's friend and loyal subject Griasj of Or, tested in the battles of Ghor River and Amn, Supreme Horse Chief of the South, trusted scout and cavalry leader, the Bird Emperor and Commander of the Winds sends you greetings. These are my secret Words to you, given to my Speaker and to be held sacred above all other Words today spoken. Let all present at this Speaking witness that I name Tash my son and heir, that he shall marry his sister, my legitimate daughter, and thereby become my legitimate son, Prince Tash, Lord of Everien, answering to no man in the empire but myself, obeyed in all things by all beings and enjoying my full support in every activity. These are my personal words as a father and my Command Words as an emperor. All hail Tash, Prince of Everien!'

Ukili flushed prettily. Even she had not known what she was getting as a husband, and her lips could be seen mouthing the words, 'Thank you, O Father.' She fanned herself, hot with excitement.

Invisible Flower

Every time I return to it, the garden becomes more overgrown. The trees devour the ground with their roots, and where there were flowers now there are weeds and saplings, and the roses have grown leggy though their blooms are still dark and true. The fountain is still. I do not have the courage to return to the house, though it stands with windows intact, roof tiles crooked and mossy but mostly in place. I know she is not there. They ripped her apart with their hands and eyes. I have seen an animal killed and butchered; I have hunted and prepared food myself, and though I do not relish the dismemberment of a living thing, it does not frighten me. But this was not the manner of my mother's death, and I did not understand it, and I could not return to the house but please don't ask me to explain any more.

In the garden I weep. She would have hated the disorder. So much work on her part, every day; so much care and attention, and how quickly it all goes back to jungle.

When last I returned to the garden, there was a man there. He had a sword and the look of one who has spent too much time using it, and he was hacking at the rosebushes, which are my favourite – they are my namesake, after all. Invisible flower, Jai-a in the original language, so named because they are most beautiful in the dark, known by their smell. When I saw him cutting them down as if they were ordinary brambles, I didn't know what to think. I stood there dumb, watching. He stooped and began gathering the blooms, cursing and sucking his hands where the thorns bit him; then I laughed.

He stopped, still crouched, and looked up at me like a startled fox.

'I do not begrudge you my flowers, but I have never seen anyone gather them in such a manner,' I said, and there was a tremor in my voice. I realized that it had been so long since I had spoken to another human being that I would do anything if it meant he wouldn't go. I cautioned myself against such an attitude and glanced over my shoulder. Blue was still there, dozing by the gate. My escape route was open.

The man straightened, dropping the flowers. He was tall, six feet and half a hand, and leaner than his broad-shouldered frame required: He had been getting by on short commons, I thought. His face was pitted and scarred, no longer young and probably never pretty, but the eyes were sympathetic. His hair looked as if he had cut it himself, using a knife and without benefit of a mirror. His boots had gaps between the sole and the leather, but the sword in his hand gleamed perfectly: it had not been neglected. He sheathed it and gulped.

'You!' he accused.

'Me?'

'Where have you been?'

'In the wood. Riding . . .' I was staring at him, trying to recall whether I knew him. My mother always said a man would come, but—

'Ah, games and riddles! How long do you intend to carry on running from me?'

I shrank back.

'I was running from them,' I said. 'Who are you?'

'Don't be funny. You have made me chase you across worlds and over bridges, under seas, between the stars themselves, and never one fucking word of explanation. Don't look at me like that!'

'Like what?' I said, baffled. It was so dark I could barely make out his features; how did he know what look I gave him?

'Like . . . like that way you do,' he stammered. 'You know what I mean.' He paused, licked his lips, shook his head a little. 'Why are you so cruel? I know I was something to you once. I remember you, I remember enough to know we loved each other. When you weren't trying to get me killed or sending me to places where man isn't meant to go.'

'I'm sorry,' I said, for he made me feel that I should be. All I was sorry for was not knowing what was going on. I felt sure that was my fault; certainly he seemed to think I ought to understand his meaning.

Then he said, 'It doesn't matter. What happens out there' – he gestured dismissively at the hedges that surround the garden on the outside of the fence – 'it doesn't matter. We're safe here.'

'I hope so,' I said.

'Where are the children? Are they here?' He looked around anxiously, his words an entreaty.

'I don't know what you're talking about.' I could hear my voice rising with a slightly hysterical quaver. It was occurring to me that there was no one else to mediate; Jihan would not be leaping out of the bushes and explaining the lesson with a jaunty wink. I was on my own. 'Who are you?'

At that he hesitated. He tilted his head to one side and scrutinized me thoroughly, like a blacksmith studying a lame horse. His voice was softer when he spoke again, and I had the feeling he was being gentle because he thought I might be hurt, or out of my mind.

'I think you had better come with me,' he said. 'Some kind of sickness has taken you.'

I took a step back.

'Tell me your name.'

'I am Quintar, known also as Tarquin the Free, and I am a man broken in ways only you know how to mend, Jaya Paradox.'

'No no no,' I babbled, for he had spoken the words like an incantation and

341

they were already working on me in places down deep, like a foul but potent medicine. 'I hate mending. I hate spinning. You've come to the wrong place. My mother might have helped you, but she is dead. They ripped her limb from limb without spilling a drop of blood; that is how They are and that is why I must leave.'

I ran to Blue and tugged the reins back over his head, preparing to mount; but he rolled his eyes at me and stepped away.

'Hush, my love,' I soothed. 'Let me get up.'

He threw his head back and his nostrils flared red. His teeth made a deep crunching noise on the bit and his throat flared as he trumpeted a challenge. Birds fell silent. I scurried around him, trying to put his body between me and the man called Quintar, and grabbed the stirrup on his offside. I intended to mount any way I could.

'No!' Quintar shouted, and Midnight Blue reared, tearing the reins from my hands. He gathered himself and shot across the garden, leaving gouges in the lawns and trailing clouds of earth. When he came to the far fence, he spun and began to circle round the other way, in a state of total panic.

Quintar had reached me by then, and he grabbed my arm. I kicked him and tried to wriggle free, but he had me by both arms and was shaking me.

'You mustn't ride him! Not now, not while I'm here. Jaya, don't be stupid. If they meet, they'll kill each other. Ice is already hurt.'

'Shut up!' I screamed, still kicking. I didn't know why he was making me so angry, for I didn't even know him and couldn't make sense of his words. Yet I was furious, frustrated – alarmed. Blue was still screaming challenges to some unknown adversary, running up and down the fence line as if another stallion were on the other side.

I could not get free, and his fingers were bruising my arms. I did as I never would have done in the old days, under the tutelage of Jihan. I did as I had seen my mother do, only once, on the night they came for her, in an act of desperate surrender. I began to cry.

'What is it? Jaya! Jaya! Are you out of your skull tonight? What is the matter?'

He pulled me to him then, and I could feel his heart pressing against my cheek. Witlessly, I clung to him as if he were a tree and I a piece of flotsam in a flood.

'Why don't you help me?' I sobbed. 'I don't know what to do, and they said you would come for me but all you do is accuse.'

I wiped my nose against his tunic, sniffing pathetically, and he pushed me away and turned my face up toward his as if trying to get a good look at me in the moonlight. His thumb traced my jawline, very lightly; but it was bleeding where the thorn had stabbed it and the blood left a cool stickiness on my skin.

'Oh, mother of Ysse,' he whispered. 'I made a mistake.'

Suddenly he let go of me and backed carefully away, his hands held up in

342

the empty air before him as if I were a vase carefully balanced and he was willing me not to fall.

'Please,' I begged, seeing that he was about to go away without explaining anything. 'Please, help me! Don't leave me alone here! Quintar!'

He was already almost at the gate, still backing away from me, one hand groping behind himself seeking the iron bars that would secure his release and my abandonment.

'I'm sorry,' he whispered. 'It was the wrong time. I'm sorry. Forget . . . forget I was here.'

He had the gate open now and I was beginning to stagger toward him, weak and convinced of my own helplessness.

'Stay here!' He said it imploringly, as if he had no faith that I would follow his advice. 'Do not ride out in the forest any more. Stay and wait for me, and hope.'

'Hope what?' I cried, but he was gone. Blue ran to the gate after him and stood looking out and whinnying. He stamped and blew, and then he began to run up and down the hedge again. The garden was in ruins.

'Hope what?' I said again, and sat down on the edge of the fountain. I drew my finger through the dust that had collected in the basin. I wrote his name.

Ixo took the Carry Eye from Gialse.

The name Quintar upset her. Until now Ixo had believed she was listening to a story of some other place and time – ancient Everien perhaps, for this would explain how Gialse and the other girls had gotten the sophisticated Knowledge from this Carry Eye. Ixo even made the connection between Jaya's reading of her father's books, and the Impressions that enabled young girls to draw complex diagrams and symbolic equations. But the name of Quintar entering into the story made everything different. Ixo didn't know what to do.

'If anyone asks you, I have never had this Carry Eye,' Ixo said. 'Do you understand?'

Gialse swallowed. She was so grateful for her position of privilege as the servant of Tash's favourite concubine that her loyalty by now was absolute.

'I have seen this Carry Eye,' Gialse said. 'It is Kivi's. He and Tash made me look in it. Then they sent me here. That is all I know.'

'Ah, Gialse, I forgive your bad needlework! I forgive you your sneezing and your snoring! You are my good little friend, are you not?'

Ixo hugged the girl, and now when Gialse smiled, she almost looked pretty.

'Now, go! I must be alone.'

After Gialse had left, Ixo put her hand on her belly and wished hard for Mistel. Then she gathered up the silk bedsheet on which she had

343

recorded Gialse's utterances. She dipped one corner in lamp oil, then went to the fire and moved the screen aside. She felt the heat on her belly, which was just beginning to swell. She started to move the silk toward the fire, but her hand stopped halfway. She was thinking.

Suddenly she pulled the screen back over the fire. She folded the silk up into a parcel, which she fitted into her corset. It would be a shame to burn it – and anyway, she'd just gotten an idea.

Liaku Spy

Liaku performed the search for the Carry Eye as Se ordered her. It was not difficult for her: Chee required attendance only twice a day, and her needs were not great. Ukili was preoccupied with decorating her rooms and issuing commands and ordering things from Pharice, and she scarcely noticed the comings and goings of the byrdgirl. And the rooftops and towers of Jai Khalar were a good challenge to Liaku. She could not say that it was pleasant to be climbing around in the winter wind, for in comparison to the biting cold and dangerous heights of Jai Khalar, the chala seemed a playground. Yet after the long march and subsequent confinement indoors, she found exploring the castle to be exhilarating and baffling, maddening and thrilling, but never boring.

Right away she learned that there was nothing to be gained by building a fixed conception of what was what or where, here in Jai Khalar. She did not try to memorize positions or coordinate landmarks. She just climbed, and looked for new ways in and out, hidden places, non sequiturs (of these there were many), and, of course, treasures. Se left her to her business, for a while, and the skyfalcon often glided overhead or taunted her from unreachable spires or invisible bridges. For a good deal of the castle was invisible even when you were in it. Liaku bumped into a wall or two this way before she came to understand the principle.

She did a fair bit of spying while she searched. She spied on Tash, for example, while he instructed Kivi on the particulars of his new regime. He had hung a number of tapestries and drapes in his audience hall, and it was easy for a person of Liaku's size to secrete herself behind them. The problem of visible feet was resolved by clinging to the wall behind the tapestry like a spider. She found herself kept relatively warm this way, both by the insulation from drafts and by muscle exertion. And with a small mirror attached to her right ear by a piece of wire and angled toward her eye, she was able to see through a gap in the curtain with her back to the room.

'I shall set a few heads rolling,' laughed Tash, and scratched his belly absently. 'Can no one do anything about the fleas in this place?'

'It is the mice, my lord, which attract them.'

'Kivi, stop looking like such a rainy day. Midwinter is past, the days lengthen, and soon you can stop acting so miserly every time I delve into the stores for food: Hezene has sent many gifts, of seed and stock as well as dry goods. Soon your Clans will be well fed, and sending me their best men for training, just as was done in Ysse's day. Believe it, for I will uphold the standards of the elite. Everien has the wrong geography for massive armies such as Hezene is prone to relying on. We will have strong, small tactical bands of men. We will hunt Sekk and wild monsters and bring back fortunes in magical substances. It will be good, Kivi.'

Kivi made a visible effort to brighten his expression.

'My one fear, that Hezene would act against me, now is swept away with a single gesture: his daughter. Did you see her, Kivi? She is fine.'

'She is very beautiful.'

'Yes, and the Fire Houses will bring us great wealth. Nowhere in Hezene's whole empire are there weapons such as those we have invented. Everien will be great again.'

'Will I ride with you, Tash? Who will mind Jai Khalar in your absence?'

'Not Evra Kiss, I tell you that much. He will come with Shiror and me, where we can watch him – and anyway, we will need a Scholar. I suppose Illyra will have to mind the castle. And you will have to help him, for he is stupid when it comes to the Knowledge, and we have already seen what a mess he made of Clan customs. Mistel can advise you there. I will make gifts to your people, Kivi. Your loyalty is everything: Keep it true, and Everien will prosper. For the rebellion cannot last long in the face of my generosity, or under the eye of so many troops. Your people will see the need to become my subjects and go about their business. No one in Everien wants more war. Of this I am sure.'

If he was so sure, why did he say it? Liaku wondered, and suppressed a powerful itch in her hindparts. Her grip could last a long time, but she was getting fidgety.

'Illyra scares me,' Kivi said frankly, and Tash laughed.

'Illyra scares everybody. But he will not interfere with the normal running of things if I tell him so. However, I shall not leave myself blind. There will be provisions made in case you slip, Kivi; you, or any of your people, especially Mistel. You will be watched. Therefore I urge you to behave just as you would if I were here. For you are right: Illyra is not a forgiving man, and he is not as patient as I am.'

Liaku thought Tash smiled as he said this, but as was his habit the war leader had turned and moved away on these last words, before his audience could fully judge his meaning. This must be Tash's way of being playful, Liaku thought, grateful when Tash flopped on his couch with his back to her and dismissed Kivi, giving her the opportunity to slip away.

After this, Liaku followed Kivi everywhere. His movements took him all over the castle, and frequently into the Eye Tower, where Liaku observed him with great caution. She never saw him with this Carry Eye that Hrost had spoken of. But she was watching Kivi on the night that Ixo went to his quarters carrying the Eye wrapped in a piece of white satin. Since discovering herself pregnant Ixo had taken up the habit of walking with one hand curved protectively across her flat belly; now she stood outside the door in this pose, listening. There was no sound within. After a moment she lifted her hand, made a fist, and hesitantly knocked.

Kivi opened the door at once. His room was well lit and she could see he had been reading. His face conveyed a vacant intensity in her direction, emotionless and distracted. There were dark circles beneath his eyes and sweat stains on the collar of his tunic. The bed was piled so high with books and papers that it was clear he had not slept there in some time.

'I'm sorry,' she stammered. 'I'm sorry, I just wanted to talk to you.'

He stood back from the door so she could enter. She shut it behind her. The room was stuffy and stale, and even the fire seemed to be burning sluggishly. Ixo, obsessed with the health of her child, marched to the nearest window and opened the shutter. Liaku had to duck out of the way at the last instant to avoid being seen. A gust of icy air blew in, and Kivi's papers lifted and cast themselves about the room at random. Kivi snatched at them and hissed at Ixo to close the window, which she did, looking more embarrassed by the second.

Kivi for his part didn't seem angry, though, so much as resigned and miserable. He picked some books off a chair by the fire and sank into it, wearily gesturing to its mate, opposite, which already bore the impression of his backside. Ixo sat down on the edge of the cushion and leaned forward uncertainly. Liaku had never seen a woman address a man in private, and on equal terms. Nor did Kivi look at the Wasp the way a man looked at a woman. He looked at her with a healthy respect mingled with dislike.

'I have come to apologize,' she said, directing her words at the cloth-wrapped Eye she held in her cupped hands. 'I have been harsh and imperious with you. I treated you as an enemy when you could have been a friend. I was wrong.'

She let the cloth spill open and the dark Eye was exposed.

'The girl who speaks, she is called Jaya Paradox. She has been cast out of her home and she rides in a dark forest, pursued by some creatures . . . Sekk, I fear. She has spoken of her childhood. I . . . I confess I developed a strong sympathy for her. But I am troubled, Kivi. I fear you were right all along.'

'I was right? How do you mean?'

Ixo hesitated. From her corset she tugged a thin silk scroll, somewhat crushed. 'I have written down some of the things she says.'

'Let's hear it,' Kivi said eagerly.

Ixo unrolled the scroll and leaning into the lamplight, began haltingly to read:

'*When I held the lamp in my hands and directed it to the blankness beyond the edge of the forest, I could—*'

Ixo paused. 'You see, beyond the forest there was nothing. She rode to its edge but it was just an emptiness.'

'I have heard this is possible, in the Liminal,' said Kivi. 'Go on.'

Ixo cleared her throat and began again.

'*When I held the lamp in my hands and directed it to the blankness beyond the edge of the forest, I could see other places projected on the sky, like shadows projected on a screen, only coloured and full of noise and feeling as well. It was as if I were looking down a long tunnel at another world, and I could see the riders, as a group and individually. I could see many other places. Depending on where I pointed the lamp, I could look at totally different things. They were as wild as the pictures in my father's books, or wilder. One was an ice-world; one was underwater. One was a place of great reptiles and insect-teeming swamps. One was geometrical and dark, and everything seemed to be made of metal; even the people didn't look like people.*

'*You must understand that I had nothing. I was nothing. How could I not look? How could I not wish for those men you gave me to act, to fight as I could not fight, to move as I could not move? They came to my call. How could I not love that?*

'*Night is my ruler, the cloak that guards me; I suppose it is my father's cloak or perhaps, as Jihan said, it is my shadow; maybe they are even the same; but it protects me from the hideous, demented creatures that live in this forest. Night's darkness, my blindness, saves me from the sight of them. My stolen eyes. The Company roaming free; but it was my desire that guided them. For when the Glass was broken at Jai Pendu, my father's lamp went dark. Now when I point it at the sky I see starlessness, pointless emptiness, like a canvas unpainted. How is that better than what was before?*

'*ARE YOU EVER COMING TO SAVE ME?*

'*This little lamp cupped in my hands, it draws on my words. It sucks my words in a little backward wind. Sometimes it seems to me that I can feel another girl's hands cupping it, as if she is holding it from the inside and I am holding it from the outside, and only a thin barrier separates it. I feel that way now. Is anyone listening? Is anyone coming?*

'Why did my father leave those things behind if he did not mean me to use them?

'What were they protecting me from, when it was I who was the danger?

'They are following me. They are calling, singing with Jihan's Music of Everything. It fills my throat so I feel I will choke on the sound.

'Time. Time is the problem. Jigsaw pieces scattered across time. Is there such a thing as my time? Is there a way to set the story straight?

'Is someone there? Talk to me.

'At this point,' Ixo said, 'Gialse let out a cry. It was as if she had been trying to answer Jaya, but the spell broke then and she came out of the Impression.'

'Jaya Paradox,' Kivi mused, and Ixo fidgeted.

'She is a Sekk,' Ixo said impatiently. 'Don't you understand? That is why they are so beautiful, that is why they seduce us with their voices. Do you feel how she would move us by pity, by sympathy, by understanding? This Eye is dark because it is still held by Night, the creature that would have marched off with every fighting man in Everien to a destiny the Animal Protectors could never imagine.'

'Is a child evil for playing with dolls? As I hear her tell, that is Jaya's only crime. The real question is, where is she, that she speaks to us?'

Ixo stared at Kivi in disbelief at his reaction. She gestured to the vast dimensions of Jai Khalar around them. 'I don't know about you, but if this is the child's dollhouse, then I am very afraid. As for play: My brother ripped the heads off my dolls.'

'We have more pressing concerns. The Fire Houses, for one.'

'I thought you of all people would understand, Kivi! Wasn't it you who told Tash you were afraid Night was still a player? This is the same Eye that Tash used to get all that information about weapons through the Impressionists. Now we know it is controlled by Night.'

'And Jaya is stopping that information from coming through. Do you think those diagrams are things she read in her father's books? Do you think that somewhere the Everien Knowledge is recorded properly? Ixo, we have to find out where Jaya is. We have to get to her. She's desperate, she's afraid, she's in danger—'

'Kivi, you *fool*,' Ixo retorted in a rage. '*We* are desperate. *We* are in danger. Can't you see that? Fuck Jaya! Let's save ourselves!'

'I'm not so sure,' Kivi said. 'If we could get more Knowledge . . . Ixo, I need that Carry Eye now. It is critical that I study it.'

'How are you going to study it? Gialse is the only one Jaya will speak through.'

'Then I will work with Gialse. Listen, Tash has been asking about it constantly. I can only blame Jai Khalar for so long.'

'I offered you the chance to work with me long ago, and you refused. You only want to take over, but it is my discovery. I have no intention of giving it to you. I only wanted your counsel.' She stood and went to the door, opening it and going halfway through before he caught her by the arm.

He whispered, 'And I am counselling you that dealing with Night is dangerous.'

'Apparently not too dangerous for you.'

'I am a Seer. You are—'

'Only a woman?' she shrilled.

Kivi spoke through clenched teeth. 'Do not take it out on me if the Pharicians treat you badly. No Clansman would lock a woman up.'

Ixo gave him a withering look. 'The Clan warriors could not save their women from this fate. Do not take it out on you? You stupid men let the Pharicians conquer you. For myself, I don't know if I'm coming or going. Tash may be my ancestral enemy, but he protects me as you Clansmen could not. And you, Kivi, you are doubly at fault for you live to lick Tash's ass. Danger! What do you know of it? I have nothing to lose, Kivi.'

Her voice was loud and clear as she jerked her arm free and stepped fully into the hall, leaving him imploring her from the threshold. Liaku took a risk and leaned in the window, ears pricked. She was amazed that Kivi had not struck Ixo by now; but the Seer continued to speak in soft tones.

'Yes, you do. Your life. Your child's life. Tash will always favour you, Ixo. But if there is a coup and he goes down, your life will not be so easy.'

'I already have a child. I have a son,' Ixo said in a whisper that had nothing to do with secrecy. 'Tash took him away.' For a moment she stood there silently and Liaku guessed that she was crying. 'I hate all you men. No matter what I do, I have lost. But *this*,' and she stroked the surface of the Eye, 'this is something extraordinary.'

Liaku had a hard time following Ixo after that. She had to move across the dark outer surfaces of Jai Khalar, and there was ice on all the stone. A renewed shower of freezing rain had begun to fall. Liaku was hungry. Doggedly she matched Ixo move for move, almost catching up when the castle made a shift and she found herself at the bottom of a flight of stairs with Ixo descending toward her. Ixo went to a grille in the floor and lay down on it. Liaku took the opportunity to slip through a window to Ixo's back and secrete herself in a recess that held the shards of a broken urn.

'Grandmother,' Ixo whispered. 'Can you hear me?'

Liaku could not hear any reply, but Ixo was speaking and then pausing as if someone were answering her. Liaku didn't hear everything that was said, and what she did hear she didn't particularly understand, because Ixo spoke in the Clan common tongue, which was a bastard of Pharician and several Clan dialects. Liaku could not speak it, and only understood about half of what she heard spoken. She couldn't be sure, but she thought that Ixo said, 'Hide it in your cunt if they come for it.'

Then Ixo stood, brushed herself off, and returned the way she had come, passing Liaku without a glance. Liaku noticed that the silk covering for the Eye was now held loose in her hand; in fact, she brought it to her face to wipe away tears and blow her nose. When she was gone Liaku went to the grille and peered in. She couldn't see anything, only darkness. An odour of urine drifted up.

The bars were just wide enough to pass the Eye through.

A Sculpture in Ice

The sound of one hand clapping woke Istar. Silence after so much noise startled her from a deep sleep. She lay in the dark, wondering what the sudden cessation of the howling wind might mean and wishing she could go back to pleasant, warm sleep with its dreams of food and colour and heat. But she could not get back into her dreams and was forced instead to lie awake, negotiating with her bladder as to whether she should move. She was curled in a ball, every inch of her ermine cloak carefully arranged to retain as much of her body heat as possible. Even the tip of her nose did not protrude; she had folded the hood so that fresh air could enter only indirectly, warmed by the ambient heat of her body before it reached her nostrils. Her muscles were stiff, for she had not moved for hours, and she even slept with some tension in her legs and back. It was necessary to generate heat. In her sleep she sometimes shivered.

But now she had to get up. She had to relieve herself. Her belly was swollen and a dull ache travelled up her back. Even so, she was loath to leave her fragile cocoon of warmth.

She stirred a little at a time, flexing and stretching her muscles slowly to awaken them. She couldn't feel her feet at first, and she began to worry, for though she kept her fingers tucked beneath her armpits, her feet had no such luxury and the fact that she hadn't changed position meant that the circulation to her toes was poor. When the sharp, stinging sensation of returning circulation made her legs jolt spasmodically, she was relieved even as she grimaced at the unpleasant return of feeling. Her teeth began chattering and she deliberately tensed her arms and back in order to create more heat. When her feet were restored, she climbed out of her nest and groped toward the dim light that marked the gap in the stone leading to the main cavern.

It was still dark. Her reckoning made it the fifth day since she had gone to earth. Most of this time she had spent sleeping to conserve her strength, while the winds and snow played out their wild tale before the theatre of impassive mountains. Now, as she dug her way out of her hollow and waded into the cavern's main chamber, which was halfway buried in drifted snow, she could hear no whisper of wind. She could hear nothing but herself shuffling and breathing, and even these sounds were muffled by the snow. She sneezed.

How have I got myself into this? she thought. It was amazing how hard she found it to remind herself that she once had moved about freely, had taken air and light and strength for granted. How spoiled she had been then, how unaware of her own luck. She thought: *I will never again complain about anything. Ever.*

The storm had raged for days. It had been a whiteout with no relief, impossible to travel in. She wondered sadly what had become of the Hawk Girls. They had dumped her here with the gift of a brace of dead snow hares, but with no means to make fire she could not cook them, and they soon froze. The rations in her own pack would have been enough to sustain her, but she had wriggled free of her pack when the boulders had trapped her. She should have gone back for it, but she had been too eager to get to the site of the wrecked caravan. Stupid; but typical. Istar was not unversed in impulsive stupidity; it was something of an art form with her, actually. She knew she was lucky to be alive.

It was dark in the cave even by day, and snowdrifts blocked most of the entrance, anyway, so she usually depended on a small Knowledge-light when leaving her nest, which she did as little as possible. But tonight there was a silvery sheen on the snow near the entrance to the main cavern, and a chink of blackness beyond. Moonlight.

Shivering and cursing and sniffling, Istar quickly undid her clothing and squatted in the corner she had been using as a privy. She regretted losing even the heat from her own piss, which she kicked snow over before bundling herself up again and moving toward the cave entrance, curious. The silence was strange and made her feel unreal, as if she were still dreaming. She waded through the snow and, catching onto the icy wall of the cave for balance, looked out into the lonely night.

The mountains were utterly empty. Tonight there was no snow, but the sound of the wind made her draw her shoulders up, and she was shaking internally, every muscle working to stave off the cold. She turned back toward her nest, and in the moonlight she saw what she had missed until now: a faint channel cut in the snow and ice, as if water had run down from the back of the cave.

Water? Where was it warm enough to melt the snow?

She moved quickly along the indentation, passing into darkness and going up a slope and around a bend in the rock. She could feel a faintly warm draft on her face. At first she thought she was imagining it; but then her skin began to sting and soon after that her boots were breaking through the ice into slushy water beneath.

A thermal vent.

The cave dried out as it went back, and to Istar's delight she came upon a shallow flight of steps. Then, in a warm niche beside a deep shaft, she found an iron box. Warm air was coming up from the shaft. The box was unlocked.

Eagerly she flung it open, hoping to find food and bandages and medicines such as Birtar had told her were customary in such hides. Bandages and medicines she found, but except for a small store of dry nuts, there was no food.

Istar sighed and leaned her head back against the wall in disappointment. Then she told herself it didn't matter. It was warm here. She would not freeze to death. And there was yet fat on her body; not much, but enough to hold off starvation for a little while.

She ate the nuts anyway. She couldn't help it. Then she fell asleep.

She must have slept all day, for when she woke and left the warmth of the thermal vent to look outside, it was dark again, so silent that she swore the stars made tiny ice-sounds as they twinkled. She breathed delicately, for the air was so cold it hurt going down. And then she saw him, and she gasped painfully.

He didn't move like a Sekk, he moved like a human hunter, deliberately and with every nerve alive. But it was the same man. She would know his frame anywhere, and he still wore the white cloak and the white braids.

Istar didn't think. She simply followed him. She trailed him across the snow, through the wind, and up. The rocks lay pitched so steeply that the snow had been blown from them, but there was a thin coating of ice over everything and Istar slithered and slipped. Above her he was climbing easily, glimpsed from time to time as the edges of his white cloak lifted and his black-clad legs could be seen beneath. Istar followed.

He squeezed into another cave. It was only a slit in the ice-wall, with icicles dangling even over the black stripe of its entrance. Istar had to grab at the ice to balance herself, for there was no level stone at the entrance. She could not draw her sword, and she could not see inside. She leaned in, her gloves still trying to grip at icicles the size of ox legs, lost her balance, and began to slide. She was grabbing at the walls of a narrow, sloping icy tunnel that plunged several yards and then disgorged her into the bottom of a large cavern, faintly lit by what appeared to be Knowledge-lights embedded at irregular positions in the walls. The cave led deep into the mountain. It was hard to be sure where the walls really were, for everything was snow and ice with hardly a scrap of dark stone visible anywhere. Protruding from the snow here and there she could descry the regular shapes of boxes or squarish chests, and when she stood and walked farther into the cave she also saw a shield sticking up from the snow; and later, a Pharician crossbow; and then, sitting on an ice ledge, a human head, frozen dark blue.

The white-cloaked figure was ahead of her in the tunnel. His back was to Istar. Though she was making her fair share of noise with her footsteps and breathing echoing in the cave, he didn't turn or show any interest in her. She drew her sword and ran after him, shouting incoherently.

'You! Sekk! Answer me! Hey!'

The warrior kept walking. He came to a sculpture carved in the back of the cave, a seahawk with its wings spread, bejewelled and fabulous, festooned with icicles. A chimney in the ice and snow admitted a yellow beam of moonlight from somewhere far above. There was a whistling of wind in that crack, and snow blew sideways across the cloaked Sekk, settling invisibly on his white hair.

She saw the flash as he drew his sword, and there was a faint grinding noise. For a moment the cave shook. Then he vanished.

Icicles came crashing down from the roof and shattered. Snow blew in and danced in the place where he had been. Istar stopped, the sword trembling in her hand, still ready to fight. But she was surrounded by skeletons and skulls, dead warriors who had come before. The Sekk was gone without a trace.

She searched the cave anyway, roaming in and out of that tunnel and, finally, when daylight came and brought more light from the chimney, checking the walls themselves. There was so much ice that it was difficult to examine the stone, but Istar judged from the shape of the tunnel as well as the texture of the exposed rock, that she was in a section of H'ah'vah tunnel. Strangely, the tunnel ended suddenly at the wall with the seahawk carving. H'ah'vah tunnels seldom dead-ended, and Istar found herself wondering if the carving hid a false wall. It would explain the disappearance of the Sekk; for although they were strange beings with many unknown properties, Istar had never heard anything to suggest they could render themselves invisible at will.

She cracked open the boxes in search of food, but all she found were scrolls and books and specimen boxes containing feathers and claws and other parts of the seahawk anatomy. Rumour that Taretel had kept a home up here amongst the birds had not been lost on Istar, although she had always thought the stories apocryphal on the grounds that Seahawks seldom came so far inland as this. Now she began to think maybe the stories had been right. And the thought that she had stumbled on the secret cave of Taretel the Animal magician would have excited her greatly if it were not for the fact of the Sekk.

In the stories, Taretel was depicted as a strapping, white-blond swordsman. But he had not been portrayed as a murderer or kinslayer. Istar could not begin to speculate as to what was going on with the caravan, or the skeleton she still possessed, or the white-haired warrior.

But she could read, albeit slowly and with difficulty, and by the wan radiance of the Knowledge-light, she did.

A good many of the documents were written in Everien symbol-language. Istar had seen many examples of this kind of writing recorded on scribestones, on walls in Jai Khalar and A-vi-Khalar, and in visions given through the Eyes. She had never seen any written by hand on a perishable surface such as paper or leather, or etched in the traditional manner on ordinary stone. So to find scroll after scroll in hand-scribed Everien was a small shock and, she suspected, would have sent Xiriel into an ecstasy of discovery. Not that anyone, Xiriel included, knew how to read or write Everien; but to find that a Clansman such as Eteltar might have known these things would surely set the Seers' imaginations alight.

Istar was not a Seer. She was cold and hungry and perplexed. Shivering, she searched for the few scraps of notes that were written in Clan-Pharician.

Power Source?
Does light get old?
Energy generated through electromagnetic imbalance across time membrane. The light which illuminates/heats the furnaces of the Fire Houses must shine from another time. It is an ancient light, or none at all.

The breaking of the law which dictates the flow of time as undirectional will release explosive and highly focused power.

N.B. Once such an Artifact is moved across time membranes it will resonate with other contemporaneous Artifacts and they will be revealed.

'Xiriel, Xiriel, where are you when I need you? Hah, if you had known about this you wouldn't have complained I was leaving your precious lake of candles. You would have personally escorted me. But what the fuck does this mean?'

Light shines through a glass that admits only ancient light. The glass has the ability to draw the light across time. This circuit creates power.

'Blah, blah,' said Istar. 'Mumbo jumbo.'
She missed Kassien. Together they might have laughed at the weird language. Alone, she found herself drawn under its spell.

Using the codes I have discovered a tile sequence that may enable me to temporarily repair a section of the bridge between the Fire Houses and Jai Pendu. Originally there was a tripartate structure: Jai Pendu, the Fire

Houses, which are themselves threefold, and a third, unknown aspect which is implied by the equations if not seen in fact. It is possible that the Floating Lands are the unknitted structure of this third aspect, but I think it more likely that they are detritus left behind by the riving of Everien. In any event, Jai Pendu will be our destination. It is there that the Everien Knowledge is surely the most intact.

There were pages and pages of stuff like this:

I am worried about the Animal aspect.
I cannot deny the drives.
Any effort at rationalization is met with an equal and stronger power of the senses.
I must have them.
Ysse, if you are reading this, I must confess to you what I never could.
I did it.
It was me you hunted.
It was me.

Frustrated by the cryptic notes, Istar gave up on reading them. In a day or two she would be reduced to eating them, anyway, if she didn't do something. The Sekk did not return. The snow had begun again, and the thought of going anywhere was impossible.

She examined the sculpture minutely. She could find no seam, no hollow space that would indicate where the white-haired Seahawk had gone. Yet it had been carved there for a reason, she was sure. In the centre of its breast was a slot, covered with ice. Every day with her breath and body heat she tried to melt the ice, but she could never do so completely and on one occasion her lips actually got stuck to the sculpture.

It was a very realistic portrayal of a seahawk. The thing seemed to be attacking, flying out of the wall with beak open and talons extended. Malevolent. Extreme.

There were plenty of bones here, Istar thought. Plenty of skulls. Had he lured them here and killed them, or had they assaulted his cave and been beaten? Or had he killed them elsewhere and dragged their bodies back here?

Where had the Hawk Girls gone, now that she needed them?

The snow stopped but she was too tired to go out. She was beyond hunger or even thirst. The temperature fell. Her mind was going. Istar could feel herself giving up. She propped herself up against the shield of a dead warrior and fell into an exhausted sleep, dimly aware that it would probably be her last.

Then, out of a dreamless darkness, the idea came to her. It was a simple idea, so simple she should have thought of it long ago. She knew what she had to do, but she didn't have the physical strength or the will to carry it out.

Stand up, Istar. Stand up now.

She tried to get to her feet and fell forward stiffly onto her knees.

Draw your damn sword.

That was a complicated motor act. Not possible.

Draw your sword, stupid. It's the last thing you're going to do anyway, so why not?

True. It would all be over soon. She drew her sword.

I said stand UP.

She waveringly rose and doddered forward. Like a very, very old woman who had never picked up a weapon in her life, she drove her father's sword into the slot in the breast of the Seahawk. She felt the resistance of the ice and leaned on it. The ice cracked and slipped away. The sword fit perfectly. It went in.

There was a musical sound. Ice cracking and breaking.

The ground beneath Istar's feet was whisked away.

The Rebel Camp

The rebels had moved into position in the very shadow of an Everien monitor tower which, according to Xiriel, was broken and disused.

'It is a perfect position,' he said. 'They will never know we are here, and we can monitor A-vi-Khalar easily.'

Stavel was anxious to proceed. 'What about your plan?' he pestered Xiriel. 'Time is short! We must strike soon. Do you see how he removes all his weapons to Jai Khalar? He is planning something. The Fire Houses spew out fumes like a dyspeptic dragon.'

'My agent will be back soon,' Xiriel said, and prayed it was true. Pallo could be such a fumbleton; but he had been the best person to send in. Xiriel was afraid that with his soft heart, Pallo had got caught up with Mhani and the other Scholars and so was delayed. He used the excuse of the winter storms to stall. For his own part, Xiriel was frustrated. He had been away from Snake country for months. Jakse sent regular reports, indicating among other things that he had 'poached' some of Tash's Clan recruits. Word came through Jakse of a Seahawk army coming down Tyger Pass, and Xiriel was cheered at this rumour of Istar's accomplishment.

But his problem here was not solved. The Wolves would not wait for ever.

Then the news came. The Pharicians had sent a great army, and it was almost upon Jai Khalar. You could see it from the high ground, cleaving the snow and leaving brown mud in its wake.

'We have missed our chance!' Stavel railed, and the men were restless and eager to act.

'Wait!' said Kassien. 'This is not the time for hasty decisions. Besides, I am not authorized to order an attack at this time.'

'Not authorized?' Stavel said incredulously. 'Whose authority do you require? That of Eteltar the swordsman?'

'No,' Kassien said. 'Dead men cannot help us now. But the king is coming.'

The name of the king still meant something. The Wolves shut up and the camp stayed as still as possible. Waiting. Stavel and his men made periodic forays against the Sekk when necessary. They returned from one of these with a Clan envoy wearing a Pharician uniform. Stavel had put him in chains.

It was all Kassien could do to keep from kicking the envoy who recited Tash's message to him. He kicked the snow instead, cursed, and shouldered roughly past Xiriel, who did not meet his eye. The Seer was intent upon the bound messenger.

'How far behind the emissary is Tash himself?' Xiriel asked.

'He has not set out yet,' said the messenger. 'He is still in Jai Khalar, settling his new wife and briefing his troops. And introducing Hezene's Scholars to the Fire Houses.'

'Prince of Everien! Son of Hezene! Ah, it makes me sick! This will kill Lerien.'

Lerien was not at death's door just yet, but he looked older. He carried too much weight, his face was misshapen thanks to the loss of his eye, and moreover some part of him had succumbed to the idea of failure. He might keep up pretences, but his whole bearing was that of a man who had already given up. Swathed in black furs and with his blond hair long and shaggy, he looked more like a trapper or gamekeep than a king – but such was the state of Everien these days.

Stavel went to see Lerien immediately on his arrival.

'We must put sentiment aside,' the Wolf pleaded. 'The Fire Houses are a tactical objective. So we must remember.'

'Aye, the Fire of Glass. It is the one remaining Artifact, and it was Ysse's. I would that the Pharicians did not have it on that ground alone. But what about the people of A-vi-Khalar? They are Deer, many of them, if not loyal to Tash, then at least not hostile to him. They are pacifists.'

'That's exactly what I mean about sentiment. But we may be able to do it without hurting too many of them. Depending on whose side they take in the war.'

'Very well,' Lerien said. 'Show me your plan.'

'Plan?'

'How are you going to infiltrate the Fire Houses? How will you overpower so many men? What will you do when you take control of the Fire Weapons? And how will you defend against the engines that Tash has already removed to Jai Khalar?'

Stavel said nothing. Plainly he had been so enthusiastic, he had been intending to make it up as he went along.

'We are working on that, King Lerien.'

'Well, work harder and work faster,' Lerien said. 'Soon Hezene will have a stranglehold on everything. Now, Kassien, what do we know about the situation in Snake Country?'

And their attention turned to other matters.

Xiriel began to plan to get back to Snake Country ahead of Tash and his troops. He was kicking himself for letting the lake of candles lie unexplored all winter. Wisdom in hindsight, he thought to himself.

Then Pallo turned up with Mhani and a Deer girl.

Xiriel and Kassien found Pallo stuffing his face with Dhien's honeycakes, pausing every now and again to belch, for the beer was also very good.

'I can get us in,' he said. 'I can get us in secretly. And there will be no need for bloodshed.'

'This is a military camp,' Kassien said sharply. 'Save some food for the soldiers.'

'Sorry,' Pallo said with his mouth full. 'It is a very clever plan, the one I've hatched. And what's more, Xiriel, there are parts of the undercity where I've been that I doubt anybody's been in since before the fall of Everien.'

Xiriel listened to Pallo's story. When it was finished, the Seer planted a loud, smacking kiss on Pallo's forehead, and then rubbed the smeared jam off Pallo's unbearded cheek with an almost maternal thumb.

'Good work!' he said. 'Good, good, good. Let's go see Lerien.'

He dragged Pallo to his feet by one elbow and called Kassien's name at the top of his lungs.

At Lerien's tent, Pallo accepted a cup of hot wine and some buttered black bread but could not eat the bread. Everyone seemed to be compulsively feeding him, and he supposed he looked half starved; but he hadn't the capacity for so many meals in such quick succession, however much he might have liked to indulge.

'Leaving morality aside for a moment,' Lerien said, sharing a private glance with Kassien that left the latter staring sulkily at the floor, 'tell me how you propose to take the Fire Houses.'

Xiriel swallowed his wine and cleared his throat.

'As you know, my lord, there are underground refuges beneath most of the old Everien towns. Some of them are ruined, some are inaccessible, and some, like the undercity of A-vi-Sirinn, are kept sealed and are used only by the Scholars. In the case of A-vi-Khalar, we have a mix of all three. Some of the tunnels and chambers have collapsed and others are unstable, probably due to some shifting of the ground during the past few hundred years. Some areas have been stripped by the Scholars and are now used by the Deer Clan for winter storage and emergency shelter. Yet others are inaccessible, not because of damage, but because the Everiens sealed them and we could never get in.'

Lerien's blue eye had been swimming hazily until now, watching not Xiriel's face, but the slow-shifting flames of the oil fire. When the Seer paused, the eye focused itself on Pallo, who cleared his throat and said,

'The chambers immediately below the Fire Houses have always been locked. We could not break in by force and the means of opening the locks were unknown to Ysse and all her Scholars.'

'I know,' Xiriel said. 'Everien doors are something of an interest of mine. They are seldom opened easily.'

'It was you who opened the doors in the Floating Lands,' Kassien remarked, interested now and having recovered his good humour. 'Have you found some way to get into the secret parts of the Fire Houses?'

'Yes. That is, Pallo has. I can get a team into the centre Fire House through the undercity. And I can shut the Fire Houses down at the source.'

'But the Pharicians will surely overwhelm you and merely start again,' Kassien said. 'That's why, short of storming the entire town and holding it under siege, your plan cannot succeed.'

'You don't know what my plan is,' Xiriel said calmly.

'I'm listening,' Lerien said.

'We will steal the Fire of Glass.'

The Wasp's Arrow

Ice's hoofbeats made the White Road tremble and lurch. Tarquin passed his hands across his eyes, straining to see something, anything. This was not the White Road that Tarquin knew; but then again, the White Road was never the same as itself. He was in a shadowless, colourless tunnel that seemed to change shape around him. He listened for Ice's stride and tried to run toward it, for there was no other way to orient himself. *I will never catch up*, he thought, but found that he didn't really mind. There was a part of Tarquin that was comforted to find himself returning to whatever part of the Liminal the time serpents' path occupied. Life in the bowels of the Earth had tested him and he had barely passed muster. His hair was beginning to grow back in uneven clumps, and the scars where he had cut his scalp when shaving it itched incessantly, and though his body was lean and hard like a young man's, he felt old. He wanted a proper meal, and a fire and sleep – wanted these comforts in a way he had never wanted them in his younger days. He was tired, and he had no place in the world.

Or did he? *Maybe*, he thought wryly, *the Liminal is my place*. For it seemed to him that the visions of Jaya were more real than his long and lonely life of journeying and trying to forget Jai Pendu had ever been. And it seemed to him that any destiny, however convoluted, had to be better than dying in some lonely field or roadhouse, unrecognized by enemies or friends, without ever knowing what his life had been about. When Jaya had looked at him and said *you* she seemed to understand what it meant – what *he* meant.

But Jaya was not here. He had had rumours of her in the world around him, but no dreams, no visions, nothing of Jaya since Jai Pendu.

The hoofbeats slowed, and there was a shuffling sound as though Ice were stepping in place, or turning around his own tail.

'Ice? Kere? Ice?'

Nothing. Then a soft *thud-thud, thud-thud thud*, as though Ice were walking on a softer surface. Tarquin followed the sound trail.

He could still hear the time serpents clicking and breathing some-where behind him, so maybe they were not dead yet. He sucked air deeper into his lungs and extended his stride. The whiteness had not yet broken up into the spilled jigsaw puzzle of worlds that Ice had carried him through on the way to Jai Pendu, but he was sure it would, and then he would be badly lost.

Ice's hoofbeats stopped. Tarquin thought he heard voices, male and female. He strained to hear better, but suddenly the Road began to plunge. He lost his footing and could not regain balance. It was as if the Road was truly made of Ice – and now it had become a frozen waterfall. He could find no purchase. In the distance he heard the hoofbeats begin again, falteringly.

White changed to black with nothing in between. Now he was in a void. He couldn't even figure out which way was down. At the same time, the hairs on the back of his neck flew up, reacting to a sudden, primal sound with terror even as a savage shriek reached his ears. His heart roared with thunder.

Ice was screaming. There was a rush of wind and a smell of damp decay: leaves, earth, rotting wood. Tarquin thought he heard a man laughing, a feral, disturbing sound, and then the musical sound of breaking glass. He was in absolute darkness, sliding out of control on a surface he couldn't see. He fetched up hard against Ice, who smelled reassuringly of horse – and less reassuringly, of blood. He scrambled onto Ice's back, and then the stallion was running in the dark. He could hear and feel Ice's hooves impacting on loamy soil transected by roots, and occasionally a fern or an overhanging branch slapped against them as they barrelled along. They were in a forest. Either he was blind or it was deep night.

Ice's stride did not feel right. He was favouring the right foreleg; Tarquin thought his breathing sounded laboured as well. Then he heard running water, and the horse careered across a stone bridge. Suddenly Tarquin could see. To be sure, it was dark, but once out of the trees the sky was exposed and a grey landscape of fields and woods revealed itself. Behind them lay a river-bordered forest like a great shadow. On the near side of the river were cultivated lands that rose steadily toward a barren moor and a deep blue sky with a thin moon and glassy, weak clouds that caught its light. Strangely, when Tarquin looked back, he saw more of the same, but nothing of the forest that they'd surely come from.

Ice broke from the road and began to climb. Tarquin was holding on for dear life as Ice galloped up a slope too steep for anything but a goat; he glanced once over his shoulder and saw that no one pursued them. There was nothing but the occasional scrub tree for cover, and by the time they reached the crest of the hill, even these had run out. Beyond the green of the river valley stretched a wasteland: first a stony country of scrub and then, beyond, nothing but white sand for mile upon mile, desert like a sheet of wrinkled paper.

Ice lurched sideways and finally came to a halt, flanks heaving. Tarquin leaped off at once, concerned. The animal stood with his legs splayed, neck stretched out in front of him, and head extended. He drew a ragged breath and coughed harshly. Keeping a hand on the horse's sweating shoulder, Tarquin moved around to the front and saw with horror that blood was gushing from a deep arrow wound in his right breast. He put his hand on the shaft to draw it out, thinking with bafflement that there had been no one to fire on them on the White Road; for that matter, he hadn't seen a single bowman among all the Pharicians in the Snake cavern. Nor was the arrow Pharician in design.

He took his hand away. Ice coughed again, spewing blood from his nose and mouth. The horse was shaking all over.

'Easy now,' Tarquin said, laying his palm on Ice's neck comfortingly. The horse seemed unaware of him, preoccupied with his own ragged, crackling breathing. He studied the arrow without touching it, and a slow chill broke across his sweaty back. It had the distinctive notch pattern below the fletching that the Wasp Clan used to warn of a barb point: the arrowhead had been designed with a flower-petal tip that would open inside the wound, rending the flesh horribly if you tried to pull it out. It was a cruel example of Wasp humour, in that even though the arrow told you what it was, you couldn't do anything about it.

But they were not in Everien. In fact, they looked to be in Pharice, on the edge of the southern desert. How had a Wasp Clan arrow gotten into Ice's chest?

After all that had occurred on the Snake island, Tarquin knew better than to think that nothing of the Clans could exist this far south. They had been, after all, a thousand years in the past. Maybe the Wasps had come from these parts, contrary to the legends that placed them in an island chain to the southeast of Hãz. Still he could not work out when the shot had been fired; but there was no time to speculate with the horse dying before his eyes. Now Ice sat down on his hind legs, toppling to the side and finally lying cast out. His flanks heaved spasmodically as he struggled to breathe.

Tarquin left him there and ran back the way they had come to see if the archer was following them. He didn't see a soul. What could he do? The arrow had to come out, but he couldn't act without making matters worse. A skilled surgeon was needed, and an herbalist to prevent infection or fight whatever poisons were in the tip of the arrow. Although, if Kere had survived the poison of the Snakes, there probably wasn't much that could hurt him.

The sun was beginning to rise. Where there was a river, and a road, there would be settlements. He would have to bring help. He glanced over his shoulder, thinking that he should tell Ice what he planned to do, just in case the horse really could understand him. But the curve of the sand was undisturbed by any form. The white horse was gone.

Tarquin couldn't believe it. He ran back to the place where the horse had been, following the tracks in the sand. There was a trail of blood leading to the depression where Ice had lain down, where there was more blood. And going off to the right, toward a stack of red sand-sculpted rocks, was a set of human footprints.

'Kere?' he called, not daring to hope. 'Is that you?'

Kere was curled up on his side in the shadow of the rocks, eyes shut. Tarquin bent over him and gently pulled his arms from his body. There was no blood, no arrow. The boy stirred and murmured irritably, as if he'd been disturbed in his sleep.

'Kere, wake up,' Tarquin said. 'Can you breathe?'

Kere moaned. 'Sure, I can breathe. Ah, I have a headache. Could you put out the sun, please?'

Tarquin laughed in relief. 'That was one hell of a dose of venom you took. I wonder if it cured your fits.'

Kere had folded his arms across his eyes to block out the light. His voice came out muffled. 'I thought I was going to die.'

'Can you remember what happened?'

'I took the venom, and I could see the future, the past, I could see across the possibilities of every move I made. It was too much. I thought I would be sick. Then Ice came, but he was . . . he had a shadow.'

'Yes?' Tarquin said. 'And what about the arrow? Who shot Ice?'

Kere swung his head from side to side.

'You don't know? You won't tell me? What? Kere!'

'Paradox! Paradox!'

The boy kicked out suddenly and Tarquin was thrown back several feet, stunned but unhurt. When he picked himself up, Ice stood there, ears erect, nostrils wide. He lashed his tail like a cat and Tarquin saw the muscles of his chest gather and bunch even though his feet did not shift. Most unhorselike behaviour, he thought. He could not help but notice the edge on Ice's hooves, which though unshod were in perfect condition, gleaming and sharp, and he recalled the glint of the animal's fangs, which though not needed for eating grass, were evidently useful in a fight. Tarquin shuddered when he thought of the power in those tightly muscled jaws.

Ice was only watching him. It was enough to make Tarquin feel insignificant. Kere is a fool, he thought. Why would anyone want to be a man when he could outrun anything on legs, outfight a black bear, and cross times and dimensions as easily as a man could ford a river? That this animal had come to Keras's call and let her ride bareback would have been inconceivable to Tarquin had he not witnessed it. For

366

the hauteur, the inherent superiority of his being, was written all over the beast. Electricity hummed along every line of his body. It was excessive, Tarquin thought. The horse was like a light you couldn't turn off. Everywhere he went he would stand out. Every move he made was a flagrant challenge.

'Now then,' Tarquin said. 'Where are you taking me? What is this about?'

Ice turned and began to walk across the sand. His body surged, rising and falling like a flowing tide, as he laboured across the dunes. Black blood had dried in thick deposits on his coat; as Ice moved Tarquin could see the gleam of fresh blood welling anew from the tear where the dart penetrated the muscle. He grimaced as he imagined the horse's pain. Ice was avoiding putting weight on the right leg, yet he gallantly pressed on, glancing back from time to time with nostrils aflare as if to remind Tarquin that pity would not be acceptable, and that he was still fully capable of killing his erstwhile rider.

'Where are you going?' called Tarquin, wondering if Kere could hear him and feeling like a fool. He had treated Kere with little patience, and now it seemed Ice was going to rub his nose in it.

If they went down into the river valley they would sooner or later find someone who might help them. Not that Tarquin had any money. Not that he looked worthy of help. From the look of the landscape Tarquin felt sure they were somewhere in Pharice, probably even the central part of the country not far south of the Jundun plateau. The river would lead them to civilization. But the desert . . . well, if they were where Tarquin thought they were, this desert stretched all the way to the Khynahi Mountains and the emptiness of Or, Ice's birthplace. He had no water. He had no food. But how could he complain? Ice was injured, and poisoned besides. Dark lines could be seen radiating from the wound where his blood was infected by the Wasp chemical.

Tarquin had the terrible feeling that Ice was going home to die.

Eteltar

It was all pain at first, and not even the kind of pain Istar understood. The pain she understood from experience was the kind you could fight, the kind that set your teeth on edge but also sharpened you and made you focus. She had never experienced the enervating, sapping, total-body pain that engulfed her now. She was sure she had broken every bone in her body. Everything hurt. Her thoughts were blurry and she drifted in and out of a nauseous consciousness, lapsing into a dark and awful sleep when she couldn't bear the awareness of her own body.

Afterward it was humiliating to learn that she hadn't broken anything, that she was only bruised and battered, with a lump on her head the size of a duck egg being the cause of most of the trouble.

Someone held her head and made her drink an awful tea that made her shudder. At first she vomited the tea up, disgusted with herself and her own helplessness and also perversely satisfied when she heard the curses of the one who doctored her – possibly because he cursed in perfect Seahawk, reminding her of Pentar. But she knew he was not Pentar, because his eyes were pale green and his face was gaunt, and his hands were dry and warm, with strong tendons and long fingers but none of the heavy flesh or sword calluses of Pentar's hands. He had a pleasant smell about him and the back of her head tingled at the sound of his voice, which she heard when he cursed her cheerfully. The reason he cursed her was because he kept propping up her head and urging her to drink, and she kept spitting it out or regurgitating it. He persisted and after a while she kept the tea down; then, after a little longer, she guzzled it, for as revolting as the taste might be, her body seemed to crave it.

She still didn't try to move. At first it was daytime. The light moved steadily across the sky. It was very hot, and though she lay in the shade of some kind of canopy or tent made of bleached Pharician linen, she could see the sun reflected off reddish brown stone nearby, and there never seemed to be any clouds. She made an effort to think. She remembered falling but not landing, yet it seemed to her now from what she could see of the rocks and the sky, and from the way the wind moved, that she was still on some kind of height. At times she wondered whether this could all be some kind of frost-induced hallucination, and whether she was still in the cave, snowed in above Tyger Pass; but she did not think she could be capable of hallucinating the person who was taking care of her.

It was evening when she got her first good look at him, for he came back to attend her. She woke from a shapeless sleep and the light was coming at him sideways, dramatizing the angles and planes of his face and setting his extraordinary form all alight. For a long moment she gaped, speechless.

His face was very like that of the ghostly warrior, the Sekk she had pursued. The same face – but older, much thinner, and the skin showing signs of wear. He wore no braids, so his hair fell in a silver cascade from the crown of his head. His skin was drawn tight across prominent cheekbones and an aquiline nose. He was pale not with the fleshy pallor of the Seahawk people, but with the metallic sheen of certain lizards, a whiteness closer to blue than to pink. Where most men had hair on the chest and belly, he had a light brushing of feathers that lay close to his skin and made him shine even more. His genitals were held by a pouch of dark feathers bound with a string about his hips, but the rest of him was bare. He still had the big frame of the Seahawk warrior, but his body was sinewy and spare, and she could see his diaphragm moving when he breathed. He looked less like flesh than like a scrap of sunlit wind.

Behind and above him, enormous and powerful, was a set of wings to put any raptor to shame. Istar could not stop staring at them. They were a smoky grey, three shades darker than his silver hair. He had a tail to match. From behind he would look like a gigantic skyfalcon; but his underbelly was human.

'Taretel?' she asked in a whisper. 'Is it true? Can you fly?'

He frowned at the name. 'Eteltar I was called,' he said.

'Ysse said you were Free as far as she was concerned. So she named you Taretel. She said you opened the White Road for her, but then you disappeared. You joined the birds, they say. Is it really true?'

'I joined the birds,' he said. He spoke slowly as if out of practice. 'But I did not think anyone had witnessed it. I hoped Ysse might come someday. If you are here, I must conclude that she will not come herself. Did she send you?'

'She is dead.'

He looked at her and his eyes were anguished with an uncomplicated pain, like a child's. She had to look away.

He recovered quickly. 'Why have you come, then?'

'I was hunting Sekk. A Sekk who looked like you.'

'Ah,' he intoned, and she thought his voice was unusually deep for his light frame. 'I understand.'

He began to laugh, and she was afraid.

'Drink more tea,' he said, and knelt to offer her the bowl. She hesitated, her body craving the strange liquid but her mind beginning to question his motives. He laughed again. 'Go on, drink it! I don't poison people. I'm trying to make you well. That fall you took, I've never seen anything like it. You should be dead, by all rights.'

'Where am I?' she said weakly, sipping and looking up at his silver face and then sipping some more, while his hands held the bowl patiently.

'These are the Khynahi Mountains, and just below is the desert that will be known as Or, but now there are no names for it. No men come here. Ever.'

'I fell. Was it a trapdoor? I put my sword into the Seahawk and the next thing I knew I was falling.'

'It was meant for Ysse's sword. Or my own.'

'Chyko's sword was modelled on Ysse's. Only it has wasps and mantises on it, see?'

'I have examined your weapon,' he said gravely. 'It is a fine one.'

'Made in the Fire Houses,' she said proudly.

'So they burn once again.'

'Yes! Don't you know? Ysse brought the Fire of Glass from Jai Pendu. I thought you knew.'

'I have forgotten much, so if ever I knew these things, I'm not surprised if they are gone from my mind. But I don't think I was there to see Ysse after she returned. I don't think I could have been.'

His brow wrinkled pensively and Istar wondered why he looked so bemused. He let loose another laugh, but it contained more unease than mirth. He explained,

'All the things I learned in my time in ancient Everien were retained by the skyfalcon, but hardly any by me. I have forgotten nearly all of it. And I fear what may happen to me if I am taken back through that door where you fell. I have tried to go and the effects are terrible.'

'You are a Sekk,' Istar said. 'The Hawk Girls led me to you.'

'I killed their family.' His tone was matter-of-fact and he took no notice of the fact that she was reeling at his revelation, her face heating, her chest tightening. He continued, 'It is what I do, what I am, out there beyond the gate. The sisters who brought you to me know it well.'

'I was looking for you anyway. You make it sound like I was a gift to you from the Hawk Girls.'

'No!' He directed a keen gaze at Istar, his eyes full of an understanding that rattled her. She had never seen someone with so much knowledge in his eyes. It was like looking at two stars, two shards of infinity. 'I think they know that you will be the death of me, and that is why they brought you.'

370

This was the beginning of Eteltar's spell, though Istar would only realize it when she looked back later – much later, when her tears had long since run dry and she was pretending she could think about it all with cold objectivity.

Days turned into a week, and then a fortnight. The bruises and aches slowly lessened. She began to move more freely, but she could not go far as Eteltar lived on a ledge set in a cliff of great height. She would have to climb in order to go anywhere other than the cave, the tent, or the strip of sunbaked rock where he was in the habit of perching. And she was not yet fit to climb. Her scabs itched. To ease her boredom she talked. She told Eteltar of the Floating Lands, and Jai Pendu and events since then in Everien. She told him about her parents, wishing he would volunteer more information; but he said he had not known Chyko and did not seem interested. Istar's initial awe and respect at finding herself in the presence of the great Skymaster quickly became exasperation at his reticence.

'I wish you would tell me more. You must remember something of Everien. And what of Ysse? Won't you tell me anything about how you learned to open the White Road, or what you found there?'

He never answered her. It was as if she hadn't spoken.

'You have to go back,' he would say. 'You can't stay here. It isn't even a world yet. Look, see those horses below? They don't even belong on that plain; they are only there because they have lost their way passing through the time serpent hole. No horse will be born here for thousands of years. That is the sort of place this is. It is not a place for you!'

'I will be happy to go back,' Istar said, although it was a lie because she was fascinated by Eteltar and the wings she never saw him use. She didn't want to leave until she'd learned more of him. She added, 'However, I can't see how I got here. I fell. But I don't know how far. Is there a hole up in the cliff?'

He gave her a weird look then: not full on. Sneaky.

'See for yourself.'

'I don't think I can climb it,' she said.

'Do you have a choice?'

'Have you got any rope? Spikes?'

'Look in the cave. You may find things you can use.'

It was a terrible cliff to have to climb, and her confidence had been badly shaken by the fall. She felt defeated before she'd begun. Eteltar was utterly neutral and unsupportive, although he did provide food for her, mostly in the form of fish from his carefully tended stock pond, below, and fresh-killed rabbits supplied by the birds. She cooked for them both over a heatstone fire ('I usually eat it raw,' he said. 'But it is very nice, the way you scorch it. Much less effort to chew.'). As her body recovered, her mind became less certain of everything she had formerly known. The sunlight and silence and emptiness of the cliffs had a way of blasting away her sense of who or what she was. She came to feel like a feeble extension of the rock itself as she crawled up the cliff face, a little higher every day as she built her route. Sometimes she froze, clinging to the rock, unable to move as the sudden awareness flooded her that if she fell and died, no one would ever know. She simply did not matter.

'I am nothing,' she whispered into the impassive rock. If the blistering heat did not destroy her, the isolation would. Being with Eteltar was not like being with another person. He was too different, too unpredictable. Nor was it like being alone – for every so often he would do or say something that made her believe they *did* have something in common. He would offer a glimpse of intimacy, and then in a flash he would take it away. No – being with Eteltar was not like being alone. It was worse.

Yet it was he – Eteltar with his wings – who had magnetized her, made her stick to the rock; determined her actions; shaped her mind. Never had she felt such a psychological tautness as that between her and the winged man. His will overpowered her. To be subject to an element or natural force she could easily accept, for these things were simple and often transient in their effects. But to be subject to another person was a different thing entirely. Eteltar eclipsed everything else in the world. Everything he did or said became the focus of her attention, not because he was seeking it, but because she couldn't look away from him. As time passed, it became so that she would have done anything for him. He was like a god to her, only without the distance of divinity, for she loved him, too, in all the small intransigent illogical ways she had never known it was possible to love.

She didn't call it that to herself, of course. She kept focused on her goal: to get high enough to pass back through to the icy cave. Istar knew she had been stupid to fall in love with Kassien, who would never love her back, but to fall in love with a man who wasn't a man would be even worse.

So then she would decide that she hated him, and she would struggle and fall while he looked on.

'Will I ever get back?' she would sometimes ask him, almost in despair, and he always said, 'Yes, of course!' or 'Don't be silly – you have to.'

But he never proposed how she should do it.

He was strangely manlike at times, and would talk of his days in the Fire

Houses, trying to make sense of them, excavating, experimenting. His falcons, he said, had followed him even into the valley of Everien where they would never otherwise have gone; laughingly he described them fishing on the riverbank, startling at their own reflections in the slow dark water. He did not care what men thought of him, he said, for the judgment of the birds was higher and more demanding, and they understood the politics of solitude.

Istar felt a yearning when he spoke of those times, a yearning to have been there not as herself, but as him. It seemed to her that Eteltar held the very essence of life within him like light in a jar; that is, he did not hold on to it, did not contain it at all, but somehow it multiplied in him and reflected off him, like a killing bolt from the heavens given form and turned to understanding by its capture. Living had not killed Eteltar. He laughed at the sharp end of life, at death its scorpion-tail sting, and Istar wanted to be him but could not. She felt like a wet incognizant lump of clay. He filled her with desire, and shame its underside – shame for all she was not and never could be.

'Teach me the things that made you what you are,' she begged, and he shrugged and threw pebbles at her.

'There's nothing to teach,' he said.

'But I have to get back to Tyger Pass! And you're supposed to be helping me.'

He shrugged again. 'I'm trying to teach you. I can't help it if you don't learn.'

Learn what? she wondered. Istar had never had a teacher who didn't state in advance what were his purposes; who didn't inform her in some way exactly what she needed to do to satisfy him; who couldn't be understood in his habits and anticipated in his actions.

Sometimes he would whistle cheerfully and encourage her.

'That's it, Starry! Up you go! Use your fingers! There! To your left, a beautiful little hold!'

'Where?' Istar, eyes shut, on the edge of panic as her strength began to give. 'Where? Where?'

'To your left and up! Come on, girl, stretch! It's got your name on it, it's calling you, *Istar, Istar, come and grab me!* Almost. Almost. Yes!'

And as she hung there by her fingertips she would hear him sighing in empathetic relief. 'Good!' he'd pronounce, his voice coloured with the same pleasure he reserved for food well eaten, and a good wind to fly on. For in his odd way, he was a pleasure addict, she soon learned. And he was as lazy as the sky was blue. He soon had her fetching water, gutting fish, catching rabbits, finding eggs, gathering brush for fire, and performing every other mundane task possible.

While she was doing all this – and doing it weakly for she had lost most of her condition and all of her fat while freezing to death in Tyger Pass – Eteltar was busy carving the cliff face.

He had a cave, to which he might have made any number of improvements to in order to increase its comforts and keep the bat shit off everything. But he spent little time there and did not seem to hoard possessions of any kind. (He usually slept outside, sometimes on a ledge, or sometimes in the tent with Istar, where he would fold a wing over her to keep her warm. He did not touch her with his hands, and he did not snore.) The cave was little more than a rain shelter, and it almost never rained. But with his chisel and any scrap of rock he could find, Eteltar spent his days chipping at the cliff.

'Are you looking for something?' she asked him in the beginning. 'Gold? Gems?'

'Nope.'

'Are they holds for birds? Handholds for me to climb?'

He laughed. She knew the latter was not true. He was more likely to climb past her and knock her down with a stray blow of a wing while she was executing a particularly difficult traverse, than to do anything to assist her in any way.

'Is it art?' she asked finally, timid because she thought maybe she had offended him by not recognizing the aesthetic value of his efforts until now.

'No,' he answered. 'It is not art.'

And his tone warned her against further probing.

She could not see the design in its entirety from below, but she knew that he was working on a large section of the cliff face and that he was often engaged in precision chiselling. When she was able to climb high enough to actually witness him at work, she saw that he was chipping out tiny flakes of rock. Where he had worked it, the smooth stone had been made subtly bumpy, so that when she glided her palm across its surface, she could feel a patterned texture.

She watched him from below. He clung to the rock like an insect, his wings and tail splayed out for balance and his bare hands and feet gripping the rock with nearly equal dexterity. His concentration was ferocious. His purpose was inscrutable. When a bird came along once and perched near him, preparing to break open a snail on a small ledge, Eteltar went after it so suddenly and violently she thought he had gone mad. He chased it off, screaming insults. Istar cowered where she was, afraid to move until he had returned his attention to his work. She made sure not to drive any pitons into the areas he was sculpting after that. She thought it might be more than her life was worth.

Occasionally he tried to help her, but he was impatient and critical on some days, kind and helpful on others. When it came to climbing, he had an instinct for knowing exactly where she was going wrong, and if she had a deficit that she used a crutch to overcome, he would happily kick away the metaphorical crutch and watch her struggle on the ground, in the dust, crippled. He attacked her bad habits and weaknesses, taking personal offence at them. There was no malice in this, just a cool kind of realism – but that didn't make it hurt less.

Once she fell rather badly and sustained a long scrape from her armpit, across one breast, down her ribs, to her opposite hip. The wound became infected, and she was fevered and then delirious. During that time he hovered over her ceaselessly. More of the horrific tea was forced down her. Dressings were changed with astonishing gentleness. Jokes were told. The tent was always positioned to keep the sun from burning her eyes.

Then she recovered and the ridicule began in earnest. She had the feeling he was insulting her to test how much she could take, so even when his remarks hurt her she didn't show it. His moods could be contagious, and sometimes Eteltar succeeded in driving Istar almost to madness with his lightning changes from resentment to humour and back. She was never sure whether he was aware of his effect on her, or whether she was reading some purpose or wisdom into his behaviour that wasn't really there. Often he acted foolishly and said outrageous things, as if trying to goad her into believing she was only his exploitee and he a maniac. And he almost succeeded. Yet there was always a gleam in his eye, a slight backward glance as he was going away, as if he could not resist giving away his own game. As if the mirth he had created for himself by torturing her actually overwhelmed him.

Torture. Yes, every day it was a kind of torture to be with Eteltar. Maybe it was because she had come so close to dying in Tyger Pass, or maybe she was just a perverse human being, but – disturbingly for Istar – she liked it.

Or

The horse walked mile after mile until all sign of humanity had been left behind and the mountains blocked the stars. He stopped. Tarquin had been keeping a respectful distance, staggering along not under the pain of a wound, but nevertheless profoundly weary. When he glanced up, the horse was gone and the boy was there. Kere didn't turn or speak to him. Like a tired soldier he, too, kept walking, dragging his bare feet through the sand.

At last the mountains, flushed with the light of dawn, grew clear. Kere was stumbling in a half-dream. The sun rose and grew strong. When it approached mid-heaven, Kere's knees gave way and he sat down in the sand. The mountains were closer, but not close enough. Tarquin stopped, too.

'I know those hills,' he said, shading his eyes to gaze at the tumble of sienna and umber mountains that cut into the azure sky. There was no vegetation on the mountains, but high on the red slopes lay snow like icing sugar. Below, the brazen desert sulked in the heat, throwing up ripples and teasing eye and tongue with phantom pools of water.

Kere said, 'I'm home,' and burst into tears.

Tarquin could get no sense out of him at first.

'What are we doing, Kere? Where are we going? Is Ice still . . . he's not . . . ?'

'He's not dead. But he's very weak. And I can't go much farther without water.'

Tarquin said, 'We must try to get out of the sun. Come on! Don't give up.'

They set off again. Tarquin thought he was in a delirium when he felt the hoofbeats, and he threw himself on the ground to listen. It was not a dream. Riders were coming toward them.

It was a trading caravan led by a couple of enthusiastic young lads on spirited desert horses. Tarquin took them in at a glance and knew they were ordinary horses, not predators like Ice. He was planning how to address them when Kere hailed them in perfect desert dialect. Tarquin had forgotten about the boy's gift for languages, and now found himself standing to one side while the white-haired freak conversed fluently with the traders.

'We are in Or,' he announced to Tarquin, his eyes sparkling. 'And they have a horse doctor among them! It is our great luck, for she is on her way home from a consultation in the mountains, or else she would not be abroad at all. She is very old, they say.'

'Can she help Ice?'

'I hope so. Come on! They will take us to her.'

They were led to a covered wagon at the back of the train. Kere asked for water and they were brought a skin of it together with some flatbread, which between the two of them they wolfed down. In the dim interior of the silk-covered wagon, the horse doctor sat on a pile of silken cushions, smoking. She was wearing a dark cowl, and the only thing they could see of her were her withered and twisted hands on the pipe she smoked.

She welcomed them in Pharician and added, 'You smell of the White Road.'

'The White Road has a smell?' Tarquin said incredulously.

'My sense of smell is keener than most,' she answered. 'I like to think of it and other gifts as compensation for my sacrifices.'

Kere leaped on the word. 'Sacrifices? Madam, have you also been given to the horses of Or?'

She made a soft sound, halfway between a laugh and a sigh.

'No. I did not speak of that. You see, I have no more eyes.' The gnarled hands reached up and let down her cowl. 'I have only diamonds.'

It was true. Where her eyes had been were two dark hollows from which gleamed two brilliant stones, each worth a fortune anywhere in the world – but here in the desert, worth more than the land and all its contents combined.

'Give me your hands, boy, I will look at you.'

Kere put his hands in hers and she directed her sightless eyes at him.

'I can see his wound,' she said without prompting. 'He has been wounded in a battle with another of the same kind. He can no longer run. When he is afraid, he will try to become the horse, but he cannot. Instead, he has a seizure.'

'Wounded in a battle with another of the same kind . . . what kind?'

'Another horse. But not directly.'

'But he wasn't wounded,' Tarquin said. 'I was with him, and he wasn't wounded.'

'You were on the White Road? That must have been where it happened.'

'But it didn't happen!' Tarquin denied. 'That's what I'm telling you. He was fine.'

'The White Road doesn't connect places,' said the doctor. She let go of Kere's hands and took a long pull on her pipe.

Tarquin groaned. 'I don't want to talk philosophy. Just tell me how we can cure him.'

'I can do nothing. I cannot cure an injury that has not yet occurred.'

'Has not yet occurred? Are you trying to wring my mind?'

'Why do I try to explain such things to you. The horse Ice has not yet encountered the bowman who will hurt him.'

'How did you know it was a bowman?' Tarquin blurted, and her head turned toward him although the glimmering stones could not fix on him.

'The arrow will wound him first, and then eventually kill him,' she said bluntly.

It was hot and stuffy in the caravan, and Tarquin had been sweating liberally. Suddenly he found himself shivering. How had she known such things? They had told her nothing, and there was no visible mark on the boy.

'You know about Kere, then,' Tarquin said. 'You know that he was Eaten.'

She smiled enigmatically and blew a smoke ring.

'Long ago the great ones defined the animals. They sculpted their forms and made them solid. You can still see the statues, deep in the desert of Or, if you go there when the majala blows. So it was that men captured creatures. And some creatures captured men; but that is another matter.

'There was only one animal the sculptors could not render in stone, and it was the horse. Alone in the world the horses of Or resisted taming. They are too swift to be seen. Even the deer were captured, but the horses of Or cannot be caught by men. They still run wild among the Animal Guardians, and some of them have powers beyond those of other animals. The people of the desert, who ride and eat their lesser cousins, worship the horses. They even offer their children to them in exchange for their protection. The horses of Or are so swift they are seldom seen at all. If you see one, remember that although they are beautiful, they are not kind creatures and must never be taken on face value.'

She patted Kere's hair; Tarquin noticed that although she was blind, her hand didn't hesitate or falter and she made no error in bringing it to the boy's funny, standing-out-straight hair.

Tarquin said, 'What kind of powers? How is it that they move too fast for the eye?'

'What you ask is a mystery. The Guardians may know the answer, but I do not.'

She pulled the cowl back up.

'All right,' said Tarquin wearily. 'I'm truly trying to understand what you say. If Ice hasn't been hurt yet but somehow senses that he will be, why doesn't he just avoid doing the thing that will hurt him?'

'He is a creature who exists in more than one place at the same time. Therefore he does not live in a straight line, but in a circular way. Whatever has not yet happened to him, this poison arrow, it has already harmed him as we see him now, and there is no taking that back . . . now. But if he can somehow make it to the time and place where the injury is due to occur, and then avoid it, then in that future he will be cured, by virtue of the fact that he will never have been hurt.'

Tarquin sighed. 'Tell me only what you think I should do. Please.'

'It is not for you to decide,' said the doctor, and the cowl turned toward Kere.

'Me?' Kere said. 'What?'

'Ice has used you as an escape route from his own death. You are his immortality. It is up to you to find the way – and to recognize and avoid the danger when it appears.'

'What way?' said Kere. 'Where? How?'

The boy was scared and trembling. The doctor reached over and laid her hand on the side of his neck.

'Why can't I just be me? Why can't Ice go his way and I go mine? Wouldn't that be easier on everybody?'

For once Tarquin agreed with Kere wholeheartedly, but he knew even before she spoke that the old woman would gainsay it.

'It is too late. You and Ice are bound too deep with each other. You have been assimilated into the fibres of his body. He is the keeper of many, many humans, and he cannot let them go any more than he can let you go.'

Tarquin could not hold back any longer. 'How do you know so many things? Are you a Seer? Do you have the Knowledge, even here in Or?'

The doctor said, 'I can smell it.'

'*Smell?*'

One slow nod. 'I can smell your history. A dog can do the same, but he cannot reason as I can. From the moment you sent the Company back to Jai Pendu, Ice was in peril. For at that moment he became a potential target for the Wasp, and no matter how he tried to avoid the archer – by becoming Kere in the Snake island, refusing to answer the boy's call or yours – he could not avoid this destiny. For once he came to you in the time serpent's tunnel, he was on the road to the forest of Paradox, where the archer was waiting.'

'But why would anyone want to shoot Ice? Ride him, sure, but shoot him? It's crazy. Why?'

'Ah, but you do not know the circumstances which led to the arrow being released. You know the end of the story but not its middle. You did not witness the act. The time serpent's venom took Ice to the time and place of his death. Literally.'

'I thought we could slip death,' Kere said. 'I thought if we were wary, we could avoid it.'

'It has been done,' the doctor acknowledged. 'But this archer is not to be fooled with. Not what you expect.'

'I see that now,' Kere said.

'Now, Ice has run back to his beginning-place, where he is safe. If time is a current, Ice is in its backwater. He cannot leave. He is hemmed in on all sides by death and paradox. Anywhere he points the road, it will lead to a contradiction, or to his own destruction. So he hides his spirit in the boy. And when the boy dies, so does Ice.'

'And while I live? Am I his to command?'

'You are faced with a unique choice. The first time he took you, it was against your will. You were a babe in arms and could make no decisions for yourself. Now you are alive, and he is dying. If you want to go free, you need do nothing. Ice will end, and you will continue. As a human.'

Kere nodded.

'Is there no way to save the horse?' Tarquin said. 'Can we do nothing?'

'You would have to return to the place and time of his death and see to it that this arrow does not penetrate him. That it *cannot*. Remove that possibility, and he is saved.'

'How can we do that?' Tarquin said. 'How can we get Ice to take us back to that place and time, so we can prevent the wound being incurred?'

'Ice will not trust you now. You have tricked him.'

'Maybe we could get him to change his mind. It is his life at stake, after all.'

'That is the choice of the boy,' said the doctor.

'What choice?' Kere asked nervously.

'As I was starting to say, you were first Eaten against your will. Give Ice your spirit freely, and perhaps he will trust you enough to come to you. But there is no guarantee you can avoid this death. If he takes you to the place it happened, he will leave you to deal with the situation. And the arrow could strike you, not him. In that event, Ice would still die, and so would you.'

Kere swallowed. 'What a mess,' he murmured.

They stayed with the caravan partway across the desert; then Kere suddenly began making his farewells and Tarquin found himself being handed food and water and then being left standing in the blinding heat as the caravan began to pick up and move off. Tarquin had no means to pay the horse doctor, so he hastily gave her the scabbard Ysse had given to him.

'If you bring it to Jundun you will find men of the Circle who will pay handsomely for it,' he said.

'I do not need money,' she replied. 'But I deem also that you do not need this, so I will take it from you.'

From then on, he had to carry a bare sword. Kere set off into the open desert and Tarquin followed him.

'I can't talk to you, Tarquin,' Kere said. 'Don't follow me.'

Tarquin kept his mouth shut, but he certainly did follow Kere. It was a waste of energy to try to dissuade the boy from madness, but he calculated their food and water and watched their distance from the hills, and he told himself that if something did not happen within twelve hours he would hit the boy over the head and carry him back to civilization.

What he did not expect was that while they dozed in the midday heat, the boy would take off without warning. Tarquin woke and Kere was gone. He had not taken food or water, and his footprints led on out into the open sand. Tarquin set off after him, trudging up and down the dunes.

He walked for hours because that was what he knew how to do; but when he stopped, he found himself at a loss for a purpose. The red cliffs and their system of roads and caves were behind Tarquin's back, and except for the outflung branch of the Khynahi Mountains to his left, the desert lay before him as wide and mysterious as a sea. There were no herds anywhere near. The sand was undisturbed and the horizon was clean. He was alone.

He didn't like being alone.

It seemed absurd to admit it, for he had spent so many years on the road with only the wind for a companion that he thought himself inured to solitude. Certainly he couldn't get along with anyone else. Kere had put proof to that statement! Maybe in the old days when he'd had his Company around him, maybe then he'd felt at ease. What he wouldn't give now for just one of them beside him, someone to crack a joke with and sit back-to-back on watch. Horses weren't the only herd animals, Tarquin thought wryly. Maybe even he was one himself.

Tarquin strained his eyes in the failing light. The sky was empty of clouds, birds, portents. There was no sound but for the slight scratching of wind on loose sand. Yet in the depths of his chest he could feel vibrations like drums, like the speech of the Snake Clan when a fight was coming. His heartbeat intensified, and there was an implied darkness in the rhythm that seemed to come from within him; whether it was imagination or not he couldn't be certain.

He scanned his surroundings for movement, for any feature at all. Now that the light was lower he could see more clearly, and he picked up the shadow of a distant figure: the boy with white hair. His heart leaped.

But something was wrong with the picture. For a disorientating series of moments he realized that something *was* moving; that the horizon itself was bending and lifting like a wave on the ocean; that the sound he could feel in the bones of his body was transferred not across the air, but across the miles of sand that was heaving and convulsing on itself – sand lifting like water, sand travelling over itself as a cloak skims a polished floor. He turned in a slow circle as the sky got smaller and the desert got taller, and wind came up as quick as light, burning across the surface of the ground and hurling loose sand at him.

'Kere!' But his voice was lost on the wind. 'Kere, you can die out here. We'll find another way to do this! Stop where you are before the sands pick you up.'

If it were daylight, the hue of the sands would be the blinding white that Keras had spoken of when she compared Ice to the majala, the white winds of Or. But there was no sun to illuminate the desert, only the terrible noise of the storm all around and the feeling of the ground beneath his feet shifting and falling away like the sands of an hourglass running down, time running out and taking him with it. If this was the birthplace of Ice, then no wonder the horse made everything else in the world seem weak and bloodless. The sand was whipping through the air like a moving tunnel, spinning into a vortex that rose and danced into the air like the backbone of a dancing snake. The flying sand gave shape to a force that was otherwise no more visible than a malevolent spirit, a demon that sucked Tarquin down and threw him up again as if he were no more solid than the line painted on the side of a child's top which spirals as it spins. The inchoate darkness whipped him every which way as no human wrestler ever could until his mind finally overloaded. Everything around him was dark, but his vision went all white, like the inside of a cloud, and then ended.

His head hurt and his ribs ached from what must have been the impact when the storm finally dropped him. He lay for a long time listening to the wind, covering his head with his folded arms to protect his eyes and skin from the burning rush of the sand. At last it was quiet, and he opened his eyes. He was lying half buried in drifted black sand that sparkled as if studded with tiny gems. It was a clear night without moon or wind. Kere was not there. A rash of stars dazzled him from a sky that was too large to be seen. He was deep in the desert, and the wind had fetched him up hard against a stone wall that rose in an irregular shape and blotted out the stars. After a moment he made out that it was a statue of great proportions, shaped like an animal. At irregular intervals across the still desert, other statues also stood, blacker than black against the phosphorescent sparkle of the sand. They did not relieve the emptiness, but rather were an aspect of it, their presence obliquely emphasizing the negative space around them. Each statue depicted an animal, but hundreds of times greater in scale: lion, lizard, bat, turtle . . . They faced different directions and seemed to be different sizes, unless the distances on this plain were not as they appeared. Most were too far away to be identified, and there was no end to them that he could see.

Later the feeling would fade as he stood back from it, but now, held in the pause of his own heartbeat, ruled by the will of the Animal Guardian, he realized what his life was, and what it wasn't, with a certainty as true as bone. It was impossible to prevaricate, and there was nowhere to hide, and if he ran away he knew it would catch and eat him and render him into usable soft tissue but his fate would never be known to him. That was the Guardian's innocence. That was its power. His eyes depicted them as gates or statues in the desert but they were only as smoke, as lightning its precursor, as cloud war noise the maker of both.

He wrenched his eyes away from the lion statue and scanned the darkness. Kere must have come here, too, but Tarquin couldn't see anything moving. The next statue was half a mile away, but between it and Tarquin there was a raised plinth in the desert, a platform identical to the one that supported the lion, only empty.

'There is no Horse Guardian, for they did not catch the Horses of Or,' the old diamond-eyed woman had said. 'The Horses of Or can outrun time itself.'

Tarquin stared at the place where the statue should be. The lion guarded something; so did the snake and the sparrow, but if this was the place of the horse, the horse was not in it. Whatever the horse was meant to guard had been left unattended and free.

The missing Guardian held the air in a state of tension like a violin string, its control as unmistakable as if it made an actual sound – but it did not. He felt he should approach the empty platform, but he was afraid of it.

'He has to come,' Kere whispered in his ear, and Tarquin jumped, his heart racing. The boy had crept up beside him.

'This is his returning-place. This is his anchor. He has to come here. And if I am here, he has to take me.'

'Kere!' Tarquin grabbed the boy by both shoulders and shook him. 'I've never been so glad to see anybody in my life.'

'It may be the last time,' Kere said, just as the hoofbeats began. 'I think this is the end of me.'

Like audible ghosts, they were coming. There were four of them, and the largest had fangs. This one, Tarquin thought, made Ice look like a palfrey.

'What the hell are you up to?' Tarquin cried, grabbing hold of Kere and looking for somewhere to run where the man-eating horses couldn't catch them.

'They can help me get enough speed,' Kere said. 'Maybe. And then Ice will have to come. Hold on to me!'

The Horses of Or swept up to Kere and Tarquin, eyes blazing, light flying from their hooves, nostrils hellishly red. With a trumpeting scream one of them lunged at Tarquin as he ran past, his teeth sinking into the pack of food that Tarquin had strapped to his back. Water sprayed everywhere; Tarquin screamed as the teeth continued to penetrate into the back of his shoulder; and the horse dragged him off at a blinding velocity. His ears popped. Kere was holding him and screaming. His feet came off the ground and for just a moment, he felt that he was flying.

Listening Walls

After Ixo left her, Mistel lay curled in a ball on the floor of her cell. There were no windows or doors, only a trapdoor in the ceiling and metal grilles in the ceiling and floor, from the latter of which came a stench of sewage. It was icy cold and she had only her shawl to keep her warm. She lay shuddering and exhausted, thinking of nothing. She could hear the mice moving about in the gaps between the stone. One of them came sniffing toward her ankle, but it darted away when she twitched, shivering.

'Grandmother Wolf!' The voice was soft but urgent.

'Ixo?' She knew it wasn't Ixo. But who else knew where she was being held? The Pharicians would never call her 'Grandmother'.

She didn't answer, but the sound of her teeth chattering now filled the tiny space.

'Grandmother Wolf, listen well!' She tried to curl herself tighter on herself, but everything hurt, and even the tough inner core of her that made her Grandmother when her contemporaries were mostly dead, even this was weakening. Was this the voice of Mother Wolf? But it could not be. A Wolf could never come to a place such as this, a terrible place where you could not see the stars or smell the water, where everything was confinement. Since she had come to Jai Khalar, Mistel's greatest fear had been to die somewhere high above the earth, unable to seek out her own resting place and make her peace with the worms before they began on her. Now, this voice in the darkness told her that her fear was coming true . . . and yet, she was not alone, for even here in Jai Khalar there was an Animal Protector to guide her to the end.

'Grandmother Wolf! Hear me! There isn't much time!'

She stirred with an effort, whispered, 'I hear you.'

'Strange matters are afoot. Messages pass across times like unguents pass through skin; whether they heal or harm is up to us.'

The puzzling words roused her mind even if her body did not wish to respond.

'Who are you?' Her voice came out like the sounds of dry grass rubbing together in autumn; but even her autumn was past, and this was her winter.

'I am the card trick that has caught the Pharicians. I am the listening walls you curse and kick; but I have led you well and you will not die in this place. My Magic is small and multiple. It will not fail you.'

At the news that she wasn't going to die yet, Mistel began to perk up. 'Answer directly! I am too old for bullshit.'

In the darkness she could hear mice stirring. Her lip curled.

'You will answer me,' said the whisper. 'In return you will be saved.'

'Ask then. I've lost one finger already.'

'When Sendrigel traded with Pharice, he sold them some of our Knowledge. He had dealings with the Circle.'

'Yes, it is well known by now that he did.'

'Who was his contact?'

'Byrd,' said Mistel.

'You mean he sent messages by bird . . . but to whom? Think, Grandmother.'

'I don't have to fucking think, I just told you. Byrd was the mastermind.'

'But where did the messages come, and how? Not through the Water of Glass, surely?'

'No, for Mhani was not to know of it.'

'Why not?'

'If you are the listening walls, how is it you know not of these exchanges?'

The whisperer was not amused. It said, 'I am the walls that can free you, or I can leave you here in the dark until Tash is ready to take another finger – or a head.'

But Mistel was not afraid of anyone. 'You do not listen well, Listening Walls,' she rebuked. 'Hear again: the contact in Pharice was Byrd.'

'A *person* called Byrd?'

Mistel nodded and then remembered she could not be seen. 'Now you finally the fuck understand,' she said tartly.

'Ah. Now I do understand!' And the whisper contained a note of dismay. 'Byrd is Chee's mate, the ears and throat of the emperor! I wish I had known this before, or I would not have let the mice send the skyfalcon's message to Jundun.'

'Then you should have asked me sooner.'

'I should have. Or maybe the mice are wiser than I know.'

'Any more questions?' Mistel said faintly.

'No more questions. Thank you, Wolf Grandmother.'

A gust of hot air and light hit her. She covered her eyes with her elbows, clutching her head as if to protect herself from an explosion. But everything around her had gone still, and the only sounds were the faint rustle of wind in the trees, and birds. Singing. She peeped out into yellow light. She had the immediate impression of spring.

I have died, she thought, sitting up. She was somewhat peeved to discover that she was not a Wolf, that there were no other Wolves to greet her, that the moon was not waiting for her nor their welcoming howls; that she was still hungry and in pain and old and weak. And she was still indoors! *What have I done*, she thought, *to deserve to die within a house of men?*

She sneezed. There was dust everywhere, and sunlight roaring in from outside, not the weak light of Everien winter, but a powerful stream of summer radiance that could soak into your very bones. There was a tin bucket in front of her, full of food; pinned to a piece of linen wrapping was a note.

'Do not leave this room. You will be safe here until I can return. Forgive the untidiness. Hanji.'

Still on her hands and knees, she fell on the food, wrapping her jaws around a chicken thigh and sucking the skin off even as she looked around, taking in the place.

It was octagonal, high-ceilinged, possibly the base of a tower. She was on the ground floor, for outside could be seen the foliage of a heavily overgrown garden. She sneezed again. There was dust everywhere. In fact, this was the messiest room she had ever seen.

A Reunion

The desert constellations spun into a starfish of whirling light. Kere's arms around Tarquin became Tarquin's legs around Ice, and the other horses were left behind as Ice, all arrogance, resumed his run on the White Road. Ice did not seem to be injured in any way, and Tarquin thought with relief that maybe everything was going to be all right after all.

But it was not to be. Ice's peril and his own were recalled to him when up ahead the White Road abruptly gave way to total blackness. Ice ran off the edge, giving a mighty buck in midair, and as Tarquin was falling he heard Kere's voice shrieking, '*No! Help!*'

Tarquin could see nothing at first, his hands scrabbling vainly in the air until they found purchase on what felt like roots, earth, and mossy turf. He identified them by feel, and then as if someone had whipped a blindfold away from his eyes, he could see the browns, greys, greens of a forest floor, and he was dragging himself up against the roots of a great oak tree in full leaf. There was a thick forest before him, but in his peripheral vision he could see that behind him there was nothing but cloud-soaked sky.

Gasping, he pulled his legs over the edge and drew himself up, using the tree for support. The air was cool and damp. If the void Tarquin had climbed from had been a natural sky, there would have been wind here, and a view from the height into the abyss below. Instead, there was only an empty stillness where the tress ended.

'Ice?' he called, listening for hooves. 'Kere?'

From among the trees there was an answering shout of many voices, and for a second he thought that the Pharicians had followed him down the tunnel. Then they sprang into view, surrounding him so that there was no retreat but the white emptiness. They were armed men, their faces painted for battle, their weapons blood-blackened where the hilts met the blades, their bodies bitterly scarred. They were men of many Clans, but they all carried swords, and they all looked at him with eyes that knew him.

Tarquin let out a cry of half joy, half anguish. His cry blotted out the sound of their voices, but he saw each of their lips moving, their expressions full of disbelief as eleven members of the Company said his name.

'*Quintar.*'

Vorse was holding Kere, his arms pinned behind his back, and Ovi had a hand over his mouth. Kere's eyes rolled wildly as he saw Tarquin, who ignored him.

'Where the fuck's Chyko?' Tarquin asked as he shook hands with each. He immediately lapsed into military speech with its abundance of curses added to sentences like salt to food.

'He left us,' Lyetar said grimly. 'Told us to fuck off, that you were the leader and he never gave a fuck about us. Every man for himself and all that. You know how he is.'

'Bastard,' said Tarquin out of habit. 'Where did he go? Back to the iceworld?'

'No.' Lyetar pointed with his sword into the trees. 'He wanted to pursue Night. Why didn't you let us back into Everien, Quintar? We fought so long and so hard, and you banished us.'

'You fought too long,' Tarquin said. 'In the Floating Lands you were killing everything you saw. What kind of protectors would you be for Everien when you couldn't tell friend from foe?'

'You have gone soft! We have fought for *years*. We have fought enemies you never dreamed of. We are owed kingships, each of us,' Lyetar said. 'Shit, we are owed kingdoms and more, and who will give them to us?'

'Not I. It is not within my power to give or withhold anything but my sword. I have nothing.'

'Then you are in good fucking form to lead us again, for we have less.'

'I cannot lead you,' Tarquin said. 'I have matters of my own, a mess to clean up, that you would do well to stay clear of. But let us remain friends all the same. Let the boy go.'

'Is he yours?' said Ovi in surprise, and took his hand away.

Kere promptly said, 'Tarquin, these maniacs haven't changed one single bit—'

'Shut up, fuzzhead!' interrupted Zeno. 'I wasn't going to shoot you. I thought you were a white deer, but as soon as I saw you were a kid I held my arrows.'

'You have the eyesight of an old man if you mistook this boy for a deer,' Lyetar said.

As Zeno struggled to respond sensibly, Tarquin decided to speak before the Company got suspicious about Kere. He could see the boy quivering even though he was yards away, and guessed that Kere had been frightened back into human form by the sight of the bowman. 'Yes, he's mine, alas. Excuse his overactive mouth. In time I will cure it.'

Ovi clapped a hand over Kere's mouth again, preventing him from making a contribution.

'How much time do you make it since I broke the Glass?' Tarquin asked.

Ovi shrugged. 'It is hard to tell time in the forest. We came out of the crystal into a house with broken windows. We had lost our horses by then. The place had been deserted for a long time and the trees were beginning to reclaim it, but there was a clear track leading into the forest.'

'This forest?'

'Yes. We stayed together as we went through the trees, but then Chyko went off when he saw—'

Riesel interrupted him. 'After Chyko left, we came to the edge of the forest and crossed the river. I would have said a year we spent roaming out there . . . but then we came back to the forest again. Time doesn't seem to pass here.'

'We hoped you would come,' Lyetar said. 'That is why we returned here, once we had seen that there was nothing great to be had in the cultivated lands of Pharice.'

'Pharice? This does not look like Pharice.'

'The forest is its own thing,' Lyetar agreed. Then he pointed out over the abyss. 'I meant out there, across the river.'

Tarquin turned slowly, half expecting to see a river. But he still saw empty sky. He turned back to his men.

'What river?' he said fearfully.

'The damn river you have just climbed out of.'

Tarquin looked down at his body. He wasn't wearing enough clothes to prove them right or wrong, and his skin was soaked with sweat. He might have been in a river, or he might not.

'So it is Pharice,' he said, looking into the whiteness and trying to pretend he could see what they could see.

'Yes, but it is not our time,' Lyetar said. 'It's another age. The emperor is dead and there is chaos in the land. They know this forest is not . . . ordinary. The Pharicians don't often come here.'

Tarquin was listening only halfway. He was fixated on the absence of Chyko. 'Why did he go after Night? I would have thought all of you would have taken your freedom and renounced battle for ever.'

'Renounced it for bloody what? Chyko couldn't live without a fight to look forward to. Night he wanted revenge on. And he wanted the girl.'

'Girl? What girl? You mean Istar?'

'She was riding a fabulous horse. And she had red hair.'

Tarquin let out an inarticulate cry. 'Damn it, if that isn't the end of my patience.'

'That's what I was starting to say before,' Ovi said. 'Chyko saw the girl on the horse, and he went off after her. I doubt he caught her up, for she was riding as if her life depended on it.'

'They will be back,' Lyetar said. 'Every so often she comes back to her house, but she never stays.'

'Her house?' Tarquin swallowed. 'Is this the house in the crystal that you spoke of?'

'It is a strange house, to be sure,' Ovi said dreamily.

Tarquin said, 'Take me there.'

Jaya's House

'We have tried to get into this house a thousand times. The rooms change. Sometimes there is food in the kitchen, and sometimes there isn't. The seasons vary. And the tower always seems to be locked.'

'It is like no house I have ever seen,' Tarquin said, taking in the unfamiliar construction, the odd angles, and the many windows – most of them broken. But his eyes were drawn to the garden. 'Are there ever any people here?'

Ovi shook his head. 'Night slips in here from time to time, but where it hides we could not tell you. It is a strange place, but it is also a kind of haven. Compared to what you will find out beyond the forest, it is safe. And it seems somehow to be the centre of things.'

'I will go inside,' Tarquin said. 'Keep a lookout for Chyko, and warn me if he comes.'

The house seemed inhabited. The stove was warm. A cat was taking a bath on a windowsill. There was a fire in embers on the grate in the library, and books were open carelessly on tables. In the sitting room, someone had left an unfinished piece of knitting.

He climbed a flight of stairs and found himself in an empty aviary on the top of an octagonal tower. The birdcages had all been left swinging open, and on the floor was a wooden box shaped like a book.

He opened the box and took out a large deck of cards. Their backs were covered with unintelligible Everien symbols writ extremely small and complex. They spilled open into his hands and he saw that each one had a picture on its face, delicately painted in rich colours. He drew one at random and looked at the picture.

It was an old man with silver wings and a shock of white hair, his emerald eyes gazing piercingly at the young woman who knelt at his feet. They were on top of a cliff. In the background was a red desert with sculpted cliffs and an azure sky deepening to dark blue as twilight came on. The girl wore no armour and she looked thin and wiry, her eyes overlarge in a gaunt face – no longer the sturdy Honorary warrior he'd known, but he recognized Istar all the same. He shivered.

At the bottom of the card were written Everien symbols. Sometimes in dreams Tarquin had been given a scroll to read and had found that the words turned to nonsense even as he looked at them; the effect now was the opposite. When he looked at the Everien symbols he knew at once what their meaning was 'The Magician'.

'Quintar!' It was Lyetar's voice from the garden below. 'Are you still there? The windows just moved.'

'Yes. I'm still here.'

He went down the stairs and then paused. The locked door was now standing slightly ajar. There was a silver key in the lock.

He touched the door and it swung open.

Fleetingly he recognized the sensation of displacement: It was like being halfway down a flight of stairs in Jai Khalar and then finding yourself up to your knees in the water of a bathing pool. He fell into a room that was very different from what he had expected. It was made of dark blue Everien smoothstone, and it was close and dim, windowless. There were three doors, one of which was blocked by rubble, one was half open with darkness beyond, and the other closed solid. There was rubble everywhere and the air was swimming with dust. He smelt fire and acid. Around the perimeter of the room he could see panels of coloured glass and the tables that the Everiens had used in the Fire Houses, the kind with symbols on them that glowed and made odd sounds that seemed to come from nowhere. Compounded with the warm air and the dimness, these details made him believe he was in A-vi-Khalar or perhaps some other Everien ruin. Kneeling on the floor with a shaving brush in one hand and a disc of clear glass in the other was a man with black skin and white hair.

Fear shot through Tarquin as for an instant he took the man for Night; but despite his unusual colouring, this was not a Sekk. He was a young, white-blond Seahawk with soot blackening his face, which would have otherwise been pale. Even as Tarquin appeared, he coughed and spat, rubbing his eyes with the backs of his hands. Though he was armed only with a dagger and wore no armour, just a loose-fitting brown tunic and light boots, he wore the paint and his hair had been battle-braided. His eyes meeting Tarquin were hard.

Tarquin glanced over his shoulder. He could still see the staircase and the rain-soaked garden through the open door, and wondered if the Seahawk could see it as well.

'Who are you?' said the youth, getting slowly to his feet and starting forward hesitantly, as if he could not believe his eyes. He carried himself in such a way as to cover Tarquin's hands, though he didn't draw his own weapon.

'My name doesn't mean anything,' Tarquin answered. 'I'm looking for Jaya. What place is this, what year is it, and who are you?'

'I am Eteltar, and you are in my laboratory in A-vi-Khalar – what is left of it. The year is one past Smoke.'

'Smoke is an accurate name!' Tarquin rejoined, coughing to expel dust. The pause gave him a chance to recover from his surprise; and to hide his amazement at the name of the young man, he resorted to making fun of him. 'Laboratory? It looks like a ruin.'

'There was an explosion,' said Eteltar defensively. 'Then the whiteness. Then *you* appeared.'

'Eteltar . . .' Tarquin said, chewing on the name. 'Did you call me here?'

'I don't know. What's that behind you? It's like a path. A white path. Am I hallucinating?' He licked his lips.

Tarquin didn't know how Eteltar could see the White Road when he himself could see only Jaya's garden. He bluffed his way along.

'It is the White Road, and you have called it here. I hope you can help us, Eteltar. For in my day you are a legend, the greatest of all Animal Magicians, and the saviour of Everien as much as any man.'

'I don't know,' Eteltar said, blinking and licking his lips again. 'I feel strange.'

Alarmed, Tarquin perceived that he held a glass vial in one hand, full of liquid. It seemed to be identical to Kere's vial, only dustier, the cork dangling from its string, black with age.

'You haven't . . . you haven't drunk that, have you?'

'I just tasted it, on the tip of my tongue. I—'

'But how did you get it?' Tarquin roared.

'I found it here in the old laboratory. There were codes laid into these panels, and the vial was sitting here with these codes on it, see? I wondered what it was—'

'It is time serpent venom,' Tarquin said, 'and I suspect you have just used it to bring me here, although I'm no longer sure who is causing what, because I thought I was meant to bring it to you.' He paused. 'Did you say codes?'

'Yes. Codes. See?'

Eteltar held up the vial, and on a white label on its side Tarquin could see a set of symbols.

'I don't know what they mean,' Eteltar said. 'I don't know how to begin to translate them.'

Uneasily Tarquin said, 'Listen, I think you had better decipher these so-called codes. The time serpents are dying, and you hold in your hand the key to their continuation. You must find the flaw in the code and repair it if you can.'

'What's a time serpent?'

'A Li'ah'vah, I mean.'

'But they are extinct!' Tarquin could see the intelligence in Eteltar's eyes as the young wizard slowly nodded. 'Or are they?' he amended thoughtfully. 'Tell me, messenger, are you saying this road leads into the past?'

'It leads many places, friend, and there is no such thing as the past on the White Road.'

Excitedly then Eteltar asked, 'Does that mean this White Road could take me back to old Everien?'

'I don't know. Possibly. But men cannot drink of the venom, Eteltar. Do not taste it again! It is for those of divided nature, like Ice.'

'Who is Ice?'

'Do not drink it! You would have to be an Animal, and you are not.'

'But this task you charge me with – I don't understand it.'

'You will. You are the most famous Animal Magician in all Everien, and you will open the White Road when Jai Pendu comes.'

'You're mad!'

'So they tell me. But I must discover how this has happened. Kere had the venom, but he is Ice on the White Road. Someone had to put it here for you to find.'

'Ah, maybe I put it here myself! If I was in old Everien.'

He was quick, this Eteltar, Tarquin realized, if he had already grasped the implicit consequences of slipping through time. He tried to imagine what a conversation between Eteltar and Kere would sound like, and shuddered.

'See to it that you do, then! But I am losing track of things. I was sure I had to give you the venom, but maybe I only had to give you the injunction. Eteltar! You must decode the time serpent venom, so that you can make more of it for yourself to find.'

'Paradoxes,' mused Eteltar.

'Jaya,' said Tarquin. 'It is all one to me. I must go. I must find her.'

'Wait!' The young man started forward, hand outstretched. 'How am I to do this? When am I to do it? What do you mean about the coming of Jai Pendu?'

'All I know is that on the longest night of the year after Smoke Year, Jai Pendu came and you opened the White Road. And Ysse rode upon it. That's all I know. But you must find the flaw in the code and make a repair.'

'You speak as if it is all in the past.'

'To me, it is. But I know you will do it. You will open the White Road.'

'But where? How?'

'That's all I know,' said Tarquin, and turning he stepped through the blasted hole in the wall, finding himself back in the stairway of Jaya's house. The door had been locked behind him. The key was gone.

'At least I am back where I started, for once,' he said aloud. He clattered down the stairs and stopped at a warped door to the lower room of the tower. It did not look as if it had been opened for a long time. 'Here we go again,' he muttered, and set his shoulder to it.

'Hanji, you should clean this place up,' Mistel muttered with her mouth full, and then, remembering the Carry Eye Ixo had given her, patted herself down. It was gone. 'Ach! Sneaky old goat of a Deer.'

She put her meal aside and dragged herself to her feet. The windows were made of thick glass and they were locked. So was the door.

I will break the hell out of here presently, she thought. *Smash the windows and get out amongst the trees and the fucking wind. I am sick of stone. But first . . .*

She yawned. She was so sleepy. It must be the food after starvation, and the warmth after freezing. She curled up on her cloak in a patch of sunlight and fell asleep.

She woke to the sound of footsteps on the stairs just beyond the interior wall of the room where Hanji had left her. She didn't know how long she had been sleeping, but when she heard the intruder she was instantly awake. She got to her feet and rushed to the door, feeling better than she had in months. The sores she had acquired in prison were healed, their scabs already peeling, and her nails had grown considerably. Excited, she shouted and pounded on the door. But she heard nothing from upstairs, though she shouted herself hoarse and bruised her knuckles on the door.

At length she lay down to sleep again. It was some time afterward, in the late afternoon of an unknown day, that the door opened and Tarquin the Free walked in.

'Ah, Quintar,' she said. 'It is about fucking time we had a madman in the madhouse. I am glad to see you!'

He did not recognize her at first, and she supposed she would be unlikely to recognize herself were she to look in a mirror. When she explained what had happened, he said, '*Hanji?* What's the old coot up to this time?'

'Tarquin, what are you doing here? Where are we?'

He tried to explain to her, but she found his words baffling. The Liminal, the White Road, a horse called Ice . . . 'Wait just a damn minute. I thought this was Jaya's house,' Mistel interrupted in bemusement. 'It looks just like her description of it.'

'*Jaya's house?* How do you know about Jaya?'

When Mistel explained about Gialse and the Carry Eye and Ixo's secret visits to her prison cell, it was Tarquin's turn to look baffled.

'Is she gone, then?'

'They drove her out,' Mistel said, recounting what she could remember of Ixo's narrative. 'It seemed from the way Gialse was talking that all of this happened a long time ago, and Jaya has been lost in the forest all this time.'

Tarquin's brow was furrowed pensively. 'What of this trickster, Jihan? He folded up the house into a deck of cards?'

'He told Jaya, "My heart is stone",' Mistel quoted. She added, 'When I was imprisoned in Jai Khalar, the walls whispered to me. Someone or something changed my prison into this room, and the Eye Ixo entrusted to me was gone.'

'Jihan,' Tarquin said again. 'Jihan, Jihan, Jihan.'

'Hanji,' said Mistel.

'Yes.'

Tarquin advised Mistel to stay where she was until he could return for her. While they stood there exchanging news, a sound had begun outside, faint at first and almost indistinguishable from the wind in the leaves; but after a time they realized it was not like any wind. It was a kind of soft, beckoning singing, now coming closer, now going farther away.

'Shit,' Mistel said. 'I don't like it.'

'I am going to find Jaya,' Tarquin said simply, not bothering to explain or even acknowledge the difficulty of the task; nor did Mistel point it out to him. She simply nodded and said, 'Yes, after all that has been going on, I think that is what you had better do.'

He made sure the Wolf Grandmother would be safe. Then he staggered out into the kitchen courtyard, his brain spinning possibilities. There were shards of broken glass mixed with dead, dry leaves that blew across the paving stoves with a sound of burning. He turned toward the garden. No one was there but Ice, standing in the overgrown grass, his neck stretched out into the thorny bushes. He was eating roses.

Night is Here

Chyko had been in a bad mood for a time he couldn't measure, because the sun didn't move across the sky in a straight line and the days were of uneven lengths making it hard to count them – and anyway he'd never been any good with numbers. Tarquin had gotten him out of the iceworld, that much was true, but when Chyko passed through the crystal at Jai Pendu he and the Company had found themselves in a wild wood that seemed to be without end.

'He said we were free,' Riesel said to Chyko. 'Free to do what? Free to go where?'

Chyko could see that the breaking of the Glass had meant nothing to them. The Company still needed to be led; they needed to be given a purpose. Chyko had never needed anyone to tell him what to do, and now that Night's spell over him was broken, he could roam unrestricted through whatever was left of the worlds inside Jai Pendu. There was little satisfaction in such freedom. There was little satisfaction in anything any more. He couldn't remember when last he had felt pleasure, even in killing. Yet he had the mind of a hunter, the habits of a warrior. He couldn't very well stop and begin cultivating vegetables or keeping bees.

At first he set off after the girl and the black horse, but he couldn't keep up their pace and soon lost them in the intricacies of the forest path. Then he resolved to find Night. Night who had imprisoned the Company, who had watched Chyko fight and taken a cowardly, vicarious pleasure in his violence, Night who had used his honest sweat and aggression to some unknown purpose. Yet Night was no longer so easy to find. Night was no longer so simple as a creature who walked Everien as a Sekk – if indeed it had ever been so simple. That shape had been like a doll or puppet – only a guise for something more strange and deep. For something worse. What shape Night might now take in the realities exposed by the shattered crystal of Jai Pendu, Chyko could not begin to guess. This did not stop him from looking. His brows were drawn together all the time now in a constant frown. He ceased to whistle. Months went by and he spoke to no one. When one day by chance he came across a merchant walking up the main road through the forest with a pack mule and several servants, Chyko had to cough and clear his throat to make greetings, for his voice had scarcely been used.

398

'What lands lie on the other side of this forest?' Chyko asked, pointing up the gloomy road in the direction the merchant had lately come from.

'Ah,' said the merchant in High Pharician, and Chyko guessed from his jovial air that he would prove loquacious and probably irritating, but full of gossip. 'That depends which side you mean. If you take the left fork in the road, when the trees stop you will come to a bridge and then a river valley, and beyond that the desert and the Khynahi Mountains, and eventually to Or. But if you take the right fork, where I have come from, then you will reach a ford; and if you follow the river upstream in time you will come to Jundun.'

'Whose land lies on the right fork?'

'That would be Baron Horas. I have just sold him my entire spring stock of painted silk. Are you headed that way?'

'Is he worth the trouble?'

'That depends what you mean by trouble.'

'Is Baron Horas himself trouble?' Chyko asked, his interest sparked. The merchant stuck a thumb in his ear and wiggled it, a pleased look on his face as he transmitted the following slanders.

'Baron Horas is a vicious sluggard with no more imagination than that required to gorge himself every night on badly prepared game from this forest, abuse the cooks who prepare it, drink himself into a stupor to disguise the flavour, and, if he's still able after all that, fuck anything that doesn't have visibly running sores or rotted teeth, although I've seen him make the odd exception for the latter by tying a rag over her mouth.'

'You speak like an educated man,' grunted Chyko, who did not.

'I come north from Jundun once a year, and that is enough. These parts were once well administered by the old baron, who is dead now. His fighting men kept order on the roads. Some of the police are still honest, and Horas has a few good captains who maintain civility in the towns and keep trade flowing. Yet brigands abound, and those whom the baron has cheated or offended now roam the woods and poach the deer when they are not getting up to anything worse. If I were you I would make haste to the nearest town, conduct your business there, and leave as quickly as possible. It is not a pleasant country, not any more.'

'Thank you for your advice,' said Chyko.

'And where are you from?' asked the merchant with undisguised curiosity. Chyko knew he didn't look like much of a threat: skinny and wearing little but tattoos, a stingnet disguised as a necklace, and his crossbow lying apparently harmlessly across his back. This apparent harmlessness was about to make it easy to rob the man.

'I am from Wasp Country,' Chyko answered cordially, and savoured the shock on the merchant's face when the stingnet came whirling over him, its needles sticking into the victim from all angles and making it impossible for him to move without extreme pain. Then Chyko swiftly got control of the servants, whom he left bound on the ground while he lifted their master's jewels and some of his food and wine. He left the gold and silver, dismissing it as too cumbersome. Chyko said, 'I would offer to see you safely through the rest of the forest but I think I would rather go and kill this baron you speak of before I take on any new jobs.'

He lifted the stingnet with a practised flick of the wrist, ignored the shriek of the helpless man as the needles hurt him a second time on their way out, and gave the baffled merchant a jaunty salute as he set off whistling. But he did not come to the edge of the forest even after several days' walking. The trees went on and on. Chyko was ever on the alert for prey – and for predators, for in the forest there were creatures he feared roaming just out of eyesight in the hidden spaces between trees. He had the feeling he was being watched.

Few others travelled the road. On two occasions bands of uniformed bowmen carrying Pharician scimitars went sweeping by on light horses. They were too well armed to tempt Chyko to attack, yet they annoyed him. There was something proprietorial about the way they rode. It made him want to cut them down to size. As it was, he was reduced to shooting rabbits and cooking them on a spit. After a few nights of rabbit and nothing else but the occasional handful of berries or cress (mushrooms were plentiful but he didn't trust them in this unknown land) he was yearning for bread and milk and somewhere dry to sleep, and he resolved that no matter how large or well armed the next party he encountered might be, he would ambush them. For the gems he had got off the merchant did him no good if he could find nowhere to trade them for food, and without a horse who knew how long he would be walking up this road?

And besides, he was lonely, and the corpses of your enemies are good company sometimes. Especially when your friends have betrayed you.

In Chyko's mind, although Quintar had freed the Company from Night's control, by banishing them from Everien he had also abandoned the men who had never been anything but loyal to him. Chyko's lip curled whenever he thought of Quintar. Yes – he was in need of a fight. Some men needed drink, but Chyko needed hatred.

Then he saw them: the girl and her black horse that seemed to tread all on silver. It breathed sparkling light, and its eyes were blue, and although it was only walking or sometimes trotting, it picked up its hooves with an energy that suggested great speed.

He wanted the horse. The girl he would have liked only in an incidental way at first, but after he followed for a time he found that she appealed to his protective and possessive instincts, especially when he observed that the creatures of the forest prowled all around her, threatening but staying just out of reach of the snapping jaws of the black stallion. And sometimes he saw shadowy figures in her wake. From time to time he heard these shadowy ones singing, as the Sekk are wont to sing – but none of them declared themselves openly. The air held a kind of implicit terror, even though no violence was occurring.

Night is here, he thought. There was something about the way the girl was beset that bore Night's stamp. Chyko knew how it felt to be tortured by someone or something you couldn't see, and this made him more sympathetic to her than he would otherwise have been. For although Night was supposed to be his quarry, Chyko understood that it had laid a trap for him in the form of the red-haired girl and her beautiful steed. And he could not help but take the bait.

She was trying to get to the edge of the forest, but whenever she came to the river, she stopped and turned back. Then she found her way to the main road, and the black horse approached the ford in the river. Open countryside lay beyond, but the horse would not step into the water.

Then Chyko saw that the ford was guarded. They came out of the trees, five of them, mounted on six-legged lizards with forked tongues. The lizards were controlled not with bridles or spurs, but with wires that protruded from within their very flesh, as if their riders were pulling on their tendons and stimulating their muscles beneath their armoured skin. Chyko felt his balls curl up toward his body reflexively. The teeth of the lizards were of a size similar to that of the assassins' daggers of Pharician eunuchs, and their eyes were multifaceted, like wasps' eyes seen under magnification. Chyko had some hair-raising memories of magnified wasps, going back to his youth and his initiation into the Animal Magic of his Clan, and he hesitated for just a moment as the sight triggered some primitive fear.

No wonder the black horse was rearing and picking up his feet nervously, foaming and rolling his eyes. Chyko darted closer through the trees and got his first good look at the rider. She was a red-haired girl in a green silk cloak trimmed with fur, and he expected her to come off at any moment. She was no rider for such a mount under the best of circumstances, and it was clear enough even from a distance that the circumstances here were not good.

The lizards surrounded the black horse. Why the girl had not fled from them on sight, he couldn't imagine. She must be stupid to allow herself to get into this predicament, especially when the horse clearly knew better than to get near those foul reptiles. The men were not pretty; in fact they were strange, doughy and pale, flat-haired and dressed all in the same dull, slatted armour. He would not have made much of them taken in stillness, as a tableau; but when they moved, they scared him. It seemed to Chyko that these men and their mounts both were moving faster than anything natural could move. There was a jerkiness to their motion; it even seemed to him that they jumped from place to place suddenly, disappearing and then reappearing so quickly that spots danced before his eyes. It was like watching mosquitoes touching down on water, or ants – too fast for the human eye to track smoothly.

Silently, he slipped from tree to tree in an effort to get close enough to overhear the interaction. He rubbed his eyes, trying to reconcile the sight of these too-swift-moving creatures with what he knew to be possible of men or animals. It wasn't right. Yet in the middle of it there was this girl, beset.

It's a trap, thought Chyko. *It's a trick. I'm supposed to see this and rescue this girl out of charity, but all it will be is another cock-sucking journey into some other world, one probably worse than this one, and Night laughing all the while. At least in this place I get to eat, and the sun rises and sets. I'm not going to interfere.*

So he watched.

'You cannot escape the forest,' said one of the men, and the others echoed his voice with wordless cries. Their voices braided into a kind of singing. Chyko thought they must be insane, all of them. The black horse was lovely, though. In a minute, he thought, this horse will leap over the backs of the damned lizards, dump the girl on the ground, and be free. *Then I will catch it and we'll have some fun.*

But the horse was out of his element. The lizards hemmed it in, and it would soon succumb to nervous exhaustion and shock. It rushed at one of the lizards as if to attack it and then sprang back, repelled, when some hissing poison shot from the thing's mouth and scalded its forefeet. Chyko smelled burning hair. The horse screamed and ran in circles.

'Go back into the trees, Jaya Paradox,' said one of the other men. The girl was not listening to them. She had let go of the reins and wrapped both arms around the horse's head, and she had a look of concentration that is beyond speech. Chyko knew it well but had previously only seen it in the best of warriors, and in his mate Mhani. He wondered how rich she was, and what she could do for him if he aided her.

No. He didn't think he wanted to take on the lizards. Best to wait about and hope to capture the horse if it lived; or possibly, to intervene and save the horse if possible, after they had done what they were going to do with the girl. His hands tightened on the bark and suddenly one of the lizards looked up.

A gout of white liquid flew at him; quick as grease he slipped under the branch and let go. Some of the stuff caught him across the back of the shoulders, but he was already involved in the act of slipping a dart out of his belt and plunging it into the neck of the man he landed on. By the time the man had expired, Chyko had already kicked him off the back of the lizard, grabbed the wires that controlled it, and jerked it savagely to one side.

It responded so quickly he thought he would vomit. Blurry trails like the aftereffects of jungle drugs smeared his vision. The screams of the horse and the girl commingled and seemed to turn around backward in his hearing. The lizard leaped to one side and he began shooting darts at the other men. He didn't have time to realize that the reason the other lizards didn't attack him was because he was riding one of their own; he simply dispatched the men as quickly as he could. He could hear tearing sounds, the butcher's wrenching of sinew and bone, whenever he directed the lizard beneath him to move. He wanted to make it stop but didn't know how. He had the inbetween feeling of being on the White Road, the shock of too much happening in too little time, his senses overloaded, his body and mind whirled into a numbness of incomprehension. The other reptiles shot off into the forest, almost too quick to see, leaving four dead men on the ground behind and carrying two with them. He leaped off the lizard and it was gone like a shadow.

The horse charged at him and he rolled out of the way and came back up onto his feet. He could not understand how this girl had not fallen off; he glimpsed her white face and stunned eyes for long enough to see that her feat was not the result of being a brilliant rider, but rather some bizarre and unaccountable luck. Yet if he didn't do something, the horse would be off and Chyko would lose out.

He didn't hesitate. The darts under his left armpit were for sedation; they worked well enough on horses, although it would take three or four to bring about a measurable result on an animal this size. Chyko blew them neatly into the horse's flanks as it was racing away along the road. He saw the horse slow, stumble, catch its balance again, and finally stand. It took a few hesitant steps forward. The girl slid from its back like a cloak from a smooth banister. She lay in the mud fifty yards from the bodies of her waylayers, red hair splayed about her. The horse's head sank in weariness. It was covered in pale foam, legs trembling, flanks moving with fluttering breaths. Chyko approached it.

Chyko ran his hands up the face of the horse, feeling each contour of bone and vein, smoothing the damp fur. He gazed into the strangely flat eye with its curling membranes. He laid his palm on the horse's pulse point and felt the action of its heart. His face changed. If he could have watched himself, he would have seen the terrible hardness seem to vaporize, and his features appearing smoother and younger. Beneath his beard his jaws relaxed. His lips parted, and his nostrils trembled as tears filled his eyes. It was a breathtakingly beautiful horse, and its heartbeat was the very stuff of life. Under his touch the stallion grew calm.

The girl was prostrate on the ground, hands still clasped over the back of her neck as if they could protect her spine from the blow of his weapon. He could hear her ragged breathing. She was dressed in silk and velvet, and her sandals were trimmed with ostrich feathers and inlaid with semi-precious beads. Her hair was the richest of all, a natural endowment of the most radiant auburn. It spilled in natural curls; unbraided and free it struck Chyko as suggestive of nothing so much as the bedroom, and he was already aroused by the fight.

He let go of the horse and went to her. He knelt at her side and said, 'It is all right. They are destroyed, and I will not hurt you.'

She didn't look at him, but when he put his hands on her she began to cry. He picked her up and held her, at first like a child but she aroused him too much for it to remain that way. She didn't look at him. Her face was delicate, cream-skinned as only the rich with their shaded rooms can afford to be, but he saw her only in profile for she would not look at him. She gazed steadily at his chest, picking at old thornscratch scabs with her fingernails, and did not attempt to get free.

'Thank you,' she kept saying.

Chyko turned her around in his arms and lifted her skirts. She gasped when she felt him between her legs and he put a hand on her throat. He let out a groan.

'Get down.'

She knelt on the leaves and he was quick about it; he didn't know when more of the Sekk might appear to interrupt them, and the horse was untethered. She turned her head to one side and pressed her face against the fallen leaves, rocking forward and back as he pumped. He put one hand in her hair, gossamer-bright and soft as a child's. She did not cry out but tears slid down her cheeks and she made snorting breaths through her nose like a young horse. When he came he gave a terrific laugh.

He felt really good afterward. Better than good – exhilarated. He didn't bury the bodies, but rather arranged them in the road as a warning to any who might overtake him. He mounted the men's heads on their spears and wedged them in the crooks of tree branches. He was pleased with the effects. Then he vaulted onto the horse. She was sitting on a log watching him and looking away whenever he turned in her direction.

'Get up behind me,' he said. 'And be quiet.'

She fairly ran to him, tripping over the edge of her cloak. He noticed that she bundled it between her legs as a cushion where her underparts met the saddle. He gave her a moment to settle and then goaded the horse ahead. He began to whistle.

Black and White Stallions

'You must be careful,' Tarquin said to Ice. 'Promise me you will change to Kere if you sense any danger. For the event we are trying to avoid is the shooting of a horse, not the shooting of a boy. And I can protect Kere easier than I can protect you. Promise me, Ice!'

The horse was not the promising type, Tarquin realized, and he wondered if his words were even being registered. Ice had let him mount and ride out into the ever-dark forest, where Tarquin felt uneasy and tense. There was no sign of the Company anywhere, but the invisible denizens of the wood could be heard slithering and clicking among the boles of ancient trees and the tough undergrowth that thrived in total darkness. Ice was far calmer than his rider, and for several hours they wandered the twisting path without incident and without a twitch of the white horse's sensitive skin.

But when the hoofbeats of another horse sounded on the forest path, Ice began to buck without warning. Tarquin had no chance. He flew and landed in a thorn brake, and Ice plunged among the trees, swallowed quickly by darkness. Tarquin picked himself up and saw a black horse come along the road, walking in a rather dejected fashion, he thought. It was a magnificent animal, but ribby and neglected.

Jaya was walking beside the horse, equally joyless in her demeanour. And the rider was Chyko. Tarquin even recognized the tune he was whistling.

He didn't know what to feel. He loved Chyko, but the sight of Jaya walking along like a subject or slave while Chyko rode her horse was too much for him. And if he knew Chyko, the Wasp was using more than just her horse for physical convenience. Tarquin's guts boiled but he didn't dare act, for he wasn't sure what had become of Ice.

After they passed, Kere crept through the forest and settled beside him.

'That horse is dangerous. So is the rider. Tarquin, what will we do now?'

Tarquin heard the blood crashing against the inside of his own skull like a high tide. His voice was clipped. 'Watch. For now we can only watch.'

He watched Chyko and Jaya for two days before he made up his mind to act. They camped for a time in a clearing, and Chyko was

405

concentrating on hunting and butchering game, which Jaya cooked at his instructions. The horse grazed the clearing down to nothing, and Tarquin hid in the trees and observed both of them. It was clear that Jaya took no joy in Chyko; but nor did she resist him. She was strangely passive, and Chyko grew impatient with her.

'It is like fucking a piece of fruit,' he snapped at her once, grabbing her hair and twisting her head. 'Try to act a little more alive, will you?'

Tarquin's self-control almost snapped at that point. He waited for Chyko to be asleep; then he stole from cover and silently put a hand over Jaya's mouth from behind where she lay apart from the Wasp. She jerked but made no sound.

'It is Tarquin,' he said. 'Don't be afraid. Come with me.'

She stood and put her cloak on. Chyko lay still. Tarquin led Jaya into the deep shadow of the trees and still Chyko did not stir. Ice was waiting, stamping nervously in place.

'All right,' Tarquin whispered. 'Quick, up you get on his back.'

Jaya looked back and forth from the white horse to the stubble-headed man. 'Who are you?' she whispered. 'Why should I go with you?'

'I will explain later,' Tarquin said. 'Trust me, I will treat you better than he.'

Ice's eyes rolled. He let out a neigh and Tarquin looked over his shoulder to see if the Wasp had heard it.

Chyko's bow was already trained on them. Even at a distance, even in the dark, Tarquin knew Chyko could hit Ice. He turned carefully.

'Ah, Chyko,' he said in a falsely jovial tone.

'*Tarquin?* I thought you were an enemy.' Chyko slackened the bow and came forward. 'What are you doing sneaking around my camp at night, stealing my woman?'

His tone was not so friendly then, and he grabbed Jaya's arm and pulled her back against himself.

'She isn't yours,' Tarquin said. 'Let her go.'

'I disagree. Would you like to make an issue of it?' Chyko's teeth shone in the dark.

'Let her go. She has a free will, has she not?'

'Not when I saved her from certain death. Anyway, she doesn't know you. She's better with me.'

'Chyko, I've never known you to resort to rape,' Tarquin said with what was meant to be a laugh but came out more like a nervous bark. Chyko barked a laugh in answer.

'Rape? How is it rape when she offers no resistance?'

'She's only a child.'

'Hah! What a notion. Come, it is plain we disagree. Let us go about it

406

like two warriors, then, two men of the Clans and nothing more complicated, which once we were, long ago.'

'I don't want to fight you, Chyko.'

'Thank you for the compliment. I always knew you were afraid of me. But perhaps I give you a great gift in my offer. To die for what you love is an honour you thought you were beyond. Is it true? For you lost your Company without fighting for us, and since then you have never loved anything, for you considered yourself unworthy.'

'Let us fight, then,' Tarquin said, angry at such an accurate analysis. 'For I am not afraid of you, and I never have been.'

'Good! In the traditional way, then.'

'What?'

'First our horses fight. If that is indecisive, then you and me.'

Tarquin was dismayed, but he tried to cover it with bravura. 'Now who is afraid? Would you sacrifice your horse to save your own skin?'

'Absolutely.'

'Well, I will not.'

'Then you go back on your word. Look at them! They are itching to get at each other. Two stallions so close together, and neither of them properly tamed.'

And with that he released the black horse, who promptly charged at Ice. The white stallion met him with neck extended and the two rose, kicking at each other with their forehooves, their teeth snapping and seeking hold on each other's necks. Chyko whooped with pleasure; but Jaya picked up her skirts and ran.

'Ice!' Tarquin shouted. 'Cut it out!'

But he was more concerned about Jaya. He charged off through the underbrush after the girl, who was small but surprisingly fleet. He heard a splash and a scream and clawing through the brush he found her up to her thighs in quicksand. A tentacle with a dog's head rose out of the shadowy muck and blinked at him.

In one movement Tarquin lopped off the head and, catching hold of the nearest tree, he extended his hand to Jaya. She grabbed it, and they looked at each other.

'Quintar!' she said. 'At last.'

Then she was in his arms and for the first time in his life, Tarquin was happy.

Chyko rode them down not long after that. Jaya had found her way back to the path, and soon they heard hoofbeats. Midnight Blue clipped along the path bearing Chyko and Kere in a miserable bundle. Kere's forearms were bleeding and his face was bruised.

'What a fight it would have been,' he said to Tarquin with the first sign of real aggression Tarquin had ever seen him display. 'That shadow horse was asking for it.'

'Let's keep this simple,' Chyko suggested, reining the horse. 'We exchange the boy for the girl, you get out of here, and we pretend none of this ever happened. It's a good offer, Tarquin. I'll even forget the wrongs you have done me in the past.'

Jaya's small hand gripped his.

'No,' said Tarquin.

'Please,' Jaya said. 'Both of you have helped me. You are friends. Let us try to find a solution. Let us go to my old house. If you can fight off the monsters that pursue me, perhaps I can get to the Knowledge I need. Please.'

'House?' said Chyko. 'Not that useless house where the windows change? Have you food there? Have you fire?'

'I . . . I think so,' Jaya stammered. Tarquin stroked her palm with his thumb, conscious of the fact that she was really only an adolescent, unsure of herself and scared. 'Chyko – please – a truce.'

Night's Eye and Poison

Kivi knew he had to get to Tash before Ixo could, so he made an appointment with the prince for the morning after Ixo had visited him.

'I have been doing much research,' he improvised. 'New Knowledge has come to light in the archives. I suspect . . . I *fear* that the Carry Eye is still connected somehow to Night. Wherever Night is. And if that is the case, then Gialse and every other girl who looks into the Carry Eye will See only what Night has put there.'

'What Night has put there since two days before the skyfalcon arrived and then disappeared again, only to return as a gift from my father. It is a confusing omen, Kivi. Could the falcon be a servant of Night? Could *it* be ruining the Eye?'

'I don't know. I have never heard of such a thing. But I do know that there are other ways of gaining Impressions. Word about the castle is that Mhani used the Water of Glass to enter the Liminal and receive Impressions, and that is how she went mad.'

'What are you driving at, Kivi?'

'Let's perform an experiment,' Kivi said. 'To test my theory. Let Gialse look into the Water of Glass. Let her use a more powerful Eye.'

'It is a thought,' Tash admitted. 'But you are always telling me that only a Seer can handle the Water of Glass. What makes you think this girl could do it? As you continually remind me, she is untrained.'

'Well, if we are desperate to finish the weapons, we must use desperate measures. You told me to solve the problem and I am using my utmost resources.'

'I am not as desperate as I was, but I am prepared to try it anyway. The falcon is here now, after all. And the Water of Glass never gave Impressions before. Your Carry Eye did. Where is it, anyway? I wanted Ixo to work with Gialse on it.'

'She did,' Kivi said. 'Some of the things she told me gave me this idea, about the Water of Glass.'

'Very well,' said Tash. 'First things first. Do you have the Eye with you?'

'No. Ixo has it.'

'Boy!' Tash summoned his servant and sent him to the harem to ask for the Carry Eye. He spoke to Kivi of other matters concerning his upcoming ride from Jai Khalar until at length the boy returned.

'Ixo says she does not have the Carry Eye. She says it is Kivi's and there must be some mistake. She has never had it except under Kivi's supervision.'

Tash looked at Kivi. The Seer wanted to say, 'She's lying,' but Ixo was a great favourite of Tash, so he merely said, 'Women! I will take care of this.'

Liaku was in Ukili's chambers attending to Chee when the word came through that Kivi had ordered a search of Tash's harem. Ukili, who had been having her hair unbraided while she sipped hot chocolate, shot to her feet.

'I will not permit it. Kivi gets above himself if he thinks he can intrude on my domain. Tell him it is the sanctified ground of the woman.'

'They are searching for a missing Carry Eye which Tash badly needs,' said Doren in his most diplomatic tone.

'Then he should apply to me and I will make the necessary inquiries among the women.'

'But . . . Forgive me, Princess, but this is not a matter for women. And those who have this Eye are not to be trusted, nor dealt with reasonably.'

'Ah! So Kivi understands that females are not reasoning beings. Therefore let him understand that he should never attempt to reason with me, either! He may not enter the harem, nor send anyone else in. The privacy of my girls from the intrusions of men is guaranteed, and even Tash shall not enter uninvited. Any Pharician would know this and would not so gravely insult me with such an absurd request.'

'It is a matter of most urgent security,' Doren pressed unwisely.

'And does Kivi accuse me of treachery, the emperor's own daughter and the wife of the emperor's son? Do not dare imply such a thing. I have said I will make my own inquiries. I suggest you leave before I become angry.'

Doren departed, cowed.

'Byrdgirl,' said Ukili, 'do you know what this thing is they are looking for?'

Liaku knew very well, but she shook her head dumbly.

'Go find out,' Ukili said. Liaku scampered off, glad to be released but bursting with unexpressed laughter. She no longer knew who she was working for and had begun to twig that once again, even though she was no longer in Byrdland, she, Liaku, was working for herself.

And Quiz, she amended mentally, and took herself off to the harem kitchens to get something to eat. She was still chilled from her climb but Ukili had not noticed her wet clothes, and Liaku intended to take this opportunity to have a little time to herself. She would find a fire and some good provender, and think things over. By now Liaku had no intention of bringing the Carry Eye to Se even though she knew where it was. She found it far more interesting to watch events unfold. And sure enough, the next morning the harem was searched on Tash's direct orders. But the search was performed by Ukili's female companions. Liaku and Chee were sent in as witnesses, and Liaku went to some pains not to reveal the fact that she knew they would find nothing.

Se was waiting for her when this job was done.

'Listen carefully, byrdgirl. You know that the black-haired woman called Ixo is Tash's favourite concubine? She is carrying his child and has considerable influence here in Jai Khalar. She is a Wasp, do you know what that means?'

Liaku shook her head wordlessly.

'It means she is expert in medicines, and especially poisons. The pharmacopoeia and kitchens are all carefully controlled by Tash's Pharician servants, and there is particular surveillance over the harem to prevent any foul play among the Clans who live in Jai Khalar and may harbour traitorous intents. Do you understand what I'm saying?'

'She got no means for make poison?'

'This is where you will help Ixo,' Se told her. 'You will approach her and tell her that if she poisons Ukili she will have the full support of the Scholars and the army.'

'Army?' Liaku said incredulously and received a slap across the mouth.

'Byrdgirl, there may be no respect for status in Byrdland, but you are on the ground now. Never address me so, nor question my orders.'

'I thought you say you Animal,' she hissed, no longer intimidated, for Quiz was at her shoulder like an Everien rocket ready for launch.

He slapped her face again. 'You will slip up in front of the Pharicians, and they are sticklers for order. Therefore do not address me frankly, even in private. Even in your thoughts.'

Liaku spat, thinking his blood would curdle if he knew the things she did to him in her thoughts.

'Tell me what you are to do.'

'Tell Ixo she poison Ukili, no punish anybody.'

'That you will drug Chee's food to make her sleep. That Ixo will be allowed to escape and return to her people. And you will provide to her this fine poison.'

Liaku took the vial and shifted from foot to foot. Why would Ixo believe the lies of murderers, she wondered, but kept her already swelling mouth closed.

'Give her this token also. She will understand what it means.'

It was a wolf paw. Enormous, Liaku thought, handling it with a reverence that came to her instinctively, for she had never seen a wolf.

'It was Sendrigel's family heirloom and is prized by Mistel. Tell her only that it is from the Circle. Reveal my identity on pain of death. And I can kill you both.' He glanced warningly at Quiz. 'I can kill you both at a distance, at any time.'

Liaku was no longer so sure of this, but she didn't show it.

'Go then! Go, and perform the mission you have been given. And don't fuck it up, Liaku.'

Liaku felt shy about going into Tash's harem without Chee on her shoulder. She was not herself a woman, although she feared that with the good food she was now allowed to eat and the rest she got, that she might begin to change to one whether she liked it or not. Among the byrdfolk only about half of the girls reached sexual maturity; the rest failed to develop at all, or developed so late that they were killed off by hunger, disease, or the dangers of the chala before they were able to attract a mate to protect them. Liaku had been told this was the case because of the lean, harsh life of the chala; but she had put on a growth spurt since leaving Jundun and was outgrowing her fine clothing. Still, she felt more like a boy than a girl, and the scents and sounds of the harem were foreign to her.

Ixo was beautiful. She was dressed from head to toe in Pharician lace, and two seamstresses hovered at her feet, pinning the hem of the new garment.

'They tell me give you this poison and this wolf paw which belonged to Sendrigel and is a sign of the Circle. They say if you kill Ukili they no hurt you, they give you free passage back to your family. They say the army support you and nobody harm you.'

'Poison Ukili!' Ixo's voice was sharper than her face. 'What's this about? How would I do that? Shiror guards her like a hawk when Tash isn't fucking her. For all I know he's in their bed as well.'

'Shiror and Tash ride out. You must wait until they leave, then you free.'

'How do you know that? How do *you* know so much?'

'I know what they tell me say.'

'Who? Who sent you here?'

'That secret.'

'What about her bird? It watches everything. It tastes her food.'

'I drug Chee, make her sleep. Easy to poison Ukili then.'

Ixo opened the vial and sniffed. She made a face.

'This is better used with a needle inserted under the skin, or on a knife to cut someone.'

'That up to you.'

'How did you get a Wasp poison? This isn't a Pharician method, not that I've ever heard of.'

Liaku shrugged. 'I know nothing.'

Ixo walked across the room and looked out across the gallery.

'How I wish we had a view of the mountains,' she said. 'We are only allowed to look in on the castle courtyards, and that little patch of sky up there through the skylight. Tell me, does Ukili have a view?'

'Ukili room look out over river. See whole valley from there.'

Ixo nodded, her back to Liaku, who could feel the sadness coming from her like a smell.

'I won't do it,' she said. Turning, she threw the wolf paw back at Liaku. 'I don't believe in this shit any more. Look what happened to Mistel – gone, taken away, and Sendrigel was a miserable traitor, and whoever the Circle are, I don't like them.'

Liaku stood there tongue-tied.

'Well? Is that all you have to say? Did they expect me to thank you for the gift? Tell your masters that I have more sympathy for Ukili than hate. And if I were you, byrdgirl, I would go straight to the princess and give her the poison and the wolf paw and tell her what you just told me. You little minx!'

Her eyes flashed, and Liaku retreated, shocked at the change in her mood.

'I saw you with Ukili, beside her litter. The emperor honours you with the feeding of his skyfalcon and his daughter's Speaker, and you are ready to betray him by participating in his daughter's murder. Isn't caring for the princess's bird Chee your first duty? Would you have drugged Chee? Would you?'

Liaku was quivering. Ixo was not what she expected. Did not a belly swollen with child make a woman weepy and dependent and capable of anything for the sake of her child? Ixo was a perverse thing, she decided. But she was also physically afraid, for Ixo looked as though she might strike Liaku, who was half her size.

'Get out. You repulse me. Get out, now, or I will tell Tash everything you have said and he will skin you and feed your eyes to the skyfalcon, and don't think it wouldn't eat them, either, you vicious brat.'

Liaku turned and fairly ran. Her eyes were full of tears. She sought out Quiz but he was in none of his usual haunts, and the sky was too dark for him to be flying. Suddenly she thought she would come apart. She literally did not know what to do next. Ixo's words had penetrated and hurt her in a way she had never been hurt. It was not that Liaku was possessed of such a high moral conscience. She simply could not bear the thought of being under anyone. She had to be ahead of the game, not a pawn in it. Her only safety had ever lain in her elusiveness, and now Se was cutting off too many of her options. Ixo had surprised her. And where was Quiz? Her one certain ally was nowhere to be found.

As for Se, he was to be found with Tash, making a pitch to be taken to Tyger Pass – without Wakhc, no less. Liaku listened at the door.

'I am the hands and feet of Wakhe, and given a Carry Eye we can surely go to Tyger Pass quite easily. If he stays here, cared for by the byrdgirl who is competent in such matters, then I can ride with you and make direct observation of everything that we find. I can then consult with Wakhe, who will be our code-breaker if any such need arises.'

'What makes you think this has anything to do with codes?' Tash said. 'My understanding is that there are rebel armies in Tyger Pass – and maybe in Snake Country above Fivesisters Lake. Apparently you know something I do not.'

'It is not that I have some special intelligence,' Se squirmed. 'But Wakhe is sure that there is something to be discovered in that mountain pass. He is possessed of a special intuition, you see.'

Liaku couldn't see Tash, so she didn't know whether the warlord was swallowing this story. In a neutral tone he said, 'If what you say is true, then all the more reason I should have the best of Scholars with me. So I will take Evra Kiss. I was going to take him anyway. I don't like him, but I'd rather have him where I can keep an eye on him than not. And perhaps he can change my opinion of him, if he shows his mettle at this philosophy or scholarship or whatever they call it nowadays.'

'Begging your pardon, Prince Tash, but Kiss is no specialist in these things.'

'I have decided, Yanse. Tell Wakhe we will have the Carry Eye and we will most certainly consult him, and you, but I deem it unwise to separate the two of you unnecessarily. Kiss is happy to go. Let him be your hands and feet, and you can stay here and be eyes and ears. It is better this way, trust me.'

'As my lord commands,' said Se, and passed Liaku in the corridor on the way out without seeing her. She shadowed him back to Wakhe's quarters. Then she waited until he had put Wakhe to bed and was muttering to himself, fully in the character of Yanse.

'Ah, the old fool, never such a fuss about bedclothes did I see! Four pillows or three, round or square, what does it matter I says to him, but—'

He saw Liaku and fell silent. His eyes questioned her.

'I do what you say,' she whispered.

'When will she do it?'

'Soon as Tash leave for Tyger Pass,' Liaku lied. 'Where Quiz?'

'Never mind about damn Quiz,' he said, his face cracking a huge implausible smile. 'This is excellent! Now go and check on Chee and make sure she is happy. And wipe that horrible look off your face. You must act as if everything is normal.'

Liaku disciplined her features with an effort. He was still smiling. 'You have done well. I have big plans for you.'

Liaku did not stay long with Chee. Ukili was already in bed with Tash, and Chee was happy with her view of the night sky. The anteroom was the temperature of a sauna, with both fireplaces blazing and several oil lamps burning, and from the sounds emerging from the bedroom itself Liaku imagined it was even hotter in there. She wondered whether Ukili was happy now that she was married to her half brother and her father's likely successor, or whether the shortage of sweetmeats was a greater concern for her.

When she got back to Wakhe's quarters, the door was locked. She continued on, seeking only a place where she could rest for the night unmolested by Se; but when she passed the room of Evra Kiss, the door was ajar. She slipped into the crack and looked around the edge of the door.

There were feathers on the floor. Evra Kiss was lying on the floor with his throat slashed apart as if by teeth – or claws.

Liaku drew breath to scream and checked herself only at the last instant, emitting instead a high-pitched wheeze of horror.

'Quiz?' she whispered. 'You here? Come out!'

But she knew the bird was not there. He disliked enclosed spaces. And the window was wide open; he could be anywhere by now.

Liaku couldn't say she was sorry. Kiss had been a right bastard and would have killed Quiz or kept him captive if he could. But she was uneasy. Why had Quiz done it now, when the Scholar was no longer a threat to the bird – or to Liaku?

'Don't be so obvious,' Se said in her ear. 'There are weapons besides a skyfalcon's claws that can rend a man's throat. And perhaps Quiz was not free to inflict such a wound, anyway. Do you understand me, Liaku?'

'Where Quiz? If you have him, you must let go!'

'Must? Ah, Liaku. You are in no position to make demands. You think it's all right to lie to me, don't you? You think I have no real power over you. But you are wrong. Very wrong. For Ixo was a test, and you failed.'

He slid from the room before she could think or act. He ran out into the hallway screaming, 'Murder! Murder! Evra Kiss is dead!'

Liaku had no time to think. She made for the open window, slithered through it, and gripping the white stone with moonlit fingers, she climbed away along the wall to the sound of shouts. Lights came on, booted feet echoed. Liaku climbed until she came to a roof, darted across it and through an open window, across a hallway and out another window, taking to the roofs again. Always she looked upward for Quiz, but she saw nothing in the sky.

At last she ended up at Duor's window. She could see him through a crack in the shutters, lying in bed and reading by candlelight. She banged on the shutters.

'Help,' she gasped. 'I no find Quiz. You see him?'

'What?' cried Duor, springing from bed and coming to the window clad in a nightshirt and a hat, shivering for there was no glass on his window. 'Come in here, stupid. If you fall it's a thousand feet if it's one.'

He dragged her inside. 'You're frozen,' he said. 'Go sit by the fire.'

She ignored him, racing about the room as if it were a cage while he dressed. 'Duor, what if they shoot him? They evil, so evil.'

'We'll look for him,' Duor said. 'Who's evil. Is Evra Kiss giving you trouble again?'

'He give nobody trouble now,' Liaku said. Duor was fully dressed now and threw his cloak over his shoulders, going to the door. Just as he was about to open it there was a sound of approaching feet.

'Duor! Wake up!' Someone banged on the door, but it was locked.

'My father,' Duor mouthed. Then, 'What is it? I'm coming.'

'Get dressed,' his father said through the door. 'Get down to Tash's audience hall immediately. Bring your sword. Hurry!'

Liaku was already scrambling out the window. Duor turned just in time to see her disappear over the sill. As she made her getaway, she could hear him calling in a harsh whisper for her to come back, but she ignored him, scrambling over roofs and walls in the frigid night until unexpectedly a hand reached out of a dark window and grabbed her around the waist.

'Got her, sir,' said a voice. Liaku kicked but it did her no good, so she went limp.

The Trial

Jai Khalar was roused from slumber and other nightly deeds. Tash summoned the Scholars, Kivi, Shiror, and Illyra with his security force to the audience hall. Ukili, invisible beneath veils and capes, was spirited away from Tash's rooms. Then Liaku was dragged in, bound, and made to kneel at Tash's feet. They had already started the proceedings. *I am dead*, she thought as the charges were spoken against her.

'She couldn't have done it,' Duor said, appearing from shadows. 'She was with me.'

Shiror cast his son a shocked look. Tash began to laugh.

'So the son is unlike the father, eh? Duor! This is only a child! If you want a woman I will lend you one of mine. You had only to speak!'

Liaku felt herself going hot with a mixture of shame, fear, anger, and relief. She couldn't look at Duor.

'We were flying the falcon on the battlements,' he said solemnly to Tash. 'It has extraordinary night vision. It hunts bats, can you believe it? What sort of bird is fast enough to catch a bat?' He was a good actor, Liaku thought, captivated by the excitement in his voice as he fabricated wildly. 'However, my lord Prince Tash, this is not to say I would not be honoured and most deeply grateful to accept your offer.'

Tash laughed even louder. 'Good boy!' he said. 'Shiror, well done. I will make a duke of this one when he is a little older.' He turned to Duor, who held his eyes steady, greatly impressing Liaku. 'Boy! Are you saying the falcon was with you?'

'That is what I am saying, my lord Prince Tash.'

'And where is it now?'

Duor shrugged. 'We left it on the north tower near the aviary, where it was grooming itself. It had stuffed itself on bats and we assumed it was roosting for the night.'

'Someone go get the falcon,' Tash said.

'It will only come to the byrdgirl,' Kivi reminded him.

'Well, catch it, then,' Illyra said, pointing to two of his men, who appeared none too eager to be given this job. 'Go on, you pussies!'

After they left, Illyra turned to Tash. 'A sated falcon does not attack a man. Not without provocation.'

Tash nodded. 'I was thinking the same thing. Let's see Kiss's body.'

Servants were sent to fetch the body, and while they were gone,

Wakhe and Se arrived. Se came in saying, 'Please do not be too harsh on her, for some might have said she had good cause to hate Evra Kiss, if not cause enough for murder. Even the princess Ukili will vouch that no love was lost between them. If you must kill her, then do not torture her first, for up until now she has been a good servant and Chee is fond of her, as is Wakhe, my master. He asks that you—'

'We're not going to kill her if we don't find her and her falcon guilty,' Tash said, and Se came up short.

'But of course,' he stammered, changing gears almost too smoothly. Liaku thought his front was transparent, but she knew it only seemed that way to her because of what she knew. The others could scarcely be expected to guess that Yanse was really Se, an agent of the Circle and an assassin. He was too chubby, too servile, too talkative. 'Oh, I pray that she may not be guilty. I merely thought . . . what other thing could make such a wound?'

'That is what we are trying to determine,' Tash said. 'Now be quiet.'

Se subsided. Liaku looked at Wakhe and saw that as ever, he seemed to be a million miles away. He had ceased all efforts to communicate. Se's disguise was surely slipping, Liaku thought desperately. Anyone who looked at the pair closely must eventually see that there was no dialogue between them – mustn't they? The Scholar was utterly passive, and Se spoke whatever words he chose on Wakhe's behalf. Poor Wakhe, Liaku thought. Trapped and unable to make his needs known. He was repulsive, but no one deserved such a fate.

She was drawn from her thoughts by the arrival of the servants with Evra Kiss's bloody body, the head half ripped off.

'You saw this murder?' said Tash to Se.

'No. I found him dead.'

'Why did you go into Kiss's room so late at night?'

'I . . . Wakhe sometimes works in the night, it is no different to him whether it's night or day. And he had to ask Evra a question. I went to see if he was awake, and there he was. Blood everywhere.'

'Hmm.' Tash made a dispassionate examination of the wound. 'He has been dead some time. The body is going cold. Duor, how long were you . . . er, hunting bats?'

'I don't know. From moonrise until about an hour ago.'

'It has not happened within the hour,' Illyra averred.

'Who saw him last?'

'I did, lord.' Kiss's bodyservant came forward. 'I spoke to him at bedtime, about midnight I guess. He didn't require anything, so I went to my own bed.'

'And you heard nothing.'

'No, my lord. I heard nothing until Yanse started shouting.'

Illyra said, 'The times do not match, then. But another weapon could have done this deed. Did he have enemies? A man in authority always has enemies.'

'He had no enemies,' Yanse cried. 'He was named Kiss because he was friendly to everyone.'

'Except, you say, this girl.' Illyra faced Se, shoulders squared, hips apart, rocking back and forth slightly with his thumbs hooked in his belt.

'He did not like the bird,' Se admitted.

'Kivi?' said Tash. 'What do you think?'

'The likely explanation is that the skyfalcon did it, with or without the complicity of the girl. It could have done it before Duor took it hunting.'

'Were there feathers?'' Illyra asked. Everyone looked at him curiously. 'In Kiss's room. Were there feathers?'

'Yes, sir,' Kiss's servant said. 'And the window was wide open. It must have flown in and out.'

'It is strange that he went to bed with the window open,' Kivi added.

'He wasn't in his bed,' the servant said. 'He was dressed, and lying on the floor.'

'Very strange,' Tash said. 'But I will ride tomorrow anyway. If the purpose of this act was to deter me from reaching Tyger Pass, I am undeterred. Yanse, you will come with me if it is to Wakhe's satisfaction that he remain here and communicate via Carry Eye.'

Liaku knew that this was exactly what 'Yanse' wanted, and wished she could get a piece of him between her teeth. Now Kiss was dead, he could go to Tyger Pass, and Liaku would be out of the way, all in one clean stroke.

Illyra's men came back. 'We can see the bird, but we can't get him, my lord. He's on top of the Eye Tower.'

Illyra said, 'Take the byrdgirl with you and get her to call the falcon. Be ready for anything; it may attack you.'

One of the men beckoned to Liaku and she was compelled to stumble after them, hands behind her back. They took her up to the aviary and one of them pointed to a nearby tower, where Quiz was still roosting, his head curling down toward them like a feathered gargoyle, utterly malevolent. Then he cut her hands free.

'Call him. Get him down here. Otherwise, we just push you over the edge.'

Liaku called Quiz, and to her amazement he came. She held up her arm for him and the guard holding her let go momentarily, probably afraid at the sight of the great bird's wings as he dropped toward Liaku. One of Illyra's other men had a net and tried to throw it over the falcon, but Quiz swerved to one side at the last instant and caught the net in his claws, throwing it over two of the men and then rising out of reach.

419

Liaku ducked beneath their flailing arms and scooted away between legs, grabbing hold of a crumbling pillar and swarming up its knobbly, rough surface easily.

The men were shouting and firing arrows seemingly at random; Liaku bit her lip at the thought of Quiz being hit, but didn't stop. An arrow slid harmlessly across a ledge toward her and she grabbed it, sticking it between her teeth. Above her she could see Se and Wakhe standing on an open bridge between towers. Se was holding a torch, and in its light his assumed face looked even fatter and more implausible, at least to Liaku. She ducked beneath an overhang as another arrow went past her.

She still had the poison that Ixo had refused.

If she were Duor, she would go to Tash or Shiror with the poison and the truth about Se, and make them test his so-called 'communication' with Wakhe, and search his rooms for secret messages and the paraphernalia of assassins. She would trust justice to prevail and take the high road.

Liaku was not Duor. And even Duor had lied tonight. So why shouldn't she commit murder? She was almost ten years old. It was time.

She opened the vial and spread the poison carefully on the tip and shaft of the arrow, putting the fletching between her teeth delicately so that the poison could not accidentally run into her mouth. Then she came out of hiding and began climbing straight up, toward Se.

They were screaming at her to come down. They were shooting wildly now; she could not see Quiz and hoped he had the sense to get above bow range. Se was waving his arms and telling them not to shoot her.

She reached his level, and he dropped the torch and held out his hands as if to help her. The torch rolled aside, leaving them in a darkness that whistled with the flight of arrows. She didn't have much time. She took the arrow out from between her teeth, let Se draw her up, and waited for him to start to say something. Then she jammed the point of the arrow into his mouth, trying to shove it down his throat. He grabbed her arms and pushed her down and away, so she could not complete the penetration of the arrow; but it didn't matter. Even as he tossed the arrow away and, one hand clamped around Liaku's wrist, began to speak, there was a change in his face. He passed his free hand before his eyes, letting go of Liaku with the other. Strange sounds came from his lips.

She didn't stay to find out the effects of the poison. She heard him say '. . . *can't see . . . where?* . . .' and then she had made herself scarce, sliding past the useless gangling arms of Wakhe on her way. She vanished among the pillars and posts of the Citadel.

Trust

Kivi did not sleep that night. He had time for only a brief visit to the Eye Tower, and to his surprise the rebel Clan troops he had been secretly monitoring were no longer visible. He tracked the immediate area, wondering where they could have gone and what they were up to, but he could find nothing. Before he could cast his search wider or inquire of Soren what the younger Seer had observed, Tash's servant interrupted him. Tash was calling another meeting. Kivi rushed to his audience hall unshaven, uncombed, and bleary-eyed. Tash was dressed for travel. He looked the better for not having slept, Kivi thought, and wondered where the Pharician had come by his seemingly boundless supply of energy.

'I used to think that Jai Khalar was a mad place, and I used to wish for more of Pharice and our civilized ways to be brought here. But now, despite the great honour done to me by my father Hezene, and my sister and wife Ukili, I find that the coming of Pharician ways brings nothing but strife and plots and even worse confusion. And although I would like to, I cannot blame the castle for these things. There is a traitor in this house. I charge you, Illyra, to find him or her and to deliver the appropriate punishment.'

Illyra, thought Kivi, appeared sanguine about being laden with this duty.

'Meanwhile, I will take *none* of you Scholars with me. I will take one of the Seers, Soren.'

Soren? Kivi thought: *What about me?*

'He may be Clan, but I don't believe him capable of murder, whereas you Pharicians are obviously more interested in killing each other than in acquiring Knowledge. You are all too interested in Tyger Pass for your own good – and I suspect some of you are trying to prevent my going there. Well, you will stay here. You can join the Deer Clan Scholars and see what you may contribute in the Fire Houses; but I do not expect it to be much.'

Then he dismissed them, turning his attention to Shiror and Illyra.

Kivi was eager to get back to the Eye Tower, but he was kept busy organizing the imminent departure of Tash. He managed to get Soren aside, and in a whisper he said, 'Have you seen anything in the Eye?'

Soren's eyes flickered in recognition of the secret. 'I have never seen anything. And recently I have seen even less.'

Kivi looked at him searchingly, trying to decipher his meaning. Was Soren admitting his collusion and saying that he *had* seen something – an event of import, perhaps? Or was he, chuffed with Tash's selection of him to ride to Tyger Pass, denying any involvement?

Or had he betrayed Kivi to Tash and this was why Tash had chosen Soren and not Kivi?

It was not until Kivi was standing at Tash's stirrup and taking his last instructions that he got his answer.

'Kivi, you are the one man I have been able to talk to since I came to Jai Khalar. I have not always trusted you, but now my home and my bride are in your hands. Illyra does not understand Jai Khalar or the Knowledge, and he is even less diplomatic than I am!' He laughed at his own assessment. 'Look after things, will you, Kivi? And see what you can do about getting the Scholars to make some progress with the Fire Houses. Who knows? Maybe the Carry Eye will turn up yet.'

With more emotion than he intended, Kivi promised. Then Illyra shouted at him and shoved him aside. Kivi raced into Jai Khalar to do his duty.

Learning to Fly

Istar fell for the fourth time in one day. She sat there on the dusty ledge looking up at the cliff and thinking: *I have had enough of this.*

She had tried her best. She did not expect favours from Eteltar, even though she suspected that he would miss her if she wasn't there and that she meant more to him than he let on. She did not expect him to carry her back up to the aperture and help her to make her way through to the cave in Tyger Pass – even though it would be easy for him to do so, she did not expect it. In fact, she scarcely allowed the thought to cross her mind, for Istar was used to self-sufficiency, and her pride prevented her from making herself dependent on the man-bird.

But after three months she had not gotten to the hole in the cliff that she had fallen through. She could not even see it. Her climbing was improving and she had climbed quite high along certain routes up the sheer face. She was beginning to wonder just how far she had really fallen, that she was still alive, for nowhere up there could she find an aperture big enough to have admitted her. To be sure, there were large sections she could not climb across, but that was mostly because she could not cross Eteltar's mysterious sculpture lest she ruin it.

And Eteltar still showed no sign of instructing her in any concrete way. She was beginning to think he didn't want her to leave, no matter how many times he swore to the contrary. Up until now, she had been patient, for Eteltar was famous for having taught Ysse sword, and she'd heard many stories about weapons teachers and their tricks and quirks. Istar half expected to be told that all this time he had only been testing her resolve; or that there was some meaning in making her collect feathers that had profound implications – even though all he ever used the feathers for was for brushing away the dust from his carving. ('Mine are too coarse,' he explained when she glanced questioningly at his own wings); or that he had been waiting for her to be 'ready' before he showed her the means by which she could return to Tyger Pass and her own time. When at last she confronted him with the fact that he had done none of what he promised, he acted surprised.

'Promised? But why would I promise to help you?'

'I don't know *why* you do anything,' she said. 'But you did, and now you must uphold your word.'

'No. That would be stupid. I'm trapped here myself. How could I possibly help you to leave if I can't leave?'

'But you said I came through a door.'

'That doesn't mean I know how you can leave through it. Anyway, you don't need to climb to do that.'

He sounded so sure that she almost believed him; then again, he contradicted himself so frequently that she sometimes suspected him of senility, and this ought to be one of those times. He had said that when she was well, he would help her to leave.

'I don't need to climb? But how am I going to get to the trapdoor? I fell, didn't I?'

'Of course you fell. Saw it myself. I was amazed you survived. Must have been all the furs.'

She wasn't wearing furs now. She was nearly naked, skinnier and browner than she'd ever been, and covered with scratches and insect bites.

'You don't need to climb,' he said again, turning his wing over and picking a louse out of the feathers with his opposite hand. 'If you really want to learn something, learn to fly.'

Istar burst out laughing and couldn't stop.

'What's so funny?'

'Me? Learn to fly?'

'What?' he asked, offended. 'The art of flight is my specialty. No one else can do it. Are you questioning my talents?'

His nostrils were flaring and the feathers on his chest stood up. Istar knew from experience that he was about to have a tantrum.

'No, no, of course not.'

'I hope not.'

'B-but . . .'

'What? But what, Istar?'

'But I can't fly. Why do you taunt me so? Why do you suggest to me ideas that are so outrageous and impossible I could never hope to achieve them? I can learn to climb, but I can't ever learn to fly.'

He looked up at the cliff and then spat into the dust.

'Climbing is wasted on you. You have the wrong body type anyway. Learn flight. I meant to teach Ysse, but she never came. I will teach you.'

'I can't possibly—'

'Ah, stupid wench. Tremble and back away. I knew you would. Never mind. Go away!'

She hesitated, lower lip starting to give way at his rebuke, which it had never done in all her years of military training, no matter what the instructor said. He was in the full flight of his anger.

'Go away, false one! Coward!'

'I'm not a coward,' she shouted, and leaped to her feet, tears of indignation dancing in her eyes. 'What you say is crazy! You cannot teach me to fly. I would only die in the attempt.'

'If that happens, at least you will have the satisfaction of trying to do the impossible. How many people can offer their deaths in this way? Precious few, I tell you.'

'But I want to live. Now, climbing that cliff—'

'—is a waste of your time and mine. I'm surprised it's taken you so long to realize that.'

'Please, Eteltar. Don't be mad. I could find you someone else. A real Seahawk. Eteltar, don't you understand? The Seahawk magic. It's not in my blood. *I can't fly.*'

'Then you might as well be dead.'

To her great shame, she had started crying. When he spoke, he spoke with such force that his words came out like divine pronouncements. She felt as though her sentence had been uttered from on high. Her own voice sounded feeble by comparison.

'But why?'

'Because flying,' Eteltar said with a snort, 'is the only thing really worth doing.'

And he cracked his joints one at a time, beginning with his knuckles and ending with his spine as he stood, silhouetted against a dark gold sky shadowed by clouds the texture and colour of auburn hair, windblown. His body arched backward and his fingertips splayed wide. He winked at her and laughed. Then, in one movement, his legs bunched, he pressed against the ground and then sprang into the sky. His wings spread and lifted once for a slow downstroke – then folded suddenly and he plummeted over the edge and out of sight. The roar of his laughter came back to her, and the burnt and stained sun went down abruptly.

Istar's breath caught and she began to cry again. She sat down and wrapped her arms around her folded knees like a child.

'Oh, loneliness,' she said.

Medicine

Eteltar had his good days and his bad days. On his bad days Istar wished for a hammer to bash herself in the head with.

'I am old,' he moaned and wailed. 'I cannot leave this place and soon the worms will come for me. I know everything there is to know about anything you could name, and I am trapped here alone with no one to tell it to.'

I might as well be a flea on his backside, Istar thought. 'Tell it to me,' she ventured on one occasion, when she was feeling bold.

'You? You can't even grip a rock without crying for Mommy. Oh, don't get into a cauldron, Istar, but you know you are only a small bit of a thing. Ah, it's useless. No one understands me. I'm doomed.'

'But in my world, I'm strong,' she tried to explain. 'I can save you. I can bring you to people who will marvel at you and hang on your every word.'

'There is no such world. It's a thing of your dreams. You know nothing about it.'

She went away, jaw trembling. She felt like a puppy whose master is throwing a tantrum about the politics of a distant country. No matter how many times she dropped her bone in his lap, she couldn't help him.

'Coward,' she whispered so that he would not hear her. 'Come with me and find out. What have you got to lose?'

Maybe he was wrong. *There's no such thing as 'doom'*, she told herself. *That's bullshit for people like Tarquin. The disease of disappointed men. But I'll throw myself against this rock as many times as it takes to break it or me.*

Easy to vow, she soon learned. Hard to do. Especially in the absence of alcohol and other analgesics. She spent most of her time on the cliff, struggling.

'You're too fat!' he called. 'Especially in the hips.'

Istar spat and didn't answer. She was hungry. She picked her braids up off her neck and mopped away the sweat that had collected beneath them. She was aware that she was squinting and red-faced in the intense heat, and the sound of her breath in her own chest was making strange, uneven noises like distant birds. She didn't know whether she wanted to cry or throw something. There was nothing to throw.

She drove in another spike.

'Remember, it's only my life at stake,' taunted the old man from the ground. 'Not yours.' He began to laugh. 'You can come down if you want. It's got nothing to do with flying, anyway – does it?'

Istar dragged herself to the next ledge. There were bones of small creatures wedged into crevices of the rock, long picked clean by the hawks and the wind and the rain. If she craned her head back as far as it would go, she could see the tailfeathers of one of the birds some twenty feet above her. They spread apart, and for a moment the light came through them. Then a shadow fell from the hawk's tail; Istar dodged to one side, but too late. The faeces hit her on the forehead. Eteltar was still complaining.

He wants me to fail, she thought, and found the will to move her arms over her head.

'Come on!' Eteltar called, anger in his tone now. 'Come down. Don't be stupid.'

Still she said nothing. A stream of refutations came into her mind, but she didn't have the energy or the nerve to express any of them to him. She felt sure they must be obvious anyway, even without her saying them. Things like: *I'm only up here because you told me to come up here, and if you're going to tell me you'll die without my help, then let me fucking help you; and if you're trying to imply that I'm not strong enough, I'll prove you wrong; and if I turn out not to be strong enough, well, I hope you'll be really sorry but I won't give in, you mean bastard.* Things like that.

But her silence and persistence only seemed to outrage Eteltar more.

'Get down from there now!' he called. 'Of all the stupidity you could engage in, and now you will not even listen to me. You call yourself a student? I might as well teach mosquitoes. Come down at once.'

She had reached an impasse. She could see the hawks now, gathered in a semicircle about a smooth bowl in the stone whose lip rested only a few yards from the curving summit. They seemed indifferent to her presence. When she looked down she could see the land falling away in terraces and sheer drops, and Eteltar was a stick figure below. He leaped into the air and fixed himself to a nearby ledge, just out of her reach.

'Your fingers aren't sticky enough,' he remarked, tilting his head and scrutinizing her. 'You'll never climb and you'll never make a thief, which is too bad considering what you've got ahead of you.'

'Thief?' She laughed. 'I'll come by my desserts honestly, thank you.'

'Too bad. Thievery's easier, less stress on the joints. You'll appreciate that if you're ever as old as me.'

He flipped neatly off the ledge, dangling by his feet.

'Show-off. Ah, fuck it.' She dropped off, landed hard on her backside, and thrust her burned and aching fingers into her mouth. 'My hands aren't like your hands, and they never will be.'

'Quitter. Stool pigeon.'

Sulking vigorously, she didn't reply.

He continued to taunt her. 'Fat ass! Whiner! *Girl!*'

'Eteltar, you bastard, I can't fly but you can't torment me into leaping off this cliff to prove it.'

'Sure I can. Jellyfish, crybaby, loser—'

'You have *wings*. I *don't*.'

'Ah, she perceives the problem. Good, Istar. I had nearly given up hope.'

'You won't tell me how you got yours, only that you're now trapped here and doomed. So how can *I* get wings?'

'Wee babe that needs its hand held, that I cannot tell you.'

But when she curled up to sleep that night in the protective heat of his feathers, he whispered in her ear. She was half asleep.

'Steal my wings. Make them yours.'

'What?' She stirred.

'Shh. Be still, and do not fart so much as last night or you can sleep alone.'

She closed her eyes, clenched her buttocks, and drifted off.

Then again, there were the good days. Eteltar flying and explaining the principles of converting one's body to reflect one's desires.

'In that case, couldn't we just convert me into a man?' she asked once. 'It would solve my life. I might not fly, but I'd settle for that, and leave the flying to sailsnakes and yourself.'

'It's a riddled world,' Eteltar said cryptically. 'I'm weaker now than ever. You punched yourself a hole and soon other things will follow. It's the way. My days are numbered.'

She looked around, trying to perceive these holes or passages that he spoke of so vividly ('The world's like a cheese, Istar, it's been eaten through in so many places') but she saw only the sun-scorched heights of the dead volcano and the red desert with its faint gilding of yellow grass below.

'I don't believe in doom,' she said.

'You don't have to believe in it,' he laughed. 'It exists whether or not you are pleased by it.'

'You can change your fate. You must try.'

He shook his head. 'There is no medicine for me.'

'I am your medicine.'

He looked at her with a sudden perception, as though she had said something he did not expect.

'*I* am your medicine, Eteltar,' she said in a voice shaking with the force of her certainty. 'You must use me.'

'Istar.' He cupped her face in his hands and only looked at her for a long time. 'You are such a small thing and do not know it.'

For once she did not bristle. Tears heated her eyes and spilled. 'Please come. We could go back to Tyger Pass together. We'll help each other. Eteltar, please.'

'It would not be what you think.'

'I don't care! Please—'

'The White Road has me, Istar. I am no longer like you. There is no going back.'

'I don't believe that's true. We can make things better in all Everien. With your history and knowledge we will right the shape of things.'

'No.'

She was about to break into heaving sobs, and kicked the wall to stop herself.

'You are too intense,' he reproached her – and without irony.

'So everyone says. They say I am trying to be my father. But it's not just about my father. Not any more. I mean' – she laughed – 'I'm one of dozens of children, he never knew any of us, not really. He wasn't that kind of man. But it's more than that now for me. Since Jai Pendu—'

'You killed me,' he interrupted.

'What?' She was pretending not to understand, but his words had hit her like an electric shock. They sang through her with dead certainty, even before her mind threaded its way through to their true meaning.

'I attacked you and you killed me. In Jai Pendu. It doesn't matter. But you can't go back there. Time runs in concentric circles, and you're not on that loop. You will have to find a new way to kill me now.'

'I'm not going to kill you.'

'Of course you are.'

'Eteltar, stop it. I love you. Not that you care.'

'Don't be stupid. You can't love what you don't know.'

'Tell me of Everien.'

'Why?'

'Because I want to know.'

'I can't tell you of Everien. Because Everien does not yet exist. It has only sowed the seeds of its own possibilities on a wind that flies backward. But I do not expect you to understand.'

Istar was not so easily discouraged. She persisted with her questions. 'If Everien does not yet exist, where did the Floating Lands come from? What happened to them?'

'That is a mystery.'

'Are the Sekk also a mystery?'

'The Sekk are not my especial study. Ysse knew more of them than I. It was how she came to seek Jai Pendu, for she had glimpsed the towers across the sea, and she believed that the Everiens had fled there to elude the Sekk. She hoped they would possess some weapon she could use in

429

Everien to banish her enemies – or if not a weapon, then a Knowledge that would help her.'

Istar said, 'But you're the one they always called a wizard. She deferred to your Knowledge. And you opened the White Road. That's what everyone says.'

'You should not believe what everyone says.'

'Set me straight then. You owe me the story. At least some of it. If we are to be trapped here forever bickering with one another, you cannot keep silence.'

'We will not be here for ever. You will get out. But I will tell you some of it, though I don't expect you to understand.'

'Good! Tell me, how did you open the White Road for Ysse? The accounts merely say that you did it, but not how.'

'While I was excavating the ruins beneath the Fire Houses I discovered a potion. Written on the side of the vial were six symbols. I recognized them as Everien, but I didn't know what they meant. I sniffed it and tasted it, and suddenly the wall in front of me exploded and light came pouring in. A man was there, bald and dirty and ragged-looking, carrying a sword but wearing no Clan colours. This messenger, he had a compelling way about him. He told me I was the greatest Animal Magician the world had ever known – and I believed him, for he seemed so sure. It is funny, is it not, how conviction grants courage. I became what he believed I already was. I had no such conviction of my own.

'He told me that the liquid I had discovered in my ruined laboratory was the venom of the Li'ah'vah, the extinct time serpent. He said my fate and his and all of Everien's depended on this time serpent. He said I must discover how to save the time serpent from extinction. Then he vanished, and the hole went dark. Later I explored it, but it only led to the surface by a convoluted route. The other Scholars who looked at it agreed it appeared to be a Li'ah'vah's tunnel. I didn't tell anyone about the explosion. I was a young man, eager for credibility, and I didn't think anyone would believe my story in its entirety.'

'You didn't even tell Ysse?' Istar asked boldly. She had heard so many rumours and tales of Eteltar over the years, and they all painted him as a mysterious, almost omnipotent character whom everyone, even Ysse herself, was afraid of. Whom no one understood.

'Ysse and I had spoken many times of how we might reawaken Everien and drive away the Sekk. Their hauntings had shaped both our lives. We each had our reasons for hunting them. I showed Ysse the venom and told her what had happened and she said, "Eteltar, this is our chance! You must learn its secrets."

'But she had little understanding of the principles of Scholarship, and though I was surrounded by the relics of Everien Knowledge, I did not know how to use them. The Fire Houses lay dormant, their codes undiscovered, their powers at rest.

'We were under tremendous pressure. Every night the Sekk circled round A-vi-Khalar and sang, and the Making equipment sometimes sang back, but in a muted way, for the Fire Houses were without the Fire of Glass. It was deep winter, the shortest day of the year, a night of no moon, and their calling was loud.

'Ysse came to my lab with her sword in her hand. "I am going to ride out among them," she said. I told her to wait, to let me try something crazy. And I went down into my laboratory, walked into the Li'ah'vah tunnel, and drank the venom. I found myself walking through walls and stone until I was back in my own laboratory – but it was not the same. It was not in ruins. It was working. There were lights and sounds everywhere. There were people there who spoke to me, and we understood each other. I was in the Fire Houses, but long, long, long ago.'

He paused, his eyes distant, his face lit from within with the intensity of memory.

'The venom I had taken had all but killed me. Had I drunk it all I would surely be dead. As it was, I entered the Liminal still carrying the vial half full, and I found myself in the Fire Houses as they were of old. With the help of the people there I received much Knowledge. I examined the venom and was able to detect its essential pattern, its code in the Everien language, by which in the Making engines of the Fire Houses the time serpent might be created. The label on the bottle with the Everien code written on it came to be written by me, and I understood the meaning behind the code. I knew how to make the venom and the creature that had produced it. I learned many things there which I have since forgotten.

'Yet my body was dying. I had the information I had been charged to retrieve, but I could not take it back with me, for I had no way to go back. I could sense the nearness of my own death. I could not call the White Road – I was too weak, and I was only a man. The White Road exists only on the borderline between the Knowledge and the Animal Magic, the realm of Paradox. It's the tissue separating reason from everything else. My reasoning parts were strong but the spark of life was weak. So there, in the Fire Houses of that time, I changed myself. I had always loved the birds and studied them, so I mixed my patterns with the pattern of the most powerful of all the raptors, the Everien skyfalcon. For they are older, and purer, and they are unclouded by human doubts. I found myself flying, and the path I tore open was the White Road. Ysse used that path – from her point of view, only a moment had passed since I recklessly entered the Li'ah'vah tunnel and took the venom. So she rode up it looking for me, but she did not find me. She found Jai Pendu, and the Fire, which she took.'

'What happened to you?'

'To those who were with me, including Ysse, it was as if I had never left. The White Road appeared for Ysse. The poison worked on my body. While Ysse was on her quest, I was making a slow and difficult recovery. When I awoke, I did not possess the memories of my time in ancient Everien. I never recovered those memories. I remember some things, but not the crucial details. I could not speak; my tongue knew no words but my throat was full of a singing I must have learnt in the old time. And I could not find my avian half. I wandered around like a ghost. When Ysse returned and aroused the Fire Houses, I was indifferent. My life's work now meant nothing to me. I had become something more, and then the *more* part was taken away. I felt like the flying part of me was the essential part, and me, my mind, the man called Eteltar, he was only an afterthought, some sugar on top of the cake. The best of me was gone. I was lost without my wings. Everywhere I sought contact with the skyfalcon. Using the Animal Magic I empathized with seahawks, falcons . . . but the Everien skyfalcon is extinct in our time, and I could not become a creature that had been dead for a thousand years. I had flown into another part of time and I could not find myself.

'I was divided. I could project my awareness into the birds, but I was ever only a visitor. I was never myself. Moreover, while I was a man I did not behave as other men. I was troubled, confused. Obsessively I searched for answers; I became more abstract and strange, even to myself. I was impatient, irascible, difficult.'

Was? Istar thought, but did not say anything.

'The birds I entered soon began acting wrongly as well. They slew things indiscriminately. I myself was consumed with unnatural urges I could not curb. I removed myself from all society, to my place in Tyger Pass, which I had discovered at the terminus of another Li'ah'vah tunnel.'

'The hills are full of them,' Istar said.

'I still had the sample of venom, and I knew now that if I took it I could again get into the tunnel of the Li'ah'vah – the tunnel that digs through time. I wanted to get back to ancient Everien, for that was the one place where I was not lost to myself. In desperation, I took the venom, and for the second time, I flew – but I did not return to the time of Everien, but to an even older time. I was brought here, and I cannot now escape. I believe I am stuck in a dead end of the time serpent trail, trapped by a paradox. I cannot get out.'

'But why are you trapped? What about your own door, the one I came through?'

'I told you, I cannot cross it as a man. I would not want to. Two doses of time serpent venom mean that I am split. And I would rather be banished from the world, and keep my wings, than be among people as I was. Just like a ghost.'

Istar said nothing for a long time. The heat of the day was fleeing, leaving behind a cool stillness and the cries of the desert dogs far below.

'Do you know how this all started? From my point of view, out there in Tyger Pass?'

He shook his head.

'They found a skeleton. The Circle of Pharice – do you know who they are?'

'I do not.'

'Well, they purchase relics of the Knowledge every chance they get, and some hunters found a skeleton up in Tyger Pass. Eteltar, the skeleton was a man with wings.'

'Me?' he squawked, his voice breaking in surprise. 'You're saying I died like this?'

He was looking at his own body, wings spread, his incredulity so sudden and comical that the mood was broken. 'Ho!' he added, waving his hands in denial. 'Do not try to trick me back through that door! I do not foresee how I will die – or even how many times I will die, since there seem to be three of me, man, animal, and . . . how you see me now.'

'I still don't understand how you got split. When . . . where . . . how did it happen?'

He was laughing. 'When, where, how? Such questions! As near as I can make it, it happened when I went to ancient Everien, and yet it also happened when I tried to return from ancient times to my natural time. And it happened when I came here. Somehow, all of those times were the same. They converged, the Liminal in between those times and places was the same to me, and it cut me in pieces. I had to send a message out into the spiral of time, with the answer to the riddle of the time serpent. As I tried to explain, I learned many things in ancient Everien. I learned the art of flight and how to project my consciousness into an object of my contemplation. That is how I flew. And when I became the bird and it became me, there was a ripping. My wings went one way, bearing the Knowledge and the message, and my human body went another – into madness. And I . . . I am what is left over.'

'But the human part of you, the Sekk that hunts in Tyger Pass—'

'I cannot help that.'

'But are you conscious of it? Do you know, are you that Sekk?'

'How could I be? He lives in another time.'

'That doesn't seem to matter with respect to anything else in this story.'

'It must have risen up when my bones were disturbed,' Eteltar said. 'For I was a man when I took the venom in my cave. I went to some pains to get it right. I found an old Li'ah'vah tunnel, I set up the locking mechanism, and I took the venom deliberately so that I could enter the White Road, and I found myself here, half man, half flier.'

'You must have left something behind in Tyger Pass. How do you know your Sekk killed the Hawk Girls' family?'

'I just know it. That is what will happen. Because when my bones are disturbed, I will be reawakened.'

'*Will* be? *Will* happen? But it already has happened.'

'For you. But not for me.'

Istar let her head fall into her hands. 'But how can you know these things? Eteltar, are you sure you don't ever pass through into the cave in Tyger Pass? Like sleepwalking? Are you completely sure?'

'I'm not completely sure of anything. But it doesn't matter.'

'Well, I think you have a responsibility,' Istar said censoriously. 'There is a Sekk out there with your face and your eyes, and it is killing my people. My sisters and I are immune somehow, for we have not been Enslaved by it – but Eteltar, you were not a poor swordsman in your time. Your Sekk is a killer, do you understand?'

'Of course I understand, you impertinent little twerp! I would put my sword against anyone and anything. I am a Seahawk and a Skymaster. I told you my story because I thought you would be sympathetic. But you obviously have not been listening to anything I've said.'

'I've listened!'

'Then go! Make an end to the story. Go out there and kill my Sekk!'

His eyes blazed. She swallowed, affected because in essence he was saying, 'Kill me.'

'Ah, you quail at the thought of it.'

'*I do not quail*. But I'm stuck here as much as you. *You* can fly! I can't! How am I supposed to get back?'

'Learn then, damn it. Do I have to spell everything out for you?'

'Well,' said Istar, drawing a breath to gather her strength. 'I see our moment of quiet understanding is past. Very well! I'm going.'

And she began to climb. She fell; scraped herself; blew her braids off her face, and then paused on a ledge and hacked them off.

'Now what you have you done?' he said in scathing tones. 'You look like a plucked chicken.'

Of course, that only made her fall. Again.

*

Then, one day, while she was dozing in the tent – for she had been banned temporarily from climbing after her most recent bout of injuries – she saw a bird disappear in midair. She had been looking right at it. It was a small alpine warbler, white with black markings, and it had flitted off a ledge near where Eteltar was busy with his carving. One instant it was there, the next it was gone.

Istar had had too many experiences of this kind to think for a second that this had been a trick of her eye. She stared at the place where she had last seen the bird. About ten minutes later she was rewarded when it reappeared.

'Hey!' she yelled. 'There's a hole in the sky.'

Eteltar finished what he was doing before he lifted his right wing and dipped his head under it to look at her.

'What?'

'There's a hole in the sky.'

'Oh, that.'

He went back to work. She stood up painfully.

'Come down here, Eteltar!'

He knew when he was caught. Afflicted with temporary deafness, he refused to come down until well after dark. She forced herself to stay awake, and when he entered the tent she said,

'It goes to Tyger Pass, doesn't it?'

'Apparently,' he said, shrugging.

'Why didn't you tell me?' she moaned. 'Why didn't you help me?'

'What? And deprive you of your right to find out?'

'It's not funny,' she wailed, punching him.

'Yes, it is,' he laughed. He did in fact convulse in a fit of giggles, momentarily unable to continue. Then he straightened and cleared his throat. 'It truly, truly is funny. And you have to make your own way. That is the closest thing to a conviction that I still possess, after all I've been through. That's the defiance of death, or the Everien version of death, which is un-life.'

'What?' She was so annoyed she couldn't take in the sudden and unexpected dose of philosophy – though she knew this was the only way he ever delivered it.

'The livingness of a thing depends on that thing making its own way. You cannot abstract the animal essence of a thing and expect it to remain alive. You will have a dead abstraction, and death only begets more death, as the Sekk have shown.'

Istar was bone tired, and she could not follow. She stifled several yawns and pinched herself to stay awake; Eteltar was so fascinated by his own words that he didn't even seem to notice she was about to doze off.

435

'The Everien codes are death codes. They contain nothing. They describe nothing. They lead to emptiness, but a real struggle for life leads to fullness. That is why the Animal Magic will always be wild. It will never submit to the measurements of man; but the more clever man's measurements become, the more elusive will be the Animal Magic, till it can scarce be perceived. The harder you try to see it, the less receptive you become. Animal Magic is not hard work, Istar the Sleepy. It comes or goes by its own grace.'

'The Knowledge is hard work,' she yawned.

'I know. I have done it myself.'

'Then what happened?'

'What happened between Ysse and me is a story it would pain me too much to tell. I am here, and I believe I am before the beginning of the world, where no one else would come. All you need to know is that the White Road divides the Knowledge from the Animal Magic, and there are precious few bridges across that divide. Beyond myself I believe there is only one other, and it is not aware of itself as such. Whereas I am too aware of myself, and so must hide here where there will be no danger I will be understood.'

'I may come to understand you. Someday,' she said petulantly.

'It is what I hope, and what I fear, small Istar. If I go with you, I will be sundered from my wings. It is my wings you love, Istar. You would not like me without them. I am not kind.'

She began to chortle. 'Are you kind *now?*'

'Kinder than you know, to refuse you as I do. Opening the White Road is not like opening a clamshell! You cannot survive without me,' he assured her. 'And I don't believe you will go alone, anyway. You would rather stay here with me.'

'And be a witness to your doom, as you call it? No.' She was bristling with indignation. 'I will set off down this mountain and into that valley, even if it is full of fire, even if I perish amongst the ruins of Everien.'

'You will not.'

'Yes, I will.'

'You will not.'

'Yes. I will. Ah, Eteltar, watch me. For I am going to fly.'

She walked to the edge of the cliff then, spreading her arms like wings.

'No!' he cried, and springing after her blocked her with his own wings. 'Don't be crazy!'

'I thought you were teaching me to fly.'

'Such things cannot be taught. A bird doesn't need to be taught.'

She groaned and growled her frustration. 'How you contradict yourself.'

'Do not jump! Go to sleep, Istar, and let me think.'

She woke to utter blackness. Someone was moving, without: She could hear the birds rustling and talking to each other. She poked her head out of the tent and was greeted by a sharp, chilly breeze. The stars punctured the darkness over the desert, and in her sleepy eyes their points stretched to lines of light arrowing toward the horizon. The air was so clear that she imagined the scene before her might snap like a thin sheet of ice, might shatter on contact, if she moved – so she didn't move. Silhouetted against the sky was a man with a sword strapped to his back. His outline was indistinct as he took a few steps toward her and stopped. He reached back and unfastened the sword, casting it on the ground. Starlight caught his braided hair; whether it was white or blond she could not tell. She held her breath.

He lowered himself so that he might pass into the tent. He picked up her hand where it was bandaged from a recent encounter with the rocks. He brought it to his lips. Light sculpted the lines of his cheekbone and jaw without reaching his deep-set eyes. His wings seemed to be everywhere.

'Have you decided? Will you come with me?' she whispered as he pushed inside the tent, bringing the heat of his body and the cold of the stars. He was laughing in Eteltar's low voice. 'Please, will you open the White Road?'

'Not tonight,' he said, and pulled her down unresisting.

It was the only night of Istar's life. Every other one before or after was now rendered so as to be without quality or weight. The ancientness of her bond with Eteltar gave a grainy truth to everything that happened, from the roughness of their coupling to the softness of Eteltar's sleep, afterward, that she was too amazed to share. She lay awake listening to him breathe. She was so full that thought could not enter her. She was filled with a sense of triumph; a sense that at last, something was beginning.

She did not know that instead, it was ending.

Sledgehammer

Like a spider suspended by a thread coming from its ass, Pallo was hanging from the ceiling of the Fire House in the climbing harness Kassien had provided for him, carefully examining the edges of the Fire of Glass where it was set in the apex of the vaulted dome. His head for heights had not improved with practice, and he was chanting to himself under his breath: '*Nice warm bed. Nice bowl of soup. All over soon. Nice warm bed.*' In the exposed control pit below, Xiriel was working his magic with the Everien code panels.

'How much longer?' Kassien asked. 'Pallo, can you pry it out?'

'I'm not sure about the best way to do this,' Xiriel said. 'When Ysse's people placed the Fire here, they used a lock made of sound, and that particular sound is associated with a symbol, which is a typical Everien way of doing things. But no one wrote down what the symbol is.'

'Shouldn't we have thought of this before?' Pallo hissed.

'I assumed people kept records,' Xiriel said in an acid tone. His hands moved across the instrument panels in the pit, and as they did so symbols lit up, as if buried within the dark stone and suddenly set alight. The Fire House began to vibrate, very soft and very deep. It was a sound that wasn't heard so much as felt in the bones.

'Why don't you just look in the history of the Eye that governs this Fire House?' inquired Pallo. 'The Eye must have recorded Ysse's people installing the Fire.'

Xiriel was growing annoyed as he explained, 'If the Water of Glass had been around in those days to activate the Eyes, maybe I could. But it wasn't. So I can't.'

'Children,' said Kassien. 'Don't squabble.'

Then came the silence of no one knowing what to do. At last Xiriel said, 'Well, maybe it's worth a try. The Eyes weren't connected to each other in those days, but they did sometimes record images individually. There are some records of Ysse from before the Water of Glass. I don't know if there are any from before the Fire.'

'I suggest you look anyway,' said Kassien tensely.

'Meanwhile, I'll just fiddle about up here, unperturbed by this dangerous height,' Pallo said. '*Nice warm bed. Fire. Nice soup. Brandy. All over soon.*'

For about ten minutes Xiriel stood motionless in front of the Eye.

438

'Someone's coming!' Kassien whispered.

'Damn it,' Xiriel said. 'Do you think the Eye Tower has noticed me tampering with this Eye? How many men?'

'Shit, it's a whole fucking delegation of Pharician Scholars.'

'Can't we just force the Fire out?' Kassien said. 'Pallo! Do something!'

'What do you want me to do?' Pallo whispered. 'Smash it with my chisel?'

'Yes, goddamn it!' Kassien answered. Xiriel hushed them both. He went to the door and listened. Then he made a sign that meant, *They're coming.*

Kassien waved at Pallo to come down; Pallo struggled helplessly with the straps and buckles; and the door opened, admitting the same Deer Clan Scholar who had given Pallo the guided tour of the Fire Houses, followed by a Pharician guard, four Pharician Scholars, and finally another guard. The Deer shuffled in, gesturing proudly.

'And this is the most enigmatic of the three—'

Xiriel leaped out from behind the door and caught the first guard in a throttle-hold from behind, dragging him out of sight of the rest behind the door. Kassien had no choice but to move to the other flank while the Scholars, confused, milled in the doorway. The first had quickly been rendered unconscious by Xiriel's nerve attack, and now the Seer started grabbing Scholars and bodily throwing them into the open space in the middle of the Fire House, where they did not know how to acquit themselves. One was particularly dispossessed of a clue, a crippled cack-eyed idiot of a man who spun in a slow circle and then fell down.

Kassien was on top of the rear guard before he could raise the alarm outside, punching him repeatedly in the head and gut and then dragging him into the Fire House and shutting the door. From above, a voice said, 'Don't move, Pharician Scholars! I've got you covered.' To put proof to his words, Pallo, still swinging upside down, blew a dart harmlessly into the floor.

'Cut it out, Pallo,' Kassien said. He and Xiriel looked at each other, at the Scholars, and back at each other.

'We have a situation,' Xiriel said. 'I'll tie up the guards before they wake.'

While he was doing this, Kassien instructed the Scholars to sit down and be quiet, which they did except for the idiotic one, who was crawling around groping blindly and drooling. Disgusted, Kassien ignored him and directed his attention to Pallo.

'It's hot up here,' Pallo said. 'Maybe with a sledgehammer I could do some damage. The chisel just bounces off it.'

There was a delay while the three argued about what to do, and from the tunnel below Stavel's voice called, 'Hey! You three! Hurry up! Our bird scout has just given word there's a Pharician tour group on the way.'

'Yes,' said Kassien, his face flushing with suppressed anger. 'Thank you for that useful and timely information. Stavel, you better get up here.'

Stavel climbed up out of the pit and took in the Scholars and the bound guards. He laughed. 'I was afraid of this. All right, look. We have to make this area secure. Otherwise the whole operation's ruined.'

One of the Pharician prisoners began to curse and shout, trying to raise the alarm, and at a sign from Kassien, Xiriel walked over and kicked him into silence.

The Wolf and the Bear looked at each other. Kassien's blood was up. He was Lerien's second, he had masterminded this plan, and yet now Stavel thought he could pull seniority and steal Kassien's thunder just because the majority of the rebels were Wolves.

Kassien said, 'This is my operation and *I'm* going to tell *you* what *I* want. Not the other way around.'

Pallo called, 'Kassien, where's my sledgehammer?'

'What do you want, then?' Stavel asked. He gestured to the crippled Scholar, who was now groping across the walls of the Fire House, feeling its surface with a rapt attention of a vinophile swilling a fine vintage in his mouth. 'More Scholars to help with the Knowledge?'

'No,' said Kassien curtly. 'I want to get the Fire and go without bloodshed. Take ten men and secure the other two Fire Houses. Lock them from without and seal the underground passages. Pallo can come down and help you: He knows all the secret ways.'

'Are we taking prisoners?' Stavel asked.

'Only if they are harmless. I would not be conservative of Pharician blood were I you.'

'And where will *you* be?' Stavel asked.

'I'm going to get a sledgehammer and take care of the Fire once and for all.'

It was a tense couple of hours as the Wolves raged through the Fire Houses, subduing and killing and chasing away anyone who opposed them, and locking the structures from the inside. Kassien and Xiriel had wanted stealth; they were disappointed.

'We can't stop now, you know,' Stavel said when he returned. 'The whole town is up in arms, and Jai Khalar will not be long in responding. We must secure the rest of the city.'

'We don't have the manpower,' Kassien said. 'The Deer are not warriors, but there are plenty of Pharicians, and A-vi-Khalar has grown strong since Tash came.'

'Not all the weapons went to Jai Khalar,' Stavel said, and when Kassien didn't immediately give in he added, 'Listen, Kassien. This is an old town, with strong walls, a safe undercity, and plenty of food. We could withstand a siege here for some time if Jai Khalar opposed us. But we can't survive locked in the Fire Houses alone.'

Kassien said, 'This is getting out of hand. It was to be a covert strike, not an invasion.'

'Maybe invasion was inevitable,' Stavel replied.

'Or maybe,' said Kassien, 'you warned us about these Scholars too late! Maybe you sat on the bird scout's message for a while.'

'Do you call me a liar?'

'It is your conscience, Stavel.'

'Only think a moment, Kassien,' said the Wolf, making one last effort to win Kassien over. 'These are Hezene's prize intellects. The Deer who run the Fire Houses are equally adept at the Knowledge. And now they are ours. We have hostages.'

Pallo protested vehemently. 'The whole point of my plan was to outwit the Pharicians without harming the Deer. Don't you understand? Take the Fire of Glass and Jai Khalar *disappears*.'

'The Wolf Grandmother Mistel is captive in Jai Khalar,' Stavel replied, red-faced. 'Tash is taking her apart bit by bit. This is the sacrifice of the Wolves. The Deer, too, must make their sacrifices.'

'Hush,' said Kassien. 'Give me the sledgehammer.'

And, ascending in Pallo's harness, he took his best shot at the Fire of Glass. But when he smashed the sledgehammer into it, the haft broke off, sparks flew everywhere, and Kassien himself was set to swinging crazily in the safety harness as all the while the Fire Houses resonated like a gigantic bell. The walls lit up in response to the sound. Symbols that had been hidden in the texture of the ropy red skin of the interior glowed visibly. And the idiot mute, blind, crippled Scholar looked like he was having an orgasm as his hands moved over the surface of the inner wall.

While everyone else was cowering and covering their ears, Xiriel was excitedly taking note of the symbols as they appeared. After the resonance died, he approached the cripple and pried him away from the wall. The man clutched him, tapping frantically upon his arms and face.

'I can't understand you,' said Xiriel. 'But I think *you* understand *that*.'

Muffled by the thick walls of the Fire Houses, the series of explosions outside came after the sledgehammer blow like a dull, delayed echo. Kassien ran to the door just in time to collide with one of Stavel's men.

'Rockets have gone off!' the man cried. 'From the stockpile outside the first Fire House, fired at random right into the city! Everything's burning!'

441

The Good Son

On the windy heights of Jai Khalar's battlements, Duor brought Liaku a cooked trout, two cold potatoes, and half a pastry. (He had eaten the other half while he was looking for her.)

'Tash and my father are in Snake Country by now. The Scholars have gone to the Fire Houses, including Wakhe, even though nobody can talk to him.'

'What about Yanse?'

'He's still very sick. They think he's dying.'

Liaku could not suppress a pleased smile.

'Why you lie for us?'

'My father.'

'Eh? What you mean?'

'Everybody expects me to be obedient, a good son. They expect me to turn out a boy-lover like him. Or to lower my eyes like a woman and take second best. Do you know, he can never have a house? He has to go where Hezene sends him, and be happy about it. And I'm supposed to be a good boy.'

Liaku laughed.

'Yeah, you *should* laugh! I don't want to be good. I want to be noticed for myself, not my father.'

'Your father kind man. Good man.'

'Fuck that.'

'You horrible boy.'

'Thanks!'

'I serious! You horrible to me in Ristale,' Liaku said. 'Worst boy I ever saw.'

'I'll go on being as bad as I like. Did you see Tash swallow my story? He loves it. He knows I've got balls and he knows I'm not like my father. I won't point my cock at him, either. Did you hear what he said? He's going to make me a duke.'

'If he come back from Tyger Pass,' Liaku said solemnly. She got up from her perch on a cornice. 'You coming?'

'Where?'

'Look for Quiz, stupid.'

Their search for Quiz took them up on the ramparts overlooking the entrance cave of Jai Khalar. They walked along the top of one of the highest walls, from which they surveyed the tiers of the city, the promenade that led from the magical entrance cave to the main gates, and the valley so very far below, with the dark streak of river breaking the white of the snow-covered meadows.

The airspace above Jai Khalar was almost empty. The messenger birds were kept captive in the aviary, and few wild birds cared to cruise the capricious currents of a disappearing castle, especially at such heights. Especially in winter. The sky seemed empty and barren to Liaku; she said as much to Duor.

'I miss crowded sky.'

'How could you know which bird was which? Jundun is a crazy place for birds,' Duor replied, stretching his arms wide as if to embrace the emptiness.

Liaku said, 'In Kukuyu, every bird look like every other bird. If you know them well, you tell difference. If you know really well, you can learn which ones have Speaker blood.'

'Speaker blood? In the *pigeons*?'

'Some. You can't see it. Their heads just like other bird head, but if you open mouth you find false roof, they have more brain than other bird.'

'What do they do with their brains if they don't Speak?'

Liaku shrugged. 'Remember people, place. Find them. Maybe talk to each other. Not talk out loud like Speakers, but maybe some other way. I find these birds easy, they like me, they gather. They come to me and we together. But I no know why.'

'You're so lucky,' Duor breathed. 'What about Quiz? I'd be scared of him. Doesn't he eat the other birds?'

'Not usually. He funny, you never know what he do. He like fish.'

Duor laughed nervously.

'And he just *came* to you?'

'Uh-huh.'

'Weren't you frightened?'

'Why?'

'He's fucking huge, he's dangerous, look at those claws!'

'He come from egg, too. And he special. Everyone fight over message he carry, nobody care about him.'

'Except you. Let's—'

'There he is!'

Quiz was wheeling almost directly overhead, having dropped suddenly from a great height much as he had done on that day when Liaku first met him. He curved sharply to the left, caught a thermal, and began slowly to rise again. Higher and higher went the skyfalcon, until Liaku couldn't see him any more.

'So that where he hide. He hide in the clouds.'

Duor was studying Quiz through his spyglass.

'Maybe he happy up there,' Liaku continued. 'I wonder what he see so high.'

She looked out across the grey-and-white emptiness of Everien. The road along the river had been trampled to dark brown by the passage of the Pharician horses, whose trail could be seen arcing off to the left and the sea gates from whence they'd come. The river itself was a frozen black sheet scored with the tracks left by the ice sail runners. Ice sailing was an Everien practice revived from obscurity by Tash when the Impressionists produced sketches for improved vehicles, faster than those used by the Seahawks and more versatile than the land sleds favoured by the Wolves. Traffic from A-vi-Khalar to the Citadel and back was routine, and even during her short stay Liaku had seen plenty of it. She observed the phalanx of ice sails glide raggedly upstream toward Jai Khalar, their sails bent hard by the easterly wind. The only trouble with using ice sails on as narrow a river as the gate stream was that it was almost impossible to tack into the wind. The vessels had stalled, and people were running on the ice.

Why didn't Quiz fly down and get a closer look? Why did he disappear to a still higher elevation?

'He must be as high above us now as we are above the river,' Duor uttered excitedly, still absorbed in his spyglass. 'Or so I make it by his relative size, which—'

Suddenly he went quiet. A feeling of alarm shot through Liaku.

'What?'

'I don't believe my eyes.'

'What, Duor? Let me see.' She crowded at the spyglass, but his body was as stiff as the parapet he leaned against. The spyglass was pointed almost directly up. '*Let me see!*'

'He's . . . it looks as if he's landed.'

'Landed? On what?'

'Nothing, that I can see. But his wings are folded and he's walking back and forth. In the sky. Liaku, he's walking back and forth in the sky.'

Liaku elbowed him hard in the ribs and wedged herself against the parapet, grabbing the viewfinder of the spyglass before Duor could reassert his hold.

'Don't move it away, or we'll never find him again! There are no landmarks in the clouds.'

'This is impossible,' she breathed, looking. You couldn't walk on a cloud, but that was what Quiz seemed to be doing. Well, actually he was walking on a perfectly level line, stopping, flapping his wings, bobbing his head, turning, and walking back the other way. Just as if there were a level perch up there in the clouds.

Liaku's neck hurt. She stepped back, shaking her head.

'He find another tower. Higher.'

'This *is* the highest tower but the Eye Tower, which is only a little taller. I've been briefed on all this.'

'How he see it? Hrost say message bird fly into towers and die, almost every week. That why aviary so high. They can't see castle walls. So how Quiz see tower half mile high?'

'We have to find it,' Duor said. 'Maybe Tash doesn't know about it. Maybe no one does. Maybe it's a secret weapons cache. Maybe it's a spy hideout. During the occupation, people disappeared and were never seen again. Important people, like the High Seer . . . come on, Liaku!'

He turned and leaped onto a stone outcropping where the castle mingled with the mountain, drawing himself up until he had gained the pitched roof, which was Everien smoothstone glazed with ice. He jammed his spiked boots into the ice to gain purchase and beckoned to Liaku. She followed him, passed him, and slithered down the other side of the roof, looking for the best path across the rooftops to the area where Quiz was. Parts of the castle could be seen and parts could not. What seemed to be rough white mountain might well turn out to be smooth man-made walls, and vice versa.

'Do you still see him?' Liaku called, but Duor didn't answer. When she turned she could see him on the peak of the roof, his head turned back toward the valley and the scene on the ice.

'A horse,' he said, turning the spyglass down. Liaku made a frustrated noise and joined him at the vantage point. Someone was galloping from Jai Khalar toward the boats along the riverside track. The running figures swerved toward the shore and there was an exchange of gestures and probably shouts. One of the figures climbed up beside the rider and the horse was whipped on the way back to the Citadel. The rest of the newcomers followed on foot, leaving the boats stalled in the headwind.

Duor was plainly torn. Curiosity piqued on two fronts, he glanced back and forth from the mysterious perch of Quiz to the scene at the gates. Which intrigue he would have chosen to pursue, Liaku would never know, for the tramp of approaching feet decided the matter for him.

'Duor! Are you up there?'

Liaku ducked behind a chimney and Duor slithered down to the

445

walkway atop the guard wall just as an armoured figure emerged from the Citadel.

'Come at once. The Wolf Clan have attacked the Fire Houses and driven out our men. It's a catastrophe. What are you doing up here in this wind?'

'Watching,' said Duor. 'How did they get into A-vi-Khalar?'

Liaku did not hear the answer, for they went inside. So much for Duor and his spyglass. She shaded her eyes and looked for Quiz. She could just make out what she thought was the speck of him, high above the castle. Well, it didn't do to stay in once place too long in this cold. She made off toward the invisible tower where Quiz had landed.

Liaku's feet were adapted to be almost as dextrous as hands, and she scurried through Jai Khalar making always up and north, toward where she had last seen Quiz perched in the clouds. At one point she crossed the gulf between towers at a covered bridge that gave a view of the gate stream, and she saw more boats and horses arriving from A-vi-Khalar. Birds were coming in, too, and there was a smudge of smoke across the valley where A-vi-Khalar was said to lie.

Liaku thought of Se and hoped he was dead by now. Continuing across the bridge, she came to the passage leading to the women's gallery (which she'd thought was behind her) where it intersected a walkway that eventually climbed to the aviary. If Ixo was right about Jai Khalar's moods, the castle's message to Liaku seemed clear: *Stay out of trouble*. But she was already in it so deep, she didn't care. She looked up but could not see the falcon from here. Where was Quiz?

She hesitated, and a mouse scurried up her leg and back down again so fast she only glimpsed it before it bolted across the bridge and disappeared – literally. Liaku stopped and examined the spot where it had vanished. It looked solid, but the mouse had gone somewhere. She felt with her fingers and there was a hole in the stone. Wary of sticking her fingers into an unknown place – for egg snakes hid in holes in Jundun, and though they were not poisonous they could deliver a nasty bite – Liaku wrapped her handkerchief around her fingers, then stuck her hand into the hole. At the bottom she felt a lump, faceted like a jewel. When she pressed against it, it yielded, and there was a click followed by a deep humming noise. Liaku's ears were just starting to work on identifying what kind of creature made such a sound when the floor beneath her knees gave way and she was falling through a trapdoor.

She could see her feet swinging and kicking beneath her. She was in a cylindrical shaft whose walls stretched down, slowly converging as if over a great distance, until there was nothing separating them but a pinprick of light.

446

Down there was death: no question.

She heaved her legs up and tried to kick her way into the aperture she'd just fallen through. Everything seemed to be happening very slowly, each heartbeat a slur of noise, each breath a lifetime. The humming had begun again, and the trapdoor began to close, not like the lid of a box, but by sliding sideways across the rectangular opening. It knocked her head down and smashed her fingers, and her feet kicked futilely at the panel when she swung them up. Her fingers were trapped and crushed and forced to let go.

She was going down.

Returning to Stone

'Down is not down,' said a quavering voice in a perfect Pharician accent. 'It is up, and not as far up as it appears. This is the first principle of relationships in a backward country.'

'Who are you?'

'I am Hanji. Welcome to my place. Company twice a day is more than I could have hoped for after all this solitude. You might not be able to tell by looking at me, but I am giddy with joy.'

Liaku's face was pressed against a stone floor that exuded a faint fragrance, like incense. She sat up slowly. She was in a round turret room, almost bare. There was a stone channel running around the perimeter of the room through which tinkled a thin stream of water, and there were hanging shells and bunches of reeds that made rustling noises. Quiz was there, on a high window ledge, blotting out most of the light. And so was the seated figure of an old man. She assumed the voice came from him, but he was so still that in the grey half-light she might have mistaken him for a statue. Quiz hopped across the floor and let out an unholy shriek. The man's blue eyes flicked open. He said,

'What if you had a symbol you could burn into a thing – say, for example, a sign that meant "ox"? If you could connect ox and this sign irreversibly, the way you brand an ox, and then you copied the symbol somewhere else, onto something else, it would still always connect you to the original ox. Yes?'

'Uh . . . yes if you say yes.'

'So you can go on using the symbol without needing the real thing. And the symbol can get up to all kinds of fun while the real ox is somewhere else. The symbol draws on the essential oxness of the ox. And the ox propagates itself in the world by means of the symbol.'

'Yes.'

'But what if the brand is then removed and the ox goes free – or the symbol goes free? What if the connection that was supposed to be irreversible is broken? Then what? Somewhere you have an ox, and in all these other places you have its symbolic deeds, and they have forgotten each other. Does it make sense?'

'No.'

'Look, to do the Animal Magic you need to have an Animal. You need to *become* an animal.'

448

'Hanji – Liaku only byrdgirl. I too stupid, yes?'

'I'm not so sure about that. Concentrate, Liaku!'

'But Hanji, tell me only. What these symbols mean? What Animal they connect to? Why everybody so excited about message?'

Quiz let out a shriek.

'Shut up, Eteltar,' said Hanji. Then he sighed. 'Liaku, I do not know. I perceive that there is an Everien code attached to it, but I cannot *remember* . . . ah, there is something, but I can't quite catch it.'

He looked around distractedly, groping in his pockets as if he'd lost something.

'What you look for?'

'A memory, Liaku, a memory.'

'In your pocket?' She laughed, then silenced herself. Perhaps he would become angry if she mocked him.

'We order our memories by association. If I want to remember something, I put it in a mental location and when I want it I go back to that location. Same thing if you build a real structure to hold information.'

'Like boomhall . . . I mean, library?'

'Not quite, because the information in a library is being stored in books, made sterile, and the books in turn are filed in a static, linear way. But if you used all the objects in your house associationally, turned them into information, and if you added rooms when you needed to hold new stuff, then you'd have something like Knowledge. And if that Knowledge got scrambled in time, you'd have a structure like Jai Khalar.'

'Ah! That why the walls move?'

'The walls are full of Knowledge. They unfold dimensionally like a deck of cards turning itself into a house of cards. But only if you see the interdimensional.'

'Can you do that?'

'No. We're only meant to go one way. We aren't meant to corkscrew through time. Our minds aren't built for it. We don't have a collection of different selves for different time shades that we can shuffle through at whim. We're not free in that way. We're locked into ourselves, and if you set us loose we go mad, same as a wild animal goes mad if you cage it.'

He retreated into his own thoughts.

'What about code?' she persisted. 'You remember yet?'

'Codes. Codes. They're the keys to memory. They're the shortcuts. If you want to remember an animal—'

'Remember an animal?'

'An animal is just taking a set of historical probabilities and letting it go. Roll the dice, deal the cards, play. But an animal that straddles time, a non-linear animal, that's an animal that can think and act in ways you and I can't.'

'Codes—?' she prompted.

'Ah, yes, the codes. I remember now. You have the codes for a nonlinear animal. Ironically, it's the creature that looks most like a line – but isn't.'

He looked at Quiz suddenly, who had reared back and spread his wings, half filling the room.

'Eteltar! Stop it!'

'What you call him?'

'Huh? Never mind. I believe that what matters is understanding the principles behind the symbols, principles that can be discovered and understood only by interaction with real things, not with other symbols. That is why a true Scholar does not live among books, except as a last resort.'

'They say Wakhe brilliant genius. He no interact anything. He no read book. He hear pattern, feel touch pattern, but nobody talk him now. Se kill his helper and now he alone.' She didn't know why she said it. Wakhe must have been weighing on her mind since she poisoned Se. Although Se had not been Wakhe's real helper but only a cruel imposter, it was the idea of Wakhe alone in Jai Khalar with no one who understood him that aroused Liaku's pity and guilt. After all, she had participated in the killing of the real Yanse. She now found herself telling Hanji about it, about the Circle and the message and the secret exchange of symbols between Se and the Circle as they travelled across Pharice. About the killing of Evra Kiss and the attempt to use Ixo to get rid of Ukili. The old man listened and at the end of it all, he shook his head, smiling.

'Skyfalcons, murder, the Circle . . . it is all a smokescreen.'

'What you mean?' she asked sharply, amazed that he could so casually dismiss her whole story. 'Se, he is great Animal Magician. Dangerous. I hope he dead, but I not sure. He take shape other people. Maybe he no can be kill.'

'Se is dangerous,' Hanji agreed. 'But do not factor yourself out of the equation. For the skyfalcon, Quiz as you call him, has chosen you. He has brought you to this place, at this time, for a reason. Look! See how the mice treat you?'

Liaku realized that a semicircle of mice had gathered around her, gazing on her adoringly. As if she were a great block of cheese about to be delivered to them, she thought wryly.

'Quiz eat them all if you allow. He only come here for hunt.'

'Quiz is more than you know.'

'Quiz is bird. He can fly higher than wind. He can see one hayseed a mile away in fog. He kill goat, sheep, horse, or maybe man. That what Quiz is.'

'That may be the end of Quiz, but it isn't his beginning.'

'You talk garbage. What Quiz want Liaku, then, Clever Man Hanji?'

'I don't know.' The old man's face greyed with thought and for a second Liaku had the impression that he really was a statue, that she had only roused him momentarily and now he would begin returning to stone. 'I don't know. But for the first time in a very long time, I begin to scent hope for Jai Khalar.'

'Jai Khalar? What about us? What about hope for me and Quiz?'

'I have something for you. I believe everyone is looking for it.'

He moved his arm slightly and his sleeve disgorged a globe of dark glass. Liaku caught hold of it as it rolled across the pitched floor.

'Not again,' she said. 'Everybody pass it back, forth, back again. Hanji, what Liaku do with it?'

'That, byrdgirl, is up to you.'

Losing his Head

When Ixo heard the news about the invasion of the Fire Houses, she couldn't get out of the women's gallery fast enough. There was a good deal of coming and going in the confusion following the delivery of the news, for Ukili sent for helpers and Illyra sent for two of his girls, and the other women all clamoured for news of their mates, brothers, and sons who were to be deployed in the counteroffensive at A-vi-Khalar. Ixo slipped out and made her way without hesitation to the cell of Mistel. The old woman was not there. Neither were the guards. Ixo went directly to the Eye Tower, where she brazenly asked for Kivi.

He recognized her, for he had seen the disguise before.

'Where's Mistel? Are they going to execute her? I must see her.'

Kivi's face was hard, whether with anger or fear or both she could not tell.

'Mistel disappeared days ago. Simply vanished. Now get back to your quarters and stay out of trouble!'

'What does Tash say? Will Illyra use the fire weapons against A-vi-Khalar?'

'That is not your concern. Now go, before I tear off your disguise. I have much to do.'

Ixo stalked back to the women's gallery to wait. She was sick of Gialse – who in the absence of the Carry Eye was about as sharp as a puddle of melted icicles – and promptly told the Impressionist to remove herself from her presence. She lay on her bed, hands on her belly, remembering Tash driving himself into her, his teeth holding the back of her neck, but softly.

For his part, Kivi was unable to explain how the invasion had occurred. Under questioning he admitted to Illyra that he had been monitoring rebel activities near A-vi-Sirinn, but he made it sound as though Tash had known about it.

'We knew there was a camp there,' he said. 'But we watched the perimeter of A-vi-Khalar at all times. Your own men must have looked out from their walls! No one saw anything.'

He then had to stand around and listen to Illyra rant about Jai Khalar, even though, Kivi amused himself by thinking, he could have written the script for the tirade, so many times had he heard Tash make the same complaints. Illyra lacked Tash's wit, however, and Kivi was forced to stand silent while the Pharician vented his considerable spleen. Kivi's bones sat uneasily between the currents of his blood. He had to press for peace, yet he felt sure there could not be peace anytime soon.

At length Illyra stopped griping. He had wandered over to the fire, where he stood with his back to Kivi, looking into the flames.

'Call all the Seers,' Illyra instructed him without turning around. 'Even the apprentices.'

'Very well. I will watch in the Eye Tower myself, while you question them. I cannot leave it unguarded.'

Illyra said, 'All of them. Even you.'

The Seers were all lined up along the wall, various ages and sizes, Clans and genders. Some looked more nervous than others. Illyra nodded for Kivi to come and stand by his side; then he drew his sword and turned toward the assembled Seers.

'Some of you seem to have forgotten what Tash does to traitors,' he said. Kivi's insides were trembling. He saw sweat break out on Soren's forehead. What did Illyra know, and how did he know it? Kivi disciplined himself not to move or show any sign. Illyra wasn't looking at him, but Kivi knew he was watching him all the time.

'Tash is not here, but I must act in his name. In the house of Tash, traitors die,' Illyra said to the people along the wall. Kivi stared straight ahead, wondering which of the scant handful of Seers would be his target. He saw Illyra begin to move his sword, but he never saw the stroke that came at him and severed his head just below the jaw. He saw the whole room spin and the ceiling come flying at him, and he saw strings of his own blood splayed out through the air before his eyes, and he saw the flagstones come rushing toward him. That was all he saw.

You Can't Build an Animal

Kassien ran both hands through his thick hair, tugging at it slightly as if he could somehow pull sense out of his own brain. 'This is all fucked up,' he said. 'We don't have enough men to hold the whole city! Is it too late to steal the Fire and begone?'

Stavel said, 'Are you crazy? Look at the new Knowledge we have uncovered! Look at the potential. Tash isn't even in Jai Khalar, his people will be totally taken by surprise, and by the time they recover we will be producing fire weapons of our own.'

Kassien looked at Xiriel for support, but to his shock the Seer said, 'It's too late to turn back now. And we could survive a long siege down here. This is where Ysse's people made their stand against the Sekk.'

'You cannot expect to run the Fire Houses without the support of the Scholars and the Smiths,' Pallo said.

'We have Scholars,' Xiriel said. 'They may be Pharician, but they can learn. They may even know things that we do not.'

'What of the Deer Clan?' Pallo was sounding desperate. 'We have inadvertently massacred innocent people.'

'You talk to them, then,' Stavel said. 'Convince them they must support us, or the Pharicians will hold Everien for ever.'

Pallo looked unhappy. 'This is not what I envisioned when I set out to rescue Mhani.'

Xiriel rounded on him then, 'What is your problem, Pallo? For the first time we have a chance to strike back at the Pharicians, drive them from our soil or at least bargain for better terms. Would you rather be driven back to die in the hills?'

'No,' Pallo said sadly. 'But I am afraid of these weapons of the Fire Houses. You have not heard the things Mhani says about the Everiens. About why whole sections of the undercity were sealed off. You don't perceive the danger.'

Xiriel started to reply but Kassien shut him up with a gesture. There was a long silence. Then Kassien sighed.

'The truth is,' he said, 'if we were not here, it would be Tash doing these things. Tash and these very same Scholars we have captured. We cannot undo the past' – and here Pallo stirred as if to say something, but didn't – 'but we can take control of the situation as it stands. Better we should have this Knowledge than Tash.'

'Agreed!' Stavel said heartily.

Xiriel said, 'I will begin work at once. The first thing I wish to investigate is the curious occurrence of the firing mechanism possibly being activated by the rhythm pattern of the crippled Pharician Scholar. We already know that one of the Fire Houses is set up to receive rhythmic patterns, and that certain patterns seem to be associated with symbols hidden in the walls. But those patterns are so intricate that we have never been able to decode them. Perhaps with the aid of this Scholar – what is his name? Wakhe? – we can begin to make some progress.'

'Only see to it you do not set off more weapons accidentally,' Kassien advised.

'I will focus my efforts on the Fire House which is designed with these sonic patterns in mind. I will stay away from the forges. Will that satisfy?'

Kassien nodded and they dispersed. Pallo for his part was unhappy, but he went with Xiriel and the Scholars so that he could keep an eye on them. He wondered how Mhani would react if she knew how Xiriel was behaving. He repeated to Xiriel the things Mhani had said about animals and the Everiens.

'I think,' Xiriel said when Pallo was finished, 'that the rhythmic patterns are a code for living creatures. Like notations on a page are a code for sound, which seems alive, these rhythms are a code for life. If you see them represented visually on those panels in the wall, you are perceiving their visual translation.'

'Visual translation of what?'

'Of the code. The code to make a living thing.'

'You can't make a living thing with a code! Xiriel, this is nonsense.'

'All right,' Xiriel said. 'But Mhani spoke of gaining Impressions from animals, and these Impressions took the form of sights and sounds. Patterns, she said. And sound and language have patterns. I think the Everiens were building animals.'

'Don't be ridiculous. You can't build an animal. Build it out of what? Thin air? Flute playing? Animals are *born*.'

'Most are born. But they still have patterns to make them what they are.'

'Aha. Patterns that form in their mothers' bellies, maybe. But if you wanted to build one, what would you build it out of?'

Xiriel had no answer for this, and Pallo left him thinking about it. Neither was satisfied by the conversation.

The rebels established control over A-vi-Khalar much more rapidly than Pallo would have predicted. The Deer Clan, by now accustomed to oppression, submitted without much opposition, although Pallo saw that a hatred burned in their eyes at the sight of the Wolves and the Bears stalking among them, laying down the law. Dzani had been killed in the incident, and Pallo was faced with the grim task of visiting his family. His efforts to explain what had gone wrong were met with stony silence.

'Enzi is safe,' he said at last as he was leaving their house. 'One day perhaps she can return. When there is peace.'

He made the mistake of turning to look back at Enzi's mother as he held the door open for himself, and narrowly missed being struck by a thrown goblet, which struck the door and shattered as he stumbled into the street. 'I'm sorry,' he murmured, and strode quickly away.

Meanwhile, the Pharicians surrounded the town, but even with their fire weapons they could do no great damage, for the majority of A-vi-Khalar was constructed of ancient Everien smoothstone, the rest being more common brick and granite. There was no straw, no wood, and, at this time of year, no crops nor gardens to be incinerated. The residents retreated underground, and the exits were all kept well guarded and fortified with the fire weapons that A-vi-Khalar retained. Production on new weapons went into swing, and Kassien had his men pitch a few bombs over the walls and into the Pharician ranks, 'to suggest to them that they might back off a few furlongs', he said.

And they did. But early one morning a week into the siege, something happened that was much stranger than bombs, although it occurred in the middle of a rocket-firing trial. The rockets were being fired from the walls, but at the same time the central Fire House with its Fire of Glass began to make loud and inscrutable noises; symbols lit up in the walls; and outside, clouds gathered around its cone so that it resembled nothing so much as an erupting volcano, only without the ash.

Kassien came running in, roused from sleep, to find Xiriel alone in the Fire House, poring over the luminous symbols in the pit.

'What are you doing?' Kassien cried. 'There's a storm brewing around the Fire House and the whole place is shaking!'

There was no need for him to say all this, as most of what he said was already obvious, and in addition the Fire of Glass was blazing and trembling in a strobe pattern. Xiriel said, 'I have been trying to figure out what these symbols mean. And old Wakhe up there, he's trying to talk to me but I have no idea what he's saying.'

Kassien had not noticed the chubby, crippled Scholar until just then. Wakhe was glued to the porous wall of the Fire House as usual, feeling its surface and tapping like a safecracker.

'You don't think he . . . ?'

Xiriel shouted, 'I have no idea. I think Wakhe's listening to the rockets. I don't know what's happening, and I don't know how to stop it.'

'Well, shit,' Kassien exclaimed, and ran outside, where he was just in time to see a full-sized sailsnake come bursting out of the cloud and whirl around the tops of the Fire Houses like an animate rainbow. Meanwhile, the clouds around the cone disintegrated, and it began to drizzle.

People cheered.

Later that day Illyra sent an envoy to negotiate for the Fire Houses.

'He's scared,' Stavel said. 'He knows we've discovered something and he's scared what else we'll do.'

'Fire off a few more rockets and let him think about it,' Kassien said. 'Then maybe we'll talk.'

Stavel gave a hearty guffaw of agreement.

Xiriel could not understand what had happened, and the Pharician Scholars were so useless that he gave up on talking to them. He would have given up on talking to Pallo, too, except that he had to talk to *someone*, and Pallo didn't take it personally if you called him stupid in the course of a discussion. Xiriel talked himself dry, to no avail. Then Pallo said, 'Pharician palm-readers know that every impulse and thought and sensation and action of a human being is expressed through the blood and nerves, which terminate in the hands and feet. A gifted reader can sense the character and behaviour patterns of a person by studying their hands because that person's history is written in their hands. On a similar level, you can look at a tree and draw conclusions about its history by examining its wood and bark and growth patterns.'

'Yes, Pallo, and what does this have to do with the Fire Houses?'

'All right. Mhani says that the animals the Everiens built have patterns. And those patterns have passed through the Fire Houses. So they must have left some impression, some memory.'

'Impression,' said Xiriel. 'Interesting choice of words.'

'If I were a Pharician palmist and I was to go about understanding the Fire Houses, I would be examining the physical texture of the Fire House. Mhani said the walls pulsed. She said the whole Fire House behaved like a human organ. She said the patterns of the mouse could be seen in the equipment like a flower.'

'That would be through this device that Mhani said was used in her Impression from the Liminal,' Xiriel said. 'But what about the symbols? What about the codes?'

'I don't know about codes. But we all heard the sounds go off when the weapon was fired. We all *saw* the sound registered in those lines on the walls. But the only one among us who *felt* what happened was

457

Wakhe. Wakhe was groping around the walls with his hands, because he is blind. And he was *trying to talk.*'

'Trying to talk,' Xiriel repeated, and stared at him, trying to understand the meaning of his emphasis on those words. 'Ysse's boots, Pallo. He was making sounds. He was making rhythmic patterns.'

'I think,' Pallo said, speaking very slowly as if trying hard to be clear even to himself, 'that Wakhe *felt* the firing pattern in the texture of the walls, and articulated that pattern with his rhythm-language.'

Xiriel ran to the Eye. 'I'm going to look at the record of this,' he said. 'Maybe we can duplicate the event.'

Water of Night Sky Glass

With a gnawing feeling of worry, Liaku surveyed the departure of Illyra and his troops, their siege engines and guns and carts full of munitions. She was disturbed not so much by the invasion or its political consequences, which she did not understand, nor even by the implications of the use of the Everien weapons built in the Fire Houses, which she barely knew anything about. What she kept thinking about was how, in the absence of Tash and Shiror and now Illyra, there was no strong authority figure in the Citadel. She felt sure that this was the moment Se had been waiting for. Was he dead yet? Was he so ill he could not cause trouble? Was he permanently blinded or otherwise incapacitated? Or was he, as she feared, beginning to recover from the effects of the poison?

Duor must be with Illyra's force, for he did not return to the roofs to report to Liaku. She was able to get by well enough, for she could get into the Citadel where and when she needed. She could steal and then disappear. In fact, her existence was in most ways an improvement over her tenure as Chee's keeper. But it was cold, and Quiz did not provide any more clues as to what she should do.

In the end, she hid the Carry Eye and went to Wakhe's room. The crippled Scholar and his servant were gone. Their rooms were empty.

So he was dead, then. Liaku's heart was so light she could have risen higher than Quiz. She made promptly for the women's gallery and Ixo's chamber.

'I bring you gift,' she said. 'You think Liaku evil. I not evil. Quiz not evil. Yanse tell me, get Carry Eye. So I get. But now Yanse gone, and Ixo hold grudge on me. I give you. You lift grudge, yes?'

Ixo's mouth fell open at the sight of the Carry Eye.

'Mistel!' she cried. 'Where is she? Is she alive? How did you get this?'

Liaku shook her head. 'No Mistel. I find Eye. In secret place.'

Ixo regarded her suspiciously. 'You're a little liar if ever I saw one, and a sneak besides. I'll bet Yanse had it. What did Yanse want with this? Wakhe can't even see, much less get Impressions.'

'Liaku no know. But Yanse never touch, Liaku swear it.'

'What about Mistel? Are you telling me she just disappeared? First Yanse, now Mistel – just vanished?'

'Yanse vanish? What? I thought Yanse sick of poison.'

'He was. Very sick. They sent Wakhe on tour of the Fire Houses without him, he was so sick. But then, yesterday morning, the servants went into his room to check on him and he was gone. No message, no sign where he went. Just gone.'

Liaku's stomach sank.

'He shape-changer,' she said. 'He can look like anybody. He not Yanse, he real name Se. He kill Yanse. He kill Evra Kiss. He try make you kill Ukili, but you say no. I hate him! Ixo, Se – I mean, Yanse – he very dangerous. Tell guards be careful. Maybe he even dress as woman, sneak in here. If he find out you have Eye . . .'

Ixo laughed. 'A fabulous imagination, byrdgirl. But thank you for the Eye. I lift my grudge. And now I'm going to the Eye Tower. The Seers must call for Tash, for I need his counsel. Now go fetch Gialse and spirit her up to the Eye Tower.'

'What I say Doren?'

'Say what you like. Bite him on the leg if you have to. Just get her up here.'

Ixo almost swooned when she saw Tash's face. His eyes were slitted shut against the cold but twin plumes of steam shot out of his nostrils as he recognized her.

'Trouble,' she said immediately. 'Kivi is dead. He betrayed us. He saw the rebels planning their attack on the Fire Houses, but he did nothing. Now there are no Seers in the Eye Tower but a couple of apprentice boys who are half dead of exhaustion, and Illyra has gone to besiege the Fire Houses before the rebels can do more harm. He does not trust the Eyes on account of Kivi, so he has sent a bird to you.'

'Ixo, what are you doing out of the women's gallery? Return at once! This is a disgrace to my honour. Is Ukili safe?'

'Yes, your wife is safe,' Ixo said shrewishly. She had planned to defy Tash's commands but now when it came down to it she could feel herself quailing. Tears started in her eyes.

'What is the matter? Who has wronged you?'

Ixo sniffed. 'I have found the Carry Eye. Tashee, I want Gialse to use it.'

Tash thought.

'Ixo, it is unlikely that this will work.'

'You can't stop me,' she said, and smiled to take the sting from her words.

'The rebels hold the Fire Houses. Even if you get information out of the Carry Eye, you won't be able to use it.'

'We could use it in barter, perhaps,' Ixo said. 'Negotiate with the rebels, until you return. Otherwise I fear Illyra will blow the Fire Houses to bits, not understanding their importance.'

Tash crushed ice in his bare fist.

'Ah, the frustrations! I never should have left Jai Khalar to chase these mountain spirits. Ixo, do what you will. But if you truly hope to find something to help you in that Carry Eye, try to use it together with the Water of Glass.'

'Together with the Water of Glass? What do you mean?'

'Ask the Seers. Kivi said something about it – it was his last idea, but it was foiled.'

'Tash!' Ixo said. 'Be careful! Return to me!'

'I'm going now,' Tash said. 'Shiror is calling me.'

Ixo turned to the boy who was running the Eye Tower and said, 'What did he mean, connect the Carry Eye to the Water of Glass? How on earth would we do that?'

'Madam, I don't know,' whispered the boy. He had bags under his eyes and he looked cold and malnourished. Ixo paced around the elliptical rim of the Water of Glass, looking up at the many Eyes hanging from the ceiling and the many visions reflected in the water. She tried not to be intimidated.

'But where is he? Are they all right? Have they had success?'

The boy started to tell her but was interrupted by the clumsy entrance of Gialse, who gazed in awe round the tower and approached Ixo, trembling.

'Don't be afraid,' Ixo said. 'Liaku, give her the Eye.'

Gialse was shaking so hard she could scarcely take it. She looked inside.

'Seer!' Ixo commanded. 'Look in the Water and see if you can find an image that matches what she says.'

Gialse was in trance. In a softer tone Ixo said, 'Tell us where you are. Are you in the forest?'

Yes. They fight over me. Tarquin cannot fight or he will lose the boy. Will no one save me? We must go to my house. We must read the books.

Ixo became excited.

'Seer!' she whispered. 'What do you See in the Eyes? Can you find her?'

'I only See the inside of the Fire House,' he said. 'With the rebels.'

'Yes, I know that is important, but not now,' Ixo answered impatiently. 'Try harder.'

Something has to change. Something must be undone. I—

'Gialse! I mean, Jaya. Can you remember the books? Can you remember the pictures? Engines, you said, remember?'

Gialse's eyes turned upward into her head, eyelids fluttering. She toppled over and let go of the Eye. It began to roll toward the water.

Liaku lunged for it and caught it. It was warm in her hands. Gialse had fainted. Liaku offered the Eye to Ixo.

'You look in, byrdgirl. You are the right age. You look in.'

Liaku obeyed.

If my desire could take a shape and go off on its own, it would not stay in this room and be content to watch, man or woman, active or passive in the movement of creation and change and destruction, my desire would never be still. Seen or unseen it would move and act in the world.

But I am protected, I can feel the barriers all around me.

Am I protected from what is without, or is it protected from me?

On that night I looked at my shadow in the water and two eyes looked back. Human or animal or machine I cannot say. But I know that what Jihan said after was right. Whether it happened in that moment or whether it had been happening for a long time and this 'magic' of the lamp was just a formality, it is not important. My shadow split from me and went roaming. And it was and is not a simple thing, a shadow. The darkened world is not simple because we do not see in it. I can attest to that, for I have ridden in the wood among the calls and shrieks and rustles of things I know not. Night is not simple. We may have only one colour to describe it but it is the colour that dominates everything.

Ixo's voice reached Liaku through a watery distance.

'The diagrams! The Fire Houses! The weapons! Think!'

Oh, the diagrams. The codes. The equations. The truths that strip down to paradox; the clothes I have worn. All the dreams of engines, all the principles I have learned. If I could describe it I wouldn't be blind in this place. If I could talk about it, I wouldn't always have this inchoate choking feeling in my throat. If I knew what it was, I could tell you. I, Jaya, have no knowledge of Night, but I am sure Night knows me all too well.

'Damn it, there must be something in here we can use.'

I won't be your tool. Do you hear me, Night? I won't be your tool.

And with that Liaku hefted the Carry Eye like a ball of lead shot and

462

with a heave, she put it in the Water of Glass. It made a deep *plunk* and sank into infinity.

The Water went dark and stars came out in it, constellation after constellation and none of them with names.

Ixo screamed and lunged at the byrdgirl. Liaku fled.

The Rescue of Istar

Istar woke, alone. The ledge was empty, the sky was empty, and the weather had changed. Months of unrelenting blue sky had given way to a bank of heavy clouds moving across the desert. A wind kicked up.

She called Eteltar's name. She called him Taretel. She climbed as high as she could but she could not see him anywhere. None of the birds were about.

The wind blew a gust of ice-cold air at her and then turned hot again; she turned on the cliff face and saw that she was directly opposite the place where the bird had disappeared into the invisible trapdoor. She was so close to Tyger Pass; but without wings, she would never get there.

'Eteltar!' she cried again.

Right before her eyes, a rope fell out of the sky, uncoiling like a silver snake until it slapped against the ledge outside Eteltar's cave. Istar looked up, astonished, but could see only the sky.

'Eteltar?' she called, hope rising in her throat.

Pentar's voice answered. He was calling her name.

'Go away!' Istar shouted. 'Do not come down here! I fell in and I cannot escape.'

Pentar's boots appeared; then his legs and torso, shedding snow that melted the instant it hit the hot, red rock. He was grinning broadly as he descended, sliding rather than climbing down the rope.

'I thought as much,' he greeted her, whipping off his gloves and beginning to unwind furs from around his neck and head. 'You went plunging in, didn't you?' He tugged at the rope, and it held firm. Tapping his forehead with his fingers, he added, 'Too bad you didn't use your wits.'

'What wits?' said Istar, dumbfounded. She flew at him and threw her arms around him. 'All my dilemmas, solved!'

She spun in a circle, looked up the cliff, and renewed her shouting. 'Eteltar! Eteltar-Taretel-Eteltar, Man-who-flies, Eteltar! Come and see what's happened! Now I don't have to fly after all.'

But there was no answer to her call.

'He is hiding,' she said nervously, and then grabbed Pentar's hands. 'I can't believe you found me! Tell me, what has been happening?'

'After the avalanche, we couldn't get back down the Seahawk side of

464

the pass, so we had to go on to Snake Country. There we had the great good fortune to rendezvous with a band of renegades like ourselves, some of whom had come originally from Jai Khalar and had much to tell about Tash and his doings there. They are in communication with Jakse at Fivesisters Lake. He has met a Wasp archer, a woman called Dario who claims Chyko as her father – she's a good shot, Istar, you'd like her. We—'

'Pentar,' she interrupted, 'how much time has gone by for you? How many months?'

'Months? I make it five weeks, no more, since the avalanche separated us.'

'But I have been here longer than that. Go on – the army.'

'By messenger bird we have been able to communicate with the whole north side of Everien and organize, to some degree, the anti-Pharician contingent. You know how the Pharicians hate to travel by winter, but the Wolves with their sled dogs are not bothered at all, and even the Snakes have come out on skis or through little-known H'ah'vah tunnels. We are poised to make an assault on the valley. There are more of us than they think, and Kassien has sent word that there is more trouble with Pharician troops – lots of them – but he is doing something to distract them in the south. Deer Country and Wasp Country will be Kassien's focal point, and we can move in village by village and restore our own outposts. We'll take out the Eyes as we go, so that they cannot be used against us from Jai Khalar. If we are quick enough, we can get into the valley basin before Tash can move to stop us, even though he'll see us coming in his Eyes as they gradually, one by one, go dark.'

'An ambitious plan,' Istar said, becoming excited. 'Then what are you doing up here?'

'Looking for you,' Pentar said. Istar laughed.

'Don't be stupid. For all you knew, I was dead. And don't tell me that Grietar's men wouldn't follow you without me, for I know they have no such loyalty to me.'

Pentar hung his head and sighed. 'All right, I'll admit, there was a bit more to it. It was the Sekk, the one you were hunting.'

'What about it?' said Istar, remembering the vision of the Seahawk warrior and realizing in a rush how much had changed since she had met Eteltar; how much more she understood about the Sekk.

'We agreed that it could not be left behind, for all of Seahawk was being left unguarded and it had already wreaked devastation in the timberland.'

'What about the sea garrisons? Couldn't they send men up here?'

'They, too, are to be mobilized toward Jai Khalar as soon as the ice clears. Anyway, the avalanche had blocked off access from Seahawk to Tyger Pass.'

'Wouldn't that contain the Sekk as well?'

'Is it your experience of Sekk that natural barriers cause them problems?'

'No,' she admitted.

He continued, 'Anyway, it had followed us into Snake Country. We kept seeing it, and it even took a few of our men. We had to kill and butcher them on the road, but we could not catch it. I had a feeling – well, I had a fear, Istar, that it might even have gotten you. So I took half the group and went after it. I told Jakse we would meet up with them in the Snake lowlands near Marauders Bridge in three weeks. We'll catch up with them, for a few can move much faster than a whole army, especially when that army must go to great pains to avoid being picked up by the Eyes. So I came here.'

'Did you catch the Sekk, then?' Istar heard the edge in her own voice, and Pentar gave her a look that said he'd heard it, too, although he didn't know the reason for her anxiety – namely, fear for Eteltar, who still had not appeared in the sky or anywhere on the cliffs. Even the birds seemed reluctant to draw close, and Istar began to feel like a traitor. She hoped Eteltar was somewhere, watching.

'We did not catch it. Not yet. But it led us to this cave, and we saw the open portal. I thought maybe it had gone through, and was hiding in here. You can't imagine my relief when you answered my call!'

Istar's insides were churning and she knew her expression was giving something away.

'It's not here, is it?' Pentar asked, looking around. 'You're sure nothing else has come through that door, either before you or after you?'

'Nothing,' Istar said. She did not meet his eye. 'Pentar, we have to talk about the Sekk—' She was wringing her hands in an effort to find words to describe what Eteltar had taught her, what she had come to feel in her gut about him. But she failed, and Pentar gazed curiously into her silence with his soft black eyes.

'What about the Sekk?' he asked gently, and when she didn't answer he prompted, 'Don't forget, I was Enslaved once.'

He might as well have said, *I was Enslaved once, too, like you are now, Istar the Betrayer,* for she reacted as if he had.

'Nothing!' she snapped. 'Never mind. We must make plans. What is it that Kassien is doing in the valley, anyway? And has anyone seen my mother?'

Pentar followed her into Eteltar's cave, where he stared unabashed at the incredible assortment of items that hung or were piled in the ruddy gloom. 'I am still pledged to kill this Sekk,' he said. 'How did you get in here, anyway? Did you pursue it? Whose cave is this? Why is it so hot here?'

'Too many questions,' Istar muttered. Suddenly she threw up her hands. 'Look, why don't you just go back. Leave me here. I have to think. Leave the rope for me, and I will come out when I am ready. I have to—' She cut herself off again. She had to talk to Eteltar, but plainly he would not come while Pentar was here.

She turned and faced Pentar squarely.

'I'm not leaving,' she said.

'What?'

'I have to stay here. I have to think. Pentar, you go. Go meet Jakse and lead the army. They are yours; you have been commanding them anyway, so just carry on. I will come out when I am ready.'

He studied her face and nodded slowly.

'All right,' he said, and went back out onto the ledge. 'But you look very thin to me. Are you sure there isn't anything you need?'

'No, nothing,' she answered hastily, turning to gesture at the storage facilities in the cave. 'As you can see, I—'

Something hit her on the head. The next thing she knew she was being roped up tight like a steer. Half conscious, she had a succession of impressions of the coming clouds across the desert, the dust blowing across the ledge, and Pentar heaving and grunting on the rope as Istar was dragged out of Eteltar's world and into the bitter chill of Seahawk.

Pentar's men were removing most of the boxes from the cave when Pentar chucked Istar in a bundle onto the icy floor.

'I wouldn't do that if I were you,' she advised them blearily, wanting to rub her head but unable to get her hands free. 'Please let me go. I won't do anything. Look, I don't even have my sword and I'm naked and it's *freezing*.'

She wasn't strictly naked, but she might as well have been for all that her climbing gear protected her from the cold. Pentar untied her and gave her her clothes back, which he had brought in a bundle from below. While she was putting her boots on, Eteltar appeared in the mouth of the H'ah'vah tunnel, blocking the way out of the main cave.

'The Sekk!' cried one of Pentar's men.

'Atar, quickly! Slay him!'

Istar leaned across the open pit and pulled her sword out of the sculpture. The floor panel slid shut as if by magic, and the vibration sent ice cascading from the ceiling.

Pentar didn't see her. None of them saw her. They had their backs to her.

Eteltar. The Sekk. There was no recognition in his face. He had no

467

wings. He was young. There was no injury on him. He wore a snow lion cloak and he was a killer. Istar told herself these things as she moved slowly down the H'ah'vah tunnel toward the Sekk.

'Let me through,' she said. 'I know what I'm doing.'

'Istar, *no!*'

'Pentar, get your men out of his way. He wants to get to the Seahawk sculpture. He's gone for a little stroll and he wants to get back now.'

'He's a Sekk, Istar. You don't know what he wants. He wants to kill us all.'

The Sekk didn't draw its sword. Istar tried not to look at his face but it was hard.

'Back away slowly,' she said. 'I know what I'm doing.'

Two of the men did so, and even Pentar looked like he was thinking about it. Now Istar was almost in range of the Sekk.

Then Atar lunged at it. He missed, but the Sekk's sword came out. Istar launched herself forward, throwing her arms around Eteltar's neck. His eyes were blank and cold and she did not let herself look at them, but she covered his body with hers.

'You will have to kill me, too,' she cried. 'I will not have him murdered.'

'Istar, you're under the Slaving. Come away at once. Come, Istar.'

'Go away, you stupid fool. Leave us! You don't understand him.' She was sobbing, weeping womanly tears such as she had never ever allowed herself in all her life as an Honorary. She ran her hands across Eteltar's impassive cheeks. 'If you will kill him, you must kill me, too.'

'Ah, this is madness,' cried Pentar in frustration, and began to pry her off the Seahawk warrior. But Eteltar was not so passive and went at him. Istar was flung to the ground and soon the two men were duelling.

'Enough!' Istar leaped into the fray, her father's sword whistling in the frozen air. She got between Pentar and Eteltar and a moment later she was facing Eteltar herself, blade to blade, the cold cruelty of those dead green eyes facing her across years, across the divide which had broken Eteltar for ever.

He was a terrible foe. She knew she had only a few seconds before he cut her down – and he would not spare her, she believed that as well. Her only hope was to distract him somehow. Behind Eteltar, Pentar's men ranged in a respectful semicircle, wary of entering his sword radius but determined to contain him all the same. Istar's dagger appeared in her left hand without her conscious volition, and she knew what she would do. She dove for his legs, aided in her transit by a patch of ice that lay in a pool beneath some stalactites; her slide took her within the arc of his sword where he could not so easily cut her, and she brought the dagger across the back of his knee where the tendons lay open. Blood slapped her in the mouth. Pentar's men had taken the opportunity to wade in. They were cutting him, knocking him down; again Istar threw herself on top of him and they had to draw their blades away at Pentar's command. Eteltar's Sekk was wounded, bleeding, but not finished yet.

'Stay down, Eteltar, you fool!' she shrieked in his ear, and clambered onto his chest. She threw her cloak over his head and wrapped it tightly round his face, twisting it and wringing it so he could not get free, then smothering him until he was still. She was surprised at how weak she felt; she was thin and the cold sapped her strength. But she didn't let go. Still holding firm to the cloak, she kicked the sword out of his lax hand and screamed at Pentar to take it.

'Istar, I'm not sure he's dead . . .'

'Shut up.' She rolled the Sekk over and pulled the cloak away. His neck was limp and his head flopped facedown into the snow. She whipped the laces out of her boots and tied his wrists brutally tight behind him. She tore the lining of her cloak and bandaged his eyes. Still he did not move. Had she suffocated him? She rolled him back over again, all the while ignoring Pentar's speeches and slapping away with her dagger anyone who came near her.

'Stupid bitch, she'll get us all killed.'

'Jump on her, hit her on the head, and put a sword through him.'

'No, wait, I think it's dead. Why's it painted like a Seahawk? And those are the braids of a high chief. Did you ever see a Clan Sekk before?'

'It might be a Slave, a Clan warrior in the service of a Sekk.'

'I've never seen him before.'

'He's fucking dangerous, did you see the way he let her bring him down? He could have killed us all—'

'He could not have done, you twat – not five on one. Look out, what's she doing now?'

She listened for his heartbeat and heard it, but he had stopped breathing. She put her mouth on his mouth as she'd been taught in childhood, before Jai Khalar, before studying warfare, when she'd still been a girl learning the Seahawk ways in the fishing town of A-Tar-Ness where people sometimes drowned. She blew air down his throat, waited for it to come out, blew again, took a gulp of air for herself, and again covered his lips.

'Oh, no,' she heard them begin, and then Pentar picked her up bodily and started to drag her off Eteltar. She struck out violently; her sword went flying out and Pentar sucked his gut out of its way in the last instant.

'Stay away!' she spat, kicking at another who tried to come in and attack the supine Eteltar. 'Don't touch him. He's my prisoner, and anyone who interferes, gets it!'

'Is she a Slave?' one of the Seahawks asked Pentar incredulously. 'She's awfully coherent.'

'She's mad, that's for sure.'

'Leave me!' Istar shrieked again, torn between the feminine histrionics she'd already given way to once, and the threatening machismo that was closer to her normal mode. Pentar was watching her very closely but he gave his men no definitive signal, and this was enough for her to get hold of Eteltar again. Now he was coughing and had begun to move; she promptly shoved another tatter of cloak in his mouth and bound it round as a gag.

'I'll let you breathe, but you won't speak or sing,' she said in his ear. 'Can you understand me, Eteltar, you bastard? It's Istar, and you'd better behave or you're dead.'

He made a sound, an inarticulate mixture of furies, and she kicked him in the back.

'Someone give me a hood. I want his whole head covered, just as if he's going to the gallows.'

Pentar took off his hood and threw it at her. She jammed it down over his head and spun him in a circle; he couldn't support his weight on the injured leg and fell down. Istar jerked him to his feet.

'Go on, Sekk bastard! Walk! Crawl if you must!'

She shoved him again with her foot in the small of his back and he lurched forward, bleeding copiously from multiple sword cuts, but especially from the leg injury Istar had dealt him.

'He'll bleed to death soon enough,' one of the Seahawks said with satisfaction. 'I've seen it happen before.'

Istar whirled, not knowing how the light caught her eyes or the way their redness made her look like a monster from legend, but seeing the horror in their faces at the sight of her emotion.

'Then tend him so he doesn't die, you big arrogant fool. Pentar, I want his leg fixed or there'll be more blood shed this day.'

She was spitting and foaming at the mouth, and she knew Pentar was only going along with her for the moment, but she didn't care. Eteltar must not die; not from her hand, anyway. She longed to speak to him, to touch him, to tell him she hadn't meant to hurt him; but she had to behave this way or the Seahawks would kill both of them. Pentar would even kill her if in the end he thought she was Enslaved and could not come out of it. Or she would kill him first. They had fought once before, but that seemed like years ago now and she wasn't so sure she would lose to him this time.

They bound Eteltar's leg and found him a stick to use as a crutch. Istar kept him close to her side, taking in the others with the wrath of her eyes.

'Let's go,' she said grimly.

'Go?'

'I have an army to lead.'

Four Parallel Waves in Silver

When Xiriel checked the Eye implanted in the largest Fire House, it refused to give him a view of the Eye Tower. At first he thought someone was controlling it, blotting it out so that the rebels would not have the use of it, for that was what he would have done were he the Seer at Jai Khalar. But Xiriel did not know that there were no Seers left in Jai Khalar. And he did not know about the Carry Eye falling into the Water of Glass. So when he looked into the Fire Houses' Eye and observed a deep, velvet darkness lanced by a field of stars, he could not imagine what had happened. *Well*, he thought, *it is of no use to us now.* He ought to turn his attention to all the wonders at hand here in the Fire House – all the wonders that he might use, if only he knew how. But for a moment he found himself pausing, still, and gazing into the Eye simply because he found it restful. A beautiful night, he thought. He did not notice that when he turned away, humming a soft tune, the stars pulsed in answering rhythm to his voice.

Liaku could not find Quiz, but she stayed on the heights anyway, unperturbed by the cold. She saw Ixo trying to organize an escape from the women's gallery, but her compatriots were not very cooperative, for Ukili had been lavishing attention on them and had even recently distributed a tin of the magical Pharician confection called chocolate, which made it impossible for any woman who ate it not to wish to eat more, and possibly even to compromise herself to get it. In comparison to such bounty, Ixo's proposition of bundling up in furs and taking chances in the open hill country until Tash could return hardly seemed appealing. Ixo packed and made her preparations, all unknown to Doren and the other eunuchs. At first Liaku had thought they turned a blind eye to Ixo's antics out of Clan fellow-feeling, but after a while she realized they were just stupid.

Soon Jai Khalar will be empty, Liaku thought. For even Se was gone. It was a great relief to her mind; now, if only she could find Quiz.

Quiz was far away on the other side of the mountains, high over Tyger Pass. The Seahawk army had taken up ambush positions in the lower part of the pass on the Snake Country side, and Tash's army was working its way toward them. Behind Tash, unknown to him, the rebel army that had swept through Snake Country now cut off his retreat to Jai Khalar and began slowly to move down the valley toward A-vi-Khalar, picking up willing men as it went along. The spring thaw had begun in the low country and the rivers were swollen with rain, but their progress could not now be stopped.

The skyfalcon could also see the small party descending the pass toward the Seahawk army: Pentar, five men-at-arms, Istar, and her prisoner. Quiz observed the prisoner intently. It was only half there: no shadow, none of the electricity of life even though it moved and seemed to have a substance. That substance was a mockery of the tall warrior it had once been. Now it was only a shell. Quiz knew what he had to do. He folded his wings and dove.

Istar sensed the bird coming in; she looked up and saw only a dot, but alarm raced through her and she gave a shout of warning. 'Skyfalcon! Heads up!'

It was coming for the Sekk.

'Get back,' Istar screamed, and pushed the Sekk ahead of her, knocking it facedown into the snow just as the bird roared by, narrowly missing their heads. The prisoner was so effectively bound that it could not resist, and as ridiculous as it appeared when Istar flung herself bodily upon the Sekk's back to protect it from the skyfalcon, the prisoner could do nothing.

'Istar, what are you doing?' Pentar had rushed several paces away and stared in astonishment as the skyfalcon made one pass and climbed again, reassessing its target. Pentar drew his sword. 'By my mother's braids, it's as big as a horse!'

'Don't approach it,' Istar commanded. 'No matter what happens, you are not to harm the bird.'

The skyfalcon made another swooping pass, its talons just missing Istar's face; then it whirled and hovered directly over her, tilting its head from side to side as it watched her first out of one eye, then out of the other.

'I won't let you kill him,' Istar whispered. 'I won't let you kill yourself. Take me or nothing at all.'

'By the lights of Jai Pendu, Ysse, it wants the Sekk! Will you get out of there?'

'Shut up!' Istar replied. Still lying faceup on the Sekk's back, spreadeagled in the most vulnerable possible pose, she drew her sword and tossed it into the snow. 'There is the sword you made the sculpture to receive. There is the sword that killed you. You cannot make me do it again!'

Beneath Istar, the Sekk shuddered violently and began to struggle. The skyfalcon drew height and plunged for a third time. It raked Istar's cheek with its talons. Four parallel cuts bled red down her temple in the sign of the Seahawk Clan. The skyfalcon began to rise. Higher and higher it rose, until the people and the Sekk were just dots below. Istar was laughing, her hand on her cheek.

'Thank you!' she called after the bird, her voice giddy in the cold air. 'I will never give up, Eteltar! I will bring you back your wings if I can! Know this one thing: I owe you your wings!'

She stood up. The skyfalcon watched as the men approached Istar hesitantly. The Sekk stood, still hooded and bound, unmoving, leaving no shadow on the white snow.

'You called me Ysse,' Istar said to Pentar.

'Did I?'

'It is the same name, you know. Ys, Is. It is the same, only she bore Snake suffix -se, and I bear the Seahawk, -tar.'

'Never mind that now. Did you see it? That was an ancient Everien skyfalcon. By the five winds, I thought it would kill you!'

Istar shook her head. She touched the scratches where the skyfalcon had superimposed on the four parallel waves in silver that showed her Clan. 'No. He wouldn't kill me, even though I killed him once. He loves me, you see.'

And with that cryptic remark in his ears, the skyfalcon rose on the thermals, turning toward sunset in the southwest. Purposefully he began beating his great wings, arrowing toward Jai Khalar. Even from far away he could see the blaze from within the Fire Houses. Faster and faster Quiz sped. There was nothing the skyfalcon could now do, unless it was maybe to save one small living thing.

A Snake by Any Other Name

After Illyra had backed off a little further and sent another messenger and he, too, had been rebuffed, Kassien was in a distinctly better mood. It was good to feel in control – for once. He stood on the ramparts of the city and watched a lone man approach the gates on foot. He wore a Scholar's robe, and signalled for a parley. Kassien took a group and went out to meet him.

'I am Kassien, commander of the Clans. Tell Illyra he must withdraw his troops to Jai Khalar before I will talk to anyone. Otherwise I have nothing to say.'

'I am not Illyra's representative,' said the Scholar, who was middle-aged and tall, lean, broad-shouldered – and trying to hide it by wearing ill-fitting clothes and affecting a stooped posture. He had compelling green-gold eyes and a soft voice. 'I am Yanse, the servant of Wakhe, your hostage, and I am the only man in the world who can communicate with him. I beg you to release him, for he will die without me to look after him.'

'I have no intention of releasing anyone,' Kassien said. 'What do you mean, you can communicate with him? The others have told us he is blind and dumb.'

'It is a special language, of tapping and touching,' and Yanse demonstrated on himself briefly.

Kassien considered this, not failing to realize that if Wakhe had triggered the explosion using his tapping language, and if Yanse knew this same language but also spoke normally, then some translation might be effected.

'Very well,' Kassien said. 'I am not unreasonable. You may enter and serve your master. But if you cause me one whit of trouble, I will kill you both.'

He ordered his men to search Yanse and confiscate anything that was potentially dangerous. He watched while they brought the Scholar inside and deposited him among the other hostages, some of whom Xiriel had been deploying to assist him. Yanse and Wakhe immediately began exchanging signs.

'What is happening?' Xiriel inquired urgently. When Kassien told him what he had done, the Seer turned white. 'Don't let them talk! Kassien, we have no way of knowing what they are saying. Besides, look, Wakhe is plainly afraid of him.'

Kassien could not see what had Xiriel so upset, but he had the two men separated. Xiriel looked Yanse up and down. He began to shake, and he was so affected that Kassien took his arm to draw him away, but Xiriel shook him off.

'*You*,' he said to Yanse. '*Se.*'

Istar's Army

Istar found the Seahawk army well rested and ready to go. Word had reached them by bird of the advent of Tash, and messages had been flying back and forth among the rebel contingents in Snake Country and Tyger Pass. Especially from Jakse's people. Even Lerien had sent word: *Stand strong. There is change in the wind, and Pharice is not as strong as it appears.*

Yet it fell to Istar to explain herself to her men. She knew she had to leave the metaphysics aside; and certainly she had to leave aside her relationship with Eteltar and all its implications. To her men, a Sekk was a Sekk – and if they thought she had been Enslaved by one, they would kill her and then they would kill it. So she thrust her own doubts deep into the bottom of her heart. She took shallow breaths of the cold air. And when she faced the assembled men, she held aloft the fur-wrapped remains of the creature she had loved only yesterday.

'I have in my cloak the complete skeleton of Eteltar, the greatest Animal Magician our Clan has ever known. It is the thing which was wrongfully removed from its resting place by Grietar, thereby bringing about the deaths of a number of men, including Thietar, brother of Birtar, who is here among us. The Sekk which did this deed and which also killed my aunt Ranatar and orphaned the Hawk Girls is now my captive. You see him here, hooded thus.'

She put down the cloak and drew the Sekk forward. Limping, it towered over her, wrapped in furs and unidentifiable. The muscles of its powerful legs shook inside their leather hose. It was cold.

Now she spoke over the men's collective noise: shufflings, swords being rattled, and the bassy rumbles of dissent and disturbance. She raised her voice.

'You wonder why this Sekk still walks and my sword is in its sheath. But that is my decision to make. I have caught the Sekk. I have as much right as any man to exact vengeance – maybe more. And I have my reasons for preserving its existence. I will not tell you those reasons today.'

More audible protests from the men. 'Outbreed. Honorary. Weakling.'

'There are those here who will question my right to my own name. Look at my face!' She pointed to the fresh cuts that scored her temple. 'Atar, tell the men how this happened.'

'The skyfalcon came to kill the Sekk, but Istar would not let it. So the skyfalcon scratched her and then flew away. It was like a sign.'

'Skyfalcon?' called a sceptical voice. 'There is no such thing. Not in this day.'

'Yes, there is,' Birtar said unexpectedly. 'I saw it. The day my brother died in Tyger Pass, I saw what I thought was a skyfalcon. I didn't believe it was possible, but now I know it is true. Istar does not lie. The skyfalcon has returned to Everien.'

Murmurs of surprise.

'I will stand by you, Istar,' Birtar continued, climbing onto the snowbank and joining her. 'Your name is known as a hunter of Sekk. I, too, have a right to kill this Sekk, but I will delay its execution on the basis that I trust your reasons are good. If the skyfalcon could wait, so can I.'

Shocked gasps. Birtar threw his head back and addressed the assembled.

'No man has greater claim to the Sekk than Istar or me! Therefore let no man who doesn't wish to meet my sword speak against the decision of a skyfalcon.'

'I will speak anyway,' said Atar. 'For it is not a matter of vengeance, but of common sense. To let a live Sekk walk amongst us is an act of suicide. I am no coward, but I would sooner sleep with a whole pride of hungry snow lions!'

'Ay!' shouted some of the others enthusiastically.

'Then go and make your own way, and I will make mine,' Istar said calmly. 'I have no need of men who will not trust my judgment. Go! It is simple. Go now, before I lose my temper.'

A handful picked up their gear and left, casting disbelieving glances at the rest; then a few more ran after them; and then finally Atar took a pack pony and began to lead it away. He stopped and turned.

'I hope I will not be digging your graves. Death to the Sekk.'

He spat in the snow.

Yanse-Not-Yanse

'What is it?' Kassien whispered, still trying to draw Xiriel away, but he began to circle the newcomer like a moth to a flame, drawing close and then springing back, unable to escape his orbit.

'I met him in the Floating Lands. He is some kind of magician or wizard.'

'I am no such thing,' said Se. 'I never claimed to be. I helped you then and I can help you now, Xiriel.'

'Help me? What do you speak of?'

'Research, that is what I speak of,' Se told Xiriel. 'It is a simple plan. I will act as negotiator. As Wakhe's servant I am beyond reproach. We will tell Tash that the Fire Houses have been made safe, and you will desist your attacks on Illyra's men. Meanwhile we will say we have negotiated for the Clans to hold this town until payment has been arranged with Pharice. Tash's coffers are full, and he wants the goodwill of the Clans. He will pay you for control of the Fire Houses before he fights for them – so Hezene will have ordered him to do. For the Seahawks are attacking Tash's forces in Snake Country and amassing a considerable army that he now must meet.'

Xiriel looked away, thinking of Istar.

Se resumed after a pause. 'But I speak of research. That is why you will keep your people quiet. So that we can learn. So that we can break these codes. I thought I was coming to Everien to visit Tyger Pass and recover the great Knowledge that Eteltar left there for Ysse, but I see now that my real destiny must lie here. In the Fire Houses. For look! I have recovered the time serpent symbols from the depths of time.'

Xiriel was far from satisfied.

'Who are you? Where do you come from? How did we meet in the Floating Lands, what did you do to me, what can you do to yourself to change forms so dramatically? Se, I will not even consider complying with your wishes until you have answered these questions.'

'That could take years,' Se uttered dismissively.

'I don't care. I have to know.'

'Very well. To tell it briefly. I was born a thousand years ago, the grandson of slaves in Pharice. My grandparents escaped to Kierse and then to a small volcanic island between Kierse and the Snake Islands, a nameless place. It was inhabited by two Li'ah'vah.'

'I thought Li'ah'vah were only found in Everien, and that they had been made extinct much longer ago than that.'

'They had fled to this island, fled across time and distance, and they hid there in the volcano, slowly dying. Until I came, and became one of them. I can change shape because I am part time serpent. And I have moved through time the way a snake moves through sand. Less than twenty years ago, I came to Pharice through the Liminal, travelling hundreds of miles and hundreds of years in an eyeblink. And in Pharice I have followed the work of the Circle, sometimes supporting it, sometimes sabotaging it according to my needs.'

'And what are your needs?'

'To save the time serpents.'

'How can you save something that's extinct?'

'By calling it through time, by making a way for it. The Everiens knew how to do such things, for they built the time serpent. It is only that their Knowledge has been lost or forgotten.'

'It sounds like a dangerous proposition,' Xiriel said. 'None of this answers what you were doing in the Floating Lands.'

'A minor incident. We merely encountered one another in the Liminal, and I was able to perceive your true nature because I could glimpse your future. You were meant to be one of us, you were meant to cross time, and you were meant to help the time serpents. So I gave you to the Snakes.'

'It was real, then,' Xiriel said. 'I thought I died.'

'You were Eaten,' Se replied. 'You now possess talents that others do not. When and how you discover them I cannot say. But I can tell you that you can no more change your allegiance to the Snakes than you can change the colour of your blood. We are your family now. You sense it. You know it. That is why you pursue the solution as staunchly as I do.'

'No. My motives are to seek the best future for Everien and its people.'

'Ah, they are pure words, but whose side are you on? Who is to say what is best for Everien?' Se probed. 'Xiriel the Seer? Xiriel the Wolf? Xiriel the Snake? Which one will it be? When I met you in the Floating Lands, you were not a Wolf, you were a Seer. Now you fight as a Snake, but continue to pursue the Knowledge. You sent your agent in here posing as a Pharician to get Mhani the Seer out because you wanted her information.'

Xiriel's face was hardening with anger, a vein in his bare temple visibly throbbing. Kassien glanced at him but didn't speak.

Se continued, 'Did you think you were so secret? But I have many spies, Xiriel, and few of them are human. Whose side are you on, my friend?'

'I have nothing to say to you. Kassien, we should kill them now. I don't know what manner of being he is, but this one is as dangerous as any Sekk.'

In a mild tone Kassien said, 'It is surprising that you want to kill them when only a little while ago you wanted to use Wakhe to trigger the weapons.'

'Use him to trigger the weapons?' Se blurted, excited. 'Is this true? How?' Instantly he began talking to Wakhe in their language. 'Wakhe says it was an accident, he simply felt a sound come from the equipment and tried to answer it.'

'What sound? I thought he was deaf?'

'Ah, but he can feel vibrations and pitches in his fingertips.'

'So what was it? What did he feel?' Suddenly Xiriel was excited.

'Someone said something in time serpent.'

'What did they say? What?'

Se shook his head. 'He is trying to tell me, but I don't understand.'

'Can he repeat it? Can he repeat what was said to him, and what he said back?'

'Probably.'

'Wait a minute,' Kassien interrupted. 'Let's think this through before we go setting off more explosions. Se, what did you mean when you said Wakhe spoke in time serpent?'

'Wakhe speaks a modified form of time serpent, which is an ancient Snake Clan dialect from a thousand years ago that was taught to us Snakes by the time serpents and then modified. But these days it is only used ritually, and I know of no one but myself who is fluent in it.'

'How did he learn such a thing?'

'Because he was born in the Snake Islands and some fragments of the language are still used there in ritual magics. Wakhe had no other way to be understood, so he learned what patterns he could that had been passed down precisely from generation to generation, and inferred the rest by analysing the patterns he already knew. Time serpent is a mathematical language. If you know a little you can construct the rest, provided you have a powerful mind for patterns, which Wakhe, for all his other deficiencies, does. That is how Yanse came to know Wakhe. For his genius for perceiving patterns had been observed almost accidentally, and Hezene's Scholars hoped to make better use of Wakhe by teaching him to communicate. Yanse was a minor Scholar who knew enough Snake to communicate with Wakhe, and he became his translator.'

'So there is a real Yanse.'

'Was,' Se replied shortly. 'He was an obstruction.'

'You mean you killed him?' asked Xiriel with heat.

'Have you never killed anyone, Xiriel? Ah, let us not waste time

481

moralizing! Look at the wealth that surrounds you! Look at the discoveries. Think what you might do. The Everien symbol language has been a mystery for years and years. Any penetration of it in the past has been accidental at best. Now, with the help of Wakhe and me, you could learn to speak it. You could reawaken lost Everien!'

No one said anything for a minute. Finally Kassien spoke.

'Xiriel, is this true?'

'It could be,' Xiriel said. 'Pallo asked me how you could build an animal without its mother. But maybe, build, isn't the right word. Maybe it's true you can't build an animal without its parents. But if you speak its language, you can call one.'

'Now I am really really lost.'

'You could call a time serpent, for example, out of the past or future.'

'And why would you want to do that?'

'To free the time serpent from its unfortunate demise,' said Se. 'To connect you to times that haven't come yet. To see the future. To correct the past.'

'But all of that leads to paradox,' Xiriel put in.

'Yes,' said Se. 'All of that leads to Paradox.'

Until now the Seer and the Pharician had been engaged in a tight dialogue, but in the background the others were growing restless. Stavel had been listening for some time, and now he walked across the resonant, tiled floor and bluntly asked, 'Enough talk. What can you do for us, Se the Scholar?'

'I can build you a weapon,' he said, 'that will make the Pharicians as if they never were born. It will not merely hurt them. It will annihilate them, make them less than nothing.'

'I don't believe you,' Stavel sneered.

'You don't have to. Just stand back and watch. Or would you prefer that your food runs out and you hurl your pathetic fireballs over the walls? As soon as Illyra gets permission from Tash, he's going to storm this place, make no mistake. You have very little time, and my offer is the best you'll ever get.'

'Don't trust him,' Xiriel said.

'I have the codes,' Se told them. 'They are come all the way from the archives of Eteltar the wizard, and they were probably bought with his very life.'

'Codes are no good unless you know how to use them.'

'And I believe I have just watched you figure that out. Or did you *intend* to make a sailsnake? Will you carry on without my guidance? Perhaps on your own, in a year you will build your first mouse.'

'Very well,' said Xiriel, and stood back from the panel with its lexicon of symbols. 'Let's see what you can do.'

Wakhe had been listening to the starry sky; but Yanse-who-was-not-Yanse had taken hold of his hands from behind and now led him away from the Eye. Wakhe was sure the Eye continued to talk but he was wrenched away from it. Yanse had become so cruel. Wakhe, distraught, began to retreat inside himself. The inside of his mind was a better place than this heat, these smells, and Yanse-not-Yanse's treacherous hands on his body, not even talking to him, only making him do things.

Then Yanse-not-Yanse placed Wakhe's hands on a dappled surface. With his fingertips Wakhe could feel the delicate alternation of complex patterns, the bumps of the tiny ampules that comprised the inner skin of the Fire House. And he understood the sense of them. Another man might have spent years trying to decipher the code, but Wakhe perceived it without any effort at all. In his mind it was as clear as the simplest thing, like putting your hand on an apple and knowing it was an apple.

Yanse-not-Yanse was tapping him urgently. *What is it? Can you read it?*

Of course, Wakhe indicated.

What does it say? Make the rhythm!

The rhythm of the touch-pattern was not a mere matter of expressions in Snake language. It was stunningly complex, it was minutely articulated, and most of all, it was not about human beings at all. It was about math, and it would mean nothing to anybody but Wakhe and – perhaps – the Fire House. All the same, Wakhe began to describe the pattern in sound, fast as a hummingbird.

Yanse-not-Yanse grabbed his hands and stopped him.

Do you know it? Can you remember it?

What a question. That was like saying, *Is your hand attached to your wrist?* Yanse-not-Yanse was stupid at times. Wakhe signalled the affirmative, and swiftly his hands were placed on yet another pattern, and then another. Wakhe drank them like wine. He would have liked to savour them more, for in all the years of his life he had never had such pleasure from a design, not even the most arcane puzzles devised by the Sleepless Mages of Aranoka. But Yanse-not-Yanse was rushing him. Wakhe could smell the fear of several Clan nationalities and two separate regions of Pharice in the air of the Fire Houses. He asked for something to eat and was hastily promised it by Yanse-not-Yanse, but his nose told him Yanse-not-Yanse was lying again. He reeked of old deaths still carried on his skin, of malice – and of something else, something that niggled in Wakhe's mind, for the smell resembled the patterns he had just committed to memory. Something in Yanse-not-Yanse's smell was *of* those patterns.

Wakhe's stomach still grumbled at him but he decided not to worry about food. He did as Yanse-not-Yanse commanded until he had six patterns in sequence. He ruminated on them, even as, through the soles of his feet, he felt the explosions outside.

Illyra, it seemed, was seriously pissed off at Kassien's refusal to negotiate. He had overextended himself in a sincere effort of diplomacy. Now, when word came to him that the Clan leaders were closeted in the Fire Houses and receiving no messages whatsoever, the Pharician lost his temper.

The rockets came in like tidal waves made of fire. A-vi-Khalar rumbled and shook, but the Fire Houses were strangely insulated, their occupants preoccupied with the drama going on between Se and Wakhe and the building itself. Kassien stepped outside and saw that the enemy were moving in for an assault on the walls. Stavel joined him and said, 'This is the showdown. We have to do something quick.'

'Lock the Fire Houses,' Kassien said. 'Get everyone underground.'

He went back inside, intending to talk to Xiriel – but a trumpeting elephant could scarcely be heard over the booming and humming of the Fire House. Xiriel was transported with fascinated exultation. Kassien could see the situation was out of control, but he did not know what to do to fix it. Xiriel seemed to have lost all reason. His face was a mask of rapture as he experienced the patterns beginning to thrum through the Fire House.

'Ah!' he cried. 'Look, the symbols in the walls are lighting!'

Se nodded as if it had all been his personal contrivance. 'Do you see how they match the symbols on the control equipment? They have been translated into Making Language. Now the Fire House will produce the matter out of the codes.'

'How could you do a thing like that?' Pallo wondered. 'You can't make a being out of thin air.'

'What do these patterns mean?' Kassien asked suspiciously. 'What's going on? Se, what are you *doing*?'

'These are Eteltar's codes,' Se said. 'And now we are putting the recipe into practice.'

Blind, crippled, and mute, the Scholar Wakhe dragged himself across the tiled floor. He could feel the pulsing rhythms in the building itself. Someone was trying to talk to him, but from where? Where were the vibrations coming from? They were subtle, but persistent.

He felt his way along the wall until he came to a metal bracket which held a smooth sphere. The bracket was vibrating minutely and he could feel the pulsing coming off its surface, like heat. *Light*, he thought, for light and heat often went together though he could not perceive the former. And together with the light, the faintest of sounds, beyond the range of ordinary human hearing but not quite beyond Wakhe's enhanced receptivity.

Wakhe passed his hands across the smooth surface of the Eye and the pulsing paused, resuming when his hands moved away. A pattern was coming off the glassy surface of the Eye and being picked up by the sensory equipment of the Fire House, which transformed it into sound. Wakhe played with the rhythms for a while, making sure that it was the Eye that was generating them. Then he crawled back to the centre of the room. He could feel the vibrations of their voices arguing in the pit: the Bear, the Wolf-Snake, Yanse-not-Yanse, and the Wolf. He felt for the panels they had removed in order to get into the pit. One by one, he replaced them, and stood on the bottom one. Now he was in a well with angled tiles on the sides, and each tile was a drum with a different resonance: an Everien mystery, for they were not much thicker than paper and where their resonance came from could not be determined.

Wakhe felt Yanse-not-Yanse pressing on the panel beneath his feet, and he stamped on it, making a deep, loud *boom*. Yanse-not-Yanse could not get up! But he, Wakhe, now he could make sound and *everyone* could hear.

The subtle message was still coming across to him, the message from Jaya asking for help. He did not think he could help her, but he listened for a while to what she was saying in his rhythmic time serpent language. And then, pounding the Everien drums with his broken, ungainly body, he thrashed and flopped his arms and legs and head to articulate himself. In a strangely graceful release of information, patterns, and feeling, Wakhe began to say the unsayable. Simply for the joy of it, for the fulfilment his brain had in that one task he could perform so well, Wakhe decoded the patterns and transmitted them in sound. To him it was a pleasure, a pure pleasure with no purpose, like singing. Across the membrane of the Eye, Wakhe gave out the recipe for time serpent.

An Unexpected Retreat

Istar sucked the ice that had formed on the fur edges of her parka.

'He's crazy,' she said.

Pentar was feeding the messenger seahawk that had just brought them word of the siege at A-vi-Khalar. He and Istar were a little distance from the bulk of the Seahawk army, overlooking the Snake side of Tyger Pass. Tash's forces could be seen making slow progress up the trail into the pass.

'Silk banners and high-strung warmbloods,' was Pentar's cryptic assessment. 'Their horses will die at altitude and they have wasted their efforts on fancy armour instead of good equipment. Word has it Tash has paid out food and medicine all through Snake Country. He has undoubtedly heard of our exploits and realizes that if he doesn't do something, the Snakes will side with the rebellion and refuse tribute to him in Jai Khalar. So he is making himself popular with them.'

'In the middle of winter?' Istar said incredulously.

'He's already got a war brewing with the Wolves. I daresay this is preventive medicine. And of course, everywhere he goes he stations fresh Pharician patrols and administrators.'

'To replace the ones the Sekk have taken.'

'Exactly.'

'But what's he doing up *here*, Pentar? Surely he's not going to Seahawk at this time of year?'

'Maybe he knows something we don't.'

'Such as?'

'Maybe it's the skeleton. *Someone* paid Grietar a lot of treasure for it, sight unseen. That person still hasn't received his merchandise.'

'You think it's Tash? I thought Grietar sold it to the Circle.'

'No one seems to know who the Circle really are. Anyway, it's either that, or the fact that he's picked us up in a Monitor Eye and is coming to prevent us meeting up with Jakse at Fivesisters Lake.'

'Are we that dangerous?' Istar said in surprise.

'We could be. Istar, I don't know why Tash is up here, but we'd be fools not to take advantage of our position.'

'I agree,' she said. 'Let's swat the bastard.'

Istar was afraid of Tash. She'd heard too many stories about him; she knew he had control of the Eyes and worried what he could See that she couldn't; and she didn't feel as secure in the command of her men as she would have liked. Moreover, she was distracted and upset by what had happened to her in Eteltar's cave, and not only could she tell no one about it, but even if she could she didn't think that a man would understand her predicament. So she positioned the men and planned the attack with extra care, convinced something was going to go badly wrong. She instructed that extra rations be given and she spoke to the men at length of what she knew of Pharician fighting methods. Still she was nervous, and she did not sleep. She was expecting a mess: casualties, weather problems, possibly having some of her force divided because of the rough geography. But she had to do it. There would never be another opportunity like this to catch Tash unawares.

It was a rout. The Seahawks waited until nightfall and then swarmed down on the Pharician fires. In their white furs, they were all but invisible until the last second, and though Tash's men outnumbered them, the Seahawks had the advantage of surprise. They stormed through the camp like an icy wind, shrieking in Seahawk and cutting down the unprepared Pharicians without mercy.

Istar was keen to get hand-to-hand with Tash, but she had to be sure the Sekk didn't get free in the confusion. Such a duel probably wouldn't have occurred anyway, for the prince wasted no time fighting a losing battle. As soon as the alarm was raised, he and his second in command were exhorting the men to pick up camp and flee. The Seahawks chased them all the way down the pass to the snowline, where finally the Pharician horses began to come into their own and the Seahawks were left behind.

'Into the woods, now,' Pentar told the men, and the Seahawks disappeared among the hemlocks like smoke. When the sun came up, Istar's army was cheering.

Gradually they regrouped under cover of the forest, while Tash's riders made off down the road into the Snake low country. Istar was guarding the Sekk, which she was doing her best to isolate from the group. It meant she, too, was kept apart from her own men, although she made sure they knew this was for reasons of their safety, not wanting to admit to herself it was also because she drew comfort from the tacit presence of the Sekk prisoner, who looked and smelled like Eteltar her lover.

Her command might have been compromised if after the melee Pentar had not effectively become acting commander. He made sure her orders were carried out. And once the men were reassembled, he came trudging through last year's leaves to talk strategy with Istar and to drink a toast.

'He was already thinking of turning back, I'm sure,' Pentar said. 'He gave up with no fight at all.'

'It's only a matter of time and equipment before he gets up there,' Istar observed. 'He'll be back. But I think we have the thing he wants, and best to get away from here as soon as we can.'

Pentar pulled a message slip from his belt. 'One of our seahawks intercepted this,' he said, pleased. 'It's a message from Kivi to Dario at Fivesisters Lake: *Tash is en route to you. He believes you are lost. Contact me at once for instructions.*'

'Shit,' said Istar. 'The cave! How does Tash know about the lake of candles?'

'Maybe he doesn't. Dario could be a double agent.'

'Xiriel will kill me if I let Tash get to his cave.'

'We cannot pursue him effectively through Snake Country,' Pentar warned. 'For one thing, his horses are too fast. We can follow at a distance, but we mustn't engage him. The Pharicians would beat the shit out of us down here. Did you see Tash? Did you see his second in command? On a different day, they would have thrashed us.'

'Yes.' Istar sighed. 'I saw, all right. But you'd better warn Jakse and make sure he's in control. I hope this Dario hasn't taken hold of Xiriel's cave. Pentar, I don't like it.'

Pentar scrutinized her for a moment and then handed over the flask he'd brought to toast their victory. 'Look at you,' he said. 'Sitting in a fern brake with a captive Sekk twice your size, a victory over Prince Tash, and the sun shining for the first time in months! Quit worrying, and have a drink.'

She did. But she made sure her army didn't relax too long, and soon they set off after Tash on the road to Fivesisters Lake. They made slow progress, stopping in a village to reprovision and detouring around spring flooding that made a local ford impassable. In the end they took to the high ground again, which was why they happened to be camped on a high ridge, with a view of Everien's slow-greening valley on their left and the snowy slopes of Snake Country on their right, when the earth began to shake and open, and even stranger things began to happen.

The Stars That Shake

'I'm not going in there,' Chyko said when they reached the gate of Jaya's garden. 'That is where she keeps all her magic. You may bring me food and wood, and I will wait out here.'

Tarquin's lip curled at the thought of serving Chyko, but he also knew that this could be his chance to slip away with Jaya. While they had ridden she had spoken to him of her time in the forest. She said, 'It has been getting worse lately. If Chyko had not come, I don't know what I would have done.'

It was not what Tarquin wanted to hear, that she was grateful to Chyko. She didn't seem to perceive his jealousy. In some ways, he thought, she was like a child. But she led them unerringly to the gate. The garden.

'Where we always meet,' he said in her ear, and she smiled.

'I will be watching you,' Chyko called after them. 'And so will all the creatures you fear, Jaya. We will all be out here, your monsters and your men! Do not try to get away.'

The garden was not the way Tarquin remembered it. The plants had grown more, and it was not a tranquil place. The wood seemed to be creeping in from above and below. The fountain was not running, but was full of rainwater and dead leaves. Jaya went inside and returned with Chyko's food. It was as dark in the garden as it had been in the forest, and she found her way by means of a small lamp held aloft. Kere eyed it curiously.

'What's that?'

'This is the lamp I used that night. Like this.'

Jaya shone the lamp on the water of the fountain. She let out a cry.

'What do you see?'

'I see stars, Tarquin. Stars that shake. Look!'

'I know those rhythms,' Kere said. 'Unless I'm very mistaken, those stars are shaking in time serpent.'

'What?'

'It is a mathematical pattern. I wonder who is making it. I will call out.'

Kere began a fierce rhythm, just as he had done when talking to the time serpents. He paused, and the stars flared at him.

'Someone's there. "*Who are you?*" they say.'

Jaya trembled with excitement.

'Night? Night, are you there? Answer me! I, Jaya, summon you.'

Kere glanced at Jaya and then tapped out a translation of her message.

'Ah!' she cried. 'The stars are talking back. See them shake? What do they say?'

'They say, "*Jaya, I am blind, deaf, mute, broken. I cannot come to you.*"'

Jaya's hand covered her mouth. Tarquin put his arms around her and she pressed against him. He drew her away from the fountain, but Kere was still tapping and clicking. 'Don't listen,' Tarquin whispered in her ear. 'Everything Night does always proves to be an illusion.'

After a few moments Kere called to them. 'I am in communication with the Fire Houses. The Clans will build or call a time serpent. Se the Snake has Eteltar's codes. The time serpent will come and eat the Fire of Glass and maybe more.'

'A Li'ah'vah at loose in Everien?' cried Tarquin. 'No! It must be stopped.'

Jaya ran back to the pool. 'Help me, Kere. Ask it. Look, how dark it is. Night. Night. Tell me who you are. Tell me who I am. Please. What should I do? What is this house? How can I get out of here?'

At length Kere translated, '"*I am not Night.*"'

'No more of this,' Tarquin said, looking at the confusion on Jaya's face. 'Kere! Let's go.'

But Kere shook his head. No Ice. Tarquin throttled his anger. The stars quivered.

Jaya gripped Kere's arm. 'What do they say?'

'"*Be careful!*"' Kere quoted. '"*If we can perceive each other, the time serpent can come to you also! Leave that place if you will not be caught by it.*"'

'You see? Let's go, Kere.'

But Jaya was almost hysterical. 'Father? It's Jaya. Jaya Paradox. Please! Night? Jihan? Anyone! Tell me. Tell me. Tell me.'

'No, Jaya,' Tarquin said, and forcibly dragged her away.

'Please,' cried Jaya.

'Believe me, Jaya, you don't want to know these things. Kere, is Chyko still out there in the wood?'

'He must be,' Kere said. 'For Ice will not come. He must be watching us.'

Midnight Blue raised his head and trumpeted a challenge. Kere trembled, his nostrils flaring. But still he did not change to Ice.

'Right,' said Tarquin. 'That's enough of that, Chyko. I'm coming to get you.'

'Tarquin, no, don't go! Don't leave me!'

'Hang on, Jaya,' he called over his shoulder. 'I'll be back. Just wait there. I'll be back.'

Jaya sobbed. 'That's what you always say.'

She followed him to the gate but did not pursue him beyond that point. The creatures could be heard slithering in the underbrush.

When she returned to Kere, he was still paying rapt attention to the fountain and the reflected stars.

'Jaya, we can call a time serpent. I don't know what will happen, but I do know that we will not escape any other way. Not without Ice, and he cannot come here.'

'I'll do anything,' Jaya said. 'Anything not to relive this. Not to go back to that forest.'

She turned and peered into the gloom. She could hear angry words being exchanged between Tarquin and Chyko. The forest seethed with watchers and other silent things. She caught hold of the black horse and tried to soothe him.

'They fight, but they don't understand. They don't know what this place is like. Kere, we have to get out of here!'

Kere said, 'I'm trying. I have received the codes. Now you will have to take me to the tear in the Liminal.'

'The what?'

'The place where the Sekk broke in here before.'

'Oh,' said Jaya in a subdued tone. 'You mean the gallery windows.'

'Show me, quickly!'

Jaya was trembling and shaking her head. '*They* will be there. I won't go alone. I won't go without Tarquin.'

Before Kere could do anything to persuade her, there was a sound from the forest like a discordant violin, and from the trees shot a live sailsnake. It rose out of the tangled branches and covered the stars in a flash. Jaya's breath caught in her throat, then the sailsnake rose and was gone. So was Kere; but a white horse ran across the garden and stood, shivering.

The gate opened and the two men came rushing in, swords out and bloody.

'They're coming,' Tarquin said. 'The whole fucking forest is alive and it's coming after us. Shut the gate.'

Chyko shut the gate and put his back to it. Strange noises could be heard from the trees.

'Don't listen,' Chyko said. 'Be careful, Tarquin. You are in peril.'

'*You* are in peril,' Tarquin threatened. 'On account of me.'

Chyko only laughed.

'What's so funny?'

'Do you remember the time the Sekk Enslaved you?' Chyko said. 'In

491

Wolf Country, a few months before Jai Pendu? Do you remember it?'

'Of course I remember. You saved my life. But that was a long time ago.'

'I broke the spell,' Chyko said. 'The Sekk will never have power over me. I don't believe in beauty or love. They can't get to me. Neither can she, the little witch.' He pointed to Jaya, who bit her lip.

'You're sick, Chyko. You are missing everything that's good in the world.'

Chyko spat. 'I don't care. You were supposed to live for me, Tarquin. It's what you should have done, when Night took us. But you didn't. Why else did I do all I did for you? Join your Company, save your life, tell everyone that it was you who had saved me so that your status would rise yet higher with Ysse . . . Why did I do these things? To give you a chance at what I never had. I even gave you my children! What could I do with them? But you, Tarquin, you had a chance.'

'You cannot hand over your morality to another man, Chyko. The blood you have shed, all you have done in your life, it lies on you. I couldn't have saved you, no matter what I did.'

'Then you should have killed me. You shouldn't have tried to use me. You see what I am. I'm a murderer, a warrior; it's all I am and it's all I know. I was made to die in battle and I can't even find an opponent worthy enough to give me that honour.' He turned and faced the iron bars that held the forest at bay. 'Perhaps now is my chance.'

'Don't be stupid,' Tarquin said. 'We have to get Jaya out of this place.'

'You have truly become the coward!' Chyko said bitterly. 'I never would have believed it.'

'I'm not a coward,' Tarquin said. 'If Jaya wants you, then take her. Better that you should have her than Night. I will not press my claim.'

'Better that I—?' Chyko broke off, shaking his head, laughing. '*She is Night*, you pea-brain! Ah, take her, Tarquin, if you want her so much. But she is silent, and she does not quicken, and she only looks on me with those great sad eyes like a cow. Take her back! Do not command me, though, nor any of the Company. I serve no man, and now that I have the black horse I will ride the worlds tearing pieces out of them. You cannot stop me; you will not, I see it in your eyes. If you wish peace, I will give you it in death. You will have none in life, Tarquin the Free. So I curse you.'

Tarquin had never wanted to take a man's head off so much as he wanted Chyko's head now. He wanted Chyko's mad head, his testicles, his virgin-blooded cock that had caused so much trouble. He wanted them all for stew which he would feed to the black crows and laugh as they burned their tongues and hopped from foot to foot. But the girl behind him was sobbing uselessly, her heels digging trenches in the mud as she tried to hold the reins of her gleaming black horse. The stallion lunged at Ice, ears back, sabre-teeth gnashing; but Ice was ever just out of reach, and the trees seemed to close in on the animals, their branches never quite where they were expected, like a moving puzzle, or like snakes.

Chyko was laughing. He slid an arrow from its quiver; Tarquin charged. He felt the surprising frailness of Chyko's body as he struck it with his own, ramming Chyko into the dirt and roots, his hands avoiding the poison ampules at Chyko's neck and going instead to the eyes. But Chyko was slippery, and he had a dagger Tarquin didn't know about, nestled between his groin and his inner thigh. It slipped between Tarquin's ribs. Tarquin could feel it moving around inside as though questing for something. He clapped his legs around Chyko's body and held him down while he groped for a chokehold, ignoring the knife for now. He felt his forearm slip across the vulnerable trachea and lock beneath the jaw, and he grabbed his own wrist to secure the hold, all the while holding Chyko in position with his legs. He clamped down hard on the side of Chyko's neck to cut off the blood supply to his head. He counted to five. His old friend was unconscious, limp in his arms.

He was distracted by a trumpeting scream.

Ice.

Bleary with violence, Tarquin looked up from his vanquished foe. Jaya had lost hold of the black horse and now the two stallions were up on their hind legs, snapping at each other's necks. Tarquin felt Chyko's limp weight in his arms and remembered how he had raped Jaya with utter thoughtlessness. He kept squeezing. He could snap Chyko's neck now and kill him. Or he could just wait, and Chyko would die from the strangle. It was a matter of only a little time.

'You bastard!' he said in Chyko's ear. 'I'd like to take you apart, I would.'

He let go. Chyko did not stir, but his pulse still moved. Tarquin cracked him hard across the jaw. Then he stood up and kicked him in the kidneys, and four times more, each harder than the next. He would have continued, but Jaya was tugging at him.

'Stop them!' she begged. 'They'll kill each other!'

Both horses were bleeding, and they were so evenly matched that Tarquin feared they would indeed inflict mortal wounds on each other. How could he stop them?

He picked up Chyko's bow and nocked an arrow. He aimed at the horses.

'Tarquin, please, no!'

Jaya flung herself into Tarquin's line of fire; but Ice had already broken free of the black horse. He sprang into the air as if to leap over the sailsnake fountain, but he landed on the stone lip with a thud of human bone and flesh.

'Kere.' Tarquin set the bow down, relieved, and dismayed at the same time. Jaya had run off to quiet Midnight Blue, and now Chyko stirred.

'I win,' Chyko said from the ground. 'Your horse ran away. Jaya is mine. Believe me, it is safer for you this way. I am doing you a favour, though you cannot see it.'

'He is right, Tarquin,' Kere said. 'The danger does not lie in Chyko.'

'Who else fires Wasp arrows around here?' Tarquin snapped. 'Kere, shut up.'

Kere sat on the edge of the fountain and began palpating himself for injuries. Jaya joined him a moment later, making a fuss over the boy such that Kere blushed and stammered.

Tarquin turned to Chyko. Through clenched teeth he hissed, 'What did you mean, *Jaya is Night?*'

Chyko got to his feet and limped across the garden. Tarquin followed. He looked up at the side of the house and saw that there had been large windows overlooking the courtyard. Their glass was broken and lay in sheets and shards on the ground. The windows of the tower where Tarquin had found Mistel were dark. He wondered fleetingly whether she was still there; but he did not let his attention slip from Chyko as his old friend picked his way through the broken glass easily, his bare feet scarcely seeming to touch the flagstones. He entered the kitchen and opened a pantry, from which he withdrew a haunch of smoked venison. With relish he bit into it, tearing off a chunk with his teeth.

'Nothing ages here,' Chyko said. 'And nothing dies. It is still good to eat.' He proffered the meat and Tarquin took it. He had been ignoring his hunger, but when the smell of food reached him, it threatened to overpower him. He bit into the salty flesh and scarcely chewed it before swallowing. Chyko was grinning and chewing.

'It is good, yes? She cannot take away physical pleasures. If anything, they are stronger here.'

He closed his eyes, a soft smile on his face, and Tarquin suspected he was thinking about Jaya's cunt. Tarquin took another bite and shoved the joint of meat into the point of Chyko's breastbone. 'What do you mean, *Jaya is Night?*' he repeated.

'She called us in Jai Pendu. She drew us into the Glass. She used us to fight them.' He gestured with the bone toward the forest. 'She wanted you, but she couldn't get you, so she used us. Out beyond this forest, there are worlds on worlds. There is no end to the battle she set us.'

'Chyko, you're talking nonsense. Night was a Sekk. I saw it. You saw it. I fought Night, goddamn it. Night is not unknown to me. But Jaya, Jaya is . . . Jaya was . . .'

'Jaya was there all the time,' Chyko said. 'But it wasn't until you broke the Company of Glass and set us free that I could get back to this place.'

Lake of Candles

'Why are so many of the Everien strongholds underground?' Dario wondered aloud. 'And the Sekk also seem to rise from the earth. All I can think of is graves, ghosts, death.'

'There may be a more practical explanation,' Jakse said. 'To hide from bird spies, for one. We use H'ah'vah tunnels for that purpose – and to protect us from the weather. But the Pharicians are well versed in communication by air, as are the Seahawks. My Clan has always favoured the earth as a refuge and a place of secrecy.'

Finally Jakse trusted Dario enough to show her the place where the Sekk came from. He was guarding it, he said, until Xiriel could return. And she knew that when that happened, she would have to make a decision. Sooner or later, Kivi would demand a report.

They stood on the lip, which was not a natural rock formation but a straight edge of Everien smoothstone, and gazed out across the black mere.

'I don't see any candles,' Dario whispered.

'They come out only at night.'

'How can the Sekk know when it is night, so deep underground?'

'They know,' Jakse said. Although she was standing a yard away, Jakse could sense Dario trembling. Her imagination was working on her. 'Let us walk around the lake. They do not rise when the candles are dark, so you need have no fear. Yet.'

He showed her the symbols incised in the walls. The lake was perfectly square, more of an ornamental pool of grand proportions than a true lake. There was nothing to indicate how long ago it had been carved: no cracks, no weathering, and very little dirt. 'Even the bats seem to avoid it,' Jakse said.

'Why doesn't the water freeze?'

'It isn't water. I *think* it's the same substance that forms the Water of Glass. It is always liquid, it coheres more strongly than water, and it never evaporates or freezes or boils. Ah! Here comes the first candle.'

Dario jumped a little, but followed Jakse along the edge of the pool without hesitation. He stopped several paces short of reaching the circle of soft illumination that had appeared near the edge of the lake. 'Leave your torch on the ground. You will see it better in its own light.'

The Sekk had Enslaved nearly every member of Dario's village. It had taken all of her family, and it would have taken her children if she had not fled to the trees and stayed there, shooting anyone who came near, until the attack was over. Dario believed that the part of her that saw beauty and felt love was dead, too. Ever since that day, there had been such a coldness in her heart that she had left her children with relatives in another village, convinced she would only do them harm with her bitterness and anger. She went off to fight the Sekk because it was all she could now do. Others thought her strong because she had resisted the Slaving, but Dario felt as if she were missing a limb. Nothing could touch her now. The Sekk had stolen the light inside her and she did not think she would ever get it back.

So it was that Dario looked at the small lamp in the dark water, curious and detached. Wary. And what she saw, she did not expect.

It was a globe made of glass or some kind of crystal, about the size of a Carry Eye. It was lit from within by what appeared a tiny flame; yet there was something not right about the flame, and when Dario bent down to get a closer look, she saw that the light was coming from a tiny figure inside the globe.

'What is it?' she breathed without taking her eyes off the globe. Dario was feeling something she couldn't explain. It was the kind of wonder a small child feels in looking into a doll's house, an innocent pleasure; and it disarmed her. Dario observed the tiny person and found herself unaccountably smiling. 'It's lovely,' she said.

Jakse had not answered her at first. Now he gently took her elbow and drew her away.

'We have to go. Night has fallen, and it isn't safe here.'

Back at camp, the word was that Tash's army had been repelled at Tyger Pass and was heading this way. The news of his princehood and of Hezene's flooding Everien with Pharician troops was met with an uncomfortable silence. Dario wondered why Kivi had not warned her.

'The Seahawks kept them from Tyger Pass. Surely this is good news!' Jakse said.

'It was the fault of their horses, and their men, being ill equipped for mountain warfare. It is said that Tash was seeking some great Artifact in Tyger Pass. He will stop at nothing to uncover the Knowledge.'

Dario shifted. She didn't have to say anything. It was obvious she was thinking of the lake, and the lights, and their seductive effects.

'Their horses will have no such trouble in these downlands,' Bellen mused.

'They must not go to the underground lake,' Dario said.

'Are you going to tell Tash that, Dario?' Jakse asked.

'He is not known to be a reasonable man,' Uven added, and the others laughed at his understatement. But the laughter did not break the

497

tension in the air. The tenuous camaraderie between Jakse's men and Dario's was now suspended as each side realized it had to make a decision.

'Are Pharice as bad as we think?' asked Bellen hopelessly, looking around at the troubled faces of his companions and the more hard-set countenances of Jakse's small band. 'I know so little about them.'

'They are stupid, if Tash thinks to solve the problem of the Sekk by marching against them en masse.' Dario's voice was quiet but certain. 'If he brings an army into this area, the Sekk will go through them like wildfire. It will be just like Night's taking of the force at Ristale, only without the Company of Glass to control the men, there will be no marching to a common destiny. There will be a bloodbath.'

Jakse said, 'It is well, then, that they are coming. Let them kill each other.'

'If that happens,' Bellen said, 'then the way will be wide open for the Sekk to filter down into the farmlands of Everien. If we do not destroy the Sekk at their source, no man, Pharician or Clan, can hope to be king.'

'Are you sure that the lake is the source of the Sekk?' Dario asked.

'Yes.' Jakse's tone was certain.

Dario drew a long breath. As her chest rose she felt as if her heart were tearing in two. 'Then we must act swiftly, before Tash finds us. We must destroy the lights. Every one.'

Don't Let Go

Jaya had left Kere beside the fountain, still receiving codes from the other side of the dark sky. Now she was standing in the courtyard, hugging herself against the cold of coming autumn. Listening to the men.

'It wasn't like that,' she said. 'I am not Night. Night is my oppressor! My shadow! Night is what keeps me in this forest.'

'You used us,' Chyko cried. 'And when you could not control us, you used our loyalty to Quintar to hold lesser men whom you *could* control. And you would have marched them right out of their world to fight your battle here.'

'But I had to,' Jaya said. 'You can't fight abstraction with abstraction. I needed something that was true.'

Tarquin only stared at her, amazed at her admission. She met his gaze and flared at him, her voice rising. 'Why should I wait around to be rescued? My mother waited all her life, baking bread and hoping for what could never be. My father never came back. I don't even believe he exists. And they looked over the wall at me. They haunted his books. Those creatures out there . . . I had to do something. Their numbers grow. They multiply. They look at me all the time. Tarquin, I had to do something. I needed a weapon.'

Chyko crowed, 'You admit it, then! Ah, you should have left well enough alone. Look! You had a house, a garden, companionship. Why did you have to go digging around? What *is* your father's Knowledge, anyway?'

'That is what I was trying to find out. I am still trying, but every time I come back here, they attack me. I'm only trying to fight back.'

Tarquin wasn't thinking about the Knowledge. He was thinking about the way she had soothed his mind, the way she could touch him secretly. The way he had thought her bound to him.

'Why me, Jaya?'

It was his only real question, and he could see from her expression that she could not answer it.

Chyko said caustically, 'Because you are the hero.'

Tarquin ignored him. 'Jaya, do you remember me? Do you know I've had visions of you? Were these tricks, Jaya? Do you remember the garden? Do you remember when you gave me the rose?'

He had to know. He held her eyes, trying to read her face.

'There was one time we met in the garden,' she admitted. 'You were picking the roses. You asked me where our children were.'

'*Children?*' Chyko let out a groan. 'Tarquin, tell me you are not falling for this.'

'Stop it, Chyko!' Jaya snapped in a sudden temper, and the Wasp looked startled and even ashamed. 'I know I did you wrong. But I was young. I looked in books and mirrors as if they were toys. I had never been hurt. I did not see the consequences.'

'She is a seductive thing,' Chyko remarked to Tarquin. 'See how she bats her lashes at you even as she admits her power.'

'Jaya . . .' whispered Tarquin in anguish.

'I don't know what to do,' she said. 'They are coming, and we are cornered.'

Beyond the garden Tarquin could see them: half-formed creatures, some with eyes and some with other kinds of feelers, questing toward Jaya. They were on the verge of entering. He kept glimpsing what he thought were Sekk eyes in the throng, but he could never make a human face resolve out of all those parts, mingled as they already were with the trees and the thorns and the wrought iron fence.

Chyko said, 'He cannot save you, Jaya. I will fight until I drown in the blood of my enemies. Tarquin only knows how to run away.'

Tarquin realized that Chyko still had the effrontery to woo Jaya, and he pounced on his old friend without warning. 'You can't have her, Chyko! You are the deceitful one, trying to come between us.'

They rolled on the ground and Chyko bit him. The Wasp got the advantage momentarily. Sitting on Tarquin's chest and pinning his arms down, he said, 'Tarquin, I'm doing you a favour. I don't love her. She can't hurt me. But you – she'll destroy you.'

'No,' Tarquin gasped, and bucked himself free, leaping to his feet and aiming kicks at Chyko. '*I'll* destroy *you*.'

'Ai!' Jaya cried, tearing her hair and looking at the sky. 'Enough! Both of you, stop!'

Tarquin's kicks missed and Chyko danced out of the way, laughing. He loved this shit.

'We have to get out of here. Kere!'

'I can't bring Ice here,' Kere said. 'It's not safe. The arrows.'

Jaya was whispering in his ear. 'We have to go. Look at them! We're surrounded.'

Tarquin put his arm around her, glaring at Chyko. 'There has to be a way, Kere. What were you two doing all that time by the pool? Jaya saw something in it.'

'The stars. Time serpent. They're in the Fire Houses and they have

Eteltar's codes to build a time serpent, Tarquin. That could be our way out.'

'Please, Tarquin,' murmured Jaya.

'I don't like it. Think of another way.'

'Tarquin, this time serpent has three corners—'

'Ah, a three-cornered snake, a one-sided road – Kere, you must be more plain, especially at a time like this.'

'It can come into being in three places. One in Eteltar's ancient Everien where he found the codes, one in Se's time on the island, and one in Everien as you know it, in the Fire Houses. I have heard the codes. They are clear in my mind. Now if only we could direct its attention here, get it to pass through us and pick us up in the Liminal . . .'

'No, Kere. A Li'ah'vah is nothing to be fucked with. I forbid it. Do you understand me? I forbid it!'

In a sudden, inspired act, Tarquin reached over and seized Chyko's bow where it was lying forgotten on the ground. He broke it over his knee.

'*Fuck you!*'

Tarquin danced out of Chyko's way as the Wasp came at him. 'Kere! Look! His bow is broken! Call Ice. Call the White Road. Do it!'

Kere shook his head. 'I can't. He won't come.'

'But Kere, Chyko's bow is broken! I have fulfilled my quest! Now stop being so goddamned chicken!'

Chyko head-butted Tarquin in the gut and knocked him down.

Kere said, 'It's not safe yet. Somewhere in time, Ice still bears the arrow. The shot has not yet been prevented.'

Tarquin kneed Chyko in the groin and got loose. He staggered to his feet and grabbed Jaya's hand, beginning to pull her across the courtyard toward the garden. 'But how is that possible?' he roared at the boy. 'I've done everything right!'

'Not everything, Tarquin, you arrogant prick,' Chyko said. He was following them with a poison arrow gripped in his hand. 'Which one of you wants to die? It's a slow poison, but the antidote is hard to find and you don't know where to look. Or should I say, when to look?'

Jaya broke away and ran up the steps to the tower. She beat on the door that had taken Tarquin to Eteltar's laboratory. 'I'll get the books. I'll get the cards. I won't be driven out without the Knowledge. There has to be a way.'

'Don't let her in there,' Chyko said. 'It will only be more tricks.'

But Jaya couldn't get into the room. Chyko advanced, brandishing the arrow. Jaya was dithering with panic. 'Tarquin, see, he is in league with them! Now we are cornered. Oh, Jihan, what are these creatures that follow me? What do they want? If this house is a deck of cards, deal me a door!'

From the garden, Midnight Blue screamed. His hooves sounded on the stones of the courtyard and they could just see him on the edge of the darkness, his silvery hooves throwing sparks on the stones. Steam puffed from his nostrils.

'They've gotten in!' Kere shrieked.

The monsters came over the fence. They came through the fence; they came under it. Half-finished creatures seeking to be finished; and ones that never should have been made seeking annihilation; and every manner of thing in between. Eyes and tentacles, wings and bodies, teeth, claws, fingers, skin. Poisons and fumes rose from them. And lurking in the shadows between them were the beautiful ones, like spirits of uncertain substance: the Sekk. It was as if Jaya's deck of cards had been shuffled wrongly. No creature here possessed its own integrity. Every one was lost. And they came toward the house like a tide.

As if in answer, from the house there was a roaring sound that rose to a musical pitch; Tarquin turned and saw glass flying from the courtyard to the windows, multiple shards becoming a single pane.

Now there was no room for conflict among them. Chyko and Tarquin and Kere and Jaya together retreated to the house, climbing the stairs that led to the corridor overlooking the courtyard, where the windows were unbroken and the night outside was absolute.

'But these windows were shattered,' Jaya said. 'I saw it happen. Just before they killed my mother . . .' She looked around, baffled. Then she put her hands up against the glass and looked out into the darkness. She recoiled as quickly, screaming, 'Monsters! Faces, and eyes, and . . . listen! Can you hear them singing? Can you hear it?'

Tarquin couldn't hear singing but he could hear a sound like drums, like the Snake Clan drums and the time serpents all going hard at it at once. Kere was leaning against the glass and had begun to tap on it in that inane Snake fashion. Useless little sod. Tarquin turned to Chyko and held his eyes. If ever there was a time for brotherhood, this was it. He thought Chyko knew it, too; but then Chyko spoke.

'I can save her,' Chyko said. 'I am the man who is come to rescue her. You cannot save her. You are doomed. If you really love her, give her to me and I will protect her.'

Tarquin seethed, for he feared what Chyko said was true. He tightened his hold of Jaya, and she leaned into him.

'No,' he said. 'Kill me if you can, but I won't give her up.'

Chyko seized Kere and wrapped an arm around his neck, pressing the tip of the arrow to his carotid artery. 'I won't kill you, Tarquin. I know you're not afraid to die. But you're fucked if the boy goes. Don't bluff me, Tarquin. I've seen you trying to protect him. Now give me the girl, so I can get the horse and take her away before they destroy everything that was ever here.'

Midnight Blue was screaming and fighting outside. Kere strangely didn't seem to notice Chyko's hold. He was beating furiously on the glass with his hands, his face a mask of concentration as he drummed complex beats. Chyko tried to pull him away, but the boy was surprisingly strong; like a cat trying to escape a basket he twisted and writhed, drumming all the while.

'Please, Chyko, don't use the arrow,' Tarquin begged, looking into Chyko's sparkling eyes. Chyko hesitated.

'I'm calling you, damn it!' Kere whispered without breaking beat. 'I am an Animal, I run on the White Road, and I'm calling you. You have to come!'

Tarquin would have slapped Kere across the face if he could. He hissed. 'Don't call Ice, you fool! Not now!'

'Come on!' Kere said, still drumming. 'Hear me. I'm calling you. One good deed deserves another and I'm calling!'

'I don't think he's calling Ice,' Jaya whispered. 'Tarquin, I think he's calling—'

Silence fell like a curtain. Jaya shut her mouth in surprise and did not finish what she had started to say. Tarquin could hear Kere panting. There was a faint stirring of wind outside, and the restless clatter of Midnight Blue's hooves. Chyko and Tarquin glanced at each other. Kere went limp in Chyko's grip. As one, Tarquin and Chyko moved toward the window.

A yellow, glowing face was abruptly pressed against the dark glass from without. It was almost a human face, yet ten times too large. And there was something wrong about it. Something wrong in a familiar way, Tarquin thought. And then it opened its mouth, and the face stretched and distorted itself until it was unrecognizable, absorbed into the sinuous shape of the monster. Its teeth gleamed and dripped toxins. The darkness beyond the windows exploded into light, and instead of the hands and tentacles and eyes of the creatures of the night, in place of the darkness there was a fluorescent yellow, striated tunnel. The maw of time.

'The time serpent!' Tarquin breathed. 'Jaya, whatever happens, don't let go my hand.'

Jaya stood paralysed, her face an inch away from the glass. She seemed transfixed by what she saw down the creature's throat; but Tarquin wasn't looking at the time serpent. He kept his eyes on Jaya. She was the treasure he had to keep. He grabbed her hand, trying to draw her back along the hallway. 'Kere, help me! We have to get her out of here!'

Chyko had let Kere go and the boy was hovering right behind Tarquin and Jaya, his eyes shining with eagerness. Tarquin didn't bother to tell him to call Ice. That had never worked before; why should it work now? Jaya shot him a terrified look. 'Not again,' she whispered. 'Not this again.'

'Don't let go my hand,' he repeated. 'No matter what, don't let go.'

But the time serpent's mouth was full of darkness now, and the arrow that flew at them came from another place. It shattered the glass, stung Jaya's hand, and kept going. Kere, standing just behind Tarquin and Jaya, let out a cry. Tarquin didn't have time to turn and see whether Kere was hurt by the arrow or just the flying glass as the window collapsed inward. For Jaya let go of him and he was scrambling to get her back; but it was too late. She was gone.

'Jaya!' Tarquin screamed – but he couldn't even see her. The dark void she had leaped into had been replaced by a fiery red vision of the inside of a Fire House, revealed at the other end of the time serpent, very close and very far away.

Tarquin recognized the figure standing in the aperture at the other end of the time serpent. It was Mavese. His arms flung wide, he cried, 'Mother, take me home,' and rushed toward them. Chyko gazed dispassionately at the ecstatic Snake leader and hurled the arrow down the time serpent's luminous gullet as if it were a spear. 'Gotcha, you bastard!' he snarled into infinity as the arrow passed through Mavese's throat and wedged between two of his cervical vertebrae. And in a flash Mavese's body was swallowed by a time he would never know.

Distracted by the loss of Jaya, Tarquin did not expect what came next. Chyko flung himself on Tarquin's back and began biting and scratching and slapping him in an excess of childish violence – for if he had wanted to kill Tarquin he could have done it with one stroke from behind, with a knife. The two went down and were rolling, into the apparition of the time serpent and then out, across the dusty hallway of Jaya's abandoned house, and then back in, damaging themselves on the broken glass more than they were damaging each other by real blows. 'Bastard!' they accused each other. 'Fucker! Shithead!' Tarquin managed to get Chyko off him for a second and they separated, panting, eyeing each other. Over Chyko's shoulder Tarquin could see the volcanic cave of the dying time serpents, the chemical fires of the Pharician attackers, and finally, running up the tunnel toward Chyko, a Pharician carrying a sword, his hair and cloak on fire. Chyko noticed the direction of Tarquin's gaze and turned to meet the Pharician.

'Get back where you came from, you piece of camel shit!' Chyko roared, and charged. Tarquin saw him pursue the Pharician back into the burning volcanic chamber, where he cut him down and then stood, half crouched, ready to take on all comers. Chyko cast a last glance back toward Tarquin. His teeth were bared – or he was smiling – Tarquin had never been able to tell the difference. He thought that possibly Chyko winked. Then the time serpent swallowed and Tarquin couldn't see him any more.

Belatedly he realized that it was he who had been swallowed; but he didn't care. He was staggering through the inside of the time serpent – which was grotesquely streaked with fluorescence and undulating like a stormy sea – as if none of it were anything new: another vortex, another trip, another turnaround in his expectations. And in his mind's eye he saw again the Wasp Clan dart come flying out of nowhere, and a sob was wrenched from his gut as he thought of all his efforts to prevent that arrow striking Ice, when in the end it had not even come from Chyko's bow. All his efforts to rescue Jaya. All he had tried and failed to do. It was not true what Kere said, that destiny lay only in the mind – that life was merely a series of accidents. *Destiny*, he thought, *leaves fingerprints. It is real. It makes things bleed.*

Jaya was gone. Thinking of that arrow, he couldn't bear to call Kere's name. He shut his eyes.

Li'ah'vah

Wakhe stayed on the drums long enough to hear the echo come back to him. Then the rumblings began, deep in the earth. They shivered up the length of the Fire House and pulsed from the Fire. Wakhe leaped up and fled. He smashed into a wall, got up, ran again, fell down, and finally, by the air currents, he found his way out of the Fire House. The Wolf soldiers tried to snatch him, but when they perceived the trembling from the Fire, they let him go and they, too, ran for their lives.

In the pit, Se finally pushed through the ceiling tiles that Wakhe's weight had been holding in position. Xiriel and Kassien and Pallo piled out and ran. The finely calibrated equipment that controlled the Making Centre of the Fire House burst asunder, and in the flash of light that came with the explosion its pieces were seen to fly glittering through the air. Then total darkness fell. There was a crunching noise as half-finished metal and gemwork was pulverized beneath some great bulk. The walls of the Fire House shook like a beaten drum, waves of sound passing rhythmically up the red membranes with a rush of sultry air. Out of the utter darkness red veins of light began to spiderweb along the walls; but something was now blotting out the view of most of the interior. In the core had formed a shadowy thing that nearly filled the conical space. It had no eyes nor limbs to be seen, and it barely moved, but the sheen of vital juices lit its gleaming, metallic skin. Someone screamed and then all the smiths were running.

'A Li'ah'vah! By the Sekk, it's big!'

The Li'ah'vah had come into being pointing toward the heat at the top of the Fire House. Its mouth yawned wide and its crystal teeth, each the length of a pike only sharper, brushed against the Fire of Glass. Sparks flew, and ghostly images of people and objects flew from the contact, falling like flower petals to what was left of the floor, where they vanished. Some of the smiths had stopped and turned, unable to look away from the sight despite the danger. They saw the Li'ah'vah turn against itself, its mouth opening wider and wider until its teeth stuck out in all directions like spikes, and then the creature turned inside out and devoured itself, its mouth rolling toward the floor like the open end of a stocking pulled off in haste. Only when the mouth reached the floor and the engorged body lay with its tail pointing at the Fire of Glass, only then did the teeth take a bite out of the ground, and with the delicate flexibility of a skinned worm, the Li'ah'vah slipped into the fissure in the earth.

The walls shook. All the city shook as the Li'ah'vah crashed through its underground avenues, taking out storerooms and residences and alleys and roads with no apparent effort at all. At length the rampage ended when the Li'ah'vah reached the middle of a marketplace and dove deeper underground, leaving a dark and steaming fissure behind, into which tumbled fragments of pottery, children's toys, baskets of dried winter fruit, and other remnants of people's lives.

Miraculously, Xiriel and Kassien not only survived, but managed to stay together. Pallo turned up in a sewer in A-vo-Manik, hundreds of miles from the Li'ah'vah epicentre, with no recollection of how he'd got there. The body of Se, cervical vertebrae run through with a poison arrow, was found a year later on the sea plateau.

Despite everything, the Pharicians held their discipline. If anything, Illyra and his men were in their shining hour, for they rode up and down the valley making order from chaos and assisting the terrified victims of the event. Most of the area in and around the Fire Houses had been reduced to a black, smoking hole. Weird sounds echoed from its depths, and the air whipped and whirled in fluky patterns. No one was crazy enough to go near. Meanwhile, the Li'ah'vah stormed on – now here, now there, displacing itself with a vengeance without regard for distance or time – carving chunks out of Everien.

How long this went on for, no one was really sure. The sun jumped around the sky like a grasshopper and the hourglasses simply shattered. Even years later, housewives were still discovering bits of broken glass and sand in odd corners and under carpets. Nothing behaved as expected.

And then, as suddenly as it had come, the Li'ah'vah was gone.

But by then, everything had changed.

Falling

Liaku screamed. She could see the Li'ah'vah's mouth: It was full of ghosts of cities, and Jai Khalar was being crushed accordion-style as the monster came on. She scrambled to the top of the aviary, opening cages so fast she cut her fingers. Hrost was long gone – didn't give a shit, probably. Birds spurted into the air like the white blood of the white city; mice leaped off the parapets in a parody of rats abandoning ship. She couldn't get any higher, and the tower she stood upon was already dropping, pulled out from beneath her by the terrible suction of the time serpent.

Her screams went dry. Her fingers clawed.

Then a shadow came over her, and sharp talons bit into her shoulders, tearing them almost to the bone. The aviary and the towers had been ripped away from her, or she from them – or possibly both, and she was whizzing through the air, legs kicking futilely. Quiz was falling fast, unable to support her weight, and they rushed toward the silver moving body of the Li'ah'vah, which had devoured Jai Khalar and now wormed its way into the cliffs, leaving a hole the size of a town, a black hole in the white cliffs. Quiz lurched on a confusion of updrafts and downdrafts, fighting gravity, and the sound of the Li'ah'vah's passing beat the flesh of Liaku's face as if her skin were a drum.

Then Quiz let her go, and she hit the ground rolling. Her right wrist snapped and her shoulder wrenched as she tumbled, coming to a halt on a ledge only a yard from the brink of the hole where the Citadel once had been. The stone was hot, and she didn't try to look over the edge. But weird melodies came out, and then a bird or two, flying in dazed circles.

And then one mouse scurried over the edge. It sat up on its hind legs, saw her, and fled.

Music

Fivesisters Lake was a dark stain far below them, and on the other side of the ridge, Everien was succumbing to the ravages of the time serpent. On their high shelf in a patch of mossy stone exposed by wind, the Sekk and Istar perched on the balls of their feet, hands outstretched for balance, fingertips touching the icy rock. It was the sort of pose that Eteltar had taught Istar to adopt when he was lecturing her on the ledges of his arid home, and although she knew it was a Sekk who now sat beside her, wingless, unspeaking, and perilous, she nevertheless felt an implicit sense of companionship in the shared pose. Istar watched the Li'ah'vah performing its strange, terrible work, breaking through the crust of rock as though it were no more dense than water, throwing great slabs of ice into the air with plumes of white snow rocketing before them, feathering the dark gold evening sky. Night and day were balanced now, exchanging places in a slow waltz of shadows, but the Li'ah'vah illumined the gloaming with its own body wherever it passed. In its wake it left smouldering rock; from one tunnel spewed liquid fire, smoke, and ash, so that the whole section of mountainside was vaporized in an instant, steam rushing out in all directions. Snowslides rumbled away beneath the impact point, and an ashen rain began to fall as the wind turned toward them. By the time the steam had cleared away, the Li'ah'vah was long gone.

Istar began to shiver. The steam had wet her face and hair, and when the harsh mountain wind picked up its usual scream, it hurt as much as a vicious slap across the mouth. She looked at the Sekk. Its hood had blown back and its head was turned toward her. The gag was brittle with ice and the blindfold hid the Sekk's expression. No matter how hard she tried, she only saw Eteltar. She took in the lines of his throat, the shape of his partially covered ears, the contours of his hairline, and she wanted to fling herself on him, press her lips to his pale skin, let his heat envelop her. It was all she could do not to remove the black cloths binding his mouth and eyes, and beg him to explain the meaning of what she had just witnessed.

'Eteltar, if you can hear me, I'm sorry,' she began. She reached through the biting wind and put her fingers on his bare cheek, in the hollow between his cheekbone and jaw, where the groove of a deep smile line made her breath catch in her throat. She wondered whether he was listening. His head was tilted slightly to one side as if straining to hear something. Emboldened, she continued. 'I'm sorry I made you come. I'm sorry I loved you. Now you are compromised and cannot fly. Eteltar, it is so bitter that I—'

The Sekk reached out and touched her wrist with one warm, firm hand, silencing her. At first she didn't know why it had stopped her, and she stared at the impassive profile, wondering if she could ever hope to understand this creature. Then she noticed that a sound was coming from one of the openings created by the Li'ah'vah – where, she could not see and had no wish to guess. For a long moment she listened, and she heard what the Sekk heard. She knew they were both hearing the same thing. They were both responding to the same strange and unlikely sound with an emotion that had no place in the snow and the displacement and the incomprehensibility of their situation. The Sekk, kin-murderer and hunter of Istar's species, and Istar, wing-thief and hunter of the Sekk, both listened to the rising and falling of the sound. It was calling them somehow. Both of their throats went tight.

What they heard was music.

Into the Neverbefore

In Everien, it was almost spring. Tarquin squinted into a high wind that ripped across the open hillside. Crocuses were starting, and streams were running underneath the snow, which had taken on a rare, semitransparent sheen like melted sugar.

Tarquin was standing in the bottom of a ditch. The Li'ah'vah had left a mole's trail of epic proportions across this field, through a patch of wood, and on in the direction of Jai Khalar. Otherwise, there was no evidence. The air Tarquin had passed through in coming here was like ordinary air. There was no hint of a doorway, no echo of Jaya's voice. Nothing. He swallowed hard. Bitterness again.

Then he saw the Wasp Clan arrow sticking in the ground. He tugged it from the earth and looked at it. This was the arrow that had pierced Ice's breast. It would not now find its target.

'Kere?'

Hoofbeats.

He turned and saw the source of the noise. A group of Pharician horsemen were galloping across the fields, away from the Fire Houses which could be seen in the distance, all alight in the middle of day. The dome of the largest cone had shattered from within and now made a jagged line in the sky, like a cracked egg.

'Kere!' he shouted again.

The boy's white head popped up from a nearby hillock. He was lying cast-out on the grass.

'Are you hurt? The arrow—'

'Missed me. I'm tired.' He yawned. Tarquin sat down, relieved and then immediately afterward, morose.

'I have lost her now for certain; but I could not kill Ice, either, and if I had stayed we would both have been trapped there. Ah, the time serpent – Eteltar has used the codes he took from us, I know he has. What have we done? I no longer know right from wrong, forward from back. Is this destruction good or bad – either way, it is beyond me.'

'The Li'ah'vah was not well made,' Kere reflected. 'She was never meant to reproduce. Eteltar may have tried to repair her, but the attempt did not succeed. For they called the same broken creature that sent us on the quest in the volcano. She devours Everien. But she opened a way for us, and we are not powerless.'

'What? Look at the mountains! Look at the sky! It is the end of the world!'

'Ice is whole now,' Kere said quietly. 'The danger from Chyko's dart, it is gone for good. We have passed through that crossroads and survived.'

Tarquin reached over and gripped the back of Kere's neck in his palm. In a lighter tone he said, 'You must have learned *something* from the Snakes. Chyko is strong and he had a good hold on you. But you squirmed! You were not defeated.'

The boy's eager young eyes turned up to him. 'Does this mean you can make a fighter of me?'

'No!' said Tarquin gruffly, and Kere's face fell. 'Well. *Maybe.*' He gave Kere's neck an affectionate shake. 'What I'm saying is that you saved my life. Again. And I won't forget it.'

Kere blushed.

'But I have lost Jaya,' Tarquin continued. 'I said I would save her, and I did not.'

'It's not over. The path made by this time serpent will cross yours, or has crossed, or is crossing. Many times. The time serpent and the flaw in its coding slice through Everien like a wire through cheese. You will have to look out for it to see it happening. It is not obvious. But it is there for you to use, if you are not afraid where it may take you.'

'Kere, I beg you,' Tarquin said, his voice cracking with sudden emotion. 'If Ice can run faster than time, make him run fast enough to take me back to her before all this happened.'

Kere hesitated. The boy was so close to coming into his own; Tarquin could not blame him if he did not want to take up the form of the horse again. After all, he had been bullied and forced into doing so time and time again, and Tarquin could not see how being Ice had brought the boy any happiness.

His eyes were full of tears of helplessness; ashamed, he wiped them away and opened his eyes wide on what was left of Everien. On the hills stained green with their escaping mountains thrusting into the sky like exposed bones. The amber of the day's end. The wind's unspoken promise, the hint of things beneath things. Every twilight in Everien was the same. This one no different. On the roads the Pharician horses moved in lines. Pharician spears, regimented; Pharician drum music an ever-present threat. From A-vi-Khalar and the close-sewn shapes of its precise and glorious houses, Everien appeared a green and possibly magical valley. But it was not entirely so.

Something else was closer and farther away. In the mountains and in the sky lay unexpressed possibilities. They lay like diamonds. Tarquin had seen them in the eyes of the blind woman, when she told him his horse was dying from a wound he had yet to receive. He saw them again now in the solid earth of Everien his home. He saw that the stone was more than stone. It hid other things.

The air had been rent like a curtain or maybe a wing, as if a bird had ripped open the sky with its very body. But the fabrication that had slunk from the discarded shell of the Fire Houses like a pupa from its outgrown shell was no bird. It had holes in both ends. Either could eat or shit. It had no centre and no directionality. It did not stand facing into time; it did not stand with its back to time. It curled around time like a parasite. In the earth beneath his feet and Kere's, Tarquin could feel it moving.

'There!' Kere exclaimed at his shoulder. 'There is it. The Li'ah'vah is a dreadful thing, but it cannot run as fast as Ice. Come, Tarquin, and I will show you. We will run faster than anything. We will run into the neverbefore.'

Tarquin turned to face Kere, but the boy had become a white blur that whipped in a tight circle around Tarquin like a garment or a personal tornado; and then Ice was there, flaring white and black and not predictable, in more than one place at the same time, and Tarquin threw himself on the stallion's back.

'Run, then,' said Tarquin. 'Do what you can do, and outrun time.'

Who Really Shot Ice

Dario was running when the world broke apart. She was running mindlessly across the uneven, icy hillside above Fivesisters Lake. She didn't care about the Li'ah'vah, though it was even now bursting into being all over Everien, its past-present-future-maybe-never-always puncturing the fabric of Everien like a needle. She didn't care. It was too late now, anyway, to change or undo what she had done. This had been decided the moment she made her personal unequivocal decision to put out the lights in the lake of candles.

They had done it early in the morning, before the sun came. Now she was running, and daylight was here, and with it the end of the world as Dario knew it. She recalled the last minutes of quiet, when Everien had lain still, a thread of moonlight drifting from the dark sky to the snow-cloaked peaks of Snake Country. Dario, Jakse, Bellen, and his brother slipped up the road to Fivesisters Lake, swords already drawn except for Dario, who had her bow. They didn't speak as they made their way back through the cave to the lake of candles, ablaze in the windless dark.

Dario did most of the work. The men took what globes they could reach and smashed them with their swords, and when the globes were broken chords of unearthly music rose from them. But most of the lights floated in the middle of the lake, and Dario had to shoot them out, one by one. Her arrows all were poisoned, even though the poison was not needed in this case, and she warned the men to stand back lest one go astray. So they retreated to the cave entrance, waiting for her without lighting torches so that she could extinguish the last few lights.

Finally there was only one left. She aimed and missed four times. She did not know how, but it was eluding her. Frustrated, she put her bow down.

She didn't want to be doing this. It felt wrong.

'*Dario?*' It was Jakse's voice. He was in the entrance tunnel but his voice seemed to be everywhere. 'Are you all right? Hurry, in case they rise!'

In case they rise. She looked again at the last light. It must be working its spell on her, playing on her sympathies. She had only one arrow left. She could not afford to miss.

She did not want to shoot this thing.

One Sekk had killed her whole village.

She nocked her last arrow and aimed. Her whole body was still, no breath, no twitch, no blink of eye.

The globe flared. The fingertip glow of a candle now became the brightness of a star. Dario squeezed her eyes shut and let the arrow go.

She heard the glass shatter, but the light was so bright that she couldn't open her eyes at first. When she did, the globe was gone. In the water was a girl, powerfully backlit by a white light and accompanied by a rush of noise: wind, shouts, inchoate crashings and clashings.

The light behind the girl was so strong that Dario couldn't see her features. Light shone through her red hair so that she seemed to possess her own corona.

Dario dropped her weapon and fled. And she ran herself into the ground, for she did not know what it was she had done.

Free

Time did a strange snake charm on me when I hesitated in the threshold of the broken window. In that moment when the Li'ah'vah came, and the White Road appeared, and Tarquin was shouting and the arrows were flying from Chyko's bow and the music of the Fire Houses was turning my brain; in that moment, my long journey through the forest was rendered as sleep, as one long night of forgetfulness; and I was returned to the time when I stood in that same place and they came for me from Outside to kill me, to kill my mother. To the time when they broke into my father's house and drove me away. Forgotten things returned to me. Hovering on that threshold, in an instant I understood things I had read in my father's books that until then had been impenetrable to me. And even as I reached for Tarquin's outstretched hand, to try to stay together in that maelstrom, at the same time I was reliving the attack that had driven me into the forest. I was looking through the shattered window to the faces of my would-be destroyers. Only now I was leaping out of the flight path of a barbed arrow as it came toward me, letting go of Tarquin's hand in the process. And now, instead of fleeing to the library where soon I would see my mother ripped limb from limb, I was throwing myself through the broken glass and out into the windy darkness. Where they were. The hunters.

This time there was only one of them. In the light that came through the shattered glass I saw the face of a wild-eyed woman, no bigger than myself. She had a bow in her hands, but her arrows were spent. She was shaking all over and crying. She looked at me as if I were not a person, but a monster, or a tidal wave, or something at any rate altogether larger than I know myself to be. And then, suddenly, she turned and fled. A heartbeat later, the light from inside the house was gone. I was not in my house or my garden or even in the wood. I was up to my hips in warm fluid, in total darkness.

My hand was bleeding where the arrow had struck it in shattering the glass, so I bathed it. I climbed from the warm water and then I was sick, for a little of the poison had got into my blood. My head spun; but darkness is no stranger to me, and I was not lost. I came out of the cave into a bitter and windy mountainscape. The dark sky was tinged with the undersea green of predawn. My assailants had left footprints in the snow, but I didn't care about them. I couldn't see Tarquin. I couldn't see Midnight Blue. I couldn't see Chyko.

But I could see my own hands in front of my face. And I could see the sky. I was very cold. And I was free.

About the author

Valery Leith is an American in England.